KINSMEN DIE

AND THE HEAVENS BURN, BOOK 1

MATT BISHOP

FENSALIR
PUBLISHING, LLC

Kinsmen Die by Matt Bishop

Published by Fensalir Publishing, LLC

PO Box 473

Lemont, IL 60439

https://mattbishopwrites.com

Cover by J. Caleb Design

Ebook ISBN: 978-0-9986789-0-0

Print ISBN: 978-0-9986789-3-1

THE KINSMEN DIE PODCAST

If you'd rather listen to Kinsmen Die, look for the podcast version, read one chapter at a time, in the player/service of your choice.

https://rss.com/podcasts/fensalirpodcast-kinsmendie/

FROM THE HAVAMAL

"THE BALLAD OF THE HIGH ONE,"
POETIC EDDA

Henry Adams Bellows translation
Sacred Texts

> 77. Cattle die, | and kinsmen die,
> And so one dies one's self;
> But a noble name | will never die,
> If good renown one gets.

> 78. Cattle die, | and kinsmen die,
> And so one dies one's self;
> One thing now | that never dies,
> The fame of a dead man's deeds.

1

Frigg

White breath pluming behind her and fear making her heart pound even harder, Frigg tugged at the edges of her cloak and flickered into her falcon shape. She shot forward like an arrow. Up ahead, the longhouse's double doors were thrown wide to release two Alvar thralls carrying a body outside on a litter, their long shadows keeping pace.

But this was no body. This was Baldr, her son. It had happened yet again.

Her sharpened sight picked out Eir, Gladsheim's chief valkyr, directing the Alvar thralls to rest the litter on the stone table in the clearing beside the longhouse.

She flared her wings, and her booted feet touched snowy earth. "Eir. How is he?"

With a quick gesture, Eir sent the shaven-headed Alvar thralls away. She dug two fingers into Baldr's wrist and met Frigg's gaze evenly. "His heart still beats, Almother. Faintly."

A broken, relieved sob came from beside the longhouse. Nanna stood in the pooling light from within the house. Her hands were cupped around her nose and mouth; her shoulders shook with the strength of her sobs. Nanna had been dealing with these mysterious, death-like dreams of Baldr's alone for nearly half a year now.

Just as she herself had been alone for the past twenty winters, ever since her husband had set out westward.

Except that Nanna's solitude had ended, while hers persisted.

Frigg blew out a long breath and laid her hand on Baldr's brow, just as she had when he'd twisted in the throes of some childhood fever. His face was stone cold.

If she tried, she could still see his pudgy, grinning child's face, smeared with honey after he and his brother Hodr had raided the larder. But she didn't try. Not with him laid out like a corpse before her.

"This is worse than the last one," she said, keeping her voice low.

"It is indeed, Almother." Eir set a cup on the stone behind Baldr's head.

How was any of this even possible? The old magic should have kept him safe against all injury. Spears bounced off Baldr as if the skymetal feared to hurt him. Even the venomous spittle of a snow bear streamed off his skin.

Eir raised a skin, popped the stopper, and poured clear liquid into the cup. A strong fruity scent assaulted Frigg's nose.

Panic beat at her like Jotunn axes on a shield wall as she felt her hand growing cold in her son's grip. She shoved the panic back and stepped calmly into the space she claimed from it. There had to be an explanation for what was happening to her son—and it was not what her visions suggested would happen. It was not.

Eir dipped a spoon in the elixir. "Excuse me, Almother."

She removed her hand from Baldr's forehead but kept a tight grip on his hand. "Should I open his mouth?"

"No, he'll choke." Eir pulled Baldr's lower lip downward with one neat, clean thumb and wet his lips with the elixir. It pooled in the hollow she'd made and ran down his cheek. She dabbed it with a cloth.

"This is the second dose," Eir said. "Hár Nanna insisted that he be brought outside to be touched by Sól's light."

Nanna had claimed that sunlight helped bring Baldr's spirit back to his body from the shores of the Gjoll. But how could Sól's light fix this?

She herself was more confident in Eir's elixir. Baldr himself had distilled it from Yggdrasil's fruits. It had brought him back before; it would do so again.

Silence descended on the small clearing, aside from her thumping heart. In that fleeting instant, Frigg wished she weren't dealing with this alone. A month ago, she'd sat on her husband's High Seat and sent her sight outward across the realms searching for him. When she'd finally found him camped beside an unknown shore, he had looked up and very distinctly mouthed the words *I'll return at once*. But he still wasn't back.

Eir again pressed two fingers to Baldr's wrist and watched his still chest and ashen face. Nanna had told her that his dreams, these fits, were worsening, but she hadn't believed it. She hardly dared breathe. Her eyes darted from Eir to Baldr and back again.

Was this it, then? Her unkillable son was dead?

And how long would they stand here waiting?

Dawn's light leaped into the silent clearing. Baldr gave a great rasping gasp as his chest expanded. Color flooded back into his face and he blew out a long breath.

"Oh, thank Aegir!" Nanna rushed the last few paces and threw herself across her husband.

Frigg felt warmth flood into her son's hand. She gave it a quick squeeze and stepped back to make room for Nanna.

Eir's eyes were narrowed. Her grip on Baldr's wrist had tightened, but her shoulders looked less like a drawn bow.

Baldr's eyes flew open. He looked wildly around and tried to sit up.

"You're all right, Baldr," Nanna said with a sob, keeping him pinned. "You're all right. Sól brought you back."

Eir took a step back, frowning, even as one of Baldr's arms came up, reflexively embracing Nanna.

Frigg watched the wildness in her son's eyes ease away. Squinting in the bright sunlight, he looked around, recognized who was around him, and said, voice flat, "So, it happened again."

She laid her hand on Baldr's shoulder, warm now as it should be. "We'll get it figured out. Freyja will be here within a few nights for Ithavoll. She can have an—"

"Excuse me, Almother." It was Gná, one of her maidservants. She braced her hands on her knees and bent over to drag in a ragged breath.

"Yes?"

"My apologies, Almother, but"—she dragged in another breath—"I bring news from the eastern gate." Hands on hips now, Gná hauled in another lungful of air and wiped sweat from her face.

"Yes, Gná," she said, forcing her voice to stay even. "What is it?"

Gná ducked her head. "The Alfather's returned."

2

Vidar

"Jarl!"

Vidar wrenched his gaze from the massive column of black smoke and ash that had piled high above the burning town and turned in his saddle. His kjolr, Garilon, rode toward him, pointing at the low curving slope of the hill ahead of them. Survivors staggered down the road, dark figures against the harsh blue of the midwinter sky.

Vidar thumped a clenched fist on his saddle's pommel. He and his warband had ridden all night to reach this mining town in the mountainous outskirts of his district. And what had he done? Spent more time staring at the smoky remnants of the town than its folk. He hadn't even seen them.

He guided Hrimfaxi off the road; light snow puffed up around her hooves. The sky's chill steeds cantered through the tall golden grasses that stretched as far south and westward as he could see.

His people, the Aesir, had been at peace with the Jotunn for more than forty winters—ever since the Last War had ended. But last night, an exhausted messenger had arrived at Vidar's hall. *Come at once, Jarl. The Jotunn have attacked Háls—they're killing everyone.*

So he'd mustered what warriors he had to hand—the sixty spears now trailing Garilon—and ridden all night to get here.

Garilon reined in beside him and spoke in a voice like a sturdy cart's creaking axle. "Odd that the Jotunn would leave so many alive."

"Doubly odd that they're not running," Vidar gestured toward the approaching townsfolk. "If it was the Jotunn."

"Indeed, Jarl. Shall we ride forward to meet them? No doubt they'll have better information than the messenger."

The wind gusted, pungent with ash and smoke. It blew Vidar's cloak open, running down the neck of his heavy shirt and past him to make his fox-head banner snap and crack. He swore, hauled his cloak shut, and leaned forward to thump Hrimfaxi's neck. She whinnied into the wind's teeth, blowing twin clouds from her nostrils. They'd ridden all night and she was tired, hungry, and thirsty. Just like every other horse and rider in the column.

His eyes went to the pack of townsfolk again, easily several hundred in number. "Let them all clear the hill first. Just in case. The town was how big?"

"Less than two thousand, Jarl."

At an itch between his shoulder blades, Vidar threw a glance at the sharp line of the ridge above Háls. Ice and snow was caught among the ridge's jagged, toothy rocks like decaying flesh in a snow bear's jaws.

He shaded his eyes again. His uncle Heimdall could easily glimpse any Jotunn tucked between those rocks, but he couldn't, even though the ridgeline wasn't that far away. The ridge itself erupted up out of the plains south of Háls and ran in a crooked line northward behind the town, then into the thick forest and the low-shouldered mountains beyond.

"Isn't there an old logging or mining road along that ridge?" he asked.

Garilon grunted in agreement. "I believe so, Jarl. Disused, though, if memory serves."

"Good place to hide."

"That's where I'd head if I were them. Only high ground around here, aside from the mountains. Good view of the grasslands here and the farms north of us. Can probably even see the Svol. I haven't seen anything moving up there, but that doesn't mean they're not there. Jotunn or outlaws, they've been here for a lot longer than we have. Days, maybe. Plenty of time to dig in."

"Or run away," he countered, lowering his hand and turning toward his kjolr. He pressed gloved hands against his saddle horn and shifted his weight. Outlaws definitely would have run, but the Jotunn?

Garilon gave a slight shrug. "Yes, Jarl."

"Scouts, then, up the ridge. Carefully." His tone took the question out of it. He pointed toward the farms, east of the town but a good distance north of his column. "And that way, out across the fields and into the bordering forest. Up into the mountains, too, if they see the need."

"Yes, Jarl." With quick gestures, Garilon sent a pair of riders galloping north toward the dark green line of trees that ran all along the mountains' base and then up its shoulders. He sent another pair west through the tall, snowy grasses to scout the high ridge.

Vidar watched them until he could no longer see the clumps of snow flying up from the horses' hooves. He ran his thumb along the carved grip of his distaff. A gift from his father, the distaff hung on his right side, a pouch with a pair of silver shears and only one charged spindle beside it. These were the tools of seidr, the magic his father had been teaching him. His sword hung on his left side. A bone-handled seax nestled at the small of his back.

He gestured with his chin toward the line of townsfolk drawing closer. "Let's go find out what happened."

Vidar squeezed his legs together and Hrimfaxi pranced forward, tossing her head, bridle jingling, happy to be moving again. Garilon fell in beside him, barking commands that kicked the double column of warriors into motion with their eyes on the ridge to the west, the fields to the north, and even the plains behind them. Not much was likely to come from behind them, but Garilon had commanded the Einherjar during the waning winters of the Last War. He knew what he was doing.

Vidar rode down the column and nodded at the warriors. Although he only said a few names—Smar and Mikill; Jalla and Hevred; Kvella and Rollo—he knew them all. He had even sparred with some of them, though that was seldom enough, given his various projects and obligations as the district's jarl.

Another itch between his shoulder blades. Vidar shielded his eyes against Sól's glare and scanned the ridge from one end to the other. Nothing but a herd of low clouds running fast, racing their shadows, edges sharp against the sky's brilliant blue. He stared longer but saw nothing but sharp rocks, patches of snow and ice, and dozens of clouds sliding ceaselessly over the ridge, flowing down the cliff and rushing eastward.

Was it those clouds and their shadows that kept drawing his attention? He dropped his gaze back to the road and the ragged clump of townsfolk a few dozen yards away.

Garilon leaned toward him. "Those scouts we sent are good men. Cautious. Thorough. If the enemy's up there, we'll know it soon. And we'll set more eyes to watching from down here once we get these folk sorted out."

Raising his voice to be heard over the clattering hooves, Vidar said, "Sound the horn for Gladsheim anyway, Garilon. I want reinforcements moving our way. I'm not confident in the Einherjar garrison's attention to duty."

Before he had ridden from his hall in Vithi, Vidar had sent a bird to the Einherjar garrison in the northeastern part of his district. Like Vithi, it was about a night's ride from Háls. If the hersir of the garrison had dispatched a column of Einherjar as he was supposed to, those warriors should be here soon.

Over the last dozen winters, though, the Einherjar had not only tripled in size, but they had also become recalcitrant to any order except the Alfather's. And since Odin, his father, had been gone these twenty winters, the Einherjar did pretty much as they pleased—unless the Almother stepped in and made the consequences of further disobedience perfectly clear. Of course, his mother had no way of knowing what was happening here in Vithi, not until the bird he'd also sent to Gladsheim arrived. Even when it did, it would take at least of pair of nights before the Einherjar arrived from Gladsheim.

Their best chance at reinforcements was the Einherjar garrison to the northeast. Or Heimdall's ears.

It seemed that Garilon hesitated for just the briefest moment before nodding. "Yes, Jarl." He reached beneath his cloak for the silver-wrapped horn.

A moment later, the horn's voice split the air like a fox's hoarse shriek. Heimdall would hear it all the way back in Gladsheim. He would tell Frigg, and she would kick the Einherjar into motion.

If Heimdall wasn't dead drunk.

But why had Garilon hesitated? Did he disapprove of calling for reinforcements a second time without having set eyes on the enemy?

The wind gusted, blowing a swirl of snow across the road.

He would rather the Einherjar be on the move sooner rather than later. It would be two nights at least before they arrived. And if this Jotunn attack turned out to be nothing, then he'd have the all clear sounded, and the Einherjar would turn back.

Simple.

Either way, it wouldn't be Garilon who would ultimately have to face the consequences—or suffer the loss of honor.

It would all be on him.

3

Odin

"I rode back as fast as I could, Frigg," Odin said, making sure to keep his tone mild. He glanced away from Baldr, who was laughing at something Nanna had just said. "And you checked his tree?"

"Of course I checked it. Lush and green during the summer, now completely covered in snow and ice."

He smiled and raised his hands, palms up. "All right, Frigg, I'm just asking. But he looks fine to me."

Frigg snorted, hot anger in her eyes. "You should have seen him this morning. Skin like bluest ice until Eir daubed his lips with that elixir he made from Yggdrasil's fruit. When Sól's light touched him, he gasped, color flooded back in, and he sat up. And you missed it."

"I belie—"

A fist pounded against the heavy wood table. "Ale! More ale! You there. Yes, you! Bring me more ale!" Tableware clattered, jumped, and danced.

Odin leaned forward, frowning, to stare past Frigg at Heimdall. The burly flaxen-haired Aesir's face was flushed with drink. His eyes were bleary, and he rubbed at his temples with the long fingers of one hand while his other hand held out his cup.

An Alvar thrall, head shaved, skin the color of gold, refilled Heimdall's cup, bowed, and flowed back into the throng of tables to meet the same demands of the hundred other guests. The late-morning gathering had grown as word spread throughout Gladsheim that the Alfather had returned.

Frigg sat back, annoyance evident in every line of her face and body. Odin gestured with his chin toward Heimdall. She didn't bother following the gesture; she just rolled her eyes and sniffed. "It started maybe a dozen winters ago, after he bested Loki."

"Bested Loki in what?"

She waved her hand in the air. "Foolishness around Freyja and that torc she wears. Does Loki get bored, is that it? Or has he always been this vicious?"

He leaned back so he could look directly at her. "What did my brother do this time?"

She touched her own necklace. "You know that torc Freyja always wears—the one her husband gave her before he vanished?"

He nodded.

She leaned a little closer, speaking to be heard over a sudden swell in the celebration. She smelled like a new-dawned day. "Well, after the Spring Festival, it went missing—"

On impulse, he laid his hand on hers, squeezed gently and kissed her cheek. She drew away, surprised, but with the hint of a warm smile displacing the lingering anger at him—and annoyance at Heimdall—on her face. He'd been gone twenty winters. It hadn't felt as if that much time had passed, but now that he was back, it felt as if twice that time had passed.

"More ale! By Rán's weeping nets! More ale!"

He leaned forward again.

Heimdall's face twisted in pain even as he held up his newly drained cup. A moment later, he crashed his fist against the table, dropped the cup, and balled his fists against his ears as if he was trying to block out some sound.

Those few Aesir still near him picked up their own cups and platters and moved toward the few unoccupied benches built into the walls.

Odin patted Frigg's hand and shifted in his seat, preparing to stand. "I'd better check on him."

She shrugged. The heat in her eyes had cooled. "Don't bother. He'll pass out in a few minutes. He always does."

He quirked an eyebrow at her. "It's not even midday."

Her gaze was the flat of a sword. "Don't give me that look. I had enough to deal with while you were gone." She pursed her lips and looked down the long, curving table to where Heimdall sat. "But he usually does wait until evening to drink himself into a stupor."

"So I should just let him drink? He seems to be in pain."

"His behavior isn't unusual, Odin. I did try to help him. Baldr, too. He rebuffed us both."

He looked again at Heimdall. The man's grimace had faded. "All right, I'll let it be." But he shifted so he could keep an occasional eye on the man whose senses had helped guard the Aesir for as long as the Aesir had existed.

Frigg gestured toward the crowd, the motion catching his eye as much as the hard note in her voice. "So this grew bigger than I expected. It's almost as if you've been gone for a long time."

"Only twenty winters, Frigg. Not that long for us. Not anymore." He ran his eyes over the crowd of folk, finding dozens of familiar faces all looking much older than he remembered.

"Not for you, maybe."

He glanced at Frigg, about to ask what she meant, but stopped when he saw her expression grow fiercer.

"So did you find them?" she asked.

"No. Not yet."

"Twenty years of searching and no trace? It's almost as if they don't want to be found. If they're even still alive."

"I wouldn't say no trace," he said in a level voice. "I came across a dozen scattered, thriving settlements of Aesir who claim descent from those who stayed put even as my brothers ventured farther away. I asked the leaders of those settlements if they'd join our realm.

They seemed to welcome the idea. I'll have to go back obviously, but—"

"What?" She shifted in her seat; her black eyes pinned him. "Go back?"

He raised his hands again. "Not now, nor any time soon. I'm not going anywhere until we figure out what's happening with Baldr." He gestured toward the rest of the hall. "And I'll start once I can reasonably excuse myself from all this. I promise."

She blew out a breath and nodded once. "Good."

"So tell me, what have you learned about what's happening to him?"

"Little enough." Her gaze lingered on Baldr before meeting his own. "He's been having dreams for months now. Not every night, but often enough. He doesn't remember what happens, but Nanna is terrified. And with good reason. I've seen it before, but this morning was the worse yet."

"Freyja can't explain them?" he asked, voice low.

"No, but then I haven't told her everything, either. I felt we should both make that decision. I sent for you when I—" She glanced discreetly around their places.

"When what?"

She leaned toward him, speaking softly. "My visions are returning. Something terr—"

Heimdall's voice cut through the crowd's din like a blast from his horn. "Just give it to me!" A loud crash followed.

Odin stood. An Alvar thrall was untangling himself from the group of Aesir he'd been flung into. Like an indrawn breath, the hall had gone quiet.

Heimdall stood, swaying slightly, a stone pitcher in one hand. His other hand beat at his ear. Each time he grimaced, gold teeth as big as a horse's gleamed behind his beard.

"Go on," said Frigg, flicking her wrist at Odin. "Best to deal with him when he gets like this."

He strode past the empty chairs on his left, chairs where Gladsheim's jarls would soon sit. Heimdall had sat back down and, with trembling hands, was trying to pour ale into his cup. He kept missing the cup, and the dark liquid sloshed across the table.

The thrall bowed deeply when he realized the Alfather now stood beside him.

Odin held out his hand. "Give me that cloth."

"Yes, Alfather," the thrall whispered, pulling the stained cloth free from his belt.

"If you're all right, return to your duties. If not, go see Eir. Tell her I sent you."

"Thank you, Alfather. I am fine." The thrall bowed and fled toward the kitchens.

Odin hitched at his breeches and sat sideways on the table's edge. Heimdall's sheathed seax lay between them, a poor dam for the pool of spilled ale. Odin threw the towel on top of the spill.

Heimdall's head came up, and he raised his cup in mock salute. "Welcome back, Alfather." Then he threw his head back and drained the cup again. His head came down, bobbing and rolling on his neck.

Odin stared down at his cousin for a long moment. "I should be shouting 'Thief! Thief!' right now."

"And why's that?"

"Because beer's obviously stolen away with your wits. You disgrace yourself."

Heimdall fumbled for the pitcher and managed to refill his cup without spilling too much more. "It's beer that does that? Ymir's tits, I've been wasting my time with ale."

Odin slapped the cup away, feeling anger's first hot flush. The cup flew, ale spraying, until it bounced hard against the platform's wood planks and rolled away.

Heimdall watched it go, shoulders slumped.

Odin pitched his voice lower, for the hall's noise had only partially returned. "What is all this about, Heimdall?"

Heimdall swayed in his seat, burped, and reached for the stoneware pitcher but instead knocked it down. The last bit of ale poured out. Odin snatched it up and moved it to one side.

Heimdall exhaled long and loud, wet lips flapping. He wiped

sloppily at a bit of drool and motioned Odin closer, pawing at one ear with a clenched hand. "It's the birds, squawking my name over and over and over. Always the birds. A dozen winters now. I can't handle it. Not anymore."

Birds?

Banging one hand against his ear again, eyes closed tight, Heimdall continued in a low, slurring whisper. "The squawking voices... always there. Always. And then sometimes, as just happened, a scream cuts through everything and now it echoes and echoes and echoes..."

He burped and weaved, hands twitching outward, searching for stability. Everything along the long wooden table rocked as Heimdall held onto it.

Odin moved the stoneware pitcher further away. "I don't understand. Birds? A scream?"

Not a handspan's movement of Sól after he'd arrived, Gná had delivered a message to Frigg. A bird had been sent from Vithi with a message: Háls had been attacked by an unknown force, and Vidar was riding to investigate.

Frigg had summoned Saglund, the Einherjar hersir, explaining to Odin that outlaws from the two western districts had banded together and begun raiding. So far, they remained at large, despite the efforts of the town garrisons as well as the Einherjar garrisons.

When Hersir Saglund presented himself, he had argued that they should wait for more details. He hadn't received any word from his garrison in Vithi. Frigg insisted that he ready a company of Einherjar, but the hersir—who Odin had himself appointed before leaving—insisted they wait for further word.

At that point, Odin had stepped in, and Saglund had backed down. Thinking about it now, he wondered if Frigg had intended that confrontation to happen.

Heimdall's muttering drew his attention back just as he drew his seax with more speed than such a drunken man should have been capable of. The knife's blade, long and sharp, glinted with reflected yellows and reds as it moved toward Heimdall's right ear.

Odin grabbed Heimdall's thick wrist, halting the seax's wavering progress. Then he swung himself over the table and came in behind Heimdall, twisting the knife hand behind him and pinning him against the table.

Heimdall struggled a few moments but then gave up, sagging against the table. His hand opened, and Odin twisted the seax free.

"Knife's too long, anyway," Heimdall said around a belch and a sigh. "Need something shorter."

Odin slammed the seax point first into the table a hand's breath in front of Heimdall's face. "What did you hear, cousin?"

Bleary, bloodshot eyes struggled upward and met his own. Heimdall shrugged. "Horn, I think? Or maybe a fox screaming somewhere, maybe?"

He frowned and gripped Heimdall's shoulders, almost in his face. "A fox? That could've been Vidar's horn. He'd sent word of trouble in Vithi. Is that what you'd heard? Vithi's horn?"

Heimdall belched again, and Odin recoiled from the stench. A moment later, he felt his cousin's shoulders go limp. A rumbling snore followed.

Odin straightened and banged the table loud enough to bring murmurs into the silent hall. He beckoned at his son. "Baldr! Get over here and wake him up."

It was hard to believe that the eyes and ears of the Aesir had come to this. No wonder Gladsheim—and Vithi—had been taken unawares.

4

Hodr

The metal butt of Hodr's spear thudded dully against the old bridge's timbers. Kona's hooves clomped beside him, his own feet a tired shuffle. The old, withered fruit, still golden and heavy in its bag, thumped against his thigh with every step.

At two hundred paces, Hodr clucked his tongue and tapped his way across to the bridge's rail. He reached and ran his hand along the smooth thick wood, then wrapped Kona's reins around it.

He leaned against the rail. It was another mild winter day. Sól was warm on his upturned face. Small birds fluttered and chirped around him. Perhaps they thought he had seeds for them.

Trade traffic was beginning to pick up. Aesir feet tramped, their rhythm conjuring days long past on a different bridge. Cart wheels rumbled past like storm clouds. Horses' hooves fell, heavy and distinct, like strikes of his brother's hammer.

But the rumbling of the bridge was not Thor summoning a storm. The sharper raps were not the lightning strikes of his hammer. And the tramp of feet was not those of his youthful comrades as he fought in the shield wall.

He sighed and turned around to gaze, unseeing, down at the

Ifing's frozen waters. The broad river gurgled faintly around the bridge's stone supports, but everywhere else it remained silent, frozen.

On impulse, he withdrew the fruit from his bag and took a large crunching bite. A warm glow spread from his stomach. He turned his back to the traffic on the bridge and took another bite, and another, hardly pausing to chew before swallowing. Juices ran into his beard, and he wiped at them with one sleeve.

The glow in his belly became a fire. Another bite. And another. The fire became a forge's blaze. He became the scrap of skymetal pounded beneath the smith's hammer. His heart became that hammer.

Bang-ting-ting-bang-ting-ting.

The noise of the traffic behind him vanished. His grip on the rail made the wood creak. Beneath that hammer, his years sloughed away. His back straightened. The ache in his knees faded. His hearing sharpened. But his eyes... Sharp knives of pain dug at the burns from the snow bear's venom. His hands trembled and shook as he remembered his last sight, the spittle dripping from the beast's jaws.

A small remainder of the fruit tumbled from his hand to the river below. He heard it hit the ice. Birds chirped angrily at him, their wings fluttering as they dove for the prize. It would be their best meal ever.

As the pain faded and the memory slipped back to whatever cave he kept it locked in, the itch slithered out. Always that itch of burned-out eyes, and always the hope that maybe this time, Yggdrasil's fruit might have restored what the beast had taken.

This time was no different. His hand darted up and felt beneath the scrap of cloth covering the thick scars. Hope welled and gurgled in his chest... but no. His fingers only met rough skin and deep hollows.

He slammed a fist against the wooden rail. It cracked.

"Hey! You there! What's going on?" It was only one of the bridge wardens—hopefully, Alara's brother.

He hung his head and sighed.

"What's going on over here?" The warden's footsteps thudded closer. The voice sound did sound like Hleven. "Turn around so I can see you."

He straightened, spread his hands palms outward, and turned. "Is that you, Hleven? I'll pay for the damage. Seems I found a bit of rot in the timbers. Sorry for the damage."

Hleven sounded surprised. "Master Hodr? Alara said you weren't due back for a pair of nights."

"I left early." He smiled and pawed the air in search of Kona's reins. "I made those trades she asked for."

"Is everything all right? You seemed upset just then."

Hodr gestured toward the cloth covering his ruined eyes. "Sometimes they hurt. If there's any damage, I'll be happy to pay for it."

"No, no, that won't be necessary. This old bridge needs so much work anyway." He could almost hear the man waving his hand in the air. "And I'm sorry to hear it. I didn't mean to pry."

"Think nothing of it," Hodr said. He wrapped Kona's reins around his hand and stepped close to her head.

"Amazes me how well you get around," Hleven said. Hodr heard him step backward. "You headed back to the way house?"

"I couldn't do it without her," he said, stroking Kona's nose. "Nor without your sister, if I'm honest."

And he was Hodr. Wasn't he always honest? To others, maybe.

5

———————

Loki

Loki leaned back against the warm wall of his longhouse, eyes closed, listening to the clink of pots, the fire's crackle, and the honest rasp of honing blades. He hadn't been home in far too long. When Sigyn set a wooden platter down beside him, he wrapped an arm round her waist and dragged her onto his lap. She laughed, pretending to resist, but he got the kiss he sought.

"Stop, Loki, there's more food to bring." More happiness radiated from her smile than heat from the fire before him. It was a shame he'd be leaving tomorrow. She squeezed his hand as she extricated herself.

Vali and Narfi had grown too quickly and were Jotunn men in their own right, having passed their trials. Trials he'd missed seeing because of his travels.

Loki forced himself to meet his sons' eyes, bright like the unmarred skymetal of a shield boss. His fingers danced through the patterns of the Jotunn hand speech. "I thought you two would be gone already, off to join Helveg."

Sigyn returned with platters for Vali and Narfi, set them down on the tables that jutted from the longhouse walls, then moved back to the cooking area, in a warm swirl of poached fish and steamed potatoes. She returned with a platter for herself.

Vali, fair and lean like his mother, answered, his fingers flickering. "We were given a month before reporting to Helveg."

Narfi just grunted, brought a spoonful of stew to his lips and blew on it.

"Well, that's surprising. I'd thought his kindness was gone," Loki said with his fingers. After his sister had been taken by Freyr, Beli had lost what few soft edges he'd ever had.

"It wasn't kindness so much as practicality," Vali said, his fingers dancing. "We couldn't have caught up with them even if we'd left right away. But they're looping down near Jotunheim before heading into the northwest. We'll meet them there—outside Jotunheim, I mean."

An interesting direction to be headed for the Jotunn's most effective warband. What was up in the northwest, which was even more desolate than the rest of Utgard, that would interest the Skrymir and Vafthrudnir? One of the sites he'd heard so few specifics about? Or perhaps it was another of those mysterious doorways Vafthrudnir had discovered.

"You'll have time to get back across the Breach?" Loki asked.

Narfi grunted again. Narfi was dark of skin, hair, and eyes. Stout, too, but not fat. He favored Farbauti, Loki's father, more than he himself did. If he dwelled on the resemblance too much, it sent a shiver right down his back. Farbauti had not been a pleasant man.

"There are still a few secret ways across," Narfi gestured, "and we can ride openly until Ifington. We'll leave the horses there with one of our people."

Loki knew he meant one of the Jotunn sympathizers who lived in Ifington, the trade town at the tip of the peninsula that stretched out toward the Breach. Ifington was a good place to blend in, as there were always new faces moving through on the ships sailing up the coast from Vanaheim and Alvheim in the southeast. Across the narrow strait from Ifington sat the Fortress at the Breach. Built and manned by Gladsheim's army at the only break in the mountains that

ringed Utgard, the fortress was the stopper in the wineskin that kept
the Jotunn from leaving Utgard.

Sigyn bumped him with her shoulder and spoke aloud. "Eat
while it's all still hot."

———

LOKI PUSHED his platter away and patted his stomach. "Thank you,
Sigyn," he said aloud. "It's been too long."

"Where have you been, Father?" Vali asked, using the Jotunn
hand speech.

"Oh, here and there," he replied with a wink.

Sigyn rose and began clearing the platters, but he touched her
shoulder and she sat back.

"I leave again tomorrow," he signed. Even if he hadn't caught the
slight slump in her shoulders, disappointment radiated from his
sons' faces. "But I can delay that, depending on what happens back in
Gladsheim and elsewhere."

He paused to savor their immediate relief. Another night, or
maybe two, probably couldn't hurt.

"Things will start moving quickly, and Helveg will be the spear's
tip," he continued in the hand speech. He held the gaze of Vali and
then Narfi, each in turn. "Are you ready for that?"

Vali nodded, quick and sharp. Narfi's nod came more slowly, after
a thoughtful dark-eyed glance at his mother. Loki reached out
and gripped Sigyn's knee, but the worry that had crept into her eyes
stayed. A wan smile was her only reply.

His fingers danced again. "And no one except Beli will know you
are my sons. Don't expect special treatment."

"Or worse," Narfi said aloud, a grin on his face. Vali just rolled his
eyes.

Loki ignored the attempt to lighten the mood. "This, right now, is
the point of no return. For me. For all of us." He edged forward on his
chair and moved his fingers more slowly, emphasizing each word. "If
we make a mistake, our spirits ride the currents back into the storm.

Even if we do everything perfectly, they still may." He looked them both in the eye.

Their expressions grew serious. They both signed to him, "We're with you, Father. And the Jotunn."

Aloud, if quietly, Sigyn said, "I am, too." She continued in the hand speech. "Every night I make an offering to Rán, that her nets may spare you all."

"Rán does have a fondness for me, even though I stole a fortune from her once," Loki said with his fingers. He pulled her into a hug, inhaling the fresh scent of her neck and hair. She had brought him back to himself after his first wife had spent her last years grief-stricken and mad with hatred for the friend who'd taken their children.

He kissed her forehead and whispered into her ear, "Your role is the hardest of all. At least we three will be busy."

She pulled back so she could look at him and rested a gentle hand on the side of his face.

A knock came at the door and a man's voice called out, pitched to carry through both wood and above the ever-present, dull roar of the waterfall beyond the longhouse. "Message from town, mistress."

Loki strode across the house and hid behind the door. His fingers flickered, "I'm not here."

She nodded, then called, "Just a moment." She smoothed her dress and stepped to the door, dropped the latch, and hauled it open.

Daylight rushed in, illuminating the tension on his son's faces. He patted the air, saying with his fingers, "Be calm. It's just a messenger. You're supposed to be here."

"Good morning, Mistress," the man said.

"And to you, Raudr," she said. Loki heard the smile in her voice. "What brings you all the way up here so early?"

"Message from Gladsheim, Mistress. For you personally."

Through the space between door and jamb, Loki watched the man hand her a small runestick.

"The bird also bore another message, Mistress. An announcement, really, meant for everyone."

"Oh?"

"After twenty winters, the Alfather's returned. Happy news!"

Loki's stomach dropped, and the bright room seemed to darken as if the cooking fire had belched black smoke.

Ygg was back?

Now?

6

Vidar

The wind blew straight from the town into Vidar's face. It tasted of burned wood, stank like lost livelihoods—and stoked his rage.

The townsfolk were not thirty yards distant now, filthy with ash, clothes torn and burned, streaked with blood. Most coughed and spat filth from their chests even as they staggered with exhaustion. Everywhere he looked, he saw babies clutched to their mothers' chests or small children, eyes vacant from the terror of the sudden flight, draped across their fathers' shoulders. Some of the older ones staggered along on their own.

These were his folk. Fellow Aesir, regardless of rank. And even if he hadn't been their jarl, he would have been upset. Hands tight on the reins, he pulled in a deep breath of wintry air, hoping to calm the rage that roiled the waters of his mind like a longship's oar.

The green slits of his fylgja's eyes slid open and glared up at him from the darkest depths of his spirit. Interest coiled in her eyes, just above the bedrock of her hate for him. Or was she simply wondering why her host—him—had become so very angry?

Keep your mind like the waters of the Bay of Thund in winter, still and cold. Until you want her to wake up, of course.

The time his father had spent teaching his son how to control the fylgja had been too brief. Not for the first time, Vidar cursed himself for allowing the Alfather to shackle him with this spirit.

The memory still angered him, which was less than ideal since he was trying to calm down. He exhaled long and slow, closing his eyes and focusing instead on the regularity of Hrimfaxi's walk. When his thoughts slid off that, he pictured himself standing knee-deep in Vithi's swaying grasses, the summer's heat rising around him, relaxing the knot in his chest even as he felt her stir deep inside his mind.

She flicked her long tufted tail once, twice, as if lazily mocking those same wind-brushed grasses. She stood, too, heavy muscles flexing as she raised her head. Dull and gray, her taloned paws clicked and tapped just as they might in a real cell. Her bonds clinked, reminding them both who controlled whom. She was his fylgja and bound to his spirit—his hugr—just as he was bound to her.

Her green eyes challenged him.

Why had he ever agreed to this? Why?

Another part of his mind answered. *Because your father convinced you.*

He breathed out, focusing on the runes tattooed around his wrists. He sang those words in his mind, plying them the way an animal tamer might snap his whip in the air above a beast. His fylgja merely blinked, laid her head back on her paws, and like a spent witchlamp, her eyes winked out. Her tufted ears flicked attentively this way and that. She'd obeyed because she had to—only a fool would think her cowed.

He opened his eyes, and awareness flooded back. Garilon was speaking to him. About...? Vidar gathered the words from the ground of his memory like leaves shaken from autumn limbs.

Ah, yes. The townsfolk. Of course. He needed to speak with them.

The sharp snap of his banner brought him back into focus, and he blinked away the daze of Sól's brightness.

"Jarl? Are you all right?" A note of concern dwelled in Garilon's rough voice.

Vidar glanced around. His kjolr must have been concerned, because there was maybe twenty feet left between Vidar, Garilon, their warband, and a clutch of townsfolk who could only be the town's leaders. They stood waiting. Fidgeting.

One older man took a step forward and removed a battered cap.

Vidar met Garilon's wary gaze. "I'm fine, Kjolr," he said with a nod he hoped looked decisive. "Let's speak with those we rode to protect, eh?"

"Yes, Jarl," Garilon said, leaning back in his saddle. "If I may, Jarl, their gothi is Dorvath. He's in the front there, the one with his cap in hand. You met him several winters ago."

"I remember him." Vidar squared his shoulders. "Send some warriors to shepherd those townsfolk to those boulders and scrabble of trees. Keep the rest on watch."

"Of course, Jarl."

Vidar reined in a dozen paces from the elders and dismounted. He cursed to himself when he heard Garilon order the warband to halt and stay mounted and alert. He should have been the one to do that.

He pushed the thought down and brought a smile to his face instead, then pitched his voice to carry the remaining few feet. "Gothi Dorvath, I am Jarl Vidar. We met several winters past after I took command of this district. I wish we were meeting again under more favorable circumstances."

Many winters had etched their cold, dark days into the gothi's face and bearing, wearing him down like a gnarled tree. His clothes, ragged and burned, were smeared with blood and dirt. He might be bent, but like that gnarled tree, he still stood, fighting the stoop of age and the weightier press of exhaustion and fear.

Dorvath was a free karl in his own right and chosen to lead Háls by his peers, but Vidar extended his right arm to greet him as an equal. To have the man duck his head seemed wrong, given the cruel doom the Norns had delivered to him this past night.

"I remember you well, Jarl Vidar." The gothi's voice was as solid as his grip. Dorvath didn't deserve to have his later years thrown into chaos by this attack—his home burned, his town and trade destroyed. None of them did, these free men and women, landowners and tradesfolk, farmers, miners, and merchants. It didn't matter who was behind the attack.

His rage crested and washed him over the gunwales of his mind, driving him back down into his mind's depths where his fylgja now circled like a wolf of the sea. Cold emerald eyes met his, and she bared white teeth—distant promise, distant threat. He gasped and swam up and up till cool reality broke around his upturned face.

His gaze refocused on the gothi and the karls of his council. To a person, their expressions were wary. A few had stepped back. Others rested their hands on the meager weapons hanging from their belts.

Odin had warned him this would happen when she was awake. She would try to influence him, toy with him and play his emotions just as Bragi plied the harp. What he should have done, he realized, was spend more time with her awake in his mind. That practice might have made his current situation easier.

She'll take advantage of your emotions—she'll play on them, try to manipulate you. She's very far from being a dumb beast. That's what Odin had told him. He had also said, *The runes work, to a point. You must learn to let her speak, but don't let her sway you.*

And that was something else it would have been good to practice. But it didn't matter right now. Let her glare and threaten. She couldn't take control unless he let her. She was his tame disir. His fylgja. She would obey him. He hurled that thought down at her. Her long, slow-swimming arcs continued.

To buy himself another moment, he raised a hand to shield his eyes against Sól's glare. He'd been too silent too long, staring off into the empty air. Who wanted a jarl prone to erratic, disturbing silences? No one.

"Your pardon, Gothi. Good karls and drangr, the sight of you and the unfortunate folk of your town has brought such grief and rage welling up into my heart that I was beside myself for a moment." He bowed slightly from the waist. "My apologies."

When he straightened, they were somewhat more at ease, eyes less narrowed with suspicion.

Still shielding his eyes with one hand, he said, "And poor rescuer that I am, I also forgot to offer what few provisions I have strapped to my saddle."

He turned to see Garilon already approaching. "Knowing you'd want it done, Jarl," Garilon said, "I collected most of the provisions the warband brought with them."

The kjolr handed several heavy bags of provisions and skins of beer to the gothi and other elders as the wind kicked up and swirled snow through their midst.

Vidar smiled and raised a hand by way of introduction. "Gothi Dorvath, this is my kjolr, Garilon. For a time he led the Einherjar during the waning years of the Last War. Now he is my second-in-command."

"Gothi." Garilon gave a respectful nod that included the karls and drangr standing just behind the town's chief.

"Thank you, Kjolr." The gothi accepted the provisions with a smile and age-knotted hands. He stepped back and handed them off to those behind him.

And with that simple gesture, Vidar noted, much of the unease drained away like water after a heavy rain.

"Jarl, as you ordered, the warriors are assisting the townsfolk as best they can with what little supplies and water we brought," Garilon said. "The others watch both for our scouts' return and for sign of the enemy. By the looks of it, we should also see what spare blankets or other gear the warband has. And if I may, Jarl, I recommend we get everyone moving."

"I agree, Kjolr, thank you." Vidar drew nearer to the gothi. "If you and your council would walk with us, we'll find what shelter we can alongside your people. And then you can tell us what happened."

7

Odin

Odin folded his arms across his chest. "How much longer is this going to take, Baldr?"

"It's not seidr, Father. It takes a little time to work." Baldr held a metal dish in front of Heimdall and wafted pungent gray smoke into his slack face.

It certainly wasn't magic. If he'd just used his healing charm, Heimdall would already be awake and telling all he heard—and probably vomiting the foul contents of his stomach onto the floor.

Frigg set a hand on his arm, no doubt a gentle attempt to urge patience. But if the Jotunn had attacked and Vidar needed help, every moment counted.

He gestured for his baresarks, Gulfinn and Rata, to approach from where they stood, watchful, by one of the side doors.

Before he had left, he'd instructed his baresarks to help Frigg. Gulfinn was one of the oldest, while Rata was one of the youngest. Gulfinn was burly, his beard grizzled and his forearms scarred above the runes tattooed around his wrists and neck. One of his nostrils was notched from a draugr's bone blade. Rata was every bit as strong as Gulfinn despite her comparative slimness, the elm to Gulfinn's stout ash, and with a glare sharper than a bared knife. Her leathers hid the blue tattoos around her wrists, but those encircling her throat were visible.

Together, though either could have done it alone, they hauled the dead drunk Heimdall upright.

He tapped an impatient cadence against his left arm. "How long before it works?"

"Not long," Baldr said.

"I'll clear the hall." Frigg strode the edge of the raised platform where the jarls sat. "Friends and guests," she began, "Jarl Heimdall's unique powers of perception..."

And that was all he heard, for he looked up toward the hall's doubled roof at the first whispers of the familiar, croaking voices inside his mind. At its highest point, the upper roof was about six spear lengths high. A gap yawned between the point where the lower roof ended and the overhanging upper roof began. That gap, maybe a sword's length tall, let smoke from the hall's fire pits rise up and out. It also let in a bit of the day's mellow, nearly midday sunlight. And right now, it also allowed his ravens to enter.

They hopped in, croaking, heads darting sharply. Then they dropped, wide black wings snapping out, to glide past the dozens of stout, intricately carved yew pillars to the table next to Heimdall. Odin drew his seax from the small of his back and cut long strips of meat from one of the blackened roasts set there. The ravens settled on his shoulders as he fed the meat to them, their beaks clacking in the hall's silence.

He whispered into their minds, *Fly to Vithi. Swiftly. Let me know when you arrive.*

Loudly, they croaked their assent.

Heimdall spluttered and coughed.

Go now. He gestured with his chin.

In a clatter of wings, the ravens launched themselves and flew out.

Heimdall thrashed, his teeth bared in a golden snarl. For just a moment, the baresarks struggled to hold him. But then the set of their shoulders changed, and they pinned his arms against the table.

Baldr sighed. He reached into one of the pouches at his waist, withdrew a pinch of something and ground it between his fingers under Heimdall's nose. Almost immediately, the flaxen-haired Aesir relaxed.

"That reaction happens sometimes with that particular mix of herbs," Baldr said. "He'll be more lucid in a moment. He'll feel like he ran ten leagues, though."

Odin shrugged. "I just need to know what he heard."

Frigg stepped up beside him again. This time, she touched his arm with a neat, tawny hand.

"Where did you send them?" she asked, gesturing toward the ceiling.

"To Vithi. Thank you for clearing the hall."

She nodded once and was about to speak, but Heimdall sighed loudly as his eyes crawled opened, showing bloodshot orbs that were focused either very far away or very deeply inward.

Odin glanced at Baldr, who nodded back. Speaking as he might to a dazed man on a battlefield, he said, "Heimdall. Can you hear me?"

Heimdall coughed. "Aye, Alfather. I can." His head wobbled, and his bloodshot eyes refocused downward to stare blankly at the table's smooth, stained wood.

At least he had some shame. "What did you hear, Heimdall? Whose horn?"

"Vithi's, I think, Alfather." Heimdall coughed again, wincing.

"You think so? I need you to be certain."

Heimdall's head fell forward, his eyes tight shut, and he doubled his fists over his ears. "Help me, nephew. The sounds, I can't keep them out."

Baldr crouched and put his hand on Heimdall's shoulder, turning him away from the table so that they faced each other. "I will, Heimdall. I'll do whatever I can to help you regain the control you lost."

"That Loki stole." Heimdall's voice was a low growl.

What *had* Loki done to Heimdall? Back less than a night, and he was already regretting being away for so long.

Baldr pinched more herbs onto a metal plate, ground them with a pestle, and poured them into a small cup of ale.

He frowned. "More ale?"

"No, this is beer," Baldr said with a wink, offering the cup to Heimdall. "Drink this, uncle."

Frigg laughed and swatted his arm. It was the first happy sound he'd heard her make since his return.

Heimdall slurped it down, and still more of the tension drained out of his shoulders.

Baldr took the cup back and held it up. "This amount is nothing compared to what's already in him. It'll just help get these additional herbs into him, and they'll ease the ill effects of the ones I already gave."

Heimdall shifted back to the table and placed his hands flat against it as if to steady himself. "I'm all right now." His voice was thick, and he looked up at him, his eyes red and watery. "I'm sure it was Vithi's horn. Whoever sounded it called for reinforcements. Twice."

Odin nodded. "Good. Thank you." He pointed at Gulfinn and Rata. "Drag Heimdall up to the promontory and face him toward Háls. Pry his eyes open if you have to, but I want him looking. One of you come tell me what he sees. I'll be with the Einherjar."

The pair of baresarks nodded. "Yes, Sigfather," Rata said. "And after? Where should we bring Jarl Heimdall?"

He shrugged. "Throw him over the wall, for all I care."

"Odin!" Frigg exclaimed.

"Fine," he said with a shrug. "Take him to his house, and let him sleep it off."

The baresarks hauled Heimdall to his feet, draped his arms over their shoulders, and dragged him to the nearest side door.

He glanced at Frigg. "Did Saglund send out the Einherjar earlier?"

"If they did, the gatekeeper didn't inform me," she said, implying that wouldn't have happened.

He frowned and thumped the table with his fist. If Vidar had called for help, the situation was serious. Probably. Vidar was smart, clever, but sometimes a little too cautious. But to call for help...

"We need to speak about him, Odin," Frigg said in a low voice, touching his arm.

"Vidar?"

"No, Saglund. We need to rein him in."

"Perhaps. But it will wait until I return."

8

Frigg

Frigg wrapped her arms around herself, containing her rising disbelief. Her rising irritation. Her rising sense that no matter what she did, Odin would do as he pleased, leaving her to contain whatever followed in his wake.

"I cannot believe you're leaving again after you literally just promised not to." She hated the rising note in her voice and forced it down. "Send the Einherjar. It's why we have them."

Odin gestured at the door through which Heimdall had just been dragged. "You heard him. Vidar called for help. I'm the only way any reinforcements can get there in time."

She guided him back toward where Baldr stood repacking his satchel. "Vidar can take care of himself. You saw to that long before you left. You are needed here."

He shook his head. "Vidar wouldn't call for help unless he felt it necessary."

The familiar weight of having to do everything alone settled back onto her shoulders. "And what about the reason I summoned you back? You're needed here."

"I'm fine, Mother," Baldr said, tucking the last pouch of herbs away. "Really."

"You weren't fine this morning. The whole reason he's back is to help you."

"Then I'll go with him. If the dream—or whatever it is—happens again, Father can deal with it then."

"What, on horseback? Or right before a battle?" She shook her head sharply and jabbed a finger downward. "No, you need to stay here."

As she glared at her son, his hair turned the same fiery gold as the witchlamps glowing behind him. The glow reddened, and a fire seemed to rise, crackling around his head and spreading above it to unfurl like a ship's sail. And then, bellying out before the wind, the vision burst into flame.

Frigg stumbled backward, shock stealing the breath from her lungs. She was... *astride a ship, flames licking at the gunwales and crawling up the rigging and skittering across the sail. The flames roared and rushed across the planks beneath her feet, but she felt no heat.*

Baldr's face swam into view behind the flickering flames. He sat straight-backed on a chair set beside the mast. The flames lay at his feet like hungry hounds. He was speaking to her, but the hounds snapped his words from the air. Grave goods littered the deck, gold cups melting in the heat. The ship's timbers cracked and popped, the paint curled, and ash swirled. Yet still she couldn't hear him. She was about to press forward when the flames leaped to her son's face, devouring his flesh and leaving blackened bone behind. And still he kept speaking, but she still couldn't hear him, not above the roaring flames and her own growing scream. He raised a skeletal hand in farewell and she stumbled backward, falling, hands...

... pressing her hard against one of the hall's wooden pillars. She thrashed against them as she heard her own voice screaming, "No, no, no..."

***

"Here, Father, give her this."

Frigg felt the cool rim of a cup pressed to her lips. The world spun, but she let the liquid pour in. Even with the tartness typical of Baldr's remedies, it coursed, cool and sweet, to her belly, where it vanished into her body's warmth.

As the spinning slowed, she forced her eyes open. She focused first on Odin's craggy face and deep-set eyes, warm with concern like the sun above a glacier. No flames danced above his head. A carving of an open-mouthed wolf yawned wide over his shoulder. Her stomach twisted, and she shuddered and closed her eyes.

Odin's calloused hand brushed her forehead and smoothed her hair. She felt whiskers against her cheek and a gentle kiss.

"Give your mother and me a moment please, Baldr," Odin said.

"Of course," he replied.

She counted his steps—eight, ten, a dozen.

Odin's voice was close to her ear, calm but tight with concern. "What did you see this time?"

She steeled herself to look past Odin to where Baldr sat at one of the empty tables. But it was just him sitting there, no flames, a concerned look creasing his features.

"Frigg?"

"How long was I—"

"Not long. Baldr had just finished that remedy when you woke." His voice roughened into a hoarse whisper. "What did you see, Frigg?"

She met his insistent gray eyes and shook her head.

He sighed, sat back, and took her much darker hand in his own. Odd how Baldr favored her coloring, but her second son favored his father's. Their daughter Hermod was somewhere in between.

"The more I know, the better I can help. If you don't tell me—"

She shifted and laid her hand on his arm, easing him back. "These visions—and Baldr's dreams—are why I sat upon Hlidskjalf and called for you to come back. That's all you need to know for now."

"All I need—" he raised his hands palms out and straightened. "Frigg, I have to ride out. If it is the Jotunn, then Vidar needs my help.

I've more than enough witchthread to speed the journey both ways. I won't be gone long."

She sniffed. "You've said that before."

"I mean it."

"You always say that, too." She brushed away the gritty residue of tears she hadn't even realized she'd shed.

She looked past Odin again at Baldr's tawny, clear-eyed face that blended the best of her features with the best of Odin's. He was watching them closely and seemed more relaxed now that she was moving and talking.

"Tell me what you saw," Odin said again. "It may help."

An agonizing doubt stabbed at her. "We made sure he couldn't die, didn't we?"

"We absolutely did. It's been proven a hundred times over—and we'll prove it yet again in two weeks' time." He gripped her hands tighter, voice taking on a worried note. "Please, Frigg, what did you see?"

When had saying what she saw ever done any good? Certainly not as a girl, when she had freely spoken of her visions. She shook her head and smiled tightly.

"Frigg, the more I know, the faster I can solve this mystery."

Unbidden, the imaginary flames leaped back across her son's face, devouring the fine, whole flesh and leaving behind a blackened ruin that framed bright teeth, white and clean. She squeezed her eyes shut and leaned back against the wall, lashing the memory down as she might a billowing sail.

Baldr could not die. He couldn't. She and Odin had made sure of it.

But if that were true, why was she seeing what she saw? Her visions had always come true—not always literally, but whatever see saw always came about. Always. So did that mean he would die on a ship? And if so, why had he been surrounded by grave goods?

Maybe he was safer in the grasslands—safer than here, where the river Silfr ran right outside the gates and down to the Thund.

"I changed my mind. Go ahead and take him with you."

"What?"

"Take Baldr with you."

"But just moments ago you were—"

She raised a hand. "I know what I said. But you're right. If the Jotunn have attacked, you do need to go."

She beckoned for Baldr to approach. He knelt and touched cool fingers to her wrist, which pulsed in time with her heart.

"I'm fine, Baldr."

"But—"

She laughed. "You two are more alike than either of you would like to admit. Listen to me. I'm fine. Yes, my visions are returning— slowly and fitfully, but they're coming back. They can't be cured, and talking about them doesn't help anyone. I see what I see. Once I get used to having them again, these little episodes won't happen. All right?"

She looked from one to the other. Odin's face was creased with annoyance. He'd never liked that she kept what she saw to herself. Baldr's expression was simple concern.

"You should go with your father, Baldr. Vidar or his warriors may need your skills."

"If the Jotunn have attacked after all this time and all the progress we've made," he said, "then we're going to need answers from them, too."

"Indeed we will," Odin said. "So we should be about our preparations. If you're sure you're all right, Frigg."

To prove it, she stood. "I am. Go swiftly."

Odin stepped close, hugged her, and kissed her cheek.

Into his ear, she whispered, "Just make sure you bring him back unhurt."

"What can hurt him?" he whispered back. "But I will, Frigg. Count on it."

When he stepped away, Baldr embraced her. To him, she said, "Keep an eye on your father. He has a tendency to wander off."

Odin frowned, but Baldr laughed and kissed her cheek.

She watched the pair of them walk across the hall to the side door. Even their strides were similar.

She leaned against the pillar, ignoring the wicked leer of that carved wolf. When Odin's hand was on the door, she called out, "Send Gná in, please. She's probably waiting right outside."

Her family appeared to be safe. But after what she'd just seen, Frigg had no desire to be alone.

9

Vidar

Vidar tugged his cloak more closely around him as a gust of wind tried to claw it open. It was difficult to appear authoritative while shivering.

He cleared his throat. "Gothi, good council members of Háls. My kjolr here reports that your people—our people—are being seen to. We'll be ready to move out before Sól rises another handbreadth. So, gothi, if you're ready, please tell me as much as you can about what happened."

The small fire crackled and popped as the aged gothi rose to his feet, his back to the largest boulder. "Again, thank you, Jarl Vidar, for coming so quickly. I take it Jako is all right?"

Vidar nodded. "Yes, Gothi Dorvath. Your man is exhausted but safe."

"Aye," Garilon added, "he ran into some merchants on the main road. They didn't believe him but let him swap out his horse so he could get to Vithi that much quicker. He would've come with us, but the Jarl forbade it."

"Those merchants were headed here to pick up my goods." Another man, tall and well groomed beneath a liberal coating of dirt and ash, leaped to his feet. A silver torc hung around his neck; more silver glinted beneath the cuffs of his shirt and heavy coat. Multiple rings glittered on his fingers.

"What are you going to do, Jarl?" the trader demanded in a sharp high-pitched voice. "Or more precisely, when will you ride into my town, extinguish the fires, and save my—our—goods? I have a warehouse stocked with pelts. They were to be shipped out this morning! I'll lose thousands of silver."

Garilon stepped toward the trader, pointing a blunt finger. "You'll put a civil tongue in your mouth when you address the jarl."

"And if I don't?" The trader waved a ringed hand dismissively toward Vidar. "We had no choice in his being jarl. Another of the Alfather's brood set up above us. Another time-honored custom broken at our expense. We pay our tribute, and this is what we get?" He jabbed a finger at Vidar. "We're paid up. Do your part, get down there, and save what's left of the town."

Before the shock at the trader's words had really hit Vidar, Garilon had grabbed a double fistful of the man's heavy shirt and shoved the trader back a pair of steps toward the boulders sheltering them.

"Stop, Kjolr. Release him."

Garilon dropped him. The trader stumbled as he regained his balance. Garilon stepped back, fists unclenching.

"Check on the warband, Kjolr, and the scouts," Vidar said.

Garilon nodded and stalked off toward where the garrison moved among the townsfolk.

That had to have been an act. You didn't become hersir of the Einherjar, even for a short time, unless you were able to control yourself. So why had Garilon done that? To cut off criticism? To remind them of Vidar's authority? Both?

And more to the point, why hadn't he himself acted as swiftly as Garilon? His father would never have suffered such brazenness.

Vidar raised his voice, loud and sharp against the building wind. "You're right, trader. I am one of the Alfather's sons. You're also right that, against custom, you had no choice or say in my appointment to this district." He stepped closer to the fire. "However, the Alfather may appoint who he wishes when he wishes. You should be grateful —and I'm sure you are—that he so seldom invokes his prerogative."

He held the trader's gaze and then looked at each karl ringing the fire.

Inclining his head respectfully to the town's chief, he continued. "None of that wipes out my obligation to this town or to any other town or village within Vithi's borders. When I received word of this calamity, I mustered the warband, sped here, and called for reinforcements from Gladsheim. The Einherjar ride as we speak."

He met the trader's gaze again. The man oozed belligerence. Vidar kept his tone even, though his own anger rattled within the scabbard of his mind. His fylgja saw it, and he felt her own rage trickle in to feed his own.

It seemed they were two separate beings after all.

He gritted his teeth, flung her anger back down at her, and forced a smile to his face. It vanished a moment later.

"I stand here ready to fulfill my duty as jarl to your town. But I won't be rash. I need to learn what happened. But so far, all you've done is interrupt your gothi and delay me." He pointed up at the sky. "Sól begins her daily descent within the eitt, at most. I need to get you and the townsfolk moving toward even the slight shelter of these few scattered trees along the road. But I also need to know how many Jotunn attacked and what clan they were—or what tribe, at least."

He took a step toward the trader and punched a finger at him. "So sit back down, shut up, and let your gothi tell me what happened."

Still belligerent, the trader looked ready to say something else. Vidar kept up his glare. The Aesir tugged at the hem of his heavy shirt, adjusted the silver bracelets around his wrists, and fingered his rings as if emphasizing to Vidar who he was. Then he shrugged and sat back down. He looked around the circle, back straight, head high, daring the other karls to say something. None met his eye. Their faces were all expressionless.

Vidar waited a long moment. Garilon stepped back into the silence around the campfire, met Vidar's eye, and shook his head.

Still no sign of the scouts. Not necessarily bad, but it didn't help him make his decision.

Suppressing a sigh, Vidar said, "Now, Gothi Dorvath, if you please, tell us what happened."

The gothi cleared his throat and shot a stern look at the trader. "As I was about to say, today—well, yesterday morning, actually—was the day I travel up to the mines for the monthly inspection. Everything was normal. A typical quiet winter morning. We reached the forest road—"

"Excuse me, gothi, but who is we?" Vidar asked.

"Apologies, Jarl. I was riding up with the next three-day shift. The mine's too far off to make daily trips, so every three days we change shifts. This was one of the switch days. Well, yesterday was."

"No permanent crew at the mines?"

"No, Jarl." He shifted his feet as if uncomfortable. "The wardens switch out along with the mining crews. There's only ever a short time that the mine's untended. The returning crew and their replacements typically meet up somewhere along the road. Come to be a game, since where the two crews meet on the road shows who got up earlier or was moving quicker. Anyway, leaving the mine untended's never been an issue. Not in my life. Not until now. But no one ever expected Jotunn to show up here in Vithi."

No, indeed. "No criticism intended, gothi. I was just trying to get a sense of things."

"A sense that maybe you should've gotten before now," groused the trader.

This time, a few other voices rumbled their assent.

Vidar let the comment pass. He gestured for the gothi to continue.

"Anyways, we were nearly at the mine when things got strange. Now, I served in the army. I've seen battle with the Jotunn and with those savages to the far south. It wasn't anything in particular— maybe how quiet it was or just that sense of eyes on you, you know?"

Vidar nodded, as did Garilon and several of those seated around the fire.

The gothi paused, took a breath, and composed himself. "Well,

Jarl, we rounded that third switchback, the wide, looping one, and right there we saw the mining crew. Dead. Arrows in most of 'em. Carts overturned. Horses slaughtered in their traces. Road blocked. We were frozen there. Shocked, you know?"

Dorvath was lost in the moment now. "And that's when they hit us. Elkin was right beside me. He dropped, screaming and coughing blood. Gefr was behind me on my other side. Another arrow took him. I'd be dead too if Rollo hadn't dragged me down and pulled me back behind our own wagons. Drengi shouted something behind us —'Form up, form up!' or something. He was always one to talk like that. He died before the rest of us could drag him to cover. After that surprise, we just kept our heads down and tried to figure out where the arrows were coming from. I knew we had to move, but there were just too many arrows flying..."

The gothi's eyes stared out past the fire. Vidar gave the old man a moment before jogging him from his reverie. "Did you see how many Jotunn there were, gothi? What tribe?"

The man blinked, shook his head, and brought a gnarled hand up to wipe at his eyes.

Vidar plowed on. "All right, that's fine. Are any of those Aesir you were with still—well, did they make it off the mountain? It would be helpful if we spoke with them, too."

One of the karls stood, leaning on a stick to help herself up. An older woman, graying hair pulled back in long braid, she held her back straight and wagged a finger fiercely at Vidar. "Just hold on now. Jarl or not, show respect for the dead. The gothi—all of us—lost many friends and family today. Lost more than that. Trader Farmann here is an ass, but he wasn't all wrong in what he said before."

This time, almost all of those seated rumbled their assent. Several threw heated glances at him. Vidar didn't know what to say. He'd thought his questions relevant enough. And time wasn't on their side. Surely they could see that.

"Good woman—"

"Karl Ynesa," she corrected, voice knife-sharp. She swept an arm in a wide arc. "My family owns most of the logging in this area, which you'd know if you didn't sit back at your fort building odd instruments and staring up at the sky. Oh, I've heard the tales. We all have. And when I first did, I said no good'll come of that. And sure enough, no good has."

The other karls nodded in agreement. Several others clambered to their feet, angry looks sprouting on their faces. Farmann looked around smugly. The gothi had regained his composure and seemed to be trying to still the rising discontent.

Vidar raised his hands, palms patting the air as if that might calm them. "Please. Karl Ynesa, Trader Farmann, and..." Panic struck as he realized that despite being jarl of the district for twenty-seven winters, he didn't know the names of those on this town's council. "... and other good karls," he finished lamely. "I assure there is no connection between—"

He was interrupted by a shout from one of the other karls. "What if those Jotunn attacked us because of—well, whatever unnatural things you're doing in that fort of yours? Eh?"

A few others echoed his sentiment.

"Don't be absurd..." Vidar began.

"Don't you talk to me like that," the karl continued. He was middle-aged, stout, and voluble. "Jarl or not, son of the Alfather or not, you're as beholden to us as we are to you. And don't you forget it."

"I assure you, good karl, I have not forgotten it—"

"He doesn't know my name, either," the stout Aesir said, pointing at Vidar and staring around the circle. "He's been jarl for what, almost thirty winters, and he doesn't know my name? Just the gothi's? I bet he had to ask his kjolr there what the gothi's name was, too."

Despite himself, Vidar threw a quick glance at Garilon.

"He did!" the stout man crowed. "You see that?"

Now all of the council members were on their feet, and their voices merged into one loud, rolling rumble of discontent. The gothi's efforts to restore calm weren't even noticed.

With a ringing clap of his hands, Garilon stepped into the circle, putting himself between Vidar and the council. In what had to be close to his battlefield voice, he said, "Karl Ynesa. Karl Gunnar. Trader Farmann. Gothi. And you other good karls. Please. Sit. We know you're distressed. Beyond distressed. Hungry. Exhausted. Grieving both for lost loved ones and lost livelihoods alike."

Garilon gestured toward Vidar. "As the jarl said, he's here. I'm here. His warband is here. You may not have heard it, but before we met up with you on the road, the jarl commanded me to signal the Einherjar. He saw that black smoke rising above your town and called for them right then. So all the way back in Gladsheim, Heimdall heard that horn's sharp cry. Reinforcements ride our way even now. But even before they arrive, the jarl and the warriors he brought will be your shield—and spear, if it proves necessary."

Vidar stood as still as the boulders around them. This must be why his father had placed Garilon here with him.

"As for Jarl Vidar's questions, Karl Ynesa, well, they need to be asked. And answered as best as possible. We need to know what we face. It's past midday now, so we've only a few more hours of good light. We need to get you and the townsfolk sorted, wounds tended, and everyone provisioned as best we can. It's a long ride back to Vithi on an empty road. So even a rough estimate of how many Jotunn we face will help us plan our next move: ride back or right at 'em. The warriors, I mean."

Garilon radiated such calm confidence that the angry tension drained away from the clutch of karls like a flood easing down from its crest. Vidar had seen Odin do the same thing when he spoke with the warriors of the army and the elite Einherjar.

Did he himself even have that talent? Based on this encounter alone it didn't seem so. Was it something he could learn? Was that why Father had sent him here? Maybe. But it had to be why his father had sent a former hersir of the Einherjar to be his second-in-command. He could never have calmed that situation down. Garm's bloody snout, he had to admit he'd created it to begin with.

"All right, then," Garilon said, smiling and rubbing his hands together now that he'd led the council back from the brink. "Now we have that cleared up, let's hear the rest, Gothi. And please understand that both the jarl and I greatly sympathize with your losses here today. Everyone's losses. Don't misunderstand our questions for a lack of caring." He pointed up at Sól, now dipping past her zenith. "Time presses."

Of course, Garilon hadn't mentioned they'd only been able to bring half the garrison. Nor had he mentioned that the Einherjar from Gladsheim were at least a full night away, even assuming they rode hard. The Einherjar from the western garrison were much closer, but he wasn't confident they would ride out—not without getting permission from Saglund in Gladsheim first.

No, it was much more likely that he and his warriors were on their own, at least for a full day. Maybe longer.

Vidar's attention fell back on the karls and the gothi. Their circle had closed around Garilon, and they were all speaking animatedly with him now. They seemed to have forgotten Vidar was even there. He didn't know quite how to take that. Part of him was relieved the pressure of performing as jarl was off him, but a large part of him remained annoyed.

Should he force them to acknowledge him?

Better not to. Garilon would get the information they needed, and then he'd inform Vidar. But what the sharp-tongued Ynesa had said dug at him. He was more comfortable staring up at the stars or tracking Muspell's sparks than touring his district and getting to know the people for whom he was responsible.

Getting angry at seeing their suffering firsthand had been a childish response. It was easy to get upset when you faced something awful. But thirty-three winters ago, Odin had dragged him away from following his curiosity wherever it led, and this was why he'd done it. Gladsheim needed leaders.

Did he have what it took to become one?

10

Odin

"And that's all he said, Gulfinn? That the Jotunn were about to attack Vidar and his warband?"

"Yes, Sigfather. And then he collapsed."

So it was the Jotunn. Odin nodded. After forty winters, they were picking another fight—which made little sense, because they could not hope to win it.

"Yes, Baldr said that might happen." He clapped Gulfinn on the shoulder. "You and Ráta did well. Heimdall's where now?"

"Ráta's carrying him back to his house, as you ordered."

"Good, good. Join her. Take shifts until he wakes. When he does, I want him looking into Utgard. And listening, too. This Vithi invasion may herald a new war."

"Very good, Valfather." Gulfinn thumped his chest in salute and turned to go.

"Hold a moment, Gulfinn."

Gulfinn was one of his oldest baresarks. Grizzled, scarred, loyal; terrifying when the spears danced. He had a strong fylgja and had worked out a balance with her—that last unteachable test of becoming a true baresark. The test that most failed the first time.

He indicated the still-gathering Einherjar with his chin. "What's happened with these men? Have they grown soft, or have I just been gone too long?"

One of Gulfinn's hands came up to smooth his beard. When he spoke, his tone was flat. "Two winters after you left, Hersir Saglund suspended the requirement that those selected prove themselves on the battlefield. Instead, he created a trial. Any may join the Einherjar so long as they pass it."

"I see."

Odin had created the Einherjar before Gladsheim had even been founded. At first, he'd just intended to honor those in his warband who fought on alone when their shieldmates fell. But after dozens of battles across hundreds of passing winters, the ranks of Einherjar had grown until they'd become a small fighting force of their own, frequently sent out to reinforce Gladsheim's army.

"The trial emphasizes weapons prowess and endurance over the span of a couple nights. Many fail, but many pass." Gulfinn shrugged and met his eyes. "Those who do join the shields. Most seem proficient and seem brave enough."

No mere trial could recreate what it took for a warrior to keep fighting when the shieldmate beside them fell to Jotunn spears. Or worse. Being Einherjar wasn't about being the best with weapons or being able to run farther or faster. It was about continuing when others gave up. Einherjar never gave up. Training might expose that vein, but no one knew how deep it ran until that moment when, faced with impossible odds, a small voice inside each warrior said, "No. Not me."

Odin nodded. Gulfinn had made his point. "And your fellow baresarks, where are they?"

"Ráta and I are here, of course. Bruni and Aldis went to Alvheim at Freyr's request. Kolbrandr still guards the Breach with the army."

"Alvheim?"

"Yes, Valfather. Several Alvar villages were sacked. Freyr feared that the Svartalvar had returned. He requested our help. I sent those we could spare."

Odin snorted. There was no chance of Svartalvar attacking. He'd taken them too far away.

"You don't want Ráta and I with you now, Sigfather?" Gulfinn asked, a brief grin shining through a beard shot through with more gray than Odin recalled.

"No, I need you here to protect Gladsheim and the Almother." He gestured toward the hall he'd built for the Einherjar. "And because I'm taking these warriors with me. Once I give their hersir the kick he clearly needs."

***

The massive iron-banded main doors of the Einherjar lodge were thrown wide. Odin strode inside without breaking pace. The light of the midday sun puddled on the wide floor planks. When the city was founded, these floors had been ash and dirt.

The hall's bowels were poorly lit with reflected light from the polished shields suspended from the rafters—the shield of each Einherjar who had died since Odin had created the group.

Saglund, the current Einherjar hersir, loomed over a table set to the right of the entrance. Tall and thickset, Saglund held a long stick with a curve at the end. Tied down at one end of the table was a thick roll of what Odin presumed were other maps.

Three Einherjar stood with their hersir. By their bearing, Odin assumed they were being groomed to lead as kjolrs. Young, too. Probably scampering children when he'd ridden out of Gladsheim twenty winters ago.

They were all muttering over carved markers and polished stones, pointing at some even as Saglund pushed them around with his long stick, grouping some while sending others off to another spot on the map.

So engrossed in their task were the men that they took a moment to realize he was there. Shock leaped to the kjolrs' faces.

"Leave us," Odin said to the three kjolrs, his gaze fixed on Saglund.

He could almost taste their hesitation as they first glanced at their hersir. To his credit, Saglund immediately made a sharp gesture toward the door.

"You heard the Sigfather."

He wasn't surprised they had first looked to Saglund; he was the only hersir they'd ever known while they'd only heard tales of the Sigfather.

That would change soon enough.

The kjolrs saluted and faded back across the hall.

"My apologies for that, Sigfather. How may I be of service?"

Odin gestured at the markers. "What are all these?" he asked, even though it was obvious.

"They show the locations of all Einherjar warbands, Sigfather."

There were four markers on the square denoting Gladsheim.

"My ravens fly west even as we speak," Odin said. "They've made no report of Einherjar riding to Vithi."

Saglund cleared his throat. "Ah, no, Sigfather."

"The Almother ordered a warband sent when the bird from Vithi arrived. That was this morning, Hersir. You might remember because I had just arrived back in Gladsheim."

"With respect, Sigfather, it takes time to ready a warband and move others into new positions to cover the gap. And as I had not yet received confirmation from the garrison in western Vithi—"

"You doubt my son's word? Or his need?"

Saglund paled, even in the poor light. "No, Sigfather. I was awaiting word while I moved the Einherjar garrisons around to ensure that all of the districts were—"

Odin held up a hand. "Has the army or the Einherjar at the Breach reported anything else out of the ordinary?"

"No, Sigfather. But the midday bird has not yet arrived. It is possible, given the attack in Vithi, that the Jotunn massed out of sight of the Breach and have already attacked. I thought it prudent to wait for the bird before dispatching warbands from Gladsheim."

Odin held Saglund's gaze for a long moment. The man had aged well. Stocky, but not run to fat. No stoop or palsy in the hands. Beard going gray, but so was his own.

"Who commands the Einherjar, Saglund?"

"You do, of course, Sigfather."

"And in my absence?"

"Hár Frigg—the Almother."

"And the Almother ordered a warband sent to Vithi, did she not?"

"Yes, Sigfather. But prudence—"

Odin leaned in, and Saglund fell silent. "Get outside and get those Einherjar moving, Hersir. I want a column formed and ready to ride before Sól's shadow shifts another hand's breadth. And you will ride with us, I think. With me. I want to see how these new Einherjar perform."

Saglund's face stiffened into a mask. "Yes, Sigfather."

***

Odin rummaged through his satchel and withdrew a pair of silver shears and a spindle. When he held it up to the sunlight the witchthread glowed yellow. His wolves, Freki and Geri, sat before him, pink tongues lolling as they waited.

He unspooled a double arm's length of thread, snipped it, and replaced both spindle and shears in the satchel while holding the length of thread to one side. The strand of witchthread floated in the breeze.

Pinching one end of the thread between thumb and forefinger, while holding the other to his lips, he focused his mind and sang. A golden glow ran down the thread. When the entire length was alight, he flung one end through Freki's chest. His fingers danced, and the thread looped back around to pierce Geri's back and emerge from his chest.

He caught that end and tied it to the other. As he did, the wolves' gray fur shimmered gold.

Go now, he whispered into their minds. *Clear the road through the city to the sundown gates. Then head to Vithi, and from there, head to Háls.*

The wolves both woofed and loped off. Odin watched them go. They would run howling along the looping road, past the training grounds and the large halls atop Gladsheim's central hill, descending next to the lower tier and the wide thoroughfare that cut through the city's shops and smithies, weavers and tanneries, way houses and markets. And as the road straightened and they drew close to the western gate they would run past row after row of longhouses like ships packed in a harbor.

The first howl reached his ears, long and drawn out in that eerie way of things receding rapidly into the distance. He stood, brushed grit from the courtyard's stones from his knee. He grinned when a second howl—Geri's—joined his sister's. It was hardly necessary, but Geri enjoyed it. He had probably also nipped at someone moving a bit too slow. The folk were out of practice, just like his Einherjar.

It was time for them all to remember that when the Alfather rode to hunt the Aesir's enemies, his wolves ran ahead.

11

Loki

Loki flung a small stone into the onrushing Franangr.

And will my plan still work now that Ygg is back?

Why wouldn't it? the river seemed to reply. *Perhaps it will even work better. Less delay.*

He frowned at that, stooping to snatch up another small wet stone. The water's voice was a rumbling counterpoint to his thoughts that swam like salmon through all the possibilities that might befall him, his sons, and his wife, because of the path he walked.

He broke his oath and cast your children out. Why would he free them now?

I've never asked. Perhaps he's learned mercy these past hundred winters.

The falling water seemed to laugh at him. *Ygg? Mercy?*

He whipped the second stone into the Franangr. Its splash disappeared into the river's spray as the water plunged into the lake below.

You gave in when you heard the Norns' prophecy, thinking that if you remained free, you might win their freedom.

That's what I told myself. Angrboda never believed me. She fought him —fought the doom he'd set. I should have, too. What kind of father am I?

The kind that still lives.

As do cowards. He hurled a third stone into the river.

You're no coward, Loki. You do what must be done. You always have. Think of all the times you saved the Aesir by doing what they would not do.

That was different.

Was it?

He wiped the spray from his face and pulled his cloak more tightly around him. *Absolutely. I lost my wife and my children because I chose not to oppose my brother.*

Former brother. He broke his oath to you. There is no bond between you anymore.

What if he was right to listen to the Norns?

Perhaps you are a coward after all.

Loki clenched his jaw at that idea, flung back at him; a spear caught and returned. He wasn't a coward. Strength against strength was foolish. But his strength against another's weakness? That was how he won, though sometimes doing that meant taking the long view.

Now that he's back, all these years of planning and preparation are wasted.

Why are they wasted? Ygg is too confident in his strength. And why shouldn't he be? The Jotunn are dying even as the Aesir prosper. But you know what the Jotunn truly plan—while he's made himself blind.

Easier to kill a plague than Ygg.

That's why your plan is perfect.

But he's back now. I'm not certain it will still work.

How can it not? And even if it doesn't, how would you want your name to be remembered? As someone who realized just vengeance? Or as a weakling who instead cowered and shivered by a river?

Loki felt a gentle hand on his arm. Startled, he looked up to see Sigyn peering from beneath a cloak glistening from the river's spray.

"Come inside," she said, her voice nearly drowned beneath the Franangr's.

He was trembling with cold. His teeth were chattering. How long had he been here?

He embraced her, savoring her warmth, and whispered, "Why are you doing this? Why help me? You know what might happen—what he'll do to all of us if we're caught."

Sigyn's arms tightened around him. She kissed his cheek, then pulled back and reached up to rest chill fingers against his brow. They sheltered his eyes from the stinging spray.

A bead of water formed on her nose, freckles dusted her cheeks, and those familiar, lovely crinkles formed around her eyes as she smiled, lines that even the fruit Idunn tended hadn't smoothed away.

She peered straight into the depths of his spirit. "Because I love you."

12

Hodr

"I won't need you this evening meal, Hodr," Alara called from the cooking area of their small longhouse, where she was preparing a midday meal for him. "I wasn't expecting you back for another day or so."

"Turned out my timing was good," Hodr said. "Why that trader won't ride another night up here is beyond me. He'd make twice as much."

He heard the swish of her dress as she moved closer, pulling the smell of warm bread and fish along behind her. He felt her loom close, and a moment later heard the clunks of the stoneware cup and the wooden platter on the table to his side. He sat on the bench built into the wall opposite the main door. It was thrown open so that fresh, cool air mixed with the warmth inside.

She squeezed onto the bench beside him and snaked an arm under his. "I'm glad you're back early."

Hodr let her statement hang in the air, then grinned and squeezed her hand. "I am, too. Kona nearly yanked me off my feet when she smelled the river."

"So you decided to wait?" Her tone was forced, neutral.

He shifted on the bench to face her—not that it mattered, since he couldn't see her. "I thought about just going, but..." He shrugged. "I'm sorry."

"Oh, Hodr," she said, touching his cheek. "It's all right. When you're ready, you'll go."

"I'm not being fair to you, and it's not—"

"You know you get like this every Midwinter, right?"

"Do I?"

"Yes." He heard the smile in her voice. "And it's all right. Really. I knew what I was getting into."

He snorted. "No, you didn't."

"Well, no, not at first. But after that..."

"Maybe I'll go after Midwinter, so I don't get all mixed up in my brother's celebration."

"You say that every winter." She patted his leg. "Go when you're ready."

"If I wait too long, my father will probably be gone again," he said, laying his hand over hers. "And I'm not being fair to you."

"But you haven't talked to your family let alone your father for what, fifty winters? I understand, Hodr, really I do."

He pulled her onto his lap. "Not a night goes by that I don't thank Aegir for sending me to you."

"And I love you, Hodr. I'm a patient woman—but not sixty winters patient," she said, smiling. He knew because he heard it in her voice and felt it in her kiss. She slid off his lap. "Eat up, before it gets too much colder. I'll be in the way house. And don't you come in tonight. I have it covered."

"Well, I have to do something to earn my keep around here," he said, reaching out to try and pull her back onto his lap. He caught nothing except the whisper of her dress.

"Go muck out the stables, then," she called from the doorway. "I can smell them from here."

13

Vidar

"You must have some of Heimdall's blood in you, Canewin," Vidar said, shaking his head. Strain though he did, he couldn't see more than a haze of snow hugging the fields to their north.

She grinned but kept her eyes on the ridgeline, maybe four hundred yards distant and twice as high. "Not that my mother's ever said, Jarl."

"Any sign of the other scouts?"

"Not yet, Jarl. Thought I saw something move up there just now, though." She pointed. "On that flatter area just south of that big sharp rock on the peak."

Sól slipped from behind a cloud and he shaded his eyes and looked, wishing for the farseer he'd built so many winters earlier. Even though it was too big to move without a cart, he could have read runes cut into the stone up there. Though they would be upside down.

"Keep an eye out," he said, lowering his hands.

Beside him, Garilon sheathed his sword with a dull thunk of cross guard against scabbard's throat. He had just flashed sunlight off the blade to tell the incoming scouts where they were.

Vidar cleared his throat. "So, Kjolr, what did the gothi tell you?"

"Well, Jarl, the gothi doesn't know how many Jotunn attacked, what tribe they were, or whether they had shamans or snow bears with them. All he could speak of was lots of arrows and maybe thirty Jotunn attacking as he and the surviving miners fled back down the road toward Háls. I asked several of the men to speak with the survivors. They might get more."

Vidar grunted. His angled shadow on the frozen road was a clear sign that Sól had begun her westward descent. "And your assessment?"

"Honestly, Jarl, based on what the gothi told me, we could be facing anything from a small group—maybe twenty or thirty—to a full warband. Or more." He pointed at the approaching riders. "But they'll have much better information."

"Your pardon, Jarl, Kjolr," Canewin said. "I saw movement again on the ridge. Same place as before."

"The scouts?" Vidar asked.

Canewin cupped both hands around her eyes. "It's—sweet Aegir. It's the Jotunn. And they're—"

Garilon whistled and gestured toward the warriors holding their horses nearby.

"Oh, no!" she said, voice rising sharply. "Jarl, they've rolled spear-throwers into place."

A dozen black lines arced toward them, swifter than birds, followed, a pair of heartbeats later, by the deep twang of heavy bowstrings.

Vidar turned and sprinted back toward the boulder and the scrubby clump of trees surrounding it. Beyond that boulder, the townsfolk had begun massing for the march to Vithi. Garilon was right beside him, shouting orders as he ran.

If the Jotunn were lucky, and had already found the correct range, the spears would kill dozens of townsfolk and wound still more.

He heard the spears shatter against the frozen earth but couldn't see where they'd fallen. No screams reached him, though, which meant they'd probably fallen short.

He looked up when he heard the whistling passage of another flight. This volley also went over the scrubby line of screening trees. A second series of splintering crashes reached his ears.

Garilon shouted at him. "It was about a seventy count between when that first release went overhead and the second. It's been twenty already. I guarantee this next volley will do far more damage."

As Vidar cleared the trees, he could see into the temporary camp. This time, shadows rippled over the ground, followed by multiple crashes as the huge spears slammed to the earth. One black spear split a young man's chest and pinned him to the frozen dirt with a broken cough and a splattering of gore across the snow.

Even some of the misses were dangerous. The spears shattered on impact and threw jagged fragments in all directions. The lucky were simply knocked down in a bloody spray; the unfortunate clutched arms, legs, or chests that had sprouted a forest of splinters.

A small group of his warband galloped toward them, leading the horses they'd left behind.

Vidar looked back westward—the next wave of spears was already arcing toward them black, wingless shapes against the bright sky. The enemy's rate of fire was improving now that they had the range. But how could they see what they were hitting?

On impulse, he looked up. Several birds wheeled in slow, deliberate circles above them. Shamans. Had to be.

The next flight of bolts smashed down. More screams as townsfolk died or were injured. His heart pounded, and his fylgja pounced upward, eager for the fight.

Young Lukr reined in beside him, dust and snow billowing around them. Hrimfaxi whinnied and Vidar mounted, nodding his thanks.

Garilon, already mounted, charged toward the clutch of warriors trying to keep the townsfolk moving southeast away from the ridge.

Vidar dug into his satchel for his spindle, heavy with thread. He unscrewed the metal cap of the hand distaff he wore opposite his sword, slotted the hollow spindle on the handle, replaced the cap, and teased free a long strand of thread. The spindle rattled as it spun free. He blew out a long breath, composing his thoughts. Then he squeezed his legs, and Hrimfaxi trotted right toward the center of the fleeing townsfolk.

In a loud voice, he began singing the galdr Odin had taught him. He forced the power of   the charm out through his lungs and his chest and his mouth.

As he sang, he flung the thread out toward the folk. Quicker than a striking snake, it darted through them, spearing each one through the chest. Not that they could see it. All they saw was their jarl riding through their midst, arms moving as if he were casting a net over and over, fingers dancing, drawing the thread back so he could knot the spell and send it out again, strengthening the weave.

He felt the coming flight of the bolts like an incipient headache. They would land any second now. They had to. He didn't so much sing the galdr now as shout it, willing power into every syllable.

Spears hammered into the panicked townsfolk. One struck a child, knocking the boy face down into the frozen earth. Another hit a young woman. She spun away sideways, her scream cutting off in a horrible explosion of air as the breath was knocked from her. Another struck one of his mounted warriors. The force threw the man from his saddle. More fell elsewhere. Behind him. To his sides. Shrieks went up all around him.

But without exception, the spears did no harm to those they struck. The boy who was knocked down stood up, his eyes and mouth wide. The young woman staggered to her feet, helped up by those near her. The fallen warrior—Helga—clambered up, a burgeoning grin on her face.

All around, shrieks of dismay and fear turned to disbelieving, raucous laughter.

Another wave of spears fell. Again, townsfolk were knocked down, but the spears caused no injury. As long as Vidar sang, as long as he had enough thread, his charm blunted the Jotunn spears and prevented them from biting.

Garilon's voice cut through the noise. "Your jarl's bought us some time. Make it count! Move. Directly east. Now! Move!"

And finally, they did begin to move. They helped each other up.

Vidar watched the birds circle lower. He kept singing, the powerful words tearing at his throat. Another wave fell, this flight clustered tight with the one prior. More townsfolk were hit, but they rose uninjured. It seemed the Jotunn were at the extreme end of their range.

As if mocking that thought, another wave of spears swooped down swifter than a cloud's shadow. He'd sat too long in one place. Throat raw, Vidar sang louder—till a tremendous impact knocked him from the saddle.

The last thing he heard before he hit the ground was Hrimfaxi's defiant whinny.

***

Vidar woke to the sound of leaves rustling in a light breeze. No, not leaves. Voices, whispering, their sibilance masking the words' meaning. He rose from the stillness deep inside his mind, slipped past the fylgja chained within and her calm green gaze, and opened his eyes—only to shut them again, dazzled by the bright blue sky.

"Take another moment or two, Jarl. One of those spears hit you." It took him a heartbeat to place the voice; it was Garilon.

"It's a wonder you're alive and unharmed," Garilon said, "though I expect it was that charm you sang, eh?"

Lying still a moment longer, savoring the earth's cold embrace, Vidar opened his eyes and saw three birds still wheeling high above in long, lazy arcs.

And then, before his mind caught up with his tongue, he said, "Well, not all of it."

Garilon squinted at him. "I've seen your brothers in battle before —the Sigfather too, of course—but never saw any of them take a hit quite like that. Except Thor, and he hardly counts."

Instead of answering, Vidar sat up. The world spun once, twice, and then settled back down where it should be. His right side ached. He moved his arm. Nothing damaged.

A dozen mounted warriors stood around him in a loose circle, facing outward. He glanced up. No more giant arrows.

He pushed himself to his feet, suppressing a grunt. Garilon stood with him, knees popping, one hand out to steady him if he needed it. He didn't. Wouldn't have taken it if he had.

"How long have I been out, Kjolr?"

"Long enough for a couple of men to drag you out of range. Sorry about that mess down your shirt." Garilon grinned briefly.

He felt it now, a wet lump dripping down his back. He loosened his belt to shake out what he could. A bit of slush and dirt was better than getting thumped with a few more spears. He re-belted his trousers, smoothed his shirt and overtunic, and tugged his leather armor back into place. The straps all along the right side of his armor were destroyed, and he pulled it off and threw it on the ground with a snort of annoyance.

"And Hrimfaxi?"

"She's all right. Bit scared when you and she got hit—and you knocked off—but she's smart and well trained. Took off around the line of fallen spears but then came back around. If she had hands, she probably would've picked you up and carried you."

"Good. That's good." He turned slowly in place to take in his surroundings, rather than moving his head. He almost didn't want to ask how many he could have saved if he'd acted sooner, but he did anyway. "How many of the townsfolk? Our warriors?"

"Best count is forty-three townsfolk dead or missing," Garilon said, his voice flat. "Of our men, only two. Rikr died on the ground. The valkyr—Noplin—tending him died too."

He gripped Garilon's shoulder in commiseration. Two men down. And more than forty townsfolk. He looked toward the high ridge. Nothing visible, though it was more distant than the last time he'd seen it—hence the lack of wood and iron rain.

"There's worse news, though, Jarl." Garilon pointed south and west where the high ridge met the plains. "You can just see it there—

that bit of blackness hugging the ground. Seems to be moving, least that's what Canewin says. Any idea what it is?"

He followed Garilon's arm and did indeed see the dark foggy mass hugging the ground. He shook his head. The stars that appeared over his vision made him wish he hadn't.

"Also, Tryggulfr and Harafn reported in. Tryggulfr says there was at least one warband of Jotunn in the forest."

"So that confirms what you guessed."

Garilon nodded. "Yes, Jarl, but I'm wondering if we're facing more than just one. If there's a second or a third..."

It was a good point. If they faced multiple warbands, they should withdraw and cover the fleeing townsfolk. If there was only one, their best option might be to attack. Might be. Successfully protecting several hundred fleeing townsfolk with only sixty warriors against a Jotunn warband that had at least twice as many warriors seemed a losing strategy.

"And one more thing, Jarl. Look at the town. What do you think it means?"

Vidar did and immediately realized what Garilon meant. The tall column of black smoke was entirely gone. It could not have burned out so quickly.

Garilon spat on the ground. "Almost as if the town had never burned."

"I don't know how they did it, Kjolr." Assuming the Jotunn shamans had. Nothing his father had taught him about seidr could explain how they might have extinguished the fires much less why they'd bother.

He looked again at the dark fog hugging the lower ridgeline and then back toward the slowly departing herd of townsfolk. They might live out the night if he and his warband could stop the Jotunn here. Or slow them.

Vidar glanced up at the still circling birds.

"What are you thinking, Jarl?" Garilon asked, tone level.

"They have shamans with them," he said, pointing up. "That's why their missile attack was so accurate. And it means they know how few we are in number."

"So we have a fight on our hands."

"I believe we do." And it was one they'd have to win to protect the townsfolk.

Or die trying.

14

Odin

   We are here, Huginn croaked into Odin's mind.

   Well flown, Odin replied , standing up from cleaning Sleipnir's hooves. *What do you see?*

   Fire and smoke, said Muninn. *Smells of food,* added Huginn.

   My son? The folk of Háls?

   Folk fled, said Huginn. *The fox readies for battle,* added Muninn.

   Odin swore to himself. So it absolutely was an attack and Vidar, riding under his banner of the fox, was about to answer the Jotunn in the only tongue they understood.

   Glancing westward at Sól's descent, he swore again. Even if they left now, they still wouldn't arrive until dawn.

   Have you seen the Jotunn?

   No.

   Keep looking. Shamans may be there, so be wary. I will arrive by dawn.

   Yes, Wing-Father.

   He looked down the long double row of armored Einherjar, all dismounted alongside their horses doing the same thing he was doing—cleaning hooves.

   A few groused and grumped that the thralls had already done it, but one of the aktaumr walking up and down the line cracked those fools about the heads. "You'd trust your life to the work of someone who might hate you? Who might have reason to see your horse stumble, break a leg, and send you tumbling into a tree?"

Even though those aktaumrs were all older, grizzled men, Odin didn't recognize their seamed faces. But they touched their foreheads with respect when they felt his eyes on them.

He bent to finish his task, running his hand down Sleipnir's eighth leg—the second rear leg on her right—past the hock to the hoof. He lifted the hoof and sent the pick round it, checking the crevices. Sound hooves, sound journey.

"And here I thought to find you impatient at my tardiness."

Odin looked up. Baldr had led his horse into the clearing where they were readying for their ride. Sól broke out from behind the lone afternoon cloud and set Baldr's dark blond hair to glowing.

"An impressive sight, is it not, Father?" Baldr gestured toward the line of horsemen behind him. Most were mounting now, heads capped with leather helms chased with silver. Even their shoulder armor, also leather, bore bright ornamentation. They all held their long spears just so, wide brown shield straps across their chests and polished sword hilts hanging from every warrior's belt. All of it glinted in the sunlight.

Clearly, much of the gold the Einherjar were granted each month was being spent outfitting the warriors. Each with a sword? Extravagance. Each with a shining helm? Ridiculous.

He grunted. "Pretty enough, but will they hold an edge? Will they stand in the shields when the Jotunn bear down upon them?"

"I've missed your poetic turn of phrase, Father. It's good to have you back." Baldr's grin seemed to add a bit of extra warmth to the day.

He grumped more. "I don't remember them taking the better part of a day to muster. We need to ride, not fool about with pretty armor, provisions, and tents."

"Forty years is a long time to go without war," Baldr said.

"And so you've all lost your edge, then?"

Baldr grinned. "It's there. Dulled with disuse, maybe—but many old blades will take a new edge." He added more quietly, "If need be."

"Do you disbelieve Vidar's call for help, then? Or Heimdall's eyes?"

Baldr shook his head, golden curls shedding sunlight like dew, his smile fading. "Of course not. I knew that not all the Jotunn wanted peace. The Skrymir's said so himself—and said that he'd dealt harshly with those who opposed the treaty."

"Not harshly enough, it would seem."

"Not even the Skrymir can control all the tribes, let alone those who have stayed away from Jotunheim," Baldr said. "I'm sure many secret places remain in that broken land. Any number of rogue tribes could hide away and we'd never know, especially not with Heimdall the way he's been. One of those rogue tribes might have attacked Vithi. But perhaps we can still find a way back to peace. Too many enjoy it for war to win out."

"Or too few," Odin replied, turning toward the approaching thud of hooves.

"You don't happen to know why the Jotunn attacked, do you, Father?"

Was that a bit of chill in Baldr's tone?

He met his son's eyes. "How would I know? I just got back. And son, the Skrymir—regardless of who holds that title—rules all the Jotunn. There are no 'rogue tribes' in Utgard."

Hersir Saglund reined in a few paces away and saluted. His armor was even prettier than that of the warriors behind him. Silver highlights glistened in the warm sun, and golden eagle wings rose from the helm, all but inviting an axe to catch upon them.

"My warband is ready, Sigfather."

The "my" set his teeth on edge, but he let it pass. He had embarrassed Saglund earlier today and he still needed him—at least until he'd figured out just how broken *his* Einherjar might be.

"Have they been trained to ride with me?" Odin asked. "A fast ride, mind you. We hunt our enemies, and my power will speed the way."

"Yes, Sigfather, they've been trained. Some have even ridden with you before. Many winters ago."

"Good. Give the order."

With a crisp salute, Saglund wheeled his horse and trotted back down the long line of Einherjar calling out the order to prepare for a fast ride as he went.

Odin hauled himself up onto Sleipnir's broad gray back, dug into his bag, and withdrew the spindle he'd just used to enchant Freki and Geri.

He met Baldr's gaze, clear and still like a mountain lake on a calm day. "Last chance, son. Are you sure you don't want to stay and help prepare for Midwinter?"

Baldr laughed. "You're right. Sitting in a dark, smoky hall, staring at the walls, listening to Mother and Nanna plan the feast would be much better. No, I'm riding with you."

Odin grunted. Midwinter was still a week away. Less planning had gone into the Vanir War than these yearly feasts celebrating Midwinter. The festival centered on the main hall in Gladsheim, but celebrations were held at every one of the smaller halls throughout the city and lasted for several nights. "Gladsheim's hall isn't dark. She glitters gold in the light of a hundred torches."

"And all her guests cough, wheeze, and wipe grit from their eyes, thanks to the smoke from all those torches," Baldr countered. "It's a wonder it hasn't burned down yet."

"Nonsense! What smoke there is—if any, mind you—rises high and drifts away," he retorted as he unwound a thread from the spindle. "Besides, Gladsheim's hall is ten times taller than the tallest Aesir. Even the tallest among us couldn't touch the spears framing her roof."

"Not that one would, slick as they no doubt are with the grease from ten thousand meals," Baldr said, a broad shining smile on his face.

Odin sniffed.

The clatter of Saglund's mount's hooves against the packed,

frozen dirt sounded loud above the creak of leather and the stamping of horses in the column. "Sigfather, we are ready."

Odin nodded. "Very well. I will check that the way is clear."

He sent his mind out, seeking Freki and Geri.

I answer, Freki said. *And I,* said Geri.

The way through the city is clear?

Yes, Pack-Father.

Good. Go quickly. Clear the way to Vithi and Háls beyond.

We go.

He nodded to Saglund. "Give the order to move out."

Hersir Saglund lifted a silver horn to his lips and blew a few sharp notes. Before their echoes faded, Odin squeezed his legs together. Sleipnir whinnied, tossed her silvery mane, and began walking. Baldr fell in beside him on his right, Saglund on his left.

And behind them, the first Odin-led warband in more than twenty winters rode out.

Odin extended his hand, and Gungnir flickered into it. He settled the dark ash shaft of the long spear into the crook of his arm and let it slide down until it was braced in his stirrup. He unscrewed the cap at one end of the crossbar below Gungnir's foot-long blade, withdrew the hollow spindle from his bag, slotted it onto the crossbar, screwed the cap back on, and teased free the thread. The spindle rattled and the thread glowed like the dense coils of Sif's hair after Loki had made good his promise to replace it.

He smiled at the memory of that mischief—remembered laughing to himself about it until Thor had returned from the east and flown into a rage. He had ordered his blood brother to make it right. Loki had done more than that. He not only convinced the Svartalvar smiths to weave new hair from the finest gold but also to craft marvelous weapons and devices. Gungnir had been one of them; his heavy gold arm ring was another.

He glanced at Saglund and nodded. The hersir blew another short, silvery sequence into the chill air. The column shifted into a trot, hooves thudding on the frozen road.

Warned by the wolves that the Alfather would be riding, the folk had lined Gladsheim's streets. Children sat upon their parents' shoulders. Older boys and girls sat on the low thatch roofs of the long-houses, smoke rising from the holes cut in the roofs. The most adventurous perched on the high, stout beams of smithies, tanneries, and stables.

He raised Gungnir, saluting the crowds of Aesir lining the street. Their answering roar rolled back from the city's high central hill. The crowds grew thicker as Odin and his warriors wound through the city, following the broad road that looped like a noose around the central hill before heading westward.

And then he had to squint to see anything beyond Sleipnir's ears as they turned into the dazzling sun along the stone road that flowed out Gladsheim's western gate.

***

Odin raised a clenched fist, and Saglund blew the staccato call for make ready. The column thundered through the West Gate, heavy timbers stretched high overhead. Broken stone filled the gap between the inner and outer row of timber. The gate itself, iron-banded wood, stood wide.

Odin braced Gungnir against his stirrup and trusted Sleipnir to lead the column straight along the road. He closed his eyes and listened close for the beat of Sleipnir's eight hooves to overlap the cadence of the other horses. Once he found the rhythm, he raised the witchthread to his lips and sang his charm.

The tip of the thread incandesced brighter than a falling forge spark. He flicked his wrist and sent it plunging forward into Sleipnir's chest. Faster than thought, the thread of light emerged from Sleipnir's side and plunged into the chest of Shining, Baldr's mount. From there, it speared through every horse in the long column until the tip came back around to Odin's hand.

With a deft flex of his fingers, he twisted the tip around itself and flung it back down through Sleipnir and around the column again. Each pass wove the loop tighter around the company of Einherjar.

With each pass, he sewed more strength into the horses. With each pass, he more strongly felt their hearts and lungs and legs beating in time with Sleipnir's.

He urged Sleipnir to move faster, a canter and then a gallop. And still he sang strength into the horses. His spindle rattled around Gungnir's crossbar as the thread unspooled. Another weave, and they moved faster than any horse could sprint. A final cast, and the sound of their hooves became like the ocean's roar. Around them, the landscape blurred into the dull browns and muted greens and brilliant whites of Asgard in winter.

15

Vidar

Vidar sang in the shields, each pounding hoofbeat bringing his warband closer to the onrushing enemy. With a flick of his right wrist, he sent out a thread of magic like a fishing line, weaving it through his warband. Just as he had protected the townsfolk, so too would he protect his warriors.

Ahead, three black longships, dark sails bellied out before the wind, hurtled toward them across the sea of tall grasses. Like embers, their prows burned a deep red where the ground swelled up meet them. The taste of ash lay heavy on the wind. Jotunn shamans had apparently learned a new way to use seidr.

Behind him, his sixty spears pounded across the plains toward the ships in a tight wedge. Garilon was on his right; on his left, Canewin bore the fox-head banner of Vithi. Far behind them, the townsfolk fled alongside the long shadows cast by the setting sun. If his warband could stop the Jotunn, those townsfolk should arrive safely in Vithi within a pair of nights.

And if he couldn't stop the Jotunn?

He blew out a long cone of white breath, emptying his lungs, and closed his eyes. Failure wasn't an option.

He sent his mind coursing inward until he saw his fylgja stretched out like one of the great-cats on Vithi's golden plains. Her green eyes met his. They reminded him of a wide, deep river whose serene surface hid terrible currents.

Which she did, of course. Odin chained disir to men and women to create the baresarks. So bound, a disir became a fylgja, and the spirit's power made a baresark capable of tremendous feats.

But we'll have none of those feats just yet, my fylgja, he whispered in his mind.

She licked her lips in the sleepy way of great-cats and leaped high toward him, green eyes gleaming.

Startled, he invoked the binding rune that his father had tattooed around his right wrist. The distraction caused him to fumble the words of the witcharmor charm he was singing to protect his warband. A gap appeared in the armor.

He panicked for a moment, exhaled hard, and then wasted his next cast on covering the hole he'd sung into the armor.

His heart jumped a second time when he realized that while he'd focused on his weaving, he'd forgotten his fylgja. A hasty glance showed her lying down, eyes bright and watchful. The rune had stopped her upward surge, but what if she'd fought it? His father had said she would test him, would always test him.

He must not stumble again. No mistakes.

He could balance controlling her while fighting. He had to, even though it wasn't something he'd ever done before. Nor was it something other baresarks did. Except for his father.

But if he failed, then his warband failed. And that meant not only the death of every remaining person from Háls, but also a Jotunn warband was free to roam unopposed through Vithi. And if their shamans could spin up these black ships from smoke and ash, and chain the wind to fill its sails, then they could sail wherever they chose. He had to stop them. Now.

The spindle in his hand rattled more loudly. Maybe a quarter of the thread remained. Time to tie it off; he'd need some for the fight itself. He withdrew his silver shears and clipped the thread, then tied it deftly.

With that done, he exhaled long and hard and closed his eyes. To his mind's eye, his witchsight, it looked as if every warrior and horse was clad in golden armor. Now he was ready to deal with the fylgja.

He invoked the rune tattooed around his right bicep. He looked down at his fylgja and met her emerald eyes, taut haughtiness in every line of her body.

Now, join me.

She leaped upward. He rocked in the saddle, feeling as if he were astride a longship bucking on stormy seas. He couldn't help but grin even as he grasped Hrimfaxi's saddle horn and steadied himself. Was this how his brother felt, Mjolnir clenched in an upraised fist and the storm's power hammering through his body?

Above the distant thundering of hooves, he heard Garilon call to him. "Jarl, we're close."

He opened his eyes. The black ships were close enough that he could see the swirling ash and smoke trapped within the net of the shamans' sorcery.

He drew his sword and held it high. He let his fylgja rise higher, like water filling a barrel.

Not yet, spirit, he whispered, *but very soon.*

If he lost his grip on her, or himself, then he had no doubt she would take over. Odin had warned him repeatedly that accepting a disir as a spirit-follower meant never, ever letting her take control. If she did, she could do anything she wanted. She could rampage through Vithi or slip her bonds and flee back to the Ginnungagap for another to claim. But until then, if ever, she was his—if he could keep from becoming hers.

16

Hodr

Hodr leaned the pitchfork against the stable wall, pressed his bunched fists into the small of his back, and arched backward. A dozen pops and cracks chased up his spine. Only three more stalls to muck out.

Were it not for the warm tingle that had spread through his body after he'd eaten the year-old fruit of Yggdrasil, he would have left those three stalls for tomorrow. But with the flush of renewed youth running through his limbs, he felt as if he could clean twice as many more.

And the odd part was he didn't mind the labor. His old self, the warrior, would never have bent his back to clean a stable.

He turned his face up to the sun, enjoying the warmth but hating the remembered yellows and reds pressing against his eyelids.

Kona whinnied at him from the enclosure behind the stable, and he made a shooing gesture. "All right, I'll get back to work. Go play. Enjoy the day."

And judging by the breeze's scrape across the stable's roof, these pleasant winter days were numbered.

His hand found the stable wall, sliding along it till he gripped the handle of the pitchfork. With the tool tapping before him, he stepped into the empty space before him until a dull thud found him the wheelbarrow. When he found its handles, he tossed the pitchfork into the barrow, but it clattered and bounced out, thudding onto the frozen earth.

He sighed. It had taken many winters before he had gotten used to getting around in the dark. Whenever he rushed, he ended up regretting it.

"Can I be of help, karl?" It was one of the house thralls that Alara kept around.

"No. Be about your own work."

"Yes, karl."

He cocked his head, listening to the receding scrape of the thrall's boot leather. He took a short pull from the wineskin hanging from its cord around his shoulders.

Shaking his head, Hodr plugged the wineskin, stepped around the wheelbarrow, and groped for the pitchfork and then placed it so it wouldn't fall out. When he refound the handles, he trundled toward the rich stink of refuse.

No, the warrior he'd been would never have done this work.

17

Frigg

Frigg folded her arms and frowned as Hermod flung her mud-stained cloak against the bench.

"He couldn't have waited?" Hermod asked. "I would've gone with him."

"I didn't know when you'd be back," she said. "And the Jotunn posed an immediate threat to Háls—or perhaps even Vithi itself by now. Your father had to leave when he did."

"Half a day would've made a difference?" Hermod flicked her long dark-gold braid out of the way and put her hands on her hips.

Frigg met the girl's gaze levelly. "Of course it would have. You've been with your uncles. You know the warrior's life."

"I know what it's like to train and ride and scout and freeze near to death—and then to rejoice when I'm back in a warm longhouse. But a full-scale battle?" Hermod sniffed. "I could've helped him in Vithi."

"I don't disagree, Hermod, and I'm sorry that you missed him, but that's how it goes sometimes. He'll be back soon."

"Did he at least ask about me?"

Frigg crossed to the bench and picked up the discarded cloak. "He hasn't forgotten his only daughter, if that's what you're getting at."

"So he didn't."

She folded the cloak in three quick movements and set it down, sat beside it, and looked up at her daughter. Tall and slim as a young elm, Hermod had been training with Gladsheim's army for the past sixteen winters. She stood as if she knew how to handle herself, and it made Frigg proud. She herself had learned to fight bare-handed and with weapons, not that she had done so since the Vanir War.

She patted the bench beside her. "I was as surprised as anyone when Gná brought word this morning that he was back. And when this whole thing with Heimdall and Vidar happened, off he rushed." She shook her head and spread her hands. "What do you want me to say, Hermod? Your father does as he pleases, when he pleases. At least this time, he had a good reason."

"While leaving us all behind," Hermod said, the aggression draining from her stance. She unbuckled her sword, wrapped the belt around the scabbard, and sat. "And what about Hodr? Did he ask about his other forgotten child?"

"I understand you're upset, Hermod. But stop acting like this. Your father hasn't forgotten you or Hodr." *Or me?*

"Really? I was nine when Hodr slipped away in the night. And Father left that same way. Hard to not feel forgotten and abandoned."

"Just because we're not constantly talking about you—or him—doesn't mean that you've been forgotten. Quite the opposite," she said, biting back the urge to lash out and say *try spending twenty winters being responsible for absolutely everything that happens in Gladsheim.* Even so, something in her expression must have given Hermod pause.

"Mother, I'm sorry, I didn't—"

She raised a hand. "I know. None of this is fair, as if the Norns give any thought to that. What matters, Hermod, is how we act. How we respond. Are you going to whine and throw fits? No, of course you're not. You've the best of both me and your father in you. Let all that show through, all right?"

Hermod leaned in and hugged her. She smelled of sweat and leather. "I will, Mother, and I'm sorry. I just wish—"

"That we'd drag Hodr back here or that I'd pitch a fit and make your father stay." She leaned out of the embrace. "I'd sooner try to stop a runaway horse than make your father or your brothers—or you—do something that any of you didn't want to do."

Hermod smiled faintly. "It's just that everything revolves around Baldr, especially these past months. I can't help but believe that's why Hodr stays away. And why Father left in the first place."

She shook her head. "Your father left all that time ago because he enjoys being out there discovering new things—wisdom, lands, people—not because of Hodr or Baldr." And because he preferred wandering to the constraints of ruling—and left her to deal with all of it.

"Do you think he knows?"

"That who knows what?"

"That Hodr knows that Father's back," Hermod said. "Wherever he is."

Frigg wanted to say that she knew very well where Hodr was, in Ifington with a young woman Hermod's age. "It wouldn't surprise me. I had Gná send birds out to all the major towns."

"It'd be nice to see him again, to be a family again. Assuming he stays."

"It would indeed. But for now, you can help me get the city ready for Midwinter."

Hermod frowned. "Ullr said I should—"

"Nonsense. You can take a break from archery or whatever else your uncle said to do. You just don't want the drudgery of planning. And in that, you're more like your father than you think."

She smiled to make sure the words didn't sting. There was time enough for Hermod to learn that she could not anchor her life on her father or her mother—or indeed, on any of her kinsmen. Hermod had to become her own rock.

18

Vidar

Vidar's mind burned as his fylgja's strength coursed through him. Yet it was as if he clutched a slick rock with wet hands in a cold, fast-flowing river. That rock was himself, his body, while his grip was his spirit. His hamr and hugr. But if his grip slipped, she could take control.

And probably would.

"Garm's teeth," Canewin shouted. "They're huge! How can—"

Garilon barked a reproof, and the standard-bearer fell silent.

The black Jotunn longships were as large as any of the ships plying the trade route to Vanaheim. Such ships could easily hold more than a hundred sailors and warriors. But spun as they were from smoke and ash, who could say how many warriors these might bear?

They would find out soon enough.

A grim smile rose to Vidar's lips. A company of Jotunn warriors numbered two hundred men. With his fylgja pouring strength into him, he felt as if he could take them all himself.

He glanced up. Only one bird drifted overhead, high above bowshot. One shaman of the three to track the Aesir's movements?

That meant the others would be using their magic to harry him until the threads he'd woven parted and the charm unraveled.

The sails of the black ships slackened, rippling as if they meant to stop. Garilon's horn sang out sharply over the heavy rumble of hoof-beats. The double column reformed into a narrow spear with Vidar at its tip. Garilon rode at his right and Canewin on his left, one of her gloved hands tight around the spear from which Vidar's fox-head banner cracked and snapped in the wind.

Maybe a hundred yards were left between them and the ships. The ashen sails slackened entirely. The ships halted and then vanished in a cloud of ash and smoke. The stench of burned wood grew overpowering.

The wedge of Aesir, horse and cold iron, accelerated to a gallop. Vidar wrapped Hrimfaxi's reins around his saddle horn, leaving enough slack for the mare to move freely. He withdrew his spindle and pulled free a double arm's length of thread.

Smoke burned his eyes, and he coughed from the thick stench. The drumming sound of hooves filled his ears. Maybe fifty yards left.

He let loose a battle cry. His fylgja slavered, flexing insubstantial limbs, and he felt his strength double again. He dug his fingers into that river rock that was himself and began reciting the runic phrases that would strengthen the leash wrapped round his fylgja's neck.

In between eye blinks, the cloud of smoke and ash condensed into a massive black sphere that spun in the air. It pulsed once. Twice. On the third pulse, it transformed into a thousand black spears that shot toward them. Garilon's horn cried out; he understood the danger.

Thirty-five yards left.

"Steady!" Garilon shouted above the thundering hooves. "Their magic won't—"

The black spears smashed into Vidar, his men, and their horses, bursting into a shower of ash and soot. Horses screamed and balked. Trained though they were, they were blinded. The men coughed and spit, dragging on reins to get their panicked horses back under control.

Maybe it had been luck, but Hrimfaxi had not been blinded by the soot. She'd barreled right through it.

The Jotunn had formed themselves into a shield wall. These Jotunn were armored in much the same way as the Einherjar: boiled leather armor covering chest and arms and split below the waist to partially cover their legs. Leather helms shining with studs. Round shields painted black. Long spears jutting forward.

Vidar realized he was hearing Hrimfaxi's hooves alone. He glanced to either side. No one. It must have been the cloud of ash from the destroyed spears. He'd ridden through it, but his warriors had been caught.

Maybe fifteen yards left. Less than the length of a warship.

He had heartbeats left to decide: Either face the Jotunn alone or circle around and wait, which would give the Jotunn warband more time to ready themselves. And more time for their shamans to bend their seidr against his warband.

No real choice, then.

He pulled witchthread into his hands until the spindle rattled empty. He cast the thread forward, singing the charm his father had taught him. The grasses and roots obeyed, surging up from the dead earth to twist around his enemies' legs.

Cries of dismay went up among the Jotunn shield wall that was four warriors deep and maybe twenty wide, their spears bristling.

In the heartbeat that remained, he drew his sword, readied his shield and charged.

Garilon's horn shrieked from behind a moment later, calling the warriors to reform.

Vidar smashed into the Jotunn. He knocked three down immediately, those in the first line who held the shields. They screamed in pain and fell awkwardly, their legs and feet bound to the ground by his power.

Those in the third and fourth lines rammed long spears into his face and chest. The impacts rocked him back in the saddle, but thanks to his fylgja, none of the blows injured him. And thanks to his charm, Hrimfaxi remained unscathed.

Though there was no pain or blood from the jabbing spears, he gripped Hrimfaxi tight with his legs so that he wouldn't get knocked off. In flashing arcs, he hewed spear blades like heads of grain, but he couldn't quite reach the warriors themselves.

A pair of spears slammed low into his right side. Rather than pulling back, this pair of Jotunn warriors shoved harder, trying to lift him out of the saddle.

He brought his sword down to cut through the shafts, but his strike was off and his blade stuck in the tough ash. Before he could free it, another pair of spears slammed into him. Rough hands reached up and dragged his shield down.

He hit the frozen ground. Breath blew from his lungs. Above him, Hrimfaxi did as she'd been trained: she went wild, spinning and kicking her heavy hooves.

Bound as they were by the grasses, the Jotunn immediately around him couldn't flee. He heard the wet *thocks* of smashed skulls and broken bones.

A howl tore free of his throat, as much the fylgja's roar as it was his own. Without thinking, he hauled on her strength like a sailor raising a mainsail. His body thrummed with new strength and he was up, hammering Jotunn warriors aside with blade and shield alike.

He screamed as he swung his sword, blood spraying as he hewed through them till it broke in his hand. He flung the hilt at a thickset, black-bearded, grinning Jotunn. It bounced off the man's helm and dropped him.

When his shield became a smashed ruin, he laid about him with his fists. He charged back and forth, trying to break free of the encircling Jotunn but there were just too many of them. They drove Hrimfaxi off and, tucked behind round shields and long spears, got around him.

Garilon's horn shrieked again, closer now. The sound pierced the battle fury that had settled into his mind.

Yet Vidar could taste the Jotunn's uncertainty—like hot blood and the sweet flesh of Yggdrasil's fruit. They might have him at bay, but they'd shortly have to deal with his warband.

One Jotunn started shouting orders, and resolution replaced their uncertainty. They began jabbing their spears at him.

And then he felt—finally—the Jotunn shamans picking at his charms. Not only were they beginning to unravel the weave that protected his warriors, but they were unwinding the grassy fetters he'd flung around the Jotunn's feet.

He slapped one darting spear aside and caught another. He yanked hard, using his fylgja's strength as naturally as his own. The Jotunn flew toward him, surprise etched into the man's swarthy, heavy-browed face. Vidar caught the warrior and broke him across his knee.

His fylgja screamed with delight.

Aesir battle cries echoed behind him. He turned toward the sound and gathered himself for a charge—and then the shamans hurled seidr at him. It cut runnels across his skin like a snow bear's venom. Pain flared, but his fylgja screamed it away until only his rage remained.

His fylgja made him slap one spear away even as another struck him in the small of the back. She spun him around, and he grabbed the spear in both hands and with it flung the Jotunn warrior aside. Then she made him sprint forward, spear still in his hands, toward the opening she—they—had created.

No, he thought at her, shouldering her aside and taking back control of his body. He needed her strength, but he would not let her control him.

She snarled like a cornered great-cat, but backed down.

Through the gap in front of him he saw his warband on foot, fighting toward him in a tight wall of their own. Most of the Jotunn seemed to be attacking them. He himself was in the middle of a noose of maybe twenty Jotunn.

He spat on the ground. He could feel the shamans further picking apart the witcharmor he'd woven for the warband. It wouldn't hold much longer.

His fylgja shrieked inside him, making his blood pound harder.

Enough, he shouted at her. Then a pair of spears slammed into his back.

He stumbled forward, fell, rolled and then came back up to his knees. He took another pair of spears full on his chest. They tore through his tattered armor, but skidded across his flesh.

As he stood, arms wide, facing the Jotunn, he saw fear in their dark eyes, leashed like hounds. They knew what he was and they lacked the weapons to kill him.

This time when his fylgja screamed, he turned to his left, pulled on her strength, and sprang forward faster than the attacking Jotunn could react. They were coming at him in pairs, shieldman on the right and spearman to his left, alternating all the way around the noose.

But they hadn't expected him to move as fast as he did. He slammed shoulder-first into the shieldman. The round shield broke, and the Jotunn warrior flew backward, dark beard parted in a howl of surprise.

Vidar then grabbed the shoulders of the spearman and drove a knee into his stomach as he pulled down on the man's shoulders. The warrior vomited blood as his torso was pulped.

By then, the next shieldman had begun turning toward Vidar. Still moving far more quickly than the Jotunn could react, he skip-stepped forward and caved in the shieldman's skull with a single clenched fist.

Seidr flared across his shoulders, hissing and burning. He staggered and went down on one knee, mind reeling with pain.

Before he even realized what was happening, his fylgja had picked him back up and was driving him forward into the next spearman. She used his arms to grab that warrior's shoulders, pull him down. When she hammered his knee upward, he felt the spearman's spine snap.

Vidar watched the dead warrior's hugr dart free like a silvery fish. His fylgja reached for it, extending bloody hands as he might reach into the mists above a lake.

And then she ate the Jotunn's spirit.

Vidar's heart nearly burst with ecstasy. He reeled backward, struggling to rein in his—no, her—desire for more. Hot horror rose like the dawn.

The remaining warriors in the shield wall attacked, hewing him with axes, slamming spears into him. None of it mattered. The thuds of their weapons against his body sounded like a heavy summer rain on a longhouse roof.

The pounding of his heart and the need for more death were all he felt. He fought that need even as his fylgja fought his enemies.

Using his arms, she slapped a spear aside, spun, and stepped in close. He watched the warrior's eyes, deep brown below heavy brows, widen in surprise. The man's lips parted, a white strip of teeth behind a black beard.

His fylgja tore the warrior's throat out with her talons.

Talons? When did she—

Renewed ecstasy flooded through him as his fylgja drank in the dead warrior's spirit.

He was losing his grip on that river rock, his fingernails peeling back. He focused on the icy manacles of his tattoos and began to invoke the runes that would restrain her—

Only to be drowned out by the fylgja's shriek, malicious and eager.

Dozens left. More food.

No! He had been a fool.

He threw what will he had left into reciting the runes. The shamans must have sensed it, for seidr incandesced against his skin, burning him with long rippling lines of venom.

His fingernails slipped from the rock, and the current took him.

No no no...

When the fylgja realized his control was gone, she surged up from the depths of his mind like a broaching whale. Dimly, he was aware of her propelling his body forward at one of the Jotunn still before him. The Jotunn's spear shattered against his chest. And with one of Vidar's hands, the fylgja ripped away the man's armor and sank Vidar's teeth, lengthened into fangs, into his neck. The warrior thrashed, trying to throw him—her—off. She broke the warrior's neck with one savage twist of her head.

Another wave of ecstasy swept him further away from the rock of his hamr.

The further away he was carried, the more control she took and the more she shifted his hamr, molding his flesh into a shape she wanted. Already his body had doubled in size, looking more and more like a snow bear with long curling horns and sharp talons, thick and black.

He had been a fool. As if from a great height, he watched his body leap toward the Jotunn shield wall that had engaged his warband. His body rampaged, opening a wide, bloody swath through the Jotunn. She drank more spirits and grew larger, altering his hamr still more.

But he no longer felt any of it. Just a lingering, vague shame as his thoughts faded.

She turned to look at him then, green eyes wild and triumphant.

Such a fool...

19

Loki

Loki stood outside his longhouse beneath the high, spreading limbs of a yew tree—scant cover from prying, distant eyes, but it was early morning. Goldtooth was probably still recovering from the previous night's drink even as he filled the next day's cups. Or maybe, hopefully, time had become one continuous dark, muddled night for him.

And all thanks to some garrulous, green-feathered birds in Vanaheim. He smiled, hoping they might teach their hatchlings well.

"Smiling? Are you that happy to be leaving again, Loki?" Sigyn's fingers flashed in the Jotunn hand speech. She stood silhouetted against the longhouse, its doors flung wide to let the air in. Melting water fell with a faint steady drip from the roof into open barrels. The Franangr's roar was a mere backdrop.

Loki replied, fingers dancing. "Not at all. We're bound together, you and I, no matter how far we are apart."

Sigyn sniffed and stepped in closer, wrapping an arm around his waist. "Or how close," she whispered.

Vali and Narfi walked toward them, leading horses that snorted, shook their heads, and stomped their hooves, eager to be out on the road. Loki saw that same eagerness in his sons' eyes and his smile deepened, remembering when a similar feeling had swelled in his chest.

He was anxious for the last part of his own journey. Despite Ygg's unexpected return, he'd decided to go ahead with the plans he'd laid over the past hundred winters. They *would* bear fruit, as would the Jotunn's plans.

Whether he lived to see it was another thing entirely.

Vali and Narfi looked every inch the young Aesir warriors they seemed to be—round shields slung on their backs, axes by their sides, hands upon long spears, heavy leather armor over even heavier woolen clothes. They wrapped their reins on one of the yew's low hanging, sparsely leafed limbs.

Loki's fingers moved. "Take care in Ifington. Remember to split up when you get there. Slip away in the hours before Sól rises, but do it separately—"

"We know, Father," Vali signed, with a lopsided grin on his narrow, sharp-featured face. "We've been over it."

Loki frowned and leveled a finger at Vali. "If the army catches you traversing the Breach into Utgard, they'll figure out who you are. Eventually. Then they'll come here."

Vali's expression grew more serious as understanding bloomed in his eyes. Narfi just nodded, every bit the counterweight to his brother's airier temperament.

"I'm sorry to be hard on you," Loki signed, smiling, "but many plans are strung together. If they find one thread, they'll find the others, and then the whole weave will come undone."

Narfi signed, "We know, Father. We won't let you down."

"That thought never entered my mind," Loki said, smile widening further. "Mine's a father's concern for his sons' welfare. The enemy has eyes everywhere, especially in Utgard."

Sigyn swatted his chest, and he glanced down at her. Her frown seemed to suggest that he should scold less and advise more. And maybe he should, since he might never see these two again. But they needed to be prepared. Not that words alone could do that.

"And when you reach Helveg, only Beli will know that you are my sons. That's for your protection as well as my own," he said, fingers dancing. "I know Beli well. He's among the best of us, so keep your eyes and ears open. You can learn much from him."

"We will, Father," they signed.

"And you be careful, too, wherever you're headed," Narfi added.

He grinned. "Don't worry about me. I've been in trouble more than I've been out of it. When it's finally thrown, you'll both be at the spear's tip so—"

"Take care of each other," Sigyn said out loud. She stepped from his side to hug and kiss both her boys.

Maybe he had been droning on, but another war was coming. He was proud that his sons had chosen his side. And should he fail, they'd be safer with Helveg than they would with him. Just as Sigyn would be safer with the Jotunn.

For now, though, he embraced both his boys, working hard to keep the tears from his eyes. Then he caught Sigyn in a fierce hug.

"Make sure you come back to me," she whispered.

He kissed her cheek and said, "I will," as if he were certain he would return. He doubted she believed him. She had hope, though. She would remain behind for a little while, doing nothing but playing the part of a devoted wife who knew little of the activities of a husband who was rarely around, and then herself slip away.

"Swift and true," he said to Vali and Narfi.

And then he shifted into the shape of a large snow owl, and in puffs of snow, left the spreading yew branches and the ground behind. After a long curving upward climb, he looked down and saw Vali and Narfi had mounted and were heading toward whatever dooms the Norns had cut for them.

Just as he was.

20

Odin

Odin lifted Gungnir free, threw a leg over his saddle, and slid from Sleipnir's back. Beneath his feet, the grass lay flat against the hard-packed earth. In some places, it had been trampled into the ground itself, mixed with blood and gore and then frozen solid. Bodies lay scattered in grotesque contortions.

Odin glanced behind him and caught a glimpse of Baldr's sorrowful expression, his lips a bloodless, tight line.

Saglund approached and bowed stiffly, disgust plain on his face. "We're ready, Sigfather."

Indeed they were. The Einherjar had formed a shield wall and had begun marching forward.

How odd that Saglund should show such revulsion. He had fought a dozen campaigns against the Jotunn and distinguished himself in the last Jotunn war. His valor was partly why Odin had given him command of the Einherjar.

"Is something wrong, Hersir?" he asked.

Saglund's expression went hard. "It's just that I understand now what you meant, Sigfather."

From high above, his ravens gave a raucous cry. Odin tapped a finger next to his eye. "It gets worse. And this will be a fight these Einherjar have never fought."

"I'm confident they are up to the challenge, Sigfather," Saglund replied, pitching his voice to carry above the tramping boots as, two Aesir deep all around, the Einherjar wall parted to engulf the stationary Odin, Baldr, and Saglund and reform with them in the center.

"Then let's go, Hersir," he said, clapping Saglund on the shoulder. He pointed north along the bloody trail. "If it weren't obvious, Huginn and Muninn say we need to head that way."

As they walked, stepping over or around the Jotunn corpses, he sent a thought back to his ravens: *Watch for falcons.*

After the shield wall crawled past a particularly large pile of corpses, he called Gungnir to his hand. "Halt here."

He lowered Gungnir so her blade was parallel to the ground and waved her tip back and forth as if divining for water. She twitched in his hand and pointed directly ahead toward the heap of wrecked bodies.

He strode to the pile, kicking broken weapons out of his way. When he was directly before the bodies, Gungnir twitched again. He slammed the spear butt first into the ground and dragged the topmost corpse off the pile. Saglund barked an order; several Einherjar sprang over to assist, as did Baldr.

When they had dragged the top layers of corpses aside and arrayed them all in a line, Odin retrieved Gungnir and held her blade parallel to the ground. He walked slowly down the line of bodies until she twitched in his hand. Swiftly, he raised Gungnir high and reversed her so her blade faced downward.

Baldr must have seen it coming. "Father, wait, I might—"

He let Gungnir slam down into the Jotunn she had selected. The warrior's ribs fractured with a sharp crack, and the Jotunn himself shuddered, moaned softly, and went limp. The spear's blade, what little of it showed, glowed golden around the edges.

"You should have let me tend him, Father," Baldr said, skidding to a halt opposite him. "Alive, he could've told us what happened. Why they attacked."

Gungnir's glow intensified and drew a mist from the Jotunn's broken chest; the glow dimmed and the mist thickened. "The Jotunn hate us, Baldr. They always have. That's why they attacked."

He ripped Gungnir back out, fresh gore dripping a crimson trail, and made small circles in the air, wrapping what was left of the Jotunn's spirit around her blade. "The real question is this: Where is Vidar and his warband?"

Baldr knelt beside the dead Jotunn warrior, removed the man's helm, and closed his eyes. Seen in Sól's long light, the Jotunn's brow appeared less heavy than he knew it was, the nose less broad. The Jotunn's skin had gone gray in death. Baldr then laid one of the warrior's thick-fingered, hairy hands across his barrel of a chest.

An eager ululating shriek ripped toward them from across the plains.

Baldr rose abruptly. Mutters ran through the Einherjar, leather armor creaking in the silence. Their weapons banged and tinged against their shields.

Odin exhaled and cast his mind upward, seeking Huginn and Muninn. Sharp-eyed though they were, all his ravens could see was a black clump not far beyond the circle of their warband.

He sent his mind toward his wolves. Geri was closest, near the high ridge. He felt a rumbling growl building in the wolf's chest. He sniffed the air: fresh blood, but something wrong about it. Geri's hackles rose, and he snarled.

Odin slipped into Freki's mind and caught the same scent Geri had, a rotting wrongness woven with the steaming stench of stomachs spilled open.

It stalks you, Pack-Father, Freki thought to him.

He inhaled and fell back into his body. "Saglund, quick, sound the horn. Form the shield wall!"

He lifted Gungnir and ignited the spirit-cloud he had wrapped around the blade. For those with the sight, it burned gold and bright.

Silvery, the horn pealed out.

A tortured shriek answered.

Geri howled a challenge. *It comes now, Pack-Father,* Freki said in his mind.

"Brace yourselves," he shouted. He rammed Gungnir into the ground, the Jotunn's spirit burning bright along her blade. It would lure the creature, whatever it was.

Odin reached into his satchel and withdrew his spool of witchthread. Working quickly, he unscrewed the cap on Gungnir's cross-brace, hung the spool, replaced the cap, and with a quick jerk of his arm, unspooled a long strand.

The beastly roar echoed again, the sound bearing down on them. Saglund called out and the Einherjar fell back a dozen paces, tightening the wall around Odin, Baldr, and Saglund.

Odin flicked his wrist, sending the thread out to pierce the back of the Einherjar nearest the approaching roar, and began to sing the charm he had taught Vidar. He pulled more thread free, directing it toward the Einherjar with one hand while the other wove it through the leather and steel circle of warriors around them. He sang in the shields, softly, the golden glow of his charm giving them strength.

The Einherjar fought in fours, two warriors in front with shields and axes guarding two behind with long spears. The pulling hooks on those spears glinted in Sól's fading smile.

Something huge slammed into the shield wall. The Einherjar roared in reply. Those in the first rank buckled beneath the impact of something wide and heavy and black. They were driven back two steps, then three. But they held. They stumbled forward slightly as whatever had hit them pulled away.

"Reform," Saglund shouted, his voice high and tight. He raised his horn and blew a silvery peal.

Odin flung another golden thread into the Einherjar, weaving it back around on itself. The weaving would lend the charm greater strength.

From your left, Wing-Father, Huginn whispered from high above.

Odin thrust an arm in that direction, the song pouring from his lips.

"Left flank, brace yourselves," Saglund cried. He dropped the horn and drew his sword.

Like a landslide, the beast struck the shield wall. The line flexed inward, shields squealing beneath huge shaggy paws that flashed with knife-sized talons. Spears bit, flexed, and then splintered with loud pops as the beast pressed forward, head low, haunches high.

The creature swung its heavy head back and forth, sword-long horns catching warriors and batting them down or flinging them upward. Odin could see the weave unraveling where the beast struck; it began looking more like the threadbare knees of trousers than whole cloth. It would tear soon enough.

The beast was trying to reach him and the Jotunn spirit swirling around Gungnir. These warriors were no threat to it. Only he was.

So he sang on, his fingers dancing as he strengthened his weave. It alone kept the bodies of his men whole, despite the fraying that happened every time the beast's talons or horns slammed into them.

With a massive crash, the beast burst through the shield wall, throwing warriors aside. Its horns glowed dark red where they terminated in a bony plate on its forehead. The eyes below those horns were green and vicious. He knew those eyes. He knew what...who... this thing was.

Odin reached for Gungnir even as the beast began her charge. Saglund screamed out a challenge and threw himself in the way. And then Saglund was down, having tripped or slipped on some soft patch of churned earth or detritus. It didn't matter either way, since the beast—the disir—would be on him in a heartbeat.

And he hadn't worked the charm on himself.

The beast swelled in his vision, gore-stained horns lowered, matted hairy shoulders making even the bone plate that stretched across its neck behind the horns look small.

And then his view was eclipsed by Baldr leaping in front of him, arms spread wide. Sól emerged from behind a low cloud and made Baldr's dark blond hair shine redly.

Odin's fingers closed around Gungnir's smooth wood. The spear fairly leaped from the ground and he swung it upward to block, however he could, the beast's long talons. There came a meaty impact and Baldr was batted sideways, tumbling away beyond his vision.

The breathy roar that washed over him stank like low tide. Odin invoked a rune word and the manacle tattooed around the beast's right foreleg seared to brightness in his witch sight.

The disir stumbled. Haunches bunching for another charge, she shrieked at him in a voice colder than the north wind.

He spun free a length of thread and flicked it toward the disir, singing a new charm. Fast as thought, the thread darted into the earth in front of the beast. Grasses climbed up around its scaly legs like grasping vines on a thick-boled tree.

The disir roared again and strained against the roots. Odin repeated the charm, and more grasses wound around her broad back, fur matted with blood and gore, and snaked around her heavy, scaled haunches and thick neck.

He met her gaze, eyes hard. "Not so easy with one who knows you, disir."

With a sound like a ship's stout mast breaking in a storm, the disir ripped one foreleg free from the grasses binding it. She roared, spittle frothing and dripping from her toothy lower jaw.

He pulled free the last long thread wrapped around the spindle. He showed it to her, doubled and tripled between his hands held arm's length apart. "More than enough here, child of the Gap."

The disir's struggles redoubled.

He spoke a second rune. The tattoos hidden beneath thick fur flared to life, and it went as stiff as if the joint had locked up.

His fingers danced delicately as he sent more thread at her. With each additional rune word he spoke, the tattoos on her legs and neck flared bluer and brighter.

In time with each flare, the disir's struggles grew slower almost as if she were underwater and swimming up, straining to reach the surface but running out of air. She roared and twitched and thrashed, her hind legs gouging great furrows in the frozen ground. Some of the grasses binding her did pop and tear, but those fetters no longer mattered. He had powered and invoked the runes. In a moment, he would revert the changes the disir had wrought in his son's flesh.

For this disir, this spirit, was Vidar's fylgja. It had known exactly what Odin was doing. Her stolen breath was hot on his face. Her chest heaved as she tried to break free. She flicked her head and tried to gouge him with her horns, her emerald eyes blazing with hatred.

Odin laughed. "You had your fun. But now I want my son back."

He cast the last loop of thread at her, singing, and the grasses dragged her flat till she lay like a dog sleeping on its side.

He knelt beside her and touched the first tattoo around her right foreleg. He spoke a word: *binda*. It cracked the air and the disir shrieked. The Einherjar warriors staggered away, hands clutching their ears.

He touched the tattoo on the fylgja's right upper leg and spoke another word: *brott*. This word bit the air like an axe striking a tree. The fylgja shrieked again. The bestial quality sounded farther away, while the man's voice sounded closer.

And more like his son's voice.

The ice-blue light from the first tattoo mingled with the loops of seidr around the second. Like merging streams, they flowed up and wound around the tattoo about the fylgja's neck, then down its other side.

The entire massive body before him flexed, trying to throw off the fetters of light. He raised a hand and they tightened further, constricting like serpents from steamy Alvheim. He touched the tattoos on the disir's upper and lower left leg and spoke the same words again: *binda, brott*.

"You are chained. By my power, disir, you withdraw and become, once again, a fylgja." He stood and held both hands over the creature before him. "I bind you. And so will my son return. Remember yourself, Vidar."

He licked his thumb and bent forward to trace a single rune on his son's forehead. He spoke the word: *muna*.

A hiss slithered from the fylgja's mouth. Her eyes darted this way and that looking for escape. Her limbs shuddered and bulged with effort, but she didn't move. Couldn't move. The wicked green light of the tempest in her eyes faded.

He wiped his thumb on his sleeve, licked it again, and raised it to trace another rune on the fylgja's broad scaly chest. The fur there was sticky with blood and sweat. He traced the rune: *hljod*.

Inside the constraining threads of light, the fylgja shuddered and its breath rasped. The beast's body faded, shuddered, and shrank, regaining its original shape. Odin's shadow lay heavy across the brown grasses and roots humped over Vidar like a barrow.

He put his hands on his hips and exhaled long and slow as he turned his face up to the sky, eyes closed. He listened to the creak of the Einherjar's armor, their harsh breathing and the chilly breeze rasping against the ground like a serpent's scales across stone.

***

"Took you long enough to get back," Odin said, turning a tired smile on Baldr. Baldr's clothes hung in tatters, but the skin beneath was whole, proving the value of the sacrifice Odin and Frigg had made—and of the old magic she'd used at Baldr's birth.

"He flung me quite far," Baldr replied, then gestured at Vidar. "So was that how they all look?"

"The disir? No, they look how they choose," he said. "I want him up and moving as quickly as possible."

"After what he just went through? I'd be surprised if he's conscious inside a week."

Time was exactly what they did not have. "He may need it, but I need him back in Gladsheim with us."

Baldr frowned. "He won't like that. And I susp—"

"And I won't enjoy dealing with your mother's anger if I take too long to get back. Get it done, Baldr. Use your new potions if necessary."

Baldr forced a sunny smile, but wariness clouded his clear blue eyes. "Potions? I haven't—"

Odin held up a hand. "Spare me. Freki smelled them and told me."

Baldr laughed. "Well, that's hardly fair."

"Long before you were born the Jotunn tried to steal Yggdrasil's fruit. Ever since, I keep at least an eye—and nose—on them. And Idunn keeps me informed."

"So if you knew and let me continue, then you don't mind how I've been using them?"

Odin shrugged. "Let me put it this way. What you're doing benefits us and may do so even beyond what you've already discovered. But make sure folk believe it's you and your arts healing them. Yggdrasil's fruit are fundamental to our grip on power. I will do what it takes to keep them secret."

Baldr's good humor slowly drained away as he understood what those words meant. "All right, Father."

"Good." He pointed at Vidar again. "Now, ply your arts."

Somehow, the Jotunn had gotten to Háls. He'd nearly lost one of his sons because of it. Could they do it again? If they could, it might not be a bad thing.

21

Vafthrudnir

Vafthrudnir opened his eyes. The sight of Vithi's wide white plains, where he'd just been—in spirit, at least—was replaced by dark cave walls that reflected the sullen red glow of his fire's remnants. He shivered , despite the heavy bearskin he'd draped over his shoulders.

Welcome back, his fylgja said. *One of my cousins had a romp, eh?*

If by romp you mean slaughtering more than two hundred Jotunn, then yes, she had a romp.

Well, what would you call it?

He sighed. Both he and the Skrymir had expected Ama's attack on Háls to fail, but not as quickly as it had. Vidar Odinsson had just moved himself from the category of known threat to deadly foe, perhaps on the same level as the Thunderer and Ygg himself.

Assuming he wrests control back from my sister, his fylgja said.

Or finds common ground with her, Vafthrudnir thought. *Makes it a partnership rather than a master-thrall relationship.*

What are the chances of that? She's got him now, and she'll fight him tooth and nail to keep control. I would.

Vafthrudnir stood, stretched, and rolled his head on his shoulders. His neck bones cracked and popped. He shivered again and wrapped the bearskin more tightly around himself.

Ygg's returned.

I saw, his fylgja said, slithering into view. She'd taken the shape of a long wyrm, complete with bony head and back spines. Not that it mattered what form she took, Fimbulthul was a disir, a creature spun from the raw stuff of the Gap itself. She had played among its currents, and when Vafthrudnir died, she would return to them.

Anything happen while I was elsewhere?

Ygg's return now complicated everything. He needed time to think on it. And he had to tell the Skrymir.

I scared away a young snow bear—a male, probably excluded from his pack. Looked strong; be a bull soon enough.

I meant anything I should care about?

Oh. No, not really.

Good. Help me move this boulder then?

Fimbulthul slid forward and wound her way up his leg. When her head was level with his own, she merged with him. Strength thrummed through every part of his hamr. Better still, he no longer felt cold.

He stepped forward and leaned into the boulder that mostly filled the entrance to the cave. It scraped and ground against the frozen soil in the groove he'd carved over the past several hundred winters. Moonlight filled more and more of the gap. With his fylgja inside him, he could feel every line and ridge of the boulder he'd just rolled back.

He remained inside the cave, though, just in case Goldtooth was watching. He knew Ygg was occupied, because his wolves and ravens were in Vithi.

Back to Jotunheim? Fimbulthul asked.

Yes.

Vafthrudnir spread his arms and shifted. He hopped forward on long talons until he reached the narrow ledge outside the cave. Then he launched himself up on snowy wings and soared away.

***

Vafthrudnir stood outside the Skrymir's hall in Jotunheim, the last city belonging to the last Jotunn. Trampled snow covered the three steps up to the platform outside the big, iron-banded doors.

The chiefs are about to leave, his fylgja said inside his mind, her airy body drifting back out through the hall's doors.

He grunted his thanks and leaned on the railing, gazing down over the snow-covered tents, longhouses, and few remaining halls of Jotunheim. The scents of cooking meat, spicy stews, and baking breads hung in the night air. The recent harvest had been unusually good, the best in nine winters.

Supplemented by the dry goods Baldr had brought during his last visit, most Jotunn would enter the long, dark days ahead with unexpected company: full bellies. That bounty had already caused several of the chiefs to argue for delay, to build their strength for another winter, maybe two, while trade grew and their people recovered.

The big iron-banded door squealed open like a happy baby, a sound this sad city hadn't heard in more than a dozen winters. Burly in their furs and wools, six figures stomped into view. These were tribal chiefs of Hill and Lake, Mountain and Plains, Forest and River. Names that had meant nothing in generations. Better to call them Squalor and Famine, Death and Dying, Lickspittle and Fear.

Follow them, please. Make sure they don't cause trouble. Warn me if they do.

His fylgja looked at him and yawned, then grew a spined tail expressly so she could twitch it at him. He sighed and suppressed the urge to rub his temples.

She settled onto his shoulder. *All six? How am I supposed to do that? And what does 'trouble' mean?*

He bowed to the clan chiefs as they pooled on the wide platform outside the door. As high shaman of the Jotunn, he was second in rank only to the Skrymir. These chiefs knew it, but they still treated him like a mere tribal shaman. But he didn't mind. Sometimes it was better to appear less than he was.

Figure it out. You know our plans. If they speak out against them or conspire with each other, let me know.

Without the continued support of these six men and women, the plan he and the Skrymir had hatched would never succeed. So he played to their egos. The stupid ones—Lake's chief was the best example—took his bow as deference. The suspicious ones inclined their heads to him in return. Of those, Hill's chief was the least trustworthy. Her tribe had profited the most from trade with the Aesir.

All the chiefs but one tromped down the steps and onto the path toward the city and, he assumed, their respective dwellings. Unless any chose to meet by themselves in secret.

Lake, however, stepped forward, bulky in his furs, his lean face deeply lined and burned nearly red by many winters wind and cold. "What do you have to report, shaman?"

He's kind of an idiot, isn't he? observed his fylgja.

Vafthrudnir replied in the hand language. "The Skrymir awaits my report, chief."

Lake scowled and replied, long fingers dancing. "I know what he wants, but it was my tribe that attacked Háls."

"I would've thought your shaman would have reported by now."

"She did. Their initial attack succeeded, and they'd spun ships to finish the Aesir. We haven't heard anything since."

"That's because Ama's failed. The warband you sent has by now been destroyed."

Lake's icy expression cracked. "What do you mean?"

He is an idiot.

"The Aesir killed Ama and the warband he led," Vafthrudnir said, his fingers moving more slowly. "All of them. If you'll excuse me, I must inform the Skrymir."

He gave a quick nod and then pushed past the chief—then stopped as if he'd forgotten to say something. Which he hadn't, of course. "Oh, and chief? Ygg has returned. Long before he was expected. I'm sure you know what that means for our people, especially considering that Jotunn axes—your tribe's axes—just felled several hundred Aesir. I hope your desire to reclaim honor lost long ago has not destroyed our people's last best chance at escape."

He gave a quick nod, set gloved hand upon cold iron, and hauled the door open.

His hand is on his axe. And the way he's glaring at you right now...

Kill him if it clears his belt.

Vafthrudnir paused in the doorway, then, without haste, stepped through and shoved it shut behind him.

Well, he obviously reconsidered. Too bad, really. Following people is such a waste of my gifts.

See where he goes. Stay with him if it's interesting. If not, find the other chiefs.

Fimbulthul leaped from his shoulder, shifted into a blob of tentacles floating on wispy wings before passing back through the closed door.

The Skrymir's bellow came a heartbeat later. "What now?"

Vafthrudnir went in, affecting Lake's imperious tone. "Skrymir, I wanted a private word about how you're setting the other chiefs against me."

The Skrymir's hall was wide and high-roofed. Aside from the entryway, it was dimly lit. The sections on either side of the entry were the Skrymir's to use. He slept on one side and worked on the other, meeting with the chiefs and charting the course of their people.

And grim work it had been for a very long time, for them both. It helped that they'd been friends even before their parents had set them before the rising of Muspell's sparks.

The Skrymir had his back to the door and was yelling over his shoulder as he urinated into a bucket. "Rán's wet, saggy tits, Lake, if they're against you it's your own fault—for what *you've* done. Don't expect me to support your stupidity." All the other Jotunn used communal jakes since the urine was used to tan hides. As the chief of chiefs this was one privilege the Skrymir accepted, but he still carried his own bucket down to the tanner.

"You still need my support, Skrymir, I don't appre—"

The Skrymir finished and spun around, a scowl on his broad face. When he saw who it was, he blew out a breath and grinned. "You bastard, Vaft. I thought I'd have to waste more of my morning with that dimwit."

"A dangerous one," he replied and then switched to signing. "I asked Fimbulthul to follow him."

The Skrymir grunted and gestured toward the chairs clustered around the single lit hearth set deeper in the hall. The hall's back wall was mountain stone itself, into which had been shaped wide tunnels that led down into larger caverns where it was somewhat safer to speak aloud. Up here, though, they mostly used the Jotunn hand language.

Once they were seated, the Skrymir's fingers began dancing. "So Ama's attack on Vithi has failed."

Vafthrudnir nodded and related what he'd seen, ending with the most important news. "And, even better, Ygg has returned. Now we'll have to—"

"I know," the Skrymir said aloud. A grin broke across his face, shedding a hundred winters' worth of worries. He struck the arm of his chair before signing, "It's great news."

So the spies in Gladsheim had reported back while he was observing Ama's destruction. "How is any of this good news? We needed Ygg to stay away until after Midwinter at least."

"I know, but I think it solves our supply problem."

"Sure it does. The Aesir march on Jotunheim within the week, or maybe the Thunderer arrives tomorrow and brings the mountain down on our hovels. No need for supplies if most of us are dead."

The Skrymir smirked, shook his head and reached for a jug of ale —passing over the wine—and poured two cups. "None of that will happen. Not that quickly, at least."

Now that the trade route had grown more active, wine had again made an appearance in Jotunheim. The richest chiefs, Hill and River, bought it thinking it somehow implied higher status. He was continually astounded at how petty his people could be. Here they were on the brink of extinction, yet the chiefs still plotted and maneuvered while exulting in their perceived higher status.

Before handing him the cup, the Skrymir signed, "We already needed another month to get more supplies. I think we can use Ama's attack to buy us that time."

Vafthrudnir accepted the offered cup. Then he set it down to sign, "They're never going to believe the 'rogue tribe' excuse. We've used it too many times."

"All we need is to buy a few nights until Loki strikes."

"I don't see how tha—"

The Skrymir raised a hand then signed, "We don't attack at Midwinter as we agreed. We wait until we're ready. A month longer, at the most."

Vafthrudnir snorted. "Loki will balk at that. He's relying on that attack as a distraction."

"Yes, but I can be very convincing."

When he and the Skrymir had been boys, his friend had staggered back from the rising of Muspell's sparks, frozen and gibbering about a vision granted by one of the wild land disir. He had convinced him the vision was real, that it would happen and that the pair of them could save their people. And a winter later, once Vafthrudnir had also been set before the Rising, he'd come back with a shaman's gifts. Just as his friend had said would happen.

"You're going to show him where the doorway in Gladsheim is, aren't you?" He didn't relish the idea of sharing too many secrets with Farbauti's son. Loki had too long a history of double-dealing.

The Skrymir shrugged. "I don't see that we have another option. Ama's failure means any new warband we muster now stands a good chance of being noticed by Ygg or Goldtooth. So we play the innocents, which, as I said, will buy us a few nights."

He frowned and looked down into the fire. Trust Loki still further? Both he and the Skrymir had known Loki before he had sworn a blood oath with Ygg and joined the Aesir. The Jotunn had been holding their own against the Aesir until then. After Loki defected, they'd lost two wars and ended up confined to desolate Utgard.

He looked up at the sound of the Skrymir knocking his knuckles against his chair. "He's not going to betray us. Not now."

"Are you so sure?"

"Absolutely. He would've done it by now. He already knows enough to wreck everything. And he's the one who approached us, remember?"

Of course he remembered. Who approached whom wasn't the issue. Nor was his problem a faulty memory.

"I have to offer something in exchange for delaying our attack," the Skrymir continued. "He'll be risking more than us at first—and trusting us to do what we said. He'll want something for that."

But the doorways? A hundred winters of planning and effort hinged on them. Literally all their hope as a people. He signed, "It would be best if I were with you when Loki arrives."

"No, it wouldn't."

"Because I don't trust him? He knows that already. I haven't made a secret of it."

"How will your distrust help me convince him to go ahead alone?"

It wouldn't.

"Just don't show him too many," he said aloud. Sometimes the hand language just wasn't forceful enough. And those words were innocent, even if Goldtooth happened to hear them.

"Only a few," the Skrymir signed, expression grave. "I promise."

Vafthrudnir switched back to using his hands. "Is he still planning to come here after Ithavoll?"

"Yes. Our spies said that Ithavoll won't happen until Ygg's back from Háls, which means we probably gain another night, maybe two, beyond what our play-acting will buy us."

"Good. That'll give me a chance to figure out what the chiefs are planning. Lake was more than usually confrontational just now."

The Skrymir shook his head. "I need you to join Beli and Helveg. He thinks he's found another doorway."

"Now's not really the best time to scout those. I'm needed here more than out there, even if I don't join the conversation with Loki."

"And what if this new doorway leads to an even better place than the others? We need every advantage to grapple with the Aesir and win. Besides, Helveg needs snow bears, and their shamans can't handle that alone. So when you get there, you can help with both."

Vafthrudnir grunted and stared into his cup of ale. He sent a thought out to Fimbulthul. *Anything?*

Lake's being verbally abused by Forest and Plains. Your hands are so expressive sometimes.

What are they saying?

Fimbulthul delivered the mental equivalent of a shrug. *Only that they're distancing themselves from Lake.*

When his gaze refocused, he found the Skrymir's eyes on him, curious. He set the cup down and signed. "Forest and Plains want nothing further to do with Lake."

The Skrymir clapped his hands. "Perfect. Aside from Lake, we're united—and he'll fall in line, too."

Vafthrudnir gave the slight upward flick of the hands that meant he wanted to talk about something different. "Let's go over this supply problem. That month you mentioned? I think I can halve it. But my solution, coincidentally, relies on the same doorways you're going to tell Loki about."

***

Vafthrudnir tapped the map spread out on the table. "We take what we need from here and here," he said, first pointing at the silver square marking Ifington and then at the one for Gladsheim.

"We don't have the numbers to hold Ifington long enough," the Skrymir said.

Not only was Ifington home to thousands of Aesir, but it supplied the Fortress at the Breach with food, drink, and weapons. The Aesir army, led by Tyr and Ullr, maintained a large presence in Ifington as well.

"We won't need to. Not if we start now," Vafthrudnir signed.

The people of Ifington, Gladsheim, and all the Aesir towns had been stockpiling food and drink for months in preparation for the Midwinter celebration only a handful of nights distant. Ifington alone probably now held enough supplies to keep ten warbands for a month, maybe longer.

He flipped through the maps until he found the one detailing the long stretch of road between Ifington and the Breach. He tapped the green disk to the east of road among what passed for trees in that section of Utgard.

The Skrymir scowled. "How is that going to work? Even if we load up the merchants, they'll be expected at the Breach. The whole caravan can't just vanish."

"No, but we already have a warband hidden on the other side of this doorway. All we need to d—"

"—is have the warband step through, seize the supplies, and step back." The Skrymir traced a finger down the long line of the road from the Aesir fortress to the silver square representing Ifington. "That doorway's completely exposed, though, right? Goldtooth and Ygg—or both—could easily see what we're doing. Not to mention the possibility of an Einherjar patrol stumbling across us."

Vafthrudnir raised a finger in the air. "Yes, but our friend has sent the loyal Einherjar elsewhere. And, Ygg is about to be too busy intimidating our envoy while also trying to understand those dreams affecting his son."

The Skrymir's frown deepened. He hadn't won him over yet.

"Here, let me show you the other half of my idea." He flipped back to the detailed map of Gladsheim. It had taken their spies months to get enough information to map the buildings and streets. He tapped a square inked into the thin hide right beside a red-painted silver square in what the Aesir called the Lower Tier. "We can also steal supplies from this storehouse. It's one street away from the building where the doorway is. A building which our friend controls. Getting in and out of the storehouse—"

The Skrymir held up a hand. "I can see loading up our caravans in Ifington. We won't be discovered there, given our allies' help. But to do the same in Gladsheim itself? To anyone paying attention, it'll be like watching ants marching back to their mound."

"It's risky," Vafthrudnir said. "But it's Midwinter. Thralls moving supplies through the city are already a common sight. A few more doing the same shouldn't attract any notice. We also don't need to rush it. We can seize the bulk of them later. But the more in the store-house now, the smoother things will go later."

"It's a risk."

He met his oldest friend's gaze. The Skrymir knew the problem as well as he did. It was taking longer than either of them had expected to reclaim the supplies from beneath the frozen lakes, and so much of what they had pulled out was ruined. They just didn't have enough food for both the colonies and all the warbands. Unless they piled another risk atop all the others they'd taken.

The Skrymir gave a mirthless smile and gestured at the maps. "You trust all those who'll handle this?"

"Absolutely."

The Skrymir stared at him for a long moment. "Do you remember when we stood beneath the night sky all those winters past?"

Of course he did. All of this had begun on that night, the last of several in the brutal cold. He waited.

"The great glory of Muspell's sparks had just cleared the moun-tains, Ymir's chill lights above us. You remember what I said to you then?"

How could he forget?

The Skrymir rapped the table and gestured at the maps. "Go ahead with it. We've risked more before this. And we will again before it's all over."

Vafthrudnir grinned. Their entire plan was one wobbly stone of risk stacked upon another. He wouldn't let them fall now.

22

Hodr

Hodr's foot thumped against the step on the low platform separating what Alara called the serving table from the rest of the way house. He reached out with his right hand to find the cool oak of the casks. With his left, he found the table's smooth, warm wood. Farther down, the stoneware cups sat in neat rows. Still farther was the door to where the cooks worked—mostly women and thralls who did nothing except cook simple foods and serve them to the traders in the large common room.

Alara's parents had built the way house, which was basically an oversized longhouse adapted to the needs of the traders constantly passing through Ifington rather than those of a single family.

"Master Hodr, I didn't see you come in," the thrall said.

"Nor I you," he replied, then held a hand up to forestall the stammered, cringing apology. "Finish what you were doing. I'll take over."

"Yes, Master Hodr."

Head cocked, he listened to the sound of beer pouring into the cups. They scraped and clinked as they were placed on the platters. And he heard the distinct swish of Alara's dress and her laugh, a bird's feathers on the air, as she approached the table where he stood.

"I'm finished, Master," the thrall said.

"Fine. Go see Cook. I'm sure she needs help." He began setting a few stoneware cups in a neat row by his right hand. It was easy enough to reach behind him, but he liked having a reference point on the table.

"Hodr, you didn't need to work this evening," Alara said. The delight in her voice brought a smile to his face.

"I know, but I enjoy it. And there's little enough I do around here otherwise."

"Mucking out the stables doesn't count? I think the traders here would disagree. As would I."

Hodr heard the heavy, uneven steps of a drunk trader approaching. A moment later, the man's hot bulk rocked the neat row of cups he had arranged.

The man thumped the table. "So my friend, what does your nose tell about the weather? Will the seas be smooth for my trip home?"

Hodr nodded his head toward the voice. "The air smells dry, Rollo. But I hear the wind building in the west. If you sail tomorrow, you'll have a swift passage. After that, I expect storms."

"It always amazes me how you know it's me," Rollo said. He slapped the table, and his laugh, thick and wet, turned into a cough.

Alara touched Hodr's hand. "I need three cups of beer."

Recovered, Rollo set down the cups he'd brought. "I could use a couple more myself."

Hodr felt for the cups, turned to the casks behind him, and began filling the cups.

"You should charge us traders for asking your man here about the weather," Rollo said to Alara. "Three winters I've been staying here. He hasn't been wrong once. Even saved my ship one winter."

"That'll be one silver then, Rollo," Hodr said, turning back with the cups in hand.

A coin clinked down. "A bargain."

"We can't accept that, Rollo," Alara said. "That's as much as you'd pay to stay for three nights."

"Maybe, but if it saves me a shipment or gets me home safe, it's coin well spent." Rollo picked up his cups and slid a step closer to where Alara stood. "Those new way houses being built, mistress, they look nice. Big. But I'll keep staying here because of my friend's nose, and because I like it. Not all the caravaners are like me, though, especially the new ones. I don't make these trips from Gladsheim to Vanaheim and back again for my health. Take it from me—I've figured out what folk want, what I can provide, and then I deliver it. You've the same thing here."

And then he was off, staggering back into the crowd of traders.

Hodr could almost hear the thoughtful expression on Alara's face. He turned away to fill the cups she'd requested.

When he turned back, she touched his hand again. "You know he means well, right?"

He shrugged. "Sure. It's fine. We can talk later. It's not a bad idea, really."

***

ALL EVENING, Hodr listened to Alara's quick step across the inn's floor. Each footfall cut through the shouts and laughs of the caravaners having a last meal under a roof before taking to the road. Ships came in from the east along the coast from Vanaheim and Alvheim and unloaded their cargo onto the wagons headed south to Gladsheim. The caravaners would set off before dawn and would arrive back before Midwinter, assuming fair weather. Most had their own homes and families to reach, where they would remain through the rest of the winter.

And through it all, Alara's feet moved lightly, quickly, surely, between the tables. A pause there to drop off a platter, three strides to the next table, a dozen back to him.

"Three more cups of ale," she said. And then she was gone again to answer a hail from another table.

Hodr reached right and picked up the first cup. Then he turned around, found the middle keg—he had notched it—and moved his hand to the right for the ale keg. He couldn't do that much around the inn to help, but he could pour drinks.

"Good morning, sir." The voice behind him itched at Hodr's memory. "I'll have some of that honeyed mead when you're done there, if you don't mind."

"Of course. Just a moment." He finished pouring the third cup and set it down with the others.

"I'm off to Jarnstadr tomorrow," the man said.

"Cup or horn?" Hodr asked. The horns held about twice as much, but they cost twice as much, too.

"A horn," the man said.

He waited for the scratch of coins on the table before him.

"Just have it added to my bill," the man said. "I'm good for it."

Hodr tapped the table with a thumb. "Rule is, you come to my table, you pay at my table."

"But I'm through here all the time. I'm Lopt, the smith. You've seen me before. So has the mistress."

"Not I," Hodr said, shaking his head, even as he remembered the man's voice.

"What? This is my second trip this winter alone—" Lopt cleared his throat. "Ah, I s—ahem—well, I meant no offense. Just a turn of phrase."

Hodr heard a coin click down on the table. He picked it up and ran his thumb around the edge and across the face. There were several types of copper coins in use, each with its own weight and markings he could discern despite being blind.

He held the coin up. "You get two horns for this weight, if you want."

Lopt slapped the table. "Well, all right, if that's the case then tell you what, why don't you join me? Consider it an apology for the offense I gave, unintended though it was. As I said, I'm through here a lot."

Hodr pocketed the coin, felt for where the horns hung from hooks behind the table, and poured the smith a drink. He held the horn out. Lopt's warm calloused fingers brushed his own as he accepted the horn.

"That's kind, but I don't drink while I'm working." He forced a grin and held up a hand, which he made tremble. "Need a steady hand for the pour. Mistress gets angry if I whet the floor's thirst."

Alara's laughter floated above the din, and then he heard her quick, approaching step.

"No? Well, have it later then." The smith's voice dropped a notch, and Hodr felt the man fade back a pace.

He heard the whisper of Alara's fingers on the tray he'd loaded with cups of ale. "Talking about me?" The smile in her voice was warm sunshine.

"Only good things, Mistress," Hodr said. The worn heel of her left boot scraped against the floor as she spun and left.

"Better be," she called back.

"The Norns smiled on you," Lopt said.

"How's that, then?" Hodr asked.

After a pause, Lopt said, "I give offense again, I see. Also unintended. I meant only that she's lovely and obviously cares for you." Hodr heard the man take a sip. "Good thing I'm not at my forge this morning. Having made this many mistakes with my mouth, Aegir only knows how many fingers I'd have hammered flat by now."

Alara's laughter drifted through the sea of voices. Hodr shook his head and offered his arm to Lopt. "I can hear an insult when one's intended. I know you meant none. I'm at fault for being too prickly. I'm Hodr."

"A pleasure," Lopt said, clasping Hodr's arm with a wrist and forearm corded with muscle. "I run a smithy in the village a day's ride east. I make weapons for the Einherjar."

"You've come through a few times this past year," Hodr said.

"Every few winters the Einherjar doubles or triples its order, and my sons and I forge enough to make Svartalvar proud and then run ourselves ragged delivering everything. This winter, my eldest's expecting his firstborn. I told him to stay home. Nothing quite like seeing your child take their first breath. My youngest son got his leg broke by one of our horses. Bit wild, that one—the horse, I mean—but strong. Pulls twice what the others do."

Hodr swirled his rag across the tabletop. "I'm sorry to hear it. He mending?"

"Oh, aye," Lopt said.

Hodr heard him take a swallow of mead. "I paid for one of those healers who trained at Jarl Baldr's fregnahol to ride out and fix him up. She's here in Ifington. Expensive, but the Einherjar pay well."

Hodr's reply was delayed by the realization that he hadn't felt the reflexive twinge of anger he usually did when his brother's name was mentioned. "I hear those valkyr are quite skilled."

Lopt snorted. "Not skilled enough. He's still flat on his back, with me running twice as many carts back and forth to Gladsheim. A bit of rest tonight then dawn will find me well on my way home. Don't fret I'll be back this way again a few nights later. Hoping to fit in another trip before Midwinter."

"Tell you what, I'll have Cook put some food together for you. For the road."

"That's very kind of you," Lopt said.

"Not so kind," Hodr said, smiling. He knocked the table with his knuckles and pointed toward the smith. "You overpaid by a few coppers, remember. I'll make sure she puts some extra in there for you, and I'll fill a wineskin. Smooth the way between us."

"Thank you, my friend," the smith said.

Hodr felt Lopt's strong, hot hand clasp his shoulder. He felt his smile, too, like the warm sun on his face. Something thawed inside him—and then he wondered why the smith was going out of his way to befriend a blind man pouring drinks in a way house. Was this what a normal life was like? If so, he rather he liked it.

23

Frigg

This morning, it was a divorce, one that had turned nasty as they too often did—at least in her experience after presiding over dozens. And so Frigg sat in the Lower Hall, Nanna beside her, listening to the wide-eyed, disheveled man gesticulating in front of her chair. He was big, heavy in the shoulders, with the weather-beaten look of those who spent their days and nights outside. She'd asked him to tell his story, how he'd come to beat his wife so badly.

The man, Harald, looked more shocked than anything else, saying how he couldn't have—wouldn't have. He'd known his wife, Bera, wanted a divorce because he was gone all the time—he was a drover—and because he'd struck her once. In public. Yes, he sometimes drank too much, but he loved her. He did. He thought they were working it out, that everything was getting better, but he'd returned the prior night to learn she'd gone ahead with the divorce after all.

"I'd stopped by the hall before coming home, Almother. I had a few cups with friends and then come home to find her packing. I knew what she was doing, and something broke inside me—but to beat her? By Aegir, Almother, I wouldn't have."

A likely story. It made more sense that he'd returned home, realized that this Bera was leaving him, and then taken his rage out on her.

Frigg regarded Harald's wife. She was blond, slight, and pale-skinned but not washed-out like the pregnant woman standing protectively on her left. They looked similar enough to be sisters. Beside the pregnant woman stood a tall man, lean and dark of hair and beard. And beside him was an older couple, jaws slack and eyes glazed as if they couldn't believe this was happening to their daughter.

Bera herself stood silently, one arm in a sling. She had a huge bruise purpling one cheek and swollen, split lips. Judging by her smoldering dark eyes and white-knuckled, clenched fists, she would fight back the next time. Not that there would be a next time.

It was clear to Frigg that as far as Bera was concerned, this divorce was final.

She raised a hand and indicated Bera to Harald. "How do you explain her face and arm, then?"

His dark blue eyes wide and wild, Harald glanced at his former wife and stepped toward her, hands outstretched.

Beside her, Nanna flinched back in her chair. Frigg frowned slightly—it didn't look threatening to her—but before she could lift a finger, Ráta had slid forward. Lean, tattooed arms corded with muscle unfolded from behind her back.

The drover's advance faltered.

Frigg raised a hand; the gesture quieted the low rumble of the witnesses. "Answer me, Harald."

Harald faltered, eyes flitting from Frigg to the baresark and back again. He shrugged. "I can't explain it, Almother."

As she thought. She beckoned to the wife. "Bera, please approach. Before us all, give your reasons for wanting this divorce."

"Yes, Almother," Bera said in a voice like fresh honey. She took three steps forward, turned toward the crowd of witnesses, and spoke. "Harald and I were married for three winters; it would've been four this Midwinter. He's always been jealous—angry when I spoke with men of any age at the market or in the trade shops. Just buying simple things and smiling in thanks would earn me a slap if he saw it. And he's slapped plenty before, but always in private, and never where the bruises would show."

Frigg couldn't tell if the mutterings from the crowd expressed agreement or outrage. Violence between spouses or among family members was uncommon, but it happened, particularly in the winter months when there was less to occupy folk.

"Just before he left on his last run south," Bera continued, "I met a childhood friend in the lower market who'd just returned from service in the army. Harald saw it and, later, accused me of having an affair with him. I denied it and explained what had happened. It didn't matter. He still beat me, but this time in public. Many others saw him do it."

Now the crowd's murmurs sounded more like agreement, so perhaps others had truly seen it. Frigg glanced at Harald, but he just stood there, head hanging, eyes squeezed shut. No one stood beside him. Was this shame, then? Acceptance? Or was he just acting like a man who'd never grow so angry that he'd beat his wife where others could see? If he ever did, by some wicked cut of the Norns' chisels, then maybe his shame would look just like this.

Aegir knew she'd seen enough of these divorces to know when a man was lying, but Harald seemed genuine. If this was an act, then he was as good as Loki.

"I told him then I would divorce him. He just laughed and said I didn't dare—but I do dare." She advanced on Harald, her good hand raised to strike him.

Frigg motioned with her chin, and Ráta unhurriedly caught Bera by the wrist and around the waist. The woman struggled, but Ráta lifted her off the ground and set her back down like she might an unruly child.

Low laughter came from the crowd, along with calls of "that's right, get him, girl." Ráta swept her eyes across the crowd, cutting the din by unspoken threat.

Bera's chest heaved and her cheeks were red. Her pregnant sister stood close, rubbing her back and whispering in her ear. Frigg happened to catch the sister's gaze, and she suppressed a shudder at the black look in those pale eyes. A hard woman, it seemed, though the parents, frail, white-haired, clung to each other and seemed more befuddled than anything else. Only the sister's husband appeared wholly present, and even he chewed on his lower lip while the fingers of one hand fidgeted at his belt.

"So that's why I want this divorce—why I declare myself divorced from Harald," Bera shouted, her voice cutting through the crowd's dull noise.

Frigg sat forward in her seat. "And your divorce is witnessed, Bera. You've already announced it before friends and family at your home?"

"Yes, Almother," Bera said with a quick nod.

Frigg turned to the husband, keeping her tone neutral. "And what do you contest about this, Harald? Every woman has the right, particularly under these circumstances, to demand a divorce."

Voice husky, he met her gaze. "Nothing, Almother. Though I still say I couldn't have beaten her. I've struck her, yes, to my shame. But not this."

He'd admitted to being a drunkard and too free with his fists. If he was honest in that, then why lie now? From the humiliation of being caught out? Bera was quite certain that the marriage had been unhappy, and she'd clearly been beaten. "Her sister and her husband witnessed you attacking her, Harald. They stopped you from doing worse."

His shoulders slumped and he shrugged again, looking down at his feet. "I know, Almother. I don't understand. I've no memory of it—no memory at all until I came to myself, shackled and under guard."

Frigg glanced at Nanna, taking in the younger woman's sad expression. She had much to learn before she could preside in the hall like this. "Perhaps it was the amount of beer you drank that clouds your memory, Harald?"

He shrugged again. "I didn't think I'd had that much, Almother."

"Were it not witnessed—both last night's beating and the public one you gave Bera weeks ago—I'd investigate further, but you understand the position you're in, yes?"

Harald nodded, met her gaze for one more miserable moment, then looked down again. "I do, Almother. I can't deny any of it, not my jealousy nor striking my wife—former wife now. I just don't remember doing it last night." He shrugged again. "I'll accept whatever judgment you set."

Despite herself, Frigg felt sorry for him. He still wasn't acting like the wife-beaters she'd judged before. No anger at being shamed here, no arrogance. No hostility toward her. Just apparently honest confusion, guilt and, seemingly, regret. Were it not for the severity of the beating, the history of it, and the unanimity of those speaking against him, she'd be inclined to leniency.

She looked at Bera. "You've demanded most of his property. That's more than either custom or law requires of him—it's more, even, than the dowry your parents gave. Why do you ask for so much?"

Bera lifted her broken arm and then gestured toward her other injuries. "For these. And for the shame."

"And he feels no shame?" Frigg said, gesturing with her chin toward Harald. "It will be a long time before he's able to find another wife. If ever. No doubt there are a dozen in this hall who'll seek your hand, fierce as you've proven it. You won't be alone long."

That earned a muted chuckle from the crowd. Over too many winters of sitting in public judgment over divorces and crimes, she had discovered that if she could sway the crowd, she could often pressure either party into accepting the fairness of her decision.

She doubted that would be the case this time. Alone, this woman might be swayed into accepting a judgment less severe than what she demanded. But with the black glint in her sister's pale blue eyes and her dogged whispers, it seemed unlikely. Even so, awarding her most of what her former husband had would be too much, and unwarranted even by his actions. Such a harsh judgement might drive the man to banditry.

Bera spoke again, but Frigg detected a waver in her voice despite the whisperings of her witch of a sister. "With respect, Almother, my sister and I will settle for half, but no less."

Frigg frowned and leaned back in her seat. My sister and I? Nanna's face plainly showed her concentration, as if she were bent over jewelry, fashioning some intricate design. It didn't help that nearly everyone present had been babies—children, at least—when Odin had left Gladsheim. None of them had even been born when she had ridden into Gladsheim as his bride. She had seen and pronounced more judgments than anyone here. She knew fairness from naked greed.

She stood, making every line of her body and face radiate disapproval. She knew the trick of becoming the Almother rather than simply being the woman in the chair.

Harald dared a glance, saw her face, and flinched away, clearly expecting the worst. Bera seemed to wilt. But curiously, the pregnant sister didn't flinch. She stood straight, a touch of hatred in her eyes.

"I am the Almother, Frigg, and I rule in Gladsheim. Hear my judgment. Bera will receive one-third of Karl Harald's property: fourteen silver total, as assessed by my stewards. She will also receive all possessions she can reasonably claim as her own and the house which they had shared. This is consistent with long custom. If any here disagree, speak now."

Her tone made it clear that no one had better say anything. And if her tone didn't drive the point home, then maybe Ráta, with her arms again crossed over her chest, blue tattoos evident, did.

No one spoke as Frigg ran her gaze over the crowd. Bera looked relieved; her sister looked as baleful as before; Harald was still broken, as well he might be. Her judgment had been severe, but not so much so that he'd turn to thievery to meet his debt.

"Very well. Since none have spoken, my judgment is final. Thank you all for bearing witness." She remained standing until the folk began shuffling toward the doors at the hall's opposite end.

She sat and beckoned Harald closer. "Are you able to settle the fourteen silvers now?"

"No, Almother. I have two silvers to my name. All the rest is invested in my business."

"And your trade earns what each month..." she asked turning toward Gná.

"Five silver," Gná answered at once.

"Yes, about that, Almother," Harald said without hesitation. "I clear about two silvers, Almother, maybe more if the drive's done sooner."

Frigg glanced at Gná, who'd only now stepped forward from her place off to one side of the platform. She nodded once, confirming the numbers.

Frigg tapped her fingers on the arm of her chair. "All right, here's my decision. You have two choices. Gladsheim's coffers will pay the sum in full today to Bera. Harald, you will then repay Gladsheim at the rate of one silver, three copper, until the entirety is repaid. Or you will pay that same amount, one silver, three copper, directly to Bera until the entire judgment is made good. My stewards will keep track."

He spoke first, without even a glance at Bera. "Almother, if it's all the same to my former wife, I'd prefer her to receive the entire payment now. I'll work hard to repay Gladsheim as swiftly as possible."

"Well said, Harald," Frigg said. "I assume you have no objections, Bera?"

Bera shook her head. The look in her pregnant sister's eyes was still wicked. Why such malice?

Frigg had never seen the woman before, nor would the coming judgment affect her except perhaps by reducing whatever amount of silver she could ultimately win from her sister. Maybe that was enough.

"Very well. Speak with Gná; she will disburse the funds. Harald, please step aside and wait. After your former wife has finished, Gná will instruct you where to go each month to repay your debt to Gladsheim."

And while you do that, poor Harald, I will sit here and, alone, dig deep to pay the price that Odin left me with.

24

Vidar

Vidar thrashed awake. He took in the bright night sky even as he heaved in a lungful of air. He was soaked, cold, and flat on his back, rising and falling with the sea on a bit of weathered flotsam just big enough for his body. He sat up; his raft shifted alarmingly. Mist clung to the wavetops, churned by a chill breeze.

A vast black shape circled the depths, and large, steady green eyes gazed up at him. He recoiled and the raft rocked beneath him.

A burning longship pushed through the mists, first its prow then its mainsail, flames skittering across it, bellied before the wind. It passed within a spear's throw of him, the heat washing over him along with the fruity smell of hot mulled wine.

Just before the mainmast, a figure sat in a chair. Flames curled around the chair legs like tired hounds. The ends of the figure's clothing were alight, the gold and silver woven in with the cloth molten with firelight. The figure's hair had begun to crisp and float away on the wind. He gagged on the stench of burning hair and flesh.

The figure turned toward him. It was Baldr. Unmistakably Baldr, his half-brother. Baldr nodded to him and began to speak, his teeth flashing bright white even as the flames ate his blackening flesh. Like ash, fragments of speech floated across the depths to Vidar.

"*... seek me out, nor my mother. 'Ere the flames come to the green wood, my doom is set. I see it now, rising, it takes wing. A long...*"

"... time since I last saw you, Brother," said a pleasingly warm voice. The smell of warm cider hung in awful contrast to the stink of ash, smoke and burning flesh of where he'd just been.

Where *had* he been?

Where was he *now*?

The pleasant, familiar voice fell away into a quiet humming that lapped at his thoughts like the waves on which he'd just been floating.

Wherever he was now, he was warm and dry. He forced his eyes open; light stabbed them. He squinted through it, trying to make out some detail past the fuzziness.

He lay on his back. On blankets. His body ached, but he could move his hands and feet. A fire crackled merrily, but it glared at him. Vidar squeezed his eyes shut and, despite himself, peered down into his own dark depths where his fylgja slept, bound by Odin's magic.

"Ah, there you are," the voice said, sounding less distant than a moment ago. It made him think of riding across Vithi's rolling grasslands in the high summer heat, with a west wind rippling through the tall grasses.

"I thought you'd wake soon, and see, you proved me right. Well done, brother." Cloth rustled and leather creaked. A cool, dry hand rested on his forehead. It dabbed his eyes with a damp cloth that smelled faintly of honey. His skin tingled when the cloth and the hands departed. They returned a moment later to lift his head slightly and place something soft beneath it.

From right above him, the now-familiar voice spoke again. "Try opening them now."

Vidar did. His eyes opened easily, and this time the faint light was easier to bear. Baldr's bright smile swam into view. They were in a long, low tent. Baldr was mostly in shadow, lit as he was by firelight from behind. Steam drifted up from a kettle over the fire, carrying with it heady scent of fruits and spices and wine.

Baldr's cool hand touched his shoulder, then folded the blanket down to lightly touch here and there. The fingers pressed in circles and in lines and several times went around his torso toward his back. Finished, Baldr replaced the blanket, set his hands on his knees, and sat back.

"You took a beating, but you suffered no actual wounds." Baldr's grin was as if Sól herself had stepped out from behind a cloud on a summer's day. Like a mountain lake, Vidar couldn't help but return the smile. Baldr favored his mother, tall and lean where she was willowy and every bit as tawny-skinned as she was. His hair, though, was as golden as Vithi's grasses before the snows came.

"How do you feel?" Baldr leaned aside to let more light fall on Vidar, his clear gray eyes focused in concentration. Baldr's clothes were simple, brown, and well made. The arms of his overtunic were rolled back, exposing arms corded with muscle.

"Well enough," Vidar said, voice thick and dry. He tried raising himself up to his elbows but slumped back again.

"I can see that," Baldr said, merriment in his eyes. "Give yourself a few minutes, Vidar. You just went through a lot, thanks to that thing inside you."

He waved a hand in the air, a gesture that succeeded in encompassing both acknowledgment of the fylgja and his disapproval. "Father wanted you up and moving quickly, so I cheated. Just a warning, he wants you back in Gladsheim right away."

"I'm not going anywhere," Vidar said. Then his brother's remark registered. "Wait, Father's back?"

Baldr brought a horn of water to his lips. Vidar drank the honeyed water gratefully, greedily, even. That honeyed scent was everywhere in the air, the cloth, the water. He sensed a theme. Based on Baldr's remark about cheating, well, it wasn't hard to puzzle out, even with his wits still scrambled.

"He is indeed, a few nights ago now. He'd ridden in at dawn and was gone again before the day ended, thanks to this attack."

Vidar rolled the sweet water in his mouth and swallowed, feeling a comforting heat bloom outward. "I'll bet your mother loved that."

"Aye, she did." Baldr leaned forward to take the horn from him. "Not too much, now."

He raised a shaky hand to rub at his eyes. "Does Idunn know what use you make of the golden fruit she plucks from Yggdrasil?"

Baldr's laugh was rich and hearty. And again, he couldn't help but smile.

"Of course she knows," Baldr said as he secured the drinking horn's plug. "She's a willing participant in my wicked plot to find new and varied uses for Yggdrasil's fruit. She'd probably hand them out to all comers, maybe even the Jotunn, if they asked nicely—and assuming Father allowed it."

"But he doesn't," Vidar croaked. And with good reason.

"No, he doesn't. Not yet. But I think I can persuade him—to let me use the fruits for healing, I mean." Baldr flashed another sunny smile as he moved to the opposite side of the small fire.

Vidar pushed himself to his elbows. More easily, this time. Every single muscle in his chest and back burned with dull pain. In a soft croak, he asked, "My warriors? How are they?"

Baldr looked up from the herbs he'd placed in a mortar. "A dozen with serious wounds. Another six with minor injuries. All being cared for in a nearby tent. They'll all recover. I cheated with them, too."

"And me? How long have I—"

"Drifted half-alive in my tent?" Baldr smiled. "Nearly two nights now."

"Two nights?"

Baldr laid down his mortar and pestle. "It's nearly midday of the second day after your battle with the Jotunn. Father's impatient to leave, but I told him you needed to wake up on your own." He spread his hands. "I can heal the body. Usually. But the spirit? That's beyond my arts, such as they are."

"I lost control," Vidar said, sighing and lying back down again. He closed his eyes and tried not to focus on that moment his fylgja's fierce glee swamped him.

"Yes, and Father brought you back."

He sent his mind inward, spiraling downward till he saw his fylgja bound by the golden threads of Odin's magic. She still slept. He swam upward and opened his eyes to stare at the rippling black fabric of the tent roof.

He wasn't sure how to ask. "How bad was it? I didn't..."

Baldr didn't respond for a long moment. When he began grinding herbs with the pestle again, he said, "Don't dwell on it, Vidar. It's done. It was always done, scratched and painted red by the Norns."

The note of quiet sadness in Baldr's voice pierced right through him. He closed his eyes again and tried to squeeze out the fragmented memories that swirled from the blackness inside.

How could he not dwell on it? He lost control.

The pestle's grind continued, harder. "And, no, you didn't kill any Aesir."

He opened his eyes, pushed himself back up, and stared down at his bare arms. At least the blood had been washed off, but he imagined he could still taste it, coppery and thick.

Baldr set his pestle aside and brushed the mortar's powdery contents into a small pouch. "Do you remember anything? From while you were shape-shifted, I mean."

He remembered that she had enjoyed feeding just as he might enjoy a good meal.

"No, not really." He shrugged and winced as pain thrilled down his arm. "Bits here and there. Impressions."

"Uh-huh." The pestle resumed its grind. "The Aesir and the Jotunn have been at peace for more than forty winters. I know that's not very long to us, not anymore, but for many Aesir alive today the times of open bloodshed with the Jotunn are just a memory."

The pestle ground on alone for a time.

"Obviously, that means the Jotunn have also been at peace. Trade grows. But although the Jotunn themselves seem to be suffering less than in past winters, they are having fewer and fewer children. Those who are born alive, arrive ill and soon perish. At least those I've seen."

Baldr set the pestle aside and brushed the remaining powder into his pouch.

Vidar sat up straighter despite the now duller aches and the popping of his joints and sinews. He glanced toward the tent flap, then looked around for his clothes.

"They're there, by my bags." Baldr gestured toward a bundle tucked behind saddlebags. He began grinding more herbs. "So I'm curious, Vidar. What's here in Vithi that the Jotunn wanted badly enough to break the peace?"

Did Baldr suspected something? If not, why ask? Father had told him to stay quiet about his work—the new weapons he'd forged, his farseer, that old, broken ironwood device, his observations of the night sky—so he shrugged and then winced at the resultant sharp pain. "Metals and timber, probably. The skymetal mines in Háls run deep and rich."

The grinding stopped. He felt Baldr's gaze on his back—now more like the sun on a hot, windless summer day. And then the pestle tapped against the mortar.

"Rich indeed," Baldr said. "But Háls is further from the Breach than probably any other mine. And why go for the raw material when they could more easily ambush any number of carts carrying weapons to one of the many Einherjar garrisons?"

Vidar stood, shakily, holding the blanket around his midsection. Stooped, he shuffled toward the stack of clothes.

The grinding started up again. "Any ideas on how the Jotunn reached Háls? Father said the Breach hasn't been attacked."

He decided not to risk another shrug. "I don't know. By ship would be fastest but more easily spotted. Over land would take months."

The grinding stopped, and the fresh silence hung for a moment. "Just after the Last War, I remember you moving out to the high peaks east of Gladsheim. You also ventured into Utgard several times?"

He began dressing. So Baldr recalled the farseer; best to not play dumb, then. "Yes on both counts. I was working on the early models of that long tube that lets you see faraway objects as if they were an arm's length away."

"I remember. You called it a...?"

"Farseer. I should ask Bragi to think of a better name," he said, tugging on his trousers. "The idea for it came to me during the first years of the Last War. I was with Tyr in Utgard, and we were riding past a frozen waterfall. Tired though I was—we all were—my eye caught Sól's light streaming through an icicle. On a whim, I broke off a chunk and played with it. Looking through it distorted how the land appeared. Some things seemed far away, some close, some blurry, some crisp. And that's right about when the Jotunn set a pack of dominated snow bears on us."

He shook his head at the memory of his younger self, so taken with his discovery that he barely got to his sword in time. "Anyway, the experience stuck with me. Many winters and many failed attempts later, I built the farseer."

"That shows the world upside down, if I remember right," Baldr said, sounding amused.

"I haven't figured out how to fix that yet."

Baldr shrugged. "I'm sure you will. My guess is you just haven't been able to spend all your time on it. I remember you working on something else in those mountains, something found late in the war and brought to Gladsheim. And then we never heard of it again—or at least I didn't, though I was preoccupied with starting the fregnahol at Breidablik."

Baldr had been a warrior once and fought alongside Hodr during the Last War when Hodr had been blinded by a snow bear's venom. Baldr's skill at healing, comparatively meager in those days, couldn't restore his brother's sight. Nor could their father's magic. After ten winters, a bitter, angry Hodr deserted Gladsheim in the night.

The whole sorry mess had compelled Baldr to give up fighting and dedicate himself to learning all he could about healing. In Breidablik, his jarldom southeast of Gladsheim, he began to pursue those arts nonstop. In time, the village became a town and then, with Frigg's blessing since even back then Odin was often elsewhere, a fregnahol that trained the valkyr. Many Aesir, Vanir, and Alvar flocked to Breidablik to learn what Baldr and his fellow healers taught.

Vidar carefully pushed his arms and head through his shirt. "I'm not sure what you're getting at, Baldr."

Baldr laughed. "You're so like Father in a hundred ways, Vidar. Except one. You're terrible at lying."

He glanced at Baldr, feeling his cheeks beginning to heat up. There was nothing but mirth in Baldr's expression—and he couldn't help but grin back at him. He shrugged. "I promised not to say anything."

Baldr slapped his knee and set his mortar and pestle aside. "Aha! I knew it! Tell me what's been going on here, Vidar. Please. Maybe it has something to do with this Jotunn attack. If it does, maybe we—I—can stop this...sickness...before more suffer."

He'd hoped to avoid this confrontation. He looked down, pretending to concentrate entirely on donning his woolen socks. His beard, no longer weighted with silver or bound up with straps, spread like a bird's tail feathers across his chest and upper arms.

"Vidar..."

He met Baldr's eyes. "I can't answer you, Brother."

"Can't, or won't?"

Vidar shrugged. "Both. I gave my word."

"Indeed he did, Baldr," said their father from the tent's opening, his voice chillier than the air flowing in.

Baldr's expression grew more resolute.

"I can heal this breach between us and the Jotunn, Father," Baldr said. "But I need to know what's been going on—what exactly might have prompted the Jotunn to violence rather than just speaking to Mother or me."

Odin fully entered the tent, dominating the entire space. Vidar straightened as much as he could and faced his father. In a way, it was a little absurd—as if he and Baldr were children caught stealing wild berries.

Odin's evaluating gaze shifted from Baldr to Vidar. "You did well, Baldr. Less than two nights, and he's whole and moving about. Stiffly, but moving."

"You did say to cheat," Baldr said.

"So I did," their father said flatly, smiling that not-smile of his.

Even after more than a hundred and twenty winters of not seeing it at all, that particular expression of his father's still made Vidar's stomach roil. He'd watched many grown men, proud Aesir, back down from that not-smile. Even Tyr chose his words more carefully in its light.

He'd only ever seen two Aesir completely unaffected by that not-smile: Thor and Loki. Thor would simply drop a hand to Mjolnir and smile back at his father. Loki never seemed to see it.

Odin looked from Baldr to Vidar, then back again. "Well, if you'll excuse us, son, there's much Vidar and I need to discuss. About this attack on Vithi."

Baldr must've heard the same unspoken message Vidar had. "Thank you, Alfather, but after I finish here, I need to check on the wounded. Perhaps later."

"Of course," Odin said. He turned and ducked out of the tent, taking the chill with him.

Vidar bowed to his brother. "Thank you for your care, Baldr."

"You are very welcome. And Vidar?"

Vidar paused in mid-stoop.

"Don't follow him too closely."

25

Vafthrudnir

Hill Tribe is not convinced that stealing supplies will help, Vafthrudnir's fylgja whispered. *But the other chiefs are, so she's fighting an uphill—*

Funny, Vafthrudnir broke in. Torso bare, tattoos a faded blue around his wrists, he sat cross-legged on a thick hide he'd placed beside an ice-covered pool fed by a meandering river in the dead forest outside Jotunheim. His heavy tunic and fur-lined cloak lay behind him.

Even before Sól had risen, he'd slipped from beside his wife and out past Jotunheim's walls. Now, with dawn striding toward him, he was almost calm enough to throw his mind down into the water.

I thought you'd appreciate that. Anyway, she hasn't swayed any of the others, but she's trying.

He remembered a time when this river had run straight, or nearly so, through this same forest. And a time, much later, when children had splashed in the pool that had gradually formed as the river bent to avoid the dying forest.

To his fylgja, he said, *Her efforts would probably have been more fruitful if Hill hadn't been so enriched from trade with the Aesir.*

He set an iron pot, full of icy water drawn from the pond, onto the stones set in the small fire before him. From his satchel, he withdrew a bundle of dried herbs and a battered metal cup. He dropped the herbs into the pot, stoked the flames, and set the cup in front of him.

That's what the other chiefs have been saying, his fylgja agreed.

The pool before him was much deeper than he was tall, which mattered because he'd be sending his hugr deep, too. And it helped that sitting here dredged up sad memories with which he stoked the embers of his hatred.

Come help me, he said, closing his eyes.

I'd really rather not. That thing is terrifying.

Vafthrudnir opened his eyes and stared at his lithe, translucent fylgja. The plume of his breath merged with the fire's smoke.

Oh, all right.

***

Down he went, his hugr slipping through the waters like a silver-bellied salmon. He swam against the current, casting his mind out, seeking an eddy. The wyrm always found him in the eddies.

A voice came to him even as the waters calmed around him.

I am here, Weaver. Why do you trouble me again?

To request a boon.

Something vast shifted in the darkness below him.

And what do you offer in return?

What do you want? Vafthrudnir said.

A way out, of course.

In granting the boon, you may find that much sooner than we planned. Vafthrudnir sent the words out into the currents, little boats set adrift by children.

There's nothing of that in the Norns' scratchings.

They limit even you?

Again he had the sense of movement—of an uncoiling; a rising.

Inside his mind, Vafthrudnir's fylgja whispered: *That was foolish. Get to the point.*

Vafthrudnir spoke again. *Ygg will soon return to Gladsheim. We suspect he'll seek counsel. That will put him close to the well.*

My broodlings dealt with his uncle, as you asked. How does revealing myself to Ygg help me?

The Norns prevent you from leaving—

They prevent nothing, shaman.

Apologies, great wyrm, I meant solely that their scratchings mark when you will break free. But does the same apply to your children? Surely some of them are old enough, strong enough, to deal with him.

When the wyrm spoke again, Vafthrudnir felt the first sizzle of venom in the water.

So you suggest I capture the little father, then send one of mine into him? I think that would help you more than me.

With respect, it helps us both. He's a threat to our plans. Yes, suborning him removes an obstacle in our path. That same action—unforeseen though it was—may be one of the steps that brings about your release.

Are you telling me, then, that you'll fail if he's present? You guaranteed success.

The venom began to sting; his mind's voice grew hoarse.

I stand by that promise, great wyrm. Our plan will succeed. But I can't see all the runes cut and painted by the Norns. Perhaps this path is the one set forth. If not, there will be others.

Now, as the venom began to burn, his fylgja wrapped herself around him like a cloak. The pain receded, and he spoke again. *Your snares have worked before.*

Partially, it agreed. Then, *I will do as you ask, but promise nothing.*

Vafthrudnir sensed a vast bulk turning and a tail flicking. The currents surged; his eddy vanished. He tumbled upward, mind afire from the venom-laced waters, until he slammed back into his flesh.

* * *

. . .

VAFTHRUDNIR OPENED his eyes to a gray sky. Back aflame from lying in the freezing snow, he rolled onto all fours, retched, and pushed himself up. He dragged a shaking hand across his mouth, beard crusted with ice from his breath, and huddled before the fire.

The water in the pot bubbled with the light fragrance of ripe apples and fresh honey. Wrapping his hand in a fold of his cloak, Vafthrudnir lifted the pot from the fire and poured the tea into his cup. The iron pot hissed at him when he set it in the snow.

Hands already trembling a bit less, he brought the cup to his lips and sipped. Warmth spread through him and he relaxed further.

If I didn't know why you did this to yourself, his fylgja said, *I'd question why I stay with you.*

26

Vidar

Squinting against the brightness, Vidar straightened outside the tent. His muscles ached, but Baldr's elixir continued working its magic. He felt stronger with every passing moment.

The cold air, heavy with wood smoke, burned in his lungs. He found himself in a makeshift camp comprised of a few dozen black tents arranged in circles around large fires. A cooking pot hung above the nearest fire. On the broad back of a chill wind rode the simmering smell of onion, garlic, and boar flesh— a typical Einherjar stew—along with the muted clatter of rattling pots, weapons being sharpened, men laughing and horses whickering.

Those sounds fell away, though, as the nearby warriors noticed him—and then rose to acknowledge him. Like that long tense moment when the strain comes on the anchor's rope, time slowed. He felt the weight of his warriors' regard, saw the respect in their eyes and felt, more strongly than ever, the absence of those he'd failed to save. Gravely, he returned the salute of those he had.

Odin's gloved hand fell on Vidar's shoulder; the anchor jerked free. Time resumed.

His father spoke quietly in his ear. "And now you have an inkling of how it feels."

Vidar stepped out from under his father's hand. "When did you return, Father?"

"Just in time, of course. You did well, son." Odin's genuine smile stole some of the sting he heard in the unsaid words—that he'd lost control of his fylgja.

"All right, you lazy oafs," Garilon shouted, approaching through the loose assemblage of warriors, kicking those who didn't move quite fast enough. "Get some warm food in your bellies, the tents broken down and your gear in order. We'll be riding out before long."

Garilon halted a few respectful paces away, but Odin waved him closer. To Vidar Garilon presented a large bundle of spare leather armor, along with a heavy wool overtunic and another cloak. An axe with its belt lay over it all. "Fresh from your packs, Jarl. Well, most of it. And if I may, it's good to see you back on your feet."

Vidar nodded his thanks and accepted the bundle. "Good to be seen, Garilon."

He felt his father's disapproval at the familiarity like heat on his neck. He ignored it. He knew he had a lot to learn, but some familiarity with his kjolr—the man who'd held the warband together when Vidar hadn't—was the least of his worries. Vidar donned his armor quickly, welcoming the added warmth of the overtunic, and finished by buckling the wide belt around his waist and sliding the scabbarded axe into a comfortable position.

"Apologies for the axe, Jarl. Your sword was lost."

"That's all right, Kjolr. Better to have something than nothing," he said patting the axe's head. "How are wounded doing? And what have I missed?"

The tent flap pushed out, and Baldr emerged, blinking, into the sunlight.

"Extremely well, Jarl," Garilon said, with a respectful nod to Baldr. "Your brother's worked wonders."

Baldr bowed slightly in acknowledgment. "Speaking of the

wounded, I'm off to check on them." And without another word he headed toward a trio of black tents to the left of the central campfire.

"I'll join you shortly, Baldr," Vidar called after him.

Baldr raised a hand in acknowledgment and ducked into the first tent.

"As for what you missed, Jarl," Garilon continued, "well, there's quite a bit. If you're feeling up to a walk afterward, it might be easier to show you."

Vidar looked at his father. "Will you be joining us?"

Odin grunted. His sharp features were impassive, and his eyes were deeply shadowed even in the bright sunlight. The sun glinted in the silver bands plaiting his grizzled beard. "Lead on. You and I need to speak, but we can do so afterward."

Vidar frowned inwardly. Baldr *had* warned him.

He turned back to Garilon. The kjolr couldn't have missed Odin's implication or Vidar's body language, but his face remained inscrutable. Natural enough, given that the last place he likely wanted to be was caught in a battle of wills between father and son.

"Well, Kjolr, lead on. The wounded's tent first, and then where you will."

"Very good, Jarl."

***

Vidar dismounted onto trampled grasses and followed Garilon across the red-stained earth, frozen into an ankle-twisting sea of peaks and valleys. Odin trailed behind them, his eyes on the sky and a pair of circling birds more than the battlefield.

Squinting against Sól's glare, Vidar forced himself to take it all in: six rough lines of mangled corpses, limbs twisted, heavy-browed faces frozen in pain or fear, more like hewn trees than the men they'd been. Almost without exception, the bodies had been savaged—great gaping rents in their flesh, white bone protruding, backs broken, limbs missing.

Wings clattering, his father's massive ravens landed on the dead and stabbed their beaks into the frozen flesh. Vidar glanced at his father, who returned the look impassively.

He knew what his father was thinking. These were the enemy. The Jotunn had attacked, slaughtered Aesir and destroyed Háls.

But he, Vidar, had done *this*. He'd torn these warriors apart. His fylgja had, really, but it had been his body. His lack of control had made this happen.

Garilon stepped up beside him. "This is what the Alfather and I wanted to show you." He thumped his boot into the eyeless corpse of a middle-aged Jotunn male whose belly had been clawed open. His shaved head was covered in blue, swirling tattoos, bright against the ashen skin, that showed he'd likely been a shaman.

Vidar squatted to look at the unfamiliar crossed spears pattern beneath the knot of tight, flowing swirls. "Lake Tribe, but I don't recognize the clan markings."

"We don't either, Jarl," Garilon said.

"Which means we can expect the Skrymir to claim it was some 'rogue tribe' that attacked us," his father said. "Have your sweeps found any other Jotunn, Kjolr?"

"Not yet, Sigfather," Garilon said. "We've been moving slowly, not wanting to overextend ourselves before the reinforcements arrive."

"Reinforcements?" Vidar asked.

"Yes, Jarl. A full warband's on its way from Vithi, and the Sigfather's directed the Einherjar to remain and assist us." Garilon gestured toward the white-shouldered mountains. "This morning, I sent a heavy patrol into the mountains. Trygg's leading 'em. I'm hopeful they'll find something despite the fresh snow up there."

"Are they headed up the mining road?"

"Yes, Jarl, to the camp. If nothing's there, Trygg will backtrack to where he and Rikr, Aegir keep him, cut trail through the forest the first time they were up there."

Vidar nodded. That had only been, what, three nights ago? Already it felt as if more than a week had passed.

"Seems you have things well in hand, Kjolr. Thank you."

"Thank you, Jarl. My pleasure to serve."

"What of the town itself and their dead? From here, it looks as if the town is basically destroyed."

"It is, Jarl. A few of the homes furthest from the northern entrance weren't touched by fire, but I doubt any of the townsfolk will want to live in them. Fear of draugr."

Vidar gave him a questioning look. "Why draugr?"

Garilon pursed his lips, looked sideways at him and away again. "Well, Jarl, some of the townsfolk died at the town's northern gate. The ground was too disturbed to tell—may Aegir preserve and protect them—whether they were dragged there and killed or if they held the gate while the rest fled."

Vidar stood blinking in Sól's light, disbelieving what he'd heard. His fists clenched, and he felt his face growing warm. His people might have been executed.

"I want to see where it happened."

"With respect, Jarl, there's nothing to see. We removed the bodies and said the words," Garilon said. "But certainly, we can ride to—"

Odin stepped forward. "No, we don't have time for that. We've spent too much time on this already."

Vidar's temper flared, but his father raised a hand palm outward. "I need you back with me in Gladsheim, Vidar."

Vidar forced his anger down past his pounding heart and gave a Garilon a tight smile. "Thank you, Kjolr. Please give me a few moments alone with the Sigfather. I'll be with you shortly."

Garilon touched his brow in salute. "Of course, Jarl. I'll wait with the horses."

***

"Why is it you need me back in Gladsheim, Father?" Vidar was careful to keep his tone respectful. He stood facing Odin, hands gripped behind his back.

"Two reasons. The first is related to why Frigg called me back—the dreams Baldr's been having. Did he mention them to you?"

He shook his head. He wasn't about to mention the dream he'd had of a burning Baldr in a flaming ship. He wanted to stay here and figure out what happened and how the Jotunn got to Háls, not return to Gladsheim at his father's heel.

Odin raised an eyebrow. "He said nothing at all of the dreams?"

He shook his head again. "He asked me questions. Some of which you heard."

"A simpler man might think you were avoiding my question, Vidar."

He grinned, spread his hands, and met his father's gray gaze. "What else can I say? No, he did not say anything about dreams he was having."

His father grunted and nodded. "All right, son. I pushed because Frigg's visions are returning. She won't say exactly what she's seeing, but she's worried. And she's already spent several months trying to figure out why Baldr's dreams are happening. Nor can Freyja figure them out."

"So, this why you're back after twenty winters gone?"

His father nodded.

Again, his temper flared. "Because of dreams? Others here, me included, could have benefited from your presence before now."

He gestured at the lines of corpses. "Maybe I wouldn't have done this."

Odin snorted. "They're the ones who attacked—and they killed at least three times their number."

"No, that's not what I mean," though of course it was, at least in part. "I lost control. She took over. If you'd spent more time training me..."

"Vidar, there comes a point with all baresarks when the only thing left to learn cannot be taught."

"Do all baresarks end up doing what I did?"

Odin grinned and gestured toward the dead. "Well, usually not with such practical benefit. But we all have lost control, usually within the first few winters of becoming a baresark. It's like riding a mad stallion toward a cliff so hidden in the mists that you can't see where the edge is. Maybe you stop in time, maybe you don't. If the baresark plunges off the cliff, the fylgja takes over. Unlike the falling man, the baresark doesn't die. Usually. The shifted baresark is contained by his brothers and sisters until the fylgja spends its strength. Then the baresark reasserts control, this time with the knowledge of exactly where that cliff's edge is. After that, a baresark doesn't usually lose control again."

He frowned. "Far too many 'usually-s' in that explanation, Father. But what you're saying is that once the fylgja ran out of people to devour, I would have reverted."

"Oh no, that's not what I meant at all," Odin said with a grin. He clapped Vidar on the shoulder. "But you're here and whole, so why dwell on it?"

So he would've stayed shifted, a thrall to his fylgja? He pushed the notion of it away. "It would've been nice to have been told all this before the disir and I were bound together."

"Yes, I'm sure it would've been. But I don't tell any baresarks. They all learn it the hard way. I did. And if I'd told you, would you have pushed as hard in that fight as you did? There's a balance point for everything, son. Too much caution or too much risk—either can end in ruin. Finding that balance takes practice, and it's something you must figure out on your own."

27

Hodr

Hodr stepped into the stable yard, his spear tapping before him. The air was thick with the sound of carts being readied, traders calling to one another, and horses stomping the ground and blowing, ready to be on the move. One of the thralls must have seen him coming, because his spear did not clunk into what should have been the closed stable door. Indeed, the earthy smell of horse manure and hay was also stronger than it should have been. He touched the chilly wood of the doorframe, heard the familiar creak of Kona's door open and then the familiar clop of her hooves on the frozen ground.

"Here are the reins, Karl," the thrall said. He smelled faintly of ale and the oat-crusted bread Cook baked every other morning.

Smooth, worn leather was held against his hand. It smelled of old sweat and horsey earth. "Thank you."

He took the reins in his spear hand so that he could stroke Kona's nose and pat her neck. They'd been together from long before the moment he slipped out of Gladsheim all those winters ago.

Reins in one hand now, spear in the other, he said, "All right, Kona, let's go." And following her lead, he walked out of the fenced yard surrounding Alara's hall.

***

A large, growing city at the tip of the northernmost point of Asgard, Ifington straddled the river Ifing where it emptied into the Great Sea. If Gladsheim was the brilliant central gem of Brisingamen, Freyja's torc, then Ifington was one of its two complementary jewels —smaller, but still stunning to the eye.

Sometimes as Hodr walked through Ifington on his way to the market, the memories of the battle that had cost him his sight slipped out like rats from a trading ship. The Ifington of then, though, had been far smaller than the spreading trade center of today.

Ifington was built on the bones of the joing Aesir-Jotunn settlement it had once been. According to his father, when the Aesir and Jotunn fled in their ships from their homeland, beset as it was by pounding, tall waves, exploding, fiery mountains and wild storms, they had all, for a time, lived in these lands. The Aesir had moved further south, leaving behind the constant fighting with the surviving Jotunn, who chose to remain closer to the icy waters of the Thund west of Ifington and the Great Sea, whose waves pounded Ifington's eastern shores.

Kona's hooves struck a sharper, harder note. A step later Hodr found his feet on Old Bridge. It was the quickest route to the market, and Kona knew it meant less time before snacking on the traders' apples and oats.

His scarred eye sockets began to burn, just as they did every time he set foot on this bridge. During the Last War, the remnants of his warband had held this bridge against repeated, vicious Jotunn assaults.

Thor hadn't been able to help; he'd been fighting the Jotunn who'd braved the failing ice of late winter to run across the Ifing to attempt to gain a foothold on the southern shore. Odin had battled the shamans' magic while Ullr and Tyr had directed the army. Heimdall had coordinated from the center. Heimdall must have seen the pack of snow bears the Jotunn drove toward the bridge Hodr held. Heimdall must also have heard his cries for reinforcements.

Hodr sucked in the icy air blew out a breath and clucked his tongue. Kona was happy to pick up the pace. Clop-clop, tap-tap across the Old Bridge—which had been new when he'd fought upon it. Since then, two other bridges had joined Old Bridge. Were the Jotunn to attack Ifington again, it would be much harder to stop them reaching what were now commonly called Asgard's shores.

Kona's hooves changed tone again as they stepped off the wide ramp onto frozen earth. A riot of voices stormed Hodr's ears; smells of sizzling fish and other roasting and stewing meats swamped his nose. It had taken weeks before his feet, let alone Kona's, knew the route to this market and those others dedicated to specific trade goods. One market had even sprung up outside the northern wall, frequented by many Jotunn traders seeking to avoid intrusive searches and petty thefts by the town's wardens. It had taken still more weeks before Kona could lead him there. Not only was it safer and easier with her, but her broad back was the easiest way to get his purchases back to the way house.

In the bustle of the marketplace, he bumped into quite a few people. He heard their sharp intake of breath as they rounded on him, about to let loose with some invective. He might have learned to hide the slight smile when that same breath faded and they apologized for jostling a blind man, but he had never learned to ignore the stab in his warrior's heart as he remembered battles he would never again fight.

He'd been strong once, his name known and respected—not like Thor or Tyr, or even Ullr with his bow, but then he'd never had a runeforged weapon to aid him much less the protection Baldr had been given.

He'd just been Hodr, a normal warrior—stronger than most, certainly, but normal just the same. The snow bear's venom had burned that all away. Neither his father's magic nor his brother's healing skills had been able to restore his sight.

"Back again, eh, Hodr?" called Uni in a friendly, familiar tone. "I thought that last catch would last longer."

"So did we, but the fish was so good that many paid for second helpings," he replied. He stopped before the trader's booth and sniffed. "Smells like you've more of the same."

"I do indeed. Loaded a full hold a pair of days ago off the coast east of here and packed them in drift ice. As fresh as can be."

"Smells like it. I'll take the same weight as before—and at the same price," he said, smiling. The haggling was about to begin.

"The same weight I can do, but the same price? It's even more expensive to get this catch up here now that the rush of Midwinter is upon us. And would you believe the fisherfolk are charging double now? Double!"

Hodr laughed. "Uni, only a moon's passed since you sold me that first hundredweight. You mean to say that much has changed since then?"

"These fish get harder to catch as winter progresses. They tell me they're sailing out farther and farther which takes more time. It's costing them more, so it costs me more—"

"So how much will a hundredweight cost me?" Hodr interrupted.

The trader blew out another breath. "For you, my friend, five silver—good silver, mind you."

"Five? That's nearly twice what I paid before. The fish better cook themselves at that price—never mind that the mistress would make me sleep with the pigs if I parted with that much of her silver."

Hodr heard the creak as Uni leaned against the stout pole of his tent. "I hear business for your mistress has never been better—and that you might well be moving up in the world..."

***

The best part about living as long as he had was that the Hodr who defended the bridge in the Last War was only a memory to most people. With his name and reputation all but dead, he was just a blind man in a vibrant town, happy to have haggled the merchant down to four silver and two copper.

Kona was less happy. Not only had she left the sweet oats behind, but she had carried the fish and other goods back up the ramp. She'd been a warrior's horse, not a packhorse.

Alara knew who he was, of course, and loved him despite it. She'd made a place in her life for a warrior who could no longer fight, whose name was lost. She'd stopped trying to convince him he could make a new name that stood for something else. Instead, she'd just shown him what their life together could be like—should be like.

Judging by the familiar sounds around him, they were nearly back at the way house.

"'Ware the horse!"

The cry rang out above the general din of foot traffic, carts, and other horses. All around him, Aesir shouted and scattered. In their haste, several bumped into Hodr. Kona whinnied. Her feet clip-clopped in a quicker cadence than usual. She was between him and the row of trade shops lining the street.

Someone slammed into him. He staggered, caught himself with his spear, and barely avoided hauling Kona's head down. She whin-nied again. Through the reins, he could feel her head turning as she faced the clamor behind them. Her hooves clacked against the cobbles marking the road's edge.

Not far off, a chorus of voices screamed, "Quick! Grab his halter!" Through his feet, Hodr felt dull, pounding vibrations. They were punctuated by the pattering, thumping sounds of booted folk scattering every which way.

A loud metallic bang sounded behind them, followed by a prolonged rumbling. Kona started and jerked her head up. Someone thudded into him and knocked him in the opposite direction. Kona's halter ripped free from his hand.

He stumbled forward. His spear caught on something, and he fell. The spear bent and then snapped as his weight came down on it. He hit the ground, and his breath left him in a loud grunt.

Thunderclaps approached, rapid, concussive blows that vibrated through his head. He hauled in a breath and got his hands underneath himself to push back up.

"Pull him back! Pull him—"

It wasn't thunder, of course, but hammering hooves.

Hodr felt hands grab his legs. He tried to push himself up, but something cracked hard against his head and sent him tumbling. The road stones dug into his back and banged his elbows and knees.

"Sweet blood of the Mother!"

He rolled up against something that smelled of wet wood and lay still. Cold stone dug into one cheek while a hot sheet of blood ran down the other and into his mouth. His stomach twisted and he vomited, the sharp stink reminding him of the battlefield.

More hands pressed against him, one cupped behind his neck, others pulling against his hip and shoulder until he felt the hard stones pressing into his back. A hammer went to work inside his skull.

A deep voice called out, "That's the blind man who works for Mistress Alara. I'll fetch her."

Another voice, closer to him, high and sweet: "You! Get the valkyr."

The pounding in his head swelled and he vomited again. His throat burned like his face had when the beast's venom had stolen his sight.

"Roll him back over," urged one voice while another, more distant, cried out, "What did they do—oh, what did my horse do?"

He knew that voice, but his thoughts slipped away.

28

Odin

Odin dismounted beside the tall, solitary tree on the outskirts of Arnheim's Forest. Behind him, the long column of Einherjar clattered to a halt.

Wineskin in hand, Odin kneeled before the shrine at the tree's base. He brushed leaves and twigs from the rune stones, poured wine into the soil as an offering and asked the local disir for her protection.

At a throaty call from high above in the darkening sky, he stood. A pair of winged shadows fell fast toward him. He raised his arms and caught them, grunting beneath the weight of thought and memory. Their talons dug in as they sidled up to perch on his shoulders.

Sleipnir snorted indignantly at the ravens. Muninn cackled at the mare and then turned, beak clacking as she swallowed a strip of meat Odin dug from his bag.

"Oh hush," he said, holding up more meat for both ravens.

Anything?

Feathers rustled as they shook their heads.

Your son reports, Huginn replied. *No enemy on the plains.*

Muninn said, *He rides into the town. From there into the mountains.*

It was good news, and some progress. *Thank you. Fly to my wife. Tell her we return, victorious. And then a rest for you both.*

Huginn launched himself into the air, fast as thought. Muninn lingered a moment and then followed her brother eastward toward Gladsheim. Long shadows stretched across the spreading land below the forest like stitching on a quilt, with hundreds of homesteads and villages sewn into it like buttons. The shimmering line of the Silfr ran a wandering line across the quilt, curled around the far hill's northern edge, and slipped out of view.

Above that quilt, Gladsheim stood, its high walls built from the tall trees of the forest that had once covered the farmland before them. He remembered the degrees by which he and his Aesir had exposed the bare land—young arms with broad axes felling old trees. Even as they had made peace with the Vanir, the First War with the Jotunn had begun. And then those same arms had felled Jotunn.

"What news, Father?" Baldr asked. He sat his horse, hands resting on the saddle horn.

"Vidar's sent word," he said and waved for Saglund to approach.

When the hersir had reined in beside him, he said, "Huginn and Muninn bring word from Vidar. He's found no trace of more Jotunn on the plains round Háls. He now rides into what remains of the town and from there into the mountains."

"Excellent news, Sigfather," Saglund said. "Perhaps now my Einherjar can return to Gladsheim. Undoubtedly they'll just be in the way."

He gave Saglund a stony look. In a quiet tone, he said, "They are my Einherjar, Hersir. They, and you, ride when and where I say. Is that clear?"

"Of course, Sigfather. I meant nothing by—"

"My son and I will ride the remaining league alone. You and the Einherjar may gallop ahead. Freki and Geri have made sure your route is clear. Huginn and Muninn will tell my wife that we will arrive soon."

A black look wormed its way across Saglund's face so quickly that it was gone before he saluted. But it had been there.

"At once, Sigfather," the hersir said. He sawed his horse's head around and rode back to the dismounted column of Einherjar and relayed the order.

Temper, temper, Saglund. He'd have figure out what exactly gnawed at the man.

Odin looked over at Baldr, who was watching him closely. "Once they're well on their way, Baldr, I will include you in an old secret."

And then I'm sure you'll wonder how many more I keep.

29

Frigg

Frigg forced herself to stop drumming her fingers on the arm of her chair. She ached to stand, to move, to do anything other than sit here and wait for word of what was happening in Vithi. After four nights, she should have heard something. Odin's ravens could make that flight in half the time—less, even. Not even the regular clamor in the hall—laughter, talking, shouting—ease her mood.

She glanced over at the dim nook into which the thralls had dragged Heimdall's inert form and shook her head in disgust. He should have been able to tell her what was going on, but whatever Baldr had given him had knocked him out for nearly two nights. When he awakened, he'd stumbled back here and began drinking. And there he lay, snoring and twitching.

She should make him sit by the casks of ale. At least then he'd be completely out of sight.

"If only Jarl Heimdall were sober, we might know what happened in Vithi," Nanna said.

Frigg smiled wearily. "You read my thoughts, Nanna,"

Nanna had come to Gladsheim with her husband, Baldr, months earlier for aid in dealing with his night sickness. Over the last few weeks she'd spent much of her time as she usually did this time of year helping to plan and organize the Midwinter festival which marked the celebration of Aegir's escape from Rán's nets. Frigg's own people, the Jotunn, also celebrated on Midwinter, but the dominance of the two figures—Rán and Aegir, who fought and fell in love as summer passed into winter and back again all through the long ages was different.

"I would know if something happened to Baldr," Nanna said, sounding more as if she was trying to convince herself.

Frigg patted Nanna's hand, knowing exactly what her son's wife was referring to. "We'll figure it out."

When Baldr was born on Midwinter's Night, Frigg had used the power of that long, dark night to guard her son against all harm. She had bled for it, as had Odin, just as they gave of themselves every Midwinter to maintain the strength of that charm.

But if nothing could hurt her son, then why was he being plagued by these deathly dreams? And why did she see him aboard a flaming ship?

Her eyes roamed over the feasting, drinking mass of Aesir and Alvar in the great hall without actually seeing them. Their revelry was like the dull, distant pounding of surf. The earthiness of their close-packed bodies was accentuated by the wafting smell of roasting cow, boar and deer's flesh, and the spices used to flavor the meat.

To her right, one seat down from Nanna, Idunn and Sif laughed at some bit of verse or song that Bragi, Idunn's husband, was composing or rehearsing. The hall was so loud that she could only hear fragments of the harp's voice. A bored-looking Tyr sat to her left. Ullr's usual seat was vacant. After news of the Jotunn attack on Háls, he'd chosen to remain at the Fortress at the Breach which guarded the border with Utgard.

Frigg's gaze next fell on the Jotunn envoy. Eldir shook his head slightly and looked away. No news from him, then.

What had happened in Vithi?

When she'd spoken with Eldir yesterday, the envoy said that he was, of course, aware of the attack and was awaiting further word from the Skrymir—who hoped to find some way to redress the Aesir's losses and thus avoid a war.

No war? She almost laughed. Not with Odin back.

Her eyes flicked away. Odin. She forced her hand to remain unclenched. She must show nothing except strength and calm control.

It wasn't enough that he'd been gone for more than twenty winters, leaving her to manage Gladsheim's affairs. No support. No key advisors, beyond aged Fimafeng. Might as give a boy an axe and make him off to duel Thor. But she had survived. She had proven herself and those in this hall, and elsewhere, did accept her as Almother.

But no sooner had she had called Odin back to deal with his own son's sickness than another problem arose and off he rushed leaving her alone. Again.

She felt the scowl on her face, and she knew it would be noticed before long, if it hadn't already. So, she forced a smile to her lips and hoped the glinting gold all around the great hall might lend some sparkle to her eyes.

A raucous cry from a florid-faced man drew her attention back to the floor. He was massive, dwarfing even his companions as he stood, black beard bristling, dark eyes shining in a bluff face flushed with drink and good humor as he lifted his ale horn in a toast. Whatever he shouted was lost in the din.

"These new Einherjar," Nanna whispered, leaning in toward Frigg, a slight frown on her face. "They seem so different from the older ones among their ranks, don't you think?"

Frigg frowned and peered into the comparative gloom at the eastern side door, where a pair of veteran Einherjar sat, grizzled and scarred. They were speaking quietly with Ráta, one of the two baresarks Odin had left to guard her.

Ráta noticed Frigg's gaze and quirked an eyebrow, but Frigg shook her head slightly.

"Different, indeed, Nanna, but those who earned the Einherjar distinction during the Last War are old now—no doubt many long for a new war before they depart for the Gjoll."

Nanna nodded and gestured with her chin toward the florid-faced Einherjar, who was now gesticulating in a decidedly lewd manner. "But I don't remember them carrying on like this one here."

Frigg was about to reply when shadows darkened the space above. A heartbeat later, amid clattering wings, the empty chair to her left rocked slightly under the weight of Odin's two large ravens. Their huge taloned feet gouged fresh cuts into the tall back of Odin's chair.

Their heads and beaks darted in quick, ferocious movements, and they called out in loud, hoarse, cough-like voices, that silenced the hall's din.

He returns, croaked one.

Soon, said the other.

Frigg's gaze darted to the Jotunn envoy. He wore no expression; his eyes were a stony blank.

Victorious, said the first raven, talons grinding against the yew chair.

Make way, said the second.

Frigg felt Nanna's hand on her arm, gripping tight. She patted Nanna's hand reassuringly without taking her eyes off the ravens. Would Odin double the spectacle by sending Freki and Geri in next?

"And what of Baldr?" Frigg asked quietly.

One of the raven's black eyes gleamed golden, and it spoke. *"Alive. Hale. My wife."*

"See, he's well," she said, giving Nanna a comforting smile even as relief flooded into the younger woman's expression.

She beckoned for Gná. "Please inform all those jarls here, as well as Freyr and Freyja, who are most likely in their respective houses, that we will descend to Ithavoll in the morning."

"At once, Hár Frigg," Gná said, with a bow.

As the din returned to the hall, Frigg leaned toward Nanna and said, "We'll have to postpone our trip down to the victualers. Who were we to visit?"

"The ale and wine sellers in the morning and the meat traders in the afternoon. They're here tonight. I'll go tell them now."

"No, no, wait until I'm done, daughter." She stood and smoothed her dress. "I must announce Odin's imminent return, though it's hardly necessary, given the entrance he makes even without entering. Well, sooner started, sooner done, eh?"

She stepped forward to the platform's edge, tugging at one sleeve and then the other, staring out at the faces in the crowd. Most were well-off farmers and merchants here with their families. All Aesir knew how to fight, but maybe a tenth of those here had actually seen a bloodied axe or smelled the stench of battle. None of them had any desire for a new war with the Jotunn.

What they wanted, for themselves and their kin, would arrive a week from now. All these Aesir—jarls, drangr, and karls—would again gather here in Gladsheim's main hall, as well as the handful of lesser halls throughout the city, for the Midwinter festival. For three nights and days, the streets would run with ale, food for all, games of skill and chance, music, and poetry, all of it to celebrate the longest night of the year.

The culmination of the festivities would find Baldr, chest bared, standing high on a stump at the center of a ring of townsfolk. After he played the role of Aegir in the Midwinter ritual, everyone would be invited to hurl weapons at him. Baldr would stand, patiently smiling, as the weapons bounced off him and clattered to the ground. That was her people's ancient blood magic at work, born of love and sacrifice and given freely every Midwinter to prevent his death.

A few faces from the nearest tables turned up to her with expectant expressions. The light from the torches, witchlamps, and braziers scattered throughout the hall—hanging from the beams above, resting on tables, or hammered high into the dozens of columns holding up the roof—conspired to lend auras of shimmering yellows and oranges around the faces of seemingly everyone in the crowd.

She sighed to herself. She still hadn't said anything. She'd been silent so long now that she didn't really need to address the revel.

Everyone knew what it meant when Odin's ravens clattered their way into the hall even if it hadn't happened in a long time.

But if she didn't play the role of Hár Frigg, Almother, adoring and loving wife of the Alfather, these wealthy, bored folk would wink and nudge and whisper of a rift between herself and Odin.

And what did that matter, really? Many of those here had been children when Odin had left. In another twenty winters, they'd be wizened wrecks, while she would remain mostly as she was. Strong. Proud. Young.

And alone.

Her stomach twisted at the thought. And it didn't help with what she had to do now. Sooner started, sooner done.

"Folk of Gladsheim, hear me!"

She waited for silence, consciously wearing a light, armoring smile. Her gaze moved from familiar faces in the crowd who turned to listen, to those less familiar to her, to those shrouded by distance and gloom.

The hearth flames had mellowed, as had the light from the many sconces hung from the tree-thick posts. Witchlamps on every other table, were bright islands in an otherwise gloomy lake.

"Hear the Almother," Nanna called out, her voice loud and clear, and oddly, for Nanna, happy.

Frigg half-turned to acknowledge her daughter—and that's when her vision began, in flames above Nanna's head. In those vision-fires, Nanna lay prostrate on a floor, shoulders heaving as if she wept.

Not now, please not now, Frigg thought.

She turned back to the hall, feeling her smile, her armor, slip. All the light, regardless of source, dropped to the floor where it puddled and pooled, doubling and redoubling in brightness till—as she drew in her next breath—flowed up every single person and turned every head in the hall into a torch.

She closed her eyes—not now, please, not now—but the vision-flames still burned above every head. Eyes open, eyes closed. It didn't matter. Only she could see them. No one knew that she, Frigg, Almother, could see their dooms in those dancing flames.

The hall looked like a windblown lake of fire. So much pain and death and grief, smiling faces heedless of what lay before them—spitted on spears, filled with arrows, swept overboard, crushed in the slavering jaws of snow bears, trapped in burning houses and more. So much more.

Perhaps sensing something wrong, Gulfinn and Ráta drifted closer from where they'd been leaning in the crisscrossing shadows of the hall's columns. She shook her head and they stopped. They could protect her from a beast in the hall, but there was no defense against these visions.

When they had first come to her as a child, her father's shaman had told her to embrace what she saw. They were a gift from the wild disir, he said, glimpses of the doom the Norns themselves cut and painted for all folk everywhere.

She'd abused the gift, as children often do, because she resented seeing death and pain wherever she looked. She had lashed out, telling friends how they'd die, even the old shaman himself. He'd just smiled sadly, nodded, and said she would learn his final lesson on her own.

A winter later while standing on the shore of the Thund watching the shaman's burial ship burn its way through the mists, she realized what he meant. All she'd done was bring more fear and sadness into the world. She hadn't ever been able change what would happen—only how it happened, and usually not even that. Better to stay silent.

It was the juxtaposition of the now with the yet-to-come she found so disturbing, particularly in these times when people lived with such heart. That golden Alvar over at one of the traders' tables laughed among friends even as a forest burned behind him and he fell to his death.

Pitching her voice louder still, she called out, "Hear me."

Finally, comparative silence returned to the hall, upturned faces afloat in the sea of vision-flames.

"As most of you are aware, except sharp-eyed Heimdall," she said, gesturing toward the dark corner where Heimdall snored, "the Alfather's ravens have returned. They spoke of victory in Vithi, but how could it be otherwise when the Sigfather and his Einherjar take the field?"

That earned a roar of approval, punctuated by the dull hammering of fists and knife butts, further denting the tables. The big florid Einherjar again leaped to his feet, arms raised, and exhorted those around him to greater cheers, even as his death fluttered down in a rain of black-feathered arrows.

Annoyance writ plain on his scarred face, Gulfinn drifted closer, clearly ready to hurl the man from the hall. In the moment her eye lit on the baresark, she saw Gulfinn falling...

... backward, a table and bench splintering soundlessly. His mouth parted in what had to be a shout. A black-haired wrist appeared that ended, not in a hand, but in a sickening white-bone spike. Less than a heartbeat later, that spike was buried in Gulfinn's chest. Blood fountained from his mouth...

The vision-flames flared she hissed in a breath and, just like that, all the vision-flames in the entire hall winked out. Nanna touched her elbow and offered her a small cup of wine.

She took the cup, smiled her thanks, then faced the crowd. Those nearby had noticed her lapse, but those farther back had not.

She gestured for the white-robed thralls to move through the hall with fresh flagons of wine and beer and raised her cup. "A toast to the Alfather—a fitting repeat of his own words, spoken many times in this hall: No great thing need be given; often, little purchases great praise. With half a loaf and a half-filled cup a full friend I've made."

She drained her cup in one quick, cool, sweet swallow. "In a week's time, Midwinter will be upon us. At that time, all those who present themselves at any hall in Gladsheim will receive a full portion—and may friendships made then last twice as long and run twice as deep!"

For they may need to rely on them soon.

The crowd's noise rose again as they saluted her in turn. She kept her smile as she walked slowly back toward her seat next to Nanna. Was the hall she'd seen in Gulfinn's vision this one? It had looked familiar. And what of the black-feathered arrows that killed the big, cavorting Einherjar. Surely that meant battle loomed. But who had shot those arrows, the Jotunn?

She pressed herself hard into the high back of her chair.

Nanna whispered, her voice sweet and concerned. "Mother? Are you all right? You're white as milk."

She smiled tiredly and touched her daughter's shoulder with one hand. "More visions. They're becoming nearly as frequent as when I was a child."

Nanna seemed to shrink inward. "Who this time? Or is it the same one..."

"No, it wasn't about Baldr," she said. Not directly, at least. Who else would Nanna weep over—only Baldr and her kin. "I think I'll sit here a little longer and then retire for the night. It's been a long day already, and Ithavoll will make tomorrow longer still."

At the council, should she hint at her visions of death and war? It seemed the right thing to do, given that their only remaining foe were the Jotunn.

She drummed her fingers against the arm of her chair. Why would the Skrymir want another war with the Aesir? He couldn't win. He had to know that. The Jotunn had only a few warbands, and all they did was roam Utgard's wastes looking for a way out. Obviously, some of the Jotunn tribe leaders wanted war; otherwise, Háls would still be standing. And just as obviously, they must have hidden that warband away in Utgard's many caves.

But why now? Until three nights ago, she would have sworn that her efforts these past twenty winters, along with Baldr's, had borne fragile fruit. In the last eighteen winters alone, Baldr had made twice-yearly embassies to Utgard. In the wake of those trips, tenuous trade had developed between the Jotunn and the Aesir. It was the first time such a thing had ever happened.

And it was the first time since she'd been wife to the Alfather that a generation of Aesir had not been at war.

In many ways, Odin's absence these past twenty winters had been a good thing. Most of those sitting in this hall had never seen an axe bared in anger. And over the past handful of winters, trade had steadily increased as the Aesir developed a craving for Jotunn trinkets: horns from snow bear, furs, spices.

Baldr had made it all happen. She'd made sure that was known. From what she could tell, the Jotunn had come to love Baldr even as they feared his father.

If she could get Odin to step down as Alfather could Baldr effect a lasting peace?

She snorted. Odin would never abdicate, particularly now. He'd want blood for the attack on Háls.

But she also knew that he hated mediating border disputes between farmers or whose flock grazed in so-and-so's field when it wasn't their turn much less sitting in judgment over thefts and murders. Or divorces.

All of that was much more common in the Gladsheim of today compared to the one he'd left behind.

No, Odin wanted to explore, to discover new things—seidr, creatures, lands, peoples.

And what did she want? To no longer be alone, certainly. She also wanted her husband back. Despite his long absence, she loved him. And, if she were honest, that was partly why she'd gotten so angry when he'd left for Vithi.

But if Baldr became Alfather, well, maybe that was a way forward for both of them.

So how would she get Odin to abdicate?

30

Odin

Odin barked his shins on a bench that hadn't been there before. So much for slipping quietly into the bedchamber from which he'd long been absent—and yet another reminder that things changed in twenty winters.

One of Frigg's thralls peeked out, her face a dim oval. She rushed to stand and bow when she realized who he was, but he waved her back.

Having defeated the apparent warden of his wife's bed—his own bed—he crept the dozen more paces to the room where he and Frigg actually slept. Wooden boards creaked beneath his weight. He slipped through the final set of hangings, pulled off his boots and set them quietly on the floor.

As his eyes adjusted, his wife came into view. Frigg reclined in their bed, her dark hair unbound and strewn around her like the spreading branches of an ancient elm. Even at rest, her natural expression gave the impression that she would bend before she broke. Not that she would ever break.

He stepped closer to the bed, and a board that hadn't creaked twenty winters ago betrayed his presence. Her eyes flew open, fierce and awake. Her hand darted to the falcon-hilted knife he'd given her ages ago.

"Frigg, it's just me—Odin."

"Odin?" She let go of the knife. "What took you so long?"

"Baldr and I had a talk on the way down from the western shrine," he said, sitting on the bed.

"About what?" she said.

"Ithavoll in the morning. And a secret I've been keeping."

She grinned. "The device Vidar's been working on, or another?"

And all this time he'd thought he and Vidar had been discreet. "How did you know about that?"

"Odin, I've ruled here—alone—the entire time you've been gone. A witch couldn't weave a curse without me knowing about it."

"Don't be too sure of that," he said, hoping this conversation wasn't turning into an argument.

"Njord and Skadi won't be here for Ithavoll, by the way. Messenger arrived yesterday. They had to stay to resolve a border dispute."

He frowned. "Their duty is to participate in the council. We have them once a year—"

"No, I hold them once a year," she said, her tone even and her gaze level. "They each rule their own lands and have done so for a long time. Just like us. Besides, we'll have enough here to decide about the renewed war you're planning. That is what you're planning?"

She was relentless, his Frigg. So much for avoiding an argument. "They did burn Háls right down to the stones. And that was a single Jotunn warband. Vidar may yet find more in the mountains."

Frigg glanced behind him toward the door and made a dismissive gesture. "You're not needed tonight. Return to your beds."

When the thralls had left, she tapped her ear and pointed toward the thrall's quarters. Beckoning for him to join her, she rose and walked to the far corner of their room.

They stood beneath a small window where the wall met the roof's timbers. Moonlight peeked through. He put an arm around her shoulders and stood beside her, head stooped, facing the door into their chamber.

"They're just gossips," she said, her tone hushed. "Nothing malicious about it. Not like that crone I sent away all those years ago."

"You're sure?"

She nodded. "As best I can be." She met his eye. "We do need to talk, Odin. And I mean really talk. Not just about where you go and what you're doing, but about me and what I'm doing. I'm all alone here. I hate it."

"You're not alone," he said, suppressing a rush of indignation. He'd left her in very good hands. "You have plenty of help. Tyr and Ullr. Heimdall. Thor. Sif and Idunn. I know Freyja and Freyr aren't here often, but—"

She jabbed a finger into his chest. "Our marriage was supposed to be a partnership. We were supposed to be together. To rule together. That's what you promised. That's what you told my father, may Aegir preserve him. I've spent more time alone than I have with you, Odin. I don't get a break. I don't get to wander off into the world's woods to do whatever it is you're doing. Night after night, I'm right here, keeping Gladsheim on track."

He hadn't left just to go wandering or avoid his responsibilities as Alfather. He'd gone out because there was so much more to learn about the realms.

"I understand, I do. But look, we need to keep pushing outward, or somebody else is going push in on us. There are many other folk out in the realms, and not all of them are descended from my brothers or the Aesir who left with them. I've come across whole settlements that could become valuable trade partners—allies, too, outposts we could use as staging areas for colonies or even places for our own to go."

He sank to the chest beneath the window and pulled her down to sit beside him. The moonlight cast her features into stark planes and prominences. Her eyes were wells of shadow. "I thought Hermod could lead our first trade expedition to them. It would be a good experience for her. She could take a company of Ein—"

She pulled her hands from his. "No. Don't try to change the subject. I'm tired of doing all of this by myself. Sick of it."

He'd borne the same burdens she had but for far longer. "I know the weight of kingship. I also know how well you rule. And how greatly our people respect you."

Disbelief bloomed in her eyes.

"I'm serious, Frigg. Do you think I would have left Gladsheim in your hands if I didn't think the folk would respect you? To love you? I saw it the other morning before I rode to Vithi, and I see it here right now. You've blossomed."

She stood, mouth a tight line, tone icy. "So you've been what? Testing me?"

He shook his head. "That's not what I meant. Look, when I left when we were first married, it was to handle all those small crises, the raiding along the coast. Then, winters later, it was those rebellious gothis out east. Then the Vanir had their Alvar problems. And so on. Each time when I returned, often after months, you'd handled Gladsheim's affairs like you do everything else: excellently. I know it wasn't easy for you, even raised as a chieftain's daughter. Eventually, I realized that the only way for you to fully blossom was for me to absent myself."

She leaned back, folded her arms, and gave a short disbelieving laugh.

He pressed on anyway. "And look how you've grown, from sapling to strong elm. You know, I heard what you said in the hall earlier, Frigg. I *am* impressed. You've become the true Almother of the Aesir, Hár Frigg, not by marriage alone but by your own actions."

"I don't need you to tell me that." She stabbed a finger at him. "You didn't leave to help me. You left because it's what you wanted to do. You didn't want to be stuck here, ruling, when you could be out there wandering around. But you should be here, where your responsibilities are. Not out there."

He stood abruptly, jaws clenching even as he tried to breathe long and slow. She stared up at him, not backing down in the slightest.

"You don't know a tenth of what's gone on here," she said. "Not just within Gladsheim in the past twenty winters, but in our relations with the Jotunn. Baldr's been going there twice a year, bringing supplies and medicines. Have you even spoken to him about conditions in Utgard? He was appalled by how the Jotunn live. Sickness is rampant. Underfed children roam the streets half-naked and shivering. Jotunn children, actually shivering!"

He snorted. "It's a play the Skrymir puts on. He could give Bragi lessons. The Skrymir knows Baldr is too tender-hearted so he orchestrates displays of misery before Baldr arrives with his medics and his food and clothing—and gold, I'm sure—and then dismantles the show after he leaves. He's laughing up his sleeve all the while."

"Maybe," she said with a shrug. "Maybe that is what happened the first few years after Baldr negotiated the truce. Why wouldn't they make themselves seem weaker after the beating our armies had delivered? But that's not what's happening now. At all. The Skrymir's respectful. Accommodating. And it's no act. I've sat on the High Seat and watched."

"I didn't mean for you to use it regularly—"

"You showed me how, remember? How else was I supposed to rule? I don't have familiars to roam about and scare everyone. I needed to see that my orders were being obeyed. Even so, in that first year, Tyr and Ullr spent more time enforcing my will than they did patrolling the border with Utgard. Thank Aegir they proved loyal. So you're right. I haven't been alone. Many of the Jarls supported me, at first out of loyalty and duty to you. But now they respect me for myself. I have grown. I have matured. But don't you dare sit there and tell me you were testing me or deliberately helping me by not being around."

Her eyes, fierce as a falcon's, didn't waver. Pride swelled in him. Respect. "If there was ever proof of how much you've changed, Frigg, this is it. Twenty winters ago, you would never have confronted me like this."

She stepped in close—a lover's distance separated them—but she had her hands on her hips. "No, I wouldn't have. But the point is,

Odin, that we're married. We're supposed to be changing together. We can't do that if we're apart more often than not."

If they had been regular Aesir maybe he could have agreed. But they weren't. His role—and hers—was to chart a course for the Aesir. Sometimes that meant being alone and doing that which others would not. Or could not.

"We've made ourselves responsible for everyone."

She smiled lightly. "No, Odin, you've made us responsible, by eating Yggdrasil's fruits and by keeping the Jotunn penned in Utgard so long that their hatred for us will never die. Let it all go. Tear down the fortress, let the Jotunn go their way while we go ours."

He shook his head. "If we ease up, they'll recover. They'll come at us. Not now, but later when we don't expect it."

"Not all the Jotunn are bad. Baldr and the peace he has fostered proves it."

"You mean the peace they just ended?"

"Interrupted," she corrected with a slight shake of her head. "We can afford to take the longer view."

"That's the view I took, Frigg. Contain them. Control them." And if they all died, well, he wouldn't shed a tear.

She sighed and moved to sit on the edge of the bed, one hand smoothing the wrinkled blankets. "Whipped hounds eventually turn on their masters. Why not let them instead make the choice to become Aesir?"

"Because I don't trust them, Frigg. Any of them." The original Jotunn, Ymir, was the worst troll that had every existed. His blood ran through every Jotunn.

A part of Odin—a small part—did wonder if she was right. Maybe Ymir's blood was finally spread thinly enough that the Jotunn had given up. If they had, then perhaps he should lay down his weapons—but only after he had settled the mystery of the attack on Háls.

31

Vafthrudnir

Vafthrudnir leaned against the broad yew table. Opposite him, one of Helveg's scouts used a long stick to trace on the map the paths she'd taken. She tapped one spot, and he tilted his head to make sense of the map's markings.

"The only difficult part is this scrabble here, High Shaman," she said with the air of one who already said it once before. "Viper and I made it up no problem, but we'll have to drop ropes down for the baggage and whatnot."

Hersir Beli looked a question at one of his captains.

The man nodded. "I checked, Hersir. We have plenty of rope."

Beli grunted and motioned for the scout to continue.

"After that, High Shaman, it's just a normal trek to the stone pillar. Less than a night's march for the warband. Viper and I rode further, so near to where the glacier dropped off into the Thund we could've dived off ourselves."

"And there was no route down," Beli said, reflexively, though he hadn't needed to.

Vafthrudnir had already guessed the answer. Not only would the Skrymir have told him, but Helveg would have been up and nearly across the glacier by now rather than idling here in camp. After more than a hundred of winters searching, he'd only ever found one safe way out of Utgard: the doorways. One of the keys to those doorways hung from Beli's broad belt.

And this new doorway—well, possible doorway—was the real reason he was here. Dominating snow bears for Helveg's use in the coming conflict was all well and good, but the doorways meant life for the Jotunn.

He cleared his throat. "If I may, can you describe that pillar you rode past, scout?"

She nodded, her long braids scattering shadows across the map. She picked up one of the small wooden disks that were piled before her, leaned forward, and placed it on the map. "It was right about there, High Shaman. It's a long, low pile of rocks, higher at the southern end, which is how I approached it."

"How close did you get?" Snow bears had extraordinary senses.

"We were downwind, so we got within probably two hundred yards. The nest was tucked right in close, so I can't say how many total snow bears are in the pack, but I saw the matron myself and counted four females."

Which meant there were probably several adult males, as well. He could handle the matron, but the rest? That depended on how good Helveg's shamans were. Having met both, he was surprised that Shaman Steinfastr had survived as long as he had. But, Adept Kali had potential. And it looked as if she hadn't quite decided on which faction within the shamans' ranks she would side with.

"So what do you think, Vafthrudnir?" Beli asked. The ruby-tipped pommel of the finder flashed in the witchlamp's glow.

"The snow bears won't be a problem, Hersir," he said, with more confidence than he felt, "so long as we're disciplined about it."

***

One of the advantages of his presumed old age was that he got to ride on a sled pulled by four young Jotunn warriors. His fellow shamans, however, had to walk—or run, as they were now—along with the rest of Helveg.

As dawn approached, the crosswise stretch of the Bifrost above them faded, no longer a bridge of white-blue stars stretching from the southern end of the sky to the northern. Beyond the running figures of his bearers, the dark lump of rocks that was home to the pack of snow bears grew larger the closer they got. He guessed they were a few hundred yards out, so any moment now, the hersir would—

A horn's sharp note cut through the tramp of feet upon glacier ice. A voice shouted. "Helveg, walk!"

Once his sled had crunched to a halt, he stood, stretched, and thanked those who'd pulled him along. Westward, clouds clung to the mountains' shoulders. Hopefully the wind would pick up and draw that cloak over their heads.

They were only risking being active in the daylight because he had received definitive word that Goldtooth was indisposed, thanks yet again to Loki's clever bit of revenge. And, the attack on Háls had the other Aesir looking everywhere except this scrap of glacier in remote northern Utgard.

Otherwise, they would have had to wait for an obscuring storm or night's cloak. Not that they would have stormed a matron's pack during a storm. Without shamans present, a lone matron could have wiped out Helveg. And matrons were never, ever alone.

How many are there? he asked his fylgja.

Just six so far, including the matron.

So far?

The nest goes down below the surface. Might be some down there also, Fimbulthul said.

All right. Let me know if you find more.

Just adults? Or pups, too?

He raised a hand and waved Helveg's two shamans over to him. Kali jogged over at once while Steinfastr made a point of taking his time.

Both, but I'm not worried about the pups.

"There are at least five snow bears in that nest. The matron makes six."

"How can you know that?" Steinfastr said.

He ignored the question. Helveg's own scout had counted that many, which meant that scout was very good indeed, since his fylgja hadn't found any others. Not yet, anyway.

"We will stand in the middle of Helveg's fighting square, so we can cover each wall as needed." Frost bears typically attacked in pairs, sometimes trios.

Helveg's signal horn blew three quick, sharp notes. The ranks of warriors closed into a large square of double rows around them. The warriors comprising the outside wall carried shields and axes; the warriors in the second row held spears, shields slung across their backs. One aktaumr stood behind each wall; they commanded the warriors in each wall. Helveg's officers—the siglautr, kjolr, and Hersir Beli stood in the middle.

As if in response, short howls that rasped like blades being honed issued from the nest of ice and stone. The snow bears were speaking to each other, no doubt coordinating their attack. The beasts were very smart which is what made them so dangerous and so valuable, once dominated.

"Once you have them dominated, make them sleep. A pack this size won't give us much time," he said, meeting his fellow shamans' eyes. "And conserve your witchthread."

Kali nodded. Steinfastr didn't bother disguising his frown. Yes, what he'd said was obvious, but it bore the reminder. If any of them failed, the warriors protecting them would die. The dominations had to happen fast.

"Good. Head to your positions." They would be a triangle inside the warband's square, with him at the front.

"High Shaman, you are ready then?" Hersir Beli called out, one hand on the finder dangling from his waist. "Our quarry will test us shortly."

"We are, Hersir," he called back. The snow bears would indeed attack soon. That was why they hadn't bothered disguising their approach. Safer to draw the snow bears out than confront them in their nest.

Have you found her yet? He asked his fylgja.

More howls ripped through the air. An eddy of wind brought the stale reek of the nest to his nose.

Yes.

Let me guess—those howls were because of you.

The equivalent of a shrug flowed into his mind. *She knows why you're here. This one's formidable. I doubt the other two shamans can handle her.*

Can I?

Helveg's horn sounded a sharp note, and the fighting square moved forward toward the rocks and the nest.

With my help, yes.

32

Vidar

Vidar and his warband rode through the broken, blackened, half-standing gates that had once protected Háls. They'd ridden down through the fields and farms, crossed the river and now clip-clopped their way through the town's scorched foundation stones and bare ribs of frames.

The town was built atop a low hill with the ridge behind it. Háls had been home to those who worked in the mines, cut timbers from the forest blanketing the mountains, or ranged far and wide trapping animals for pelts.

A few piles of thatch or...worse...still smoldered, despite the fresh snow that had fallen during the night. The air was crisp, and Sól was warm on his back. Were he not leading a warband through a dead town, it would have been a perfect day – aside from the dull, empty thud of hooves and the occasional sharp tang of burned wood. Although the town had burned down, there was no ash anywhere—the Jotunn shamans had used it all to spin those black longships.

Háls was laid out in a circle, with four main streets and smaller streets running in concentrically smaller rings. He led his column up the main street that ran from the southwest entrance, through the town and then up the mountain's shoulder to the mine.

Something shifted and fell with a clatter in the shell of the building to his left. Hrimfaxi danced sideways, and Vidar shot a quick look into the shadows—nothing there. He frowned at his own jumpiness and snuck a glance sideways at Garilon, whose only reaction had been to drop one hand to his sword's pommel. He clucked his tongue, urging Hrimfaxi forward again, and led his column leftward around the broken, scorched bones of the large council hall at the village center. The remaining beams and columns stood like nithing poles, their scorn and curses focused on him.

Rán's hof loomed on the northern side of the street, black and empty. Smears of mud, soot...or blood...crisscrossed the temple's stone floor, along with fallen scorched rafters and columns. This was one of a few dozen buildings in Háls that used—had used—stone foundations, lower walls, and floors. The heavy thatched roofs and wooden frames were gone, their ashes scattered across the plains.

An approaching clatter of hooves drew Vidar's attention up the street leading northeast. A pair of scouts approached fast, horses blowing and lathered. Even the scouts were winded.

"Jarl, we've found the trail—and it's fresh."

* * *

"Do they know we're here, Skeggi?" Vidar asked, settling in beside the scout on his left and Garilon on his right. They were well hidden inside the snow-laden firs a couple spear lengths from the road the miners used—the very one so many had been killed on.

Vidar had rushed out of Háls, driving his warband, and the thirty Einherjar his father had left him, up the mining road till they reached the mining camp just as Sól was nearly down below the western mountains' teeth; Máni was on his way up. The damp, sharp air made him think snow would fall during the night.

"I doubt it, Jarl," Skeggi said. "But they must know their warband's been destroyed. When we snuck up on 'em, they were tearing down some of the longhouses to build those barricades you can just see...there."

A low barricade of rough-hewn stakes blocked the entrance to the mining camp itself. The Jotunn had positioned it between a pair of longhouses.

He frowned and squinted, trying to spy any Jotunn warriors squatting behind the first barricade. If there were any, it would take sharper eyes than his to spot them.

The chill evening wind blew low swirls of snow across the road.

"Attacking now would be foolish," he said, glancing at Garilon.

"I agree, Jarl," his kjolr said in his axle-creak voice.

Vidar gestured along the forest's verge, which ran a ragged path within a dozen yards of the nearest longhouse. "Have you scouted along there?"

Skeggi nodded. "Yes, Jarl. The ground falls off quick the further you go, so much so that we only saw one group of Jotunn watching that whole approach. They have a barricade in place there too, but it's sparsely manned, either because they don't expect an attack or they don't have the numbers."

"Or both," Garilon muttered.

"Could we attack along that unprotected flank?"

Skeggi shook his head. "It's a sheer rock face covered in ice, Jarl. Only way up is with grapnels and ropes, and even if they somehow didn't hear us, they'd see us once we were up top."

Vidar caught the slight nod from Garilon which meant, he guessed, he should trust the scout's assessment. "All right, Skeggi, thank you."

"With your permission, Jarl, I'll scout the far side of the camp." Skeggi pointed back down the slope. "We'll work our way up to where the steeper slopes begin. There's plenty of boulders to use as cover."

"And if they have their own scouts there?" he asked.

"We kill them quietly."

Again, the slight nod from Garilon.

"And you're certain you can do that without raising an alarm?"

"Yes, Jarl. Absolutely."

"All right. Go ahead. Take a few men you trust and send word back when you're done. We'll be ready."

33

Vafthrudnir

"Left flank, brace!" cried the aktaumr.

Vafthrudnir glanced left in time to see a dark shape hammer into the shields of the outer wall. The Jotunn comprising the inner wall leaned into their shieldmates, bracing them. Steinfastr moved to stand behind that section of the shield wall. He would dominate any beasts that attacked there.

The warriors grunted with effort, the white clouds of their breath billowing around their heads. The snow bear's claws scrabbled and scraped on the glacier's ice as it pushed inward trying to break the line. Warriors on either side of the beast thrust and jabbed their long spears into its shaggy flanks.

It slipped away.

"Right flank!" cried an aktaumr on the right just as another snow bear slammed into the shields. That was Kali's side. She was prepared, at least, hands already up, witchthread dangling between them like slack fishing line.

A heartbeat later, a pair of snow bears hit the shields on the left. The line bowed inward under the impact. One of the beasts tossed its

long-horned head back and forth, trying to pry shields away, while
the second went low, trying to hook legs.

Even as the bears tried to force a gap in the shield wall, others
struck elsewhere—the rear section, from the sound of it. Which
meant that he should probably expect—

Eyes front, his fylgja whispered.

With a thunderous boom, another pair of snow bears hit the wall
in front of him. It too bowed inward, the warriors roaring with the
effort of holding the line.

Thanks to his fylgja's warning, he'd already cast his witchthread
outward. The fingers of his right hand danced as his left pulled more
thread from his spindle which swung, spinning, from the short hook
protruding from the left side of his belt.

The pair of snow bears before him savaged the wall, horns grating
and banging against the shields. The warriors held.

As soon as his witchthread settled onto the first beast's horned
head, he began to sing. His fingers flicked and sent the thread
spearing sideways into the other beast's head and then tugged the
thread back to him. It flew fast as thought. He wove it around the
thread he'd pinched between thumb and forefinger, and then flung
out another long loop, doubling the strength of the first weave. Then
he dropped his left hand to his silver knife and whipped the blade up
to sever the witchthread.

He sang louder, sending his will flooding down through the
thread. Too many shamans tried to dominate with brute strength,
pounding on the beast's mind like a smith on an ingot. That tech-
nique worked. He'd used it himself. It was quicker than the seductive
method he'd come to prefer, and it took more effort. His approach
was a lullaby. Slower, yes, but he wouldn't have to throw loop after
loop of witchthread. The two he'd sent would suffice.

Still singing, he felt the beasts' resistance falter. He sang lethargy
into their limbs. *Sleep,* he encouraged.

Watch the left flank, his fylgja whispered, even as another pair of
beasts again slammed into them.

I almost have them. Can you—

But his fylgja had already leaped down from his shoulder and streaked across the dozen spear lengths to land on one of the snow bears. He could feel her bite deep into its shaggy neck, drinking its essence like a thirsty cat.

The beast spun, flailed its barbed tail, and bucked, shrieking the whole time. Then it bolted back toward the nest. The other beast followed.

He felt the pair of bears he'd snared collapse. Their wills were his, and they were asleep. He looped the witchthread around one of the small bone hooks set into his belt, and finished his song.

He glanced over to where Kali stood, her own dominated snow bears asleep just outside the shield wall. She wore a curious, thoughtful expression, as if she'd been studying what he'd had done.

Four down. Two to go.

* * *

Helveg advanced to within several spear lengths of the nest's outer edge. The matron had yet to show herself, but her pack were all dominated and asleep where they'd fallen.

Any sign of her? he asked his fylgja.

She's south of where you are, hunched down.

Given the size of the snow bears they'd taken, this matron was very old and very big and very cowardly. Each beast was bigger than one of the scout's wolves. But where the wolves were rangy, the thick-furred snow bears were bulky with powerful limbs ending in wickedly hooked claws. Their heads were topped with black-tipped horns that curled down to project on either side of their broad, heavy-jawed snouts. Bony plates ran down their backs, some with clubbed tails some with barbs.

The matron's deep roar rumbled over the warband. Maybe not so cowardly.

"Steady now, Helveg," Beli said, pitching his voice to carry above the building wind.

The clouds he'd seen earlier had moved in very quickly, changing a bright sunny morning into a gray snowstorm.

"Hersir, she's south of us," Vafthrudnir called. As his fylgja whispered new directions into his mind, he added, "And moving eastward."

"You heard the High Shaman," Beli said. "Stand firm. This will be over soon."

The square of shields tightened still further, now three warriors deep. Helveg had reversed face so that three sides of the shield wall faced the bare glacier. The section facing the nest was only a single row deep.

He stared out into the swirling snow. Every dozen heartbeats, he saw a dark shape flicker past. The aktaumrs on the sides would occasionally shout "Brace!" only for nothing to happen.

His fylgja gave a heartbeat's warning before the matron roared out of the screening swirls of snow. The matron slammed headlong into the shield wall's corner, knocking warriors aside even as she flung two up and over her shoulders. She was bigger and heavier than any of the other females in her pack.

Thanks to that moment of warning, he'd cast out his witchthread sooner than either of the other shamans. But almost as one, their fingers danced, pulling their threads back even as their voices found a harmony in the enthralling charm. He found it interesting that Kali imitated the lullaby he sang, while Steinfastr hammered out his charm.

The matron slid to a halt, snow and ice fountaining up around her massive clawed feet. With a roar he felt in his belly, she tossed her head back and forth in an attempt to sever the unseen lines of magic with her black-tipped horns. Snow bear horns were prized for their ability to disrupt sorcery. During the First War with the Aesir, the Jotunn had made snow bear horns into bone blades that could kill a baresark where skymetal could not.

The matron abruptly changed direction and charged Steinfastr.

The man dove aside, losing hold of his witchthread in the process. Before he'd even pushed himself up, the matron's clubbed tail came around like a ship's boom and slammed into his chest. He flew a dozen spear lengths, skidded bonelessly across the ice and lay still.

Fimbulthul leaped onto the matron's back. She had taken the shape of a long-toothed cat from the southern plains.

Kali ran right, widening the angle between herself and Vafthrudnir. He cast out another quick loop of glistening witchthread.

Fimbulthul bit into the matron's neck. The matron bellowed and twisted, but Vafthrudnir went the opposite way to Kali, further opening the angle. He sent another loop, as well, making his song more commanding. Lulling would work, but this beast might well snap the threads first.

He could feel his fylgja greedily drinking the matron's essence.

Kali tugged and hammered at the matron with her song, and the matron staggered. The reaction should have been impossible, given their relative sizes, but the seidr bound the matron's spirit more powerfully than her body.

Vafthrudnir went with the matron's stagger, but then tugged just before the matron tried to charge Kali. Massive cords of muscle rippled beneath her densely furred hide, and the matron staggered back toward him.

Kali threw another loop and sang louder. Then she tugged as he had done, and the matron's huge head snapped downward.

He tightened his loops of witchthread, his own song now a hammering, and stepped closer, taking up slack while also tugging downward. The matron tried to rear, heavy shoulders bulging, but he and Kali leaned into their threads, straining, and kept her down. Her clubbed tail thudded against the frozen earth, swinging wild, smashing great dents in the frozen ground.

He and Kali took turns stepping in and taking up slack, their voices pounding the air like surf. Close now, an arm's length away, the matron could have gutted either of them with a flick of her head, but Kali laid her hand on the matron's head.

Fimbulthul opened her jaws and stepped back, licking insubstantial lips with an equally insubstantial tongue.

Vafthrudnir put his hand on the matron's bony skull a moment later. Each of them made three quick looping gestures above the matron's head. Her neck went limp, and they stepped back.

He met Kali's eyes, the blue-ice glare fading from them, just as a similar gleam no doubt faded from his own. He nodded once to her, then turned to the Hersir.

"It is done."

34

Chapter Thirty-Four

Odin

Odin sat heavily in Sleipnir's saddle; perhaps slipping out of bed had not been the best decision. Whatever anger Frigg had set aside last night might burn all the brighter for waking alone in their bed.

Sleipnir's hooves clopped a dull eight-hooved rhythm against the ramp that led down alongside Yggdrasil to Ithavoll. The Alvar had fashioned the ramp in that prior time when the Alvar and Svartalvar had used their skills alongside one another instead of against each other.

The faint scents of the dewy grasses into which Yggdrasil sunk her roots wafted upward on the back of the ever-present, ever cool breeze. Odin dragged his hand along the trunk, his skin alternately gliding across and then tugging on the rough bark. Life drummed through Yggdrasil's ancient trunk as strongly as through his own limbs.

Unbidden, memories arose of those distant days when he and his brothers had found a crack in the rock of the hill that they eventually named Gladsheim. The crack led to a tunnel, which they followed, losing track of time and location, until they reached this world, and its impossible sky, beneath their realm.

His palm crossed a too-soft patch of bark, startling him back to his surroundings. He clucked his tongue, and Sleipnir stopped. A soft patch?

He touched the reins to Sleipnir's neck, and she turned around—the ramp was wide enough for three of Thor's chariots to ride side by side. He rode upslope a few paces, his left hand dragging along Yggdrasil's trunk, searching for that soft patch.

There it was.

He pressed his thumb into the bark; it crumbled and broke away. He coughed at the rot-stink that assaulted his nose. Rotting bark on Yggdrasil? Its outline was several handspans wide and maybe a spear's length tall, though it was difficult to measure.

He drew his knife and pressed the blade into the wood. It sank in easily right to the hilt. He turned his head from the stench of decay and it occurred to him that he had no idea how thick Yggdrasil's bark was—at least the length of his knife, but it must be thicker. He wiped the blade and sheathed it. And did the rot go deeper, all the way to the center? Was it elsewhere?

He craned his neck to stare up Yggdrasil's trunk. All he could see was the bole. Thousands of stars glinted in the blackness above, behind, and below him. By their absence, he knew where the branches to the other realms, and his High Seat, lay, dark headlands in the sea.

He withdrew one of his spindles, charged with witchthread, and called Gungnir to hand. He unscrewed the cap on Gungnir's cross guard, slotted the spindle, and replaced the cap.

Sleipnir clomped her hooves impatiently on the heavy wooden planks of the road. He thumped her neck. "Just a few moments more, then we'll be off again." She shook her mane and snorted. "Yes, I know you're thirsty. I'll be quick."

The spindle rattled as he unspooled several arm lengths of witchthread. Holding the thread pinched between thumb and forefinger, he withdrew his silver shears. He clipped the witchthread, replaced the shears, and let one end of the thread dangle free.

Beginning to sing, he cast that strand up toward the rotten bark. His fingers danced and the thread tangled intricately to form a rune. As he finished his song, the rune incandesced. Now he would be able to find this spot when next he sat on his High Seat and looked out over the realms. In finding it again, maybe he could discover something about it that would let him find other areas of decay. It seemed unlikely that he had stumbled across the only bit of rotten bark.

Sleipnir whinnied and stamped two of her forefeet in equine impatience.

"All right, all right," he said. He patted Yggdrasil's bark. *Don't worry. I'll figure out what ails you.*

He clucked his tongue, and Sleipnir turned again down the path toward the misty grove from which Yggdrasil grew. She surged into a brisk trot. Odin laughed—uppity horse—and reflexively tightened his legs. Like Sleipnir's hoofbeats, his laugh was quickly swallowed by the surrounding emptiness. They were in no real hurry, but Sleipnir wanted to move, so he let her. More time before the council wouldn't hurt. Not that additional time with the Norns meant more answers— or any at all.

He snorted. He would be lucky to get one question answered.

And so they rode on, Sleipnir's hooves beating a regular cadence against the stout planks.

A swirl in the air brought the smell of fresh, clean grass. Sleipnir whinnied and tossed her mane. She smelled it too, apparently. She increased her speed, and Yggdrasil's trunk on his right blurred. He crouched lower over her neck and let the rhythm of her eight pounding hooves clear his mind.

Soon, Sleipnir turned into the last gentle curve as the ramp followed the course of one of Yggdrasil's massive roots. With the loom of the trunk behind them and a straight path before them, she moved smoothly into a gallop that echoed throughout the glade.

· · ·

***

With a thump that jarred Odin's teeth, Sleipnir landed in the damp, tall grasses. The scent of crushed grasses burst around him. Inhaling deeply, he grinned and drank it in. White mists flowed above the thick green grass, each looking more vibrant because of the contrast between their colors. White moths fluttered among the mists.

Sleipnir began to slow, almost prancing with eagerness as they headed toward the Norns' dwelling. Odin peered ahead. Urdar-brunnr, the wide knee-high stone well in which the waters from Nifl-heim's roaring cauldron bubbled up, appeared first out of the undulating mist. Next, the gold-topped peak of the Norn's longhouse broached the mist like a ship's prow. The *scratch-scratch-scrape* of the Norn's chisels at work reached him.

Stopping before the wet gray stones of Urd's Well, Sleipnir tossed her head and stomped her eight hooves, then turned in a half circle.

"Well, hold still so I can get off."

She snorted but stopped moving. He threw a leg over the saddle, slid down, and thumped into the thick grass. He looped the reins around the saddle horn and strode the few paces to Urdarbrunnr.

He sat on the cool stone, his trousers growing wet with the damp-ness. Beside him stood a lean, elegant ewer and a wide low dish, both of untarnished silver. Across from him, white moths, wings opening and closing, covered the stone like snow as they drank from the drops of water dotting the well's rim.

He picked up the ewer, leaned forward, and dipped it into the rippling water. The water burbled and popped, tiny echoes of Hvergelmir's giant roar, the ultimate source of the world's eleven mightiest rivers and more besides. He lifted the full ewer out of the well, picked up the platter, and set it on the thick green grass. Sleipnir whinnied and moved closer. He began filling the platter even as she clopped forward, nose lowered, to drink noisily.

"Watch it, you big cow," Odin said, scratching her ears.

She flicked her tail, dismissive. She raised her head, whinnied again, and pawed the grass next to the now-empty platter.

"Thirsty indeed, eh, girl?" He refilled the platter, emptying the ewer.

She bent to drink. Odin set down the ewer and stroked her neck. Left hand trailing across her gray hide, he undid the girth strap and pulled the saddle, its pad, and the bag with the device in it from her back. He retrieved a brush and ran it through her matted, sweaty hair.

Finished, she raised her huge gray head and sighed horsily as he removed her bridle and bit. He thumped her side and stroked her nose. "Off you go. But come when I call, eh?"

She snorted, shook her mane, and trotted off. He grinned as the immense eight-legged daughter of Loki's loins gamboled through the green grasses, trailing a roiling cloud of white moths. As ever, he shuddered at the thought not only of Loki's becoming a mare but of submitting to the builder's horse. He couldn't argue with the results, though. Loki had gotten them out of their bargain, just as his efforts had gotten them out of—and into—many similar situations.

With the fading of Sleipnir's gambols, the faint scratching and scraping noises of the Norns' tools pressed back in on the glade. Grin now entirely gone, he squared his shoulders and strode toward the sound's source amid his own cloud of white moths. He shooed the one that perched on his shoulder.

Before long, the low golden roof of the Norns' longhouse became visible, nestled into the corner of Yggdrasil's vast trunk and the immense root on which he had just ridden.

He strode more quickly when the house itself came into view, along with the stone table set to one side and close to Yggdrasil's bole. Three black-clad figures stood behind the table. The ever-present scraping and scratching noises grew louder the closer he got. The sound was oddly heavy, as if some giant were piling stones on his chest.

Ages ago, he'd often come with questions for these three women, these Norns, supposed priestesses of the Slaughtered Mother. He had never found their temple, though he had looked. Unless this was it— the stone table, the well, and the tree.

His hands bunched into fists so tight it took effort to relax them. As he understood it, the Norns scraped the doom of all folk into the bits of Yggdrasil's bark that they removed and replaced. What he knew from experience, though, was that they never directly answered his questions. When they answered at all, it was in riddles that only became clear after the fact.

There had only been two exceptions, the threat to Baldr and the threat Loki's children had posed. "Beware the children of Loki, for they will cause even the heavens to burn." And, "In the golden bough shall Baldr find shelter from death and life."

Even as those remembered words arose in his mind like a black wyrm from the depths, he wondered if he had made the right choices all those winters ago. They'd done what the Norns had advised. But now, with Baldr's disturbing dreams and corpse-like stupor, he wondered just how sheltered his son was from death. If the Norns were wrong in that, then perhaps they'd been wrong in other things. Which meant he'd been wrong, and that idea kindled his anger at being here at all into a blazing fury—him, a supplicant to these three.

Pack-Father, is there danger? came Freki's thought. As ever, Geri had acted more impulsively and was nearly to him, having sprinted.

We come, Wing-Father, spoke Huginn. Muninn's mind-voice echoed her brother's.

No, I'm all right. All of you stay where you are. Turn back, Geri.

Odin felt the wolf slow until he sat, panting, to wait.

Huginn and Muninn, fly to the Breach. Tell me what is happening there.

We go, said Huginn.

Freki and Geri, stay at Ithavoll. Wait for the jarls. They'll arrive soon. Do not come to me while I speak with the Norns.

He felt Geri's growl rumble through his mind, and then Freki, her mind like a whip, put Geri in his place. *We obey,* she said.

Thank you.

He resumed his slow walk forward and forced a light smile to his lips. Wisps of smoke curled up through the roof-holes of the Norns' house.

Their stone table stood so near to Yggdrasil's immense trunk that the Norns could walk a few paces behind them, tug free a fragment of bark, return to the table to scratch and paint their runes onto the bark, and then return to the tree, pressing the borrowed bark back into the bare spot.

How they always pulled off a fragment free of runes was a mystery. The tree couldn't be growing that quickly. It never moved. Never swayed. It just...was. There was some subtle magic at work behind this place and this tree and these Norns. The thought tugged at the edges of his forced smile.

He stopped a spear's length from the table and clasped his wrists behind his back. The Norns wore simple dresses of earthy browns and blacks with little in the way of ornamentation, the slight gleam of a necklace here or an earring there. One tucked a loose strand of brown hair back behind an ear. Each moved spryly, as if they were young, but the Norns had worked in this glade since some time after Ymir's death more than three hundred winters ago.

Their brushes clinked against the stoneware that held the red paint they used. He waited a dozen heartbeats for them to acknowledge him.

Could these be the same three women as all that time ago? He was still here, thanks to Yggdrasil's fruit, so why not them?

He waited another dozen heartbeats. They still didn't look up. By degrees, his smile grew colder.

If they were different women, the older ones must have instructed the newer ones in how best to infuriate him.

So he spoke the usual formal greeting. "Three maidens, mighty in wisdom, I greet you and beg pardon for my interruption. As ever, I come seeking knowledge."

Immediately, three very different voices spoke all at once. The first was high and piping like a child. The second, mellow and strong, was the voice of a mother who had brought life into the world. The third's voice sounded like tree limbs creaking in a winter gale; she sounded like one who'd witnessed many lives passing back into the Ginnungagap. Not unlike him, in a way.

"And we greet you, father of the slain, Valfather, in the old language."

"Why do you greet me so? 'Father of the slain?'"

Scratch-scrape-scratch. They still hadn't looked up at him.

The old-sounding one spoke. "You call yourself Alfather. Does that not mean 'father of all'? And if all, does that not also mean the father of those slain?"

He waited for more, forcing the smile back onto his face despite the muscle that clenched in his jaw. That's not what his title meant; which they must know, if they knew anything at all. "But why greet me so when you must know why I came?"

Heartbeats passed. When no answer came, he pressed forward. "I come with questions, as always, wise Norns. May I ask them?"

He waited. His cheeks began to ache from holding the smile. When no answer came, he asked. "First, I ask the meaning of a dream —or insight into it, at least. It is a dream of the impossible, the death of my son Baldr. Do you know of this dream?"

"We do," the Norns said.

"Does it mean what it seems to—that my son will die? Or does it hint at something else?"

"May it not do both?"

"But Baldr cannot die. Frigg and I prevented it, as you warned...as you advised...so long ago. Just a few nights ago, he was struck a blow that would've killed nine Aesir, that might have even killed me. But he lives."

"And yet all things die, Valfather."

Not if he could help it.

"So you're saying he will die, then? That runs counter to what you said all those winters past. Has the doom you've seen changed?"

No response, but the scraping of their chisels. His smile slipped a little further.

One hand locked around his other wrist. "Have you now scratched his death rune?"

Tools clinked dully against stone as the Norns set them down. In that moment, the glade's quiet became oppressive. Sweat beaded on his lip. It dripped cold down the small of his back.

The Norns stared at him, three women, long brown hair braided, all wearing identical simple clothing and identical expressionless faces—despite one being old, one middle-aged and one young.

"I ask a second time, Wise Norns. Have you scratched the death rune for my son Baldr?"

Their faces were more still than the lake east of Gladsheim. They seemed to reflect his own forced smile and his rage, contained like a bear in a deep pit.

"His doom hasn't changed, Valfather. No more will we say. To silence, we would return."

He spoke through a clenched jaw. "You will not say?"

"It is not so marked that you learn the dream's true meaning from us."

"Marked?"

"Here, upon the bark," said the old one, tapping the piece before her even as all three spoke. The three-toned chime of their voices was more difficult to understand now. It was as if he'd been struck on the head and everything around him was a little off—a ripple through one's reflection in a lake.

"I don't care what's etched where. A third time I ask—I demand—that you tell me what Baldr's dream means."

"And a third time, we say no." The Norns picked up their tools and went back to work.

Odin blew out a long slow breath. He unclenched his hands and rubbed his palms, using the few moments to steady himself. Like a shield, his smile went back up. Spear-like, his words struck out.

"Then tell me then why the Jotunn attacked Háls. Three times I ask it."

The old-sounding Norn, the one on the right, looked up. In winter's voice, mocking the unpreparedness of men, she said, "Is it not obvious, Valfather? The Jotunn hate the Aesir."

"Yes, but why did they attack now? With this peace in place?"

The middle Norn spoke with the mother's mellow voice. "Peace between Aesir and Jotunn is merely the time between conflict." She looked down, dipped her brush in the red paint, and with quick, sure strokes, painted runes upon the bark her sister had placed before her.

"So war comes again?"

The sound of their work answered him.

Fists clenched tight behind his back, he asked his last question. "On my ride down here, I found a patch of rotten bark. What caused it?"

The first Norn put down her chisel and looked up at him. Her high piping voice clashed with her grave expression. "As a child, did you learn more from doing or more from being told?"

A smile wavered across the unshadowed lower half of her face, then hid itself as she looked back down and resumed her work. She was dismissing him. Him.

So that was it. Again they refused to answer his questions?

Quicker than an ill-made sword, his temper snapped. His sight dimmed at the edges, and he surged forward, riding the wave of his anger like a warship grounding against the shore. His hands came up almost by themselves, as if he meant to slam them down on the table or maybe reach across it to grab one of these hens by her neck and wring an answer, a genuine answer, from her clucking throat.

All three Norns looked up at him then, hands raising, fingers dancing as if along a witchthread. A wind whipped up around them, visible only in the flapping of their dresses. It caught him around the waist and flung him away—but not before he heard one of them say, "Nor is it time for that."

35

Vidar

With false dawn upon them, Vidar looked back along the line of Einherjar kneeling in the snow behind the miners' longhouses. The last man in the column raised a hand and made a sharp downward chopping gesture, which meant the scout from the opposite side had just slipped back across and told them the warband was in place.

Vidar raised his axe, swung it downward, and then he was sprinting alongside the warriors toward the barricade. Two dozen pounding heartbeats later, they were all in the open space that stretched before the sharpened pine stakes.

Surprised shouts went up from the Jotunn. A few heartbeats later, a flight of black-feathered arrows thumped into the snow ahead them.

As he ran, panting as his feet sank ankle-deep into the snow, he again considered the wisdom of not unbinding his fylgja. She slept still, compelled by Odin's magic. Without her power protecting him, these arrows could kill him. But if he lost control again, he was a danger to everyone. And his father wasn't around to save him a second time.

His father had given him another spindle charged with

witchthread so once they were a little closer he'd sing the protection charm that would render these arrows as deadly as the pine needles scattered atop the snow before him. Besides, Skeggi and the other scouts had counted only thirty Jotunn. The combined strength of his warband and the Einherjar was more than double that. Add the charm to the mix, and victory was assured.

A pair of arrows cracked into his shield, one after another, staggering him. Despite his laboring breath, he bellowed. Those warriors around him, all with shields, along with those carrying spears behind them, echoed his battle cry.

He risked a peek over the rim of his round, scarred shield. Six archers, arms moving smoothly, plucking arrows, nocking, drawing, sighting, then releasing. Five hard thwacks resounded from the leather-covered shields his warriors held.

The morning was noticeably brighter, and more details about the Jotunn came into focus: short, recurved bows; dark leather caps on wide heads above broad bearded faces. The Jotunn fought in much the same way as the Aesir, which made sense since they had been at each other's throats for hundreds of winters. Shields and spears comprised the main battle line, with hand weapons—axes, swords, hammers, and clubs—for close quarters. Archers were fewer but could turn the tide of battle.

But not this battle.

He and the Einherjar were nearly upon the Jotunn barricade, maybe three spear lengths away. No need for the protective charm. Not yet, anyway—which was good; witchthread unspent meant more for when he truly needed it. The snow wasn't as deep here, so he could run faster—another dozen paces now, so close he could taste the pine sap from the stakes.

The ground collapsed beneath his weight. He hit the far wall of the pit and bounced off. Blood bloomed in his mouth as he fell sideways to the bottom, his armor caught on something that gashed his side. The wind exploded from his mouth when he hit, and his vision dimmed. Some of those nearby weren't so lucky, as several agonized screams attested. A body landed on top of him, pinning him. Hot blood spattered across his face.

The pit was dark. The smell of frozen earth mixed with the hot tang of fresh blood. He shoved the warrior off him, his side screaming in protest. He needed to get his shield up between him and the sky before—

Black-feathered arrows showered down. More screams from around him. The arrows all missed him, except for one that cut a deep line of pain along his thigh.

To his left, an Einherjar twitched on a wooden stake. With each convulsion, he slid a little further down the gore-stained wood.

More arrows fell. Thuds and screams marked where they missed or struck flesh. He was just as lucky this time. The one arrow that did strike him drove the metal banding of his helm into his brow, drawing blood and painting stars before his eyes.

He blinked, wiped the blood away with one filthy glove, and hauled on his shield, bringing it above his head as he tried to stand on the now-slick earth, ready for more arrows.

But the expected arrows didn't fall.

Which meant that, maybe, Garilon's attack had just hit—or fallen into its own pit.

Keeping the shield above his head, Vidar counted a handful of long, rough-cut pine spikes on which were pinned the four unluckiest Einherjar. How long had the Jotunn been here that they could have dug such a deep pit in frozen ground?

Above, screams and battle cries and shouts mingled like rolling drums. He had to get out. Had to see what was happening. He dropped his shield and tried to climb out. A moment later he was sliding back down, having found no purchase.

He'd have to sing the charm from here.

He glanced right and left. At least ten warriors had survived the fall. He shouted at them, beckoning them closer. Harafn arrived first, hunkered beneath his own shield.

"I'm going to get us out of this, Harafn, but I need you to help me."

The man looked blankly at him.

"Harafn! Help me and we live."

Harafn shook his head, and his eyes refocused. "Yes, Jarl."

"Good. Now when the others get here, I'll stand on my shield. You must lift me up. You hear me?"

"Yes, Jarl."

He gripped Harafn's shoulder. "Good man."

He produced the spindle and yanked free an arm's length of witchthread. He brought the tip to his mouth and sang, casting the witchthread first into himself and then outward into Harafn and the warriors grouping around him.

And none too soon, either, for the black rain of arrows fell again. Two struck him, one on his upturned face and one on his shoulder. Both staggered him, but from surprise, not pain or injury. He regained his balance and kept singing.

"Jarl, we're ready," Harafn shouted.

He nodded and stepped onto the shield the warriors held awkwardly in front of him.

Another sheet of arrows fell and bounced off them. And then, wobbling, he was lifted up.

Once his head was above the pit's lip, he again cast out his witchthread. It flew, faster than thought to where Garilon stood behind a tight shield wall that slowly advanced toward the defending Jotunn.

The Aesir spearmen were probing the ground ahead of the shields. Garilon must have seen Vidar's warriors fall.

Vidar flung more witchthread at Garilon's group of warriors, but he couldn't see the Einherjar column, so he couldn't protect them.

Harafn shouted up at him. "Jarl, we can't hold you much longer."

A pair of Jotunn archers drew on him, deliberately, and let their arrows fly. He braced himself; the arrows struck like hammers, but they fell to the ground.

Vidar looped the witchthread around itself and then tied it off. He drew his knife and slammed it into the ground, using that bit of leverage to pull himself onto the ground outside the pit. As he got to his knees, a black arrow broke against his shoulder.

The men in the pit and the warriors with Garilon would be protected for a time, but he had to break the Jotunn line.

So, he sprinted at them, hoping that there wasn't another pit. The Jotunn spearmen behind the barricade saw him coming and leveled their spears. The archers turned from releasing volleys at Garilon's warriors to loosing another flight of arrows at him.

They were too slow. He barreled forward, slamming his shoulder into the barricade. His charmed skin deflected the outward-facing wooden spikes. The force of his charge knocked down one of the stakes, he stumbled, and then he was through.

Jotunn axes slammed into him so hard he was driven this way and that, but though the sharp metal cut his armor, it only slid across his skin.

He punched the nearest spearman; the man flew backward in a spray of blood and crackling bone. He caught the thrusting spear of another beneath his armpit, pivoted, and ripped the spear out of the Jotunn's hands. Vidar flung the spear at the nearest archer, killing him.

What felt like three spears jabbed him in the small of the back, driving him stumbling forward. But now he was within grappling reach of several more spearmen in the Jotunn line. He clubbed the first one with his fists, but the ones farther away scrambled backward.

Vidar spun, only to be struck again by those same three spears— two in the chest, one in the neck. He grabbed one spear that was withdrawn too slowly. He yanked it toward him, bringing the spearman with it. He elbowed that Jotunn in the face, knocking him down. Vidar jerked the spear from him, spun in a tight arc and jabbed one of the attackers through the neck. He stomped on the fallen Jotunn till he felt bones break. The remaining spearman ran.

He stood there, chest heaving, breath white in the cold morning air, long shadows of the trees draped over the camp.

It was over. Five bodies at his feet. Only five? It had felt like more.

Garilon and the warriors in his section of the warband charged toward the mountain's rocky face and the wide black mouth of the mine entrance. A handful of Jotunn fled before them. The remaining Einherjar, having pressed through the barricade, covered Garilon's left flank. The mine swallowed the Jotunn.

Garilon called a halt. Best to not charge a prepared position without more scouting. Vidar glanced back at the pit that he and the others had fallen into. With the blood still pounding through his head, he couldn't hear the cries of the wounded—the warriors he'd so foolishly led. But he couldn't have known the pit was there, nor could he have scouted the open area without betraying his warband's presence. Maybe he'd just made the best decision he could have, with the information he had. But because of that, his warriors had died.

And now, some Jotunn had escaped. Maybe they'd simply fled. Or maybe they'd run to warn another warband. Now they'd have to be even more cautious when they walked into the mine's black gullet.

* * *

"ULTIMATELY IT's my failing that caused their deaths, so let's hear no more talk of it," Vidar said, meeting Garilon's eyes and then those of the Einherjar kjolr. "All those who fell here will be remembered on the stones I cut and paint in Vithi."

He, Garilon, and the Einherjar kjolr, Jorundr, sat before a fire set outside the longhouse closest to the mouth of the disused mines. The Bifrost stretched overhead, a broad, white-and-blue sparkling road between the southern and northern skies.

"Hersir Saglund needs to be informed of what happened here," said Kjolr Jorundr.

"I'm sure the Alfather will do so after he's read my message," Vidar said. "The birds should be in Gladsheim within two nights, by which time we'll be in there."

He jerked a thumb over his shoulder at the mouth of the mine. Garilon had set guards and built makeshift barriers. He'd also had torches placed along the entrance's walls so that light flickered fitfully all the way down to the first large cavern.

"You mean to go in tomorrow, Jarl?" Garilon asked. He leaned forward, picked up a long branch, and stabbed the fire. A tongue of fire licked up, curled around the hanging pot, and sank back down again.

"I do. You said the scouts didn't find traces of the Jotunn elsewhere, so either they were very good at hiding their tracks, or they've been here for a long time—which doesn't quite make sense since Háls was attacked less than a week ago—"

"Or maybe they found another way into the mines," Garilon said.

"Exactly."

Kjolr Jorundr broke in. "There may also be another warband that's now marching toward us. Or there could be one headed back from across the plains. Or both."

"Neither the Alfather nor my scouts found any trace of additional warbands near Háls, Vithi, or here," Garilon said.

"What if your scouts, or the Sigfather, missed something?" Jorundr said.

The young Einherjar had seen maybe thirty winters, which meant that the first time he'd probably ever seen the Sigfather was when he'd ridden with him to Vithi. If that fast ride hadn't been enough to convince him that the Sigfather could do things that others could not, well, nothing Vidar said now would penetrate the young man's skull.

Great feats in one area didn't make Odin infallible, of course, just worthy of a bit more respect.

Garilon simply continued. "We also haven't found any supply caches yet, not even on the warband we destroyed. One of our warbands operating this far from a camp would have to carry everything they needed, particularly food and drink. During the Last War, our supply lines stretched for miles. The Jotunn would—"

"Maybe they've just stashed all that inside the mine," Jorundr said.

"My point is that they had to get all of it here—and might even have foraged and hunted to supplement what they brought. And yet no one in Háls had any idea the Jotunn were less than a night's ride distant?"

"Maybe some in Háls did know," Jorundr said.

"That had occurred to me," Vidar interjected, "especially since that person or persons was probably among the survivors and is now warm and well fed in my hall. However, the Alfather traveled back to Gladsheim through Vithi. He and the Einherjar with him would've prevented another attack. Not that he'd found even a trace of additional warband, anyway."

He leaned forward, scooped some stew out of the steaming pot and poured it into a bowl. He handed it to Jorundr, then filled two more bowls for Garilon and himself. This wrangling was getting them nowhere.

"You and your Einherjar will remain here, Kjolr Jorundr, along with those wounded among my own warband."

The man's expression flickered quickly through a range of emotions that Vidar couldn't quite track. But if anything, he sensed more relief from Jorundr than anything. Which was odd for an Einherjar. Jorundr settled on a simple, "Yes, Jarl."

Vidar turned to Garilon. "You've already picked out those of ours who'll remain behind."

"Yes, Jarl."

A reserve force might prove unnecessary, but it was better to be cautious when headed into the unknown—and if they had to move fast, the wounded would slow them.

He continued. "Let's focus on the immediate problem. We know there's a handful of Jotunn inside the mine. Maybe more. So, what do we know about the mine itself?"

"Just that this branch has been disused for ten or so winters," Garilon said. "The gothi said they abandoned it for the richer, higher-quality finds beneath the western slopes."

"Do any in our warband have experience working in a mine?"

"I don't know, Jarl, but I'll find out."

"If we do, they should lead the way—not too far ahead, but far enough they can make sure the rest of us don't fall into an open mine shaft or something. I know it's not that type of mine, but it couldn't hurt. And the Jotunn may have placed traps. We'll also need trackers up front to spot any trail the Jotunn may have left."

"Makes sense, Jarl," Garilon said.

"And how long will our supplies last? Enough for a fortnight?"

"Yes, Jarl. More, actually, if we ration, which I wouldn't recommend—not yet, anyway. Even if we're in there for a week, this camp should be reinforced and resupplied by then."

"Good." Vidar scraped the bottom of his bowl and stood. "Let's get some rest, then."

36

Odin

Odin slammed against the soft green grasses and rolled, moths scattering from his path. He leaped to his feet and called Gungnir to his hands. She settled in, a familiar weight. Chest heaving, he crouched in the glade, his sight dim and red around the edges. But Gungnir's tip was sharp and clear, the bright smile of her long blade a promise.

Thoughts swam through that red haze like darting, silvery fish. Go back... Teach them some respect... Kill them where they stand.

But atop the waves, a seabird bobbed, the waves passing under it, their red weight smashing against the shores of his mind. He focused on the seabird. She rose, she sank, the red wave rolled beneath her, she rose again, sank again, an endless succession of waves. He fought his way up through the heaving waters, filling his chest to float beside the bird. When she rose, he did. When she sank, he did. The pounding in his ears receded, the red haze drew back, and calm returned.

He stood straighter and looked down at himself: grass stains on his knees and elbows, wet streaks across his armor, clumps of grass crushed into its seams and angles. Laughter bubbled up, surprising him. At first, he thought it was the Urdarbrunnr gurgling behind him, but then it grew into a normal, hearty laugh like the one he'd shared with Frigg before falling asleep beside her last night.

And with the thought of his wife, fleeting though it was, the last of his fury receded like seawater from the shore. He released Gungnir, brushed off his knees and elbows, and walked the few paces to Urdarbrunnr.

He sat on the well's low rim, wet though it was, and dipped the silver platter in. He raised it to his face and drank some of the water, pure and cold.

He began plucking out the bits of grass stuck in his armor. He flicked them away while the water in the well burbled and hissed.

When he finished, he reached out to Freki and Geri.

Have the others begun to arrive?

No, came Freki's response. *You are well? We wanted to help, but obeyed.*

I'm fine. Just the clucking of hens. Stay there. I'll be along shortly.

He reached again for the ewer and filled it with the well's cold water. With the silver ewer in his hands, he walked to where Yggdrasil rose like a wall from the green grasses—a portion not near where the Norns worked.

He emptied the ewer on the tree, the bark darkening as it grew wet. He brushed his free hand along the tree, the rough bark snagging on his skin, as he stared upward, searching for more rot. Yggdrasil was everywhere—to each side and above—craning his head back he grew dizzy, he felt like he clung to the tree, as once he'd done, until remembered pain stabbed him in the side. That pain blossomed beneath his right armpit and spread diagonally through his chest, just as that ancient spear had poked through his ribs before emerging from his other side.

Fool.

He staggered back, left hand pressed against his ribs, trying to force away the memory. He felt again the spear's smooth wood inside him even as he slumped against Yggdrasil's rough bark. He'd been so high in the tree, having flown on eagle's wings until he had found the right place for his sacrifice, himself to himself.

In his mind's eye, the dark expanse in which Yggdrasil grew shattered beneath his feet. And then, impossibly, he was falling through it, plunging into the Ginnungagap—the void where blazing sparks rose, hot from Muspellheim's fires, to mix with the ice falling, always falling, from Niflheim's chill mists. Where those two mixed, Hvergelmir churned around and around, like a cauldron stirring itself. From that avalanche roar, eleven mighty rivers poured forth.

Even in this memory he was again lifted higher on a wave that would never crest or break. He remembered his screams, ragged, hoarse, and almost unending, tearing from his throat just as the living rivers erupted from Hvergelmir. He remembered the patterns forming like the interlinking branches of trees, of roots, till he lost sight of them as they sank back into the mists and darkness surrounding that roaring cauldron. He memorized those patterns, those secrets, those hot spikes of fire and ice and pain. He named them runes and, with hands bloody and slick from driving the spear through his side—the spear that pinned him to life and to death—he again reached out and, shrieking, took up the runes.

* * *

Back at the well, Odin splashed cold water on his face, spilled it down his neck and chest, until it took his breath away, froze his hands and numbed his face.

He stared down past his reflection, his face distorted by the clear, rippling water, to count the rows of cut stones from which the well was made. And count he did, the numbers giving him something to think about other than the dull throb in his chest or the memory of what lay beneath, above and around Yggdrasil.

At twenty-seven rows down, pain's sharp spear in his side withdrew. Calm returned at forty-five; his shoulders no longer ached. At fifty-six, he remembered the chisel jumping in his hand as he worked the stone for this well.

At sixty-three, he cocked an attentive ear. Was that a voice?

He held his breath and listened harder. Beneath the faint gurgle and slap of water on the wide well's walls, he thought he'd heard— yes, there it was again. A voice from below, calling out to him.

That was not possible.

He closed his eyes.

There it was again. A sibilance from the depths, calling to him.

Without thinking, he sent his spirit out on his exhaled breath so that it swam downward through the cold, clear water. The voice was more distinct now that his spirit was outside his body. It was stronger, as if his flesh and bones had kept the voice away like stout walls providing shelter from a biting wind.

Come, the voice whispered. *Swim,* it encouraged.

Curious, he dove deeper still, pushing harder against the upwelling waters.

It reminded him of his youth, when he'd swum with his brothers in the many lakes and rivers that had vanished when the world broke after Ymir's death. His old homeland had been as warm and welcoming as a lover's arms after a hard-fought battle while this glade at Yggdrasil's feet was akin to a sword's blade at dawn, weeping with the dew.

His spirit might have wept with the warm memory of playing with his brothers, learning to hunt from his father, watching his mother cook their kills. Perhaps most of all, the feeling of Audhumbla's hot breath on his face and his own laughter when her coarse tongue licked him. His father, Burr, had called that cow Grandmother.

His spirit might have wept with joy had those happy memories not been eclipsed by the shadow that had fallen too often across his youthful fields. He remembered that ancient giant who, looming over his father and mother, too often made them cringe. He remembered the hot words exchanged, his father's last cry, and the snow hissing as it boiled away beneath all the blood spilled that day.

His spirit might have wept not in grief but in fury when, on that distant day, he and his brothers had stood over what remained of the bodies of their parents. Even now, with all he'd seen and done, his mind shied from what Ymir had done not just to them, but to Grandmother.

Yes, he had wept, first with grief and horror, but then the rage had come and burned all that out of him. He'd called the strongest disir to him. She'd filled him like a flood filled a dry lake. Then he'd bound her to him with his new-won runes and made her his fylgja. Back then, she had brought all the fury and clarity of a river breaking its banks. For a time, he'd ceased to be completely himself. He'd been a leaf swept up in the disir's flood until, eventually, she exhausted herself and he found himself again.

No, he wouldn't weep. Not again. Never again. Not for anything. His last tears had fallen on his parents' cooling bodies.

And had he known what would come after he killed Ymir, he still would have done it.

What's that, little father? No regrets for your first murder, the one that started it all? The sibilance uncoiled from the depths, flickering into his mind. *Sing, then, for I was born that day.*

Had his spirit hackles, they would have raised. Had it flesh, it would have prickled.

In an instant, he saw the silvery net into which his spirit had been lured. He saw its edges closing like a noose. He'd been lured from his body and drawn within a place he'd only ever seen from a distance.

With a flick of what would have been a tail, were he a fish, he fled back up the well—just fast enough that he slipped free of the net. Faster he swam, back up the well's waters, until he cried out in pain through physical lips. He fell back from the well's edge to land, gasping and dazed, in the thick grass.

A shadow fell across his chest. He scrambled up, then realized it was Gungnir standing tall beside him. Had he called to her? She flickered into his outstretched hands. He lowered her tip, facing the well as he might a Jotunn shield wall.

"Who spoke?" he shouted, his voice loud in the glade.

At first, only silence answered him. That and the incessant, faint *scratch-scratch-scrape* of the Norns' tools on Yggdrasil's bark.

Pack-Father, we come!

No, Freki. No, Geri. Stay. I don't know what I face. I'll call if I need you. Be ready.

Water bubbled and popped in the well before him, slapping and rasping against its stone sides. A thrill rushed through him. He shuffled forward, spear tip poised, his entire body tense.

"Stand forth!" he shouted.

No response, save the slap of water on stone.

He waited several pounding heartbeats and then shuffled forward again till he was at the well's rim. He shifted Gungnir high, ready to thrust down into the water. Only his reflection in the rippling water stared back at him.

But something was down there.

"I know all the creatures who shelter beneath these wide branches," he said. "Ratatoskr and the eagle. Heidrun and the four harts, always hungry. What manner of—"

Ah, but you don't know them all, especially if you don't know me, hissed the voice from the well's depths. *Come back. Visit me and mine, little father. I'll introduce you.*

"Visit a serpent in its den? I don't think so. If you know me, then you know how I deal with serpents." His arm tensed, but Gungnir didn't waver. "Come out, instead, and face me rather than hiss words from the cold dark."

I won't be as easy to deal with as Loki's son.

"Then you are serpent, eh?" he replied, smiling. "But less subtle."

If I were, then what shame would that be? You've taken that shape before. Poor Gunnloth. While she lived, her shame was like nectar.

He lowered Gungnir and stepped back a pace. How did this thing know about that? Thoughts raced like horses before the cart of his rising anger. Perhaps a change of tactics?

"You know me, spirit, and have somehow followed my deeds. Come out and let us speak as men. Face-to-face."

A moment passed without response. Still the water popped and bubbled, and still the faint *scratch-scratch-scrape* of the Norns reached his ears.

"Or can you not face me? See, I release my spear." He opened his hand, and Gungnir swayed back into the shadows. He spread his arms wide. "I am unarmed. Don't be afraid."

The voice that rose from the well carried the hint of a smile. *No, little father, I am not afraid. But if you knew me, your knees would tremble.*

Odin sneered and waved a hand. "If, if, if... I haven't been afraid since Ymir loomed high above me. He was a true terror. And yet here I stand, his killer. I ask a second time: come forth and speak with me, spirit."

And I invite you again. Come back down. Visit me and mine.

"Oh, I think not. I've not traveled into that darkness beneath Yggdrasil. Were I to go now, knowing that some spirit lurks there, I would bring my sons and daughters."

So you fear facing me alone? You must, having fled so quickly. I didn't think a coward lurked inside you.

He laughed. "Name calling? I think that perhaps you cannot meet me here. So a spirit is all you are? Or maybe it's just that you fear me. Is that it?"

It is not yet time for us to meet, little father.

"Then why did you call to me and try to trap me?" He stepped closer to the well. "No, I think that you cannot meet me here."

The Norns have decreed the time of our meeting. We may converse, but to meet, face-to-face? Not yet. The current carried what might have been a touch of anger.

He laughed. "So I'm right, you did try to lure me down there. Clever, trying to circumvent the doom scratched by those women. But let me tell you something about the Norns, spirit. They're hens in a yard, scratching and scraping, thinking that all world ends at their fence. So they rebuff those who come with honest need and intent. More power in secrecy and vague words—easier to claim they were right regardless of what actually happens."

Hens? No, little father, what the Norns write is what will be, what has been, and what is becoming. Those scratchings bind you as completely as the runes you use to enthrall others. They bind us all.

"Nothing binds me," he said. "Where were the Norns when my

brothers and I slew Ymir? Where were they when I led the Aesir to Asgard and fought the Vanir for the land above? No, I make my own doom."

Why not ask them?

"Ask them what?"

Where they were, before.

"I have. They avoid answering, just as you do. Do you know why? Because they didn't exist. Maybe Ymir shat them out before he died. Or maybe they crawled, wriggling like maggots, from his flesh. Perhaps that's where you came from."

The voice did not reply. Had that barb pricked flesh?

He stepped back from the rim of the well. "I'm tired of this, spirit. I have business elsewhere, and you've kept me too long from it."

Wait, little father. You asked why I drew you to me? I bring a warning. Hold your council and chart your course, but it means nothing. Your doom is set. As is the doom of all your children. I have read them all in Yggdrasil's bark.

He snorted. "That's not much of a warning. What doom is set for me and mine? Why is it set? And by whom? If you mean the Norns—"

They've been right before.

"Have they? True, we avoided one doom but caused another— which they didn't warn us about. I've come to wonder why that is."

If you doubt them, then why ride down alone, ahead of your family, to question them?

He shrugged. "When I go sailing into unfamiliar waters, I seek those who've sailed them before."

So you admit the Norns see more than you can.

"So does the man who climbs the mast and sights land before those astride the planks do. Another may do the same—and if he climbs a taller mast, he'll see still farther."

But the distant land is the same, regardless.

"It's not a perfect metaphor, spirit. If you imply that the Norns' prophecies always come true, then you and I disagree." He turned and began to walk away.

Your death yawns like a wolf's hungry jaws, as does the death of your sons and your wife, and all you—

"Rán's nets will catch all the Aesir before that ever happens, little voice." He threw a laugh back over his shoulder and kept walking. "Go away, or come forth."

The column of water sizzled as it struck him, blackening the grass and knocking him down in the roar of a crashing wave. It flowed around him so that he drifted with it, his entire body burning with the water's touch. His leather armor smoked as if a snow bear had spat venom on it.

He twisted his head to look back. The water rose from the well in a waterspout. It gripped him in a fist stronger than the ebbing tide and dragged him back toward the gray stones.

I told you, it is not yet time for me to venture into the realms. You can join me here, though. That is unwritten.

Odin fought the water's pull and struggled to his feet, calling Gungnir to his hand and leaning into her to brace himself. Once he was steady, he swung the spear through the water pulling at him. Golden light exploded where Gungnir struck. The watery limb lost its form and parted with a pop. He staggered backward and nearly fell.

Another column of water whipped out and coiled around his leg. *Come, little father. Come down and meet my children.*

The water gnawed at him, hissing and burning the bare skin of his face and hands. His vision went red as he drew on his fylgja's strength. With another roar, he cut this new coil. Then, staying balanced and low, knees bent, he shuffled toward the well even as a new thick coil of water reformed. Gungnir was out in front of him, her tip bright and steady.

The single coil split into a dozen or more watery limbs that lashed out at him. He dodged, spinning Gungnir in quick arcs that blew apart, in flashes of golden light, whatever seidr animated the tentacles.

The flattened grass where he fought was wet and blackened. His soaked armor and clothes weighed on him. His flesh sizzled. The pain grew maddening. The red edges of his vision grew thicker and thicker the more he drew on his fylgja's strength. Conscious thought receded.

The long watery arms were everywhere. He sliced through one coil around his leg only to find another pair of tentacles wrapping around his upper arms. He whirled Gungnir up, blasted through those coils, then brought her blade lower to sever the arm wrapping around his waist.

He pulled still harder on his fylgja's strength, and his vision narrowed until his entire world was dodging, ducking, striking, getting struck, and getting burned and burned again.

He backed away, trying to gain distance. But the thing below the well changed tactics, hammering blows like Jotunn clubs against his chest and back and thighs, deadening his muscles and staggering him. The water flowed down his neck, delivering burns on top of scalds.

A club of water struck his knees from the side, and he fell. The thing began to drag him skidding across the seared grass. He jabbed Gungnir against the gray stones of the well to stop his slide. He levered himself up and, like a drowning sailor on a lifeline, hauled on his fylgja's strength.

More water blasted into his face; the glade vanished behind a red wall of pain.

37

Frigg

On outstretched falcon wings, feathers fluttering, Frigg shrieked with the sheer exhilaration of flight. She burst from the dim tunnel into the bewildering, expansive night sky in which Yggdrasil lived.

A deep voice called to her. Her sharp eyes spied dark-haired Tyr near the ramp's top, the spike he wore in place of his devoured hand raised in greeting. Tyr led Gladsheim's army, alongside Ullr.

She shrieked again, folded her cloak-granted wings, and dove. The stars blurred into white streaks alongside the billowing trails of Muspell's fiery sparks. The wind howled past her ears like Odin's wolves.

As she dove, she tried to leave behind her annoyance at awaking to an empty bed. She had thought she and Odin would ride to Ithavoll together. More time to talk, especially after the confrontation they'd had last night. It hadn't ended badly, though it could have ended better. Even so, she'd still awoken alone—then washed, dressed, eaten, and dealt with the never-ending urgent matters. All alone.

Plummeting now, she thought she might never remove the cloak. The falcon's shape brought unfettered delight at the feel of the wind rippling through her feathers. She spied the first hint of mist, flared her wings and rode them into a swooping, wheeling, much more patient downward progress.

Odin had said he would speak with the Norns before the council. She looked for the golden gleam of the Norns' longhouse. She spotted the prow of the roof jutting from the swirling mist like a ship's sun-touched figurehead and, the wind still howling, drifted toward it.

Maybe this time Odin would wring some answers from the Norns. Or maybe she should try. They'd never acknowledged her before, but being women themselves, maybe they'd sympathize.

The wind's howl rose even higher until she realized it wasn't the wind at all but the baying of Odin's wolves. She'd heard them often enough, clearing the way through Gladsheim's streets or, in earlier days, fighting. Which is how they sounded now.

She beat the air with her wings, darting forward, till she passed through the white mists and the vibrant grasses swelled before her, white moths fluttering above them.

Another series of short barks and long howls were split by Odin's rage-drenched voice. Stark shadows were stamped upon the mist by flashes of golden light.

There he was, several dozen spear lengths away, Gungnir spinning in long arcs, glinting in short jabs, as he fought long grasping, watery limbs rising in ropey coils from the waters of Urd's Well.

Odin fought them all, his spear flashing in quick thrusts and wide sweeps. Where the spear struck, golden light flared and blew the limb apart. Where the water splashed down, the grass hissed and blackened.

She flared her wings, and they became a billowing, feathered cloak even as her booted feet touched the thick grass.

Her eyes grew wide as she watched. "Odin!" she screamed.

He gave no sign that he heard.

But Freki did. Her big head, with its white strip of fur like a scar across one eye, swung toward her. She woofed then dashed toward her. Geri slipped into the spot his sister had vacated. She slid to a halt, butted her head into her belly, and started pushing.

She ran a hand through her wet fur. "No, Freki, he needs me."

Freki pushed again, driving her back a few paces.

"Freki—"

Welcome, daughter of earth, a voice said, resounding both in her mind and, oddly, the air around her.

She spun, head lowering even as Freki's growl rumbled out.

A long tendril of water, stood before her, thick and coiling like the snakes that hung in Alvheim's wet forests. *Have you seen me yet in your visions?*

Freki backed away, her growl deepening. Shocked though she was, Frigg held her ground.

No, you haven't. I see it now. The voice, slippery like a damp rock, came from the rope of water. *That's all right. You will soon enough. When you do, tell the little father that though we fight, I'm not his enemy. Not really.*

The tendril shifted slightly, as if looking back toward the battle. Gungnir boomed, scattering water like leaves before the wind. Except where the water struck, the grass sizzled. Odin's leather armor was black and steaming from the burning water.

You can't prevent what's coming, Almother. None of you can. The voice spoke with the hiss of water boiling away. *But you'll try. And those efforts will accomplish as much as the Alfather's does now. Fighting water, indeed. When hatred strikes, Hár Frigg, remember that we spoke.*

The tendril of water burst. Droplets popped and sizzled on her skin like animal fat that had leaped from a hot stone.

At the same time, the tentacles Odin fought collapsed, dousing him. He roared as the water burned him. Gungnir's tip whirled about, dragging Odin along behind it, looking more like a hound hunting for prey than a Svartalvar-forged spear. When it pointed at her, the blade lifted, seeming to curve upward in a wicked, wet smile that, a heartbeat later, was mirrored on Odin's face.

Even at this distance, Frigg could see no trace of her husband in the golden glow that bled from his eyes. It was his fylgja, a realization made all too clear by the predatory hunch of his shoulders and the sharp, quick movements of his head.

Freki woofed, looked up at Frigg, and made a "go away" gesture with her head.

Odin charged, spear lowered, his booted feet making no sound on the thick wet grass. A ragged yell tore from his lips.

Her world narrowed to Gungnir's tip.

"Odin, stop!" Frigg shouted, her voice a scream as she blurred into the falcon's form and flew upward out of his way.

Freki launched herself toward Odin. Geri moved to block his master.

With powerful beats of her wings, she rose higher, spiraling in quick, panicked arcs, again looking for gleaming roof of the Norns' dwelling.

There it was.

She risked a glance down and saw Freki slam into Odin. Gungnir spun away and vanished. He'd been about to throw his spear. If Freki hadn't—

No, she couldn't think about that. She had to focus on where she was going. But would the Norns even help? She didn't know, but she had to try.

The mist swirled apart and she darted through it, streaking downward toward the long stone table where the Norns worked. She shrieked for their attention, but none of the three even looked up.

She flared her wings, her boots touched the earth, and she fell against the stone table. Pots of ink wobbled and nearly spilled until stained hands stilled them.

"Please, help me!" she cried into their faces.

Too close behind her, Odin's raw scream ripped through the glade. One of the wolves yelped.

The middle Norn looked up. Her skin was smooth and brown; her eyes were cold chips of emerald. "I think not," she said. She looked back down to the chisel in her right hand and the bark in her left.

Her sister Norn, white as snow, looked up. Her coal-black eyes yawned like a pit. Her voice squeaked like frozen hinges. "You'll live to see sadder days."

The third sister, skin a rich blue-black and eyes a startling wolfish gold, pointed with a red-tipped brush to a spot behind Frigg. "Prepare yourself, Hár Frigg. Your husband, ever faithful, approaches."

She spun, her hands gripping the table's cold stone. Odin sprinted at her, spear lowered, a roar pouring out his mouth and eyes glowing gold. His wolves ghosted along behind him, snapping at his heels, trying to slow him, distract him.

The scrape of the Norns' chisels resumed as if none of this were happening.

She glanced to her left, gauging the distance to the Norns' house. If she could get there, maybe the barred door would give her enough time to talk Odin out of his fury—or maybe he'd calm down on his own.

Maybe.

She bolted for the house, spying the welcoming glow of a low fire through the open door. Gray stones of the foundation, wet with dew. Logs piled lengthwise above. Daubed between. Low thatched roof, golden brown against the ever-present white mist.

Two dozen strides, if that. Almost there.

Gungnir slammed into the ground before her and she tripped, reflexively rolling like she'd been taught ages ago by some of the nastiest warriors her father had been able to find. She sprang back up and launched herself at the open door.

Odin knocked her down with a sweep of his arm and she rolled and banging her head against the foundation. The world shuddered; warmth bloomed on her head. She pushed herself to her knees, the door's welcome still extended.

As she stood, a dark blur cracked into the stone beside her. Wobbling, she tried to push past Gungnir into the house's dubious safety.

A big hand dropped on her right shoulder, tightened, and then flung her hard against the wall. Her breath whooshed out again. Blackness spun around her head. When it receded, she saw Odin's bearded face, distorted, scalded, and swollen. The golden-eyed fylgja leered out from behind his deep-set eyes.

She kicked at his crotch. He smacked her leg aside and she nearly fell again, only just catching herself with one hand on the wet, rough stone behind her.

His other hand darted out, but Freki clamped her jaws down on it with a landslide rumble from her belly. Frigg saw in an instant that Freki was biting hard enough to dimple the thick leather but not hard enough to draw blood.

Odin hammered a fist into Freki's belly. Frigg heard a forge bellows whoosh followed by a harsh yelp. Odin pried Freki's jaws open, grabbed the thrashing wolf by the scruff of the neck, and flung her tumbling away.

Geri darted in low, trying to clamp down on his master's leg, but Odin spun and struck such a blow that Geri seemed to bounce off the grass. He too was flung away.

Free, Frigg darted to her left, banged against the forgotten Gungnir, and tried to duck underneath, but she'd bungled her chance. Odin grabbed her by the neck and slammed her against the wall of the Norns' house. She kneed him in the side, but it was like hitting a tree. She chopped at his elbow, but it didn't buckle. She glanced left, caught Gungnir's bright smile and, beyond the blade, the low fire burning cheerily in the house.

She brought both hands up and clawed at his hand, her nails opening long red wounds. But the grip didn't loosen. It tightened.

She was gasping for air. "Odin, it's me."

She dragged again at his hand, trying to break his grip. Again, she kicked, but he didn't even grunt.

He leaned in toward her then, his arm flexing until his breath was hot on her face. The fylgja's golden light danced behind his eyes, and it used her husband's face to grin at her.

Odin yanked Gungnir out of the wall.

She writhed again, kicking, fingers clawing long flowing lines of red down his face. She ripped at his throat, dragged on his bent elbow, tore at the hand around her throat. Nothing worked. She might as well claw at the wall behind her.

Freki and Geri sprinted back in. Their jaws clamped around his legs, this time drawing blood. She could see it, bright around their teeth. Odin ignored them. His grip tightened.

Her vision was graying at the edges now, narrowing with every breath she was able to drag in.

She stopped struggling and, instead, stroked his face. She wiped the blood from his forehead, caressed the burns, and cradled his cheek in one hand. "Odin. It's me, Frigg. Your wife."

The water on his skin seared her hand, but the pain was distant. She looked directly into Odin's eyes, trying to look past the fylgja, to see her husband.

Her voice was a croaky rasp. "Odin... please..."

The golden haze behind his eyes flickered, surged, and vanished, replaced by Odin's own eyes.

"No! It's Frigg!" he shouted.

His fist unclenched from her throat. She slid down the wall, gasping and coughing. Air burned sweet pathways into her chest.

He tried to catch her, but she slapped at him until he pulled back. She realized her feet were on the ground and she slid away, staggering, one hand dragging along the wall until she fell onto all fours by the open door, hauling in breath after shuddering breath.

Freki and Geri released his legs, and Odin crashed to his knees beside her.

A too-ragged breath later, he said, "Frigg, I'm back. I'm—"

She held a hand up, demanding silence, and dry heaved into the vivid green grasses. The Norns had been right. Today was not her day.

38

Hodr

As always, Hodr woke to darkness. He tried sitting up, but an anvil pounding in his head drove him back down with a tight hiss of pain. A damp cloth was wrapped tightly around his head. He smelled earth, sage, and grasses. Gingerly, he probed with his fingers at the spot where the smith's hammer kept striking his head. The damp poultice that was there did little, it seemed, to dull the ache.

Familiar sounds reached his ears: the creak and bang of shutters, voices rising and falling as they moved around outside. Familiar scents reached his nose: cooking food and—

"Alara, are you there?"

"Yes, Hodr," she said, sounding as if she'd just woken. "I'm here. Don't try to move."

"I just found that out...my head feels like an anvil in Thor's shop. What happened?"

He heard her move, and a moment later the bed creaked as she sat beside him.

"You don't remember?"

"I was coming back from the market," he said, his mouth dry.

Memories began to emerge from the ringing in his head. "There was a horse..."

"Yes, you were knocked down. Trampled. You hit your head."

"Least I hit something I rarely use." He edged into a less reclined position. Pain flickered like lightning among dark clouds.

She gently smacked his shoulder. "Don't joke. I watched the valkyr press the bones of your skull back into place. She wasn't sure you'd ever wake up—not that she said it."

"Could I have something to drink?"

He heard the smile in her voice. "Of course."

In a rustle of skirts, she fetched a jug of wine. The wine gurgled into a cup. She sat back down and touched the cup to his lips. Light and sweet, the wine eased the dryness and warmed his belly.

She took the cup away. "Not too much at first. Are you hungry?"

He edged up a little higher, wincing as the lighting's flicker threatened like his brother raising Mjolnir. His stomach growled. "Yes, I could eat. How long have I been asleep?"

"Three nights now. I would've said it'd be a fourth, but you surprised me." Relief was evident in her voice and in the tight grip of her hand in his.

"Did the valkyr really push my skull back together?" If so, that explained the pounding—and the hooves that had cracked it to begin with.

"She did, yes, though I could barely watch."

Idly, he wondered if it was that withered, year-old fruit his father had sent that had helped him heal. Usually, it's power lingered for several nights before fading away.

The words leaped from his mouth before he'd even realized he was going to speak them. "Alara, I broke my promise—I ate that old fruit my father sent. I think that's why I'm still alive."

He felt her draw back—not much, but his heart skipped a beat anyway. Her silence was worse. Alone in his darkness, dread built like a storm.

But then she kissed forehead and a smile rang in her voice. "Well, in that case, I forgive you. Rest. I'll be back later."

***

He dreamed he was lying in a pasture, much as he'd done as a boy. The smell of crushed grasses all around him—and the evidence on his knees, elbows and down the front of his shirt. He was sure to be red-knuckled and scrubbing them out by evening, unless he hid them well. That might buy him a few more nights. But with a sky bluer than a robin's egg and the sweet scent of wildflowers hanging in the air, he didn't care.

A woman's voice called his name—not his mother's with its harsh edge, nor his sister's with its exasperated air, but sweetly, as if she wanted to see him. To talk to him. To be with him. The wildflowers drifted closer, and he smiled.

A hand touched his shoulder and he sat up, startled, the darkness snatching away the sky.

"Who's there?" Even to himself, his voice sounded slurred. He licked his lips.

"It's just me, Hodr," Alara said. "And the valkyr, but she just left."

He reached up and touched the bandages and the wet poultice beneath.

"Are you hungry?" she asked, sounding further off. Then, as if over her shoulder, "Keep your hands off those. They're fresh."

Her quick steps approached and the bed creaked as she sat, the wildflowers just within reach. He smelled porridge, then a weighty tray pressed the bed down.

He tried a nod and regretted it. "How long did I sleep this time?"

"Not too long. Sól's moved maybe an eitt. The valkyr was pleased that you'd woken and were yourself."

"What?"

"She didn't say anything about your hearing."

"No, what did you mean, 'not myself'?"

He heard the shrug in her voice. "Apparently, it can happen. Sometimes those who get hit in the head are never quite the same afterwards." Then he heard the smile. "Maybe you'll be better."

"Funny."

"I brought some—"

"It smells great. Will you?"

He felt a spoon pressed into his hand, and he pushed himself up a bit further. Her hand, cool and dry, touched his. Then a warm stone bowl settled into his lap.

While he ate, she said, "The smith whose horse struck you sent a messenger asking how you were doing. I sent the boy back, said that you had died."

He coughed and spluttered. "You did what?"

"I'm kidding," she said, the smile rosy in her voice. "I told him you'd woken and would probably be up and about in a few days."

"That's what the valkyr said?"

"She told me if you keep the first food down, you'd be up inside two weeks, but she doesn't know what we do. Just don't push it, all right?"

He grunted, swallowed another mouthful, and asked, "What about the way house? Shouldn't you be there?"

"Hleven's running it. With any luck, we'll still have chairs come morning." The bed creaked as she sat.

"So it was a smith's horse?"

"Yes, that Lopt fellow you were talking to a few nights ago."

"You know, he told me he had a wild horse in his team. Broke his son's leg—or his brother's. I don't remember." He ate another spoonful. "What happened to all the fish I had bought?"

"You worry about the strangest things. It's here. Kona wouldn't let anyone near you but me. That smith said he'd be back through here in another few nights. Asked to speak with you when he does. Apologize in person both for the accident and having to leave."

Hodr shrugged, then winced at the streak of pain. "Sure, no harm in that, I guess."

39

Vafthrudnir

A long black tunnel stretched out in front of Vafthrudnir. He ran his hand along the tunnel wall; it wasn't rough stone. It was smooth glacier ice that glistened in the light of the witchlamps. And it led, like a gullet, down to the belly—a reeking nest he could smell from here—that had been home to the matron and her pack.

Shall I run ahead? Fimbulthul asked from her perch atop his shoulder.

Are there more snow bears down there?

There were some pups. But I took care of them. He got the impression of a full belly.

Go on, then, he said.

Fimbulthul leaped down, taking the shape of a great-cat as she landed. *Keep an eye on Kali. I'm pretty sure she can see me.*

I suspected she might.

Fimbulthul looked back over her shoulder. *Why didn't you say something? I would've been discreet.*

Vafthrudnir snorted.

"High Shaman?" Hersir Beli asked as he offered him a forked

device made of smooth witchwood that looked like a sword with two hilts set at an angle to the blade. All three ends of the device were capped with a gold setting that each held a single dark ruby.

"No thank you, Hersir."

Beli nodded, twisted the gold settings in turn, each clicked, and the device began to emit a quiet thrum. Beli extended the device in front of him so that the single end would show them which way to go. He turned slowly in a circle; each ruby glowed faintly and then faded as he passed through one direction in his rotation.

Well? Fimbulthul persisted. *Why didn't you say anything about Kali?*

I wanted to find out if you thought the same.

Well, she's pretending otherwise, but she seems very curious, Fimbulthul said.

Beli completed one full rotation and again faced in the direction where the device had faintly glowed. He moved it up, the glow faded. When the device pointed down and to the right, the rubies glowed like the cheeks of an angry child and the tip bounced up and down.

"Down it is, then," Beli said.

What a surprise, Fimbulthul said. She darted ahead.

"I'm ready," Vafthrudnir said to Beli.

The hersir nodded and motioned for the warriors to proceed. The front row of three fighters held axes and shields. The second row extended their spears in front of the shieldmen with witchlamps swinging from the ends. The darkness retreated as the small formation began moving forward.

He followed, with Beli and Kali beside him. Another knot of a dozen warriors followed behind. The rest of Helveg was topside, sweating and swearing as they dragged the dominated, still-sleeping snow bears back to the nest and its shelter—Goldtooth might be a drunk and unlikely to hear or see them, but he'd spent too many winters being cautious to stop now. When Kali returned to the surface, she would wake the snow bears and Helveg would be that much stronger.

But for now, the tunnel beckoned.

***

The long dark glistening gullet of a tunnel ended in a cavern somehow carved into the glacier itself. Bones rolled, clinked and crumbled underfoot as the party stepped from the tunnel into the cave.

Even within the short reach of the witchlamps' light, Vafthrudnir counted the skulls of three types of animals, none of which had ever lived atop a glacier. Particularly the fish. The air itself was warmer than he'd expected. It tasted wet and stank like stranded seaweed on a hot day.

He squatted and ran his hand along the cave wall where the ice had been deeply scored by the passage of the beasts. A well-traveled gullet.

As they slowly walked further into the cavern, Beli again raised the device moving it through an arc before him. As it pointed toward the cave's center, the three-pronged wand bucked up and down in his hands as the red glow from the rubies threw bloody shadows across his face.

"Ahead and to the left, Kjolr," Beli said to the warriors before him, a curved sliver between him and the darkness ahead.

"Yes, Hersir," the big-shouldered kjolr said. "Advance. Slowly."

The warriors with shields stepped forward two paces to the edge of the light cast by the witchlamps. The spearmen followed. Then the shieldmen took another two steps.

Vafthrudnir and Kali followed just behind. Every step across the bony field was treacherous. Ancient bones crumbled and crunched while newer ones clinked as they rolled and shifted underfoot.

A hundred paces in, it became obvious that the cavern was both huge and empty. If there had been more snow bears, even pups, they would have attacked by now.

There's nothing in here besides all these bones and the doorway, his fylgja said.

I'm not going to interrupt them, he thought back to her. *Their caution is commendable.*

The device in Beli's hands bucked like an unbroken stallion. The rubies' glow intensified, pooling in the lines of strain across the hersir's face. "We're nearly on top of it, Kjolr."

"Yes, Hersir," the kjolr replied. Then to the warriors around him, he said, "Look for the shimmer of heat in the air. It's not hot—well, it never has been—but that's what you look for. Call out if you see it before I do."

Tense moments passed as each warrior slowed to a single step every few heartbeats. The light cast by the witchlamps swung back and forth.

"I think I see it," one of the warriors called over her shoulder. "Bit more than a spear's length ahead."

"All right," the kjolr said. "Everyone another pace forward till it's visible."

This really isn't necessary, his fylgja said. *There's nothing here or on the other side.*

You went through already?

Of course. Looks like a lakebed.

Another pair of steps, and the witchlamp exposed a shimmering in the air. "There it is," said one of the warriors.

"I see it," the kjolr said. "Shake that witchlamp off the spear right beside the shimmering. We'll walk a quick circle around it."

Having found the doorway Beli turned around so the device stopped bucking. He twisted the gold settings and rubies' glow faded.

***

Led by Kjolr Yngvi, Helveg's warriors drove their spears butt-first into the bones. They hung witchlamps on them, making a wide, well-lit circle around the shimmering doorway. Using their shields as shovels, they cleared a rough circle around the doorway and a wide path back through the bones to the tunnel. Below the bones, nearly a sword's length deep in places, lay the grainy gray-blue of glacial ice.

Once they had room to work, the warriors cleared the bones that concealed the lower portion of the doorway. Next, using the longer bones, spears and rope, Yngvi had a crude frame built for the doorway—to prevent "idiots from going where they shouldn't."

Vafthrudnir sat on the piled bones beside Kali. She was wide-eyed, staring at the doorway. It glimmered like a bead of dew in the witchlamps' light.

"First time seeing one?" he asked.

"Yes, High Shaman." She was probably just past her twentieth winter. The swirling blue tattoos on her shaved scalp showed her as an adept, the appropriate rank for a shaman serving as a second.

"It's safe on the other side, so you can step through after me," he said.

Maybe I was just trying to trick you, his fylgja whispered.

Mmhmm.

"You don't seem too surprised at that, Adept Kali," he continued, keeping his tone friendly and casual.

She stiffened.

He gestured toward the doorway. "It's all right. She said you were probably able to see her."

"I'm not sure I understand—"

He laughed. "Not all shamans can see the disir—of those who can, very few have the strength to call one to them." Or go to them. Not that it would matter if they could. Except for two, Ygg had claimed them all for himself and the Aesir. "I also noticed you studying the charm I used to dominate the snow bear. And then you adapted it for yourself, which certainly helped with the matron."

A line of sweat had formed on her upper lip. What was he doing that made her so uneasy? Or was it simply that he, the Vafthrudnir—the name taken by all those who became high shaman—was talking to her, an adept?

"High Shaman?" Kjolr Yngvi called.

"Ready for me, then?"

"Yes, High Shaman."

"I'll be along in a moment. Thank you."

He stood and brushed bone dust from his cloak. "I'm in need of a second, Kali." He gestured toward the doorway. "I have work to do there—on the other side—so Helveg will be moving on without me. You'll go with them, of course, since you're the only one who can manage the snow bears, at least until the replacement First Shaman arrives. I'll eventually rejoin Helveg, though, and when I do, I'd like you to begin training with me. That you can see the disir is reason enough..."

That's not quite true, his fylgja whispered.

"... and you've shown a willingness to depart from what the masters in Jotunheim have no doubt pounded into your head."

Nor is that, necessarily.

She has potential, all right? But it needs to be shaped, like an ingot.

Or thrown back in the fire, if that shaping goes awry.

I won't know till I try.

Kali stood, wariness evident in the set of her shoulders and tight-pressed lips. But hope was in her eyes, too. "I would like that, High Shaman."

"Good," he said, with a quick nod. "We'll start now. Follow me."

***

They stood ankle deep in puffy snow on the other side of the doorway from the glacier cavern. The doorway itself glimmered behind them, the dark cavern visible through what looked like a rippling sheet of water.

"Where are we?" Kali asked aloud, turning to take in their surroundings. Her eyes shone with barely contained excitement. "It looks like Utgard."

Hauling in a deep breath, he also turned in place. Nothing but cold air whistled through his nostrils—no odd smells at all. They did seem to be standing in a drained lakebed, just as his fylgja had said. In the distance, thick layers of wooly clouds lay draped across the mountain's shoulders. Sól was much higher in the sky than she should be if they were in Utgard.

He blew out a lungful of air that he was among the first two Jotunn ever to breathe. Probably. "Speak this way," he said using the hand language. "It does resemble Utgard, but that's not where we are."

"How can you know that?"

"You tell me," he signed.

She took her time looking, shading her eyes and examining the mountains, stooping to taste the snow. Then she looked up at Sól and immediately down at her shadow. "The sun's in the wrong place. My shadow's too short."

"Well done. And having observed that, any guesses as to what the night sky might look like?"

She pursed her lips. "Different stars, I'd guess—some of them, at least. Maybe all."

"And do you have your instruments with you?" All shamans were trained to study and measure the stars' movements, including the rising and setting of Muspell's sparks.

"No, High Shaman." A pained expression crept across her face.

He grinned. "I don't, either. Normally I would, but I have an advantage most don't."

Find anything interesting? He sent the thought winging toward his fylgja.

I went eastward, about as far as you could walk in a day. Nothing out here. I'm coming back now.

He had the impression that she was bounding closer, covering huge distances.

"So we have a little time. What questions do you have for me?"

Her expression shifted from careful study—apparently, she was observant enough to see when he was speaking with his fylgja—to the first genuine smile he'd seen from her. She pointed at the doorway. "What is that? How does it let us travel so quickly from one place we know to another we don't?"

"No one's entirely certain, but here's what I've figured out. The doorways appear to be natural. They just exist. There's nothing I did or can do, as far as I'm aware, to make one appear. Having stepped through many, I don't think we're traveling—not like we would across land or water on a wolf—or sea-wolf," he added with a lopsided grin. "I think it's more like an actual doorway. We just...step from inside a hall, as an example, to outside. Or the reverse."

Her head tilted slightly to one side and her eyes narrowed. "But even then, there's space being crossed—the threshold itself, right?"

He nodded and motioned for her to follow him. First, they stood and examined the doorway. It was maybe twice the shoulder width of a large man and roughly a spear's length high. Big in comparison to many of the others he'd passed through.

"What do you see?"

"Just the doorway," she signed. "The cavern, too, but it's difficult to make out."

"You noted how wide it is?"

She nodded.

He motioned for her to follow him again. Now they stood looking at the doorway edge-on. "What do you see now?"

"It's barely visible," she signed, moving back and forth to view it at different angles. "But how can that be? It's thinner than spring ice."

"You expected what?"

She glanced back at him. "I... well... I don't know. A tunnel? It would make more sense."

"More sense than a magic doorway that lets us step without delay from remotest Utgard to wherever this place is?" He gestured grandly around him.

His fylgja chose that moment to slide into place between them, startling Kali so that she took a quick three steps backward.

That proved it. She could see Fimbulthul.

"Kali, meet Fimbulthul. She's my fylgja. You're the first in a very long time to see her."

Wonder crept across Kali's face, displacing the surprise. With a deep bow, she said, "I am honored, Fimbulthul."

I like her.

So do I.

Are you going to get this one killed, too?

Not on purpose.

Kali cleared her throat and asked, fingers dancing, "If I may, High Shaman, that device the Hersir used—it finds these doorways? Or makes them? And where did it come from?"

"From here," he said, tapping the side of his head.

40

Frigg

The low rumble amid the sound of approaching voices meant one thing: Thor was coming.

Frigg's hand tightened on Odin's knee. "I'll handle him."

Odin shook his head and hauled in a breath that crackled like dry leaves underfoot. "Let me—"

She gently squeezed his hand and smiled up at him. "You can barely move, let alone speak. He'll listen to me."

Without Sleipnir's help, she'd never have gotten Odin to the table at Ithavoll where the jarls met. Ithavoll was really just a place in the glade not far from Yggdrasil's trunk where they'd set a large round table, open in the center, with a dozen chairs around it. Nor was it that far from where the Norns worked. Every Midwinter and Springtide, the jarls of the Aesir met and discussed the realm's affairs. But it was only at Midwinter that they partook of Aegir's Bounty.

She patted Odin's knee and stood. His face, normally lean and lupine, was swollen, scalded, and covered in red welts. He looked like he'd been whipped. Beneath what remained of his blackened, wet armor and sodden clothes, his body was similarly injured. She didn't like the way he clutched his chest with one arm or the way his breath crackled and popped. He needed Baldr.

She didn't look much better. Her light green dress was torn and stained with crushed grasses and crumbled tree bark. She'd ripped off one sleeve to daub Odin's wounds, then torn the other off as much for symmetry as to have more cloth handy. The jarls would be upset at seeing her disheveled. But it was her neck—with light fingers she touched the heavy bruising—that would anger them.

But most would listen first. And once they saw Odin's state, they'd realize that something else was at work.

Thor, however, would react first and listen later.

She finger-combed her hair, braided it roughly, and draped it over one shoulder, where it might partially hide her bruised neck. Then she tugged her feathery cloak forward to cover her goose bumped arms and walked toward the pair of burly figures pushing out of the mist.

Thor, red-bearded, tall and broad-shouldered, looked at her, a smile spreading across his expressive face. Beside him, Tyr strode black-bearded, black-eyed, serious.

She stepped to one side to make Odin clearly visible. If Thor saw how injured his father was, maybe curiosity and concern would restrain his temper.

Thor raised a hand in greeting, "Ho, Mother. Gná's message reached me just in—"

He'd gotten close enough to see the marks around her throat. Like clouds on a windy day, confusion flew across his face.

"Thor, thank Aegir, have you seen Baldr? Your father needs him. Quickly."

"He laid hands on you?" He growled the question having leaped, of course, to that conclusion. He towered over her, a thunderstorm, beefy fists clenched and red beard bristling.

Tyr looked more like a man calmly bracing for rough seas. His left hand rested on a sheathed knife that balanced the scabbarded sword hanging from his right hip. The knife was hung to be drawn more easily with that hand—the one Fenrir had not taken.

Thor's hand dropped to Mjolnir's leather-wrapped grip.

"Thor, take a moment and listen," Tyr said. "Your father's never laid hands on the Almother before. And look at him. Hár Frigg can fight, but she couldn't do that to him."

Thor's blue eyes flickered like stormy skies as he looked from her to his father.

Frigg kept her voice calm and steady, an Alvar sooth-woman approaching a wild stallion. "Baldr. We need Baldr. Have you seen him, Thor?"

It must've helped, too, that Odin's crackling breath, dimly heard where they stood, changed to hacking coughs. She looked back and saw him dabbing bright blood from his lips and beard.

Freki and Geri limped in from the mists, concern and pain evident even in their golden eyes.

"So, Mother, what did happen?" Thor asked, his brow clearing quicker than the sky after a summer storm. She wasn't his actual mother, but he called her that anyway. He disliked complicating things, especially familial bonds. And apparently, he'd decided to listen.

"Your father left early to speak with the Norns. When I arrived, he was fighting a spirit that had quickened the waters of Urdarbrunnr. I don't know how long they fought, but you see what it did to him. His battle fury took him. Freki and Geri tried to make me leave, but I remained—"

"And that's when he did this to you?"

"He wasn't himself, Thor. His eyes glowed golden."

"Lost control, eh, Father?" He walked around her and squatted beside Odin's chair. "I warned you about that when you took that thing into you."

Odin's glare was evident even through the pain. He tried to speak, but he convulsed with a cough and all he produced was more bright blood. Frigg knelt beside him and daubed at his mouth with her former sleeve. His lips were blue, as if he were cold. She wadded up the remnants of her other sleeve and put it behind his neck.

"Did either of you see Baldr on the way down?" she repeated, hating the note of panic that had crept into her voice.

Tyr shook his head as Thor rumbled a negative.

"I did," a sweet, soft voice replied. "They're not far behind me. But maybe I can help—or what I carry with me can."

"Oh, thank Aegir you're here, Idunn," she said, rising and holding out a hand. "May I?"

"Of course," Idunn said, smiling.

With one slim hand, Idunn flung back the leather cover of the saddlebag draped over her shoulder and withdrew a single golden fruit twice as big as her palm. She laughed as a white moth lit upon it.

Frigg smiled her thanks, snatched it, and sank back to Odin's side. Her knife flashed a piece from the fruit. "Odin, bite into this," she urged. "Suck the juices, at least. Just get some of it into you. Quickly!"

Odin coughed again as pushed himself up a little straighter. She halved the slice she'd cut and pressed it into his open mouth. Color crept back into his face; the tautness in his shoulders eased. He chewed once, twice, then swallowed.

She fed him the other half. He sucked on it, chewed, then swallowed. Several ragged breaths later, he groaned and shifted. His ribs rasped against one another; the sound raised the hair on her arms.

Then he sagged back against the chair with a sigh, eyelids fluttering. "That's better, Frigg. Thank you."

His lips were no longer blue, and the red weals and blisters covering his face and hands had faded. Even the swelling began to recede. She smiled and stroked the side of his face.

He covered her hand with his own. "I'll be all right." He sat up a bit straighter, with less obvious pain, and spoke in a stronger voice. "And thank you, Idunn, both for your timely arrival and the fruits you brought."

He coughed again, deep and scratchy, and spat it out. "I'll take my place now, I think," he said, gripping the arms of the chair and forcing himself upright. Sweat beaded on his brow.

"I really think you should wait until Baldr gets here," Frigg said, frowning even as she moved to help him.

41

Odin

Leaning more heavily on the table than he'd admit if asked, Odin gestured with his chin toward Idunn. "If you would, Priestess, please pass Aegir's Gifts around the table and let us begin. I remain in more than usual need of Yggdrasil's fruit."

"Of course, Alfather." Idunn flipped hair the color of fresh-turned soil from her face and removed one large golden fruit from the basket, set it down slid the basket to Freyr. He stood, took one for himself, and passed the basket to his sister Freyja.

When the basket came to Odin, he took a second fruit. With Frigg's help, he dropped that fruit into a sack and handed it down to Geri. The wolf took it in his jaws and trotted off into the mists. Freki watched her brother go and then lay beside Odin's chair.

Frigg then took her own fruit and passed the basket on to Thor. From there, it went to Heimdall, then Tyr, and then back to Idunn.

With a graceful nod, Idunn thanked Tyr, glanced around the table, and raised her own fruit to shoulder height on an open palm. Everyone around the table stood and then did the same.

Odin's already cut fruit waited for him on his palm, ripe and golden. It smelled of honey, fresh from the hive. Of clean sea air. Of a winter's crisp dawn. Of apples mulled in wine. The juices flowed in his mouth.

In a clear, cool voice Idunn spoke. "With each bite and swallow of this apple we renew our pledge to Aegir, keeping ourselves yet another night, another day, another winter, from Rán's chill home. Aegir's Gift brings renewed life, just as the waters from the Roaring Cauldron swept life into the realms. And yet those same waters may also bring death. Should we fall in the dance of spears, should Rán's weeping nets clutch us tight, we will go proudly, joyously, remembering that what we do in life outlasts our death."

Along with everyone else, Odin spoke the response. "Cattle die. Kinsmen die. But our names will never die, if we win good renown."

Idunn bit deep into the golden fruit, its juices flooded down her chin. One fine hand darted up to catch those juices, she slurped them up and sucked at the fruit.

Though his wounds burned and throbbed, and his hand trembled, Odin he resisted for one thunderous heartbeat, then a second, as he watched his family—through blood and alliance—tear into their own golden fruit just as Idunn had done.

He couldn't resist any longer. He bit deep into the fruit's sweet, crisp flesh. The golden skin parted with a pop that sent a shiver through him. He devoured mouthful after mouthful, trying to slow down, to chew and savor, but instead he gulped them down.

Each bite of the fruit was like a hammer blow on a spike of fire driven through him, but this spike brought relief from pain. Heat grew in his belly and his limbs shook.

He felt caught between twin spirits. One nuzzled his ear and stroked his hair, whispering that it was all right to be tired, that she would comfort him. The second agreed with the first, saying that surrender was success, and failure was success. And both would feel good. Just take another bite.

He nearly listened.

Nearly.

He fought the spirits as if they were real. He kicked like a child learning to swim, wild to stay at the surface but sinking all the same.

Another bite. Finish the fruit.

He nearly screamed with the effort.

Nearly.

He forced his right hand to his satchel. The spirts pleaded, sweet as the fruit, hot as his loins, but he fought them. He tore his satchel open and drove the hand holding the fruit down and away from his mouth. The whispering spirits became beasts that roared and clawed worse then Fenrir had when he'd realized Gleipnir wouldn't snap.

Sweat poured from his face, but his hands obeyed. He shoved the half-eaten fruit into his satchel, ripped his hand out, and sagged forward, hands flat on the cool wood of the table.

The twin spirits flailed and roared, mouths frothing as Fenrir's had—and still did—then, having failed, they slipped back into the depths of his hugr and merged with the darkness.

He dragged in a deep breath and looked at Frigg. Her chest heaved with the aftermath of the same struggle.

But the deep bruises around her neck were gone, as were the scratches on her arm. She was younger, healthier, the movements of her head sharp and quick. Her smile was as warm as her deep brown eyes.

His own wounds were gone, dried up and vanished like puddles in the hot sun.

Frigg dropped her own uneaten half of fruit into his satchel. Their shared sacrifice, given each winter, powered the magic that protected their son.

All around the table, the jarls were recovering—some trembled, some rubbed their faces, some smiled and licked their fingers clean —but returned youth and strength sang in their every breath and movement. If these fruits had tough, bitter brown-black seeds, the jarls—and himself—would have eaten them too. But only once in all the hundreds of winters they'd eaten these fruits had he seen a seed —a pale, frail thing that not even Idunn's tender care could coax into life.

All the jarls stood straighter now, age's weight shed. Thor's beard and hair were again forge fire red. Freyja's bronze skin glowed golden now, as did Freyr's. For once, Heimdall didn't look drunk, though as Odin watched, the pale Aesir grimaced, his large gold teeth glinting, and he groped for the wineskin before him. He would have to deal with that when he had time.

Unbidden, the memory returned of the time Thiazi had captured Loki and forced him to steal Idunn and her fruits from Gladsheim. Like snow on a mountain, age had piled its weight on these faces around him—and his own. If not for Loki, they might all have perished. If not for Loki, they would not have aged like that at all.

***

Odin remained standing as his jarls sat down. "When I left Gladsheim twenty winters ago to not only seek my brothers but find new lands for the Aesir, I did so without fully appreciating what I'd left behind. You have all thrived in my absence. Our city is greater than it was, and it's all thanks to your efforts."

He looked down at Frigg and invited her to rise. "I must thank my wife in particular. Her leadership during my wanderings has surpassed even my wildest imaginings. I knew she was more than capable, mind you," he said, grinning, "so thank you, Almother, for your care of our realm. Gladsheim couldn't have a better mother—or a more absent father."

Frigg took his hand and stood, the surprise on her tawny face deepening to a blush. He pulled her to him and hugged her tight. When they separated, he tenderly kissed her on the lips. The jarls thumped the table and called their approval.

Raising a hand for silence, he spoke again. "When I was attacked this morning—an encounter I'll relate presently—I was gravely wounded, and I succumbed to the battle fury as I fought this spirit. To my shame, I attacked Frigg and nearly killed her. I truly and deeply regret those actions. I can only say that I was not myself."

Into the silence that followed, and with a mischievous grin, Frigg said, "I forgive you, Odin. And don't worry, I won't divorce you. Not this time."

After a moment of surprise and some mild laughter from the jarls, he inclined his head. "Thank you, Frigg."

She squeezed his hand and smiled. "Why not begin with your encounter with the spirit? Then we'll discuss the rest—but quickly, for time presses."

***

Odin spread his hands. "So, questions?"

Freyja leaned forward and spoke. "Why did the waters burn you, Alfather? All here have drunk from the well, and we've never experienced anything similar."

If he knew that, then he'd be a step closer to knowing what the thing was. Amazing how he could explore for twenty winters and still be surprised by something beneath his feet. "I don't know," he said. "I suspect that what I fought has a body—a hamr—and lives below the well. Perhaps it animated the water with magic, or sent its spirit to do the same. You and I are capable of that, Freyja, so why not another?"

Freyja's green eyes narrowed like one of the long-toothed cats that roamed Vanaheim's plains. She played idly with the gem-crusted torc that lay heavy on her chest. "But that begs the question. Is there a place—"

The slither of leather upon the smooth table interrupted her as Heimdall dragged his wineskin to him.

Odin banged a fist on the table. Heimdall looked up, startled. Odin jabbed a finger at him. "Were I to rip your spirit from your body, Heimdall, it would sever the link between it and your body. Not only would this kill you, but if I were strong enough—and I am—I could wear your corpse like a shirt. Not that I would, since you've befouled your body with so much drink."

Thor chuckled. Heimdall glared at him, but Thor just stared back, a bored expression settling on his face.

Freyja cleared her throat. "As I was saying, is there a place beneath Ithavoll? There must be, right?"

He blew out a hard breath. How much had they missed because

of Heimdall's drunkenness? Deprived of his cousin's watchfulness, he could now see how greatly they had leaned upon it. Curse Loki and his pranks.

"Just as normal trees tap deep, fertile soil, so too does this one." Odin gestured with one hand toward Yggdrasil's looming bulk. "When last I looked—and that was a very long time ago—my sight could not pierce the darkness beneath us."

"What about when you..." She too gestured toward the giant tree.

Drove a spear through his side and hung himself up among its branches for nine windy nights? He gave a quick shake of the head. "My attention was elsewhere."

Thor thumped the table with one beefy fist and looked around the table. "Why don't I just swim down there and kill it? When I come back with its head, I'll tell you what's down there. Mystery solved. Can we now—"

Freyr laughed. "I don't think it's that simple, cousin. You can't just swim down the Urdarbrunnr."

"Why not? If I want to cross a river, I either fly over it in my cart or walk through it. If there's a boulder in my way, I break it."

"Refreshingly direct, but whatever this thing is, how can a realm exist literally beneath our feet?" Freyr leaned forward, a light smile brightening his golden features. "The Alfather just said there's nothing beneath Yggdrasil."

Thor frowned, his red brows meeting in the middle. "That's not what I heard him say. Besides, we ride down Yggdrasil from a tunnel atop Gladsheim, and yet there's a star-filled sky above us. If we ride down to here, then maybe there's more below. Or maybe up and down don't always mean what they think we do. I think Vidar's said something like that before, right?"

Odin grunted to himself. Vidar had said that. And he himself had thought much the same thing when he'd hung from Yggdrasil's upper limbs and stared into the Ginnungagap's roaring heart.

"Ah, well..." Freyr sat back, pursed his lips, and considered. "You have me there, I admit."

Satisfied, Thor folded his arms over his chest. Chuckles ran around the table.

Odin couldn't help but smile. It wasn't often that his plodding son wrong-footed those quicker of wit. He rapped the table. "It's clear we need to know more before we act. I see only one course before us: I will sit upon my High Seat and when I pierce the shadows beneath us, we will ride into that darkness astride Skidbladnir's sturdy planks."

He caught Frigg's frown, cleared his throat and said, "But that would take more time than we have now, so let us set this particular mystery aside, frustrating though that is, and focus on the one that caused Frigg to summon me back."

For a moment, he considered asking Frigg to tell what she'd seen in her visions. She had to know more of what was going on than she let on. How many threats to the Aesir could he quash if he could only see half as much as she did—or if she would confide in him?

Instead, he invited Baldr to speak. "If you would, son, please tell everyone what you've been experiencing."

Baldr quirked his lips but sat forward, addressing everyone. "Several of you know this already, but since early summer I've been having dreams—increasingly vivid, disturbing dreams."

"They cause his body to grow corpse-cold," Nanna said, tears leaping into her eyes. "And the only thing that wakes him is Sól's light falling on him."

Baldr reached out and took her hand, and their fingers twined together. "I don't remember that, but of course I take Nanna's word for it—and mother's. Freyja has seen my...dreams, too. All I do remember are glimpses. I'm sitting in a chair astride a ship, the sail bellied before the wind. The ship creaks and flexes upon the waves. Then I'm cold, colder than the cellars beneath Heimdall's tower. Then I wake, shivering and shaking—thanks, apparently, to having been dragged to wherever dawn's light would fall on me."

"It's the only thing that rouses him," Nanna said again.

Baldr smiled reassuringly, patted her hand and kissed her brow.

Odin glanced sideways at Frigg. Her face was drawn and tight, her hands clasped in her lap, knuckles white. She knew something more. What else had she seen in her visions?

He pressed on. "And how often do you have the dreams, Baldr?"

"At least once a week. Sometimes more frequently." He glanced at Nanna, who nodded agreement.

"But no dreams at all when we rode to Háls and back again?"

"None. Nor last night."

He grunted. "Grim though it sounds, it would be useful for me to see one." He looked across the table at Freyja. "What did you think of them?"

"I've only seen a few of them," Freyja said, with a solemn nod. "We did try to solve the mystery without you, Alfather."

Another weak barb about his absence. Weren't any of them the least curious about what waited for them in the world beyond their current borders—a world so vast that his brothers had vanished into it? "He's my son, Freyja. I'd set the heavens ablaze for him. For any of you. What have you learned so far?"

Freyja shrugged. "Very little, Alfather. I looked within Baldr's dreaming mind. When his dream came, I watched it unfold. All was as he said except more detailed. Lengthier. I looked for witchthread leading into his mind but found nothing."

"So it's not a sending," he said.

"I don't think so," she replied. "But you might have more success than I."

"I doubt that," he said with a quick grin. Freyja had taught him much about seidr, both when they'd fought each other during the Vanir War and then afterward when their two peoples had become one.

"I'll say further that it both looked and felt similar to the ritual you Aesir conduct when you send your dead off in a burning ship, but without the fire."

"And that's when you sent for me," he said, glancing at Frigg. Her expression was guarded. She was absolutely keeping something to herself.

She shrugged. "There was nothing else we could try."

He had other options. The Norns had failed him, but he could still speak with his uncle. And if that conversation produced no answers, the dead knew many. The difficulty lay in finding the right questions to ask them. "Calling me back made perfect sense."

Thor impatiently slid his hands forward on the table. "I'm not sure I see the problem. They're just dreams, right? They can't hurt him, and he's dreaming about something that's not possible. If killing Baldr were possible, then I alone would have done it a hundred times over."

In their younger days, Thor had often made a game of hurling Mjolnir at Baldr. All the hammer had ever done was knock Baldr down—or through a wall—before returning to Thor's hand. Baldr would then stand up from the wreckage, dust himself off, and grin. Over time, the amusement had faded, particularly once pelting Baldr with weapons had become an integral part of the main Midwinter ritual.

"But dreaming of the impossible is exactly what's worrisome, Thor," Frigg said. "Why would he dream of that? And why does his body become corpse-cold?"

"And the dream itself suggests that I can die," Baldr said, voice steady. "So maybe it is possible."

That wasn't necessarily true. Dreams didn't always make sense, nor were the confusing ones always visions.

Odin pushed back in his chair and exchanged a quick glance with Frigg. After she'd nodded in agreement he said, "The magic we used at his birth makes it impossible for him to be killed."

"But when Thiazi forced Loki to steal Yggdrasil's fruits, I aged just as everyone did," Baldr said. "Could I have died from old age then?"

Was that possible? Frigg had used an old Jotunn magic to place Baldr's spirit—his hugr—into a living sprig of mistletoe. They'd set that mistletoe in a young oak growing in the glade atop Gladsheim's central hill. So long as tree and mistletoe lived and the magic was fed like a fire, nothing could harm Baldr—no weapon, poison, stone, venom, or magic. That's what the Norns had promised. Thor had even blasted him with lightning. It had burned his clothes off and scorched the ground, but Baldr had been unharmed.

Freyja cleared her throat. "Perhaps, Alfather, if you shared the nature of the magic that was used, we could provide some—"

He shook his head. "Not possible."

Her smile was like a summer breeze. "Everything's possible, Alfather. All here would take that secret to our graves."

"I know that, believe me. But secrets have a way of getting out, which is why only Frigg and I keep this one. If three or more know a thing, well"—he spread his hands—"so dies the secret."

In the silence that followed, the white moths flitted and the mists flowed around their feet. Yggdrasil's bulk was weighter than the loom of an unseen shore.

He broke the silence by saying, "I've already asked the Norns about these dreams. They ignored me, just as they'd begun doing long before I left. There is another I can consult. Beyond that, I know another, more dangerous way of getting at the truth, which I will gladly hazard should it prove necessary."

He looked directly at Baldr. "I will find out what's happening, son. I promise you that."

***

"So, our last piece of business. The attack on Háls," Odin said. "Does anyone have any ideas on how the Jotunn might have gotten into Asgard in the first place?"

Tyr spoke first. "With respect, Alfather, I doubt they slipped through the Breach. Even the outposts along the mountain's shoulders have overlapping sight lines, and any passable slope is regularly patrolled."

"They couldn't have crossed even in ones and twos?" he asked.

"It's not impossible, but I think it very unlikely. Some of our best warriors stand watch upon the Breach's walls."

From across the table, Freyr asked, "What about by ship?"

Frigg shook her head. "That's also unlikely. We've a dozen longships patrolling the open sea east of Ifington and another dozen in the Thund to the west. And there are probably hundreds of fishing craft and trading vessels plying those same waters. Even if they found a harbor along Utgard's shores, then they probably would have been seen crossing."

Odin threw a glance at the still-snoring Heimdall. Obviously she meant seen by the fisherfolk.

"Improbable, then, but not impossible?" Freyr said, keeping his tone light.

She shrugged. "Let's assume they found a place to beach their ship on our shores—there are probably many such places that we don't know about—they'd still have to cross leagues of harsh lands where there's little to forage or hunt. They'd need a small fleet just to carry the necessary supplies."

Tyr leaned forward. "With respect, Almother, the sympathizers could have helped—even just stowing supplies along an out-of-the-way route. It would have taken considerable planning, of course, nor would it have been easy, but..."

"Sympathizers?" Odin raised an eyebrow at Frigg.

She nodded. "They call themselves the Sons of Muspell. We're not quite sure when it started, but they have been petitioning for us to aid the Jotunn."

Odd name. Muspellheim was the fiery counterpart to frigid Niflheim. His father had said that one had poured fire and the other ice into the Ginnungagap. From that resulting clash—that storm—had sprung Hvergelmir and, eventually, all that was.

Baldr cleared his throat. "We think that some of those I brought with me into Utgard started the group. They're the only ones who've seen firsthand how the Jotunn live—"

"How the Skrymir lets them be seen to live," Odin said. He'd known a dozen Skrymir during his long life, including the one for whom they were all named. Most had been clever, intelligent, and quite willing to strike without warning. He'd respected them.

"I'm not so sure of that, Father. Maybe that was the case many winters back. But now?" Baldr shook his head sadly.

"In any event," Frigg interjected, sitting forward, "we're straying from the topic at hand. While sympathizers could have aided the Jotunn in crossing Asgard—maybe supplying weapons, food and clothing—their *possible* involvement doesn't explain how the Jotunn got into Asgard to begin with."

"Unless the Sons are far better organized than we suspect," Tyr said.

Nanna coughed, smiled hesitantly, and asked, "Have we considered the trade route? I know the Einherjar count those going through the Breach—or they're supposed to—but do those counts balance out?"

"If they don't, I'll know the reason why," Frigg said, her voice steelier than he'd ever heard. "But that's a question we can't answer now. You and I, Nanna, will look into it. Good idea."

Nanna blushed. "Yes, Almother. Thank you."

Tyr spoke again. "If Hár Nanna is right—and even if she isn't, I suppose—even a few complicit traders with ships could transport the Jotunn along the coast to a point near Háls. No one would question small ships that appear to be fishing."

He couldn't believe what he was hearing. The Jotunn inexplicably grown strong enough again—it'd only been forty winters since the Last War—to destroy one of their cities? If they could do that, what else might they have done? Maybe they had leveled some subtle magic against his son, as well. If that was the case, Loki would answer for what he'd done to Heimdall.

"So despite our best efforts to keep the Jotunn contained in Utgard, it is possible that they've found a way out, either due to their own ingenuity or by playing on the sympathies of our people," Odin said.

"Or both," Frigg said. "Either way, we need to look into it further —Ullr at the Breach, Nanna and I here. And if this ends up being the precursor to a larger attack, then I take full responsibility for trusting them too much."

He nodded sharply in acknowledgment. He wasn't about to berate his wife in front of everyone. Whatever the reason for the attack, there would be time enough to cast blame. Not that he'd need to. Frigg wouldn't be tricked a second time.

He withdrew the smooth, cold ironwood device from his satchel. It clunked when he set it on the table. Vidar had spent so much fruitless time working on it. "Since we cannot figure out the how, I can at least present a possible reason for the attack."

About the length of his forearm, the device was made from hollowed-out ironwood the width of a sword's grip. One end held a dark ruby in a gold setting. From the other end, broken and scorched, dangled a melted length of gold.

"Even from where I sit I'd say that was crafted by the Svartalvar," Freyr said, his voice a mixture of curiosity and the first wisps of hot anger.

"And you'd be right," Odin said with a nod. "Since the Last War, Vidar has been studying this device. He gave up just this past summer."

He paused, expecting someone to ask just how he knew that. Clearly they remembered some things after his absence.

"You may recall that this device was seized toward the end of the Last War. An Einherjar patrol surprised a small group of Jotunn in the deep forests north of Gladsheim. The Einherjar attacked the Jotunn and destroyed them. Based on what the Einherjar patrol leader said afterward, the Jotunn were uncharacteristically frantic. The shaman with them used seidr to drive a small fire hotter and higher, then she smashed something and began throwing the pieces into the fire. Only this and a few other useless fragments remain."

"I remember," Freyja said, leaning forward. "So this is...what?"

"The fruit of Vidar's labors. He has succeeded in rebuilding some of what the fire had destroyed." He picked it up and handed it to Baldr. "Please pass it down to Freyja."

He continued, "When that piece and the other fragments were first brought to me, I knew it wasn't Jotunn-made. Long ago they were capable of producing such fine work, but not during the time of the Last War. That said, I was curious enough to inspect the place where it was found in case there were some clues regarding its function. I found nothing out of the ordinary, aside from a few never-explained oddities."

"Like what?" Freyr asked, glancing up from watching his sister examine the device.

"Climbing gear—ropes, rope anchors, iron wedges, harnesses."

"What were they climbing?" Freyr asked, with a puzzled frown.

He shrugged. "I don't know. There was a sizeable outcropping near their camp, but I climbed it without gear. Nothing up there but tree roots. Their camp was northeast of Gladsheim, so maybe their plan was to scale the city's northern cliff. At the time, we were busy finishing the war, so I didn't give these fragments further thought. Jotunn shamans to use staffs and wands just as we do."

Freyja handed the device to her brother. "Assuming Vidar didn't radically alter the materials used, I agree with you and him. This device was made by the Svartalvar."

"Any idea what it does?" Odin asked. The Vanir were even more familiar with what the Svartalvar smiths could accomplish than the Aesir were.

She shook her head. "Not a clue. Did Vidar?"

"No. All he said was that the device 'clicked' when he turned that setting on the end."

Freyr immediately turned the setting. The click was audible, even across the table. Freyr grinned and shrugged. "Worth a try. Should we expect Gladsheim to be attacked now?"

"They could try," he said. "But yes, Vidar and I both suspect that the original click led to the attack at Háls. The problem, of course, is that Vidar worked on the device in Vithi, not Háls. And he didn't sense any magic when the device clicked."

"Nor did I just now," Freyja said. "So maybe it was coincidental?"

"But there could be other reasons Háls was attacked, Alfather," Tyr said. "Maybe they sought the ore mined there, or it was a diversion—a prelude to another attack."

The thought had occurred to him—and to Baldr—when he'd shared the secret of the device on the last leg of their trip back from

Háls. If another attack was coming, the Jotunn would face a much more prepared opponent no matter where they struck.

Baldr repeated the same argument he'd voiced last night. "But how does any attack help them? All they've done is break the treaty and anger us."

"And given that we'll muster our reserves to scour the countryside looking for other hidden warbands," Tyr added, "we're more prepared for another attack than we would otherwise have been."

Baldr shook his head. "It doesn't make sense. Our standing army alone dwarfs whatever few warbands they can muster. And we're better armed and better fed. They couldn't hope to defeat us in a direct battle."

"Which is why they attacked by surprise," Tyr said.

Frigg spoke. "When you returned from Jotunheim in late summer, Baldr, you told me they'd grown desperate. Not enough food, few children in sight, everyone thin and haunted-looking. Perhaps this attack is just that—a desperate last stroke."

"I don't believe the Skrymir would risk compromising what we've been negotiating with him," Baldr said. "And this attack failed. Surprises only work against the unsuspecting."

"And what exactly have you been negotiating with the Jotunn?" Odin asked.

"Now's not really the time—" Frigg began.

"Oh, now I'm curious."

Her smile looked forced. "We can discuss it later."

"If it's relevant to why they attacked, shouldn't we address it now?"

"It argues against their attacking, Father," Baldr said, "even though they obviously did. My guess is that one of the tribes disagrees with the Skrymir's proposal."

He tapped his fingers on the table, waiting for the answer. "Why not tell me—tell us all, assuming they don't already know. What negotiations were you engaged in?"

Frigg had the look of a woman bracing herself for the crash of a huge wave. "That we let some Jotunn out of Utgard and allow them to settle in specific places within Asgard."

His laugh startled a dozen moths into panicked flight. "Let them out when we spent thousands of Aesir lives penning them up? The goal was to eliminate the Jotunn. We'd nearly done that." Until now.

"Another generation and there won't be any Jotunn left," Baldr said, his voice growing hot like a poker too long in the forge.

"Baldr, that was the point," he said. "End their threat to us."

"By killing them all?" Baldr made a cutting motion with one hand. "You couldn't have intended that. If we let them out, give them a chance to become Aesir as we've done with some Jotunn already— or become our allies, as we did with the Vanir—then that, eliminates them as a threat."

"Or it gives the clever ones a new chance to strike at us. As some have clearly done in Háls," he said, keeping his tone level. "The Jotunn understand strength. We cannot ever show weakness."

"In a night's time, I can be back over Utgard," Thor offered. "I'll show them what it means to kill Aesir."

Odin nodded. "I think that's exactly what should be done, but only after we speak with the Jotunn envoy. If we get the 'rogue tribe' excuse we've heard so many times in the past, then a demonstration of strength will absolutely be in order."

And if Thor and his hammer don't get their attention, then they will weep when I step upon the field.

42

LokiA white moth flitted away into the swirling mists, leaving behind the broad table around which the Aesir sat and spoke. Higher and higher it flew, until the white mist below it undulated like the sea.

The white moth changed, then, becoming a dusky snow owl that, on broad wings, silently higher along the brown boredom of Yggdrasil's rough bark until, after a time, the prominence of a branch became evident. The branch pointed outward—eastward, maybe—into the speckled darkness. The owl followed the branch, keenly searching until it dove into a pool of water.

With a crack like the sound of breaking ice, the owl burst into Utgard's night sky. A freezing wind caught the owl, spun it around and flung it downward. Still silent, the owl rode the wind's swells and troughs, feathers fluttering, wings cupped and then drawn in, then fully extended till the buffeting eased and, like a longship emerging from a gale, it began to glide.

The owl stared down at a wide expanse of snow and ice, dotted with frozen lakes, and ringed by mountains. It soared downward, flaring its wings to slow, the ground grew larger and larger, it reached taloned feet toward a snow-covered ridge and, in its shadow, thumped down onto four massive paws in a spray of ice and snow.

The bear lifted its black nose and sniffed. White fur ruffling, it shuffled in a tight circle, nose to ground, snuffling, seeking scents. It was alone. The bear lurched into a shambling run that soon brought it to a rock strewn ridge above the wide mist-wreathed lake.

Máni hung above the eastern mountains' sharp teeth like a morsel of meat held above a wolf's teeth. Overhead, the Bifrost split the sky in two, from the deep north to touch down beyond the Aesir's fortress in the south. Low in the west, a storm sulked.

In the faint shadows, the bear became Loki. He stretched and popped his neck while watching dozens of distant figures moving back and forth between the lake and a spot at the base of the cliffs that towered over the eastern shore. The Jotunn were going into and out of the same deep cave that was his destination.

They had to know how risky it was to work beneath clear skies, even if the forerunning clouds, the stray ships of the sky, were beginning to gather. They must have a way of knowing when Ygg and Goldtooth were looking. Thanks to his efforts, Goldtooth had seen nothing but the bottom of a cup for the past eighteen winters. The Skrymir must know Ygg had returned to Gladsheim, so the fact that this work was happening at all suggested the Jotunn had well-placed spies—other than himself, of course. Not that he was spying for them. It was a mutually beneficial arrangement.

He shivered, exhaled into cupped hands, but became the thick-furred bear again anyway. He still had a long way to go—and he needed to think on what he'd learned at Ithavoll. Better wrestle with his thoughts now, when he had time, than later when he might not.

Ygg's return to Gladsheim well before Midwinter had not been part of anyone's plan. As he'd just learned, his quarry's unexpected dreams had caused Frigg to send for her absent husband. Were those dreams the result of what he'd done or was something else involved —like that spirit from the well?

He blew out a beary breath. It didn't matter. He had two immediate problems. Ygg would expect his blood brother Loki to show up at some point. He had a good excuse as to why he hadn't yet—traditionally, he visited his wrongfully exiled children during the weeks

before and after Midwinter. Ygg knew that, so he would be patient—
to a point.

The other problem was the idiotic, failed attack on Háls. Why had
it even been permitted? Not only had it betrayed the Jotunn's hand,
but the Aesir had been jolted from their complacence. And now Ygg
was more motivated than ever to wipe out the Jotunn.

He stared up at the Bifrost, as if he could find the answer in the
milky ribbon.

The Skrymir would play for time hoping to lull the Aesir. He'd
have his envoys grovel and blame the attack on a rogue tribe. It
wouldn't work, of course. The Skrymir must know that. But they did
need time; there was no way the Jotunn's forces were in place yet.
Attacking a prepared Gladsheim would be stupid, but that's what the
Norns had scratched and painted.

He had planned to strike during the Midwinter festival—and
then escape during the confusion and panic of a full-scale Jotunn
attack.

Would they call off their attack? He needed them to move
forward. It was his only chance to escape. Murder was only half his
plan. It had to be now. He'd committed himself after winters upon
winters of patient planning...of enduring humiliation after humiliation. And once winter receded, his handiwork would be discovered
and Ygg would take steps to fix it.

He snorted, breath blowing out in a huge cloud. He'd delivered
the distractions he'd promised and that had furthered the Skrymir's
plans.

He *needed* the Jotunn, but maybe they no longer needed him. If
they simply delayed their plans...or canceled their attack entirely...if
he went ahead with his plan, he'd be exposed. No confusion to mask
his escape. Even worse, the Skrymir might betray him to Ygg. Sure,
that would eventually lead to the Skrymir's own plan being
revealed...but betraying Loki would be one way to get the time they
needed.

But how to convince the Skrymir to attack Gladsheim anyway?

He stood and shook his shaggy, massive sides like any bear might.

Down below, the figures toiled, oblivious to anything except their labor and the icy water.

He had to learn what the Skrymir and Vafthrudnir planned before deciding what best suited his own purposes. If they tried to kill him tonight, he could escape—maybe even kill one of them in the process. And then he could return to Gladsheim with news of a Jotunn plot against the Aesir.

But then the Jotunn might reveal what Loki plotted. Ygg probably wouldn't believe the enemy over his blood brother. Probably.

The bigger problem would be that half his plans would be wrecked because of short-sighted, timid Jotunn. And he'd have to get his boys safely out of Helveg. Beli would kill them without hesitation if he thought Loki had betrayed the Jotunn.

The Jotunn must still attack on Midwinter.

He let loose a frustrated roar and then ambled down the long slope leading down to the lake. A cloud of snow and ice trailed him like all of Ygg's broken promises.

***

Loki leaned against the back wall of the cave entrance he had glimpsed from above the lake. Three longships stem to stern would easily span the cave's low mouth. It was at least that same distance back to where he stood beside one of several tunnels that disappeared into still deeper sections.

The cave floor had been smoothed; the ceiling and walls were natural, untouched stone. Dozens of braziers set along the curve of the inside wall cast an uneven, ruddy light throughout the cave. Still more braziers, one every few spear lengths, lined the tunnels. The hulking, wild shadows thrown against the walls made it seem like a tribe of giants labored silently in the cave. Their task was gigantic, but the Jotunn were not.

After descending from the ridge, Loki had shifted to his Jotunn shape and presented himself to one of the outlying sentries. Since he was expected, the sentry had escorted him to the cave, delivering him into the custody of the stocky warrior who stood beside him now.

During the short walk along the cliff face, he had observed a handful of workers standing waist deep in the frigid lake amid chunks of thick ice. With long poles, they pulled dark shapes up from the black water and then pushed them back toward those standing in shallower water. More Jotunn floated those shapes onto rafts, which they shoved and prodded toward shore. On shore, still more men dragged the laden rafts free from the water, up the shore, and into the cave.

Now, he saw the other half of their labors. A pair of workers emerged out of the tunnel to his left, casually dragging an empty wooden sledge toward the mouth of the cave. They passed another pair, bent-backed, hauling a laden sledge toward the tunnels.

But it was the cargo on those sledges that really interested Loki. As one passed by, he got a good look. As if deeply asleep, two Jotunn laid side by side on it, each wrapped tight from head to foot in sodden, wide strips of brown cloth still flecked with ice and frost. A metal disk sat above the heart of each figure with a single rune pulsing slowly in the center.

"Awe-inspiring, isn't it?" The voice was quiet, deep, and calm, much like, in a way, the frozen lake from which these bodies had been dragged.

Startled, he forced himself to incline his head in greeting before saying in the Jotunn hand speech, "Indeed it is, Skrymir."

Long ago, he had journeyed with Thor into Utgard and battled with the first Skrymir, the one after whom all the other chiefs were named. This Skrymir and that one looked similar, but that had been long ago—before he'd even met Angrboda and had children with her.

"You are late, son of Farbauti." The Skrymir's fingers moved smoothly as they formed the words. Fewer lines and wrinkles marred that lean face than Loki would have expected of so aged a Jotunn.

"I've come as we had agreed. And I bring important news."

The Skrymir's fingers danced. "But were you pursued? Does

Goldtooth even now listen for your every word with ears keener than a hound's? Does he seek you with eyes sharper than an eagle's?"

He shook his head. "Goldtooth primarily concerns himself with finding the bottom of a cup, as you well know. When I left, the Aesir were still at Ithavoll."

"So you *were* with Goldtooth, then?"

Loki gestured toward the string of sleeping Jotunn being dragged into the cave's depths, then signed, "If you're so concerned about Goldtooth, then why does the work continue under clear skies?"

The Skrymir threw him a shrewd, sly look that cast Loki back across more than three hundred winters to when the first Skrymir had thrown a similar sharp-eyed gaze at a young Thor. The similarity was uncanny. But this man before could not be that Skrymir. Ygg protected Yggdrasil's fruits more closely than Frigg did her—

"We knew that the Aesir were in council," the Skrymir signed. "Not that we aren't grateful for how completely you've blunted his sharp eyes and ears."

And so that confirmed it: the Jotunn had other spies among the Aesir.

The Skrymir smiled, teeth flashing white in the gloom. "Yes, Loki, we have other sources of information. None quite as capable as you or with as much access, but they are helpful. You'll find them of use soon, too, I should think."

"Are Jotunn sympathizers so easy to find?" he asked. "I'm hurt. I thought I was unique."

"Oh, you are," the Skrymir said aloud. He gestured down the tunnel from which he'd emerged, and his fingers danced again. "But come, the cold's setting into these old bones. Let's slink into our warren. We have much to discuss."

***

Loki ran his fingers along the smooth, warm wall. Utgard was much warmer deep below the surface, as the Jotunn builders had discovered long ago. Given the slope of the floor and the developing ache in his legs, they were already deep and headed still further.

Deeper into the stone gullet, the warmth began to drag on him, dampening his armpits and the small of his back. He was acutely conscious of the tall warden behind him, as silent as the stone around them, and the warden leading the way. Had he been right? Was he headed to his own death?

He threw back his cloak. "These tunnels are impressive work, Skrymir," he said with his hands.

The high chief didn't break stride. With his hands, he said, "Just wait."

They rounded another bend, and the heat seemed to plant itself on his chest.

"Why so many twists and turns?" he asked.

"Because Vafthrudnir's mind is nearly as devious as your own," the Skrymir signed, twisting toward him so his fingers could be seen. "Can you not guess?"

The Jotunn lived in constant dread of Goldtooth—their name for Heimdall—and his hearing. Heimdall's eyesight was supernal, too, but no matter how far he could see, he couldn't look through solid rock any more than Ygg could. But sound always had a way of sneaking out. Loki swore Heimdall could hear the grass growing, but he couldn't hear everything all the time.

He'd proven that himself when he'd taught a flock of green-winged birds how to repeat Heimdall's name. His theft of Freyja's necklace, which had led to the fight with Heimdall—the one he'd made sure to so spectacularly lose—had provided the perfect excuse for what everyone still called a bit of mischief gone horribly wrong.

"I assume they help trap sound beneath the ground?"

The Skrymir nodded. "Well done, Loki. They do indeed—at least we think so. Very hard to test."

"Then why does the one tunnel up top run straight?"

"Heavy doors stand between the surface and that tunnel. This one too, for that matter." The chief halted beside a blank wall, while the tunnel ran on. He banged the butt of his seax against the smooth rock beside him. "See?"

With a clunk and a long grinding, the wall pulled away from the Skrymir. Light peeked out around its edges, and then it slid to one side. As it moved, yellow light fell in a widening slant across the corridor. When the door clicked to a halt, the chief stepped through.

As soon as Loki stepped out of the hot, close tunnel, it felt like a weight on his shoulders had vanished. No more roof an arm's length above his head, only the feeling of a great, shadowed height up into which he might, as an owl, soar.

"We're careful to only engage in the work when we're confident Goldtooth is otherwise occupied." The Skrymir waved a hand toward the empty space. "Have a look."

Loki took another step out and realized he stood on a wide pathway cut into the living rock. The path ran level off to his left and dipped down on his right to wind gradually down the cavern's perimeter. Just as the ceiling rose upward, so too did the ground plummet away beneath. It made his head spin.

As his eyes adjusted to the sheer scale of the cavern, he was able to pick out more details, particularly with the twin glow of the braziers behind him. The heat was less oppressive here thanks to the gently flowing air that carried with it the acrid tinge of smoke and the richer smells of cooking meat.

From what he could see, none of the cavern except the path where he stood had been shaped with seidr. The cavern ceiling glimmered as if it were the heavens themselves and not just the reflected light of the thousand fires scattered among the stalagmites below. And around those fires, figures moved.

He turned around and saw only one warden now, facing the stone door and working the metal levers that moved the door along its track. The door clicked shut.

The Skrymir caught his eye, smiled faintly, and stepped up beside him. In a sweeping gesture, he indicated the huge cavern and the fires below. "This is one of many such chambers scattered throughout Utgard. As we wake our brothers and sisters from their long sleep, they live, train, and prepare in these places until they are called upon."

The older Jotunn's eyes were a weighty black in the low light. "And, remember, Loki, these are your people. I know how badly you and your family have been treated by the Aesir, but consider these many thousands more who've been similarly treated. What you do, you also do for them."

He stared down into the cavern, nearly a reflection of the night sky he'd sat beneath earlier. Of course the Skrymir was trying to make sure that he, unpredictable Loki, stayed loyal to the Jotunn cause. And trying to make him see that despite his very personal need for revenge, the coming conflict wasn't just personal.

But none of that meant the Skrymir was also trying to deceive him.

Actually, he was being shown the truth in much the same way Ygg had brought him before the Norns so that he could hear their prophecy with his own ears.

He glanced back at the Skrymir. Loki knew—he knew it—that this man before him would not break his word like Ygg had done, if for no other reason than what the Skrymir did, he did for his people.

The Skrymir held out a hand to him.

Loki took it.

***

Loki stepped into the high-ceilinged room, well lit by witchlamps set in sconces. The floor was smooth and covered by rugs. Heavy-looking wood furniture was clustered in a few areas, including a large wooden table flanked by witchlamp braziers.

"Excuse me for a moment." The Skrymir stepped in behind Loki and tugged the heavy door shut.

He then lifted a long metal rod from where it lay flush against the wall and rotated it up like a man raising his arm. The action of the metal arm pressed a leather skirt tight against the door's edges. With a scrape and a muted ting of metal on metal, the Skrymir shoved a hefty pin through a pair of holes in a bracket bolted to the wall. It appeared to keep the metal arm in place.

Loki waved a hand at the door. "What's that about?"

"Vafthrudnir says it helps keep the sound in."

"Yet another precaution, eh?"

"If we're overheard, the Thunderer will crack the mountain and scoop us out. But deep as we are and with this door sealed, we are safe to speak aloud." The Skrymir gestured toward a nearby clutch of four chairs set on a big red rug. A small table was set with an array of food and drink. "So please, Loki, refresh yourself. Sit."

The Skrymir crossed the room and took one of the chairs that faced the door. Loki was forced to either show trust by sitting with his back to a door that he had seen took a pair of nights to open or show distrust by sitting beside the chief.

He delayed making the obvious choice by helping himself to a small cup of wine and filling a small platter with some dried fish and bread, as much to quell the rumbling of his belly as to buy a moment to think.

The Skrymir leaned back. "Before you arrived, I was reviewing the last information we received from the shaman with Ama's warband—before he was killed and we lost that warband. Do you have any more insights into that fight?"

How much to tell him? So far, this reception was going as he'd expected. But he was also locked in an underground cave with a man who might be planning to kill him.

He gestured toward the small table. "Can I bring you anything?"

The Skrymir made a dismissive gesture. "No, I'm fine."

Food and drink in hand, Loki sat down opposite the Skrymir, back prickling, and took a deliberate swallow of wine. Why show himself a liar over something so easy to verify? And a bit of truth might win some tidbit in exchange and help him figure out who the Jotunn spy, or spies, might be. He could use that to his advantage.

The Skrymir betrayed no annoyance at the silence. If anything, his black eyes twinkled as if he knew exactly what Loki was doing. "Perhaps it will save time if I tell you what I know. Ama attacked Háls in Vithi. The last communication we had was that the town had been razed, its people driven out, and his warband was preparing to engage with Jarl Vidar's. We've heard nothing from him since, but..."

Loki nodded. "Vidar's warband wiped them out. And based on what was *not* said at Ithavoll, Vidar used some seidr to make the victory possible. Ygg avoided the subject entirely."

"Vafthrudnir said as much." The Skrymir's expression was sour. "Ygg was there at the battlefield?"

"He was, along with a full company of Einherjar. They arrived the morning after Vidar's warband."

The Skrymir's fingers drummed on the arm of his chair.

Loki frowned. "What are you not telling me?"

The Skrymir gave him a shrewd look. "I suppose it doesn't matter now—or at all, really. Vafthrudnir watched the battle. He said that Vidar is a baresark and that he lost control of his fylgja."

"Really?" The prickling of his back redoubled.

"You didn't know?"

Was this entire conversation a ploy to test how truthful he'd be? "I'd no idea—not about that, at least. I knew that Ygg had taught Vidar some of the old charms, but a baresark, too?" He blew out a breath. "That means Eldr is dead, then, eh?"

"For many winters now, yes. I'm surprised you hadn't heard."

"I'm not much for gossip."

The Skrymir's laughed boomed off the ceiling.

"How did he die, if I may ask?"

"He went through one of Vafthrudnir's doorways, looking for the Sons. We still don't know what happened to him. Nothing good, obviously." The Skrymir waved the subject away. "But tell me, why do you think Ygg wouldn't want it spoken about?"

"Simple enough, really. Making Vidar a baresark meant that Ygg had broken yet another promise. The next baresark was to be a Vanir. I assume Freyr and Freyja know but are keeping quiet until there's something else they really want."

But if they didn't know, then he might be able to use that issue to drive a wedge between the Aesir and Vanir. It would take time to break that alliance apart, but enough hammer strikes split even the thickest trees.

"What are you thinking, Loki?"

He sat up straighter. "Just that I share the Aesir's confusion over why you let Ama's warband attack in the first place. They seemed to settle on their pursuit of some device Vidar partially reconstructed."

"So he did succeed in that?"

"Partially, yes. They believe it's Svartalvar-made, which Freyr and Freyja weren't happy about. Does that device what do think it does?"

The Skrymir nodded. "They haven't guessed?"

"Not yet. They think the warband slipped across the Breach or smuggled themselves into Asgard via the trade route."

"Good."

Loki snorted. "Vidar has stayed behind in Háls. He'll figure out how the warband got there soon enough."

"Before Midwinter, I expect," the Skrymir said, frowning.

"Then why did you let Ama attack?" Why betray your biggest advantage long before you needed it?

The Skrymir's frown deepened. "We don't think Ygg already knows about the doorways—or even their possibility. But even if he does, he cannot find the doorways without a functioning device."

"You're that certain Ygg doesn't know about any of this or that he can't, through other means, find these doorways?"

"Reasonably so, yes," the Skrymir said.

So, not at all certain. "How can you be confident that your attack will still surprise them? Because they're preparing for the worst right now."

The Skrymir spread his hands. "That's one of the reasons why I wanted to speak with you face-to-face."

Loki raised an eyebrow and sat back. Here it was.

"We cannot attack on Midwinter as planned. But we still need you to go ahead and kill Baldr."

They weren't going to kill him after all. They were setting him up to kill himself.

43

Odin

Odin kept his expression stony. Frigg was right. They would have to deal with Saglund. The man stood there respectfully enough—they were in Gladsheim's main hall—but his every response was contradictory.

"No, battle does that," Odin repeated, his words clipped. "Something the Einherjar have seen too little of these past winters."

"With respect, Sigfather, we haven't been at war since long before you left," Saglund said. "The ongoing training is critical to maintaining the Einherjar's fighting edge. Every warrior fights every day. They feast and rest at night, then rise and do it all over again. And if I may, they fought well when they faced your son with you."

"Fair enough. But how would they have done without my charm to bolster them?"

"They would have held, Sigfather. Or fought and died. All through this long peace, I've had them training with your baresarks, as you ordered before you left. They have a sense for how to stand against foes with superior strength."

Odin thumped his chair. "That's exactly what I'm saying, Saglund. Having a sense of it is vastly different than living it. Say this skirmish in Vithi blossoms into the bloody flower of war. Are you telling me that all the Einherjar stand ready?"

"I believe they do, Sigfather, despite the ongoing peace."

He gritted his teeth. All this talk of peace and training. Einherjar were born in battle, tempered in blood.

"Hersir, you do remember how the Einherjar came to be, yes?"

"Of course, Sigfather."

"How many warriors now join the Einherjar each year?"

"About three dozen, give or take."

"That rivals the number I added to the original Einherjar during the entire First Jotunn War, which lasted nearly ten winters."

"With respect, Sigfather, those who try to join the Einherjar are already among the very best warriors in Asgard. I take only the very best of those."

"Becoming Einherjar isn't about being the best," he said, staring evenly at Saglund. "Training and practice cannot prepare anyone for that moment when they must choose to keep fighting, standing alone above the bodies of their fallen shieldmates, and holding off an enemy wild to exploit the opportunity. As you well know."

During the Last War, Saglund had earned his place among the Einherjar by standing beside Baldr and holding the Old Bridge after Hodr had been blinded while he himself was badly wounded.

"The Einherjar are the spear's blade; me, my sons—and my baresarks—at the very point," he continued. "Yes, they kept my son at bay. And yes, maybe they are good with weapons and keeping formations. But do they have what it takes here?" He tapped his chest.

Saglund nodded immediately. "Sigfather, I ask that when time permits, you watch the Einherjar drill at any of the three compounds inside the walls. Or elsewhere. They will impress you, I promise."

He hid a frown. Was Saglund oblivious to his point, willfully or otherwise? Either way, this wasn't how he remembered the man. But the warrior before him was twenty winters older, grayer, and stouter. For himself, the time had passed like a pair of heartbeats to him— less, even, after eating Yggdrasil's fruit.

The hall's side door creaked. White-haired Fimafeng shuffled in.

"Even a well-kept sword will turn in the hand if it's disused," Odin said, his voice even. He thumped the arms of his chair and stood. "Hersir, you will prepare plans for the Einherjar to join the army on regular patrols of our border with Utgard. I will review them tomorrow."

"Very good, Sigfather." Saglund clearly understood that the meeting was over. "And if I may, please convey my best respects to the Almother."

"Of course. Thank you, Hersir."

Odin gestured for the waiting Fimafeng to approach as Saglund left.

"Your pardon, Alfather, but the envoy sent a runner with his deepest regrets. He will be late for his audience with you and the Almother."

He turned. "Did you hear that, Frigg?"

"Of course. I heard all of it." Frigg stepped out from the darkness behind the platform, screened by hangings from the hall's main area. "What reason did he give, Fimafeng?"

"Only that his own daily communication with the Skrymir was delayed. He is waiting to make sure he has the most current information."

"Fair enough," she said. "Fimafeng, Hersir Saglund was...?"

"Your last obligation of the day, Almother. Until evening, of course."

"So we have plenty of time to accommodate him," Frigg said. "Please tell the envoy we excuse this imposition on our time and that we expect him to present himself when he does receive word from the Skrymir."

"Yes, Almother." Fimafeng bowed, took a step back, then made his slow way back to the side door.

When the door had closed, Odin turned to her. "You're too lax with these Jotunn."

She shrugged. "What would we have gained by making him come now? We still would've had to wait while he hurried here. When he arrived, he would have been annoyed and claimed that he couldn't answer because he hadn't spoken with the Skrymir. Which would further annoy us." She smiled an overly bright smile. "And just think, we now have plenty of time to talk about that idiot who just left."

"Fimafeng?" He gave her a teasing smile.

"Very funny. I meant your Einherjar hersir." She settled into her chair.

"I know," he said. Saglund had grown too confident in his role, evidently forgetting the Einherjar hersir served the Sigfather.

"You made him hersir what, two winters before you left? Without you here, he realized if he did whatever he wanted, no one could stop him—not completely, at least. I've made him stumble as much as I could."

"This doesn't sound like the man I promoted," he said, sitting beside her.

Her dark-eyed gaze, warm though it was, seemed to suggest that the Gladsheim to which he'd returned was a great deal different now.

He rubbed his face and sighed. He did not want another argument. "All right, Frigg, your thoughts? On Saglund."

"Remove him from command," she said at once.

"Just like that, eh?" He smiled. "I am concerned about how the ranks have swelled, but I'm not sure that warrants his removal."

"What use is a quiver of warped arrows?"

He looked at her sharply.

"Have you noticed how young most of the Einherjar are?"

He pursed his lips and thought back to the column of warriors he'd led to Vithi. "I'd assumed they were relatively young, based on what Gulfinn told me. The aktaumr of the column I led to Vithi were older. Experienced."

"Yes, and most in their last winters of service, I'm sure," she said. "Gulfinn told you about the testing the warriors go through to become Einherjar?"

He nodded. "He said that Saglund was recruiting from the army. What are you getting at?"

"That as of maybe twelve few winters ago, most new Einherjar are the same age as children fresh from service in their garrisons. In many cases, Saglund's swelled the Einherjar's ranks at the expense of the army."

That's not what Gulfinn had told him.

"Before you get upset, Gulfinn didn't know. Most don't. Except for Tyr and Ullr, of course. They told me."

"So what are you telling me, Frigg? I've already decided that these new Einherjar don't deserve the distinction."

She shifted in her chair and leaned forward. "That's the least of it. We're looking at a generation of warriors—of Einherjar—who are personally loyal to Saglund, not to the Sigfather."

He snorted. "That won't last long."

"Odin, Saglund's established sixteen garrisons around Asgard, four within Gladsheim's walls alone, with one hundred Einherjar per garrison—"

"That's more than ten times larger than when I left."

She thumped the arm of her chair. "And that's not even counting all the support staff—cooks, grooms, blacksmiths, armorers and the rest. You see the problem."

What he didn't see was how this could have happened. "How did he grow the ranks so swiftly?"

She laughed. "It's your fault, Odin."

"What?"

"You gave the Einherjar hersir direct access to collected tariffs. Not only has trade with the Vanir and the Alvar continued to grow, but dozens of new towns have sprung up along the road to Ifington, along the Silfr, too, downstream and even upstream to the summer pastures near the Franangr. Trade with the Jotunn is also surprisingly strong."

"But they have nothing of—t"

"Not true." She raised a hand and began ticking off the key products. "Ivory and bone, pelts and leathers, gems..."

"And what goes into Utgard?"

"Mostly food and drink."

He shook his head. "That is not good."

"And here I thought Baldr had convinced you to give the Jotunn a chance," she said with a faint smile.

"We can discuss that later. For now, let's stick to the Einherjar."

"All right."

"So Saglund's access to gold allowed him to swell the ranks and build all those garrisons."

"His unrestricted access, yes. Obviously, I stopped it when I became aware of it, but by then he'd amassed quite the stockpile. In a way, I understand how it started. Without a war, the Einherjar ranks would dwindle—"

"That's exactly what I intended," he said. "The Einherjar were meant to exemplify the very best qualities of our warriors. Just knowing how to swing a sword and hold a shield isn't the point."

"I know that," she said, "but you put an ambitious man in charge of a powerful organization. He made it bigger and, in his mind, better. I don't think his intent was, or is, malicious. I just think it's become more than it needs to be. Far more. I've hampered most of his plans, and now that you're back, we can finish it."

"And you've done what so far?"

She smiled. "I declared all land property of Gladsheim. All land, everywhere. Anyone who wants to use land for any reason—a new town, a road, a wall, an Einherjar garrison—must get my approval first. Or yours, of course. And then pay us."

He couldn't help but smile back. "Bold. Clever. How do you enforce it? Tyr and Ullr?"

"Yes. And Heimdall, when he's sober. Your baresarks have helped, too, though only Ráta and Gulfinn are here in Gladsheim."

"Even so, can I assume that Saglund's still increased the number of Einherjar?"

"Yes, but it's slowed. He can't claim more recruits than he does already, since that would pit him directly against Tyr and Ullr. And he doesn't want that."

He glanced out into the shadowy hall, lit only by what sunlight streamed through the gap between the two roofs. Clearly, he had to rein in the Einherjar, and the Aesir needed to expand their borders.

The solution was obvious. "So you heard me order Saglund to have the Einherjar join the army in patrolling our border with Utgard?"

"Yes."

"Based on what you told me, I'll place those Einherjar under the direct command of Tyr and Ullr."

She sat back. "That won't sit well with Saglund."

"No, it won't. But the Einherjar are mine. The sooner Saglund recalls that, the better. Beyond that, I'll order some of the Einherjar garrisons closed down, and those warbands will be sent out into the wilderness from which I've just returned."

"Under whose command?"

"You think they're not loyal?"

She shrugged. "I don't know, Odin. But I think it makes sense to be selective about those we do send."

An ill thought that was—disloyal Einherjar. "Agreed."

"And you'll replace Saglund?"

"Why bother? He won't live forever." He shrugged. "And I'd rather have him where I can see him."

"Maybe, but as hersir, he could still drag his heels, take months to prepare or brief subordinates, hamper supplies and preparations—anything to delay. Probably in the expectation that you're likely to soon leave Gladsheim again. He'll just wait you out."

He wagged a finger at her, trying to keep the gesture playful. "Now, now, let's keep this friendly."

She went along with it, answering with a wicked grin. "There is precedent."

"Fair point. Barring me leading a warband into the wilds, I really don't think it makes sense to remove Saglund. I hear what you're saying, but I'll keep an eye on him."

"It's not as easy as that. Believe me. We may keep ourselves young, but I think we miss how important the little things are. The lives of those around us go by so quickly."

Now that was an interesting way to put it. And how did those they ruled see their rulers? *We must seem as constant as rocks in a fast-flowing river.*

44

Frigg

Frigg watched her words sink in.

"You left me in charge, Odin. I enforced your will and made my own felt in many ways, once I got used to holding the reins. There's no doubt I've been very effective in some areas. But at the same time, the folk have an ebb and flow much different than ours has become."

"We lead, they follow," Odin said, spreading his hands wide. Draupnir's heavy, intricately detailed coils of gold glittered around his wrist.

"Says the man who hasn't been here." She made sure to smile as she said it. Even so, his features darkened.

"I don't say that to anger you, Odin, but to remind you that things here have changed. Take the sympathizers we mentioned at Ithavoll – the Sons of Muspell. The wardens have standing orders to break up the crowds who gather to hear the Sons speak, but they've been doing that for nearly ten winters now. The crowds have gradually grown bigger and less easy to disperse."

"Let me guess, these so-called Sons want peace with the Jotunn."

She nodded. "In part, yes. Can you blame them? For forty winters, all they've known is peace. Only the aged—and us—remember the Last War. And only we jarls remember anything earlier."

"And what if our bloodied nose in Háls blossoms into war? Will this peaceful generation of Aesir fight?"

"My point is that most don't understand the old hatred and fear of the Jotunn. They've grown comfortable in their lives."

"That'll change when their children are spitted on Jotunn spears and their homes are ablaze," Odin said harshly.

The flames of her vision danced around Odin's head, even as the shadowy hall gaped around him like a wolf's maw. She closed her eyes.

"Frigg? What's wrong?"

She opened her eyes to a field of fire that stretched out behind Odin. Black smoke billowed into a gray sky. His face in her vision was bloodied and black with soot. His gray eyes were furious. Gungnir gleamed golden in his upraised fist.

"Frigg?" His voice was more earnest now. He touched her hand, her shoulder.

She shook her head, blinked, and the vision winked out. "Can we not speak of peace now, Odin? We have all of us grown too old for war."

"What did you see?"

She forced herself to sit straight-backed and looked him square in his deep-set eyes, chips of flint above sharp features and a beard graying despite centuries of eating Yggdrasil's fruit. She had strands of silver in her own hair, of course. That was what sacrifice meant. She'd gladly pay more to keep Baldr alive.

He surprised her by leaning back and saying, "Tell me what you and Baldr have achieved with respect to the Jotunn."

She'd expected him to press for details of the vision she'd just had. Instead, he was asking her to share her knowledge, to further tell him what had been happening. It felt like a good sign, not that he was ready to abdicate but perhaps that he'd acknowledged that Gladsheim had changed. Or he simply didn't want another argument.

"Probably the first thing to understand is that all trade with us goes through lands controlled by the Hill tribe."

"That can't be making them popular with the other tribes."

"No, it isn't. But it's also giving them the means to persuade the others of the futility of opposing us."

"And are they convinced?"

"Baldr thinks so. And he thinks that the carrot—letting them out to settle in the lands to our south—will sway the argument. He truly believes the Jotunn are dying out. He says their women haven't borne living children in several winters. He's held their stillborn in his hands. If it continues—"

"But you said food has been flowing into Utgard for a long time now."

"It hasn't made a difference. Baldr can't explain it."

"Even Hill's been affected?"

"All of them." She nodded, not bothering to keep the sadness from her face. She had been born into the Hill tribe.

Odin frowned and looked away, but not before she glimpsed satisfaction in his face. Best to try lancing it now.

She leaned forward. "I know that none of us except Tyr and Heimdall can even hope to understand what you experienced at Ymir's hands, but I think Baldr's right. Even the Sons are right in their misguided way."

"What if everything's been an act, Frigg? Everything. They trot out all the old men and women while hiding the children. Heimdall may as well be blind and deaf with all he drinks, and—"

"And I've sat upon the High Seat, Odin. I've looked, as you taught me. I don't think they're deceiving us. If they are, then I still don't see how they could have maintained the deception for so very long. We're talking hundreds of winters in total."

"So your point is what? Even if they have deceived us, we can still defeat them?"

"Absolutely," she said. "At most, they have a thousand warriors. Eight hundred or so now, given what Vidar just did. We have nearly two thousand Einherjar and more than six thousand in the army. We can muster double that if we call up the garrisons between here and Ifington. If it comes to war, we'll destroy them."

"You say the sweetest things," he said with a smile.

She smacked him on the arm.

His face grew serious. "After Ymir murdered my parents and slaughtered Audhumbla, I saw him for the devouring monster he was. We had been one tribe—but after he did what he did, and I did what honor demanded—that tribe splintered, me and mine against them and theirs."

She reached out and took his hand. "We have an opportunity to move beyond all that horror. To set a better example and heal the old wound that divides us."

"I'm not sure I'm the best person to do that."

"Then step down," she said immediately. "Let Baldr become Alfather and Nanna, Almother."

Her words hung in the air like arrows nearing the top of their flight. Disbelief danced on Odin's face. No, not disbelief; he was dumbfounded. But she'd said it. She hadn't planned on it—not this soon, anyway. But now that it was said, she felt as if a boot had been lifted from her heart.

A loud knock came at the door, and the side door swung in.

Fimafeng slipped through. "Your pardon, Hár Frigg, Alfather. The Jotunn envoy has arrived. What shall I tell him?"

Odin shifted in his chair, a thoughtful expression in his eyes as he looked at her. He hadn't seemed to hear the steward, so she answered again.

"Please ask him to wait. With our apologies and respect. The Alfather and I will be just a little longer."

"Yes, Hár Frigg."

Moments later, after a creak of hinges and a soft thud, Odin blew out a long, low breath and, quite mildly, asked, "Are you joking?"

She shook her head. "I'm quite serious."

He shoved himself up from the chair, a lean gray wolf, and stalked several paces away. "Abdicate? Now?" He thrust an arm out toward the west. "Vithi attacked." His other arm waved toward the door. "And their envoy is here to shower us with apologies and platitudes about it being some rogue tribe that hates Aesir, and they can't control every individual tribe. Everything we've heard a thousand times." He snorted. "If we show weakness, they'll attack again. They've proven they can get a warband through to us. What if they can do it again with two or three warbands? Or more? Even three hundred warriors rampaging through Asgard would kill thousands. They hate us, Frigg. Hate me, for all I've done against them since Ymir did what he did."

He raised a hand, one finger pointed up. "But they also fear me. And that keeps them in check."

She rose and faced him. "And that's exactly why you must step down."

He gave her a look that said she was out of her mind.

"We need to show them a different way. That we can change."

"But... why? If they are in fact dying out, why not just wait? Keep them contained, and the problem solves itself."

"You're all right with all of them dying? All of them? Is that what you've wanted all this time?"

He waved a hand dismissively and turned away.

"Don't you turn away from me." She grabbed his arm. "I'm Jotunn, just as you are. And your children are at least half Jotunn."

"The 'one people' argument? Did you get that from Baldr or the other way around? I forget."

She grabbed his arm and looked him right in the face. "We can't let them all die, Odin. It's wrong."

He wouldn't meet her eyes, so she knew that her strikes were hitting home. "Say Baldr and Nanna ascend to Gladsheim's throne. You remain leader of the Einherjar. Some of them go with the folk we send to settle those new western lands you found, and you mark out the places in the south we'll permit the Jotunn to settle – but always near a loyal Einherjar garrison."

"The only message we'd send by my abdication is that we're weak."

"Between you, Thor, and now Vidar, along with all the other jarls, are we actually weaker with you off that chair?" She pointed at the seat he'd just vacated. "With the Sigfather unchained, so to speak, I'd argue we're stronger."

He pursed his lips and looked thoughtful.

"Consider what we gain if we expand our borders to the west and south. Maybe new trade with those other Aesir you mentioned. New settlements. And we bleed some of the tension from this locked-shield contest with the Jotunn. They get to settle new lands, surrounded by us. How long do you think it'll take to integrate that first colony? A hundred winters? To us, that's nothing."

"So what you're really saying is that we hold one hand out in peace but the keep the other clenched and ready to fight?"

"If you want to put it that way, yes. At least it's better than what we've been doing for the last few hundred winters."

"We'd have to completely control where they settle," he said. "That's not negotiable."

She could feel him giving grudging way. She nodded. "Of course. Not even Baldr will disagree with that. It's safer for the Jotunn, as well."

"And only one settlement at first. Maybe two."

Was she actually convincing him to both step down and let the Jotunn out? "I think that would work, but only if we promise more over time—maybe one every three winters or something. Each in a place chosen and controlled by us. They won't like that, but maybe we designate a larger region and say that anywhere within it is acceptable."

"So long as we can control the ways in and out, that would be all right," he said. "You don't give a dangerous wolf a long leash. You gave him a short, strong one."

"We have nothing but time, Odin. They don't. They'll be anxious to make a deal."

He held her gaze for long heartbeats. "I'll think on it, Frigg," he said finally.

He must have read disbelief on her face, for he took her by the shoulders, looked right at her, and repeated, "I'll think on it."

Had she really just taken the first step toward freeing herself from the burden of ruling? It couldn't have been that easy.

A knock banged on the door. Fimafeng stepped in and shut the door behind him. "Your pardon. Are you ready now for the Jotunn envoy, Alfather, Hár Frigg?"

She looked the question at Odin, and he nodded.

"Yes, we're ready," she said. "Please show him in."

"Very good, Almother."

The steward bowed, hauled on the door, and slipped through, pulling it shut behind him.

She turned and found one of Odin's sunnier smiles directed at her. "You really have grown used to ruling in my absence, haven't you?"

"I've had little choice, Alfather," she said, sketching an elaborate bow.

He snorted, gray eyes twinkling. "Then you'll join me now and not skulk behind that curtain."

"That was my idea," she reminded him. "Saglund would have acted differently if I had been here. He would have been insulted I was present while he, the great Einherjar hersir, and you, the father of victory himself, spoke."

He frowned and stepped back toward his chair. "And will the Jotunn envoy be similarly insulted?"

She shook her head. "We're used to one another. It'll be best if you sit, though. It might make you seem slightly less intimidating."

"As you command, Almother." He sat down just as the door creaked open while she remained standing.

45

Loki

"You're serious?" Loki asked. Attempting to kill Baldr while Ygg was present, without a distraction—the Skrymir was mad. Even if he succeeded, he'd be dead moments afterward. He was prepared to sacrifice himself, but not until his children were free.

But the Skrymir's expression remained steady. Implacable. And oddly familiar.

"You are serious."

"Yes, Loki, I am," the Skrymir replied evenly. "Our problem is timing. We're not ready. We need another month before we can get all the warbands positioned and supplied. And despite the problems created by Ama's attack, we believe that if you go ahead anyway your plan will help buy us that time."

Loki couldn't stop shaking his head. A month? He wanted to stand up, to pace, to throw his hands up. He couldn't wait. It had to be this Midwinter. He'd already set his plan into motion. Ygg would soon discover what Loki had done and then cover that chink in Baldr's armor. Unlikely though it was, Ygg might even puzzle out who was behind it all.

"We agreed on the first night of Midwinter. This Midwinter.

Seven nights from now. The whole idea was to strike at the same time."

The Skrymir spread his hands. "We're not attacking in seven nights, Loki. If we did, our own plan would fail. The blow we strike— and I do mean *we*—must end the war even as it begins."

Was he hearing this? It was bad enough that Ygg had come back. And now, after he'd planned for dozens of winters, after he passed up several opportunities, the Jotunn now asked him to risk all of it. He laughed. "*We*? This is not what *we* agreed, Skrymir. It jeopardizes my goals to further yours."

The Skrymir raised a hand. "Listen for a moment. We don't have the supplies in place to maintain any advantage created by a surprise attack. You saw the number of wakened Jotunn out there. There are another nine strongholds just like this one. My predecessors planned for this time by submerging supplies in the lakes alongside the sleepers. The seidr preserving some of those supplies failed—"

"And you didn't plan for that?"

"Of course we did. But we lost more than expected, along with many fine Jotunn. And the Sons of Muspell were supposed to funnel more weapons and armor, food and clothing to us. Ygg's return and his scrutiny of the Einherjar stopped all that. If we attack at Midwinter, they'll roll us right back to the Breach, and then the Thunderer will come knocking."

"He'll do that anyway," Loki said. "If there's any delay after Baldr's death, then—"

Then what? Would the plan still work? Originally, it had been about his brutal, impossible strike followed by an all-out Jotunn assault, which would cripple the Aesir and let him safely escape in the confusion. If there was a delay between his strike and the Jotunn attack, what would happen?

He'd always intended Baldr's murder to be a way to make Ygg feel the pain of loss as deeply, as completely, as he and Angrboda had felt the loss of their own children. Would giving Baldr's murder time to sink in be a bad thing?

It would mean more time for Ygg's grief to build—and his rage.

And then just as they sent Baldr's corpse off to the Gjoll's shores, the Jotunn army would attack. And maybe during that confusion he could attempt the second part of his plan—freeing his children. Much less ideal than doing so as he'd originally planned, but that was no longer an option.

It could work, assuming he escaped after he killed Baldr.

And while the Aesir would certainly be distracted, they'd also have time to pick apart how it happened.

The Jotunn would not attack. So, he'd only have his own wits to rely on. He'd always extracted himself from whatever trouble he got himself into. This was no different—aside from the stakes being literally everything.

Did he have a choice?

He did, but delay was the coward's path. He was many things, but not that. Never that. And even without the Jotunn attack, he would never have as good a chance as now.

Seeming to have followed his racing thoughts, the Skrymir said, "I told Vafthrudnir you'd see advantage in changing the plan."

"Potential advantage," he said. "Assuming I succeed and their reaction is as we hope, you don't have a month—maybe a fortnight, at best. Vidar will have backtracked that idiot's warband long before Midwinter, at which point Ygg will send Thor. A few nights later, Jotunheim will be smoking rubble. Then the Einherjar and the Aesir army will sweep in to kill everyone else. You're better off attacking during Baldr's funeral."

The Skrymir shook his head. "That's all likely. Eventually. And I'll consider your proposal—attacking during Baldr's funeral. But we have planned for it, Loki. We're counting on it."

"You're all right with letting Vidar find the doorway?"

"No, but I also couldn't stop Ama's attack—too many of the tribal chiefs supported it. Now they'll understand why I opposed it, which makes me look better." The Skrymir sat back. "Besides, Vafthrudnir is with Helveg now. With his help, they should be able to kill Vidar, should he set foot in Utgard."

Loki ignored the twisting of his guts. That put Vali and Narfi in the baresark's path. If the Norns had cut an early death for his sons, then so be it. But he would have liked them to experience more of life before rejoining the Ginnungagap.

"When, Skrymir, not if. Vidar will find the doorway. He will step through it. He's every bit as curious as his father—and he has more to prove."

"I know your sons are with Helveg, Loki. You asked for them to be placed with the best warband—"

"And the best is most often used for the toughest tasks." He gave a quick grin. "I know that. They knew the risks and what they're fighting for, just as those thousands you just showed me know."

He stared down at his scarred hands, at his spread fingers. They, and he, could be anything he wanted. Too often he'd let himself become a tool—a weapon—wielded by another's hands.

Not this time. Nor ever again.

He would pursue this course no matter what doom the Norns had cut for him. He was not a coward.

"If I fall, Sigyn knows where I've hidden—"

The Skrymir stood and, again, offered his hand. "I give you my word, Loki. The Vafthrudnir, Beli and I will do everything in our power to free your children and shelter Sigyn, Vali and Narfi, from the wrath of our enemies."

Loki stood and, again, took the Skrymir's hand. "It is fitting that I strike the first blow against the Aesir, and that I steal from them their favored son."

46

Odin

"Four. Hundred. Dead." Odin thumped the arm of his chair, emphasizing each word. "Háls numbered maybe nineteen hundred people. What explanation does your Skrymir offer, Envoy?"

The envoy, Eldir, took it well. No tensing in the shoulders or sweat on his forehead. He stood before them with legs slightly spread, arms clasped behind his back.

"Jarl Odin, Hár Frigg, the Skrymir has directed me to say that the attack on Háls was not made at his behest, nor does he know who carried it out. He suspects that it was a—"

"—rogue tribe that hates the Aesir and wants to exact vengeance for..." Odin rolled his hand in the air. "We've heard that story before, Envoy. Quite often before the Last War. One of those attacks even began that war—isn't that right, Hár Frigg?"

"Indeed it is, Alfather," Frigg said.

"Is it another war that your Skrymir wants, Envoy?" he asked. He thumped the chair again, and Draupnir clunked dully against the wood. Frigg had said the Jotunn wanted peace, but he didn't believe it. "Because only my son Baldr's mercy stays my hand. Thor is prepared to rain lightning down upon Jotunheim, and my hersirs prepare our warriors to march on Jotunheim."

"I understand your anger, Jarl Odin. I made exactly your point to the Skrymir and told him you wouldn't accept that explanation. Nor would he, if the situation were somehow reversed."

Frigg's tone was as smooth as a rolling river. "You delayed our earlier meeting because you expected communication with the Skrymir. Is the answer you gave just now the result of that conversation with the Skrymir?"

"Yes, Hár Frigg." The envoy nervously touched his scalp, which was devoid of tattoos. "Of course, it was my shaman who spoke with his counterpart in Jotunheim. I did not speak directly with the Skrymir."

For some reason he'd yet to puzzle out, there were more shamans among the Jotunn than among the Aesir. Most of them could spirit-walk, too, which meant that they could speak across the many miles just as he and Frigg were speaking with the envoy now.

He had always believed that the shamans who spoke not only exchanged their own secret orders, but also kept certain information from the envoy. There were battling factions among the Jotunn. In that, at least, they were like the Aesir.

"Of course," Frigg said. "Can we assume that there will be a more complete answer forthcoming, Eldir?"

The envoy nodded sharply, his black top knot falling forward and back again. "The Skrymir assured me that while he does not know who attacked or why—or why now, given the long peace and growing trade between our people—he is looking into it."

Odin allowed his flush of anger at those words into his voice. "Looking into it? Tell me, Envoy, exactly how many rogue tribes are there?"

The envoy stared back at him, meeting his gaze without any hint of a challenge. "Dozens, Jarl Odin. And they range in size from a few families to many."

"Why has the Skrymir not brought these tribes into Jotunheim?

He seemed more than capable when I met him after I killed his predecessor in the Last War."

"We are a broken people, Jarl Odin. It's all the Skrymir can do to hold those in Jotunheim together. He doesn't turn away any who seek refuge there, but he also doesn't seek to add those who would cause trouble."

"Better to let them raid Aesir towns, eh?"

The envoy smoothed his black beard with one hand and bowed slightly. "With respect, Jarl Odin, that's not what I meant. As I'm sure Hár Frigg has told you, the Jotunn have suffered greatly since the Last War. Utgard seems to grow colder every year, crops refuse to grow, rivers run foul, game is scarce. Saddest of all, our women no longer bear live young. Truly, the Norns have cut a wicked doom for us.

"The trade that has since developed between our peoples, along with the twice-yearly visits by your son Baldr, have brought a small measure of renewed health to the Jotunn. We hope that in time and with the continued generosity and mercy of the Aesir, children's piping voices will again be heard in Jotunheim.

"So I beg you, Jarl Odin, before you send the Thunderer to rain storms upon us or send your armies to spit us upon spears, consider that we Jotunn have no reason to slap away the hand the Aesir have extended in friendship. It would be madness for us to countenance such a raid as you've described to me, let alone carry it out. Both I and the Skrymir are appalled by what happened, and he is, believe me, searching hard for an answer that will stay your hand."

Odin sat back in his chair. That was quite the plea. He didn't feel that the man was lying or exaggerating. It all fit with what Frigg and Baldr had told him. But if it had been meant to move him to pity or lower his guard, then this envoy was a fool.

Frigg broke the growing tension. "We suspect that the 'rogue' warband slipped into Asgard either via the trade route or by ship, perhaps over several months. My son's wife is checking back through the records we keep on Jotunn merchant movements."

Eldir nodded. "Just between us, Hár Frigg, we believe that the trade route is the most likely explanation. There's really no other way, given the nature of the fortress and the sea patrols."

"At what point did the Skrymir become aware of warriors sneaking into Asgard?" Odin asked, leaning forward.

"I don't understand, Jarl Odin. With respect, we're still not sure how it was done. The trade route seems a good guess." The envoy spread his hands. "If I may—and I apologize, for this is a delicate subject—but have you considered the possibility that this attack was aided by some among the Aesir?"

Odin kept his expression fixed. This envoy did indeed have a spine. And it was a clever statement, given that it mirrored exactly what they had discussed at Ithavoll and not long ago in this very hall. It forced them to suspect their own, whether or not there was cause.

"We're looking into that possibility," he said. "And should we find a link, we'll pursue it wherever it leads."

The envoy nodded gravely, concern radiating from every pore in his body as he hid what had to be a deep-seated satisfaction that his blow had struck flesh.

Frigg added, "If we were to suggest that we resume inspections of all carts moving between Utgard and Asgard, how do you think the Skrymir would respond?"

"I could convince him, I think, that doing so would show good faith and an earnest desire to root out whatever troublesome element exists within the Jotunn people."

Odin noted Frigg's glance at him from the corner of his eye, but he kept his expression neutral.

"Tell me again, Envoy, just how many rogue tribes are there in Utgard?"

"A handful, Jarl Odin," the envoy said, shifting slightly. "But by definition, we don't have a good count."

"We know within a few thousand how many Aesir live in Asgard," he said. "You mean to tell me that the Skrymir cannot do the same?"

"With respect, Jarl Odin, the Aesir have many good roads, wardens to keep the peace, an army to deal with threats and, of course, the Einherjar. We Jotunn have none of these things. Well, roads, yes. To an extent. Not like here in Asgard, though. Our best road is the one linking Jotunheim to Ifington, and even that one is maintained by funds paid by the merchants traveling it."

"Jotunheim collects substantial tariffs from all trade along that route, yes?"

"I'm not privy to the details, but yes, I believe that's the case, just as it is here."

"And what does the Skrymir spend that gold on?" Odin asked, conscious of Frigg folding her hands in her lap.

Eldir smiled. "Where are you going with this, Jarl Odin?"

"I'm just curious as to how much gold the Skrymir has spent acquiring weapons from the Svartalvar."

Like a startled blackbird, surprise flitted across Eldir's face. Then he had it under control and caged. "I'm afraid I don't understand, Jarl Odin. Haven't the Svartalvar been gone for more than a hundred winters?"

"So I thought," he said. "And I should know, since I'm the one who herded them onto Skidbladnir and sailed them far away. But during the Last War, which you seem too young to have fought in, we captured a Svartalvar device from a Jotunn warband that had ventured within a night's ride of Gladsheim's northern wall. Do you happen to know anything about that? The warband or the device, I mean. Or both."

"I've never heard of either, Jarl Odin. My spirit hadn't even been drawn from the Gap at the time of the Last War, let alone when the Svartalvar were still a force to be reckoned with."

"We also think it curious that the Jotunn attacked Háls. Do you know my son, Jarl Vidar? He rules in Vithi."

"I have not had the pleasure, Jarl."

"It was Vidar who wiped out the Jotunn warband. Him and a handful of his garrison. He is also the one who determined that this device was of Svartalvar make—and as it happens, that device was in Vithi. Did this 'rogue' warband raze Háls while on its way to retrieve the device?"

"I don't know, Jarl Odin. Until now, I didn't even know of this device," Eldir said with an earnest shake of his clasped hands. "What does it do?"

He ignored the question. "Do the Jotunn have more of those devices?"

Eldir spread his hands. "I don't know that, either."

"Did Jotunn spies inform the Skrymir where the device was? Or was it Aesir traitors bought by the Skrymir's gold?"

"If you mean spies, Jarl Odin, that would violate our treaty," he said. "And even if we had them, I'm the last person who would know about it."

Odin stared hard at the envoy, searching for any sign the man knew the answers and was trying to hide it.

The envoy looked from him to Frigg and back again. "Jarl Odin, I don't know anything about these matters you raise. I will speak with the Skrymir, though, and try to get the answers you seek. But I suspect it will be difficult. We don't live as long as you do. No Jotunn alive today was alive during the Last War, except perhaps a few ancients."

"You will return to us no later than tomorrow evening with two pieces of information," Odin said, raising his hand to count off the two points. "First, you will provide the name of the rogue tribe or clan that attacked. Second, you will provide their location."

"I will do everything I can to provide you with that information, Jarl Odin," the envoy said.

"I hope so, Envoy Eldir. For in two nights, Thor will fly to Utgard and destroy one of your people's few remaining villages. I would prefer that he destroy the one responsible for the death of my people and the crippling of one of our mining and timber operations. But you do understand that I cannot let the Skrymir believe that the Aesir have grown weak since the Last War."

In the moment before the envoy opened his mouth to reply, Odin finally saw the glimmer of hatred he'd been certain lurked behind the envoy's calm expression.

When the envoy spoke, though, his tone was even. "I understand, Jarl Odin. If I may have your leave?"

Odin nodded.

"Before you contact the Skrymir, Eldir, please speak with Baldr," Frigg said. " Just yesterday, Baldr presented the Alfather and myself with extensive plans to have Aesir craftsman enter Utgard. There, under the Skrymir's direction, they will help build or rebuild roads, longhouses, storehouses—anything that might help the Jotunn. Naturally, the expense will come from Gladsheim's coffers. Baldr has many other ideas as well that may prove beneficial to both our peoples."

The envoy made no effort to hide his confusion as he looked back and forth between them. "A very kind offer, Hár Frigg. I assume Gladsheim's generosity is dependent on our providing the information you require?"

Frigg shook her head. "No, Envoy. The offer stands regardless of your Skrymir's decision."

"I see. Well, I will relate both... offers... to the Skrymir when I contact him." He bowed to each of them, backed away three paces, then turned and left the hall.

Frigg turned to Odin. "You were a little rough on him, don't you think?"

"I wanted to see what it would take to rattle him."

"Well, you did."

He grinned. "I know. Took quite a lot, though."

She frowned. "Can I also assume you wanted him to tell the Skrymir that, yes, Ygg is every bit as awful as he'd be warned, but that Frigg is still the reasonable one?"

"No harm in that, is there?"

She sighed. "Do you really mean to have Thor attack? You know the Skrymir won't provide a name or location."

"Aesir died, Frigg. We must show strength." He met her steady gaze. "And how better to show them your new way than to remind them of how harsh mine is?"

47

Loki

The door boomed shut behind the messenger, and the Skrymir shoved the lever into place, sealing the large chamber off from the tunnel. Loki felt the air grow still.

The Skrymir sat again. "Here's the generous offer from mighty Ygg and his blood-traitor wife. We either tell them who attacked Háls, or they send the Thunderer against us."

That was hardly surprising. Loki shrugged. "Give him the name of Ama's clan. Let the Aesir pluck that thorn."

"Tempting though it is, I can't do it. Neither I nor my predecessors have ever divulged that type of information. Ygg knows that, and he'd be suspicious if I provided it. He'd probably have their spies spread rumors that I had betrayed my fellow Jotunn." The Skrymir shook his head. "Besides, we expected immediate, violent retribution against any one of a dozen targets. The council was well aware it would happen. But naming the tribe that did it? They'd blood eagle me."

"Then be more subtle. Have one of your spies in Gladsheim spread the rumor of which tribe was responsible. The alternative is to tell Ygg what? That you're looking into it?"

The Skrymir's frown deepened. "Essentially, yes. I said we can't divulge what we don't know, meaning the identity of the 'rogue tribe.' I told our envoy to plead for time so that we may investigate who attacked. We will then punish those responsible and invite the Aesir to witness, should they choose."

No wonder they needed him to go ahead and kill Baldr. This was their brilliant plan to gain a month's time? "Tyr and Ullr are mustering the army's reserves, and with Ygg back, the Einherjar might again become effectual. When I strike on Midwinter—"

"Ah, but I haven't told you all of the message."

"You have a gift for suspense, Skrymir."

The high chief smiled like the winter sun. "Not only did Baldr offer to come here and negotiate a peace, but his mother told the envoy that Gladsheim would spend its own resources to extend the trade route as the Jotunn chose."

"Your envoy heard Ygg agree to that?" The Ygg he knew would use that same amount of time to prepare an attack that would only end when every Jotunn was a steaming corpse.

"Yes. We expected to gain a little time by pretending to investigate the razing of Háls, but this offer is even better," the Skrymir said, beginning to count on his fingers. "Baldr offered to come here to negotiate peace. He's not going to leave during Midwinter—and that lasts three nights. Call it four total. Then it would take another few nights for him to prepare to leave. But that'll never happen because you'll have killed him."

Loki frowned. "That's a week, if we're generous with time. It is quite possible that Ygg will simply order an all-out attack on us."

The Skrymir feigned innocence. "But why? The Jotunn are entirely innocent of Baldr's murder. Has gentle Baldr not healed our sick? Comforted our mothers who bear only stillborn children? Why would we murder someone we love as much—more, even—than the Aesir do?"

Clever. One more reason why the Skrymir had been so welcoming of Baldr's visits. "Ygg will never believe it."

"So what? His wife will. And with one strike of your knife, you'll provide what we cannot: Confusion. Demoralization. Perhaps even fear."

"And you think all that translates to a month's time?"

"Not precisely a month, but even two weeks would help. The more time we have, the better able we'll be to press our attack. And if Ygg marches on us? He'll find Jotunheim defended only by the aged and infirm."

Loki leaned further back into his chair and steepled his fingers before him. The Skrymir must mean the doorways. Everything hinged upon them. He might escape Gladsheim on his own, but a doorway would make it easier to avoid Ygg's wrath.

The Skrymir slapped his knees and stood. "Come with me. I promised to show you something that'll help you escape Gladsheim."

***

The Skrymir tapped a small silver square sewn into the hide map. It had a blue rune painted on it. "You can use that to get out."

Loki rested one hand on the big table's smooth top and leaned forward. He touched the cool silver square and lifted its edge to reveal a rough-inked outline beneath. "And what do these lines this mean?"

"That's the building above the doorway—it's one of the places they store food," the Skrymir said. He swept a hand above the map indicating the other outlines, squares and rectangles, and dozens that looked like longships seen from above. "These are all buildings— smithies, longhouses, tanneries. That one is the Lower Market. Up here is their temple and the grove."

Loki quirked an eyebrow at that but keep his expression blank. "And so the doorway's where, exactly?"

"In the pits beneath that larder."

"Well, at least it's in a convenient spot." He tapped another black-inked square. "And this is the main hall?"

The high chief nodded.

"That's quite a way to go." He traced the curving line he assumed was the road leading down from Gladsheim's main hall, through the gates of the upper tier, and then down into the lower circle.

The Skrymir shrugged. "It's another way out. But if you're closely pursued, I ask that you not use it."

He laughed. "Then why even tell me?"

"Let me rephrase. If you're being pursued, evade them first—convincingly—and then go through the doorway. If you just run into the building and vanish, even a blind fool would know where to search. Eventually they'd find it."

"If I can convincingly evade them, why would I need it?"

The Skrymir frowned, eyes narrowing, but Loki held up a hand. "Look, it's my life on the line here. You dangle an escape but then tell me not to use it? That makes no sense. They're going to find out about these doorways anyway. Vidar's probably already close to finding the one used to attack Háls."

"Finding one is different from finding several. If we keep most of them secret, they may think there's only one."

"If they were all idiots." Loki shook his head. "Ygg and Vidar are far from that. Blind in some ways, perhaps, but they'll figure it out—especially once Vidar finds that doorway he's headed for."

"So two things," the Skrymir said. "First, yes, Ama's regrettable attack robbed us of the chance to keep the Háls doorway secret until the war starts. Second, the devices are more important than the doorways themselves. A working device, I should say."

"If that's the case, how did you find the doorways in the first place? You couldn't have just guessed at their existence."

The Skrymir spread his hands and smiled. "How is that important right now, Loki?"

It wasn't, and he knew it. Still, it had been worth a try. Instead of answering, he leaned forward and tapped the silver square with its blue rune. Then he gestured toward the other silver squares sewn into different spots on the big map.

"All these silver squares are doorways, then?" he asked.

Three of the squares had a blue rune painted on them. One had a yellow rune, and the fifth had a red rune. Each of the silver squares sat on top of drawings that must describe something about where they were—long blue lines, wavy green lines drawn crosswise to the blue, green lines straight up and down. Brown lines ran from the big circle representing Gladsheim to a smaller circle up at the top of the map. That circle bordered many blue horizontal wavy lines. If those meant water and if the black circle was a city, then that was Ifington.

"What do the colors mean?"

"On the silver squares or the map?"

"Both, actually." He tapped one silver square with a blue rune amid a cluster of upright green lines. It was just outside the circle representing Gladsheim. "But explain this one."

"The blue runes mean the doorway connects back to Utgard. Those straight green up-and-down lines mean a forest. So that's the forest just north of Gladsheim. That particular one was discovered by Ama's tribal warband at the end of the Last War."

Loki blew a silent whistle. "So you can put an army right outside Gladsheim's gates without marching there?"

"Without marching through Asgard," the Skrymir said.

So now he knew where five doorways were. If Sigyn couldn't avoid going to Gladsheim, she might be able to use the doorway inside the gates or this one outside them.

As could he.

"And how do you find them?"

"Are you asking how we discovered them?" the Skrymir asked.

He shook his head. "Say I evade pursuit on Midwinter, but I can't get to the doorway beneath the larder. How would I find this one in the forest?"

"You'd need the exact location. That one, for example, is about fifteen yards off the ground. It's only accessible if you can fly—which you can—or by climbing the cliff nearby and jumping into it. Both of those options have the same problem, though."

He raised an eyebrow. "Which is?"

The Skrymir held one hand up sideways and touched it with the forefinger of his other hand at a right angle. "You go through the doorway this way, but when you come out, it's like this." He rotated his hands so that the hand representing the doorway was parallel to the table. Then he turned his forefinger downward as if he were falling. "In this case, it's merely disorienting, since you come out sideways onto a gentle slope of snow. Other doorways are much more dangerous."

"How very interesting," he said. This was exactly what he needed. He tapped the silver square marking the doorway inside Gladsheim. "And what happens with this one?"

"Nothing unusual, except that we had to tunnel up from it," the Skrymir said. "We discovered it from the other side, Utgard, and just got lucky as to where it led. The doorways exist where they exist. Sometimes they're usable, sometimes not."

"That's too bad. I can see how useful it'd be to choose where you want to go."

"Indeed it would, and we've tried, but it's not possible."

"You're sure?"

"Pretty sure, yes, as are those who crafted the devices."

Interesting. So Vidar and Ygg were right, the devices were made by Svartalvar. "That's unfortunate. How do you know where they are? With respect to each other and on the land itself."

"How do we know when Midwinter is upon us? Or when to plant what few crops still grow here?" The Skrymir pointed up. "We look to the skies—at Muspell's sparks, the stars, Máni and Sól, and where they are relative to each other. And we send scouts through the doorways, or shamans who can spirit-walk. They come back with the information we need to locate the doorway exits."

Or sometimes they didn't return, like the Jotunn baresark Eldr.

The Skrymir tapped the silver square above Gladsheim, then indicated the black runes beneath it. "Vafthrudnir invented a system using these runes that gives directions from a good reference point. These say, 'One night's walk north from Gladsheim's northern wall. At the river's bend, sight the tallest western outcropping. Ascend. One spear's length out from the naked rock. Safe.'"

Loki raised an eyebrow. "Naked rock?"

"I'm told it's obvious when you're there." The Skrymir tapped the silver square that sat inside the walls. "As for this one, the larder has three tiers, one at ground level and then two beneath. Those are accessed by a ramp that winds downward. The second tier has three stone arches. The bottom-most has four arches. Go through the arch opposite the ramp; it leads to a short corridor. There are four rooms there, two on each side. When you reach the corridor's dead end, there's a small storeroom on the left. The doorway is beneath the back-right corner of that room beneath a false floor."

He looked up and smiled at Loki. "If you shift into something small, you should be able to squeeze through and drop into the corridor. The doorway itself is down much deeper, but follow the tunnel and you can't help but find it."

So much in these realms lay in the darkness beneath other things. His wife's corpse beneath heavy black soil. His slumbering son beneath deep, icy seas. And his own hatred, his own as-yet unrealized revenge, beneath the heaviest thing of all.

Time.

48

Frigg

Frigg climbed back up into the chill morning air. This new trading vessel's hold was wider and deeper than those in the older ships plying the coast.

"Very impressive, Shipmaster," she said over her shoulder. "You say it can carry twice the cargo?"

She stepped off the ladder and blinked. The morning was clear and bright. A pair of men stood in front of her. One was short and swarthy and had a wild beard. He held a burning brand.

"Oh, hello," she said.

The second man had clay pots hanging from his belt and a stout stick in one hand. His grin was more feral than the wicked light in his eyes.

"Good morning, Almother." He brought up the cudgel in swift backhand blow.

She got her right arm up in time to block some of its power, but the club still cracked against her head and sent her reeling sideways. She fell hard against the gunwale, bruising her shoulder.

"Mother!" Baldr cried, his head just clearing the deck.

The man with the pots kicked her son in the face. Baldr gave a cry and fell backward. The man turned toward her, club brandished.

"Leave her," the first one said. "We have work to do."

The second man threw a black look at the first, but he obeyed. He threw the hatch shut, latched it, and pulled one of the clay pots from his belt. He raised it high and flung it down on the deck.

It shattered with a sharp stink of oil.

The first man stepped across the spreading pool and lowered his brand, turning the liquid into a merry sheet of fire. "Another one. Two per ship should do it."

Fists beat against inside of the hatch, but the skymetal pin held the solid wood frame down. Urgent, muffled shouts came from below.

Another pot shattered against the base of the mast, and the fire rushed to follow it. Frigg coughed, inhaling a lungful of smoke.

The first man shouted down at her above the fire's swelling voice, "The Sons of Muspell will rise from heaven's fire!"

The second man pointed his cudgel at her and added, in a voice like the wind's shriek, "They will rise, burning, and free their cousins from thralldom to the Aesir!"

They ran toward the opposite gunwale, vaulted it, and vanished.

Her head was spinning. The fire was already hot on her face. She had to move.

The thumps against the hatch were louder, more solid sounding, as if those below had found something better than their fists to batter it with.

She lurched toward the hatch, swerving around the spreading fire —it hadn't yet reached the hatch or the rigging behind it—and fell against it.

She pounded her fist against the hatch. "I'm going to pull the pin."

The steady thumps stopped. She yanked the pin and threw the hatch open.

Baldr was through a heartbeat later, Hermod right behind him.

The shipyard master came next, followed by the ship's kjolr, a stocky woman who took in the spreading fire in a single glance and then pushed her way to the same gunwale the two men had vaulted.

"What happened, Mother?" Baldr's voice was level but tight with concern. He had his back to her as he took in the hungry fire's progress. Nearly at the mast now. And the rigging.

She put a hand to her head. It came away red and sticky. "A Son of Muspell hit me; another fired the ship. They're probably at the next one already."

"I see them," Hermod said. Two long strides later, she was over the gunwale.

"You're bleeding," Baldr said, kneeling to look at her head. He dug in his satchel and produced a white square of cloth, which he pressed against the wound. "Hold this here."

"We need to get off this ship, Baldr," she said.

The fire's heat had redoubled. Another glance showed that it had spread to the rigging and was climbing the mast.

"I know. Can you walk?"

She pushed herself up. He took her by the arm, and together they hurried to the gunwale.

***

Frigg had her back to the burning trade ship and was nearly alongside the next ship—a long, sleek, black-hulled warship—in the line, one of the three the shipyard master had invited her down to see. Already fire sprouted like weeds along its low, sleek gunwales.

Each ship sat on rollers roughly thirty yards apart, held in place by heavy posts rammed into the shore and ringing each ship, placed under the gunwales to keep the weight off the keel. The frigid water of the river Silfr lapped maybe five yards beyond the stern of each ship. When the Silfr flooded with the early summer rains, the ships would be afloat.

Hermod was nowhere to be seen. The two Sons of Muspell had

probably moved on to the third ship, which meant that Hermod had likely followed them.

Frigg was leaning less on Baldr less now as the pounding in her head faded, driven back by the sip of the elixir he'd given her. Between that and having so recently eaten Yggdrasil's fruit, even half of it, she'd be healed by midday.

Gná, who had stayed on shore, was nowhere to be seen either, which probably meant that she'd run to fetch the wardens. There was a post just inside the city walls a few hundred yards away; they might already be on their way. If she could taste the ash, they surely could as well, even if the black smoke didn't make signs of trouble blindingly obvious.

A terrified, high-pitched shriek split the air. A child's cry. Frigg's gaze snapped back to the warship. The weeds of flame bloomed with a whoosh just as she spotted a child back by the steering board. Why was a child aboard a warship? And why had she remained aboard after two madmen had set it ablaze?

Through the fire, she saw the child tugging at something, pulling hard. The Sons had lashed her to the ship. She didn't have long, judging by how quickly the flames were spreading.

"Mother—" Baldr's voice was urgent, his eyes intense.

"Go." She suppressed a flutter in her stomach. Her vision had placed Baldr aboard a burning ship, but there was no time to worry about that now. "I'm fine."

He pulled his satchel off, pushed it into her hands, and sprinted toward the ship, feet kicking up puffs of sand and snow.

She blew out a long breath and slung his bag across her shoulders and picked at the wide leather strap, trying to distract herself from thoughts of her son's flesh roasting from his bones. He'd be all right. He had time. Besides, if a snow bear's venom ran from his skin like water, then fire shouldn't harm him either.

She closed her eyes against the memory of his white teeth clacking in a blackened face.

Shouldn't.

When she opened them again, she focused on the shipyard

master's waving arms. He was organizing the workers—laborers, plank cutters, and stem smiths—into a long line to bring buckets of water to the burning ships. Men on the banks of the Silfr slammed spears against the ice to reach deeper waters.

To her left, a clutch of men were standing around doing nothing.

"Over here," she shouted at them. One of them heard and thumped his mate on the arm. Then they were all running toward her.

She turned back to the warship as Baldr hauled himself up and over the bow, one of the few spots not yet burning. He turned, lifted his hand, and shouted something she couldn't hear.

A coil of burning rigging dropped on him like one of the gigantic snakes from Alvheim's wet forests.

Before the gasp had cleared her throat, his cloak and clothing ignited. Fire leaped up around his shoulders.

She threw herself toward the ship. This was her vision. Why had she let him go? Someone else could have saved the child.

Restraining hands clamped down on her shoulders. "No, Almother, you'll be burned alive!" The gruff voice was loud in her ear.

She tried to shake herself free and surge forward, but another pair of hands joined those holding her. She pushed harder, freeing an arm, but the men dug in and stopped her.

Baldr whipped off the coil and flung it, burning, from the ship. His head was a shadow inside a wreath of flame as he whipped off his cloak and threw it aside.

It was her vision—Baldr, burning on the ship—wasn't it? And yet he wasn't burning. Just his clothes. He was unmarred.

Panic released its grip on her heart. She threw her hands up. "Release me. I'm not going anywhere."

The hands opened, and she rounded on the men surrounding her. "You, get to the ship. Baldr can hand the child down to you." She jabbed a finger at another pair of men. "You two help those with the buckets. Wet the gunwale closest to them."

A sharp crack echoed off the city's walls; she spun back to the ship

Baldr was on. The mast had broken. It seemed to fall slowly at first and then, with a sound like an entire forest falling, smashed through the gunwale and slammed into the shore.

Sheets of fire leaped heavenward, cutting Baldr off from the child. She couldn't even see the child anymore.

In a swirling void between flames, she saw Baldr standing tall, gesticulating. Now his clothing ablaze. His teeth flashed white as he shouted and looked sideways, pointing.

The line of buckets had reached the mast, and the workers had started throwing water on it. With the sharp hiss of a cornered cat, the fire began to give way.

Another loud crack came from the ship, and it dropped a few feet downward. Baldr stumbled, lost his balance, and fell forward into fire's blazing heart.

Before she even realized it, she was running toward the ship. This was it. Her vision had snuck up on her. Addled by the cudgel blow, she hadn't been thinking right. She'd let Baldr go to his death. No, she'd told him to go.

Any moment now, his burning corpse would stagger from the flames, the flesh melting from his bones. His white teeth would clatter with a message for her, but she wouldn't be able to hear it.

A figure stepped from the wall of fire, put a naked foot on the fallen mast and stepped up onto it. It was Baldr, hunched tight around a small figure clutched in his arms.

The mast shivered and shifted. She watched as Baldr staggered. Then he got his balance and ran down to the ground. He fell to his knees and lay the child out before him.

He convulsed with a hacking cough that bent him double, and he spat something black and wet onto the sand. He heaved in a breath. "Mother, my bag. Quickly."

She ran the last few steps and fell on her knees beside him, holding out the bag.

A moment's rummage and he had his elixir out and dripped some into the child's mouth.

He pushed her lips shut, massaged her throat, and then opened her mouth again. Another drop went in.

"She'd collapsed by the time I got to her," he said, his voice already less hoarse.

She gripped his unmarred, unscorched, untouched shoulder. "You're all right?"

He grinned like a second sun. "Of course. What fire can hurt me?"

49

Vidar

"I could've done without seeing this."

Vidar held the witchlamp higher so that its dim glow made the expanse of excrement roil with the panicked crawling of more insects than he'd ever seen in one place before. Pale-bodied, sinuous, and with the sound of ten thousand dry leaves burning, they fled the light, burrowing, sliding, or skittering their way across and beneath each other.

He suppressed a shudder, lowered his arm, and backed away from the jakes. Mikill and Smar swam up into the light, hands on their weapons as if finding a big pile of Jotunn excrement heralded an attack. More likely their tension stemmed from the low rustling of the insects; even six spears distant, the sound made his skin itch.

"Let's head back," he said, gesturing back down the tunnel to the main chamber.

Mikill and Smar fell in behind him, his Garilon-appointed personal protectors. The big one, Smar, had a round, cheery face and a scraggly beard. A sword-length shorter, Mikill moved like a whip. He had a scar down the left side of his face from brow to thick beard.

At Vidar's order, everyone here moved as a single large group or in groups of threes. Always at least one set of eyes to watch. They had yet to come across the Jotunn who'd fled into the mine. They also had yet to find the Jotunn base and its expected cache of supplies.

As the trio returned to the main cavern, their light merged with the torches held by Garilon and his two companions.

Vidar gave Garilon a wry look. "I see why you didn't want to go back in."

"Jakes are a bit different topside," Garilon said with a quick grin. "I'll never put them close to a camp again, I can say that much."

Behind Garilon, a circle of torches and witchlamps brought a dusk level of light to the big cavern. Their camp was laid on top of the wide-planked oak hub about six spears across that the miners had built as a staging area for the nine tracks that ran like spokes on a wagon's wheel to the individual tunnels from which skymetal ore had been extracted.

"I don't even want to think about how much shit is in that pile," Garilon continued. "Especially since the miners probably used that same spot for who knows how long."

"I wouldn't hang my ass over that," Mikill said, his voice a lean rasp just audible above the trickling stream of water a spear's distance from them.

Smar laughed and wriggled, frantically brushing his hands across his rear as if something had just crawled on it.

Garilon jerked his head back toward the camp's pool of light. "Why don't you four head on back? The jarl and I will be along behind you. We'll be safe enough."

Mikill nodded, Smar grinned, and the two with Garilon, Lukr and Harafn stepped over the stream and headed off.

The water ran back to a small, shallow pool fed by a sheet of water flowing out of a crack in what they'd started calling the cavern's back wall. From what Vidar could tell, the cavern was roughly egg-shaped. Any of the walls could be the back wall; it just depended on where you were headed.

When the four warriors were out of earshot, Garilon said, "So do we keep going, Jarl?"

They were maybe three nights from the surface. Figuring out how much actual time had passed by normal means, the rise and set of Sól and Máni, was obviously difficult. It was an interesting problem which he might try to solve once things settled down.

"Any word from the other groups sent into the mine shafts?" he asked.

Garilon shook his head. "Only three groups have returned. Nothing yet."

Vidar pursed his lips and switched the witchlamp to his other hand. They had followed the fleeing Jotunn's trail signs—scraped walls, footprints, dust disturbed, broken rock—but it wasn't until they'd come this far that it became obvious the fleeing Jotunn were not only following the only route down, but they were retracing the steps previously taken by a much larger force—at least a full warband, possibly more. But if there was a second Jotunn warband, it had vanished into the mountains or headed straight west, away from any Aesir settlements.

"So one of few things happened," he said, extending a thumb. "The Jotunn snuck across the Breach, stole across Asgard, then slipped into this mine and marched all the way down here and hid— though they might not have camped in this deep cavern the whole time."

Garilon nodded, eyes narrowing. "Makes a certain amount of sense, if they arrived so early they needed to hide. But why not just time it better and attack right when they arrived?"

"Exactly," Vidar said. He extended a forefinger. "Another option is that they came across the Breach but found a way into this mine somewhere east of here. Up in the mountains southwest of Ifington maybe."

"The gothi didn't mention anything about other entrances."

"Maybe he didn't know about it, or maybe the Jotunn just got lucky." He extended another finger. "A third option is that they sailed across the Thund, marched over the mountains, and hid in here. Or maybe they found an entrance along the northern cliffs that face the

Thund. This mine could run right through the mountain to the Thund."

"In my opinion, Jarl, that makes the most sense—even though the gothi didn't mention other entrances. It also explains how they had enough provisions. Much easier to carry them aboard ship, or several ships, than on your back or on horses. Unless..."

Unless they had help from someone in Háls or elsewhere. He couldn't pursue that alternative now, not down here. And since he was here, it made sense to look into the other possibilities.

The question was, which tunnel led north? Above ground, he could tell. But down here? He kicked the wooden track that ran past his feet. And these tracks would have provided an easy way to transport supplies offloaded from ships. Or from the surface.

He knelt beside the tracks and held the witchlamp close to them. They were dusty and worn—they didn't look recently used.

He pulled his sweat-soaked shirt away from his chest. It was inexplicably hot down here. He and everyone else wore their lightest shirts. Still he'd insisted they carry their winter gear wherever they went. If one of these tunnels emerged on the mountain's northern flank, they'd be glad for the warm clothing.

"The three groups, did they go to the end of the shafts they were exploring? Or did they just turn around?"

"If they didn't go to the end, I'll have them mucking out that pile of shit and bugs," Garilon said, looking back at the camp's glow. "But I'll find out for certain, Jarl."

Garilon stepped slightly closer and lowered his voice. "You should know, Jarl, that the warriors dislike being down here. They'll go where you lead, of course. Just uneasy is all."

Vidar nodded. "Thank you, Kjolr."

He was, in fact, already aware of it. Maybe it was the edginess gained from constantly watching his fylgja. Or maybe it was from slogging alongside the others. Either way, he was more attuned to his warriors' moods than ever before. He didn't want to spend more time down here, either. It was unnatural.

But stay they would, until he had some answers.

50

Odin

Odin stood just outside Gladsheim's largest hall looking down on the river Silfr. With Sól nearly touching the western mountain, the shadows of the walls and gate towers bridged the river. Hours earlier, Baldr had stepped onto a burning ship and saved a merchant's daughter. His daughter Hermod, who he barely knew, had fought a pair of Aesir who thought that burning longships was a way to drum up sympathy for the Jotunn.

Twenty winters gone, and his city had almost doubled in size under Frigg's leadership. Their daughter was a young woman. Their son Baldr had become beloved not through strength of arms, but through his healing. It was certainly a different approach to leadership than his, but maybe Frigg was right. Maybe Baldr's approach was better suited to the times than his own. Except the Jotunn had attacked.

He'd also been back a full week and still hadn't dealt with the dreams plaguing Baldr. Too many other things kept interfering. Tomorrow he would, though. For certain.

A knock came at the door; Fimafeng shuffled into the dying light. The steward cleared his throat and said, "Your pardon, Alfather. The

Jotunn envoy requests a meeting. I left him waiting in the usual place. I also bring word from Hár Frigg."

Odin nodded. Frigg and Nanna had left early to continue organizing the Midwinter celebration. Shortly after midday, Frigg had sent word that she had been asked to judge several divorces. Everyone in the city had the right to ask for the Almother's judgment —or his—in any case of divorce, murder, or rape. Otherwise, judgments were handled by individuals appointed within each city district, who also presided over matters such as theft, disputes, damage to property, or other comparatively minor issues.

"She says that the last divorce hearing is still going on and that you should not wait for her. Máni will rise before she is finished."

Frigg had told him this particular divorce was complicated by the husband's influential family, the large dowry, and the brevity of the marriage itself.

"Very well, Fimafeng, thank you," he said. "Please show the envoy into the hall. Do you know where Thor is?"

"After he returned from Ithavoll, I believe he returned to his quarters. Shall I send for him?"

"Yes, please do. Any word from Gulfinn regarding Heimdall?"

The elderly steward stroked his long beard which, twenty winters ago, had been more blonde than gray. "Not yet, Alfather. Shall I send the wardens out looking?"

Odin shook his head. "That won't be necessary. Gulfinn knows where I am; he'll find me once he gets Heimdall sorted."

"Very well, Alfather." Fimafeng inclined his head with more stiffness than he remembered seeing before. "I'll show the envoy in."

"Thank you, Fimafeng."

"My pleasure to serve, Alfather."

When Odin re-entered the hall, he found the envoy standing on the platform, hands clasped behind his back.

Odin stepped up onto the platform and clasped the man's hand in greeting. He gestured for him to sit and took his own chair.

"So, Eldir, what does the Skrymir say?"

The envoy sketched a bow but did not sit. "Jarl Odin, the Skrymir regrets that he cannot provide what he does not know. He expresses his deepest condolences that the misguided actions of a rogue tribe caused such harm to the Aesir. He has launched a full investigation into the attack, led by none other than Vafthrudnir. Whatever they find will be relayed to you through me. And, finally, he hopes that you might show some mercy toward his people."

Odin held the envoy's gaze for a long moment. The Jotunn seemed earnest enough, even down to the beaded sweat on his brow and upper lip.

"Very well," he said. "You are dismissed."

The envoy hesitated, wanting to ask the obvious question, but under his flat gaze, he withdrew.

Huginn and Muninn, Odin called out with his thoughts.

We are here, they both answered. A pair of hoarse croaks filtered down from the gap in the roofs, their preferred perch when he was in the hall.

Find Thor. If he's not already on his way, ask him to join me.

We go.

Hammer and lightning, then.

51

Frigg

"Hár Frigg. Hár Frigg! Please wake up. It's your son!"

Frigg lurched forward, bedclothes falling away. Light from the thrall's witchlamp stabbed at her eyes. She blinked, thoughts scrambling like startled rats. It was Baldr, she knew it, had he finally—

It was Gná. A witchlamp blazed in her hand. "Lady Nanna sent me, Hár Frigg. It's happening again. She can't get Jarl Baldr to wake up!"

Frigg surged out of bed. "Odin! Wake up!" She kicked the bed frame even as she whirled her cloak around her shoulders. She bent and tugged on her boots.

Odin was already awake, a knife bright in his hand. "Get that light out of my eyes." His eyes narrowed like they did when he spoke with his familiars. "What's wrong?"

Of course he'd be unruffled. And where had the knife come from? "Baldr needs us. Get moving!"

She spun on her heel and dashed out of the bedchamber. Behind her, she heard Odin say, "Go with her! I'll be along."

Three thuds of her feet on the planks and she was in the hall, running between pillars that rose like ships' masts. Her feet beat a quick rhythm across the platform where their chairs stood empty. Thralls beginning their work looked up in shock before bowing low. She ignored them, swept past the fire pits, dodged between the last pair of pillars, and slipped through the middle doorway into day's first promise of light.

Baldr and Nanna were staying in a small house down the road. Smaller longhouses sat on the eastern quarter of the Old Hill's bare top.

She stretched out her arms, winter's breath cold on her skin, and flickered into her falcon shape, the rapid rhythm of her feet became the beating of her wings.

Hadn't she just made this same flight a few nights ago? This had to stop. They had to figure out what was happening.

There. Third on the left. A thrall beside an open door.

She flared her wings before the house, booted feet touching frozen earth. She set one hand on the low roof, and turned back, looking for Odin. She saw only the long shadows thrown by Sól's first rays.

She ducked inside.

Nanna sat sobbing into the embrace of an older Aesir, a house thrall. The woman looked up when she heard Frigg approach. Gray hair peeked out below her simple white cap. She gestured with one hand toward a second thrall, a golden Alvar, who stood, hands clasping and unclasping, between the weeping Nanna and the recumbent form of her son.

Frigg inhaled sharply. The room seemed to spin, and she staggered forward to kneel beside her son. His skin was white. His mouth sagged open, and his eyes stared sightlessly.

"Where is Eir?"

"On her way as well, Almother," Gná gasped from behind her. "I sent Fulla to fetch her."

She reached out a hand, caressing his brow as she had when he was a boy. Cold as stone. "Is any of that elixir here?"

Trembling, she laid her other hand on his chest and pressed it down, feeling for something. Anything.

There. Yes. Just—there. The slightest movement.

The door banged open. Startled, she glanced over her shoulder. Odin stepped in, stooping to avoid the lintel.

"It's like he's dead, Odin," she said. Again.

Was that her voice? So calm. And yet what was that roaring in her ears, that pounding in her chest? She must push it away, push back from it, like standing in a skiff with one foot on the dock. Just push back and float. Let the current take her. Maybe the wind. And drift.

"Get that cover off him, Frigg." Odin jabbed a finger at the Alvar. "You there, thrall, keep these doors open."

Frigg stood slowly, drawing the blankets back. Baldr wore a knee-length tunic. The drifting skiff on which her mind had embarked rocked on the steep swell of her emotions.

Odin stepped closer and touched her shoulder. She met his eyes.

"I'm going to take him outside," he said. "I want clean ground beneath my feet and Sól above me."

She nodded.

The Alvar thrall slipped behind her, pulled the pins securing the second half of the main door, and shoved it open. Light and chill air swept in.

Frigg's eyes fell on the older Aesir. The woman held Nanna tight and smoothed her hair.

Odin got his arms under Baldr's knees and shoulders and easily lifted him out of bed. He staggered slightly, caught his balance, then turned and walked quickly from the longhouse out into the light.

Frigg hurried to a clear spot and spread the blanket. Odin knelt and eased Baldr's body down.

He looked up at her. "I can feel his heart, Frigg. It beats slowly, and it is fading."

She knelt opposite Odin, their son's body like a corpse between them. Odin set one hand on Baldr's brow. With the other, he reached out for hers. She gripped it like she might a rope thrown from shore, riding the growing waves, her little skiff tossed this way and that.

Eir hadn't believed that Sól's light had anything to do with reviving Baldr; she'd said it was the elixir that had revived him.

She looked up from her son's pale body. Odin's face, stony at the best of times, was like the ice-covered cliff beneath Heimdall's tower. This dream—this nightmare—of Baldr's was even worse this time.

Odin gave her hand a comforting squeeze then dug in his satchel. He withdrew a spindle and shears and unspooled two arm lengths of thread. The thin strand of witchthread luminesced in the wan light of dawn. He clipped the thread, tucked the spindle and shears away, and brought one end of the thread to his lips.

He spoke a word, and the thread flared gold. He began to sing.

As he did, he caught up the other end of the thread and touched it to Baldr's chest, plunging it in and then pulling it back out as if he were sewing. He passed the string up to Baldr's head, plunging it into one temple and out the other. Then he brought the thread back down to Baldr's heart and tied it off.

He came up onto his knees then, one hand on Baldr's chest and one on his forehead and kept singing as melodiously as the songs he'd sung to their children.

A golden glow ran round and round between his hands along the thread. With each pass, color returned to Baldr's body.

The glow faded. The thread vanished. Odin stopped singing. He removed his hands, and Baldr gasped. With that intake of breath, color and warmth rushed back into her son.

Baldr's eyes flew open, and he tried to sit up.

Odin supported the back of his head, looked into his son's wild eyes, and said, "It's all right, Baldr. You're back."

Yet again. She flung her arms around Baldr and hugged him tight. She had brought him into the world; why did someone—or something—keep trying to steal him away?

From the door to the longhouse came a familiar shriek. Nanna rushed toward them, the old thrall following stiffly in her wake. Nanna flung herself at Baldr—Odin barely moved in time—and hugged him to her.

From within Nanna's embrace Baldr smiled tiredly and croaked, "I'm all right, Mother."

She wiped her tears away and smiled. She was so very tired of hearing those words.

***

Frigg's eyes lingered on the thralls bustling in the middle section of the house, where it bulged like a longship's waist. She closed her eyes and stepped again into that sturdy skiff where, not an hour ago, she had tried to ride out the storm of her fears. Now, to the sound of pots clinking and brushes scrubbing, a gentle wind filled the sail and carried her softly home.

"I remember a line of torches leading up from a sea over which fog drifted," Baldr was saying, his voice rising. "I could hear a river's rush, and I felt the press of folk around me."

Frigg opened her eyes. No visions danced above her son's head.

"That's it?" she asked.

Odin just grunted.

Baldr's eyes fell on her, somewhat distant as if they sought to pick more details from the memory. "I think so. I felt that someone was waiting for me. And I kept looking over my shoulder."

He rubbed his eyes, yawned, and with a wry grin said, "So, yes, that's it."

Nanna patted his chest with one hand, then let it rest above his heart as if loath to be away from its reassuring beat.

"More might come back to you," Odin said. He sipped from his cup.

Frigg kept her hands folded in her lap. She looked from Nanna to Baldr and then leaned away from Odin's warmth. A draft from the open door snuck down the back of her dress, and she shivered. Did none of them want to ask the obvious question? Fine.

"What if this happens again tomorrow morning? And the morning after? And the morning after that?" Concerned expressions met hers. "We need to do something about this."

"By 'we' you mean me, of course," Odin said. He leaned forward and set his cup down beside him.

"Of course I do. At Ithavoll, you said you'd look into it, and you've done nothing about it since—"

"That was the day before yesterday, Frigg. We've been a bit busy since then," he said. He shifted on the bench to more directly face her. "Let's ride down to speak with my uncle this morning."

"Now." She made no effort to hide the impatience in her voice.

Baldr leaned in, the firelight gleaming in his eyes. "I'd like to come with you. If not to speak with Mimir, then perhaps I could talk to the Norns."

Odin shook his head. "Leave Mimir and those three hens to me. Stay here, rest, and deal with whatever you need to on our behalf."

"I'm sure the envoy would prefer to deal with you and Nanna," Frigg added, "particularly now that your father's sent Thor to fulfill his threat."

"Can I call him back? Such provocation will make it harder to reach an agreement," Baldr said in a neutral tone.

"Perhaps it will make them more eager to deal with you than with me," Odin said.

Before her husband could say anything more, she added, "And you can discuss your plan to improve their roads and access to Ifington. Perhaps even more than that—a settlement outside Utgard itself."

Baldr's eyes went wide and he looked from her to Odin. "You've agreed to that, Father?"

Odin's frown deepened. "I've only agreed to entertain the possibility, to discuss the plan and its details. I have not yet approved anything at all."

Frigg gripped Odin's hand hard, and he looked down at her and winked.

Then he looked frankly at Baldr. "Approval would actually be up to you and Nanna—assuming, that is, that I step down as Alfather."

52

Hodr

Hodr threw another split log on the fire and leaned back against his tree, listening to the snap and crackle of the log between the fire's teeth. His head still ached, and his ribs were sore, but at least he'd been able to get out of bed and breathe fresh air before Sól had fled beyond the mountains.

Alara had urged him to come back inside, but he'd refused. A night beneath the stars would do him good. She'd protested, but since the night was mild she'd finally relented—after having the thralls build him a fire, set wood beside it, fetch him a stool and now, with a rucksack full of food and a pair of ale jugs to hand, he was well set for the night.

Alara had always thought it odd that he enjoyed spending even the coldest nights outside beneath what was now the lone tree in the yard where their few animals grazed. Beyond the fence lay dozens of other longhouses and workshops—weavers and clothiers, mostly. The louder and smellier trades, such as the smithies and tanneries, were on Ifington's other side, closer to the docks.

What Alara didn't quite understand was that having spent many winters wandering with only Kona for company, he enjoyed knowing that at any time, he could kick snow and dirt over the fire and be welcomed inside her home.

He wasn't alone anymore.

So he sat outside, kept the chill at bay with heavy clothes and a warm fire, a reminder to himself of everything he had gained. Then, too, he was reminded of everything he might lose should he stay with Alara.

The animals in their pens squawked and snorted. Kona's whinny joined the chorus, but she didn't sound frightened. Even so, Hodr reached for the long stick that had replaced his broken spear and cocked an ear toward the night. Out beyond the fire's crackle, the silence swelled like an ocean wave until his ears rang.

He caught the sound of snow breaking under feet. Four feet. Padded feet, landing on the inside of the tall fence that enclosed the yard.

"Come out," he called, leaning back onto the tree. "I hear you well enough."

Loud panting sounded in front of him, followed by a happy, muffled woof.

Hodr smiled and threw another log on the fire. "I thought it might be you. I suppose it is that time of year again, eh, Geri?"

Geri dropped a bundle next to him. It thumped and rolled into one of his booted feet. Geri woofed again, louder this time, and bumped his shoulder, nearly knocking him off his stool.

He laughed and caught himself. "Careful now, you'll roll me right into the fire." He ruffled his ears and scratched his side. "And yes, I missed you too."

Geri licked his face, whined twice and woofed again.

He wiped his face with his sleeve and threw an arm around the big wolf's shoulders. "Oh, I doubt that's the case. But it's nice of you to say."

Geri sat and leaned into him.

"And where's your sister at?" Hodr asked, cocking his head. Freki usually tried to outdo her brother.

Geri slid down to lay beside him. He yipped and growled.

"Sent elsewhere? Well, I'm sure you'll be back together soon enough."

Hodr felt Geri's low rumble of agreement against his shoulder.

"You know," he said, "I was thinking I might come back this winter. Maybe."

Geri woofed—approvingly—and laid his head down on his paws.

***

As night wore on, a light wind soughed across the yard and stirred the bare branches above him. Protesting, they creaked and clacked like old bones. Hodr shrugged himself deeper into his cloak and even deeper into his thoughts.

Colder now that his father's wolf had left him, he tossed the last logs onto the fire. Heat blossomed, and he edged closer, burrowing still deeper into his cloak. His stomach rumbled, and he felt for the bag Geri had brought, just as he, or Freki, or both of his father's wolves had every winter since he'd left Gladsheim. He withdrew the large, heavy fruit, which distant memory told him was the color of Sól's rising light. He held the fruit to his nose and inhaled: grass after a light rain, the hint of flowers on the wind, and the warbling cry of songbirds.

Just a bite, maybe two. Three at most. Then the rest for Alara.

His mouth watered at the thought of the golden skin breaking beneath his teeth and the burst of juices filling his mouth, sending fire through every part of his body.

Hodr opened his mouth to bite into the fruit. The wind gusted and blew wood smoke and ash into his face. He coughed and spat, turning aside. He dug in his rucksack for the jug of ale, took a swig, swirled it in his mouth, and spat it out.

Had the Norns just made their will plain? Even as the thought rattled in his mind, his father's words came to him: *The Norns can scrape and paint all they want, but I was alive long before they were. My doom is mine to set, not theirs.*

Hodr shoved the fruit into his rucksack and stood. He kicked dirt and snow over the fire, snatched up his stick, and tapped his way toward the house. Toward Alara.

53

Frigg

"Was he dead, Odin?"

Frigg rode beside her husband along the Upper Road. Sól slipped behind a cloud, and she shivered. The path they took led up from the longhouses, the clutch of buildings where the city elders gathered, and Gladsheim's main hall to the hilltop clearing in the old forest that had become Idunn's Grove.

He looked sideways at her, one eye lost in shadows. "I was able to bring him back."

"But was he dead?" Her heart skipped a beat as her horse, Haukr, slid on a slick stone.

Sleipnir whinnied. It sounded too much like laughter. Haukr shook his mane and whinnied back, indignant.

A glint of ice on the old, crumbled wall to her right caught her eye. That wall had once been all that stood between the newly settled Aesir and the Vanir warriors who had stormed up Gladsheim's central hill. Eventually, the Vanir and Aesir made peace. But from what Odin had said at Ithavoll, such a peace would never be possible between the Jotunn and Aesir—even though that's exactly what had grown between their peoples since he'd been gone.

She tore her eyes from the wall and found Odin's gray eyes had settled on her. A light smile graced his lips.

She shrugged and waved a hand toward the wall. "Just thinking about war." And death. And a consuming fire. But she kept those thoughts to herself even as a small voice inside her wondered why she had yet to see a vision of Odin's death.

Odin followed her gesture and grunted, his gray eyes as cool and as unfathomable as deep water.

"So?" she asked.

"Eh?"

"My question. Did Baldr die this morning?"

Odin frowned and stood in his stirrups, one of Ullr's wonderful inventions, to stretch his legs.

She reached out and swatted his shoulder. "Would you just answer me!"

His wintry version of their son's grin broke across his face. He settled back into his saddle. "His body was alive. I could feel his heart thumping, but his spirit had slipped away. I had to draw it back."

"So he was dead." She drew her feathered cloak more tightly about her shoulders.

He shook his head. "Not entirely. His spirit hadn't yet embarked for the Naglfar; it can't until his body dies. So he was trapped on the shores of the Gjoll, which is why I asked what he could remember."

She shuddered. After their marriage, he'd taken her up to the High Seat, shown her the scar in his side and told her what he'd done to get it and why. Then he'd taught her how to sit upon the High Seat and shown her where to look—and where not to. Where the Gjoll poured back into the Ginnungagap was one of those places.

She shook off the memory. Odin was still speaking. "… stop by Baldr's tree on the way."

"Wait, what?"

He winked a bright gray eye at her. "With all that's happened, I wasn't able to slip away—and you certainly weren't. And after this latest dream of his, planting new fruit may help."

Every Midwinter since Baldr's birth, she and Odin (or herself alone) would ride to Baldr's tree to bury some of Yggdrasil's fruit. Just as the fruit kept them young, so too did it keep the tree vigorous and the mistletoe it sheltered.

"I didn't realize you'd brought them with you," she said. Which proved how distracted she'd been thanks to all that'd happened in the last two nights.

"And this trip down to Mimir is worth the time?"

"Absolutely. Mimir spends most of his time swimming through the realms. He sees much that's hidden."

And yet he cannot pierce the future's veil. Apparently that burden is mine, shared only by those three witches below and the dead.

***

They left their horses tucked behind a still-green clutch of bushes and walked into the intermingled grove of green yew trees, bare ash and oak trees, and tall rune-carved stones. Fresh snow and old ice clung to the trees, stones and made the footing treacherous. She could taste the threat of new snow in the cold air.

Three paths led through the thick grove, one to Aegir's Temple, one to the stone arch marking the road down to Ithavoll, and the third to Heimdall's tower which, a mere sixteen winters ago, had been his daily post. Heimdall stood there looking and listening for the glint of spears or the thudding of boots that meant enemies of the Aesir were on the march. Now, he listened from beneath a table and saw nothing but the bottom of a cup.

She and Odin walked a winding route around and around the hill's crown, making sure to confuse their path. The precaution was probably pointless, but since no one was barred from the grove, it was still the safest course.

They passed dozens of random trees. "Good enough?"

A pair of birds called out from high above, black against the cloudy morning sky.

"Yes, no one's around." He motioned for her to lead the way.

She looped around another pair of yew trees until she reached a tall oak, its bare limbs reaching high. Loaded with snow, golden mistletoe nestled in the main fork of the trunk.

Odin knelt and began clearing the snow so he could dig. She tucked her hands beneath her armpits as the small shovel bit the frozen earth.

She looked around the tree and at the ground, and then she ran her gaze up the trunk, along the main branches, and to the golden crown of mistletoe.

"Something wrong?" he asked.

She shook her head. "I'm always rushed when I come here alone, anxious to bury the fruits and get back before I've been missed. Not an easy feat."

He grunted and went back to digging.

She laid a gloved hand on the tree's thick bole and began walking around it, sometimes looking up to the spreading branches and the cloudy sky and back down again. "How long will it live, do you think?"

The shovel's bite stopped. Odin rested his forearms on the shovel's handle, considering. "As long as we keep burying Yggdrasil's fruit, they will live as long as each other."

The shovel bit again. He made another neat pile beside the hole.

"And us? Will we also live forever?" She was thinking of the new silver threads that appeared in her hair every Midwinter and vanished after she ate the fruit. But always a handful remained behind. She'd noticed, too, that frost had also touched Odin's hair and beard.

He shook his head and made one last pile of dark earth. "Not as long."

Sól chose that moment to break through the morning's clouds and shine down on them. Shadows sprang up, stark against the snow. A squirrel chittered down at her, maybe lured out by the sunlight. She smiled up at the fat, indignant reddish-brown thing—and then hissed in a sharp breath as she spotted the raw edges of severed branches in the mistletoe's heart.

She leaped into the lowest branches. The bark dug into her

fingers even through her gloves as she hauled herself up, feet scrabbling on the trunk. The squirrel fled, jumping from one branch to
another.

"What's wrong?" Odin called out.

She planted a boot against a higher branch and stood, climbing
higher toward the mistletoe. Her boots skidded here and there
against the snow and underlying ice, but she kept going.

His voice came again from below. "Frigg! What did you see?"

"I'm not sure," she called back down. But she knew exactly what
she'd seen. She just couldn't believe it.

What remained of the mistletoe hung just out of arm's reach.
She grabbed high and pulled herself another body length up
into the tree. Snow, lichen, and bark crumbled beneath her
boots. Level with the mistletoe now, precariously perched, she
tugged off her gloves and dropped them. Below, she heard Odin
spit and curse. She glanced down and saw him following
her up.

Sól slipped out again and illuminated the full extent of the
damage done to the mistletoe.

The world seemed to spin around her. She must've cried out,
because, distantly, she heard Odin swear again. "I'm nearly there," he
shouted.

But it didn't matter. What could he do?

She breathed out, closed her eyes. When she felt steadier, she
opened her eyes to take in the damage. It had been well disguised—
unnoticeable from a distance and from below thanks to the heavy
snows of the past weeks—but the cuts were there, just the same. The
mistletoe's heart had been cut out. How had she not seen this
before now?

She leaned in. The bare stems were weathered from exposure.
Beneath her thumb, the raw edges felt smooth, not rough as they
would have been from an animal's gnawing teeth. Cut. By someone
who knew not to use skymetal.

Odin's shadow opposite her dimmed the mistletoe's gold. "Probably used silver, either a knife or maybe shears like mine." He leaned

in closer. "Done a while back, I'd guess. Maybe in summer, when the cuts would've been hidden by the tree's leaves."

Two nights ago had been the first time she'd come to Baldr's tree since last winter. She only ate Idunn's fruits once each year, so there was no reason to come more often. There was good reason to *only* come once each year—less chance their secret would be discovered.

"Is this what the dreams were showing, then? That his mistletoe was cut?"

His gray eyes, serious and thoughtful, met hers. Reflexively, she reached up and brushed her cheeks. Dry. That was good.

"I don't know. It does seem likely, though."

"How can you not know? All that time you spend away, seeking new wisdom—always seeking." Always away.

His expression softened slightly; his fingers gently gripped her arm. "This was your people's magic, not mine."

"Our people are one and the same, Odin!" She hadn't realized she'd shouted until the echoes came back at her.

"Not if they hurt our son."

She blinked. No, of course not.

"You think the Jotunn are behind this?"

"Who else?"

"Don't talk to me like I'm an idiot, Odin."

But who else was there? The Jotunn and Aesir had been fighting each other ever since Odin and his brothers had killed Ymir—until the end of the Last War. The Vanir were friends, as were the Alvar. Odin had taken the Svartalvar far away. And it was Baldr's missions of mercy to Jotunheim that had helped foster the current peace.

"The Jotunn are just the most *obvious* culprits. You've met this Skrymir and Vafthrudnir. They're not stupid. And harming Baldr isn't in their best interests."

"No, they're not," he said. "But we have several hundred winters of experience behind us. What's obvious to us may seem the height of intrigue to them."

"Maybe, but why destroy Háls? The Skrymir had to know sending Thor to level one of their towns would be the least of our responses."

She gestured at the cut mistletoe. "And, again, why do this to Baldr? He's helping them. And most importantly, how would they even know to do this?"

He shrugged. "Spies."

"I don't talk about what we did or where this is, and we've only ever had a single conversation about this tree that could've been overheard." Aside from Heimdall. He knew their secret.

"Maybe that one mistake was enough. Maybe you were followed."

But not him? She bit back a retort and instead thought back over the past twenty winters. Twenty visits here. She tried to push her memory further back. Maybe she'd seen an old woman when she'd ridden back down or a few groups of people. Maybe. Gladsheim's main temple was up here; people were free to come and go.

"It's not impossible, I suppose, but I'm careful."

"I know," he said with a quick, mirthless smile. "Come on, let's climb down."

As she clambered down, bark and ice crumbling beneath her boots, she turned the question over in her mind. Who else could mean Baldr harm? Did he even have enemies? After his brother had been blinded, Baldr had laid down his weapons. Every warrior he'd ever fought had long ago passed back into the Gap, except those few among the Aesir and Vanir. The Jotunn loved him nearly as much as the Aesir did.

The only person she could think of was Hodr—and she hated herself for the thought. Hodr had been angry because Baldr couldn't heal his eyes. He had always resented his brother's invulnerability. But he never would have wished real harm on his brother, much less acted on it, would he?

No. He wouldn't. Nor did Hodr know about this oak tree or the mistletoe. Aegir's love, Hodr had only been a baby when she and Odin had had that one thoughtless conversation.

She pushed the idea away. She'd sat on the High Seat and watched Hodr long enough and often enough to see that he'd had found a place for himself. A woman. And, hopefully, some peace.

As her boots hit the ground, a thought struck her. "What about that thing that attacked you?"

"From the Urdarbrunnr?" Odin dusted his hands off, considering. "If it can reach through waters besides those directly linked to the well, then maybe. If it can't, then it would have to possess someone, as I assume it meant to do with me. And it would still have to have known our secret."

"Could it have witnessed the ritual?"

He shrugged. "It's not impossible."

"I can't think of anyone else. That conversation we had was nearly two hundred winters ago. Even the thralls who might've overheard are long dead."

"They could've passed the secret on, but why would they have wanted to harm Baldr?" He gave a wan smile. "Now, if it were me..."

She looked up into the crook of the tree at the cut mistletoe. "One thing's certain. Until we figure out who cut the mistletoe, we need those we trust to stay very close to Baldr."

***

Frigg held the witchlamp as high as she dared. Odin walked just in front of her, back bent with the effort of keeping the Alvar-made shaper pressed against Yggdrasil's root. Under the shaper's magic, Yggdrasil's wood flowed like water. They walked inside a moving bubble of the shaper's magic. The tree's guts opened before them and then closed behind.

"Almost through, Frigg," Odin said over his shoulder, voice tight with effort.

Sweat rolled down her back. More sweat beaded on her upper lip; she wiped it with her sleeve. She rolled her shoulders, trying to relieve the ache of holding the witchlamp.

But nothing could relieve the ache that had built in her heart during the ride down Yggdrasil into Ithavoll. Baldr had come through the fire on the ship unharmed. That meant he was still protected. It had to. Yet now he'd had another dream, perhaps the worst one yet.

Odin said that the damage to the mistletoe was the likely cause of those dreams. So Baldr was protected still, but still dying? Was that what her visions meant?

With a creaking groan, the root in front of them ebbed to reveal Mimir's glade. Odin stepped down into the knee-high grasses and turned around, keeping the shaper pressed against Yggdrasil. His face dripped sweat.

Would Mimir have answers for them? Could he have seen who or what was behind all this? Too many questions. Too many mysteries. And why was all this happening now?

She lowered the witchlamp and reached out a hand to steady—

"Stop!" Odin said. "You'll lose your hand to the shaper's magic."

She snatched her hand back and stepped unsteadily into the cool freshness of the glade.

Odin relaxed, pulled the shaper away and the tunnel closed with the rushing sound of waves rolling in. Or of fire devouring timber.

But she mustn't think of flames. Or ships. She walled those thoughts away. "I'm sorry. My mind's elsewhere."

"I can't imagine why." The corners of his eyes crinkled. He wiped his face, replaced the shaper in his satchel and met her eyes, his smile already gone. "You ready for this?"

She nodded. As useful as Mimir's counsel could be, speaking with him usually tried her patience. She straightened her shoulders and put on the calm face she had learned to use for meetings with Gladsheim's various factions.

Together, they walked toward the glade's center, where Mimir waited. The glade looked like a longship—a sharp bow where they had entered, a wide belly, and a tapered stern—except that the root rose much higher on either side than the low gunwales of a longship.

The grass was the same brilliant green it was everywhere in Ithavoll. The sky above was the familiar black, dotted with starry specks and the long, glowing trails of Muspell's sparks.

Very long ago during the Aesir-Vanir war, Odin had not only shaped this glade, but he'd also shaped channels in the root along which water flowed in a series of waterfalls. Mimir's head sat in one of the notches like a carved statue set against a wall. He and Odin looked similar: strong nose, high cheekbones, and deep-set gray eyes. Mimir's beard was very long, though, and it clung to the bark.

She waited beside Odin, both of them expecting to hear Mimir's voice, deep and slow. But no greeting came except the water's song. It flowed over Mimir's rune-etched head, across his closed lips, and down, where it pooled in a wide stone bowl set against the root. From there, the water fell again, creating a stream that flowed to a wide pool maybe a pair of spear lengths from the root.

Cool mist brushed the bare skin of her neck. She glanced sidelong at Odin. His expression had grown concerned. Mimir's eyes were closed, red runes bright on his closed lids.

"Uncle?" Odin asked.

No response.

He released her hand. "Stay back," he said. "Keep watch." He stepped quickly to where Mimir's head rested and put his hands on the wet wood.

She turned and drew her knife, holding the long, bright blade at the ready, and slid into the fighting stance she'd learned so long ago. Not that she'd used it recently. Her palm was damp on the leather-wrapped hilt. Her eyes darted around the glade, from the tall slab of root ringing her in to the lush green grass spread underfoot to the sharp reflections in Mimir's pool.

Had that spirit attacked from the pool again? The waters here were all one with the Urdarbrunnar. She edged closer, heart thumping faster. Had there been a warning before it attacked the last time? Odin hadn't said. All she could see was the bright-speckled black sky, a few moths flitting about, and—

"He's not here."

She held her stance and kept her eyes on the pool. As long as she'd known Odin, the head of his dead uncle had rested here. "What do you mean?"

He sighed, and she heard him step back. "Well, he's here, obviously, but his spirit is elsewhere. And has been for some time, I'd guess." He touched her arm. "What are you doing?"

She gestured with her chin at the pool. "The spirit..."

"Probably not. Mimir has a bit less to offer than I."

She glanced at him, took in his smile, and relaxed. He was *joking*. "Really?"

He shrugged. "Just trying to lighten the mood before I tell you what I have to do."

"You're going after him."

He nodded. "Have to. Even if we didn't need his wisdom, he's family, and he's in trouble."

"So, you're what..." She gestured toward Mimir, wiggling her fingers. "Going wherever he did?"

He nodded, quick and sharp. "I can follow the link between his flesh—what's left of it—and his spirit. Think of it as a rope between a cleat and a sail."

She sheathed her knife. "All right, what do I need to do?"

He looked at her, one eyebrow raised. "Stay here."

"No. I'm going with you."

He smiled and shook his head. "You don't know how."

"Teach me."

He laughed. "It's not that simple."

She put her hands on her hips and set her jaw.

"Can you send your spirit out into the world?" he asked, his tone infuriatingly gentle. "Can you find your flesh again once your spirit is realms away? Can you trace the flow of Yggdrasil's life? Do you know how to protect your spirit? Or how to fight as one?"

They both knew she couldn't. "I can learn."

"Maybe in a few winters' time, but not in a single morning," he said. "Look, if you're here with my body, I can focus on finding Mimir. You may think that staying here isn't helpful, but if my body is killed while I'm gone, my spirit will flutter away like that same sail blown free in a gale."

"Why not pull my spirit from my body, like you threatened Heimdall?"

He shook his head. "The shock would probably kill you. And if it didn't, I'd have two problems instead of just this one."

"So I'm supposed to just stand here and wait?"

"Call it that if you want, but keeping my body safe is important. I wouldn't do this without someone standing guard." He pointed down at the water. "You were right to suspect the spirit's involvement. These waters are the same as those beneath Urdarbrunnr. I don't know if it's responsible for this, but maybe it can sense where I am."

She gestured at the rippling pool. "That thing nearly killed you. How am I supposed to fight it? All I have is my knife."

"You saw how effectively I fought it. Use your wits."

The spirit had told her they would talk again—or had it said she would see it in one of her visions? She frowned, trying to remember its exact words.

"Look, there's no need to be afraid. I'm sure Mimir's just gotten himself caught in a current and can't get back. It can happen."

She snorted and met his gray eyes. "I'm not afraid, Odin. I just don't like standing around and waiting."

"Who does? In this instance, it's necessary." He unclipped his cloak and tossed it aside.

"And what if you don't come back?"

"Leave and get Baldr." He dug in his bag, withdrew the shaper, and handed it to her. "And send word to Freyja."

Realization struck. He wasn't patronizing her. The thing in the well wanted his body. If it possessed him, he needed her to kill him.

"I understand," she said, her voice serious.

He kissed her quickly on the cheek. "I thought you might."

He crossed to stand in front of Mimir, glanced back at her, and winked. "Just don't strike too quickly. I know you're still angry with me."

She answered with a faint smile. "How long will this take?"

"I'll be back before you know it."

***

Frigg shuddered as Odin leaned forward and touched his lips to Mimir's forehead. It looked too intimate. His hands tightened on the wet, rough bark of the notch in which Mimir's head sat. Then his body stiffened, and he went completely still.

She took a few steps to one side. Mimir's withered, wet, rune-covered face was slack, as if he were asleep—or dead. Water ran from the bark above onto Odin, wetting his face and beard and pouring down his chest.

She sighed, turned away, and threw a wary gaze around the glade. Nothing but swirling mist, dancing moths, and the steady trickling noise of water.

She began walking the oblong circle of the glade from where Odin stood, lips pressed to Mimir, to the rune stone that marked the entrance, then around to the rune stone at the opposite side. The stone was cold beneath her trailing fingers. She ran her hand against the rough, damp bark of Yggdrasil's root. It rose maybe twice her height above her. Climbable, but with a thought, she could take a falcon's shape and fly up the bole to the passage into Gladsheim.

She stopped by the aft rune stone to check Odin and Mimir. Bubbling pops from the wide, clear pool in the center of the glade called for her attention. As she stared, the image of Baldr's burning face kindled in her mind. She pressed fingertips into closed eyes, trying to press the memory away.

When she opened her eyes again, the grass was so green it hurt. She turned her back to the pool and stared up at the soothing brown of Yggdrasil's root. She was an ant staring up at a longship's mast.

A particularly loud pop made her spin round, her hand falling to her knife. She glanced at Odin and Mimir. They hadn't moved. She strode to the pool and hesitated for only a pair of heartbeats before looking down into the clear water. Aside from the ripples caused by the upwelling water and the inflowing stream, she saw only the reflected sky, her face, and the small stones lining its bottom.

The pool's center was black and deep, like a throat leading to some gullet. Was there another world beneath her feet? They had ridden from Gladsheim down Yggdrasil to this place where the Norns lived, but when she looked up, she saw the sky—which obviously couldn't be possible if they were actually under Gladsheim's hill.

A bubble popped again. Startled, she jumped back. After a heart-pounding moment, she glanced at Odin. No change. So much for this happening quickly.

The thought of his stepping down as Alfather bubbled up in her mind. Now that would be a change. They could leave Asgard in Baldr's and Nanna's hands—both were inexperienced, but capable. Then she and Odin could ride out, or maybe sail on Skidbladnir to see new shores. Set foot on new land.

The first twenty winters of her life had been spent in the heavy tents and deep stone caves of wintry Utgard. The last several hundred had been spent in the comparatively lush green forests and spreading plains of Asgard. She'd ridden the waves southward along the coast to warm Alvheim and steamy Vanaheim. But Odin had told her of still hotter places where the ground itself, burned and dusty, rolled away into the horizon.

She glanced over at him, still locked in that too-intimate embrace, and suppressed a shudder. She hopped over the stream and moved toward the cloak he'd thrown against Yggdrasil's root.

Odin would never step down. But if she could help Baldr and Nanna succeed, maybe he would truly consider it. Maybe.

She looked down at her hands, smooth, long-fingered, and tawny —so unlike her father's blunt, calloused hands. At first, she would have a hard time working Skidbladnir's ropes, but once her hands toughened, it wouldn't be a problem. And she could always work the steering board, setting the course she wanted.

That thought brought a smile to her face even as a gurgling pop from the pool drove it away again. When nothing more happened, she looked back at Odin, where nothing was also happening, and then back down at her hands.

They could always bring a crew of thralls to work the ship. No, not thralls, not more mouths to feed. Not more ears to overhear or eyes to stare back at them. Just the white-and-red patchwork sail snapping in the wind, the rise and fall of the deck beneath her feet, and her husband working the sails, smiling back at her while she worked the steering board, warm frothy seawater spraying up over the gunwales and into her face.

She closed her eyes and tried to fix the rippling sail in her mind's eye, aflame with Sól's fleeing light. It slid into the charred and tattered sail, driving her son's death ship upon the Gjoll's choppy waters. She gasped, trying now to push the memory away, even as Odin's smiling face twisted into their son's, white teeth bared in a rictus grin below hair that burned brighter than a torch.

A sob ripped its way out, and she covered her mouth as if there were someone there to overhear her. She brought her knees up and hugged them tight, ducked her head, and let the tears flow.

Abdicate and sail away? Not when her visions—those forced upon her—always came true.

54

Odin

Like a thunderbolt, Odin fell through branches and green leaves
that left him untouched. He burst into an icy-blue sky, snowy mountains wheeling beneath him. On the wings of a golden eagle he
soared downward in a wide, swooping arc.

This high, the world curved away beneath him. In the east, a
storm rumbled through the mountains. The sea glittered just beyond
those peaks. In the west, Sól sank behind jagged peaks, a morsel
dangled above a wolf's jaws.

So, Uncle, your trail leads to Utgard.

He folded his wings and fell faster until shabby trees sprouting
from a rock-strewn mountainside filled his vision. Beneath him, a fat
thread of shimmering gold wove through a snow-covered forest, a
river catching the last of Sól's light.

He reached out with long talons and lit upon a ragged branch of a
dead tree. It was all pretense, of course. His spirit was insubstantial.
He would pass unseen through Utgard, unless he happened upon a
Jotunn shaman or witch. Or a disir, roaming wild and free in these
stormy mountains.

Perched now, he found the thin gray trail of his uncle's spirit. It stretched farther east, deeper into the forest, following the river. The only forest this size in Utgard was the Iron Wood—Jarnvidr, in the old tongue. The last time he'd flown here, either as spirit or in his real, shape-shifted flesh, had been just before Loki's first wife passed back into the storm.

**

Dusk swallowed Odin. He had retaken his shape outside the crumbling waist-high wall that ran around all-too-familiar long-house. Snow dusted the ground in the drab clearing, heaved into a dozen lumps by the frost. Tall ice-coated trees rose all around him; the rasp of their ice-laden branches grated like the stone of a barrow's door.

He drifted closer to the longhouse—broken, he could see now, by a tree rising up through its center. With a thought, he clad himself in armor. He longed for Gungnir, but instead brought her semblance to his hand. He could no more touch the physical world around him than the things of it could touch him.

Only things purely of spirit or living things that had died and were then enchanted in specific ways, were a threat. The former dweller of this broken home had probably drawn spirits as rotting meat drew flies. If any lingered and contested his trespass, his armor and weapons would be as effective against them as they were dangerous to him.

He hovered by the ragged break in the wall. Mimir's gray trail ran right through it and the scrubby trees and bushes that clutched the longhouse walls. One of those walls had fallen in, carrying the roof with it. The empty doorway was a screaming mouth.

When he'd last looked in on Angrboda, she'd kneeled in green grass, face to the sky, wet from weeping. He'd sent her children away, but he hadn't killed them. He made sure Loki was aware of what the Norns had said—he heard their foretelling from their own lips. It hadn't mattered, though. Angrboda blamed them both, her husband for cowardice and himself for oath breaking.

Several winters later, she passed back into the storm. Loki had borne her body away without help and without saying where he'd buried her. Odin had never asked, but Heimdall had seen.

So much pain in this place. He drifted forward along what had been the path from gate to door. Dozens of small holes pocked the frozen ground, the black dirt frosted and mounded as if something had pushed its way up from underground. Mist slithered and pooled in the hollows and clung to the lumps of dirt, as well as the larger mounds of snow-dusted earth heaped between the trees.

Mimir's trail, much stronger now, led up the path between the fallen stones and through the ragged opening into the house.

He examined all of it again: the stones of the wall, the small, odd holes in the ground, the ragged hole in the house's side, and the gaping door. No signs of seidr woven into them. Still, there was something odd about Angrboda's dead home. Was he about to drift into a trap? Had he already?

He scanned the tree line again, seeing nothing but the darkening spaces between the trees. It would be a clear night lit by a quarter moon. A light breeze had sprung up, stirring the dark green, needle-like leaves of the scrubby trees framing the door.

He drifted forward again, avoiding the holes in the black earth. He stopped before the ragged opening and looked for traces of protective seidr woven around the house. Nothing. A pair of ward staves had been painted on either side of the gaping entrance, but they were so worn away by weather and time that he couldn't identify the runes.

Mimir's trail hung before him, grown as thick as a ship's rope. It led in and to the left, toward the house's bow, were it a longship.

Instead of following it, he moved to the left side of the entrance and peered in at the house's aft quarters. A black mound of dirt loomed there; a large slab of stone lay across it. He swore to himself. If he was still here at nightfall, which wasn't far off, the sleeper beneath that stone would rise to greet him.

He drifted to his right, examining as best he could the house's wide middle section, where the food had once been cooked and eaten. He ducked below Mimir's trail and slowly slid into the house itself.

The glowing rope of Mimir's trail led left to a tree that had sprouted up where the roof had fallen in. Its roots, spread wide across the longhouse floor, wrapped like an egg around a seated figure, its white-haired head bowed.

"Mimir?"

At the sound of his voice, the figure regarded him. Maybe two spear lengths separated them.

Mimir gestured a lean hand toward the roots entangling him. Some hung above his head; some reached up from the ground. "You know this is a trap, right?"

Relief washed over Odin. "I figured as much. Who set it?"

Mimir shrugged. "I've been told you have two choices, stay or flee. If you leave, they're allowed to kill me. If you stay, well, they get a chance to kill you. I would've warned you off, but I couldn't sense your approach thanks to these roots."

"I assume you can't just leave?"

"Wouldn't be much of a trap if I could." He gestured with his chin toward the sky. "Night approaches. Choose quickly."

"Draugr?" He jerked a thumb back toward the stone slab.

"More than one. You saw the other barrows, right?"

He paused. He hadn't, unless those snow-covered lumps among the trees were the barrows. "Of course."

"It's amazing that some folk can't tell when you lie." Mimir pointed at the darkening sky. Night always came quick in the winter months. "I'm not joking, Odin. You can still flee when they wake, but it'll be more dangerous."

"I'm not leaving you here." He strode forward, his spear becoming an axe. He couldn't chop the physical roots, but he could sever the sorcerous threads woven through them.

"Stop!" Mimir had both hands up. The roots surrounding him trembled like a wolf's jaws about to snap shut.

He paused, axe held at waist-level, blade down.

"If it were that easy, I wouldn't be here."

"How else am I going to free you?"

"I don't know." Mimir pointed behind Odin. "Prepare yourself."

Mimir's words blended into the groan of the stone slab shifting. Odin spun and faced the far end of the longhouse. An armored figure shoved the stone aside. It fell sideways and slammed into the wall; dust and dirt rained down from the ragged remains of the roof.

The draugr then stepped free of its barrow. Taller and broader than Odin himself, the dead thing was armored in dark leathers and a helm obscured its face. Where visible, runes covered its sallow flesh.

"There are two others," Mimir called. "They'll be here in moments."

Odin formed a shield on his other arm, faced the draugr, and took a fighting stance. He'd need to get outside, especially if there were more.

The draugr ripped a sword from its scabbard and swung it in a fast crisscross pattern, dead sinews crackling and popping. A swordsman, then. It charged just as fast, with just as much control.

He countered by stepping into the charge. He used both arms to slam his shield into the draugr and shove it past him. It crashed into the long tendrils of root. The hair-like mesh around Mimir trembled but didn't react like it had when he'd almost used his axe.

Interesting. I'll have to make this look convincing.

The draugr shoved itself off the root, which trembled still more. It charged him, its sword swinging in a hideous arc he just avoided. He lashed out with his axe, but the draugr flowed behind his sword, its dead feet light on the uneven floor. The sword came back around, and he barely ducked beneath it.

"Two more at the door, Odin," Mimir called, his voice tight.

He had his back to the root now. The draugr stood between him and the doorway. He spun his axe in one hand, glanced quickly at Mimir, and nodded slightly. He hoped this would work—and that Mimir understood what was about to happen.

Movement flashed, and he just got his shield up in time. The draugr's sword banged off his shield, his mind creating the expected sound. He might be a spirit, but the draugr was both dead and alive, powered by magic and its own relentless will. And its weapon was bone, etched with runes. It could wound, even kill him.

The draugr was on him again, sword darting like a snake's tongue. He stood his ground. He deflected another hammering blow with his shield and then lashed out in a counterstrike. He made sure his next block was slightly too slow and his follow-up strike inaccurate. He built deception into every attack and defense—but quickly. The other draugr crowding in through the entrance would shortly overwhelm him.

Another ringing block. This time, he tried to drag the draugr's bone blade down with the beard of his axe. It didn't work—nor had he expected it to. But it was a convincing-looking move. The draugr hauled its sword back and turned the motion into a spinning strike that he deflected even as he stepped back.

He was in position now, with the root that trapped Mimir just behind him. If he had a body, he would have felt the rough bark tugging against his clothing. All he had to do was force the draugr to strike at him in the way he wanted.

He swung his axe at the draugr's exposed waist. The dead man was so fast that it leaned back and spun again. It brought its bone blade arcing down in a strike meant to cleave him from shoulder to groin.

Perfect.

Rather than block the sword, he stepped back through the root. The draugr's bone blade thudded down, severing the thick root.

The tendrils trapping Mimir quivered and went still.

"I'm out, Odin, I'm out!" Mimir's voice filtered in through the broken roof and open door.

It had worked.

And then the two draugr from outside vaulted the severed root and crowded him, pressing him toward the back of the house. He blocked a flurry of white blades and stepped backward through the longhouse wall, just as Mimir had immediately done when he'd been freed. There were advantages to being pure spirit.

He stopped maybe a spear's distance from the wall. He looked quickly around, trying to find his uncle.

Máni hung bright above the tall trees, his white light stark on the ground. Mimir was another two spears distant and throwing seidr around him in sweeping arcs that burned the white worms flooding up from the holes in the ground.

"We need to get out of here, Odin. You ready?"

"Yes, I'm—"

The wall of the longhouse exploded outward.

Odin spun. All three draugr followed in the splinters of wood and cloud of dust.

The swordsman he had maneuvered into freeing Mimir led the small wedge of dead warriors charging him. A heartbeat later, they were on him. The lead draugr's blade flicked out.

He brought his shield up just fast enough to deflect the draugr's blade from a strike at his heart. The bone blade grated along his shield, then juddered free to rip a deep trench across his forehead.

Fire raced from his eyebrow to hairline. He roared with pain and stumbled back, fighting to deflect the flurry of attacks from all three draugr. His shield thudded beneath a handful of heavy blows while several more knocked his axe down and away.

When he felt a strong arm wrap around his chest, he let the darkness take him.

55

"Again, I simply cannot apologize enough for the injuries my horse caused," Lopt said in a voice that made Hodr's skin crawl. "I am hugely relieved to see you up and about."

Hodr shifted in his chair, his fingers tapping the cool sides of his stoneware cup. Behind him, Alara's way house was in full flow for the evening. Many traders were bustling through Ifington, trying to finish one last trip to Gladsheim before Midwinter or get home before the bad weather set in. And if the tickle in his nose was any guide, they were right to rush.

"It was an accident," Hodr said. "Had I been paying more attention, I would've heard the warnings sooner."

"Maybe, maybe," Lopt said. "Still, I regret it, particularly since it happened to you."

"I'm not sure what you mean." He hoped the man wasn't about to say what he dreaded might be coming. He heard Lopt edge closer.

"You're Jarl Hodr, hero of the Old Bridge."

How had this smith recognized him? He shook his head slowly. "Named for him. But I'm not him. I'm far too young."

"I heard the story from my father who had it from his older brother who was there, in the very battle that saved this city. You absolutely fit the description." Lopt edged closer still, and when he spoke, his voice was hard for even Hodr to hear. "Hodr, son of Odin, held the bridge alone against a warband of Jotunn reinforcements. Alone! He didn't fall even when a snow bear spat its venom into his eyes, searing them from his head. Only when he had killed the beast, with hands as strong as the Thunderer's, did he fall."

Holding a forced smile, Hodr cocked his head to listen for any murmurs from the crowd behind him—whispers that might suggest Lopt had been overheard. "I'm not him," Hodr said. Not anymore. He was Hodr the Blind. Hodr the Wanderer. Hodr the Outcast. He could no more wield a spear and stand in the wall than he could dodge a wild horse. But even as he thought it, the wiser part of his mind objected.

He'd left Gladsheim angry, jealous, and ashamed. And now that he was here in Ifington with Alara, he was becoming Hodr the Happy.

Lopt's fingers drummed an odd rhythm on the table. "Your secret is safe with me, Jarl."

Hodr leaned in. "Don't use that title. It's not mine."

"Only because you walked away from it, or so the stories say."

"I am not him." His whisper cut through the laughter and conversation surrounding their table. "And why would it matter if I was? Why is it important? Jarl Hodr, if he exists, is not important."

"Not important?" Lopt barked a short laugh. "If it wasn't for him, Ifington would probably be a Jotunn stronghold now. Again. No, his sacrifice—your sacrifice—helped make this town what it is today."

"That's ridiculous."

Lopt rapped the table once. "No, it's not. Everything comes down to the actions of a few people who are in the right place at the right time. The Norns scratch and paint the doom of all into Yggdrasil's bark—yours, mine... everyone's."

Hodr shook his head. "The Aesir make their own doom."

Lopt grabbed his elbow, his hand rough and strong, and gave a warm squeeze. "Only a son of Odin would say that. So I am right?"

A warm flush spread up from where Lopt grabbed him. Hodr frowned it away and pulled his arm back. "Lower your voice, smith."

"Of course, Jarl, of course," Lopt said, delight shining in his voice. "And may I say it's an honor to meet you."

"An honor to meet a maimed warrior whose name has withered in the shadows cast by his brothers?" Hodr sniffed. "The jarl I was no longer exists. I'm simply blind Hodr. Just a man. It's taken me a lifetime to make my peace with it. But I have, and now I'm ready to reforge my name just as you might a broken blade."

Alara's laughter floated above the rougher sounds of the traders. He smiled as he heard it realizing, in that instant of her mirth, that what he'd said was true.

"I can see that, Jarl—"

Hodr raised a finger.

"Apologies," Lopt said, his voice heavy with respect, like an overladen cart. "It's clear to me that you have. I'm honored to have met you. I wish you continued long life and every happiness."

Hodr's smile faded. He followed the sound of Alara's voice around the wide hall as she moved among the traders, laughing with them while delivering food and drink.

"Did I say something wrong?" Lopt asked. "If I caused offense..."

"It's nothing," Hodr said with a shake of his head. His thoughts fled to the heavy, round burden in his rucksack. He hadn't eaten any of it, nor had he mentioned it to Alara.

"My wife and I have two boys," Lopt said. "Honestly, I'm surprised she hasn't divorced me by now, what with the time I spend away or in the forge banging away at metals. Woodworking too, these days, as my strength's begun fading. But I've taught my sons the trade I learned, so that, at least, will continue. Hopefully, I've driven all the flaws I see in me out of them, but who knows what new ones I've hammered in, eh?"

Hodr nodded, but his mouth watered at the thought of the fruit's skin popping as he bit into it.

"If you don't mind me asking, Jarl, but are you two—you and the mistress here—you know..."

"Married?" Hodr shook his head.

"You seem happy with her," the smith said, as if he hadn't heard, "and I'm sure her father would be thrilled to have her marry so well—"

Hodr raised a hand, cutting off the smith's words. He shifted slightly so he faced Lopt.

As if anticipating a rebuke, Lopt said, "Jarl, if I went too far, let me—"

Hodr shook his head. "It's not that simple. For one thing, she doesn't have any family except her brother."

"I see, but that doesn't necessarily complicate a marriage. If I may, Jarl, do you get along well with the brother?"

The smith squeezed Hodr's forearm, his hand warm and strong, in a companionable gesture as he asked, in a hushed voice, "And does he know who you are?"

Hodr flushed as he remembered the strength that had burned through him as he fought the Jotunn vanguard to a standstill on the Old Bridge. He'd held the bridge alone with a spear till it had shattered, and then axe and shield until they, too, had broken—

His eyes burned anew as the sight in his mind's eyes shifted to the snow bear and its spit, that thick blob of green-black venom as it seemed to take forever before it splattered across his broken shield and then burned through it. That shield, broken though it was, had saved his life...and ruined it as much as the venom that had eaten his eyes and ravaged his face.

A sudden need for the taste of Yggdrasil's fruit rushed through him. His stomach gurgled and his mouth watered. He picked up a cup and turned toward the kegs, breaking contact with the smith's hand, and poured himself a mouthful of the sweeter of the ales. He drank it down quickly and wiped his mouth with the back of one shaking hand.

"Ja—your pardon—Hodr, are you all right?"

He wiped sweat from his face. "Of course. Just thirsty. Can I pour you another? On me."

"Don't mind if I do. Thank you, my friend."

Hodr listened for the scrape of Lopt's cup on the table, picked it up and filled it. He ignored the sweat dampening his lower back and armpits. He daubed at his upper lip and forehead with his sleeve.

"It has grown warm in here," Lopt said. "Feels like my forge right before I really get to work."

The smith took a loud sip from his fresh cup. "If I may, in all the many winters I've stayed at this way house, I can't say I've ever seen the mistress as happy as these last few. Have you thought about putting yourself forward to the brother? I bet he approves."

"It's not that simple," Hodr repeated.

"What could be simpler? You like her, she likes—"

He made his tone sharp and struck at the humor in Lopt's voice. "How old am I, Lopt?"

Lopt was quiet for a long moment. "I see what you mean, Jarl."

He leaned toward the smith. "Do you? I held the Old Bridge before it was called 'old' – and it was dozens more years before there was a New Bridge. And that alone was probably twenty winters before you were born. Nothing is simple for me or my family."

Lopt said nothing. He could barely hear the smith breathing above the anger pounding in his ears. He might curse Rán for taking his eyes, but her husband had strengthened his other senses.

"Apparently I have a gift for offending you," Lopt finally said. "Which is the opposite of my intent, especially since I've already caused you much injury. But if you'd allow one further piece of unasked for advice—no matter how strong the magic that keeps you young, you're still a man, with a man's needs and a man's desire to have his name remembered."

The smith tapped the table twice and stepped away. Alara's sweet voice rose above the crowd's din and the pounding anger in his ears. She bid Lopt a good night.

Did he still wish to be remembered?

In a quiet voice, Hodr said, "Yes, I think so."

56

Vidar

"This is not the answer I expected to find," Vidar said, gesturing with his chin toward the shimmering barrier in front of him. A blizzard raged a sword's length in front of him, but without the wind or the cold.

"It's where the Jotunn trail ends, Jarl," Garilon said. "Doesn't make any sense to me at all."

They had never caught up with the Jotunn who'd fled into the mine. Probably because they knew where they were going, whereas he'd made his warband move slowly, fearing traps or even an ambush.

Vidar stepped back from the swirling white-gray of the barrier in front of him. He ran his hand along a wide, smooth vein of exposed skymetal in the tunnel wall. He brought his witchlamp up close to the long, wavy line where skymetal met stone. No seam, no roughness. It was as if an axe had cleaved through bone and flesh—but here, bone was metal and flesh the rock.

"Very strange," he said.

He gestured for Garilon to join him. Together they walked down the smooth-walled passage, their footfalls echoing before them, till they reached its intersection with the mine shaft. Mikill and Smar stood guard on either side of the opening.

He brought the witchlamp close to where the smooth passage met the one cut by the miners, though he hardly needed to. Even at a distance, he could tell the difference. The wall cut by the miners was ragged and rough, tool marks evident on the stone.

The smoothness of the tunnel made him think of the Alvar-made shaper he'd seen Odin use to bend back Yggdrasil's living wood. Where the Alvar had mastered using seidr to control things that lived, the Svartalvar had mastered similar control of stone and metal. It was one of the many reasons they had been feared, hated, ostracized, and finally exiled by the Alvar and Vanir—with the help of the Aesir.

He walked quickly back down the tunnel to where the skymetal vein lay exposed, smooth and glossy amid the surrounding stone. He ran his hand across the surface. No snags. He laid his cheek against the cool stone and peered down along the face. No chisel marks whatsoever.

What if the ironwood and metal device he'd been trying to make work, so obviously crafted by Svartalvar hands, could shape stone and metal just like the Alvar's shaper affected wood?

The Jotunn with the device had been discovered near an outcropping. Maybe they had planned to tunnel into it and burrow under the stone on which Gladsheim was built?

He turned and stared at the shimmering doorway, not really seeing it. He and his family used a tunnel into Gladsheim's hill to reach Yggdrasil. Had it been dug, shaped like this one, or was it natural? If it was natural, perhaps there was a whole system of caves beneath the hill.

And that Jotunn patrol during the Last War had been found north of Gladsheim's walls. Had they intended to tunnel beneath the wall? And when they were surprised, they tried to destroy the device to stop anyone from figuring out what it did.

Then he remembered the climbing gear found along with the Jotunn. Maybe it was going to be used for descending, not ascending

—which might explain why his father hadn't found anything when he'd climbed up the outcropping.

He spun and walked back to where the smooth tunnel met the ragged mine shaft. He stepped out into the mine shaft, Garilon a few steps behind, and pointed into the blackness. "What did the scouts report about this shaft?"

"Nothing, Jarl. They're not back yet."

Vidar contemplated the darkness. "All the other scouts are back?"

"Yes, Jarl."

"Send the most rested group down this shaft to fetch them. I want everyone back here."

With a quick nod and a gesture, Garilon relayed the orders.

"What are you thinking, Jarl?"

Vidar didn't answer. He strode back down the too-smooth tunnel until he stood directly before the white blur. He looked at it from several different angles, crouching and looking up, looking sideways along it. The view didn't change—still that white, snowstorm blur.

All around the circumference of the portal, the mountain's bones bore the sharp marks of having been worked with wide chisels. He crab-stepped along in front of the barrier, staring at the floor, then rising to his feet to examine the wall and the ceiling as best as he could see above his head.

Why use chisels when they had the stone-shaper to hand? Assuming that's what the ironwood device was.

Hands on hips, he stared at the barrier. Except for within a knife's length of the barrier, the tunnel rock was as smooth as if water had flowed over it for centuries. So they used both.

But what was this barrier? How did it get here and how had the Jotunn found it?

He reached out to touch the white, swirling wall.

"Jarl!"

Vidar nodded sheepishly at Garilon. "You're right, of course. Hand me a spear, please."

He pushed it through the barrier with no more resistance than he might feel plunging the spear into a lake. Though it was dark on the other side, the spear had that bent-seeming quality of something viewed through water. He grunted and pulled the spear back.

The blade was frosted, icy cold to the touch. A bit of snow clung to the shaft. He grunted again, ground the butt, and stared at the swirling barrier. No, that wasn't right. The barrier wasn't swirling; it was clear. He was seeing snow behind it.

Moving quickly, he thrust his hand through the barrier.

"Jarl!"

"It's all right. I'm fine. It's cold. Very cold on the other side." He rotated his wrist, flexed his hand, and waggled his fingers. The same bent quality of water distorted the sight, but he felt nothing wrong. Just cold.

He took a breath, and then he stepped through.

Snow blinded him; cold attacked. He began shivering immediately. There was a vague sense of rock above him, but it felt more open ahead. He wrapped his arms around his chest and shuffled forward a few steps, feeling resistance around his lower legs. He was knee-deep in snow.

Another shuffling pair of steps forward, and the blowing snow parted long enough to glimpse a wide, white expanse beyond a stony roof. Then the wind whipped the snow back into his eyes.

He was shivering harder now. A thought struck him, and he spun around.

What if he couldn't just step back through?

He staggered back toward the barrier and saw Garilon beyond it, shouting down the smooth tunnel. He lunged back through the portal and landed on the hard rock, shaking and covered in snow.

Of course he could get back. What an idiot. How else had the Jotunn gotten here?

That thought almost drowned out Garilon's shout: "Quick, bring some cloaks!"

Then the kjolr thudded to his knees beside him. "Jarl, are you all right?"

He managed a nod and forced a smile past his chattering teeth. He had been completely wrong. There had been no spies among the folks of Háls—well, probably not. But this... doorway... explained why they hadn't found tracks or supplies or anything that might have betrayed the Jotunn presence.

"Beg your pardon, Jarl, but that was foolish," Garilon said.

He didn't bother trying to shrug, even though the shivering was slowing down. He could feel his smile growing. "The good news first? Or the bad?"

"The good news."

Vidar's trembling grin widened. "That's Utgard."

***

Vidar leaned in close to the barrier again. The air on this side didn't feel cold no matter how close he got to the barrier.

"If that being Utgard is the good news, Jarl, then what's the bad news?" Garilon's question hung in the air like smoke drifting up from a fire.

He met Garilon's eye. "We need to step across or through or however you want to say it and make sure I'm right. I know it sounds dangerous, but we have to. I have to."

He couldn't very well run back to Gladsheim without learning more. And, besides, this... threshold... was fascinating. How far did it extend through the rock around them? What had he stepped through between here and there?

"But how can that be Utgard?" Garilon asked, indicating the barrier with a quick jerk of his chin and taking a few steps back as he did. "We're deep beneath a mountain outside Háls, which is a night's fast ride northwest of Vithi, which is several nights' ride west of Gladsheim, which is itself several nights' ride south of Ifington and the Fortress of the Breach. And, the waters of the Thund lie between us and Utgard's ice cliffs and glaciers."

"I don't have an answer for you. That's why we must go through." Vidar spread his hands wide. "And consider that the Jotunn trail leads here—not just those few we've been chasing, but their entire warband. Inexplicable though this doorway is, its presence solves all the oddities we've been trying to explain using ships and the trade route. This must be how their warband got here. It's how they sent provisions. And it explains why no one saw or heard them crossing the hundreds of leagues between the Breach and Háls."

"It doesn't explain how this tunnel got here, Jarl," Garilon said. He stomped a booted foot against the smooth stone.

"That's simpler. I suspect Svartalvar devices were involved in its creation."

Garilon barked a laugh, then raised a hand. "Apologies, Jarl, I meant no offense. The Jotunn are one thing. Stepping into Utgard is another. But going ahead when the Svartalvar are involved..."

"Their devices, not them," he said, silently adding an *I hope*. "We don't need to worry about the Svartalvar. The Alfather took care of them. I suspect what we found—the device I was working on—is one of their shapers. What I don't understand is how this doorway got here. Or how the Jotunn even knew it was here."

Garilon's expression clouded with confusion. "A shaper?"

"You haven't seen my father use the one he has?"

"No, Jarl."

He held up his hands about a knife's length apart. "The Alvar fashion wands that shape living wood, making it flow and move like water. My guess is that the Svartalvar-crafted device I partially rebuilt did the same thing but for stone—which makes sense given their affinity with things dug from the earth."

Jotunn possession of a Svartalvar shaper probably also meant that they'd been in contact with each other. And if they had one such device, they obviously had more else this tunnel would never have been made.

"Could this stone shaper be used to make that doorway?" Garilon asked, gesturing at the barrier.

Now that was a very good question. "I doubt it. For one thing, and as you suggested before, there's no way this stone here connects directly anywhere in Utgard. Unless they tunneled all the way from there to here, which is absurd. And besides, I entered into a very short tunnel that leads directly outside—that's snow causing that blurry whiteness. For another, the shaper my father uses doesn't leave this barrier behind. He uses it to create a hollow space he can walk in. And then he closes it behind him. This stone shaper might work in the same way."

Stone wasn't alive, so perhaps the shaper could make the tunnel permanent. Maybe the Alvar wood shaper could, too, but his father had never used it that way.

"That all makes sense, I suppose, Jarl, but how did that doorway get there?"

He smiled and pointed triumphantly at Garilon. "Exactly. I have no idea. Except that I suspect I've encountered this phenomenon before without ever knowing it. Many times, actually."

"What?"

"Have you ever ridden down to Ithavoll?"

Garilon shook his head. "No, never."

"Atop Gladsheim's hill, there's a huge tree in Idunn's glade, near the temple. Beneath the tree, there's a path."

"I've been to the temple and seen the tree," Garilon said, nodding. "But never elsewhere."

"Doesn't matter. When the jarls meet at Ithavoll, we ride a path down into the hill itself, winding down and down until we emerge into an immense space. It's as if we were to walk out of this mine into the mountains. It's the same feeling. Yggdrasil grows in that place. But it can't be underground, because it just can't—it doesn't make sense. And believe me, I've tried to make sense of it. I've stood on the ramp and studied the stars, even convinced Thor to fly me around Yggdrasil in his cart. We never even reached the curve in its trunk."

He looked through the barrier and at the swirling snowstorm in what had to be Utgard. Unless it was somewhere else entirely. "But now that I see this barrier, I'm wondering if the same thing isn't at work beneath Gladsheim."

"I don't understand how that helps us now, Jarl."

"Eh?" He shook his head. "It doesn't, except if I'm right, passing through this barrier is perfectly safe. Though I suppose I just demonstrated that."

"Assuming there isn't a Jotunn warband on the other side."

"Well, there is that. But it's been more than a week now. If they were going to attack, they'd have done so."

"Unless they're still marshaling."

"All the more reason for us to go through, make sure that's *actually* Utgard and track down where the Jotunn came from. That's all good, solid information I can bring back."

Garilon's gaze shifted to the blurry white field beside them. He waved a hand in the air. "With respect, Jarl, how will you know it's Utgard? Maybe it's just a door to, I don't know, higher up in these same mountains. Or some other place in Asgard where it's snowing."

Vidar dropped one hand to his distaff, drumming his thumb on its grip. "That is possible. But one look at the clear night sky and I'll know either way. Even if it's not Utgard, just a different part of Asgard, that's vital information too. This doorway means the Jotunn can do something we can't and know things we don't."

Garilon's cheeks puffed out as he exhaled. He ran a hand across his head, rippling his graying hair.

"Talk to me, Garilon. What gives you pause?" A flicker of doubt ran through him. Should he have even asked his kjolr's opinion? He wasn't sure his father would have done the same.

"Your pardon, Jarl, but Utgard does. I've fought there, as you yourself have."

He had, on several occasions. Vidar raised a hand. "I know what you did during the Last War. I've no wish to lead my warband into death. But if the Jotunn can march through this doorway, they could turn this mine into a stronghold. I don't know why they haven't already, actually. But if they're planning it and we can stop it or provide warning to my father, that's all the more reason to go through."

"I understand that, Jarl. I do. It's just that our warriors aren't ready for what's on the other side of this...whatever this is." Garilon gestured with his chin at the shimmering wall. "They're loyal, willing, and brave, but they mustered out of the army for a reason. And the younger ones, well, they know which end of a spear is which, but to march into Utgard..."

"They did well enough against the Jotunn who razed Háls."

Garilon nodded. "They did, Jarl. You inspired them. But it was your magic that shielded them, and it was you who destroyed that warband."

He didn't miss Garilon's unspoken words. They both knew what had actually killed all those Jotunn. As he looked inward at her, he knew it could happen again if he let his control slip—which he wouldn't.

His jaw clenched and he looked at the swirling gray-white doorway. "Maybe they're not ready. But we're here. It'd be weeks before anyone else could get here—and by then, it could all be over. I'll go through alone if I must, but I'd rather have you and a willing warband at my back."

"Going alone won't happen, Jarl. When I took this post, you asked me to speak plainly. Your father often did."

Vidar felt as if he'd been struck with a hammer. His father had sought other's opinions? The Sigfather himself?

Garilon continued. "But if that's Utgard, the weather alone might kill us within a day, and we'd have learned nothing. Or worse yet, we'd have learned whatever it is but not be able to make it back."

"That's a chance we'll have to take. If it comes to it, we'll raise such a din with Vithi's horn that Heimdall won't have a choice but to pay attention."

"May I suggest then, Jarl, that we fortify where the mine shaft meets the cavern? That way, we'll have someplace to fall back to should things get rough on the other side."

Vidar nodded. "That makes sense. And pick four warriors to send back to the surface. They can then dispatch four from up top to relay word back to Vithi and then to Gladsheim."

Just in case.

"And you have my promise," he added, "I won't squander our lives."

But to himself alone he said, and I will do everything I can to learn how this doorway works and what actually lies over there.

57

Frigg

At a thud like a sack of barley hitting the ground, Frigg's gaze snapped down from the distant canopy of stars above Mimir's glade. Her husband lay on the ground.

The whites of Mimir's eyes rolled away, replaced by his familiar, sharp gray eyes. In a hoarse, urgent voice, Mimir said, "Quick, help him."

She pushed herself up and stumbled toward Odin. He lay on his side, water from Mimir's little waterfall splashing against him.

"Check his head," Mimir said.

She grabbed Odin's shoulder and rolled him gently toward her. He flopped over limply. One side of his face was a bleeding ruin.

She fought down the shock—he'd said it could be dangerous—but she hadn't expected this. He hadn't been so injured since...several nights ago when he'd fought the spirit from the well.

"Sword wound," Mimir said. "Draugr's bone weapon. The thing was deadly. Odin was lucky."

She grabbed Odin under the armpits and, grunting with the effort, dragged him out from under Mimir. She propped his head up on his discarded cloak.

"Frigg, cut some rags and bring them to me," Mimir said. "Quickly."

Heart pounding from hauling Odin the short distance, she glanced back toward the bubbling pool even as she slipped her slender knife from its sheath. What could she do if that spirit rose now or sent the draugr after her? She didn't even know if that was possible. And why had Odin fought draugr? She cut off the sleeves of her dress, the wet fabric twisting and bunching under the knife.

"Good. Come here, but get more cloth first," Mimir said. Then he opened wide to let water pool in his mouth.

The bottom third of her dark red dress fell victim to her knife's bright, narrow blade. When she'd torn it free, she brought all the rags to Mimir. A smell like burning pine and stewing apples assaulted her nose, making her want to sneeze.

Not sure what to do, she lifted her hands toward Mimir's wet, withered skin, which was entirely covered in fine runes of varying sizes. His thick gray hair was plastered against his skull. He looked right at her, winked, and then spat the water onto the proffered cloth.

She recoiled, anger bubbling up. Even in a time like this, Mimir was disgusting.

"Oh, stop it. It's the fastest way to transfer some of the effect of the charms keeping me alive to the rag. Hold that cloth higher." Then his mouth snapped shut, and after a moment, he spat again.

Rags drenched, she stepped back to Odin and began cleaning the gore from his face. He moaned quietly, his hands flexing and twitching each time she gently pressed around his cheek and eye, then moving up to wipe around the wound's raw edges.

Gradually, she revealed his forehead's ruin. He'd been cut to the bone, and it looked like his skull was itself scored, maybe even broken. His skin was swollen and bruised; blood flowed freely. She packed the wet cloth against the wound and applied pressure.

"How bad is it?" Mimir asked.

"Pretty bad. What happened?"

"A draugr stabbed him in the face."

She threw an angry glance at him.

He blinked. "Oh." He quirked his lips, which she realized was his version of shrugging. "It was a trap. Both for me and him. I suppose I was the bait."

She wiped her red, wet hands on her dress, picked up her slender-bladed knife and cut more cloth from her dress's shrinking hem. She sheathed her knife, undid her belt, whipped it through the sheath's loops, and then dropped both belt and blade to the ground. She gathered the fresh rags in her hands and stepped back to Mimir. "More water."

Moments later, she was back at Odin's side, removing the bloodied compresses and tossing them into the stream below Mimir. She set the new ones in place, snatched up her belt, and ran it around his head, cinching the compresses against his wound.

"Looking any better?" Mimir asked.

She laughed, short and sharp. "Better? I suppose. The bleeding and swelling have slowed, but the bone feels broken. I need to get him to Baldr."

"You're on your own there," Mimir said.

Frigg threw another angry glare at him.

"What? How am I supposed to help?"

Of course he couldn't. And she couldn't move Odin alone. "How did this even happen? You were both spirits."

"What happens to the spirit happens to the flesh," Mimir said, as if that explained everything.

She sighed and rubbed her eyes, shifting so she sat cross-legged to ease the growing ache in her knees.

"He fought draugr, like I said. And they were all wielding bone blades. When made right, those can cut spirit as easily as flesh."

She opened her eyes and looked at Mimir. "None of this makes any sense. Why were you captured? By whom? Where were you held? And why were draugr there?"

"I can't answer all of that for certain," he said, blinking to clear streaming water from his eyes. "But I know where I was."

"And where was that?"

Odin groaned and tried to sit up as he woke.

She put a restraining hand on his shoulder. "Lay still."

Odin moved his head slightly and winced, lids drooping back down again.

"Help me lean against the root." He pressed his hands into the wet, flattened grasses around them. He pushed himself up, trying to hold his head steady and grimacing as he did, his face grayish green.

She frowned but helped him move backward. His face grew grayer with every heartbeat, even as the rags tied to his head reddened. She ran a hand tenderly across his dark hair.

Once he was settled, she said, "Let me change those rags out now. You're not looking well. I think that sword cracked your skull."

He reached up and touched the rags around his head. "These were soaked in the waters?"

She nodded.

"Apparently, the healing charms I cut into Mimir's flesh can be transferred to others. At least somewhat."

"And they'd probably work better if you'd be still," she said.

He gave a small shrug of assent and winced. "So, Uncle, Angrbo-da's house?"

"Why not wait a bit until some color comes back into your face? You look more like your uncle than you should," she said, pressing gently down on his shoulder.

Mimir sighed. "Angrboda's house."

⁂

Frigg hugged her knees. Angrboda had been Loki's first wife. They'd had three children, all of whom had been banished from Gladsheim because of a doom foreseen by the Norns. After that exile, Angrboda had declared herself divorced from Loki and vanished deep into the Iron Wood. After a little while, perhaps ten years, she'd died. It was one of those topics that was never mentioned.

"So, you were trapped in Angrboda's house?"

Odin had slipped back into unconsciousness. His color had improved to a yellowish gray and his lips were a bloodless line.

Perhaps she should just try to fetch Sleipnir now. It's a good thing they'd brought the big mare rather than simply flown down here as they often did.

"Indeed. It was a clever trap, first for me and then for him," Mimir said.

She looked up at Mimir. "Set by whom? Was it that thing that attacked Odin before?"

"I don't know what you're referring to. Odin didn't have a chance to explain. The draugr attacked right after he found me. What attacked Odin?"

She nodded and laid a hand on Odin's cheek. "Before Ithavoll, several nights ago, he rode down alone to first speak with the Norns—"

"And wasted his time, right?"

She nodded again. "He said he stared down into Urdr's well. Something came up—I saw it—and he said, Odin I mean, said that it had lured him...his spirit...down into the well. But Odin resisted and turned back. That's when whatever is below us attacked him. Nearly killed him."

Mimir pursed his lips. "Aha, that's interesting. There is a dark place underneath us into which Yggdrasil extends her roots. Or maybe it exists because of Yggdrasil's roots. Either way, it's there. And it's not a place I go. Not anymore."

"But something does live down there?" She hugged herself and glanced back over one shoulder at the bubbling pool, as if the very thing they were talking about would choose right then to appear.

"Yes. I don't know what it is, but I've seen its effects on Yggdrasil. Rot and decay have spread throughout her trunk and branches. Maybe it's that thing below, or maybe it's something else. I can't say for certain because—like my nephew who is, apparently, smarter than he looks—I've always fled when I sensed it stalking me."

"So is this thing below the one threatening Baldr? The Norns told us once, told Odin—"

"I know what they told him. I believe the gift you and Odin gave

to Baldr at his birth prevented the death they foresaw. It also probably caused Hodr's blinding, but—"

His words hit her like Thor's hammer. She and Odin had caused
Hodr's blinding?

"Stop, Mimir. What do you mean?"

He flashed a quick grin. "Baldr should have died when that snow
bear spat venom on him. It was a matron. It would've killed any one
of us."

"But Baldr didn't die because we protected him."

"And where did that stream of venom go?"

Right into Hodr's face and burned his eyes from his head. Guilt
leaped over the gunwales of her grief.

She had done it. She had saved Baldr only to blind Hodr.

"You couldn't have known, Frigg. And it's just an idea that we can't
prove. Maybe Hodr would've been blinded in some other way, if it
was his doom to be blinded. But never mind me, I shouldn't have
even said anything."

Never mind? She stared down at her hands, stained with Odin's
blood. No, she couldn't have known—unless she had thought to ask
what else would happen because of her choices. Unlike the Norns
she could only glimpse the future. If she could see more, though,
maybe she could have…. No, that wasn't true. She'd tried to change
the dooms she'd foreseen, but those she'd sought to help had still
died in the manner she'd foreseen. Unless, it was her choices, her
actions, that had set those dooms in motion.

"No," she said, "I don't believe that. I won't believe it."

"What's that?" Mimir asked.

"You're saying that our choices don't matter."

"No, Frigg," Mimir said, a sad expression on his wet face. "I'm
saying that we might not have any choice at all."

If that were true, then she wasn't responsible for Hodr's blinding.
But then she also wasn't responsible for anything good, either. She
couldn't believe that. She would not. Odin wouldn't, either.

Nor did dwelling on any of it do any good. She had to focus on
problems she might be able to fix. If that were possible.

"So, Mimir, tell me again how you got trapped in Angrboda's house."

A light smile that stopped just short of mocking her graced his lips. She fought the urge to knock his head into the pool.

"Black worms erupted from the ground and attacked me—simple to avoid, but they were the distraction. The real threat was a warped bit of root. The worms herded me, and before I realized what was happening, the roots peeled off the ground and ceiling and tangled around me."

"And you couldn't leave?"

"No. The tree's roots were magicked. They kept me from leaving," he said. "And every night, the draugr emerged. The first few nights they tried to kill me, but the worms kept them away. Then they stopped."

"I'm confused. The worms and roots were the trap? Or the draugr?"

"I think the draugr were just there, maybe part of Angrboda's coven. The trap for me was certainly the worms and the roots. Regardless, I was held prisoner before a set of shelves that Angrboda or maybe one of her witches had cut into the wall."

This was getting harder to follow by the moment. "Shelves? Mimir, I don't see how—"

"There were six recessed shelves, each with a different symbol carved in oak," he continued, ignoring her. "The first was a wolf sitting upright. The second was a sleeping serpent coiled around itself. The third was a woman, judging by its shapeliness."

That was obvious enough. "So, carvings of Angrboda's three children?"

"Yes, and believe me, I had plenty of time to inspect them. Though I do wonder how long I was there." He rolled his eyes and under his breath said, "Not that it matters, since this is the joy I return to."

She held up a hand. "So you went looking for the origin of Baldr's dreams and ended up trapped inside Angrboda's house?"

"Yes."

"I still don't understand." Angrboda had every reason to hate Odin. But Baldr? Baldr had still been in her belly when Angrboda's children had been exiled. If Angrboda were somehow involved or behind it all—and she was dead now—then that begged the question: What role had Loki played? He'd submitted to the exile of his children, but only after Odin had made sure that Loki heard the prophecy from the Norns' lips.

"I don't either, yet, but if you'd allow me to finish?"

"Of course, Uncle. My apologies."

"Thank you. Now there were several other carvings, too. One was a cauldron. I'm guessing it was the Roaring Cauldron itself since, well, I don't see why a regular pot would be included in a ritual, if that's what this was, except if one—"

"Uncle...."

Mimir cleared his throat. "Of course. On the top left shelf rested a finely woven net—the only one that wasn't a carving—and nets are usually one of Rán's symbol. The top right carving looked like a fang. I don't think it was a wolf fang, since Fenrir was already represented, nor was it her other son, Jorm, for the same reason. Probably."

"So the fang refers to something else, then?" she asked. "And is there a reason why you're telling me all this?"

"Because I think it was a spell, focused by, empowered by, the symbols and what they represent," he said, triumph in his voice.

Her stomach clenched. Was this, then, the origin of Baldr's dreams? Angrboda was behind it all? She'd certainly hated Odin enough, but the timing was all wrong. Not only was Angrboda a hundred winters dead, but Baldr's mistletoe had been recently cut.

"Was there any mistletoe in this shrine?"

"Not that I saw," Mimir said. "Why do you ask?"

"Because the heart of Baldr's mistletoe had been cut out. Recently. We discovered it right before we rode down to see you. Odin said that was why Baldr was having those dreams."

Mimir pursed his lips and closed his eyes. She averted her gaze from the livid red runes cut into his eyelids. "No, I don't recall any mistletoe. It didn't look like anyone had even been in the longhouse —or that section of it, at least—for a very long time."

"You're sure you didn't see any?"

"Yes. I agree with Odin—these episodes of Baldr's are likely a result of his mistletoe being cut. Whoever did it physically removed a large portion of his spirit. That he's still alive suggests they haven't destroyed it."

She heard the unspoken 'yet' in his tone.

Then Mimir carried on as if he hadn't just contemplated the death of her son. "No, I believe I was looking at an old spell. And at the center of the design, where you put the spell's target, was an arm ring of gold. It was dusty and begrimed, but I recognized it. I'm sure you will, too. One end had a pair of raven heads, and the other—"

"A pair of wolf heads." She glanced down at Odin's right wrist even as her fingers traced the heavy coil of gold that looped around her own arm. "Draupnir?"

"Draupnir."

Why would Angrboda use Draupnir to target the spell? All the jarls wore a copy of Draupnir as both a mark of their loyalty to the Alfather and their status. Angrboda had worn one herself, before she'd flung it at Odin.

"Wouldn't a charm with Draupnir as its focus target everyone wearing the ring? And what was the spell supposed to do?"

"I don't know, and yes," Mimir said. "In reverse order. The fang statue was in the spot where you'd place the spirit being entreated. The rest of the carvings were to ground the caster, to show their reason for making contact, so to speak, and provide additional power, beyond whatever witchthread the witch used to create the spell in the first place. Figuring out what that fang symbolizes is the first step in puzzling out the spell's effect."

"And how are we supposed to do that?"

Odin spoke, his voice a startling, angry rasp. "I'm going to drag Angrboda's spirit out of the Gap and ask her."

***

Frigg tightened her belt around the freshly wetted rags and brushed her hand across her husband's cheek. Then she leaned in, kissed him, and made to stand. "I'll go get Sleipnir now."

"How's it look?" he asked, his voice tight with restrained anger.

It was no wonder he was angry. If Angrboda were involved somehow in all of this, what did that say about Loki? It certainly had looked as if he'd put his past behind him by marrying Sigyn and having children with her, but Loki was as inscrutable as her husband.

"Better, but I think these waters have done about all they can," she said. She waggled her fingers, miming what he did while singing one of his charms. "Couldn't you just..."

"Heal myself?" He shook his head and tapped his satchel. "I could, but I used the last of my power on Baldr this morning."

"You don't carry extra spindles?"

"I do, but I used them all, first getting to Vidar and saving him, then saving Baldr." He opened his eyes and grinned weakly. "It's been a busy week."

True enough. Nor was she fooled by his grin. The wicked glimmer of anger was too visible in his eyes.

He dug in his satchel, withdrew the shaper, and set it in her hands. "I've called to Sleipnir. She'll be right outside this glade."

"You'll be all right here while I do that?"

"What could go wrong?" He gestured at Mimir. "Besides, I have my uncle to watch over me."

She kissed him again, impatient to get moving now that he was awake again. "All right. Just rest. I'll be back shortly."

He smiled again and closed his eyes. "Be sure to hold the shaper high when you bring Sleipnir through. And push hard against the root. The tree pushes back."

Doesn't everything?

58

Odin

Angrboda. Loki's first wife. Witch. Mother of three monsters who, the Norns said, would someday cause the death of the Aesir. But they hadn't said why or how, and Loki's three children were just newly born when the Norns spoke their prophecy.

Odin had taken Loki to the Norns so that he could learn for himself what lay ahead for his children—the doom of the Aesir. Loki's expression on hearing those words was still etched into his memory. Shock. Anguish. Anger. Yet as he'd turned to face Odin, hope had burned in his face like the summer sun.

But had it been hope?

He'd thought so at the time. It had not been fear. Loki didn't fear anything. Loki had grabbed his shoulders, his hands hotter than his intent gaze, and simply said, "Please. There has to be another way."

Loki hadn't invoked their oath of brotherhood, which lay between them like the blood price covering Otr's corpse. But how could he have kept that blood oath if doing so meant the future destruction of the Aesir?

So they stood before the Norns, their old, well-tested vow conflicting with this future doom. He didn't say anything to Loki. He didn't need to. His blood brother was completely aware of his turmoil. It was as plain on Loki's face, as it must have been on his own.

He didn't break his oath. Instead, he bent it. Rather than kill his brother's babies because of the Norns' prophecy, he let them grow up, hoping—foolishly, as it turned out—that because Loki and Angrboda knew the prophecy, they could steer their children from that doom.

Besides, he had reasoned, he could always kill them later. But you could never unbreak a jug.

With each passing winter, the three children had grown increasingly monstrous. And every Midwinter, he and Loki returned to the Norns and asked again for the prophecy. It never changed. Many of his jarls bent his ear, urging him to do what the Norns bid.

He resisted their counsel for a long time, but once Loki's children nearly reached their full growth, he knew he had to act. Loki had known it, too.

Even now, the memory of Loki's face was fresh—his friend's eyes bright with unshed tears and his hands, hotter than forge-tongs, gripping his shoulders.

Again, he bent his oath. He merely banished the three children. The three monsters. Two he'd bound with his power, but the oldest, Fenrir, shook off his charms like dust. Trickery and Svartalvar craftsmanship eventually prevailed, though not without cost.

Loki had said he understood, that the Norns were as cruel as they were kind. And then he asked a boon: to know the way to his children.

Of course he'd shown Loki how to reach his children. How could he not? It was a small thing to grant, considering he'd just robbed his blood brother of his children.

It wasn't until many winters later, after Hodr's blinding, that he'd begun to distrust what the Norns said. Kneeling here now, wounded and bleeding, he wondered if he should have distrusted their prophecy about Loki's children.

Unlike her husband, Angrboda had never accepted her children's exile. She never forgave him, either. But what mother truly forgave any injury done to her child? Within ten winters of her children's exile, Angrboda rejoined the Gap, shrieking with hatred for him.

And yet Loki had forgiven him?

Did that make sense?

He conjured up the memory of Loki's blazing-hot hands on his shoulders. He saw it from afar, like he'd climbed a longship's tall mast and he was trying to figure out if the ship on the horizon was friend or foe even as Sól set behind it.

As he focused on the memory, fingers pushing hard on his temples, ignoring his pounding head wound, a bit of sound shook loose, the wet thwack of rope on sail. It was Loki speaking to him, but he couldn't make out the words.

He splashed cool water from Mimir's spring upon his face. Immediately, the memory clarified. Loki spoke: *I can't stop you, Ygg. We both know that. Yet I'm strong enough to do this.*

The memory skipped and sputtered, water on a pan. He splashed more water on his face and he swam into cool shadows beneath a darkening sky. The memory of Loki's voice returned...

Oath breaker! I saw it in your eyes. You would have murdered my children, had I not convinced you to exile them. And on the word of those crones? How many boons have I brought to the Aesir? How many humiliations have I suffered? How much mockery? I'll endure more, "Brother," since I can't stop you. But I will have my revenge—maybe not within a tenspan of winters. Or maybe even a hundred. But I will have it. And I say this knowing that someday you'll pierce this veil I draw over your memories. I will free my children. And when I do, we will destroy everything you've built. We will set such a fire to your works that the heavens themselves will burn.

With a gasp, Odin flung himself back from the bubbling spring. He thudded against the grass and his head pounded, both from his wound and the utter horror of his own blindness. His own stupidity. How could he not have remembered this?

"Odin! What is it?"

He was so lost in himself that it took a moment before he recognized Mimir's voice.

"It's Loki, Uncle," he said, his voice sounding dead and horrified even to his own ears.

"What?"

He pushed himself up and faced Mimir. "Loki. He's behind all of this."

"Behind what?"

"The trap you were caught in—and those draugr."

"That's absurd. He doesn't have the power to trap me, let alone you."

"I'm not so sure. He set a charm on me that I've only now broken. He swore to destroy everything I've built—because I exiled his children. And you were caught in his wife's house."

Mimir stared back at him, eyes thoughtful.

"He said I broke my oath of brotherhood with him. I had told him I could not—would not—trade the future of the Aesir for three lives."

A frown creased Mimir's face. "The Norns' prophecy put you in an impossible situation, Odin. You bent as far as you could while accommodating your loyalty to Loki."

"In this memory, Loki said that the exile was his idea, that I'd intended to kill his children."

"Only you can say if that's true."

Was it? He cast back through his memory, but the events and words and faces were like dappled sunlight on a forest floor. He shook his head, and the wound across his forehead flared like sunlight on spears...and then the pounding began. He gritted his teeth, trying to think clearly despite the pain.

"Maybe there was another way out of the doom the Norns foretold. I've since learned the tricks they play with words."

"They do," Mimir said. "But their prophecies also come true, as we all learned with Baldr."

Odin glanced down at the rippling water and then back up at his uncle. "But they didn't say Hodr would lose his sight *because* we protected Baldr. They only said that to save Baldr, we'd have to protect him. It was Frigg's idea to set his spirit in the mistletoe."

"Perhaps Hodr was doomed to lose his sight no matter what you did to protect Baldr. All that happened was how the events played out. Or maybe—"

"Hodr was never meant to be blind, but by protecting Baldr we traded one tragedy for another." Or was it that he'd been told about Baldr's potential death as a way to get him and Frigg to use that old Jotunn magic to protect him? If the Norns could see what would happen to Baldr, then they could certainly see how they'd choose to protect him. But why would that matter—and how did it make any more sense than the other explanation?

He splashed more water in his face and let it soak into the bandage on his head and run through his hair and down his back. But the pounding, the hammering, continued.

Mimir seemed to understand what he was thinking. "It's impossible to see how all events unfold. Maybe there are multiple routes to the same doom and we just get to pick between them without ever realizing what choices we're making. Or, as I said to Frigg, perhaps we have no choice at all."

Impossible. No ability to choose? He refused to believe that. If he knew more, he could pick better paths. The Norns saw the paths. Why not him?

There were many ways across a sea. Some past great floes of ice, others on warm currents to lush islands. The more he sailed, the more routes he knew. The same must be true of the future. The more he knew, the better the path—and thus the better doom. And if that weren't true, he'd make it that way. He shaped his future, no one else.

He shook his head, laughed despite the hammer pounding against his skull, and leaned over the spring to stare at his bandaged, bloody reflection, distorted by the ripples. All his power, all his sacrifices, himself to himself, had clearly not been enough.

"What are you thinking, Odin?" Mimir asked, a wary note in his voice.

"Just that nothing I've done is enough. Hanging upon the tree wasn't enough. Seizing the runes and commanding the dead and learning seidr and mastering all those charms you taught me, Uncle —none of it's enough."

"Much of it has helped. You brought me back—"

"To a life that you hate."

"Yes, but what I see helps you, helps our people."

Odin snorted.

"Do you trust these new memories, Odin? I watched you splash water on your face. Frigg told me of the trouble you had with the creature who calls them home."

He looked up at his uncle's wizened, tattooed head, dripping wet, long gray hair clinging to Yggdrasil's bark. Could he even trust Mimir, immersed as he was? If that thing below the well could nearly destroy him, surely manipulating his uncle's mind—as well as his own—was also possible.

But if that were true, he couldn't trust anyone or anything. The fruit that kept them young came from Yggdrasil, and its roots drank from these same waters.

No. Nothing was that powerful. Not Aegir. Not Rán. And if not them, then certainly not some creature lashing out at him from the dark.

Even so, he'd been a blind, stupid fool. Had he been charmed by Loki? Or had it been this...serpent...from the waters? Neither was preferable. Both alternatives meant that he'd been weak-minded. Blind.

He laughed again, mocking himself. He *had* been blind? No, he **was** blind.

His gaze lingered on Frigg's slender knife, still lying where she'd dropped it by the spring.

He stared down past his distorted image into the cool waters that had seemingly brought clarity. If those memories were false, he needed to see through them, too. If he couldn't trust this place, he'd have to reclaim it.

Pain flared in his side where the spear had bitten. That had been his first true sacrifice, himself to himself; there had been many since then. He and Frigg continued to give up unlived years to preserve Baldr. Just like the eyes Hodr had given up unwittingly so that his brother would live.

Tyr had given his hand; Freyja, her body; Freyr, his sword.

What had he given? Not enough.

He snatched up Frigg's blade and bared it.

"Odin, what are you doing?" The worried note was back in Mimir's voice.

Don't worry, Uncle. Hodr gave his sight. Tyr gave his hand. He would give an eye so that he might see more clearly.

With one hand, he pulled his eyelids back. With his other, he raised the slender blade. A part of him tried to shrink back from the approach of the cold skymetal, but he grabbed that cowardly fragment of his mind and held it steady. Just like his hand and the unwavering blade.

"Odin, stop!" Mimir shouted hoarsely, the death scrabble of a man's heels upon stone. "Frigg! Get back here now!"

He didn't flinch when the cold blade touched the tender skin just below his eye. But in that chilly instant, his inner coward almost won, almost made him fling the blade far away.

Myself to myself.

I shape my own doom.

The slender blade's first cut was a nibble. The second, well, he hauled in a ragged, shaking breath. Guided by his own distorted reflection, he cut true. And he did not scream.

Not when the blade bit deep nor when the blood flowed or when sharp skymetal severed his eye's root and it popped free. Nor did he scream when he held his slick orb in the palm of one hand.

His blood pattered on the crushed grass beneath his knees and then dripped into the pool, red ripples spread outward. His empty socket pounded like one of Bragi's largest drums, but the beat was a friend to the agony that visited him when he'd pushed the spear through his own ribs.

From outside himself he looked down at the bloody white-and-gray orb in his hand, but he did not scream. Soon he would see more with it outside his flesh than when it had been a part of him.

Holding the slender blade steady, he cut the rune for "life" into the back of his eye. He whispered the rune word and breathed upon his eye, giving of his own life so that the rune would live and would, in turn, give life to his dead eye.

Then he cast his sacrifice into the waters.

He didn't scream when it splashed into the water. He watched it sink, spinning slowly, trailing blood, the hair of a drowning man. Hot coppery blood pooled in his mouth. When his eye struck the pool's gravelly bottom, he spoke the rune again.

His sacrifice flared golden and took root. Only then did Odin scream.

59

Frigg

A scream like a snow bear at bay echoed through Ithavoll. Frigg knew it was Odin. A thousand questions ran through her mind, but with her hand on the shaper, she had to stay focused. The tree fought the shaper's magic as she made a tunnel big enough for both her and the massive Sleipnir who docilely walked behind her, huge head hanging low to pass through.

At last, Mimir's glade opened before her. Hands trembling, sweat running into her eyes, she said, "Go, Sleipnir, quickly."

Eight hooves pounded the grasses flat, and then Sleipnir stopped to wait for her. She slipped out, made sure her body was clear, and removed the shaper's tip from the root. The tunnel became a hole, then a deep dimple in the wood, and then it vanished.

Mimir called to her. "Hurry, Frigg, he's not responding. I think his face is in the water."

Shaper still in one hand, she sprinted to Mimir. A puzzling clump of dead leaves, brown and tan, lay beside the pool beneath Mimir. Her mind reeled at the sight. The fresh scent of broken grass mingled with the metallic tang of spilled blood.

With a bowstring snap, everything became recognizable. Odin was the lump of browns and tans.

She rolled him onto his back. The ragged wound where his eye had been gaped, and she recoiled as if she'd seen a snake. Blood wept from his empty black socket.

Odin drew in a hissing breath and coughed.

"Frigg, it's all right," Mimir said. "He did it to himself. Just drag him free and pack the wound."

"But—"

"Look at me, Frigg," Mimir said.

She dragged her eyes away from her husband's ravaged face. Looking up at Mimir was hardly better. Blue and red tattoos glistened in the watery light, and lichens clung to his long gray beard. "I don't understand. He was fine. Why wou—"

"Frigg," Mimir snapped like a tree branch.

Of course. Time enough later for why.

She grabbed Odin by the ankles and pulled him back from the pool's edge to lean against the brown root, just as he had before. The left side of his face was a black-red, swollen ruin.

She had to get him back to Baldr. But first, pack the wound.

"Frigg, stop for a moment and listen."

She flung herself to where she'd left the rags of her dress soaking in the pool right beside where she'd found Odin.

"Frigg, I wouldn't—"

An unblinking gray eye stared up at her. She gave a hoarse yell and staggered back from the gently rippling waters, hands coming up to cover her mouth and nose.

"Will you stop now?" Mimir said, his voice stony.

Had he been attacked again? She hadn't been gone that long. Had it been the spirit again? Or maybe that draugr had, in fact, followed him back.

"He carved out his eye, cut a rune into it, then cast it into the spring," Mimir said flatly. "He was mumbling, raving about having been blind, that he'd never be blind again. He used a magic similar to what he used on me."

"He cut out his own eye?" She didn't like how incredulous her voice sounded.

"I tried to stop him, but..." Mimir waggled his eyebrows in that odd, shrugging way.

Of course he couldn't stop Odin. She couldn't have, either. Had he intended to do this all along? Had he sent her for Sleipnir on purpose?

"But why?"

"He seems to think Loki's behind everything. That Loki threatened him in a memory he dredged up."

Her thoughts whirled like leaves on the wind. Behind all of what? The attack on Háls? Baldr's dreams? Did it even make sense for Loki to be behind everything? That he wasn't around now wasn't unusual – Loki had been a rare presence in Gladsheim since Odin had left. It was a little odd that Loki had not returned to greet his blood brother, but this time of year Loki always visited his three exiled children.

And threatening Odin didn't make sense, either. Loki didn't posture or threaten or warn. He just attacked, much like Odin. That's actually how everyone knew when Loki was joking, however malicious his mischief. If you walked away, then Loki hadn't intended harm...though sometimes harm came anyway.

Loki's prank against Heimdall was a good example. Loki had taught some bright-green birds in Vanaheim how to say Loki's name. Then they took to repeating it over and over—which had been the point. Annoy Heimdall. But who could've guessed those birds would teach others in their flock, and presumably their offspring, until the forests rang with HAME-DALL, HAME-DALL.

Loki had effectively deafened Heimdall, which led to the watchman drinking himself into insensibility...which effectively blinded him, as well. But Loki couldn't have known his small mischief would end up causing so much harm.

"But what made him do this?" She pointed at Odin's wrecked face "What did you say to him?"

"Me? Nothing. I tried to talk him out of it. He wasn't interested in listening to me any more than you seem to be right now."

She held Mimir's gaze for a long moment, then raised her hands, palms out. Mimir was right. She wasn't thinking.

She kneeled beside the pool, ignoring the naked eye staring at her, wrung out the remains of her dress, and brought them to Mimir.

Again, he soaked them with more healing water spat from his mouth. Again, she whipped her brown belt around Odin's head and cinched it tight, holding the compress in place. Again, again, again.

She sat back on her heels and tucked loose hair behind her ears. "All right, Uncle, what did he say about Loki being involved?"

"He said Loki charmed him long ago—before, after, or during the whole sorry mess with Loki's children. I'm not clear what he meant. He was a little unhinged."

Unhinged? His cut out his own eye.

"Did he say anything about what exactly Loki was supposed to be behind?"

Mimir pursed his lips and looked upward, clearly trying to remember. "All he said was that Loki had sworn to destroy everything he—meaning Odin—had built. Vengeance for breaking his blood oath by exiling his children."

She stared down at Odin, not really seeing of the slow rise and fall of his chest...and refusing to look again at the pool of water. The fresh scent of crushed grass and spilled blood made twisted knots of her stomach.

Her spies among the Jotunn had confirmed everything Baldr had witnessed in Jotunheim. The Jotunn were dying. They had a few warbands which did not pose a threat to Gladsheim's armies or the Einherjar, let alone the two forces combined.

Still, Heimdall's crippling had made it easier for the Jotunn to launch a successful surprise attack. That attack meant that either the Skrymir had been lying all this time—which wasn't impossible—or that Loki had allied himself with the tribe that had destroyed Háls. Which also wasn't impossible.

Either could be true...and both could be. Perhaps Loki had intended to cripple Heimdall.

So why would the Skrymir allow an attack when he had to know how severe retribution would be? And why would Loki ally himself with the tribe?

And yet they still didn't know how the warband had gotten to Háls. Vidar hadn't reported back, and with Heimdall in his current state, Odin would probably have to send his ravens and wolves to Vidar.

Which left Baldr's dreams.

Nobody beyond herself and Odin knew of Baldr's tree and mistletoe, not even Baldr. Yet it had been cut. Which meant that somebody did know.

Was that somebody Loki? He could shapeshift. He could have followed her or impersonated someone she trusted. But she never spoke about Baldr's secret—and she always, always, slipped away at night to bury the fruits at Baldr's tree.

Maybe it was Angrboda who'd learned the secret. Odin and Mimir could walk as spirits, as could Freyja and who knew how many Jotunn shamans and witches, so why not her, as well.

Her eyes strayed to the waters that hid Odin's eye. And what of that creature from Urdarbrunnr? What role did it play in all this?

"What are you thinking, Frigg?" Mimir asked.

She frowned at the wizened head. "That until I get my husband back to Baldr, I won't get any answers."

She clucked her tongue and beckoned for Sleipnir to approach. The huge mare lifted her head from grazing and walked over. Frigg squatted beside Odin, grabbed him under the arms and lifted him. Heart pounding in her ears, muscles screaming, she dragged Odin toward Sleipnir. Her breath rasped in her lungs, but she got him beside the big horse.

"Sleipnir...kneel."

Sleipnir lowered herself awkwardly, front four legs bending so that her forequarters and shoulders were roughly even with Frigg's chest.

Muscles burning, Frigg pressed Odin against the mare's shoulder, braced him with her body so he didn't slip too far down. With a gasp, she squatted and pushed him up. His shoulder caught on the saddle.

She swore and changed her footing so she could push him up at an
angle. Sleipnir leaned away, trying to make it easier. Frigg squatted
again and heaved until she got his shoulder past the saddle and then
his stomach above the bulge of Sleipnir's thick shoulders.

"Up, Sleipnir," she said. She struggled to hold his body in place as
the mare slowly stood. When the big mare was up on all eight legs
again, with Odin slung like a blanket across her withers. Frigg staggered back and wiped her brow.

"Better lash him to the saddle," Mimir said.

She glared at him, breath still heavy.

"Just trying to help," he said, waggling his brows. "After I sleep, I'll
send my spirit out and look for Loki, though he's quite good at hiding.
When my nephew wakes, have him send his ravens down. I'll tell
them whatever I find."

She nodded once. "Thank you, Uncle."

Then she stepped back to Sleipnir and dug through the saddlebags for some rope.

Like gnats in the summer, too many unanswered questions
worried her thoughts. She was certain of one thing, though: she
would not be played for a fool. Not by anyone. If the Skrymir was
truly behind the deaths of all those men and women in Háls, then
she'd have Tyr and Ullr take Jotunheim apart piece by moldering
piece. And if Loki were involved, well, she'd make sure he paid, as
well.

And regardless of what Mimir had suggested about future events
being as fixed as whatever the Norns cut into the chips of Yggdrasil's
bark, whosoever should harm Baldr would pay dearly.

60

Vafthrudnir

An arrowhead of black clouds, lightning flickering among them, hurtled toward the Jotunn village where he'd hoped to rest for the day. Vafthrudnir spread gray wings and launched himself back into the air.

Several nights earlier, when he was with Helveg, he had stepped through a doorway into a distant land wrapped in a deep winter, just like Utgard. But that land appeared fertile, unlike Utgard, where only dwindling patches of healthy land still existed.

Lightning flashed.

And so it appeared that Ygg had sent the Thunderer against them. As expected. And, of course, his own route back to Helveg happened to cross the town Thor had chosen to destroy.

After he'd used the stars to locate the doorway's distant exit—many of the stars were unfamiliar, but others were not—and after he explored the immediate vicinity, he stepped back through into Utgard. Then flew back toward Jotunheim to meet up with Helveg.

Which had led him here.

Thunder rumbled toward him, cart wheels against stone.

If he hurried, he might still help the villagers to safety.

***

He was too late. Smoke's black curls were already rising above the trees. Thunder gnashed the air like a goat's teeth above the peak into which the villagers had driven their mine shafts. He could just make out the Thunderer, made small by the distance, astride his flying cart with the storm dragging along behind him like a whipped hound.

Lightning blasted from the Thunderer's upraised fist. A dozen ragged tendrils of fire leaped into the forest below his circling cart.

The crash of the sky reached Vafthrudnir a dozen heartbeats later. At the smell of burning wood, he knew he needed to take shelter somewhere. He folded his wings and dove toward the snow-laden treetops below, then toward the valley's walls, hoping to find a boulder or cave. Dry as it was, the forest wouldn't be safe.

The sky flickered and thunder crashed again, the sound bouncing off the valley's walls. Then he was blinded by a brilliant flash of white light. A heartbeat later, the air convulsed and flung him downward, tumbling.

Instinctively he shape-shifted into a long-armed, brown-haired creature like those he'd seen in Alvheim. His vision cleared in time to glimpse the bare forest below, branches rattling against each other like bones, approaching too quickly.

The air roared past him, hot, wet, and filled with debris. He was cut a dozen times—legs, chest, arms—and blood flowed.

He slammed into the rough bark of a tree limb. It snapped, and he fell further, but dragging leathery hands and feet against the trunk he slowed enough to drop to all fours on the forest floor.

The frozen ground twitched and flicked him off like a cow did a fly. Another violent crash rolled over him. He leaped back into the trembling trees, climbing fast.

Another crash, sullen and rumbling. He was high enough now to look toward the village. Dust hung in the air even as a cloud roiled toward him, faster than he could think.

He wrapped himself around the opposite side of the tree, putting what little protection he could between himself and the cataclysm, and hung on.

It hit like a sea wave, but gritty and dry. He felt the tree break, and then he was tumbling backward with it, hoping he would live.

Don't worry, his fylgja whispered just as he sank beneath the wave.

***

He could tell his body was moving, but he wasn't in control, and he thrashed—

Stop that, his fylgja whispered. *I'm getting you to a safer place where you can watch what's happening.*

What is happening?

Look.

High above them, Thor rode in his cart pulled by two shaggy, long-horned goats. The wheels and hooves clattered and rumbled like the wagons across a stone bridge. Vafthrudnir's eye was drawn to Thor's right fist, held high, where his hammer glowed as hot and red as if recently plucked from a forge.

Thor flung Mjolnir downward at—

Vafthrudnir traced the arc...it was easy to do, Mjolnir hurtled like a burning arrow toward the dominant mountain peak behind the village. It had been a peak. Now it was a broken tooth.

The hammer shot through the heavy-hanging dust and grit, and turned it a brighter red than even Muspell's sparks during the Rising. Its arc was impossibly slow, an ingot gripped in tongs brought from forge to quenching bucket.

Just before Mjolnir finally struck, Vafthrudnir squeezed his eyes shut. White light pressed against his lids, the earth thrashed in agony and his fylgja again took control of his body. She dropped him below the forest's shattered remains, faster than he could've moved on his own, and took shelter beneath the debris of ancient oaks and fir trees and broken boulders.

The roaring wave passed overhead. The earth's twitches slowed.

Thor had just leveled a mountain.

Framed against a gritty sky, the Thunderer rumbled around the remains of the mountain and, presumably, the devastated village nestled at its base.

Were the villagers all dead, then?

With each slow circle, the wind from the Thunderer's passage beat down the cloud of dirt and smoke. The hooves of the goats pulling his cart added their own smithy-din to the sky, while lightning flickered like sullen children banished to a hall's darker recesses. Cold rain fell.

Thor himself became visible, chest and shoulders wide above the bronzed rim of the cart. His red hair streamed out behind him, Mjolnir held at arm's length, a white-hot ingot that steamed as the rain hit it. Abruptly, the Thunderer turned his cart south and rumbled away.

Yet his storm remained along with all the ruins Vafthrudnir must now investigate.

61

Hodr

With Sól's smile warm on his face, Hodr hefted another spear, feeling its weight and finding its balance point.

"And this one? How does it feel?" Lopt asked.

It was the morning after he'd spoken with the smith and received Lopt's apology—and unasked for advice about Alara. This morning, Lopt arrived early and asked Hodr to meet him in the way house yard, saying only that he had a gift for him.

Hodr twirled the spear and slammed it into the frozen, packed earth. He felt the spike drive deep. He tugged it free. He could feel the clump of dirt clinging to the spike. He knocked the spear against his boot and felt its heft and balance return.

"Excellent yet again, Master Lopt," he said. "But still not quite right. It's the butt-spike. It catches on the earth."

"No problem, no problem," Lopt said. "We'll find the right one for you. I've dozens here—dozens. A man like you knows his weapons. And of course, a spear serves double purpose for you, which I hope you won't mind me saying."

Hodr heard Lopt replace the spear, the haft rattling against the others. Metal clinked.

Kona whickered at him from her stall. She hadn't suffered at all from the accident in the street.

Lopt's mutterings drifted in the background. "Ah, let me see. Yes... No, not this one. Too like the first. Hmm... No, not this one."

The smith blew out a long breath. "Well, there is this one."

Hodr heard the long sinuous slide of wood against wood, the dull clink of metal against metal. Then he heard Lopt's voice, even quieter than before. "But am I ready to part with it?"

Hodr turned his head as if his attention were elsewhere. He always tried to hide just how good his hearing was. He was no Heimdall, but he often overheard private words and even slight noises like quickened breath or the sound of a knife clearing its sheath. The latter had saved him several times during his winters upon the road.

Lopt walked closer, but only a step or two at a time, like he was hesitant. "Try this one, Jarl."

Smooth wood slid into Hodr's hands. He ran his hands lengthwise along the shaft; lightly oiled. Metal cap at the butt. No spike. Good. He ran his fingers up toward the blade; the wood was scored. His fingers traced the markings. Runes, but none he knew. He touched the blade lightly. Oily and oddly warm to his touch. When he touched the light etchings on the blade's face, the blade cooled beneath his fingers, sending a chill down his spine. Strong magic. He wrapped his hands around the wood; it seemed to have its own heartbeat.

"Those scratches I see you lingering on are runes, cut to add strength to both the shaft and the joinings. They help the hands keep a solid grip and guide one's aim. The blade has runes, too, though you may not be able to feel them by touch alone. Meant to preserve sharpness, keep it strong, and further guide the strike. The oil just helps keep the blade sound during travel—the shaft, too. This spear's very old. Its crafting made me a master smith."

"I cannot accept it, then," Hodr said reluctantly even as he spun the weapon. It responded like he imagined a living branch might as it flexed in the wind. For a moment, as his hands gripped the spear, he felt he could see where he stood—the stable's outlines, Lopt himself

—but dimly, as if through shadows or gray mist. Then he balanced the weapon on his palms and presented it back to its maker. "The weapon I had was a soldier's weapon. No great value."

"Nonsense, Jarl," Lopt said.

Hodr felt the man's hands touch his own and take the weapon back. His hands felt empty, and he wiped at the sudden sweat on his brow despite the chill weather. The rumble and bang of the street and the squawking of the inn's washerwomen intruded into the short silence between them.

Lopt's voice dropped in volume. "It's hard to give away what's probably the finest thing these hands have ever crafted, but..."

Hodr made a noise, trying to interrupt, but the smith spoke over him. "Please, Jarl, let me finish. You've been nothing but gracious toward me, despite the injury I gave you and the difference in our station. What's more, well, as fine as this spear is—I wish you could see it. The blade glints gold even in the shade. It feels alive. I kept all the wood dust and shavings, you know. Made from the heartwood of an old ash tree. Used them in a ritual handed down, father to son, for"—he blew out a long breath—"well, since the first of my line learned to work metal and wood. This weapon has always felt called to a purpose, ever since I set eyes on the wood it came from."

Hodr heard Lopt spin the weapon; it sang through the air.

When the weapon fell silent, Lopt spoke again. "I always thought it was shaped for something significant—a hero's weapon, or maybe some rich karl would pay a life's wages for it, give it to his boy, and I'd hang up my hammer, give the shop to my own sons, and wait out the end of my days, well fed and with enough gold to help my family in their own lives. Instead, I've kept this spear hidden away in my house. I would take it out and oil it every few months, but I never mentioned it to anyone beyond my kin. Could never bring myself to sell it or even display it to prove my skill."

When he spoke again, his voice had some humor in it. "Foolish, right? But here we are. One of the great Aesir, a son of Odin, in need of a great weapon. Because of me. You would honor me by accepting it and carrying it."

His scratchy voice ended on a prouder note than it had begun. Hodr heard Lopt step forward, and he knew the spear was held out crosswise before him.

The silence of the moment stretched between them, undisturbed by everyday sounds—the cries of traders in the streets, wagons rumbling past, the washerwomen's laughter.

Hodr shook his head and held up his hands. "I can't accept your masterwork, Lopt, though I'm honored that you think me worthy to carry it. It's too fine a weapon for me. It deserves to be used in battle, not as a crutch for a blind man. I'll never fight again, but maybe one of my bro—"

"Take it again. If you don't feel it call to you, then I'll find a mere warrior's weapon for you. Or make one. But if you feel the heartbeat of the golden bough from which this weapon was crafted, well then, I'd say the Norns bade me to make this spear for your hands without me ever knowing it till now."

Before he realized it, Hodr set his hands on the spear. His fingers brushed the smith's hard hands, hot like a forge's fire. A longing ran through him, cooled by the ash beneath his hands.

He closed his fists around the spear and stepped back, falling into the fighter's stance he hadn't used in more winters than he could remember. Sight crept in from the sides, like a prowling beast. As it stole closer, the stout wooden supports and beams of the stable slid into view like the barest evening light revealing the trees. He looked down and saw—or thought he did—the packed earth of the courtyard.

He spun through a remembered series of attacks. The spear whispered through the air. It sounded like a word. He strained to hear it, but it fled each time he halted the spear's motion. Even so, the wood throbbed beneath his hands.

There, it seemed to whisper. *Across the way.*

He spun through a defensive whirl, his feet kicking up dust as his whirl became a confident, shuffling attacking lunge.

In this new sight he glimpsed, darkly, the washerwomen gathered round tubs of water set on grates above low fires. Their arms, just a blur, coming up toward their heads, maybe to pick long strands of hair from mouths and tuck it behind ears where the breeze would pluck them free again.

He couldn't be seeing. He was only imagining the women, stitching the scene together from dim memories of other places and other people. Even if he had eyes rather than a mass of fused flesh and scars, a cloth covered where they would have been.

But there they were. Washerwomen. The smooth side of the inn wall, and a black sketch of what he knew was the kitchen door.

He thumped the spear to the ground and spun to face Lopt. The smith was a lean shadow against a backdrop of the sky's warm white and the layered grays of the ground, the cart behind him, the fence in the farther distance, and the rounded bulk of the stable.

Could he now see with this weapon in his hands? If so, he couldn't refuse it.

He walked back toward Lopt, not tapping the spear to find his way as he usually did but almost like he used to. When he'd had eyes.

"You see! I knew the spear was meant for you." The smith clapped half-seen hands; his eyes burned like happy embers. "Use it well, Jarl Hodr."

The smith's words echoed his own thoughts. He had seen. His hands trembled. He concealed it, and the sob that wanted to unman him, by snatching the wineskin from where he'd left it. He leaned the spear against the half-seen cart. The moment his hands left the weapon, his gray sight vanished, as if devoured by that original beast whose venom had taken it, all those winters ago.

He covered the sudden shock by lifting the wineskin in both hands. The cool, sweet liquid ran in a torrent down his upturned throat. He sucked in a breath, wiped his mouth with his sleeve. "I haven't moved like that since..."

He groped for the spear. His fingers tingled when they touched the wood, and the world around him returned, half-lit, as he closed his hand around it.

"I saw the hero in you dance again!" Lopt said. A bright shadow slid across the smith's dark face, as a sunbeam might fall on a rock. Hodr realized it was a smile.

"When I hold the spear, I can see again. Dimly, like through a remembered fog, but I can see." He faced the smith. "Did you know that would happen?"

The sunbeam faltered. Lopt shook his shadowed head. "I—what? You can see?" He ran a hand across the top of his head, shadowed grass rippling in a sudden wind.

"It must be the runes I used," the smith said, his feet rasping on the ground as he turned away. "I never thought—never conceived—they might have that effect. But then, how could I? I've never done more than hold this spear. It's never been used. Not really. Not like you will, now that it's yours."

Hodr said nothing. He forced his hand to open and rested the spear back against the cart, his new sight fell away.

Lopt continued as if talking to himself. "It must be the runes. Must be. Unless you've some"—his voice lowered—"some sorcery you keep hidden." He coughed and continued with a laugh. "But those runes...they're only meant to guide the wielder's aim. Who'd have ever thought they'd give sight to a blind Aesir—"

"Half-sight," Hodr said, picking up the spear again. His own body, Lopt, the cart, the ground, the stable, the way house...all of it, and more, appeared around him. All gray, but he *could* see.

"Surely in this case, half is better than nothing?"

"Indeed it is," he said, answering Lopt's enthusiasm with a grin. He held the spear before his sightless eyes. Mist like that rising from a frozen lake streamed off the blade. "I suspect it may prove an equal to those famous weapons carried by my father and brother. All it lacks is a name."

"Oh, I assure you, Jarl, it has a name. Most weapons do. Keep it with you, and I've no doubt it will reveal its true nature."

62

Odin

Odin sat motionless, his head tilted back under the light of a dozen witchlamps. Through a big circle of curved glass banded with silver, Baldr peered down at his father's ruined eye socket.

Odin ran the fingers of one hand round and round the heavy coils of Draupnir. Loki had brought him the arm ring after a hugely lucrative sojourn into the Svartalvar smithies.

Loki.

His eye fell on the copy of Draupnir looped around Frigg's wrist like one of those huge snakes in Alvheim's hot, wet forests. Baldr wore one, too, as did his assistant, Eir.

Angrboda must have another gotten a copy of Draupnir, since she'd flung the one he'd given her back at him. Loki had his own duplicate of Draupnir, so she hadn't used his for the ritual Mimir, and he, had discovered in Angrboda's decrepit house.

Draupnir magically created a duplicate of herself every nine moon risings. Unless they needed one to mark the promotion of a jarl or as a reward for honorable service, every copy was melted down and turned into coins. Each of the copies that had dropped while he'd been wandering were accounted for: He gave most to village chiefs he'd met during his journey; the others he buried or flung into deep water.

"Hold still, Father," Baldr said, voice stern.

So where had that copy of Draupnir come from? Perhaps she stole one. Or Loki had.

"And why exactly did you cut your eye out, Father?" Baldr asked, his tone both respectful and incredulous.

"To see more clearly." The new hollow in his face felt like a never-ending yawn.

"Seems counterproductive," Baldr said. He handed the glass to Eir and looked across the room to Frigg. "You did well, Mother. The bleeding's stopped, and the swelling is less than I would've expected."

Frigg stood and stepped closer. "May I have a look?"

Baldr nodded. "Eir, if you don't mind?"

"Not at all," Eir said.

Odin turned his head so that his one eye could see his wife. "I'm not some—"

"Oh, hush," she said. "I want to see how Vidar's creation works."

Frigg leaned forward and looked through the thick glass Eir held out. She slipped both hands from beneath her feathered cloak and took it.

"Move it back and forth between yourself and the Alfather," Eir said. "When his features become sharp, clear, and much bigger, hold that spot."

Frigg nodded and then she was gone, having moved into his blind spot. He could feel her breath on his forehead, though.

"Fascinating," she said finally.

"Isn't it?" Baldr said. "I've no idea how Vidar made it, but the sight it grants has given me a dozen new ideas on how our bodies work."

Frigg straightened and handed the glass back to Eir. "So Baldr, how much unhealable damage did your father do to himself?"

"The bone above his eye socket has already begun to knit, as is the nasty sword cut, but this part here needs a couple of stitches. He did surprisingly little damage to his eyelids and socket, so those should heal well too." Baldr extended one cool finger to touch Odin's forehead. "Those waters seem to have an effect similar to my own elixirs."

"The song I sung over Mimir is the same as you had from me," Odin said, shifting in his seat. "And it helps that the waters flowing over Mimir are the same as those that nourish Yggdrasil."

He raised a hand to touch the empty hole in his face. He could just barely sense the link to his eye, left behind in the pool. Over time, it would grow stronger.

Baldr caught his wrist. "Don't touch the wound. It's clean and not bleeding. You touch it, and you risk doing more damage. So you're saying what, that those waters heal?"

Odin lowered his hand and shrugged. "Not exactly. They encourage it."

Baldr was about to ask more, but Frigg interrupted him. "Last night, you said you'd have to replace the eye with something?"

Baldr nodded. "Nanna left before dawn for the goldsmith's shop, the one that sells her jewelry. She said she had something that might help, but that it would likely be evening before it was ready."

He turned back to the table and spoke over his shoulder. "Until then, I suggest you both rest, either here or back at your house. Just don't move around too much, and definitely don't touch the wound. At all."

Baldr withdrew the compress he'd left soaking in a stoneware bowl and squeezed it so excess elixir dripped back into the bowl. "Eir?"

Gladsheim's chief valkyr gave a quick nod and picked up a long cloth bandage.

"Put your head back again please, Father," Baldr said.

Baldr placed the compress gently, packing it both into the empty socket and on his forehead. Then Eir wrapped a bandage around Odin's head, tying a knot over the compress to keep it in place. It smelled of wildflowers, berries, and hot rainy days.

With a quick, efficient nod so much like his mother's, Baldr said, "That's all I can do for now. I'll check in with you later. Get some rest."

***

Back at their longhouse, Frigg helped him remove what remained of his clothes and then get settled in their bed. The frame creaked as it took his weight.

She stroked his hair. "How's the pain?"

He shrugged. "Hurts, but whatever's in the compress is dulling it."

"Good," she said.

She turned at a sound from the door. Gná stood there, hands folded before her. Frigg nodded and sighed, and Gná slipped away.

"It seems I'll have to leave shortly to handle some things." She poked his chest with one finger. "Funny how the Alfather gets all the respect but hasn't actually ruled in Gladsheim for quite some time."

"*All* the respect? That's not what I've seen."

She reached out and brushed his temple with gentle fingertips. "Odin, why did you do this to yourself?"

He closed his eye and let out a long breath. A glib answer wouldn't let him avoid her question. "Long before our marriage, I hung myself upon Yggdrasil, seeking power I might use against Ymir."

Her hand drifted down, brushing his neck where the scars from the ropes still lingered and then running down to where the spear had split his side.

He nodded his head slightly, winced, and said, "I've realized that we now face a different challenge. I don't understand what's happening. The Norns have refused to guide me, Mimir was deceived and trapped, and apparently, the same was done to me ages ago by Loki. Or something else."

"So Mimir said," she replied. She sat down on the edge of the bed and pushed him gently back against the piled pillows. "He told me what you said, that Loki was behind everything."

"That's what I saw after I broke the charm he'd cast over me like a net. He vowed to destroy everything I'd built. That we've built."

Her brow furrowed. "Does that sound like Loki to you?"

"What do you mean?"

She leaned back and shrugged. "You know Loki better than I do, but neither of you are much for threats."

He frowned and met her eyes. "Meaning that if I were planning revenge, the last thing I'd do is announce my intention beforehand—especially to the one I meant to harm."

"Exactly," she said with a quick nod.

"So what are you suggesting, then?" He suspected he knew exactly what she was going to say. It was the same thing Mimir had suggested—and he suspected it himself, which was at least partly why he reclaimed that glade.

"I'm not saying Loki *isn't* behind some or maybe even all of these...events...but is it possible your memories were changed by that thing beneath Urd's Well? You said yourself those waters all have the same source. If it attacked you once through them, then why not again?"

He grunted. "I'm not convinced it could have altered my memories."

"But Loki did—and without you knowing? Seems to me that creature, whatever it is, has more to gain by making you distrust someone you've always trusted. It keeps you off balance and pursuing threads that lead nowhere, while also maybe turning a friend into an enemy."

"The problem is, Frigg, that I *can* believe Loki's responsible for all this. I did exile his children. What he said in those veiled memories struck a hard note. Maybe he really does plan revenge."

She raised a hand. "Let's assume that's true. How did he alter your memories? He's never shown that type of seidr before. Also, how did he learn of Baldr's mistletoe? We've protected that secret like no other. Even if he did learn of it, what good would it do to cut only some of it? You can't make a weapon from mistletoe—that's one of the reasons we chose that plant. If he really wanted to kill Baldr, why not cut the tree down along with the mistletoe and burn it all?"

Those were good points.

"Also, his involvement doesn't explain the Jotunn attack—not that they're necessarily connected. He would've had to convince the Skrymir along with all the other chiefs to go against their own best interests. If he'd done that, then why did only one warband from Lake attack us? All that does is invite the hammer's strike."

And that, too, was true. The Skrymir would know that. "So you're saying Loki's not involved in either plot? That this is a false memory?"

She shook her head. "All I'm saying is we shouldn't blindly accept it."

Blindly. He succeeded in keeping the smirk off his face.

It always came down to how much he knew. All his life, he'd sought and acquired power—but not knowing where to strike made that power useless.

He needed to know what was going to happen without relying on the Norns or his uncle or even the shade of his friend's dead wife ripped from her slumber. But until his sacrifice took root and he could swim the realms like his uncle while still striding through them in his flesh, he'd have to rely on the tools at hand.

"You asked why I cut out my eye, Frigg."

She nodded, brow furrowing.

"When we consulted the Norns at Baldr's birth, they uttered a prophecy which we acted on by protecting him with your people's magic. We never dreamed that protecting him might cost Hodr his sight. And maybe our choice did and maybe it didn't. But if I had known more, if I had asked questions instead of assuming the Norns were kindly disposed to us, perhaps I could have prevented both dooms from happening."

"So how does cutting out your eye help that?"

"By freeing my sight from my body's constraints," he said. "By giving me—us—an independent source of wisdom. If I know enough, if I keep asking questions, keep exploring, then I can guide our doom just like strong backs with shovels can change a river's course."

"Even assuming that's possible, you'll what? End up choosing a doom for everyone like the Norns do? There are many thousands living in Gladsheim alone, and many thousands more throughout the realm."

He met her eyes and waited until he saw understanding hit like his son's hammer.

She stood and backed away, shaking her head. "I've tried that, Odin. It never worked."

"But you didn't have me then, did you?"

"It never worked," she said again. "I used to tell what I saw, but those I told still died."

"I'm not talking about preventing death, Frigg. Even we just prolong our lives. I'm suggesting we use that time to pick and choose among dooms we find beneficial to our people rather than blindly accept whatever the Norns decide. Us. We will decide what happens, not them."

"You're talking about changing the course laid out for everyone. Is that even possible? What happens if what we choose is different from what the Norns have already carved into Yggdrasil's bark?"

"No, not everyone. We start with our son. You think your visions foretell his death, yes?"

She grew very still, her eyes wide and her hands folded neatly in her lap.

He reached out and gripped her hands. "It's all right. We know he's at least threatened, right? Both from the cut mistletoe, his dreams, and your visions." He gestured at his missing eye. "Once Baldr finishes with this, I'll ride down to the Gjoll and summon Angrboda's shade. She'll tell me how she's involved—and how her husband's involved, if at all. And once my eye takes root, I'll see as much as Mimir does. Between him, your visions, and my own efforts, we'll chart a safe course through the future's shoals."

He smiled and leaned back into the pillows. "Mimir thinks we don't have any choice at all. That everything is set, start to finish. When I get back, we'll prove him wrong. You and me. Together."

***

Head throbbing, Odin craned down at the small gold orb lying at the bottom of the bubbling cauldron. "What's that?"

"The fruit of Nanna's labor," Baldr said. He lifted a hand to trace the silver torc he wore around his neck. "Just as this is."

Odin glanced at Baldr's wife; she ducked her head and smiled shyly. "Meaning what, exactly?"

"Be nice, Odin," Frigg said, thumping his arm. To Nanna, she added, "Don't fret, dear, he's always like this when he cuts out his own eye."

He glared at her.

"This is the orb I'm going to put inside your empty eye socket. Nanna made it."

"Actually, I just recast something I'd already made," Nanna said, a faint blush coming to her pale cheeks. "If I'd more time, I could have made it nicer."

"Don't be silly." Baldr bumped her gently with his elbow. "It's beautiful work. The runework alone is impressive."

Her blush deepened, but Odin didn't miss the quiet smile that crept onto her downturned face.

He turned to look at Baldr. "So we're doing this now?"

Baldr nodded. "If you're ready. Just sit here. I have to make sure the eye socket can handle it."

Odin sat facing Sól and lifted his chin. Baldr stepped up behind him and unwound the bandage. The air was chill on his skin when the compress came off.

Baldr's fingers pressed and pushed all around his missing eye. "Any sharp pain?"

"No, just a constant pounding, as if Sleipnir were trampling my head."

Baldr held up the glass he'd used the night before and continued to poke and prod. "There's no bleeding, the swelling's considerably reduced, and the flesh is healing nicely. Putting in the false eye should be fine. Are you ready for it?"

Odin shrugged. "Why are you doing this exactly?"

"Because if we don't, that side of your face is likely to sag and droop. The flesh inside your eye socket may grow and push into places it shouldn't, which could cause pain and future problems. I've seen both happen before. You'd be surprised at the number of eyes lost during the Last War. Wearing the false eye should help prevent all that from happening."

He looked down at the gold orb. It shouldn't interfere with the sight his sacrificed eye would grant, but if it did... "Will I be able to remove it?"

"Not until the socket fully heals with the false eye in place," Baldr said. "And even then, I'd advise against it. You'll have to clean it—and yourself, ideally—before replacing it."

He grunted. Weekly baths were enough.

"Nanna, would you take the orb out and place it in the cold water for a moment, please?" Baldr asked.

She reached into the cauldron with a pair of cloth-wrapped tongs, removed the orb, and placed it in a smaller pot of water. Steam hissed free. After a dozen heartbeats, she used the same tongs to set it in the white cloth Baldr held out.

"May I see it?" Odin asked.

"Of course," Baldr said, "but don't touch. The cloth and my hands are clean."

He peered down at the orb and the fine runes cut into the gold. It was slightly egg-shaped with swirling, interlinked knots that straightened into three interlinked triangles right where the pupil would be. More runes were etched between the curved lines. They were the words of the healing song he'd taught Baldr. On the opposite side of the golden orb, Nanna had cut smaller patterns similar to those etched into the front.

Very promising. Once he'd harvested more witchthread and had the time, he might be able to use these runes and patterns to reinforce the link he'd already forged between himself and the eye he'd sacrificed.

He looked up into Nanna's eyes and saw the nervous concern clearly etched into her features. "Excellent work, daughter, both in your runes and handiwork."

Relief and pleasure flooded into her expression. "Thank you, Alfather."

Baldr smiled at her. Then his expression grew more serious. "First, I'm going to drip some of my elixir into your eye socket. That'll continue the healing. I'll then insert the orb and place a new compress and bandages. It will feel cold at first, but your body will warm it up."

"No galdr, then?"

Baldr shook his head. "There's nothing that song could do at this point that my elixir and your body aren't already doing. Now lean your head back, please. And hold still. This will feel uncomfortable."

He did as he was told.

Baldr pulled back his eyelids with one hand, and he could no longer see anything happening on that side. Warmish liquid dribbled into the gap...the hole...where his eye should have been. He flinched despite himself.

"Hold still, Father."

Frigg took his hands, bunched into fists, into her own. Her fingers were cold.

"I'm putting the orb in now," Baldr said. "Nanna, please hold his head."

Nanna wrapped a cloth around his head, leaving his face exposed. Then she took firm hold of his jaw and the back of his head.

At the first touch of cold metal against his eye socket, he suppressed the urge to draw away. Nanna held him steady, anyway. Baldr pushed, gently, and Odin felt cold metal settle into his head. Not uncomfortable, but the weight felt wrong. That side of his face grew wet as his new eye displaced the elixir.

"Any pain?" Baldr asked, daubing up the elixir.

"No. Just feels odd. Cold, as you said."

Baldr's fingers pushed this way and that, shifting the false eye's position. "I'm placing the compress now."

The compress came down, warm and damp. This time it smelled like fresh tilled earth. Nanna's hands left him, along with the cloth. Then Baldr was winding the bandage around his head again.

Baldr placed a hand on the back of his head and gently raised him up. "Well, how does it feel?" Baldr asked.

He turned his head left and right. The eye had warmed up, but the weight still felt odd. He cocked his head to one side, then the other. Already, the anvil pounding was slowing down. That elixir Baldr made from Yggdrasil's fruits worked wonders.

"Feels fine. Little heavy, maybe."

Baldr smiled. "You'll get used to it." He stepped to the cauldron, dipped in a ladle, and began mixing a drink in a small clay cup.

Frigg squeezed his hands and stood up, smiling. He pulled her in close and held her beside him, arm wrapped tight around her hips. He stared out at the setting sun, reddish gold behind a haze of red clouds.

Behind them, Baldr hummed as he ground herbs. Metal and clay clacked against each other. "All right, Mother, make sure he takes this when you get back to your hall. It'll help him sleep." He handed her a small clay jug.

"He's okay walking?"

He stood up and stretched. "I'm not an invalid, Frigg. Come on, let's head back while there's enough light for me to *half*-see by."

"Funny."

He stepped around the stool and caught his son in a tight embrace. "Thank you, Baldr."

"My pleasure. You did more than this for me not two nights ago."

"What else should a father do, eh?" He smiled and stepped away. "You haven't mentioned it, so I assume you've had no similar recurrences?"

"None. Eir stays nearby, though, just in case."

"Then have her remain nearby until I return," he said, looking at Frigg. "And if she has family, why not have room made for her up here through the feast day? They'd enjoy it."

"She does, and they are already here," Frigg said, her smile tight. He couldn't tell—and didn't want to ask—whether it showed worry or mild annoyance that he was issuing orders on matters she'd already handled.

"Ah, of course," he said.

Baldr said, "You're leaving again? I thought you were back for a while—at least through Midwinter."

He ignored Frigg's obvious displeasure. "I'll be back before then. Just a short trip to wring some answers about your condition from a witch." He pointed at the silver torc around his son's neck and held out his hand. "And I'll need that, if you don't mind."

"I... what? Why?"

He ignored the question. Baldr sighed, unclipped the torc, and handed it over.

Odin winked his good eye, turned to Nanna, and bowed very slightly. "And thank you, daughter, for my new eye. The fit is perfect."

63

Hodr

"Are all the thralls out of the house?" Hodr asked as Alara stepped into their private area, where the bed was. His new spear in hand, he sat on the bench along the side wall. His other hand rested on the bag containing the fruit his father's wolf had brought several nights earlier.

"What's this about, Hodr?" Her voice sounded alarmed. Her face was a misty blur in his new sight. "And why do you have your spear in here? You know where everything is."

"Come in and pull that hanging shut, in case someone walks by," he said, smiling. "Everything's fine."

He heard the heavy fabric hanging whisper along the wooden rod, but better yet he saw it move—dimly, a gray cloud drifting in front of a thunderhead—but he saw it.

"Now come and sit," he said, patting the bench beside him. "Please light a witchlamp too. I couldn't find the flints."

"You're making me nervous, Hodr. Are you feeling all right?" He heard her doing as he asked and he saw her pale hands strike a brilliant spark that shone as bright as the remembered moon. The spark moved to the wick, the light steadied and the beams above their heads appeared as did the squared posts that held them aloft.

She sat beside him, her shoulder brushing his. He put the fruit in her lap. "Unwrap it."

Her hands froze in the air above the packet. "Is this what I think it is?"

Hodr nodded.

"But... how? When did you get it?"

"Geri brought it several nights ago." He touched her hand. "Go on, take a bite."

"Who came?"

"Geri. One of my father's wolves—that's his name."

"Ah."

She toyed with the bag's drawstrings. "Did you know Geri was coming? Is that why you insisted on being out in the yard?"

He smiled but shook his head. "I'd no idea. But I told you, Freki or Geri bring me one of Yggdrasil's fruits every winter, usually around this time. Just good luck it happened to be the night I sat out."

Alara slipped the fruit out of the bag. She held it up so it caught the light of the witchlamp. "It's beautiful."

Indeed it was. They always had been. It was the first thing he'd seen that appeared to have some color to it—a hint of golds and reds, like the sky just before Sól slips away.

"Idunn tends the branch of Yggdrasil from which they grow—the only place they do grow, so far as we know." He touched her knee. "Go on, take a bite. Actually, wait—let's cut it in half first. Once you start eating, it's almost impossible to stop. But cut it in a bowl to save the juices."

She took three quick steps toward the cooking area before she stopped. He heard her shoes slide on the wooden floor as she faced him. "And eating this will make me young again?"

"Well, it's not like you're old now—but yes, it will. I don't know how it works, but my father says eating it makes the waters of the Roaring Cauldron flow through your body. They heal and restore, stripping the winters away like a woodworker's plane exposes the fresh wood underneath."

"Hodr, I..."

She stood, an icicle in the dim light. He set his spear aside and moved across the small room to her, two steps to her three. His hands found hers and the fruit they held.

"You're trembling, Alara. What's wrong?"

"I can't eat this, Hodr." She pressed the fruit into his hands.

"But why not? It's the only way we can be together."

"If I eat it, then I won't age, right?"

"Well no, not really. You still age, but each time you eat the fruit, it restores you—makes you whole. Younger. Still you, but always the you when you first ate the fruit."

He saw her head shake. "So when I eat it, I'll outlive everyone I know? My brother will grow old and die while I stay young?"

He nodded, not knowing what to say. That's exactly what would happen.

"And if we marry and have children, they'll also grow old and die while we stay young?"

Again, he nodded. "But only if we keep eating it. If we stop, we will grow old and die."

She stepped back. Her hands left his. He no longer felt her breath on his face. "That's not right, Hodr. My brother's the only family I have left. I could maybe handle him dying while I kept living, maybe. But to outlive my children? To see them age, have their own children, and then see all of them, child after child, take the ship to the Gjoll's shores? I'm crying just thinking about it."

She leaned in and kissed him, and he felt her tears on his cheek.

"But I thought you wanted this. For us to be together."

"I do. But not like this."

"What if I asked my father to give fruits to you, as well? And to any children we have? He's done so for my whole family. Would you change your mind then?"

"And then our children's children? How many fruits grow on that tree?" She stroked his cheek. "I honestly don't know. Would he even grant me that gift?"

"I...I don't know." Especially since he hadn't spoken with his father in more than forty winters. He sunk to the bench. His hand found his new spear, and the room drifted into view.

Like a longship's prow, her face edged into his vision. Memories flooded his mind of tracing her features with his fingers—the straight, bold nose, the high cheekbones and the creases at the corners of her eyes, full lips and a strong chin, her long hair pulled into a braid. She looked entirely different from how he'd imagined, and yet she was entirely the same.

"How many fruits have you eaten?"

He shrugged. How many, indeed? "More than a hundred, I suppose. I ate my first when I completed my first service in the army."

"Hodr, I wasn't even alive then. My grandparents were probably my age. Maybe their parents. I don't even know."

Unbidden, a memory of sparring with Thor leaped to mind, along with the first gut-punch his half-brother had landed. That's what he felt like now. It was all he could do haul in his next breath. When he did manage it, all he could think to say was, "I hadn't thought of it that way."

"Why would you?" He heard the slight smile in her voice. "Let me ask you this. How many has your father eaten? Twice as many as you?"

"At least. Probably more. What's your point?" He winced. "I'm sorry. I didn't mean that like it sounded."

She twined her fingers with his. "I know. I guess my point is that you take your long life for granted because you've never known anything different. But for me, it would change everything. I'd even have to leave this way house behind eventually, just as I'd outlive the children we had—and then their children's children."

"We could stop eating them, whenever we choose."

He watched the corners of her full lips turn ever so slightly downward. "Yes, maybe we could."

By which she of course meant no, they never would. He hadn't, and he'd lost everything. The spear slipped from his fingers and his sight vanished as if it had never been. A howl was bubbling up inside him. What *did* she care about? If it wasn't long life with him, then what?

"What do you want, then?"

He felt her shrug. "I want you, Hodr. A life with you."

"And then death." The words lashed out like a sword before he could stop them. "I'd have to give up my life to share yours."

She moved away from him, abruptly, their bodies breaking contact.

"I'm sorry. Really. Again." He fumbled for the spear, and Alara swam back into view. "I just... It's just that I don't know what to do. With this, I feel like a new man. Like I have something to offer again, whereas before, I just drifted from one winter to another."

"With what?" Her brow furrowed so prettily. So that's what she looked when she was confused.

"The spear. Lopt gave it to me as recompense for the injury he dealt me. When I hold it, I can see a little bit. It's like I'm looking through a fog."

And yet even that dim sight only showed her in broad strokes and rough outlines. She'd stepped too far away. "You can see now?"

"Not like I used to. It's only when I hold the spear. It's like when Máni's full—everything's drained of color. I see well enough to make out your face, especially when you're close."

She stepped toward him, boots lightly scraping, and there she was, dress flowing and rustling, concern creasing her brows, hands clasping and unclasping.

She seemed hesitant to come closer. "And it's safe?"

Odd question, but he'd grown up around seidr. "I think so. Lopt was surprised his runes gave me sight. He hadn't expected or even thought that it was possible, but it is. And it's certainly better than spending every living moment in the dark. You seem..."

"Scared?" She laughed, holding herself. "Yes, quite a bit, actually. I'm surprised you're not."

"Alara, my father regularly changes into an eagle. And like him, one of my uncles can shift into any shape he chooses. Even Heimdall can change his shape—only a seal, but still. When you've seen all that or stood your ground while your brother brought lightning down on your enemies... well..." He shrugged again and tapped the spear against the floor. "This seems a small thing."

"What can you change into?" she asked, her voice small.

"Me? Just a mole."

A double heartbeat passed. Then she took two quick steps toward him and smacked him on the arm.

He grinned and pulled her down beside him. She kissed him hard and said, "I'm happy for you, but this—the fruit, your new sight—is so much to take in all at once. I'm not as used to magic as you are."

"I'm realizing that now," he said, nodding and gently squeezing her hand. "I'm sorry I sprung it on you."

"You should also realize that your being blind doesn't bother me—never did. I came to love the man you are, not the man you wish you were."

What could he say? "I know it, Alara. And believe me, I love you too."

She leaned in, kissed him gently this time, and snuggled into him. In a quiet voice, she asked, "How long have you been blind?"

She knew very well how long it had been. "Since the Last War—more than forty winters."

This time he saw her smile, so sad and sweet it would have made him cry, if he could.

"I've only lived through about twenty winters, Hodr," she said.

He knew that. Of course he knew that. But something about the way she said it hit him like one of his brother's hammer strikes. He'd been blind twice as long as she'd been alive. The snow bear had spat in his eyes before she'd even been born.

Before the silence could grow louder than even the rushing Franangr, he said, "I may have lived longer, but I've only begun valuing my life since I met you. I don't want to give that up. Not ever."

She smiled gently and held his arm a little tighter. "But you won't be. Everyone sails upon the Gjoll sooner or later. You and your family have just found a way to postpone that journey. I don't want to walk on and on in a life without end. I want to spend the years I have left with you here, bear your children, watch them grow and thrive. And then, when the Norns have decreed it, I'll walk down to the dock, take ship to the Gjoll's shores, and either join you or wait for you there."

"But if we eat the fruit, we won't ever have to do that."

"With the price being that I see our children die?" She shook her head again. "No. I won't choose that."

"I can't just stop eating the fruit," he said, because he never had. "He'll keep sending them, winter after winter."

"He can't force you to eat them."

He ventured a grin. "You haven't met my father."

She let the comment go. "Nor am I saying you should confront your father or your mother."

"It feels like you are."

She sighed and wiped tears from her cheeks. "Maybe I am. I don't know. You've been talking for several winters now about how you need to put your past behind you and make peace with your family. Maybe now's when you do that."

"By choosing life with you or without you?"

She slid toward him, kissed him, and wrapped her arms around him. "I love you, Hodr. You've made these last few winters a joy to me. Your choice is no different now than it was when we met. You're just at the crossroads now."

64

Odin

Odin felt the drumbeat of every one of his many winters in every limb, despite having eaten the fruit Idunn had brought to Ithavoll. The drum pounded strongest in his eye socket—and the weight of the golden orb Baldr had placed there was a nuisance.

He slipped slowly from his bed to avoid angering the drummer, and his wife. His bare feet whispered across the smooth wooden floor, half the room unseen. When he bumped into the chest where he'd thrown his clothes, he sat and began to dress.

"Odin?" Frigg asked, voice drowsy. "You're leaving now?"

"I'm just dressing. I wasn't going to leave without waking you first."

He unwound the bandage and compress from around his head, sighed with relief as that additional weight lifted, and set them both on the chest beside the leather patch Frigg had given him.

"Your son said to change that, not remove it," she said, sleepy amusement in her voice.

"I can hardly ride through Gladsheim or go where I'm about to with that thing wrapped around my head." He tugged on a pair of thick wool socks. "Bad enough I'll have to wear that patch."

"Maybe you shouldn't have cut your eye out." She lit a witchlamp and sat sideways on the bed. "You know, since you've been back, I think most of our conversations happen in the dark while you're getting ready to leave."

He threw his best scowl at her, but she slapped it away like a wobbly arrow. He pulled on his breeches and sat. "It's a long ride, even for me. And I have to stop along the way."

"Why not just wait until after Midwinter? It's six nights away."

"We need answers. If Loki is behind all of this or even some of it, and if Angrboda's set something in motion—"

"All the more reason to leave after Midwinter. A baresark goes everywhere with Baldr now, but he needs the most protection on that first night when he's out among the folk. If something's going to happen, you ought to—"

"If I leave this morning, I'll be back just before Midwinter begins." He tugged on his shirt. "I'd rather be here with answers than without them and wondering what's actually going on."

"I'd ask for your promise, but you've no problems breaking your word when it suits you."

He stopped dressing and stared at her. Was he referring to Loki? She stared right back, unflinching. He broke the tension with a sharp nod. "I suppose that's true enough. But never deliberately. With you."

She snorted. He couldn't tell what it meant, so he stood and pulled on his overtunic, then stepped to the pegs in a post and took down his belt.

"Why not send for Loki?" she said. "Order him to come here."

"That would be a mistake."

"She was his wife. He might be able to help, assuming you don't reveal your suspicions. Assuming the memory you had was genuine."

He buckled his belt and started tying on the various pouches. "His absence now has nothing to do with whether or not he suspects that I suspect him. You sent a bird to Sigyn when I got back, right?"

She nodded. "She sent a reply saying that Loki wasn't at Franangr but she'd let him know when he returned. Was she lying?"

He shook his head. "This close to Midwinter, he's probably visiting his children."

"I don't understand."

"I showed him how to reach his children."

Her eyes widened and she leaned back, the obvious question forming on her lips.

"He visits them all, often, I think. This close to Midwinter, I'm sure he's either with one of them right now or on his way back to Sigyn and his boys."

"You never told me that," she said. "Shouldn't they all be—"

"Dead?" He shrugged again. "They should be. I don't understand why they aren't. They don't eat Yggdrasil's fruit—not that I'm aware of, at least. Idunn keeps careful eye on the fruits, as do I, so we know they're not being stolen. Jorm's asleep most of the time but grows bigger with every passing winter. Fenrir's growth stopped, but how he continues to live, I don't know. There's nothing to eat on that island. And how Hel's lived this long—how any of them have—I don't know."

He sighed and only just stopped himself from rubbing his face. "I've made so many mistakes."

"I'd no idea." She blew out a long breath and sat beside him, putting her arm around his shoulders.

"Why would you? I tried to keep it secret, though I suspect a few know. Heimdall obviously does."

"Odin, I'm starting to believe those memories of yours were genuine. Whatever rage Loki felt at the time has probably grown like a wildfire over the winters."

He met her eyes. "It does appear to be the best explanation."

"But you're having a hard time accepting it."

He nodded. "Loki and I were very close once—obviously, given the oath we took. But if our positions had been reversed, I never would have accepted the exile of Baldr, Hodr, and Hermod."

"Nor would I," she said.

Oddly, he didn't feel as angry as he expected. Just confused, as if he'd hit his head. "So all the mischief he's been up to these past hundred winters takes on quite a different light, eh? Crippling Heimdall makes a great deal of sense if you're up to no good."

"So he stole the Brisingamen, knowing Freyja would ask Heimdall to help her find it. And then he lost that fight to Heimdall so he'd have a plausible reason for a particularly nasty revenge?"

"Yes." All of Loki's mischief had been simple, brilliant, and completely deniable. Whenever it got out of hand, as it often did, he'd always been able to claim it had been accidental or that he'd been forced into it.

Frigg pursed her lips in a silent whistle of amazement. "But why delay? He's probably had a dozen chances to plant a knife in your back."

"I'm not that easy to kill. He'd want to make sure his first strike would be fatal. That's what I would do. Or maybe he's going after our children, since I went after his." He tugged on his boots and stomped his feet deeper into them.

"Which is why you want to summon Angrboda sooner rather than later."

He nodded and stood.

She rose with him, embraced him, kissed him, and stepped back. "Ride swiftly, my husband. Safe may you travel, and safely return. And quickly."

65

Vidar

Vidar stepped up on a bit of crumbling stone and balanced himself with one arm against the tunnel wall. Witchlamp light danced across the faces of his warband. Most were young, but plenty of weathered faces peppered the neat ranks.

He met their eyes. Smiled faintly to some, nodded to others. He tried to project that same confidence his father exuded. Garilon did, too, actually. They seemed to do it naturally, whereas he had to force it. He hoped it was something he could learn. If not, he'd never be able to do it.

He was certain, though, that his warband needed a clear reason to step through that doorway. Their misgivings were like bad fruit in a hot shed.

"We have discovered what I believe to be a doorway from this mine to icy Utgard. I'll be honest, I don't know how it works. Yet. I don't know what awaits us on the other side of the doorway. Yet. But I do know this."

He pointed down the mine shaft that led to the doorway. Save for the slight shifting of feet and bodies, the warband was silent.

"The Jotunn warband that destroyed Háls marched through that doorway. They'd have done even worse had we not stopped them. So we will step through with three goals in mind." He held up one fist and extended his thumb. "Backtrack the Jotunn warband to wherever they came from, report on their strength and, if possible, their intentions. Was this just a random attack, or are they planning more?"

One finger joined his thumb. "I believe that's Utgard on the other side, but I need to be certain. And for that, all I need is one good look at the night sky."

Another finger joined its brothers. "Investigate the doorway. I need to figure out how it works. That'll take time, but I've no intention of staying longer than necessary. Once we've accomplished the first two goals, we will fall back to the comparative security of this side of the doorway."

He fell silent, surveying the faces. Still mostly calm, a wind-kissed lake. Rumors being what they were, they'd already known they were going through. But he'd needed to give them the reasons why it was important they risk themselves. Had he said enough to air out that hot shed?

"The doorway works both ways, as I discovered when I stepped through and then came back," he said, trying to make his smile feel genuine. "So don't worry about that part of it."

He spied a few smiles here and there, maybe some crinkling at the corners of eyes. "And be assured, we won't be there for too long. With rationing, we have enough food for more than two weeks. We still need to get back to the surface here in Asgard, so we've also planned for that."

He surveyed the dirty, tired warriors staring back at him. He felt he'd said enough. A frank, clear assessment of what they had to do and what obstacles they faced. Talking too much would make him look weak. Indecisive. Best to shut his mouth and expect they'd follow his orders.

"Kjolr Garilon."

"Yes, Jarl."

"The four messengers already left for the surface?"

"Yes, Jarl. Right after breakfast."

"Good. Please have everyone wear all their clothes. Everything they can and still move. Whatever's left, bring with them. Once they're ready, meet me at the doorway."

"Yes, Jarl."

Vidar stepped down from the scrap of rock and walked past the loose stone wall they'd erected at the entrance to the mine shaft. It would offer some protection if it came to defending the mine against a Jotunn warband pouring through the doorway.

He turned into the smooth corridor and stopped a few paces before the doorway, snow swirling behind it. He threw his mind's eye inward and sank until he seemed to float right before his fylgja.

She still slept, head on her paws, tufted ears flat against the bony ridges of her skull. The golden knots his father had tied hung before his mind's eye like tiny suns.

He undid the first one, whispering the rune word his father had taught him, then the second. When he untied the third knot her eyes opened and she stared at him, feline eyes flat and intensely green.

I expect I'll need your strength soon, he thought at her.

She yawned, fangs bright white.

He whispered the rune word his father had taught him, and the bindings around her front legs and neck flared blue, just as his did. Her glare darkened like treetops before a storm.

I won't make the same mistake again, he thought. *You will obey me.*

Her lips drew back, clearly a smile, and bared that same forest of gleaming teeth she'd shifted his own into—and then used to tear the life from two hundred Jotunn throats.

***

The wind's screech doubled in Vidar's ears and tore his hood away. It tugged next at the wool cap he'd tied around his head, failed to rip it off, then blew snow into his eyes and howled its frustration.

He tugged his hood back on with a gloved hand, wiped his eyes, and held the hood low, trying to keep the snow out.

In his other hand, he held a spear. He probed ahead with it through snow nearly waist deep. The spear banged against what he hoped was solid ground, and he trudged forward another step. With the weight of rock above him and the wind clawing at him, he was bent nearly double. Perhaps a storm had blown in since the previous night.

His spear again thumped against hard ground, so he took another step forward. And another. The rope tied around his waist went taut, and he looked back through the doorway. Two figures stood there—Mikill and Smar, unless others had taken their places, made indistinct by the swirling snow and what was probably the doorway's own way of distorting sight. He tugged the taut rope twice to let them know he was fine. The rope drooped as they gave him slack. Then he turned back to his trudge.

Nine steps later, the wind ceded the contest. Vidar stumbled forward, straightening as he realized just how bent he'd been. He realized too that the rock no longer hung over him like a witch's curse.

He tugged the line, asking for more slack, then trudged forward a few more paces. Out here in the open, the wind was still strong, but weaker outside the tunnel's confines. The snowfall too was steady but not blinding. Everywhere he looked, the sky was a heavy gray wool and while there was enough light to see by, he couldn't tell if it was night or day.

Behind him, a snow- and ice-covered cliff rose like a building wave. It stretched away into the dim light on either side of the tunnel from which he'd emerged.

He scanned the sky again, hoping for a break in the clouds. Nothing. They would either have to wait out the storm or trek farther afield. Or both. From what he'd experienced in Utgard, these storms could last weeks. Maybe they could find other landmarks that would let him say for certain they were in Utgard and not some equally snowy region of Asgard's far north.

He took up the slack in his line and gave the three sharp tugs that signaled the warband to follow him through. Then he lurched into motion again, probing with his spear, stepping, probing, then stepping again. He angled back toward the dubious protection of the high cliff. All of the ground was probably safe, but it would take time for the warband to come through and while they did, moving helped him stay warm.

***

A bit of stale bread in one gloved hand, Vidar sat on a snow-covered rock and stared up at Aurvandill's toe shining blue-bright in the night sky. He'd know that star anywhere. In Gladsheim, it hung low on the horizon. In Utgard, though, it rose somewhat higher, dominating the northern sky with its clear blue shimmer.

By his best guess, it had taken most of evening for him and the warband to find their way out of the deep chasm where the doorway to Asgard was. The way up had proved relatively easy once the snowstorm had blown through, and they found a ramp leading up to the rocky tumble they now huddled in, warming themselves by their witchstoves.

Garilon had cautioned against even the use of the witchstoves for fear that their slight smell would betray their presence. Vidar had agreed it was a risk but had allowed their use for warmth, not for cooking. They had set aside a week of supplies for this journey—but were only planning for a total of four nights exploring the region near the doorway. That should leave enough to spare should something unexpected happen.

Vidar stood, stretched, and turned in place, staring up at the gradual fading of the green-blue filaments undulating like eels in the depths. No clouds in sight—a rare thing in Utgard. In the east, Sól's warm glow bathed the sharp teeth of the distant mountains.

Garilon stood up beside him. "Shall I get the warband ready, Jarl?"

"Yes, Kjolr. You still agree that two groups able to fight independently is best?"

"I think so, Jarl." Garilon nodded. "Gives a bit more maneuverability. Wouldn't want them separated too much, though."

"Never more than a few spear lengths, Kjolr."

"Head west first?"

Vidar nodded. They had no idea where the Jotunn were, so any direction would work. Even the faint trail they'd been following since entering the mines had vanished once they'd stepped through the doorway.

Garilon had advised heading west so the rising sun wouldn't be in their eyes. As the day progressed—they were shorter in Utgard during the winter than in Asgard—they would swing north and then head back east.

Garilon had also advised staying within a night's march at most of the only way they knew back—the doorway—particularly since the rugged terrain, apparently endless snow fields, and lack of trees suggested they were nowhere near Jotunheim itself. They were most likely in the wilds of Utgard, which only Thor had ever seen—and from high above no less—or Heimdall, back when he'd stood watch.

"Even if the Jotunn only marched those two warbands up here, there should be a fort or settlement or *something* nearby. We could learn a lot if we find it."

"I don't disagree, Jarl," Garilon said, "but that's exactly what worries me. If there are more warbands up here—even not at full strength—we'd be hard pressed to defeat them. And if they're preparing to attack Asgard again, they may have snow bears to loose on us. Those beasts will tear through us."

Vidar frowned, chewing the last bit of his bread while he thought. Above, the undulating bands of green and yellow light had faded to a sea-green. Sól's fingers gripped the eastern mountains' teeth.

"If I may, Jarl, I know our situation seems favorable now, but the Jotunn probably know we're here. We never did catch those we pursued through the mines. If we're careful and quick, then maybe we can gather some useful information before they can oppose us. We can probably defend the mine...for a time...but I've seen far better positions turn to shit faster than I would've believed possible. I know you have, too."

Deep inside Vidar's mind, his fylgja flicked her tails and bared her teeth. Indeed he had.

66

Vafthrudnir

Vafthrudnir threw back the flap of Beli's tent and interrupted the hersir's war council.

"Hersir, we need to move. Thor's just destroyed Akrton. We must help the villagers who survived. I've already informed Jotunheim, but it will take them several nights to respond. We're much closer."

Beli put down the knife he'd been pointing at the map with. "Everyone, please give us a few moments to speak alone."

When everyone had left, Beli stepped around the table and said with his hands, "We can't aid them, Vafthrudnir. We've been ordered to the northern doorway."

Vafthrudnir laughed. "I wasn't clear enough. I don't mean that Thor burned the town or knocked some houses down. He broke the mountain. It buried the town. It's all gone."

Beli's eyes widened. "He's never done anything close to that."

"I saw it myself. A handful of strikes with his hammer. Mjolnir burned like one of Muspell's sparks when he was done. But he did it."

Beli leaned against the table. His fingers danced in the Jotunn hand language. "We still can't go help them, Vaft. A message came from the Skrymir this morning. The shaman watching the northern doorway reported that a small Aesir warband has stepped through and is marching away from it. So the Skrymir's turned us around and needs us to double our pace. I was just asking the new shamans to spin a snow ship for us."

"So Vidar made it through?" Vafthrudnir replied with his hands.

"That's my understanding, yes," Beli said. "Not many in his warband, but..."

But, indeed. He'd watched Ygg's son succumb to his fylgja—and then slaughter two Jotunn warbands. With him and Beli opposing Vidar, though, they stood a good chance of sweeping this Odinsson from the tafl board.

Beli continued. "So far, Vidar has only walked through a mine and stepped through the doorway. But this march outward he's embarked on could complicate things."

"He found the doorway," Vafthrudnir corrected. "That's problematic enough."

Beli waved it away. "We expected that."

"But not before the assault on Gladsheim." Ama's destruction of Háls had betrayed one of their greatest secrets. But there was more at risk than just the doorways. If Vidar should reach the frozen lake near the doorway then the Jotunns' second secret would be exposed. "Which way does Vidar march?"

"Toward the lake."

Vafthrudnir swore and struck the table. The marker stones jumped and clattered. He and the Skrymir had spent more than two hundred winters planning all of what was now happening.

Maybe it had been foolish to continue the work knowing that Vidar would find the doorway, but the work couldn't be stopped. Not now. And not until everything they'd sunk into that lake was reclaimed. But just because Odin's son saw the work didn't mean he would understand it—or be allowed to report on it. The villagers would have to fend for themselves after all.

"Show me to the new shamans and my adept. I will help spin the ships."

67

Frigg

At the sound of boots approaching, Frigg wrenched her gaze away from the patches of bland sunlight scattered across the hall's floorboards. She'd finished the morning's business early and now had a little to time to herself—which she'd squandered by staring blankly at the floor.

"Mother?" Nanna called, her light voice floating across the intervening distance.

Worry crashed over her like a cold wave. She was on her feet saying, "What's wrong, Nanna? Is it—" before Nanna said, "Baldr's fine. He's okay, I just came to check on you, Mother."

"Oh, good." Relief flooded in. Of course he was all right. It was nearly midday; it would've happened already if it were to happen again—no, *when* it did. Odin said he couldn't heal Baldr, not with the heart of the mistletoe cut out.

Nanna continued. "You've been through so much in the past week, and yet you're still here, dealing with everything that's gone undone. I don't know how you do it."

How, indeed?

"It comes with being Almother," Frigg said, which is what Nanna would discover for herself if Odin...no, *when* Odin returned with answers. "Thank you for taking over the preparations for Midwinter. That alone has helped."

"That's partly why I've come, actually," Nanna said, her expression serious.

"The last batch of wine's arrived. I thought you'd want to escape this"—she gestured around the hall—"and ride down into the city with me to taste it."

"I would like nothing better, Nanna. Let me get my cloak."

***

Just being outside the dim, stale hall lifted Frigg's heart. The day was more beautiful than the patches of sunlight had promised. Astride her horse, she had a fine view of the light-dappled, snow-covered tops of the fields and forests surrounding Gladsheim, along with the silvery river snaking in and out of view.

Nanna rode beside her while Gná rode before them both holding the Almother's banner, a falcon's eye. As they clopped slowly down the curving road to the second tier, through the market and then beneath the second gate, she was in among the bustle of Gladsheim itself. People, carts, animals all moved this way and that amid the swirling smells of cooking meat, wood smoke, baking bread and the nose-wrinkling acridity of animal waste.

The crowds made way for their small group, the free men and women touching their foreheads or stopping to bow and greet her. If they'd been walking, they wouldn't have gotten a spear's throw before being stopped. But astride a horse, they were clearly on important business.

"So tell me, how did your meeting with the Jotunn envoy go?" she asked Nanna. "You and Baldr met with him, what, two nights ago?"

"We did, Mother," Nanna said, her fingers toying with reins. "But with respect, I'm not the right person to ask."

"You were there, weren't you?"

"I, uh, well, yes, Hár Frigg."

She touched her daughter's shoulder. "Don't say, 'uh,' Nanna Neprsdottir. You were taught better. In his own way, your husband is just like his father—let me guess what he's doing today. He rose early and visited the healers at Aegir's Temple to help them in aiding the many folk unlucky to be sick this time of year. And then, if there's time before evening, he'll check in with the city wardens or the Einherjar."

"Or both," Nanna said.

"Leaving you to do what?" Frigg said. She answered her own question silently: to be as alone as I am.

Nanna shrugged.

"I'll tell you what. Today, at least, you relieved me of a full helping of boredom, but I won't always be able to slip away." Frigg gestured toward the crowd of people around them, moving, bustling, laughing, yelling. She turned the gesture into a wave, acknowledging all those around her. "Have you ever walked through a cloud of those little spring flies?"

Nanna gave her an odd look but nodded. "Not in a great while— but yes, as a child, I'm sure I did."

"You're much closer to your youth than I am, Nanna. I've been in Gladsheim many times longer than I spent growing up among the Jotunn. In some ways, I am more Aesir than these around us. Yggdrasil's fruit has so extended our lives that we move through this press of people much like your younger self did that cloud of spring flies."

She took in her daughter's shocked expression. "It is a brutal thing to say, but how many new generations have you already seen, Nanna? Two? Three? I've seen six, maybe seven. And now that I say it out loud, no wonder Odin's always leaving, always out doing something. My point, Nanna, is that we both need to find something that links us to all these folk around us. If we begin to truly see them as flies, why bother ruling?"

And would we still be ourselves if we view our fellows as annoying bugs soon to die.

The crowd began to press in around them more tightly as the gate that led to the first tier loomed ahead. Wide though it was, with all the traffic passing through, the streets near the gates were always crowded.

She glanced sideways. Her daughter's eyes were clouded with thought. "So tell me, Nanna, what drudgery did you discuss with the Jotunn envoy?"

Nanna clucked her tongue and brought her horse closer to Frigg. "Is it safe to—"

"No one's listening." It was hard enough to hear Nanna's soft voice above the noisy bustle around them. It would be still louder once they reached the trade district.

"We spoke to him right after Thor destroyed that town."

"I'm sure the conversation went well, then," Frigg said, wondering if Odin would be proven right, that exerting force would indeed make the Jotunn more tractable.

"I wouldn't say—oh, I see." Nanna's cheeks colored. "Baldr tried to smooth it over as best he could, the more so because Thor didn't actually kill anyone."

"He didn't?" Normally, he didn't care. Why had he been careful this time?

Nanna shook her head. "Baldr had gone to Thor and asked him to spare the Jotunn in the town. Thor said he'd think about it. When Thor returned, you and the Alfather had ridden to speak with Mimir so Thor told Baldr what he'd done—and what he hadn't. Baldr was relieved to hear that his brother had honored his request."

That was well done. "And did Baldr send Thor back out again?"

Nanna smiled, brief and genuine. "No. Thor left shortly after he arrived. By now he and Sif are likely back in Thrudheim for Midwinter."

Since they lived farther away, Freyr and Freyja had left right after Ithavoll. Tyr had remained, as had Heimdall.

"And so what did you discuss with the envoy after the Thor incident?"

"Baldr discussed the plan you and the Alfather proposed—sending craftsmen to build and improve their roads. Baldr expanded on it, talking about building a waystation along the route between the Breach and Jotunheim where Jotunn could come for healing. He talked of sending valkyrs from Breidablik to staff it."

"How did Eldir respond to that?"

"He seemed amenable, but then he would, I suppose. Something for nothing. Baldr also mentioned some Jotunn settling in Asgard. The envoy was less intrigued by that idea. He was mostly concerned that those who do so might be threatened or killed—used as a cudgel to bring the Skrymir to heel."

That was one reason behind the idea. Frigg nodded. "Aside from that, what else did he say?"

"That he'd convey the proposals to the Skrymir but that nothing was likely to happen until after Midwinter."

"That's fine. We've enough to deal with now, anyway." She glanced sideways at Nanna. "And you? What did you add?"

"I don't understand, Mother."

"Everything you told me involved Baldr doing or saying something. What did you contribute?"

The horses' hooves thudded into the silence between them. Nanna glanced at her, cheeks rosy. "I said little, Mother."

"I thought so. Next time, you and I will talk before another such meeting. You've a sharp mind, Nanna, but don't be afraid to nick your edges. All good weapons are battle-tested."

"Weapons, Mother? I don't under—"

Frigg touched Nanna's arm, stopping her daughter even as she reined in. At first it seemed a trick of the sunlight, but flames descended on Nanna's head, roaring downward in the first exuberance of a bonfire.

There was no heat, but Frigg flinched as if she had been scorched. She squeezed her eyes shut, but the blazing red light danced just beyond them. Why was it always fire?

"Mother?"

Nanna's hand touched her shoulder. Their horses' shoulders brushed against each other as the animals shifted, nervous, anxious to be moving again.

"I'm all right," Frigg said, forcing her fingers to unclench. "Another vision."

"Of me?"

Frigg opened her eyes—the flames were gone—and shook her head. She hadn't answered questions like that since her youth, not even when Odin asked and more recently than that. She wasn't about to start now. "War burns at the edge of things."

From in front of them, Gná called out, "Almother, a warden approaches." She pointed back down the way they'd come.

The crowd parted around the warden like a river around a rock. He reined in and touched his brow in salute.

"Apologies, Almother, Hár Nanna. There's been a murder."

***

"Fimafeng, tell me again what happened." Frigg sat and gestured for Nanna to do the same. "From start to grisly finish."

Despite the braziers Gná had just finished kindling, the hall was cold and dim with evening's approach. Frigg shivered beneath her heavy falcon cloak. The halls flickering shadows reminded her of her father's tent, flaps thrown open so the spirits could lend their guidance to all the hundreds, perhaps thousands, of judgments her father had pronounced during his long tenure as chief over all the winters of his life before sunset.

"Yes, Almother," Fimafeng said, stroking his long beard far whiter now than gray. "The divorce you witnessed nearly a fortnight ago ended in the woman's murder. But not before..."

He coughed and looked down at his feet.

"You can say the word, Fimafeng. It won't be the first time I've heard it."

Or had to deal with its consequences. She glanced sideways at

Nanna, who sat, composed enough, hands folded in her lap. Nanna's eyes were wide, though, as if she were shocked to be where she was. Frigg briefly touched her daughter's knee. She'd had Tyr to guide her through her first dozen judgments...and all the time spent watching her father do the same. Nanna had Frigg.

Fimafeng continued. "Apologies, Almother. It seems the woman, Bera, was raped before being strangled."

"And this is known how?"

"By the sister's word and her husband's. Said she heard screaming; her house is near to her sister's. Said she went running, with her husband, to her sister's house. They flung the door open and found the former husband, Harald, on top of his former wife, Bera. The sister's husband pulled him off while she, Yelena, ran for the wardens, screaming 'Murder!' the whole way."

"And how did Yelena's husband come to be stabbed?" Nanna asked.

"After he pulled Harald off Bera, the husband claims that he fought with Harald," Fimafeng said. "The husband, Klakki, was carried to Jarl Baldr's longhouse—the one he uses for the care of the hurt and sick, I mean. I don't know how badly the husband's wounded."

"Claims?" she asked.

"Yes, Almother. The wardens told me that none witnessed the gruesome events inside the longhouse except Harald, Yelena, and her husband."

And the dead wife, of course. Were Odin here, he could have coaxed the words from Bera's corpse. But of course he wasn't here.

Frigg gestured for Gná to approach. "Take a warden and visit my son's hall. See if the sister's husband lives. If not, Karl Harald may have two lives to answer for."

"Yes, Almother," Gná said, nodding.

"Tell me what the wardens said they saw when they arrived, please."

"Both are here, Almother. They could—"

Frigg raised her hand, smiling. "I know, Fimafeng, and I'll hear them shortly. Right now, I want to hear it all from you. Your memory has always been flawless."

The old thrall bowed slightly, thanking her. "Of course, Almother. They told me they found the husband, Harald, in the corner, bruised and bleeding, dazed. His former wife, Bera, was dead on the floor, dress up around her waist, neck badly bruised."

"Did they seem drunk to you? Or like they had been drinking? The wardens, I mean."

Frigg caught Nanna's surprise and shrugged. Drunken wardens were common enough.

Fimafeng shook his head. "No, Almother. They'd just started their watch."

Which meant their first patrol through the area had been done while sober, or mostly so. Had it been later, the sister might not have come across them at all.

"Very well, Fimafeng. Is there anything else we need to know before the accused is presented?"

"No, Almother. Shall I fetch them?"

Frigg nodded and the thrall stepped away, boots hardly making a noise as he went.

In a low voice, Nanna asked, "We, Mother?"

The far door creaked open as Fimafeng hauled it open.

"I told you what was required, Nanna."

"Yes, but in front of them all?"

She turned toward her son's wife. "We rule, Nanna. We make the decisions when the karls and even the jarls cannot. Were this the murder of a thrall, we wouldn't have been summoned. Nor would the rape and murder of one karl by another necessarily require my involvement. But I'm sure that since I was involved in their divorce, Fimafeng thought it important I be party to this foul outcome. When you and Baldr come to rule, you'll need a steward like Fimafeng."

At the clink of chains and scuff of boots, Frigg glanced down the hall. Then she looked back at Nanna, smiled, and set her hand on her shoulder. "For now, just pay attention. I won't throw you to the wolves just yet."

The younger woman gave a quick smile of thanks.

Harald stumbled through the open center of the hall, his hands bound before him. Short though the walk was, it felt as if it took a month for him to approach and fall to his knees. If anything, Harald looked even more hard-ridden than he had during his divorce. His big shoulders were slumped, and his weather-beaten face had been further beaten by fists. Purpling bruises and crusty blood covered half his face.

The wardens behind him, however, made their prisoner look small. They were both older men, judging by their gray-shot beards, with hard faces made more severe still by the dim light and strong shadows.

The murdered woman's family crept up in the wake of their daughter's killer. The parents looked like empty, hollow trees that somehow still stood. Their second daughter had a black glint in her narrowed eyes, made somehow more wicked by the pregnant rounding of her belly. Fimafeng dragged a bench in behind her; she sank slowly down onto it but gave no sign of thanks. None of three were much changed from when Frigg had seen them last.

When all parties stood before the platform, Frigg addressed the parents and the sister. "My deepest sympathies for your loss—"

"It wasn't me, Almother, I swear," cried Harald.

One of the wardens struck him a sharp blow on the side of the head, knocking him sideways.

Frigg ignored it and continued. "My deepest sympathies for your loss. Who speaks for your departed daughter?"

"I do," the pregnant woman said. She was slight of frame and favored her mother's washed-out look, but with more backbone. And that black glint in her eye. "I'm her sister, Yelena. It was my husband this one stabbed."

Harald was struggling back up, shackled hands rubbing his head. "And you, who speaks for you?"

The man stared down at the shadows pooling on the floor. "No one but myself."

"What do the lots say, Fimafeng? Who speaks first?"

The old thrall closed his eyes and tossed a handful of wooden lots before the platform. When they rattled to a stop, he knelt and examined them with great care. "This one here," he said, gesturing at the man.

"Go ahead, Karl Harald," Frigg said, as Fimafeng gathered up the sticks.

Harald's lower lip was split and still bleeding, and beneath the beating he'd taken, he had the unfocused look of a man recovering from too much drink. She'd seen the signs often enough to know. "I didn't do it, Almother, I swear that—"

She raised her hand, and Harald fell silent. "Tell us what happened—tell true, mind you—and it'll go easier for you."

He swallowed hard, looked down at the floor and then back up at her, eyes intense and pleading. "I was home early, two nights early, from driving a herd south. Weather was fine so we made good time. Everyone wanted to be back, I think, you know, for Midwinter. Anyway, I came in through the south gate before evening. Met up with those few friends who'd stuck with me after the divorce and started drinking—had earned more silver for such a quick run, so I had a little to spare. I made my payment to Gladsheim first, Almother. I spent what was left on myself."

Frigg raised her hand again. "Fimafeng, is that true? Did the karl pay on his debt?"

Fimafeng nodded once. "Yes, Almother."

"Good. Continue." Truth on one point might point toward truth in others.

"Yes, Almother. My friends had their families to get back to, so we settled up, and I headed home. Guess I was drunker than I thought, cause my feet took me to my old house—the one I'd shared with her. The one I had to give up. Not that I disagreed with your judgment, Almother. I realized my mistake when I set eyes on it, but the door was open. I could see movement inside—shadows, really. It was late —moon high—but no one was around. So I wondered if there was maybe someone inside, trying to steal what she had—maybe knowing of the judgment and the silver she got.

"So I run forward, throw the door open, and see this one's husband on top of my wife—former wife, I mean." He gestured at Yelena with his chin but kept his eyes down.

Frigg almost expected Yelena to say something, but she didn't. She sat silently, arms folded across her belly, still with that murderous gleam in her eyes. There was also something satisfied about her expression, like someone sitting back after a good meal.

She glanced at Fimafeng, who shrugged slightly, and then the wardens, checking their expressions. They were totally impassive.

To Harald, she said, "Go on."

A fierce note entered the man's beaten voice. "So I went at him. Tried to get him off her. She was crying—I remember that—but the rest is blurry. He threw me off, and I must've hit my head. I wasn't steady on my feet; like I said, drank too much. I remember fighting, though. I had my knife at my side. It's not there now, so maybe I did stab him."

She looked at the wardens again. "How did you find him?"

The warden on the left spoke, his voice a hoarse rumble. "In the corner of his house, unconscious. Breeches undone. The knife Jarl Baldr took out of the husband's side fits this one's sheath."

"I see," she said. "Do you have anything else to say, Karl Harald?"

The man shook his head. "Only that I didn't do it. I wouldn't have. I'd done wrong by her, I know that. Your judgment hit me hard, Almother, and I didn't think about much else on this last drive." He clasped his hands in their bindings. "I didn't do it, Almother. By the Departed Mother, I didn't."

She lifted a hand. "All right, Karl Harald. And you, Karl Yelena, what say you?"

The woman's venomous gaze met hers for just a moment before she dipped her head to her chest, as if collecting her thoughts. When her eyes came back, they were cool and restrained. Her lip curled, and she gestured with her chin at Harald.

"Only that my husband and I saw this pig murdering my sister. We saw it."

Frigg nodded. "All right, Karl Yelena. How did you happen upon the—"

"We heard the screams." Yelena's voice was icy like a winter's night. "So we rushed over—not that I move so quick these days, heavy as I am."

Frigg looked at the wardens. "Did anyone else hear the screams?"

The first one spoke again. "Not that we know, Almother. I asked around while I waited for the other wardens to arrive, but no one said."

Yelena spoke. "My house is right next to my sister's. My parents live several houses from me. It was late, so maybe everyone was already asleep."

"But not you?"

Yelena shook her head and held her belly. "I'm close to my time. Sleeping's hard."

"I remember how that was," Frigg said with a smile that had no effect on Yelena's chilliness. "So tell me what happened when you and your husband got to your sister's house."

"Well, I had a club in my hand, just in case, you know. And when we got there, I froze up. I must've screamed myself. This one here"—she pointed at Harald—"was on top of my sister, hands wrapped around her neck, yelling at her. I could tell she was already dead by the way her arms flopped around as he shook her."

She broke off and hid her face in her hands. Her parents remained silent, white-haired and stooped, seemingly numb to what was happening.

Harald remained on his knees, staring down at the shadows.

Yelena coughed, looked up, wiped her face with her fingers. There was a note of pride in her voice. "My husband didn't hesitate, though. He ran right in and pulled this one off her. They started fighting. I dropped the club and ran out, best I could, screaming for the wardens. I found them a few streets over. I told them where to go, and they ran back. I couldn't keep up, so I just got there when I could."

"Thank you, Yelena," Frigg said.

She looked at the pair of wardens before her. "Now, wardens, what did you see when you first entered the house?"

The two men exchanged a glance. The one on the right shrugged, so the one who'd spoken earlier spoke again. "As we said, Almother. This one here was in the corner dazed, breeches undone. Karl Yelena's husband was on the floor, knife in his side, moaning, blood all over the place. We found the club, too, hair and blood on it. The wife's dress was hiked up, but she'd passed on by the time we got there."

"I see. Anything else?"

The second warden spoke up. "Just that the house looked like someone had gone through it—jars on the floor, chairs overturned, chests thrown open."

"From the fight, maybe?" Frigg asked.

"Could be, Almother. But it looked odd to me."

Yelena spoke, her voice angry. "It was probably him looking for the silver. Figured he'd steal it and pay back his debt with it. Make himself even richer."

Frigg ignored the outburst. "Wardens, did you ask at the way house where he was drinking? Find out if his story is true?"

"I did, Almother," the second one said. "The owner said he saw him leave not long before he closed up for the night."

"I see."

She was about to say more when Gná slipped into the pool of light cast by the braziers. She beckoned her forward. "A moment, please, while I hear this message."

Gná stepped up on the platform and whispered in her ear, "Jarl Baldr says that the wounded husband will fully recover. The wound was bad, likely would have killed him, but he used some of his elixir."

"Is the husband awake now?" she whispered back.

"Yes."

"And how did he seem to you?"

"More like a frightened deer than angry, as I'd expect a man who'd just been stabbed would be," Gná said.

Now that was an interesting observation. Why fear? Gná had a gift for seeing right through a person's bluster to what they were really thinking. She glanced around the room, her gaze passing over what seemed like a thoughtful look in Yelena's eyes. None of this smelled quite right to her. Perhaps a little deception was needed.

She kept her voice low. "Did my son say we could speak to the husband tonight?"

"He said it would be better to wait until morning but that tonight would be all right, were it necessary."

She nodded and gave her instructions, voice still low. "All right, Gná, thank you. When I dismiss everyone, bring one of these wardens back to Baldr's house. Make sure the husband sees the warden. Then go to the wardens' barracks and tell the kjolr there what I've done. He is to send another pair of wardens with you. Make sure it happens, Gná, all right?"

"Yes, Almother," Gná said.

"Once you have, find Gulfinn. Tell him to look for Heimdall and then report to me here in the morning. Once you've done that, come find me at Baldr's sick house. And keep those wardens with you, too."

With a quick nod, Gná left.

Frigg beckoned for Ráta who'd been standing by one of the columns. "You'll come with me to Baldr's. Then I want you to also look for Heimdall. When you cross paths with Gulfinn, which I'm sure you will, stay with him and report back to me here in the morning."

"Almother, I really think th—"

"I know, but I'll be fine. It's a short walk, and I'll have the wardens with me."

Ráta set her jaw and was about to protest further, but Frigg shook her head. "I need Heimdall, Ráta. Please find him for me."

The baresark hesitated a moment more, then nodded, bowed, and left.

Frigg cleared her throat and addressed everyone present. "I have good news from Jarl Baldr. Your husband should recover, Karl Yelena, but he says the next hours are particularly critical. Your husband is sleeping and has been drugged so that he will remain asleep through evening tomorrow. I've asked my servant Gná to make sure you're informed the moment Jarl Baldr says you can see him."

"Thank you, Almother," Yelena said, a wariness in her eyes. "My parents and I are so very grateful both to you and your son for taking personal interest in this. Please convey my thanks to Jarl Baldr, if you see him before I do."

"I will indeed," Frigg said, inclining her head.

68

Odin

Odin shivered back into wakefulness at the rushing sound of fast-moving water. Sleipnir clomped to a stop beside the Gjoll and bent her head to drink. He yawned and slid from her back onto the slippery stones littering the river's bank. The river itself rushed past, gray beneath heavy, low-lying clouds. About nine yards downstream, the river turned frothy and white as it reached the rocks before the falls.

When Sleipnir finished slurping water, he walked her back up to the pair of boulders he always camped beside. His breath a fog around him, he dug in Sleipnir's saddlebags for some oats, removed her saddle, and attached the feed bag to her bridle. She whickered her thanks, and he began to brush her.

Afterward, he kindled a fire, sat on cold stone and drank thirstily from a wineskin. He closed his eye, rubbed his temples and, ignoring the dull throb from his missing eye, leaned back against the boulder, and just for a few moments enjoyed the fire's heat. Normally when he traveled, his familiars went with him, but they were out in Asgard doing his bidding. Besides, for what he had planned, they'd be more hindrance than help.

And for that task, he needed seidr. Which was why he'd stopped here. He cast an eye toward the Gjoll's fast, dark current and the dozens of partially submerged rocks comprising his route to the river's center. Just beyond them, to his right, the Gjoll fell hundreds of feet to flow beneath the rude bridge onto the shores where the dead lingered. None living besides him knew this path, besides Sleipnir. They had it from Ratatoskr who himself knew many secret ways through the realms.

Odin called Gungnir to his hand, walked down to the river's edge and set booted foot upon the first broad, slick stone that lay belly up along the bank like a washed-up corpse. He sprang to the next rock, used Gungnir to vault to the next stone and the one beyond it. From here, the path grew more dangerous. A dozen rocks waited for his feet to slip. If they did, Rán would certainly cast her net and try to snare him.

Not that she ever would. He'd dodged that net more than once in his many winters.

***

Two rocks left. The first a leap, the second just a step.

On his blind side, the water fell away into a mist that obscured the height of the drop—what he risked falling into. He held Gungnir sideways before him for balance and turned his head to look down. Memories stirred of when, as a much younger man, he'd stared into the Ginnungagap and felt a deep, belly-clenching awe.

Now, he almost wanted to throw himself over the edge, to experience the rush of wind and then, the snap of his wings when he shifted at the last possible moment.

Instead, he returned to his task. Sól picked that moment to throw a spear of light on the remainder of his path. The next rock was wide, but pitched just slightly toward him, so he'd be jumping onto a sloped, slick surface. It glared at him that rock, a snow bear at bay.

He jumped, the wind's chill fingers plucked at him. His cloak billowed and he hit the rock at an unplanned angle. His feet slid, he grabbed the sharp stone—Gungnir clattered away and vanished into the darkness of his blind side—but he held on.

Gasping, clothes wet from the spray, beard dripping, he hauled himself upright. Teetering and tired, he made the short step to the final, mercifully flat-topped boulder at the river's center. In the past he'd tried to simply fly to this rock. But there was something perverse about the Gjoll. It didn't like him, this river into which the blood of both Ymir and Audhumbla had once flowed. It didn't want him here, doing what he was about to do. No matter his shape, it was always a struggle getting to this cold, wet rock in the middle of a chill, gray river that emptied into the sea where the dead took ship for the Gap.

He unclipped his cloak and dropped it beside him. He called Gungnir to him; she flickered into his hand, ice cold and frosty.

He marshaled his strength, eye shut, face upturned to catch what warmth he could from Sól. As he listened to the Gjoll's thundering passage, he slowed his breathing and extended Gungnir over the foaming, rushing water. He plied the long spear in rhythmic movements parallel to the water. Stiff with cold and frozen clothing, his first efforts were jerky. After several long passes, he eased into the motion, his entire body moving along with the spear as he plied it above the gray river.

Again, he closed his eye and focused on seeing the flow of witchblood with his mind's eye. It coursed within the torrent. He caught a tendril and slowly spun Gungnir in his hands, curling that tendril around the flat of the spear's blade. He brought the spear back to catch another, and another, wrapping the mingled blood of both the Departed Mother and Ymir around the blade.

On and on he went. Sometimes he caught a tendril. Sometimes it slipped away, pulled down by some current in the Gjoll. He kept going until the witchblood was wrapped around Gungnir's blade like a cloud around a mountain's peak.

***

Back on shore, he stared tiredly into the fire and sipped his wine.

Sól had retreated behind dense, gray clouds. His hands were red and raw from the wet and cold—and from scouring, straightening, cleaning, sorting and then flattening the witchblood like women did with batts of sheep's raw wool. Such was the price of seidr.

Now that batt of witchblood, fluffy, coarse and damp, was wrapped around Gungnir's blade and ready for the next stage.

He picked up one of his mostly depleted spindles and unspooled a knife-long strand of remaining thread. With Gungnir in the crook of one arm and the spindle pinned beneath his armpit, he teased free a bit of the raw witchblood and drew it down in a wispy tuft.

He brought up the thread and, between his thumb and forefinger, spliced the witchblood to the finished thread. That done, he withdrew a heavy soapstone whorl inscribed with runes and affixed it to the bottom of the spindle. Trapping Gungnir securely between his arm and body, he set the spindle spinning and dropped it.

With his right hand, he drew the witchblood down from where it was wrapped around Gungnir's blade. With swiftly dancing fingers, he spun it into a thread of magic that he could use to power his charms. He could use the raw stuff if he had to, but the refined witchthread lent much more precision.

And so he stood there, fingers dancing delicately up down and the thread of magic running from the batt to the spindle whirling before him. Firelight danced across his face and threw wild shadows on the landscape around him. The wind cavorted past, occasionally blowing gray smoke into his face, but with his eye closed, he held his breath until the wind shifted again.

69

Frigg

Frigg pulled back the cowl of her falcon-feather cloak and nodded to the warden standing outside the longhouse where Baldr treated the sick and injured. Beside her, Nanna wrung her hands.

"So, Nanna, are you ready for this?"

Nanna shrugged. "I suppose. You're just getting the husband's version, right? To check it against what his wife and the killer said?"

"Are you so sure Harald is a killer?"

"It seemed clear to me, Almother. He certainly had reason enough to want her dead."

"You were also at the divorce with me. Did he seem like a killer then?"

"He struck his wife several times, and in public," Nanna said. "That suggests he can be violent."

So could Odin, though that wasn't fair. The spirit within him had been in control when he'd attacked her. "I don't dispute that. But murder? It certainly can happen—I've seen it—but I'm not entirely convinced Karl Harald is as guilty as he appears."

"That's not what the witnesses said."

"No, it wasn't. But tell me, Nanna, did anything at the questioning strike you as odd?"

To her credit, Nanna thought before replying. "The sequence of events seemed disjointed."

"How so?"

"Well, if Harald left the way house when he said he did, he likely could have spent a long portion of the night alone with his former wife. The crime wasn't discovered until well after midnight."

"True, and a good point. But there's more, too. First, Harald was struck a heavy blow above his forehead." She tapped a spot above her right brow in her hairline. "When the wardens took him from the hall, I had Gná look, as well. She said the back of his head had dried and crusted blood, which you'd expect if he was struck by surprise from behind."

"Maybe he was hit first from behind but not hard enough? And when he got up, he was hit in the face. Or the wardens hit him at some point."

"Maybe, but it could have happened the other way around, too. He entered the longhouse, like he said, got hit, spun around, and then was knocked out by a blow to the back of the head. The wardens said the club had hair and blood on it."

"But that would suggest that Karl Yelena and her husband were lying about something. Why would they do that?"

Frigg spread her hands. "I don't know. But that's why we're here. I'm hoping the husband, Klakki, will let something slip."

***

Frigg settled into a chair a long arm's length from the bed where Yelena's husband, Klakki, lay propped up. His side was bandaged and his face was very pale and drawn. Sweat beaded his brow, his eyes darted from her to Nanna to the warden in the shadows by the door and back again. He wiped sweat from his upper lip and wiped it on the blanket covering him. Baldr assured her that he was well enough to answer questions, yet something was clearly not right with Klakki.

She'd met many lawbreakers over the past hundred winters and had sat in sole judgment of thirty-one in the past twenty winters alone—thirty-two, including Harald. That wasn't even counting the judgments she watched her father mete out when she was a child.

This man stank of guilt and, if she wasn't mistaken, fear. But of what? She herself was hardly intimidating, but she could have him killed. Or worse.

"My son says you're recovering quickly, Klakki," she said, offering a warm smile. "Before we begin, can I get you anything?"

"Begin?" His eyes darted from her to the door and back again.

"I wanted to ask you about what happened last night."

"But without anyone else here to speak for me?"

"Do you need someone to speak for you?"

Klakki coughed and glanced sideways at Nanna who gave a comforting smile. "No, Almother, of course not. But I want my wife here. Because, you know, she was there, too."

"But she said you ran ahead because of her condition?"

"Her what?" His eyes flicked toward the door. He wiped the sweat from his lip.

"Your wife's pregnant," Frigg said, letting a hint of amusement waft into her voice.

"Oh, yes, that. Of course," he said with a weak laugh.

"So did you get to Karl Harald's house first?" she asked again.

"Yes, Almother, I did."

"Good. That's what I'm interested in. You're the only one who saw Harald raping Bera."

He flinched. "My wife said that?"

Now that was interesting. Frigg leaned back in her chair, thumb tapping on its arm. "Not directly, but she implied it, saying you got there before her because she was moving so slowly."

"But Bera's house is right next to ours. Yelena was right behind me. I wasn't by myself for very long." He flashed a quick smile.

Frigg frowned slightly. "I admit to some confusion, then. You're saying she was with you the entire time?"

"Can you send for her, please? If she was here, we could clear this up right away."

"Was Harald raping Bera when you walked in? Or had he finished and was killing her?"

Klakki's face went even paler than it was; sweat dripped down his temples. He hunched in on himself. "Look, I tried to stop him. I did. And I took this"—he leaned to his right, presenting his wounded side—"when I was trying to get him off her."

"I understand that—and thank you for it—but I'm trying to better understand what actually happened in that house from the only person who was there besides the man who did the deed."

"My wife told you what happened."

"What she saw, yes. But she said you got into the house first and implied you were there for a short time by yourself, aside from Harald and your dead sister-in-law. You seem to be saying that's not accurate, that your wife was there the entire time."

"Not the entire time, but she couldn't have been more than a few steps behind me."

She wasn't getting anywhere with these questions. Still, she had the feeling that something wasn't quite right. He was too uneasy, too defensive, too insistent on having his wife present. What man wanted his wife present to speak for him—especially one who'd subdued a rapist and murderer. He didn't seem proud of his actions. Perhaps he was ashamed that he hadn't stopped Harald? Either way, she needed a different tack.

"Did Harald and his wife fight often?" she asked.

"What?"

"When they were married, did they fight often? Yelling, screaming, hitting, that kind of thing."

"I don't know. No more than any other who's newly married, I guess."

"But with your houses so close, you probably would've heard them, right?"

"The houses aren't that close."

He had just said their houses were next to one another. "But you and your wife said you heard Harald's wife screaming?"

"We told you, the door was open. I'm sure that's why we heard it."

"Then why didn't anyone else hear the screaming?"

New sweat leaped to Klakki's brow. "I'm not lying, Almother."

"I didn't say you were, Karl Klakki. I'm just curious as to why, if the screams were so loud, none of your neighbors heard them."

He shrugged and glanced at Nanna, then at the door and back at her, all in a heartbeat's time. "It was late. They were probably all asleep."

"Of course," she said. "I'm sure that's it. But the open door still confuses me, since it seems unlikely that a man intent on having it out with his former wife would leave the door open. Wouldn't he have made sure it was closed, expecting that shouting would be involved?"

"He was drunk. Maybe he forgot." He wouldn't meet her eyes.

"That's quite a thing to forget, not closing the door before an argument, or worse, starts."

"I don't understand why I'm being questioned, Almother. I caught him. I wish I'd gotten there sooner, but I didn't."

And there it finally was, the bit of spine she'd expected. "That's why I asked what was happening when you ran into their house. Was Bera still alive?"

"I don't know. I didn't get a good look at her. And what does it matter? She's dead now."

It mattered because there was something not right here. "To get Harald off your sister's wife, what did you do?"

"I don't really remember. You know how fights can be."

She nodded. "Indeed I do. But surely you remember some of it. Did you grab him by the shoulders or hit him or maybe throw yourself against him?"

Klakki's eyes flickered toward the door. "Could you send for my wife, please? She was just steps behind me. I'm sure she could say exactly what happened."

"When my servant arrives, I'll send her to fetch your wife." But

Gná wouldn't arrive until she heard Frigg specifically tell her to step into the house. And that was assuming Gná had finished what she'd been asked to do.

"What about the warden outside?" Klakki asked. "He could get her, right?"

Frigg stood abruptly. "Who rules here in Gladsheim, Klakki?"

He seemed to shrink into himself. "You do, Almother."

"I've been lenient with you because you've taken a wound in stopping a lawbreaker. But you're not answering my questions, and that's not only making me curious, but it makes me think I've been lied to. Have I been lied to, Klakki?"

"Aren't I allowed to have someone speak for me, Almother?"

She let her frown deepen. "Are you guilty of something? You're the hero here, right? You caught him, you and your wife. He'll hang because of you."

"Hang?" Some emotion flickered too quickly across his face for her to identify.

She forced a tight smile, the icy kind her husband used often enough. "That's the punishment for murder. If I could, I'd hang him a second time for the rape. It happens often enough, but rarely do we have a chance to make an example of them. Perhaps a blood eagle, then. Those always seem to calm the waters for a while."

Klakki's gaze dropped like a stone to the floor.

"Look at me, Klakki."

He gave no sign that he heard. He pawed at the side of his head, eyes squeezed tightly shut, and rocked slightly back and forth.

She glanced at Nanna, who was resting her arm in the crook of her elbow, one hand cupping her chin. Frigg gestured slightly toward the man.

Nanna looked questioningly at her, so Frigg repeated the gesture. Comprehension dawned on Nanna's face.

Nanna edged forward in her chair and touched the man's arm. In a low, gentle voice, she said, "Please tell us what happened, Klakki. We're only after justice, we're not looking for you—"

Klakki's eyes snapped open and, in an urgent voice pitched far too high, said, "You have to protect me from her, please. You can do that, right?"

"Of course, we can, Klakki," Nanna said in tones she might use to comfort a child. "You're safe here. The warden's right outside—"

His laugh held a tone of hysteria. "The warden? After what she did to Bera? She could tear him apart if she wanted."

Klakki's voice dropped to a whisper. He banged the side of his head with his unbandaged hand. "She's a seidkonur. She cast her net over me and made me do things I didn't want to."

Frigg frowned. There were any number of minor witch-women selling charms and cures, some of which might even work. Genuine witch-women who commanded seidr like Freyja and Odin could were rare among the Aesir.

"Like murder Bera?" she said.

Klakki's surprise was nearly comical. "No, Almother, by Aegir, I swear I didn't. It was Ye—" he coughed "—her, I mean. It had to be."

"You saw your wife kill her sister?" Nanna asked, sounding nearly as surprised as Klakki had.

Klakki's mouth snapped shut. His gaze flickered to the door and back again.

"She can't reach you here," Frigg said.

"What if she's listening? She can do things. She knows things. Things she shouldn't."

She needed to put his fear to rest, even if it meant a lie. "Hear me, Klakki. The Alfather wove charms into the very beams of this house. No mere seidkonur can pierce them."

"Really?"

She ignored Nanna's surprised expression. "Absolutely. Now please, tell me what you know."

＊＊＊

Klakki set the cup of wine aside and wiped his mouth with the back of his hand. He looked calmer, but his eyes were still a little too round, like a spooked horse. He glanced nervously up at Frigg, ducked his head in an odd sort of bow, and then looked at Nanna.

Frigg smiled at him as if she were soothing a wounded man even as she edged out of the overlapping circles of wavering yellow light by the bed. Klakki had responded better to Nanna's gentleness than her own impatience.

He spoke after a long exhale. "I remember meeting her last Midwinter. You know how it is. One thing led to another, and by summer we were married—Midwinter to Midsummer. I remember joking about it, but even those memories are hazy."

"Just tell us what you do remember, even if doesn't seem to make sense," Nanna said.

Klakki rubbed his temples and grimaced. "I remember going with her...Yelena...to her sister's house to meet her parents. But then I also vaguely remember her telling me last Midwinter that she was an orphan. When we walked into her family's house, the folk sitting around the fire looked shocked. Harald stood and reached for his knife, but my wife,"—Klakki shuddered—"lifted her hand. And then that's it. That's all I remember."

"Until now?" Nanna asked.

He shook his head. "There's other bits and pieces. I remember being on a drive with Harald and when I got back, Yelena had picked up a bag of..." He closed his eyes and tilted his head slightly, thinking hard. "It's odd. I remember most of the cattle drive with Harald, but as soon as I set eyes on Yelena, the memories jumble and fade. Everything's broken up like the pieces of a shattered cup."

Nanna continued her soothing tone. "That's all right. If they're clear enough, describe those pieces. With enough of them, we may put that cup back together. And I know the Almother will be grateful for anything you do remember. Even the smallest piece may help."

But none of this seemed at all related to Bera's murder. Nanna had the man talking, but she needed to focus him on the relevant events, not his life story.

Klakki nodded. "I'm not sure when it happened. During the day, I think, because the door was open. We were sitting around the fire, eating and talking like family does. Then Yelena, her belly big like the baby was near, stepped in. I'm not even sure when I got her with child. I don't remember any of that—not finding out or her being sick or anything."

He reached nervously for another sip of wine. "Another time, we were in the market. Evening had just fallen. Still enough light to see by, though. We passed through the old quarter where the houses are tight together. She made me turn around and watch the street while she did something."

His face twisted as he tried to remember.

"Do you know what she was doing?" Nanna asked.

Klakki shook his head, eyes squeezed shut. "There were voices. Deep. Two or three, maybe. I wanted to turn around—thought she was in trouble—but I couldn't. Literally couldn't move."

"Did you hear what they were saying? Or maybe they passed by—"

"No, none of that. Just the deep, hushed voices. Some clinking, too, I think. I'm sorry."

"It's all right." Nanna patted his arm. "Maybe your memories will come back the more you rest."

"More are coming back just being away from her," he said with a weak grin. "But I do remember what happened after that. I think it was the same night, but I'm not entirely sure."

He licked his lips and looked down at the floor, thinking hard.

Frigg took the opportunity to catch Nanna's attention. She made a rolling motion with one hand and mouthed, "The murder. Get him talking about the murder."

Nanna nodded—and smiled reassuringly at Klakki when he looked up at her.

"It was a hot, moonless night," he began. "I remember how much I was sweating. I was carrying a bag that clinked with every step. We were going slow, making sure not to be seen, which was unlikely because it was late."

She suppressed a sigh. This had nothing to do with the murder.

"Was it the same sound you'd heard when your wife spoke with those men?" Nanna asked.

"Maybe?" His voice rose slightly.

"Don't worry about that now," Nanna said. "Do you remember where you were going?"

His gaze flickered back up to Frigg, then back to Nanna. "We went into Idunn's Grove."

Frigg's heart skipped a beat. All her impatience drained away. There was no law against entering the grove, but to do so stealthily at night? That was suspicious. Or was she suspicious just because of what she and Odin had hidden there?

"We stopped at a tree. I don't remember anything else except Yelena smiling at me, singing softly. My stomach was twisting like I'd drunk too much."

Frigg came off the wall, swamping the light. "Which tree was it? What did it look like?"

He shrank back into the bed. "I... I don't know. It was just a—wait, an oak, I think. Yes, it was an oak tree."

An icy hand gripped her around the throat. She knew what he was—

"And it had mistletoe in it, high up, and she..."

The flames of a vision roared to life above Klakki's head. This time, she willed the flames to burn higher. She needed to see. Maybe they'd show her a...

... man crouched behind a shield wall, spear in hand, the other arm braced against the crumpling, headless body of a warrior right in front of him. Even as he drew back his own spear to throw, another spear caught him in the chest and flung him back, coughing blood. A Jotunn warrior stomped a boot onto Klakki's side and yanked the spear free.

"No," she murmured.

Seeing this man's death was useless. She needed to see where he'd been and what he'd done and who his wife had met in the dark. She tried to keep the vision flames alight, but they flickered and withdrew.

Clarity rushed back along with the warm yellows painting the long-house's interior. She found herself leaning against one of the columns. Klakki wore a horrified look, while Nanna's was creased with concern.

She pushed herself off the column and tugged at the hems of her sleeves. "I'm fine. But Klakki, I need to know more. What else happened at the tree?"

Like a fish breathing air, he gaped at her, eyes comically wide. He glanced at Nanna, who gave a quick, encouraging nod.

"Well, I'm not sure. Yelena stopped singing. She told me to drop the bag and catch what she dropped."

Frigg ignored the cold sweat that had gathered on her lip and brow. A heavy bag that clinked? Drop what she caught? Staring up at mistletoe? The picture was drawn for her. This man and the witch who'd trapped him were the ones who'd cut her son's mistletoe.

But she asked anyway. "Do you remember anything else?"

"No, Almother. Just a few fragments: walking back, how heavy the bag was, collapsing into my bed."

"And the bag, where did it end up?"

"I don't know, Almother. Between then and now, there's just more fragments. Staring at a blank wall while Yelena sang. She might have been sitting on the floor naked. I remember that because her belly was flat." His face twisted with worry. "Is any of this helpful, Almother? I'll do whatever I can to make up for whatever I did."

"Whatever you did, it was not by your own choice," she said, trying to keep her voice calm while a shriek scrabbled at the back of her throat. "Nanna, would you keep Klakki company? I need to speak with Gná."

"Of course, Almother," Nanna said, smiling past the confusion in her own eyes.

That confusion would be stark fear if Nanna knew exactly how important these bits of memory were. She had just uncovered the plot against Baldr.

***

Outside, the moon had dipped low. The cold night air slapped Frigg hard in the face, banishing the house's warmth.

A pair of wardens stood next to a pair of witchstoves. Gná rose and the wardens saluted even as Frigg gestured for Gná to join her a few paces away.

When they were alone, Frigg leaned in close and said, "Just before dawn, take a warden with you and go to the sister's house. Tell her that her husband woke, confirmed everything she said, asked for her, and then passed out. Jarl Baldr said he'd be fine and that she may see him at midday tomorrow. Instruct her to be at the Lower Hall at dawn. That's when I'll pronounce sentence against Harald. Tell her that exactly."

"Yes, Almother," Gná said with a quick nod.

Frigg gripped her arm. "Say nothing else to the sister. Nothing. This is extremely important, Gná—and make sure the warden stays beside you. Give the message, and then leave. From there, fetch Karl Harald from the stocks and bring him to the Lower Hall. But come through the back entrance. We will meet you there."

"What's all this about, Almother?"

With a quick shake of her head, Frigg gave Gná a reassuring smile. "It's best I just tell you when we meet at the Lower Hall. Oh, and Gná, once you've brought Harald to the hall, find Gulfinn and Ráta. I don't care if they haven't found Heimdall yet. I'm going to need them."

70

Hodr

After a pair of nights on the road to Gladsheim, Hodr had grown thoroughly tired of the rumble and scrape of the ironbound wheels of the smith's cart on the road stones. The relentless sound had driven him inward and made him dwell on his failed attempt to persuade Alara to share Yggdrasil's fruit with him. That same fruit now rode heavy in the bag looped around his shoulders. He still wasn't entirely sure why he'd decided to visit his father except that it felt right to end what troubled him before trying to start something new—whatever that might be. Which in a way, he supposed, answered his own question.

"So quiet, Jarl Hodr," Lopt said.

"Don't call me that," he said, reflexively. He still hadn't donned his gold arm ring; it hung by a cord around his neck. All of the jarls and sons of Odin wore the same arm ring, a heavy, doubled loop of braided gold, one end a wolf's head, the other a raven's. It was a copy of Draupnir, the arm ring Odin wore.

"My apologies," Lopt said, "but I don't know what else to call you. With every mile we draw closer to Gladsheim you grow that much more...gruff...than you were in Ifington. It doesn't suit you, my friend."

Didn't it? In Ifington he been free of his family and his past, though, were he honest, he'd often felt its shadow looming—family and past both—like an approaching storm on a hot summer's day. He'd left Gladsheim blind and furious, but he was returning with his sight if not healed, then...replaced...was maybe the best word. And his anger?

As he sat, jostled and bounced by the cart, listening to the dull clunk of spears and swords, he didn't feel any of that same rage that he'd taken with him from Gladsheim.

Maybe he would glimpse Gladsheim's tall gates and Heimdall's tower atop the sharp cliff that marked the crown of the city's hill. The crown to which he must ascend.

One of the cart's wheels banged hard against the road and jarred him to say, "I'm not a true jarl, Lopt. I don't rule a district."

Lopt flicked the reins, the leather slapping against the broad back that loomed hazily before his half-seeing eyes. "Maybe, but you're still one of the Alfather's sons. That commands respect, as do your deeds in the Last War. You should wear that arm ring I've noticed beneath your shirt with pride."

"Pride?" Hodr laughed. "People don't want crippled heroes, especially if they're an Odinsson."

His blind eyes could see the lean gray shapes looming tall beside the road, with leafless fingers intertwined like bones on a battlefield.

He rolled his new spear, the smith's gift, between his hands. "Yet as I hold this spear and see even this horse's ass in front of me—the one that broke my skull, I believe—I thank Aegir that our paths crossed. The horse and yours."

He thumped the spear's butt against the planks of the cart beneath his feet. "My father will ask how you came by its runes, you know. Are you prepared for that?"

The cart creaked and rumbled down the road for a long time before the smith flicked the reins and asked, "Do we have to tell him?"

Hodr laughed. "You've never met my father, have you? My friend, the moment he sees this spear, he'll notice the runes. I've no gift for magic, but he taught me the runes he knows. Most of the ones you used, I don't recognize. He'll insist on knowing where you got them."

The cart banged and clattered along again. In Hodr's spear-granted sight, Lopt looked spun from gray clay.

The smith flicked the reins again. "Maybe you could just use another spear while we're there."

"Well, now you have me worried. What magic did you use? My father and brother both failed to restore my sight, yet I stumble across an unheard-of smith from a small village—and I mean no offense by that—who succeeded where they did not?" He shook his head. "No, my father will demand an answer. My brother will be nicer about it, but he too will want to know how you did what you did."

After another dozen heartbeats of rumbling, rattling cart wheels, Lopt's shoulders slumped and he blew a long sigh. "I knew it couldn't last, but at least you'll speak for me, I hope. I have a Svartalvar chained to my forge."

Hodr stiffened, and his grip tightened on the spear.

"I joke, of course," Lopt said, grinning widely and glancing side-long at Hodr.

The smith's next words were drowned out by the banging rumble of an approaching cart. This close to Gladsheim, and with Midwinter only two nights away, many traders were heading home. And from the way this oncoming cart leaped and lurched, this particular man was anxious to be there. He raised a hand in greeting, shouted something, and was gone again, his rumble trailing after him like one of Thor's storm clouds.

When it was possible to again be heard, Hodr said, "Don't joke like that with my father."

"Not funny, eh?" Lopt threw him a shadowy, lopsided grin.

Hodr snorted.

Lopt's voice slid into the silence between the rumbles of their own cart. "The truth is, I don't know where the runes came from. I learned my trade from my father, as he learned from his. The runes were a part of what was passed down—from my grandfather and his father before him. My father knew what the runes meant and how they should be used, but he was killed before passing all of what he knew on to me. When he used the runes on the weapons he crafted, he hid them—beneath the wrap on a sword's hilt, on the inside of the axe's head, by the wood on the spear's tang. When he started doing that regularly is when the Einherjar started buying our weapons. And then I just kept doing what he'd done."

Hodr exhaled a breath he hadn't realized he was holding. Joking about the Svartalvar was not a good way to approach answering the Alfather's questions. But, Odin would accept that the knowledge of the runes had been passed down over generations. That was how everyone learned. He would press for more detail, though. Just imagining how his father would hone in where the runes came from made him want to itch the scars where his eyes had been. Instead, he asked, "Who among the Einherjar accepts delivery of your weapons?"

"Their quartermaster. Man named Geirleikr. You know him?"

Know a man who'd probably been a baby when he'd last been in Gladsheim? Hodr snorted. "I might've known his mother or father. Who commands the Einherjar now?"

"Saglund, his name is. Met him once."

"It was Jarnsaxa when I was last in Gladsheim. I heard that Garilon briefly took over after her."

Lopt flicked the reins. "Saglund's the one who started buying our weapons."

As another cart rumbled closer, heading away from Gladsheim, Hodr fell silent. He took a long look at the dim shapes all around him. The tall trees. The hazy ground. He raised his hand in response to the salute of the trader approaching them—and then laughed aloud because he'd *seen* the man's wave.

"I know what you're thinking, Jarl." Lopt's voice was loud over the receding rumble. "The spear was a gift. I'll stand before your father and brother and take whatever punishment they deal out."

"Punishment?"

"For using those runes."

"Have you provided weapons to our enemies?"

"I only sell to the Einherjar, like my father did. Well, maybe a weapon here and there to those who come asking, but they're all Aesir. And I don't put runes on those weapons."

"Then I don't think the Alfather will punish you. And if he tries, I'll speak for you." For all the good it would do. "He'll certainly require you to show him all the runes you know and explain how you've used them."

Lopt grunted, but said nothing. He flicked the reins again.

Hodr clapped his hand down on the smith's heavy shoulder. "And if I know my father, he may even require you to move here and start teaching what you know. Better weapons to fight the Jotunn."

"Move? Teach? My father said these runes should be kept secret."

Hodr shifted the spear to his left hand and held it out to the smith. "Then take it back now, drop me at the gate, and ride away home again. I'll keep your secret."

The moment seemed to stretch out longer than the road they had left to travel. Hodr saw the smith's right hand release the reins and move slowly toward the spear. He drank in the sight, hazy though it was, knowing that if the smith took back the spear he'd never see anything again.

He brought Alara's face to his mind's eye and savored it, too, like that last bite of the fruit he'd eaten. And might not ever taste again.

What would he do if Lopt took back the spear? Alara said she loved him as he was—blind and broken. Without this new sight, imperfect as it was, he could become the warrior he'd once been. He need not return to Ifington or to Alara. Did he only love her because he was half the man he'd been?

The smith's hand closed over his.

"Keep it, Jarl," Lopt said, quietly. "I said I'd face the Alfather's judgment. I meant it."

Relief bloomed in Hodr's heart—and he realized that, if he was honest, he still had no idea what choice he'd make.

71

Odin

Astride Sleipnir, Odin rode down the winding trail from the rocky heights toward the snow-covered forest below. The Gjoll wound half-seen through that forest and, eventually, into the cold, misty land where Loki's daughter Hel had been exiled. And in that land was a bald hill where he had watched Loki raise a barrow for his wife, Angrboda. That was where he would raise the dead witch to speak with her.

But for now, his eye was closed and he looked inward. Angrboda knew him, and though he would compel her speech—true words, as he'd told Frigg—the Norns also spoke true words. As did he, usually. But both he and the Norns hid meaning within those true words, as could the dead. Particularly those dead spirits who hated him.

He would need a disguise.

Trusting himself to Sleipnir, he stepped from his mind into a spirit-skiff that rocked beneath his weight and from the slapping waves of the misty waters. One hand on the steering oar, he leaned forward, and unfurled the sail. It dropped, banging limp against the mast. The wind picked up, stirred his cloak and then bellied the sail. Gathering way, this skiff of his mind smacked against the rushing water and threw a fine white wave. Beneath the sail, he guided the skiff toward the one longship—a dark blot beneath a white sail—that always sailed these waters.

His disguise would not only have to fool the witch but Garm, too. It would be best not to let the hound's mistress, Hel, know that he tread the shores of the Gjoll. Not that he feared her—much less a coven of witches—but why antagonize without need.

His mind-skiff thumped against the longship's tall, long side. Rope in hand, he clambered up the ship's toenail-colored, slick side, slipped through a gap in the racked shields and dropped to the deck between two rows of dead crewmen hauling on their oars. He tied the rope off, then traced a rune on the inside of the nearest shield to mark the spot. It began to shed a faint golden light.

Most of the dead men and women around him worked the ship in the finery their families had provided. Some were arrayed for battle, while others wore embroidered robes—traders, maybe, or rich farmers. They sat shoulder to shoulder with thralls clad in filthy shirts and trousers who looked as if they might have dropped dead in a field and been rolled into a pit. Most of the dead he could see were old, but he knew from experience that once he moved about the longship, he would see all ages. Some of the dead were warriors who had died upon the battlefield, armor rent and ragged, skulls split, limbs missing. Yet they, too, hauled upon their oars.

He touched the foreheads of several nearby. It wasn't the face that mattered but the thoughts and memories. He needed those to run strong and deep, like a fast river, so he could submerge his own mind beneath theirs and not be discovered. But none of these would do. Simple lives of simple people—nothing wrong with that, but he could hardly hide himself beneath their memories.

Odin sidled out into the aisle between the port and steering-board side of the longship. The rows of the dead stretched fore and aft along both sides. The tree-like mast was behind him and obscured his view of the ship's bow and the wyrm-figurehead mounted there.

He held his hands out to each side, moved down a row touching his fingers to the foreheads of those in the next row. Memories mingled with his. This one died upon the gallows; this one in alley, alone, cold, and shivering. He stepped forward. This one died in a blaze of pride, blood painted across his face; this one beneath a slaver's whip; this one because she'd lost hope. He stepped forward again. More deaths. Forward again. More deaths.

This was taking too long. He had to be back and disguised before Sleipnir drew Garm's attention.

He looked over the dead as he might a battlefield, looking for that betraying glint of sunlight upon a spear. He strode through more death, just as when he'd hung himself upon Yggdrasil, pierced and screaming, and found that this place, this river upon which the dead sailed, existed.

He strode on, a hundred faces behind him and a thousand or more to go. He walked on through the terrible, terrifying, sobering field of grinning death.

A hat caught his eye, wide-brimmed and unusual. He remembered seeing its like among his brothers' peoples to the west. He strode toward its wearer. The dead man's face was deep brown even in this light, his nose broad and his lips full. His belly was split wide open.

Odin touched the man's brow. Memories of sailing across a tumultuous green sea foaming with tall, white-crested waves. The man's ship...his ship...bucked beneath him—up, down, and sideways. In the memory, he looked over the man's shoulder...his shoulder... and saw a black thundercloud stacked high. Dark green waves chased him. The ship ran fast, bow plunging and surging like a racing stallion's head. Sailors clung to lashed oars and ropes. Some were aloft, trying to reef the sail so it wouldn't split or, worse, snap the mast. This man whose memories he beheld, this wayfarer, clung to the sternpost and watched a long, sleek vessel in their wake turn broadside to the pursuing waves and founder. The Wayfarer shouted orders and flung himself against steering oar.

Sleipnir's whinny bubbled up into Odin's awareness. He was needed. Odin sprinted forward through the man's memories to the moment of his violent end—and reeled back in surprise. Them? How?

Sleipnir whinnied again, more urgently.

Odin shook himself free of the Wayfarer's memories and then sat down *into* the dead man, shaping his own spirit so that it fit within the dead man's. When he stood, he wore the dead man's spirit as if it were his own. He'd plumb this man's memories later but now, he must return to his body.

He focused on his rune he'd drawn between the shields and drew himself toward it as he might drag himself along a length of rope. The entire distance he'd traveled aboard the ship of the dead passed by him in an instant. When he reached the golden rune, he dropped over the side into his skiff and pushed off.

Again, Sleipnir whinnied.

He swore, exhaled, and summoned a gale that sent him careening back to the shores of his mind.

***

The world rocked about Odin. He steadied himself against Sleipnir's strong neck, arched before him like a ship's prow. The mare stood still on the path. A hound's baying, deep and loud, throbbed in the air.

He patted Sleipnir's neck. "It's all right, girl. Thank you for bringing me back."

He reached into his satchel for one of his newly charged spindles. He unspooled nine arm lengths of thread, clipped it free, and flung it outward, fingers dancing. He crooned a song, pulling the dead man's thoughts, memories, and appearance from within his mind and made them real and substantial with the witchthread he wove around himself. He also cast his net around Sleipnir so that her appearance would also change. When he had it right, he spoke a word and tied the knot.

The hound bayed again, much closer now.

But he and Sleipnir were hidden. With one hand, thick-veined and deep brown, he lifted the dead man's wide-brimmed hat and ran a hand across his bare scalp. A weight of rings tugged at his ears, and they jingled as he moved. He had left the patch over his eye, thinking it might aid his disguise. He now wore a heavy, red tunic over a lighter blue shirt with yellow stitching beneath. His thick white breeches were tucked into knee-high leather boots.

Sleipnir stomped in place and shook her new mane and whinnied in evident displeasure. She had shrunk in size, her eight legs blended into four.

He patted her neck again. "Just a temporary change." His voice was more melodic than his usual scratchy rumble.

In the near distance, the deep-throated howl sounded again. He should have enough time for one more necessary change.

He clipped free another arm's length of thread, replaced the spindle and shears, and called Gungnir to him. He sent the thread out, fingers dancing, new voice singing. When he spoke the final word, Gungnir shimmered into a plain wooden staff.

He tugged his broad-brimmed hat low over his eye, sagged in the saddle, and clucked his tongue. As Sleipnir started forward, he sank his spirit down beneath the dead man's and let those borrowed memories float upon the surface.

***

The dead man, a former sailor, stared up into the hound's eyes that burned black with canine rage. The hound's huge nose twitched. The slavering jaws parted, threatening with huge white teeth.

The nag the sailor rode had stumbled to a halt. Only his hands, tight on the reins, kept her from bucking and panicking. It wasn't so much the hound's sudden appearance that stoked his own panic but the stench of old blood, black and matted, upon the hound's chest. It roiled his stomach worse than the dead fish reek of his ship's deck, worse than the open-gut gore of the towns he and his crew had often sacked.

What kept that panic from blooming into a raging fire was a calm whisper from very deep within him. It wasn't his own voice that whispered, though. It was another's.

Be calm. You're a messenger. Show the token.

So he did, holding up the silver token that even this hound must respect. He was proud that his hand only shook a little.

Foul coppery breath wafted over him. His nag shied, but he kept her under control. The huge teeth loomed closer, rotted flesh visible in the nooks and crannies. Sharp-nailed paws dug into the road, gouging furrows in the packed dirt and small stones.

This is Garm. He wards the path, but you have my token.

Even as he heard those words, the disc caught the light and shone silvery. Garm drew back. He sniffed again, a small windstorm. Then as quickly as he had appeared, Garm ran down the ravine and vanished in the gloom and firs.

Well done, Wayfarer, the voice whispered.

The Wayfarer stood in the stirrups and peered over the trail's edge. He could just make out the hound leaping back down the rocky slope to the low road that wound among the fir tree on the valley floor. A procession of witchlamps lined the low road that led to the bridge. Shadowy figures marched along the road. Every so often, some bundle or another would catch the witch light and gleam gold or silver—treasures laid by the wayside.

These are the recently dead. You've nothing to fear from them nor anyone in this land, for you carry my token. Ride on.

The Wayfarer tapped his heels on his nag's sides and slapped the reins. The frightened horse refused to move, so he kicked her sides. The nag seemed inclined to buck, but instead snorted and clopped forward on the road down to the sickly trees, drab grasses and the mist-covered river.

Death behind, death ahead, with me the bridge between.

72

Frigg

"Midwinter is when we celebrate the triumph of life over death," Frigg said from the platform in the hall where she dispensed punishments and rewards to folk of Gladsheim. Her heart thumped beneath her formal robes, dark blue with silver thread woven around her cuffs and bodice. She had posted city wardens at the hall's three entrances: west, east and the south-facing, double-door entrance. "It pains me, then, that I must pronounce sentence on one of our own for a horrible crime committed during this season. We should be celebrating life's promised return, not grieving its loss."

She raised a hand and beckoned. "Wardens, bring the prisoner forward."

Manacles clanking and chains dragging across the planks, Harald was shoved toward the front of the hall. Two wardens walked before him and, when Harald stood before her, they forced him to his knees.

"Let the family come forward to hear my judgment," she said, gesturing for Yelena and her supposed parents to stand opposite Harald. A pair of wardens stood behind them.

Yelena wore a satisfied smile, and the wicked gleam in her eyes shone like a fresh-honed knife. If she was the one threatening Baldr's life, then betraying her presence with this murder made no sense. Perhaps her role had simply been to get the mistletoe and, now that she'd done so—assuming her husband, Klakki, was right—she was now about her own business.

Frigg glanced at Nanna. Her son's wife appeared composed, aside from picking at the hems of her sleeves. And biting her lip. Not that anyone was focused on her.

Everyone in the hall—from the front benches to the rear doors—was looking at Frigg or Harald. Gladsheim was home to thousands, but it was also comprised of smaller communities. Probably every member of the community Harald and his family—former family—had belonged to were in the hall waiting for the judgment they expected: hanging.

Frigg turned her attention back to Harald, who knelt with his head bowed. The wardens behind him had their hands free and looks of preparation on their faces. She glanced at the pair of wardens who stood behind Yelena and her family.

"Rise, Harald," she said. And at those prearranged words, the wardens behind Yelena each grabbed one of her arms, while the two behind Harald rushed forward with leather straps.

Yelena began thrashing the moment their hands closed around her wrists. Slight though she was, she nearly flung them off. Even so, they staggered into her parents and banged into the nearby benches.

Yelena, her pretty face flushed and made ugly with fury, opened her mouth to scream something, but before she could do more than haul in a breath, a warden shoved a leather strap so hard into her mouth that her jaws opened wide and her lips pulled back in a grotesque smile. The other warden stomped on the back of her knee and forced her down, binding her arms at the elbows and again at her wrists.

Nanna rushed from the platform to help the old parents up and out of the way. Harald stood slowly, dropping the manacles and chains that had never been locked shut. Anger blazed in his eyes.

Frigg raised her voice and her arms above the commotion and shouted, "Everyone, be still. All will be explained."

***

Braced for the vision she expected, Frigg stared at Yelena who sat on a bench. Yet no vision came. Yelena's seat on the bench was the only consideration given to her pregnancy because, slight though she was, she radiated a venomous rage.

Wrists bound in front of her, the wardens shoved Yelena's hands into a leather bag and cinched it tight. She gurgled some word from behind the wide leather strap in her mouth. The wardens flinched, then rechecked the leather strap binding her elbows together, making sure it was tight enough to prevent her arms from moving. They had already taken a charged spindle off her, along with silver shears, and set both well out of arm's reach.

Frigg lowered her arms as the many-voiced rumble drew quieter. "Hear me. No doubt you are all curious. Well, my friends, we've likely captured a seidkonur."

Shock rippled through the confused din. She pointed down at Yelena. "This is the witch-woman, right here. From what we've been told, she cast a charm on her husband and family, and compelled her husband to abuse and then murder her sister Bera."

The onlookers, held back by several wardens, began muttering and murmuring. Several made signs of warding with their hands which she knew, having been told by Odin, were complete ineffectual.

Frigg gestured toward Karl Harald. "I believe this man is blameless. The Norns who carved his path made sure he happened across the witch's plot. I believe he tried to stop it, but not expecting seidr, was quickly overwhelmed and then blamed."

"How do you know that's all true?" shouted one man. And another yelled, "Looks like you've just bound a pregnant woman." A third: "We know 'er! She's no witch!"

Frigg squared off against the crowd. "You don't believe me? I've lived three times longer than the oldest one here," she said, hands on her hips. "I've seen more witches than I can count. I know the signs."

The crowd's mood hadn't changed. If anything, her words had

made them more sullen judging by the scowls and glowers. Vision-flames flickered above the heads of some among them, particularly a tall, broad-shouldered blonde man with ugly teeth who, noticing her eyes upon him, gave a disgusted snort, turned, and bulled his way through the crowd.

"I see you doubt me," Frigg said. "Stay, then, if you choose. Wardens, push them back another spear's length."

***

Yelena's long, pale-yellow braid lay over one shoulder and within easy reach of her bagged hands. And though she couldn't touch her hair, one of the wardens yanked it away and put the braid behind her back. These wardens knew how to deal with seidkonur; it was simple enough to braid witchthread into long hair. Yelena glared sideways at the warden who averted his eyes. Most witches needed thread to work magic, but Odin didn't—nor did Freyja, not always, at least.

"Remove the gag, please," Frigg said. "She needs to answer my questions. But stand ready."

The same warden undid the strap and pulled it from Yelena's mouth. He let it drop to the floor, careful not to let any of the spittle touch him.

"Who are you, witch?"

Yelena retched, coughed, and looked up, eyes bloodshot, tears welled up. "I'm no witch, Almother. It's that old woman who left with Hár Nanna. She charmed me just as she did my husband and Harald."

Doubt wormed its way up from her gut, but the claim was easy enough to check. Nanna had just taken the parents into the small room behind the hall's platform. "One of you go check on my daughter, please."

A warden saluted and moved quickly toward the room.

"Almother, she lies," Harald said. "She must be the one who charmed me. I saw no one else that night."

"I believe you, Harald, but it doesn't hurt to check." Particularly since a seidkonur need not have been present at Bera's house to work magic.

Yelena retched again and gasped, a long line of spittle stretched from her mouth to the floor. The gag hadn't been in that long.

Frigg turned when Nanna's voice came from behind her. "Both parents are asleep, Mother. If that old woman's a witch, then I am as well."

"Thank you, Nanna. Stay with me, please—"

A slurping sound interrupted her, and she turned in time to see the witch spit at her. Though she stood nearly two spear lengths distant, the spittle stretched out in one unbroken line. It struck her in face with a wet, sickly splat.

The witch shouted a word, and the spittle flowed down Frigg's face and tightened around her neck like a noose. It wasn't spittle at all, but witchthread.

Reflexively, her hands shot up to pull it away, but there was no space between the wet thread and her throat. And it was cinching very fast.

Frigg fell to her knees, breath rasping, heart pounding, the edges of her vision already blackening like a leaf thrown on the fire. She heard Nanna shout, "Silence her, quickly, she's choking the Almother!"

There was a crack like an axe striking wood, and fresh air rushed back into her chest. From her hands and knees, she looked up to see the witch sprawled across the bench, her forehead streaming blood. Harald stood over her, his knife in his hand.

Nanna's wildflower scent grew rich in her nose as her daughter knelt beside her and wrapped an arm around her waist. "Can you stand, Mother?"

She nodded, got her feet under her, and stood. Her throat felt worse than it had when Odin had choked her, but she stopped herself from rubbing it. Fresh bruises would shortly blossom. She'd need a high-collared dress for Midwinter now.

She stepped toward Yelena.

"Clever to swallow the thread, witch. Less clever to be caught."

When Yelena didn't respond, Frigg motioned to the wardens. "Haul her upright."

"Yes, Almother," one said.

The other continued. "Our apologies for—"

She held up her hand. "It was a clever trick. Make sure to tell your fellow wardens of it so we won't be caught again. But just to be safe, cut off her braid and burn it."

She turned to Harald. "Thank you for your quick thinking."

He nodded. "I'm at your service, Almother."

One warden held Yelena by the nape of the neck, face down, while the second sawed his knife through her braid. Surprisingly, she didn't resist, nor did she speak. When they were finished, they hauled her upright and shoved her back onto a bench.

"Club her if she tries another charm," Frigg said.

"Such cruelty, Almother," Yelena said, her voice a wet rasp. "I never would have guessed."

"Who are you, witch?"

"Can't you tell, Almother? I was told you saw the doom of all men and women."

Frigg frowned and put her arms on her hips. "At my word, these wardens will gut you."

"But you promised the good people of Gladsheim a hanging, Almother," the witch said, nodding toward the crowd whose gasps and horrified cries had subsided. The wardens had pushed them further back

"So I did. But I'm not afraid to break that promise if it means a better spectacle," Frigg said, her voice even. "Now, answer me. Who are you, and how long have you been in my city?"

The woman smiled and shrugged. "Long enough, Almother. Rán herself would be jealous of how far I cast my nets."

"And what have you caught?"

The witch grinned. "Oh, many fish."

"I want names—everyone you swayed with your seidr."

Yelena's grin widened.

"Break one of her fingers," Frigg ordered. From the corner of her eye, she saw Nanna blanch.

The warden in front of Yelena ripped the bag from the witch's hands and snapped her littlest finger like a twig—and with about as much emotion. Yelena's shriek echoed off the ceiling, and she hauled in a sobbing breath.

"Names, witch. Speak them, and you'll die quickly."

The sobbing gasp turned into a hoarse laugh. "But what about the hanging?"

Frigg gestured at the warden. He broke another finger.

This scream was longer, but it roughened again into a ragged laugh even as Yelena sagged in the wardens' grips, forcing them to bend further forward to support her weight.

Nanna edged forward. "Almother, I don't think—"

Frigg held up a hand. "Not now, Nanna."

Across the hall, the door banged open and Gulfinn and Ráta rushed inside. Frigg beckoned them over. The crowd had backed away still further, all but pressed against the opposite wall of the hall. Many were rushing out through the side door.

She looked down at the witch. "Keep your names for now. Tell me instead why you let yourself get caught. Was it sloppiness or stupidity?"

"Neither." Yelena sagged still further in the wardens' grips and coughed bloody phlegm onto the floor. "My mistress came to me in a dream. She asked me to."

"Who is your—"

Yelena surged up on thickening legs. Her shoulders swelled, bunched tight with new, inhuman muscle, and flexed outward. With a snap not unlike the sound of her fingers breaking, the leather strap binding her elbows parted, followed by the snap of the bindings around her wrists.

The wardens who had been holding her stumbled, thrown off balance by her changing shape. Yelena threw her arms upward as the wardens stumbled on either side, grabbed one by the collar, spun in place, and flung him across the hall. He slammed into a pillar to Frigg's left.

The witch finished her spin by driving a knee into the second warden's belly. He hit the wall, already limp, and slid into a heap.

Frigg stumbled back a few paces, and her heels banged against the platform's edge. She caught her balance, arms whirling. To her right, Nanna's sharply indrawn breath became a shriek like metal dragged across stone.

The witch's body continued to shift, shoulders swelling and hunching as her arms lengthened and thickened. Her dress tore in long, harsh splits, exposing coarse black hair that pushed up through her skin like grass.

A moment later, Gulfinn slammed the witch. They slid across the floor, limbs tangled in a single, horrid mass. Tables and benches splintered and flew up like spray before a longship's prow. Yelena just laughed. It sounded like seabirds above the waves.

The warden who'd bounced off the pillar to her left lay unmoving at its base, face down. The bronzed hilt of his sword was just visible between his arm and his side. Frigg ran toward him and fell to her knees, tugging his arm out of the way so she could draw the blade.

She glanced back toward Gulfinn, hoping to see how much time she had. Instead, she saw the witch's black-haired hand come up, a repulsive spike of white bone where her fist should be. The witch buried that spike of bone her hand had become in the baresark's broad chest.

Gulfinn roared in pain, red fountaining from his chest and mouth. Sweet Aegir, her vision had just happened. She'd seen it but not known when it would occur. If Gulfinn's death had come so soon, did that mean that Baldr's wasn't far off, either?

The witch gave a triumphant, coughing cry, ripped her reddened spike of bone from Gulfinn's chest, and spun toward Frigg. Blood spattered from the spike, and black fur rippled down to cover fingers that split out from the bone with stomach-twisting crackles.

Heart hammering in her ears, Frigg shoved the fallen warden's arm aside, grabbed the worn, sweat-stained leather grip of his sword and she swept the blade out in a flashing arc. She rose into a fighting stance. The last time she'd fought for her life was at the Old Wall, staring down at Vanir spears—but even so, the sword felt alive in her hand.

Yelena's face had become brutish and leathery, seamed and black, like ancient, oiled leather. Her large black eyes burned with hatred. Her body, fully transformed, had long, heavily muscled arms, covered in coarse black hair. Yelena grinned, baring thick, yellowed tusks, and broke into an unbelievably fast, lopsided charge, black-haired arms thumping against the planks beneath them. The planks flexed beneath Frigg's feet as Yelena closed the dozen spear lengths between them.

Frigg attacked, slashing at Yelena's shoulder, trying to sever the thick arm. Yelena swayed to one side and the flashing blade passed harmlessly by. Yelena skidded to a stop, grabbed her by the neck with her other arm and flung her backward against a nearby post.

The air whooshed from Frigg's lungs and the sword flew from her hand. Before she could even regain her footing, Yelena's rough, leathery hand closed around her throat and slammed her onto the floor, pinning her down.

Frigg ripped and tore at that tree-trunk arm. Yelena's arm felt like a ship's anchor rope, soaking wet and taut beneath all that coarse black hair.

Yelena leaned in, breath hot on Frigg's face, sharp yellow teeth gnashing as she spoke in a guttural, inhuman voice, "It seems my mistress was wrong."

Yelena raised her right fist, the bone spike again emerging from amid the sound of tearing flesh and breaking bones. She stabbed downward, but a dark shape slammed sideways into the witch.

The weight pressing Frigg down was gone. She bolted upright in time to see the witch's body slam down a dozen feet away and skid across the planks. Then she was up on all fours again, long arms planted knuckles first against the floor.

Between Frigg and Yelena, Ráta sprang up from a neat roll and squared off against the shape-shifted witch. Across the hall, Gulfinn had staggered back to his feet and lurched toward the witch's flank with what looked like a broken table leg in his right hand. His left hand was pressed hard against his chest, and when he roared a battle-cry at the witch, the sound was ragged and wet. He broke into a stumbling charge, but blood fountained from his mouth and he collapsed, twitching on the planks.

At almost the same moment, Ráta rushed the witch, hands open to grapple.

Yelena avoided Ráta's charge by leaping into the air and catching one of the columns in her rough, coarse-haired hands. She clambered up more quickly than Frigg would have believed possible for such an ungainly beast, paused about two spear lengths up and stared at Frigg with unsettling, hate-filled eyes.

The witch bared her yellow fangs in a horrible smile and in that gravelly voice said, "My mistress was right after all. I suppose I was foolish to disbelieve her—but I had hoped the Norns had given your doom into my hands. Even so, Almother, I will one day drink your blood."

Ráta flung a hand axe at Yelena, who batted it aside. The witch raced further up the column and leaped casually upward to grasp the lip of the inner roof. She hauled herself up and through and vanished without a backward glance.

73

Vafthrudnir

Vafthrudnir woke when he heard the disir's triumphant roar as it dove back into the Ginnungagap. A free disir could only mean one thing: one of Ygg's baresarks had died.

He threw off his blankets and rolled to his feet. Ygg and Freyja would have sensed the sudden freedom of the disir, too, and would even now be rushing just as he was. He had very little time, and only one option.

Wake Kali, he called to Fimbulthul. *Bring her down to the river. I'll get started.*

He dressed quickly, slung his satchel around his shoulder, and stepped from his tent into the dark, snow-laden forest. A short, slippery run later, he arrived at one of the low-burning campfires. Six Jotunn sat with their broad backs to it, staring out into the dark forest. Another dozen or so slept in tents pitched beneath the snow-covered trees. They'd seen—and heard—him coming, so those six weren't surprised until he snapped out an order.

"You and you," he said, pointing at two of the warriors, "Build a small fire down by the large rock in the river. Go!"

"Yes, High Shaman." They said, hastening to where the tinder and wood were stacked.

"You," he said, jabbing his finger at another warrior. He switched to the hand language. "Go to the hersir. Tell him I'm conducting a ritual down at the river. I want sentries, but under no circumstances are we to be disturbed. Even if the Thunderer himself rides overhead. Understood?"

The warrior blinked, mouth working soundlessly.

"Do you understand?"

The warrior signed his response, "Yes, High Shaman."

"Then move. Now!"

The warrior scrambled to his feet and ran toward the hersir's tents.

We're on our way down to the river, his fylgja whispered into his mind.

I'll be there shortly.

The two warriors had finished gathering the materials they needed. He snatched up a small pot that sat beside the fire and a witchlamp.

"Follow me. Quickly."

***

The fire crackled and popped. The pot sat above it, his ink soaking within. Kali sat to his right, naked to the waist, awkward and trying not to shiver. Her skin was smooth with youth, goose-prickled, and devoid of tattoos—but not for long, if all went well.

Have you found her?

Yes, it's Gunnthra, his fylgja said, sounding distant. *She's not interested.*

That's not acceptable. We need her. Did you explain that she won't be free for long?

She believes she can defeat them this time.

He snorted, opened his eyes, and dug through his satchel. He withdrew his charged spindle and silver shears. He unspooled as much witchthread as he dared—three arm spans—clipped it and began to sing. He sent the thread first through his own chest and then, fingers dancing, spearing through Kali's back.

She arched her back, eyes widening in surprise and then recognition of what he was doing. He sent the thread around and around, tying them together and giving them each more strength than they would have alone.

When he finished, he extended his hand to Kali. She looked at it, her gaze lingering on the blue tattoos around his wrist. She would soon have similar tattoos, if they succeeded.

"Time is short," he whispered. "Take my hand and release your spirit. We need to walk. I'll explain once it's safe."

A dozen questions leaped and danced in her eyes, but she took his hand. They both exhaled and sent their spirits out.

Don't let go of my hand, he thought to her, her hand—spirit though it was—still in his. Their bodies sat cross-legged in the snow behind them.

Where are we going?

You'll understand once we're there. He raised their joined hands and spoke a word, and the world broke like ice.

She screamed, and he pulled her downward so they fell into the widening crack. Stars swam around them, as if they were caught amid a school of silvery fish. Below them, a river of milky stars flowed outward like a sea monster's tentacle from the Roaring Cauldron.

The Cauldron itself churned around and around like a thick soup. At this vast distance, the Cauldron rumbled like a distant avalanche and growled like a distant storm. Eleven tentacular arms stretched out from the Cauldron and lay across the face of the Ginnungagap. From above, a never-ending cascade of white and green mist flowed into the Cauldron. From below, red and yellow fire blasted up into the Cauldron. And at its center, half-hidden by the maelstrom of swirling, burning tendrils of fire and smoke and sparks, those two colliding streams made up its thrumming, beating heart.

It was beautiful, terrifying, and mesmerizing every time he saw it. Those same emotions radiated from Kali through their linked hands

—along with shock and disbelief. She had spirit-walked before, but never to this place.

He shared his comparative calm with her even as he sent his thoughts out to Fimbulthul.

Is Freyja here?

Yes, she prowls out there, his fylgja replied, drifting overhead like a giant gray sea-wolf. *And there is another with her.*

Likely one of her blood-drenched priests.

Kali sensed Fimbulthul and recoiled, trying to tug her hand free. He gripped it tighter. *Let go before I tell you and you're dead. You feel the cauldron pushing us?*

Hvergelmir churned on; its eleven limbs flowing ever outward. He and Kali were salmon swimming upstream. Fimbulthul had taught him how to move in this place, and assuming they bonded, the newly freed Gunnthra would teach Kali.

Wide-eyed, gulping, Kali stared back at him. *Where are we?*

This is the Ginnungagap. And that is the Roaring Cauldron. I've brought you here sooner than I should have, but I had no choice.

He pointed ahead of them where a great-cat, long fangs bared, circled in place, facing off against an unseen foe.

She is why we're here—she is Gunnthra, a disir. If you can convince her, she'll become your fylgja just as Fimbulthul is mine.

By force of will, he began swimming toward the disir. Fimbulthul kept pace.

But I'm not—

No, you're not ready. I've no choice but to offer you the chance. Ygg's enslaved all but two of the mightiest disir. Gunnthra's back in the Gap, so that means one of Ygg's baresarks has died. That's why we're here—and that's why Freyja is here, too.

New shock rippled from Kali at the mention of Freyja's name.

I'll confront her, he said.

With my help, Fimbulthul added in a gnashing of teeth.

Kali glanced up the sleek gray sea-wolf. *Why can I hear her?*

Our spirits are linked, and we're in the Ginnungagap. Here, the spirit is the body. This is why so much of a shaman's training is spent honing the mind. We are preparing for this place.

But not all shamans have fylgja, so...

Some have found lesser disir, but one need not be a shaman to bond with a disir like Fimbulthul. Besides me, only one other Jotunn alive today besides me is so bound. You would be the third.

What if I don't want to bond with Gunnthra?

Then Freyja takes her, and our enemy is further strengthened.

He wasn't giving her much of a choice, nor was he being at all fair. He wasn't trying to. The Jotunn needed another baresark. But at least he was being truthful.

But how can she just take the disir? You and Fimbulthul will fight her.

There's no guarantee we'll win. Freyja is very strong, and her power doesn't come from this place. If she captures Gunnthra, she'll drag her back to Vanaheim—or wherever her body is—and then either bind Gunnthra to herself or that Alvar who's ventured here with her. Probably one of her strongest priests. Ygg showed her how to do it.

He could feel her interest warring with her fear.

If it helps, I didn't plan this. I would've chosen you regardless. You're quick-witted and brave—stepping through that doorway with me and figuring out we were somewhere else proved that. You've also demonstrated a willingness to change how you practice seidr. And Fimbulthul likes you.

And if I don't want to do it?

Then I'll send you back.

While you stay to fight. She only hesitated another pair of heart-beats. *What must I do?*

Anchor your thoughts on Gunnthra. Cling to her like you would a rock in a raging river. And fight that priest like you've never fought anyone before.

He spun in place and hurled Kali down toward Gunnthra.

***

Neither he nor Freyja spoke a word to each other. If she got past him, Gunnthra and Kali were lost. Every moment she fought him, the better chance Kali had to save Gunnthra.

So, he kept himself between Freyja and the grim, silent fight below them. Freyja had given a golden net to the Alvar priest while Kali had nothing but a silver spear formed from her will.

How is she doing?

Better than us, Fimbulthul said, dodging a harpoon streak of ragged energy Freyja flung at her.

Vafthrudnir surged in and grappled with Freyja, trying to get an arm around her neck. She was strong like the hot sun and a throbbing, beating strength flowed through her, like when blood pounded in his head. Then she flowed like tall grasses in the wind, slammed her elbow into his stomach, and pivoted, flinging him away.

Watch out!

A line of fire creased his back from shoulder to hip. He turned in time to block a slash intended to disembowel, and he took a deep cut across his forearm. What happened to the spirit happened to the body, so he would be bleeding now, perhaps badly—not that it mattered to his spirit form. But once his body died, so too did his spirit.

Fimbulthul slammed her gray, slab-like side into Freyja. That sent her tumbling up and away at a wild angle.

Thank you.

Instead of replying, his fylgja went after Freyja like the sea-wolf she resembled, buying him time to look down and see how Kali was doing. His fight with Freyja needed to end quickly. Even bolstered by the witchthread, his strength was limited—yet Freyja seemed as fresh as when they'd started. She didn't have a fylgja—had never needed one, not as long as he'd known her—nor did she have any other helper-spirit he could sense. Her power came from somewhere else.

Below, with the glittering river of icy stars as a backdrop, Kali kicked the Alvar priest in the stomach. He soared backward, arms spread. Kali followed, yanking the golden net out of his hand.

From above and behind him, Freyja's shouted "No!" rang like a bell.

Vafthrudnir grinned as he watched Gunnthra's cat-like shape shift till she stood upright like a Jotunn and then grew taller still, taking on the same color as the river of stars behind her. Gunnthra swelled still bigger, like a sail before the wind, and then vanished into Kali.

Gunnthra had chosen.

Freyja spun on him, her eyes a blazing red. A long beam of reddish light formed in her hands. Before he could do more than recognize the threat, she shoved the spear of light into his stomach.

74

Vidar

Sól peeked out from beneath heavy, gray clouds. She was low on the horizon; evening approached. In the wan light, Vidar watched dozens of Jotunn strain to haul bundles out of the frozen lake. He could not tell what those bundles were, only that they appeared heavy—it took two Jotunn to lift each bundle, place them on the sledges and then several Jotunn to drag them from the shore to the base of the towering cliff north of the lake.

"Are you watching this?" he asked Garilon.

Garilon shook his head. "Your eyes are better than mine, Jarl. I see dark shapes moving around, but I can't tell what they're doing."

Vidar pointed toward the northern shore, where the lake was mostly unfrozen. "Down there. North shore. Jotunn, pulling... bundles...from the lake and moving back and forth between the lake and the cliff's base."

Sól's light speckled the rocky, ice and snow-covered land. At the clink of metal behind him, Vidar squinted back down the slope to where his warband, hunkered in cold discomfort around low-burning witchstoves, threw faint shadows on the ground.

Garilon's shoulder thumped against his own. "Can you see what they're moving?" Garilon asked.

Vidar looked back at the lake. Now the sunlight happened to lay full upon the laboring Jotunn. "The bundles are long, maybe a spear's length, and round, like a log, and heavy. And they're stacked three... maybe four...to each sledge. There's easily...fifty Jotunn moving back and forth."

Obviously, the Jotunn assumed that neither Heimdall nor the Alfather could see through clouds, which might even be true. Even if it wasn't, both would have had to know where to look—not easy in a land where one icy cliff looked much like another.

As he watched, a group neared the lake, set their sledge down, and took up another. Whatever those bundles were, they were very heavy. The Jotunn bent hard into the traces before their burden began moving. The moving patch of sunlight fell on the cliff itself and Vidar watched the sledges vanish into the ridge.

He swore and caught Garilon's eye. "They're going into the cliff."

The gap in the clouds closed up and gloom once again lay upon the land.

Of course they went into the cliff. There was nothing else up here. Going into the cliff meant that beneath it—or this section, at least—lay a Jotunn outpost. Possibly one of their old stone-homes. By itself, that wasn't unusual. Many Jotunn had once lived underground. Some still did; Jotunheim was itself built as much into a mountain as it was on its lower slopes. He knew of five other caverns that had once been home to Jotunn.

This place was not among those he knew.

So, these Jotunn were engaged in mysterious work at a previously unknown outpost that also happened to be near a doorway that, somehow, connected to the mines beneath Hálsberg that had been used to launch an attack on the town of Háls itself. And this work, whatever it was, was important enough that the Jotunn did so during the day when they could be seen by Heimdall. If Heimdall wasn't a drunk.

He caught Garilon's eye. "None of this is good."

Garilon frowned, rubbed his gray beard, glanced down at their weary warband and back at the Jotunn laboring beside the lake.

Vidar understood what Garilon meant. But he needed to get closer. He needed to see what they were doing.

Garilon gestured westward past the break in the ridge to where gray clouds scraped the ground like a short-legged hound's full belly. "That storm's moving fast."

"Good. I can use its cover to get down there."

Garilon rested one ice-crusted glove on the silvered horn hanging from his belt. "With respect, Jarl, isn't it enough that they're doing something? If we move fast, we can get back to the doorway, sound the horn, and wait till Thor arrives."

He gave Garilon a significant look. "We can't rely on Heimdall hearing that."

Nor could he wait for his big brother to arrive—it would take several days, at least. He was here now.

"I need to see what they're doing," Vidar said. "Dragging things from a frozen lake under cloudy skies isn't something Heimdall would skip over, even if he were still looking. And this is probably where the attack on Háls originated. None of this seems like coincidence. Nor can it be good for the Aesir."

Garilon nodded once. "Very well, Jarl. What are your orders?"

Vidar winced internally at Garilon's formal tone. "There's a break in the ridgeline north of here and probably enough cover among the rocks to make it unseen to the bottom. We'll bring the warband there, and you'll wait. If I'm not back within a reasonable amount of time, you'll bring the warband back to the doorway and sound the horn. Maybe Heimdall hears and sends Thor. Maybe not. Either way, you keep the warband alive. If that means retreating through the mines, then do so. Use your best judgment—but keep the warband alive. Any questions?"

"Yes, Jarl. Two. What's a reasonable amount of time? And, what about you?"

"The first is easy enough." Vidar drew his knife, held it up so that its faint shadow fell across his body. "I'll show you."

***

Vidar crouched in the shadow of a boulder, maybe a long spear's throw left between him and the empty bowl-like depression that led down to the frozen lake. The Jotunn still toiled. Whatever was hidden in that lake, there was a lot of it.

Each sledge was loaded with three or four long bundles of something heavy. He couldn't tell what because the man standing chest-deep in the water beside the sledges kept getting in the way. There had to be shamans about, because there was no way even a Jotunn could so casually withstand the temperature of that water.

Once each sledge was loaded, four workers dragged it from the water, bent double over their ropes to haul it up the shore to the ridge. The workers returning unladen sledges stood upright, their sledges gliding along behind them.

He wiped snow from his eyes and squinted through the increasingly heavy snowfall. The storm was nearly upon them; it had arrived faster than those his brother dragged behind him.

Crouching, he darted forward to the next boulder, another dozen spear lengths down the slope. This one gave a better angle on the ridge's base, the likely entrance to the Jotunn outpost.

Other than the steady stream of workers back and forth from the lake, he hadn't learned much more than when he'd been atop the ridge. Which meant he either needed to get still closer—which might be possible as the snowstorm fully hit—or turn and leave, unnoticed.

Sól peeked out again between a break in the clouds, she was just kissing the horizon now, and her light seemed unusually bright in advance of the coming storm. It was bright enough that he spied a slow shadow gliding across the rocks between him and the shore.

He swore to himself and glanced back over one snow-covered shoulder to the ridge behind him. Another shadow glided quickly across the route he'd taken down. He'd been careful, but he hadn't been able to avoid crossing some open areas. And though he had dragged his cloak behind him to obscure his tracks, but even so, in this light it was obvious that something had come down from the ridge.

He rolled to one side, very slowly, and looked up. A black speck on wide wings glided high above. If he hadn't already been spotted, then he might soon be. Either way, and regardless of what was happening here, it was time to go.

75

Vafthrudnir

Vafthrudnir woke trembling. He was in a tent, wrapped in a bedroll on hard-packed snow, chilly despite the obvious layers between himself and it. Where was he? And where was—

Fimbulthul?

When she didn't respond immediately, he began counting his own, increasingly rapid heartbeats. When she still didn't respond, he pushed himself up—and then pain drove him down to his back. Cold sweat broke across his forehead.

She could not be dead. Disir couldn't be killed, so far as he knew.

He forced himself to sit up, growling through the pain, hoping that he hadn't just learned something new.

The tent flap opened and a pair of figures stepped through: Hersir Beli and Kali. Their respective fylgjas, Hríd and Gunnthra, followed behind.

Kali held a satchel in one hand.

"You're in my tent, Vafthrudnir," Beli said with his fingers. He gestured toward Kali, "She ran you here."

"Where is—"

Beli raised a hand, stopping him.

"Badly hurt," Kali said aloud. She switched to the hand speech. "But Gunnthra says that what's in here will—should—heal her. And you, as well, High Shaman."

"Hrid agrees," Beli said. "She also thanks you for saving her sister."

So Beli had told Kali. Or Gunnthra had sensed it. Fimbulthul could, after all.

"Several more adepts have arrived, High Shaman," Kali said in the hand speech, "bearing word that you and I must return to Jotunheim at the Skrymir's request."

He grimaced. "All this back and forth is really, really tedious."

Beli gave a sour smile and signed, "Our scouts have found Jarl Vidar and his warband. They've stumbled across one of our staging areas. The shaman there says he's certain the Aesir saw the work underway but that he was probably too far away to make sense of he was seeing."

Probably. "Will you attack him?"

"Of course," Beli said, holding up one hand to forestall the obvious objection. Vidar had wiped out one warband. Inadvertently, perhaps, but he was intelligent and had, quite likely, learned from his mistake. He could also command whatever ancient charms Ygg had taught him. Best to not underestimate him.

"We have the snow bears—more than when you left us, actually, thanks to Adept Kali and the others. And now more shamans have joined. Moreover, the jarl's warband is small, hungry, tired, and about to fight on unfamiliar ground," Beli said. "We have the advantage. But it's time for you and Fimbulthul to recover—and to return to Jotunheim."

Beli reached into his satchel and withdrew a small golden fruit.

Vafthrudnir's mouth watered, and his stomach growled. He hated it, but the sacrifice was necessary. His people needed him.

76

Odin

The Wayfarer stood on the hill's crown, which was bare except for the barrow of gray stones. A chill wind stirred his cloak and blew wisps of mist down toward the river behind him. He'd left his nag cropping sparse grass by a stand of trees that had retreated from the hilltop. The rain-slick cliffs of stone behind where Hel dwelled loomed in the far distance.

The Wayfarer knelt, removed his wide-brimmed hat, and ducked under his satchel's strap. He rummaged for the four witchlamps, lit each of them in turn, and set them in large square. Then he drew his knife from the small of his back and cut deep, wide runes into the sparse grass and wet soil just behind each witchlamp. He placed his token, Baldr's silver torc, in front of the barrow.

He rubbed his sleeve across his mouth and walked back to his horse. He grabbed a wineskin, took a long swallow, and trudged back up the hill. He rummaged for the second token, a hammered golden disk the size of his palm. At the center of the disk was a design of three interlocking triangles. Runes etched into the edge spiraled in to touch the corner of one triangle.

As they had on the road, the whispers in his mind surfaced: *Read the charm. Ask the questions. Tell your story.* Then like a whale that had finished breathing, the voice sank back down.

The Wayfarer raised his staff in his right hand. His left held the disk before him. He began to read the runes aloud. His voice was hoarse and weak, but it strengthened as he spoke. The dank wind rose, whipping around the hilltop. He shouted the last runes, sending them out as a fisherman might cast a line.

When he finished, the wind subsided. He dropped the disk and waited.

A mist rose from the barrow and coiled around the witchlamps like a sea serpent. The runes he'd cut in the earth flared with golden light; they kept the mist contained. The mist tested each one, then swirled toward the barrow and coalesced into the shape of a tall, lean woman garbed in a white dress with her hair pulled back from a gaunt face.

The woman knelt and with long-fingered hands lifted Baldr's torc. She turned it this way and that, inspecting it closely.

She spoke, words falling like slabs of ice into the sea. "Long was I dead, snowed under, smitten with rain, and drenched with dew. Why have you, whoever you are, made me travel back along the troublous road?"

The Wayfarer stood straight, staff in his right hand, hat pushed back. "Call me Vegtam, great lady, for I have traveled all my life."

"You would have me call you Wayfarer, then? That's not a fit name for an enchanter. You know my name, else you couldn't have summoned me. What may I call you?"

"Your pardon, great lady. I may have spoken the words, but I'm no enchanter. Another's power drew you."

She narrowed her eyes and then darted toward him, hands extended like the talons of a plunging raptor.

The Wayfarer stumbled back and raised his staff to defend himself. The air between himself and the charging spirit flared golden, and she was flung back. She darted forward again, crashed into the unseen line between two witchlamps. Again, she was flung back in a shower of golden sparks. She dragged one white hand all around the barrier; sparks followed in her wake. When she had made a complete circuit, she drifted back to the square's center, expression thoughtful.

"So, Vegtam, the father of enchanters taught you well."

"He taught me nothing. He gave me detailed instructions and a token, much like that one there," the Wayfarer said with a shrug. He gestured toward the silver torc on the dead grass.

Angrboda looked down at it, then back up at him. "And what did he ask of you, Vegtam?"

"As you well know, great lady, he commands the dead. He didn't ask."

"He treats the living in much the same way."

"That, I wouldn't know. I lived out the arc of my nights in another land."

The spirit drifted closer, expression interested. "And where are you from, Vegtam?"

"My people issue from his brother's loins. We live upon the coast far from where the father of enchanters sits watch."

"How curious." She drifted forward until she stood opposite him. "You know, we find ourselves in a similar situation, both required to do something we would not, had we a choice. May I have your name? You have mine, after all."

A wide grin spread across the Wayfarer's face. He shook a finger at her. "After he told me the questions he wanted answered, he specifically warned me not to tell you my name, great lady. Not that it would do you much good, dead as I am."

Angrboda's eyes narrowed. She leaned in closer still. "You are Einherjar, then?"

The spark of Odin deep within the Wayfarer twitched at her words. *What? Einherjar?*

Her lips pursed and she cocked her head slightly, as if straining to hear a whisper.

The Wayfarer gave voice to Odin's thoughts. "I don't understand, great lady. Einherjar? Those are his warriors, living men and women, while I am—"

"But you are Aesir, yes?" she asked, waving a translucent hand toward him. "And he plucked you from the ship of the dead as it sailed here, to my daughter's realm?"

"You know he did, great lady."

A wicked grin spread across her face. "I could ask my daughter for your name. She could learn it and then give it to me. And once I had it, I could find out why you're really here."

"I'll tell you exactly why I'm here, great lady, if you'll let me," he said, spreading his hands wide. "And besides, what you threaten would take time—time enough for me to tell the Valfather of what you attempt. I believe his anger would be boundless, as would his vengeance."

Angrboda eyed him sharply then shrugged. "What else can he do to me? He's already taken everything I loved."

"I don't know your story, I'm sorry to say. I only know what I've been required to do." Then he added, "But in my experience, there's always something worse that could be done."

"And what is your task, Vegtam?"

"The Valfather wants me to ask you about his son Baldr."

Her expression gave nothing away. "Why ask me?"

"I only know what he told me to ask."

The spirit pursed her lips and slowly walked back toward the barrow, her pale feet leaving the barest impression on the cold, wet ground. She lifted Baldr's silver torc. "I knew whose this was the moment I looked at it. But tell me, Wayfarer, why should I answer the Valfather's questions after what he did to me and mine?"

That spark of Odin deep down within the Wayfarer again stirred at her words. *Whose it "was"? My son lives still. Ask her what she meant.*

Again, Angrboda's head cocked to one side as if she were trying to hear something far away. Without warning, she flung the torc at him. The silver missile flew straight through the barrier.

He caught it neatly in his free hand. "You have no more choice than I do, great lady. He's given me the power to compel you, should you refuse." He thrust the torc into his satchel. "Just now, you said 'whose this was.' What did you mean? Baldr still lives."

"Of course he does," she said easily, smiling as she drifted closer. "Tell me, Wayfarer, why should I answer questions about Baldr? Or about anything? I am unwilling to speak and would again be still."

That's not good enough, the spark of Odin said, drifting higher.

The Wayfarer shook his head and extended his hand. "Great lady, I am not permitted to leave here without answers, true answers, to all the questions the Valfather bade me ask. I don't wish to use the power he gave me, but I will. I fear his wrath more than your daughter's."

"Nothing he says can be trusted." She crossed her arms and lifted her chin.

He dug in the bag and brought the torc back out. "You may have this as a gift."

Angrboda laughed. Crows fled into the air from the withered trees surrounding the glade. "And what would I do with it? I am unwilling to speak and would again be still."

The Wayfarer shoved the torc back into his bag even as the spark of Odin inside him burned hotter. The Wayfarer spoke a word, and golden light shone from the tip of his staff. He took one step forward and held the staff higher, as if the spirit before him couldn't see it.

A smile played about Angrboda's lips. "The carrot having failed, you switch to the stick. How like your master. A third time I say, I am unwilling to speak and would again be still."

A long moment of stillness hung over the hilltop, like a dark bird riding high on the winds. The flame of Odin's anger inside the Wayfarer's mind dimmed, and he lowered the staff. *Hold off for a moment. This is the time to offer her the story of your death—that which I saw in your memories which so intrigued me. If that doesn't work, use the power I gave you.*

"A thought occurs to me, great lady. Perhaps you would instead be interested in a trade?"

The witch said nothing. She stared at the Wayfarer arms crossed beneath her breasts.

"I offer you this: the story of my death. In return, you tell me what you see of Baldr's doom. Tale for tale. True telling for true telling."

Angrboda began drifting back toward him. Her expression was

thoughtful, her gaze piercing. Finally, she said, "Tell me, Wayfarer, why should I care about your death?"

The Wayfarer nodded slowly, but inside those memories, Odin smiled. *We have her now. Tell her why I chose you.*

"I am an Aesir, but as I said, my people are descended from Vili, one of the Valfather's brothers. I was born to a seafaring clan. My people and I plied the coasts of a new land for more than two hundred winters before the Alfather found us."

"Interesting. I knew that Vili and Ve had left, but not where they had gone. Even so, you offered the tale of your death, not your life."

The Wayfarer smiled and raised a hand. "I know. I'm coming to that. Have you heard of the Exile?"

"And the war that preceded it. Yes, I know of it," she replied, drifting still closer.

"Well, I know where the Svartalvar ended up." The Wayfarer's smile became a grin. "I know because it was they who killed me."

She pointed at him, her expression fierce. "If you lie, I will know."

"I will not lie," the Wayfarer said. "Do we have a bargain, then?"

Eyes narrowed, jaw clenched, she nodded.

"Speak the words then, wise woman. You know how this works. I offer the true story of my death in exchange for your true telling of Baldr's doom."

"And I offer my true telling of Baldr's doom in exchange for the true story of your death."

"The deal is struck." The Wayfarer drove his staff into the dank earth. He tucked his cloak beneath him and sat cross-legged on the ground and scooped up his discarded wineskin. He took a long pull, wiped his mouth, and began.

***

The Wayfarer's Tale

"Before I died and ended up here," the Wayfarer said, with a gesture that encompassed both the hilltop and the drab forest below,

"I sailed, traded, and raided all along the coast of my native land. A hundred Aesir in three ships followed me.

"Aegir and Rán sped my wooden steeds across the waters for many winters. I was never too ruthless nor too kind, and I sacrificed often. Many a bog and lake are home to the bent swords and shattered spears of my enemies—offerings to Rán. To Aegir, I offered those few prisoners I took. Many times, I gave my own blood just as my followers and kinsmen did. And some gave their lives. But their names lived on, and our reputations grew in the telling."

He fell silent for a moment, composing his thoughts. Memories swamped him like a foundering skiff. Then, as if he felt a favorable wind at his back, he set his hand on the tiller, nodded to the spirit, and said, "And so I begin the tale of my death.

"We had just raided a fortified town and were fleeing back down the wide, fast-moving river we had sailed up from the sea. We had won some treasure, but the town had fought harder than we'd expected and their seidkonur had sent a towering column of spinning wind and water after us—"

"Their sorceress conjured a cyclone, eh? She was a strong," Angrboda said. "Was she Alvar? That sounds more like their sorcery."

"No, she was an Aesir. I only mention the seidkonur and her storm because I believe it related to what happened to us. You see, it chased my ships down the river. The air boomed with the storm's voice, lightning crawled across a sky that ran from black to a greenish, sickly yellow. When the storm struck, the river itself heaved like a bucking stallion. Warm white water poured in through the shields. We rose high, shuddered sideways, and then, a heartbeat later, we slammed down again. Our mast went by the board and we began to spin, my men sliding and stumbling across the flexing deck.

"To larboard, one of my companion ships rolled broadside to the wind and foundered. Just like that." The Wayfarer snapped his fingers. "To starboard, my other ship shot round backward, slammed into the wreckage of her sister, and began sinking. And we were about to follow that same awful course.

"I cried out for Aegir and Rán to remember my many sacrifices and spare us a watery doom. Maybe they heard, for the winds diminished and the river calmed. I took on what survivors I could find, shipped a new steering board, and manned the remaining oars, alongside those men we'd pulled from the water. And so we few survivors continued our flight downriver to the sea."

The Wayfarer fell silent and stooped, catching up his wineskin. He took a long pull, head tipped back.

"Odd that you drink, seeing as how you're dead," Angrboda said.

He lowered the wineskin and wiped his mouth with the back of his hand, then replaced the plug and met her cool gaze.

"The Valfather said it would keep me whole during my task. I don't know why." He shrugged. "I'd do so even if it spilled from the hole in my belly. It reminds me of my living days."

Angrboda replied with a smile that could have meant anything. "The Valfather did have a fondness for wine. He never consumed anything but wine, at least as long as I knew him."

"I never had that pleasure—of knowing him while I lived, I mean," the Wayfarer said. "Shall I continue?"

"Oh, by all means." She drifted backward and gestured with one pale hand even as her smile returned.

The Wayfarer sketched a bow. "The wind had left us, but a thick mist took its place. We couldn't see an oar's length beyond the ship. And it had grown hot, hotter than it had been when we sailed up the river, but we were hard at work so didn't think too much of it. The current took us fast toward the sea, which was a good thing, since most of my warband were knotting and splicing the ropes, plugging holes, and shipping new oars. The sailmaker plied his craft, too, though we needed a new mast. The trip downriver seemed to take longer than it should have, but time seemed fuzzy in that mist—and we were busy.

"When we finally reached the delta, a huge stone outcropping loomed from the mist. It had not been there when we sailed up the river. I exchanged a long glance with my kjolr. That's when we knew something was very wrong. But what could we do? I'd lost most of my warband, my ship needed more repairs, and the townsfolk might have set out after us.

"So we put the ship before what wind there was and rowed down the coast—or maybe up it. Who knew at that point? We rowed all through that long, hot day. When the mist finally burned off, it became even more clear that we were lost. In every sense of the word. The shores were thick with heavy green foliage and even thicker with strange, unknown sounds. Shapes swung through the trees, seeming to track our progress. And merciless Sól was hot on our backs.

"Eventually, Sól rode down beyond the forest. Several of my warband chose that time to question my decisions, so I put their corpses over the side in offering to Rán. Their bodies were quickly torn apart by spears-long, scaly-backed monsters that bumped and jostled our ship long after they'd devoured our dead. To starboard, the land began leaning away from us to form a great bay. In the failing light, I spied a smooth, sandy shore, so I took us in. Setting foot on an unknown shore blanketed by a dark forest turned out to be a bad decision, but at the time, we needed water and food."

"And a mast."

"That, too. The ship beached, we armed ourselves and ventured into the forest. We didn't go far, gathering what fallen limbs we could for a fire. I wanted to build a wall between us and the forest. We felled several trees, working to finish before Sól fled, and dragged them back to make several fires and rude barriers. There were maybe three ships' lengths between our camp, just beyond the high-water mark, and the tree line. Come dawn, we'd deal with our ship."

The Wayfarer snorted and looked up at Máni, which hung like a silver coin above the scraggly trees. "As it turned out, none of us would make it to the dawn."

"You have my interest, Wayfarer," Angrboda said. "Take a moment, if you need it. Or perhaps another drink?"

He smiled and doffed his hat. "No, great lady, I'm fine. But I do appreciate your concern."

She smiled in reply and mimicked his gesture.

He settled his hat back on his head and gestured up toward the moon. "Once Máni's face had risen full above the sea, the forest went deathly quiet. The only sound were the waves pounding the shore. We knew something was coming. We formed a shield wall and began withdrawing to the ships. We hadn't reached the waves before massive beasts unlike anything I'd seen stepped from the forest. Armored. All scales and teeth and claws. They were arrayed in a long line before us and to either side. I stopped counting at fifty.

"Sharp-eyed Tothir gasped and pointed. 'They carry riders, Jarl.' I looked again. Riders, indeed. One of the beasts lurched forward. A man-shaped figure slid off its back and came slightly closer. It stood in the open, clearly staring down at us. It said nothing. My heart pounding in my chest, the sea's scent thick in my nose, I stepped forward and spread my arms wide, hands open. 'We were ship-wrecked,' I called out."

The Wayfarer smiled and met Angrboda's gaze. "Fool that I was."

"Those were the Svartalvar, I take it?"

"Oh, yes. Though I didn't know it at first."

"But Ygg and the golden Vanir had exiled them to another realm," she said, frowning. "You're saying you ended up there yourself?"

"I'm not sure what happened, great lady. All I know is what I told you: the river we sailed down was not the same one we sailed up. And that coast we clung to?" The Wayfarer laughed, the sound short and sharp. Birds scattered from the hilltop's withered trees. "It wasn't the same. I spent my life at sea and all along the coast of my birth. I went farther than most, found new lands. But I never saw any like that. Ever. Until that storm."

"Curious," she said. "And so how did you die?"

"You still want to know?"

"Certainly, Wayfarer. You have my interest, as I said. And more than that, we struck a bargain."

The Wayfarer inclined his head, raised his wineskin in salute, and took another pull. "The figure stood there by his beast, staring at us. A familiar creak reached my ears, and moments later, a heavy cart trundled into the gap in their lines. It was pulled by another of those armored creatures, except this one walked on four legs. It looked as if they had put a small forge on the cart. Flames danced behind a grating, and warm yellow light fell across the sand. A man-figure passed through that light, walking toward the first figure, its shadow long and narrow across the sand.

"Behind me, my warband stirred. They'd guessed what was happening. Had we not raided a hundred towns together? Sometimes a town would strike a bargain and pay us to leave—treasure, food, sometimes women. If they seemed too strong, I'd agree. But they always made some show of force. That's what was happening here. But the towns that preferred to talk always sent someone forward after the display, and these folk had yet to do that. Battered as we were, facing these scaled beasts and their riders, I suspected we would have to fight. And probably die. But I took the other option."

"You ran."

"Oh, yes," the Wayfarer said with a big grin. "Tried to, anyway. To my warband, I whispered, 'Fall back to the ship. Let's get her afloat.' As we backed away, I kept my eyes and ears on the pair of figures silhouetted before the forge-wagon. They might have been arguing, arms swinging up to gesture toward us. 'Run, before they make up their minds.' We turned and ran, maybe twenty yards to the ship. We'd beached her high, to be safe. 'Free the rolling logs,' I yelled, and a few men jumped to it. The rest of us set hands on her sides and began to push."

The Wayfarer paused. "You know that sound a fire makes when it first catches?"

Angrboda nodded.

"Well, imagine that sound passing directly overhead. A ball of fire struck our ship square amidships and burst. We fell back with a yell. Even before the second fireball hit, my ship was ablaze. I spun round and saw one figure standing before the forge-cart. He reached back as if he was about to throw a spear, and the fire in the cart dimmed. Then he made a throwing motion, and fire swept out of the wagon and streaked toward us. Then the forge fire danced merrily until he threw again."

"Imaginative use of seidr," she mused. "And what did these figures look like? How do you know they were Svartalvar?"

"Oh, I'm nearly there, great lady. I didn't last much longer." He took another quick drink. "A pair of my sailors died when the ship went up. Burned alive. My warband had numbered one hundred twenty-eight before the raid on the town. Thirty-six stood with me now, staring at our ship's flaming ruin, the heat baking the wetness from our clothes. 'Well, boys, we've had quite the time together,' I said, meeting each man's eyes. I knew them like brothers. I wouldn't trust them with a widow's fortune, but with my life? Sure.

"'Cattle die, kinsmen die, and so will we—on this beach, no less. But one thing that will never die is the fame of our deeds. I will make sure of it,' I said to them. I drew my axe as a last fireball impacted the burning ship. 'I'm going to kill at least one of these bastards. Are you with me?'"

Angrboda murmured, "And so you kept your promise, Wayfarer."

The Wayfarer nodded, but didn't break the beat of his story. He raised his hand as he'd done his axe. "I didn't wait for them to answer. I spun and charged toward the tree line, feet sinking in the sand. From the shouts and grunts of effort, it sounded as if many of the warband had followed. My eyes were still dazzled by the light from my burning ship, but as I ran, my vision cleared. The line of riders to my left rippled like a stirring snake. Their leader shouted something, and the whole line of warriors charged us.

"I say 'us' because my warband had caught up with me—most of 'em, from what I could tell in those few heartbeats of time between their forming a small shield wall with me at its center.

"The beasts charged us, heads lowered, weaving back and forth like swimming snakes. Their riders were perched high, and each leveled a bright-pointed spear. A dozen hit our attempt at a shield wall and went right through it.

"My shield shattered on my arm. Broke my arm, too. I remember screaming out as the world flew out from under me. The clawed foot of one of those beasts slammed into my head. My warband's cries rang around me as they fell, just as I did. I ended up on my back staring up at Máni's blank, pale face—the bastard. I wheezed for breath, twitching like a turtle trying to regain its feet.

"I blinked, and a second, much closer, pale face loomed into view above me. Large eyes that reflected the light gazed down into mine. A foot hammered into my side and I rolled with it, my broken shield arm screaming. But I came up to my feet, scooping up an axe as I did.

"The figure before me was tall, stocky, and pale like the underbelly of a snake. He wore a mix of black armor that glinted dully in places but otherwise seemed to be leathers. His lips were a tight line across his face. In one hand, he held a long-handled weapon with a spiked metal ball on the end. His hair was dark and pulled tight against his head.

"One of his compatriots came up beside him. His head was completely covered and many-faceted gems glittered where his eyes should have been. This second one had weapons on his belt but none in his hands. The first warrior raised his weapon in challenge and shuffled across the sand toward me, while the hooded one moved forward behind the first.

"As the first one got close, his spiked club swinging up, I splat blood into his face. He dodged most of it—he was quick—but I kicked him in the stomach. He folded over, and I smashed my axe into his spine. I ripped it out and spun into an attack that the second hooded figure blocked with a small shield.

"From that figure's other hand, a cold bit of night lashed out and buried itself in my belly. I remember looking down at a black blade. When the warrior twisted his sword, I gasped and met his eyes, they were large and shiny, like silver platters, though they were hidden behind large blue gems. He shoved me off his sword, and I fell back onto the sand.

"I don't know how long I lay there, clutching the hole in my stomach and staring up at the moon, until a new figure stepped into view above me. This second one kicked me in the ribs and then squatted to hiss, 'Tell your Valfather and his Vanir bootlickers that Eitri sends his greetings. We are coming for him.'"

The Wayfarer leaned forward on his staff. "I must have died then, for I remember nothing else until Odin pulled me from Rán's ship, gave me my task, and set my feet upon the road here.

"And thus have I upheld my end of our bargain."

77

Frigg

"Look again, Heimdall. You can't see Odin anywhere?"

Frigg stood, cloaked and hooded, on the promontory above the city. The night was clear, chill, and windless. Muspell's sparks glowed in the western sky, while the stars above were barely visible beside Máni's glow.

"I can't see him, Almother," Heimdall said, gloved hands gripping the waist-high stone battlement—the post, the watch, he had abandoned nearly two dozen winters earlier.

She glanced at Ráta, who leaned against the battlement, arms folded across her chest, with no expression on her face. The faint buzzing of bees emanated from Ráta.

"Again," Frigg said. "Try harder. Listen for him, instead."

His ice-blue eyes fixed on her. "Just let me have a drink and I will."

She laughed. "I'd sooner break every cask in Gladsheim than let you near another cup of wine or beer or whatever else you swill down."

"Please, I can smell the beer you brought. Just give me a cup, and I'll look again."

She stepped forward and slapped him so hard her palm tingled and the bones of her hand throbbed. He rocked back several paces, eyes wide in surprise. His fists clenched.

The faint buzzing sound from Ráta grew louder. Heimdall shot a wary look at the baresark and then made a show of unclenching his fists.

She massaged her hand. "Last night, a witch attacked me in the Lower Hall. I don't know how long she's been here, nor do I know what seidr she might have woven throughout the city. But I do know she's murdered at least one woman, maybe just to get to me. Maybe not. And then she killed Gulfinn. You should have been standing here watching her flee so you could tell Ráta where to find her."

Shame crept across Heimdall's features as he glanced a second time at the baresark.

"Instead, the witch escaped – and since she's a shape-shifter, she probably didn't even leave the city, but I haven't been able to find her because we couldn't find you. And now that you are where you're supposed to be, you can't find the witch nor the Alfather, who isn't where he should be." She gave a disgusted snort. "All I see before me is fire and dea—"

Heimdall dropped to his knees before her, big hands clasped together like someone pleading for her mercy. Frigg thrust out a hand, telling Ráta to stay back.

She put her hands on her hips. "Well, Watcher, what is it?"

His broad, pale face with its scar across his nose, was a battleground between indecision and hope. He seemed to shrink into himself. "I've heard you and the Alfather talking, and just now you said 'see.'"

Her heart sank. She knew what was coming.

"Tell me my doom, Almother, please. Will I ever be free of this curse?" He hammered at one side of his head; the other pounded his thigh.

With a thought, she conjured the vision-flames above Heimdall's head. In them, she saw a sword's bloody tip emerge from between his shoulders. She tried to change her perspective, to see whose hand held the blade, but the vision wouldn't budge.

She sighed. "In my youth, I always answered that question. If someone wanted to know, and I could see it, then didn't they deserve to know what lay ahead? I always saw their deaths but sometimes other...events...would creep in. Mind you, I never saw—nor do I see —the when."

She squatted so they were face-to-face. She laid her hand on his shoulder. "Only much later did I realize that telling them made some people stop living. It made others reckless. Sometimes that ended up causing the deaths of many others. But I wonder now if perhaps everything was already doomed to happen no matter what I said or did. Mimir seems to think so. Did my telling alter anything at all? Or was it just a part of the greater weaving?"

"None of that will happen with me, Almother. I swear it."

She smiled sadly at him. "Won't it? Say I tell you that I see you die from falling from a cliff. Perhaps you'd take that to mean you pitch yourself over it. Or that, drunk, you fall accidentally. Or maybe there's a battle at a cliff's edge, and you take a wound and fall over. Would you not live every moment in anticipation of your death? Would you avoid all cliffs? Or seek them out?"

He shook his head. "You don't know what it's like. All I hear is my name, endlessly croaked from a thousand throats. I welcome the silence that comes with death."

And all she saw were the deaths of everyone she lay eyes upon.

Frigg laid her hand on his cheek. "No you don't, Heimdall. If you did, you'd be dead already. But you're right, I don't have any idea what it's like. Loki went too far."

She stopped herself before mentioning their suspicions regarding Loki's involvement in the threat on Baldr and the Jotunn attack on Háls—although perhaps Heimdall had overhead that, as well. Even the witch's obvious participation didn't necessarily absolve Loki. There was still the matter of those male voices the husband had heard. For all she knew, Yelena and Loki were the same person—he, like Odin, had been known to take a woman's shape. And the witch had mentioned a mistress. Could that have been Angrboda? Or maybe the mistress *was* Loki.

"It never stops, Almother. Never. I try to sleep, but their croaking keeps me awake. And then all the other voices—crying, screaming, laughing, whispering. I hear it all. I used to stand post here, trying to hear what the Jotunn plan. I used to be able to block out almost everything I didn't want to hear. But there was something about those birds and their constant croaking. It drowned everything else out. I try not to listen, but all they do is say my name over and over."

His ice-blue eyes burned into hers. "The drink is all that gives me some peace."

"If that's peace, Heimdall, then let me put a knife in you now." She lowered her voice to a whisper only he could hear. "You and I are kindred in more than ways than one—we both perceive things we'd rather not. But drifting in a drunken stupor through every moment is not the answer."

"Then tell me of my death, Almother. Give me a destination."

"Before I married Odin, I once told a woman that she'd die in her bed at night, coughing out her last moments. I described her pallid face and blood-flecked lips. So what did she do? She joined the Jotunn army and fought against the Aesir. She took a spear through the chest and died in a bed, coughing up blood."

Heimdall looked at her, not seeming to understand.

"My point is that the vision came true but not in the way either of us expected. She assumed it meant she'd die of some sickness or maybe old age. Not wanting that, she went to war. But here are the questions that keep me awake...if I dwell on them. Did my words cause a different outcome? Might she have died of a sickness if I hadn't told her what I did? Or was she always meant to die in battle? If the former, then I can change outcomes with my prophecies. If the latter, well, then I'm simply an instrument of doom.

"The Norns claim they've seen, scratched, and painted the doom for all of us: Jotunn, Aesir, Alvar, Vanir. Are they right? And if our doom...our destination, as you put it...is fixed, does that mean the route is, too? I know what I prefer to believe."

And she knew what Odin preferred. She let her whispered words hang in the air and put her hands on his shoulders. "I'm not going to tell you what I see ahead of you. You must decide to stand up and help me, or keep staggering drunkenly down the long hall of your life. To the Ginnungagap with everything else."

She gave him a little shake, a small, sad smile and stepped back. Heimdall's pale face was intense, his eyes burned brighter than the hottest witchlamps. His gaze dropped to his hands, clenching into fists and then relaxing again.

A wispy cloud passed before Máni's face and then drifted farther eastward. Far to the west, there was nothing but stars and the red glow of Muspell's sparks.

Ráta stood by, impassive, until she caught her eye. The buzzing sound had faded away. The baresark nodded slightly. Approvingly?

Heimdall chose that moment to breathe out long and slow. His ice-blue eyes settled on her, he gave a small nod, and then he stepped to the northern battlement where he stared in that direction for several long heartbeats. Then, he turned slowly in place, gazing first westward, then southward, then to the east, until he again settled on her.

"I still see no trace of the Alfather, not along the shores of Gjoll nor anywhere in the realms between us," he said, voice distant.

He cocked an ear. "Nor do I hear him."

"How is that possible, Heimdall? Even when he was gone these past twenty winters, you could see and hear him." When he was sober enough to look.

Heimdall shrugged. "He's vanished before. If he's taken another's shape, I would see him but not know him. If he's in among Yggdrasil's branches, as he's been before, I can't always see him there, either."

"What if you sat upon the High Seat?" she asked.

He shook his head, golden teeth gleaming in a quick smile. "I tried only once before, when the Alfather first found it. Had he not been there to pull me off, it would have killed me."

"What of Sleipnir? Freki and Geri? Huginn and Muninn? Can you see or hear any of them?"

"They are harder to spot, but I will look again."

She laid her hand on his arm. "Thank you, Heimdall. Will you stand watch through Midwinter? I'll have food brought. And water."

Pain flickered across his face, followed quickly by something new. Resolve. "I will, Almother."

She gripped his arm a little tighter, smiled, and left, descending the snow-covered stairs down to the ground. Ráta followed behind.

When they reached the bottom, Ráta hefted the cask of beer she'd carried up the hill.

"No, leave it here," Frigg said, knowing Heimdall would hear. "The jarl seems resolute, but even a reforged blade needs tempering."

78

Odin

A faint smile lurked in the corners of the witch's eyes. The silence grew bowstring-taut between them. She seemed to savor it. Máni had slipped behind the western sea even as Sól's fingertips first brushed the low curve of land in the east.

The Wayfarer's voice clattered in the still air like a pebble across an icy pond. "With respect, great lady, you know the power of the bargain we made. I would prefer you speak freely, but I will compel you if you force my hand."

"Oh, I'll speak, Wayfarer. I'm just wondering, do you truly want to know what I know?"

"What I want has nothing to do with it. The Valfather bade me ask—and return with answers."

The witch smoothed her wispy hair. She caught it up in the spectral circle of thumb and forefinger and draped it over one shoulder. Her fingers began to plait its length.

The gesture was so like that of a living woman that the Wayfarer chose to wait for Angrboda to continue. That spark of Odin's mind submerged beneath as the Wayfarer's ocean of memories swam higher, spiraling up like the dead-eyed wolf of the sea.

Dawn's reddish rays broke behind the witch, lending her a bloody aspect. Her sharp gaze seemed to pierce the veil of Wayfarer's memories and stare into the dead black eyes beneath them.

She finished her braid, and a smile broke across her ghostly face. "Know my words as true, Wayfarer. Our bargain compels it. Gjoll's mistress prepares a seat of honor for Baldr."

The spark of Odin beneath the Wayfarer's memories thrashed as if from a harpoon's bite. The Wayfarer himself gaped and stumbled backward.

"Oh, yes, Wayfarer," Angrboda continued, emphasizing his name, even as she drifted closer to the barrier that had flared when she had tested it before. A hand's breadth away, she said, "The mead here is brewed for Baldr. Hel prepares a welcoming feast. The long benches have been dragged into her drab hall, now made bright with rings of gold and silver. She adds a tall chair atop her own platform to honor Ygg's bright, beautiful son. Eljudnir will, for a time, be warmed with gold's yellow glow."

Lit by the red dawn, her smile reminded the Wayfarer of the bloody froth that lingered on the ocean after a shark claimed its victim. As if she could sense the turmoil within him, her smile widened.

"That's not possible," the Wayfarer said. "All know that bright Baldr cannot be harmed."

She laughed. "Of course it's possible. All things die. Aesir. Jotunn. Everyone and everything eventually sets sail upon the Gjoll."

The Wanderer's face contorted as the spark of Odin within him flew from shock to naked rage. Golden flames ran along his staff. He brandished it as if it were a spear. "How? How does the Valfather's son die?"

"A twig." Her eyes lingered on the staff just as the smile lingered on her face. "The merest branch cut from the golden bough. Far-famed will that branch become."

The Wayfarer shook his head. "What? You speak in riddles, witch."

But that spark of Odin's mind beneath the disguise knew

exactly what Angrboda meant. Through the Wayfarer, he spoke still more loudly. "But who? Who would kill Baldr? Who wants him dead?"

"Oh come now, father of magic, I know you," Angrboda said. "I can sense you there below the surface of this dead wayfarer's memories. Clever, father of the slain—and it might have worked on some witch who hated you less. But show yourself, and let's end this game, for unwilling have I spoken. I would again be still."

The dead-eyed wolf of the sea flexed its tail and broached the surface of the Wayfarer's memories. Odin stepped from the Wayfarer's guise as one might step from shadow into light. The dead man's ragged clothes and cloak shimmered and fell away as Odin's leathers and dark blue cloak reappeared. He kept only the broad-brimmed hat.

Back to the ship of the dead, Wayfarer. You served me well, and I will reward you for it.

Golden fire burned brighter along the rude staff the Wayfarer had held, and Gungnir emerged. Odin drove the spear into the barren soil. Golden fire kindled in the grasses and raced out to find and merge with the patterns and runes he had carved earlier.

Angrboda flinched within the burning square. Her gaze darted from corner to corner, rune to rune. She had nowhere to go.

"And I know you, Angrboda, mother of three monsters," he said in a voice as hot as the flames he'd summoned. "I seek from you all the answers to my questions. Tell me this, who wields the branch? Who kills my son? Is it your husband?"

"Unwilling have I spoken. I would again be still." Her eyes remained defiant as dawn spread across the hilltop.

"You will speak, Angrboda! You will answer all my questions!" He raised Gungnir, and the golden flames tightened around Angrboda.

She squirmed from the heat, clutching herself tight. "Unwilling have I spoken. I would again be still."

He lowered Gungnir's blade toward her, and the golden flames embraced her like a lover. She collapsed, screaming, a writhing tangle of spectral limbs.

"Does Loki kill my son?" he thundered. "Speak, witch, and the agony ends."

He let her burn for the space of nine heartbeats. Her shrieks reverberated atop the bare hill. Then he grounded Gungnir, and the golden flames retreated to pace like wolves around her.

Angrboda gasped, clutching smoky wisps of mist to her like tattered clothing. She sat up and turned to meet Odin's eye. When she spoke, her voice was rough. "Your eldest son by Frigg wields the far-famed branch."

Odin staggered away from the specter and the golden fire. He stared unseeing at the tops of the trees, at the rainswept, distant mountains to the north. His eyes moved westward toward the windswept sea, whitecaps just visible—that same sea over which the ship of the dead sailed.

Hodr would kill Baldr?

She turned away, cupping bare spectral elbows in trembling, wispy fingers. "Unwilling have I spoken. I would again be still."

Her words barely registered. No matter which way he turned, he found no answers to the questions reverberating in his mind. Hodr would kill his brother? It couldn't be true—must not be true. Why would he kill his brother? Because Baldr was protected yet he was not? Because he lost his eyes yet Baldr lost nothing? How had he even learned Baldr's secret? No one knew it except Frigg and himself.

No, Angrboda had to be lying. He spun back and lowered Gungnir. The flames roared in.

Her screams echoed as she thrashed and burned.

His roar drowned out even the flames. "Tell me the truth, witch!"

He withdrew the predatory golden flames and she lay still, breathing heavily among the tendrils of mist that wriggled across the blackened circle.

She pushed herself up on sagging limbs, bolstered by the mists that slithered into her form. Her spectral dress shifted like a limp sail. Head lowered, her voice in tatters, she whispered, "Unwillingly have I spoken, Ygg, but every word of it was true. You know the power both of your summoning and our bargain."

She lifted her head and met his gaze. "And know that I saw through your disguise almost immediately. Why do you think I agreed to hearing your Wayfarer's tale? I wanted you to know in this moment that my words were true—were twice true. Three times true."

He said nothing. Even if she was lying about seeing through his disguise, his power and their agreement ensured anything she said had to be true. And how could what she'd said be more clear?

Hodr would kill Baldr.

He stared unseeing at the mist that flowed across the hilltop from the lifeless trees.

If that were true, then it meant Hodr had figured out that the mistletoe harbored Baldr's spirit. He also must have figured out a way to turn a fragile plant into a weapon.

But that was the how.

The why escaped him. Simply because Hodr had been blinded while his brother was spared? Or was it that Hodr resented—hated— that his father and mother preferred their firstborn over him?

Odin dismissed the golden flames and pulled his power back from the runes. "One last question before I allow you to rest, mother of grief. In your vision of what's to come, who wins vengeance for this deed? Will I do it?"

Angrboda floated up to her feet, mist gathering below her. Venom tinged her words. "You would hear the rest of my prophecy?"

"Of course I want to hear the rest." How else could he stop it?

His missing eye throbbed, and something furtive danced in the edges of that eye's sight. The eye he'd sacrificed was beginning to open.

Learn the future. Stop it. Change it. Whatever was necessary. He'd need three nights—fewer, if he pushed—to return to Gladsheim, but since he had no further need of a disguise he could call Huginn and Muninn and send them ahead to Frigg with what he'd learned. She could then protect Baldr—and send someone to Ifington to stop Hodr.

His heart began to pound again, not with fury as it had moments before, but with hope. Even so, that feeling was nearly swamped by confusion when Angrboda spoke again.

"Rind's son—your son Vále—at one night old will win vengeance for your dead son. He will not wash his hands nor comb his hair till he brings the slayer of Baldr to the flames."

Odin stared at her. This was the rest? Who was Rind? He would have a son by her?

He opened his mouth to demand more, but she spoke first.

"You've had your prophecy, son of Burr. I will say no more. No matter what you do. Ride home now." She drew herself up, her eyes flashing like knives. "And be proud, Ygg, for no one shall seek me again till my lover wanders free from his bonds, and his cousins, the devourers, come to the last strife."

Angrboda raised a hand, but not in farewell. "May your path home be long and fraught with peril, oathbreaker."

Too late he realized what those tendrils of mist she'd pulled in had been. Even as he raised Gungnir, a dull throbbing struck him in the head. He staggered. His hands grew heavy, as if he'd spent a day plying the oars.

A cloud passed before Sól and threw gloom like a net over the hilltop. Over his mind. Something black in the trees squawked and clattered up into the dull air. It sounded like laughter.

He used Gungnir to steady himself and looked up at Angrboda. She floated, unmoving, an inch above the scorched grasses, her face a mask of smug hatred.

"What did you do, witch? You can't bind me. Not in life, and certainly not in death."

"No, I can't—but I didn't need to bind you, Ygg, just delay you." A triumphant smile spread across her face.

He spoke a rune word that rumbled like distant thunder. "Back to your barrow, witch!"

He turned his back on her dissipating form.

He looked up, seeking Sól, but she was lost behind the heavy pall of gray skies. His head throbbed, and his feet dragged in the dead grasses. His shoulders hunched beneath the burden of the colorless clouds.

He leaned heavily on Gungnir. He just needed to reach Sleipnir. Then she could carry him to... to where, again? Gladsheim. Yes. Home.

Sleipnir rose like a gray cliff before him. She whinnied as he placed a hand on her neck and brought the reins back over her head.

"Let's ride quickly, Sleipnir, back to..."

A heavy, cold rain began to fall. The man settled his broad-brimmed hat more firmly on his head, set one foot in the stirrup, and hauled himself up onto the giant horse.

The horse shook her mane and pranced.

"Easy now, girl," the man said, thumping her neck.

He clucked his heavy tongue, and the gray horse started forward, picking a muddy road through a dark forest. That was the way back to...

Where was he headed?

Anywhere would do.

For he was a wanderer and this gray horse, his ship.

79

Vidar

A faint smile lurked in the corners of the witch's eyes. The silence grew bowstring-taut between them. She seemed to savor it. Máni had slipped below the western sea; Sól's fingertips brushed the eastern sky.

The Wayfarer broke the silence. "With respect, great lady, you know the power of the bargain we made. I would prefer you speak freely, but if you force my hand I will compel you."

"Oh, I'll speak, Wayfarer. I'm just wondering, do you truly want to know what I know?"

"What I want has nothing to do with it. The Valfather bade me ask—and return with answers."

The witch smoothed her fine black hair, caught it up in the circle of thumb and forefinger and draped it over one shoulder. She began to plait its length.

The gesture was so like that of a living woman that the Wayfarer chose to wait for Angrboda to continue. Odin's mind, submerged beneath the Wayfarer's ocean of memories swam upward, a dead-eyed wolf of the sea.

As dawn's reddish rays clawed their way through the sickly trees behind the witch. Her sharp gaze seemed to pierce the veil of the Wayfarer's memories and stare into those dead black eyes beneath them.

She finished her braid, smoothed her dress, and clasped her hands together. "Know my words as true, Wayfarer, for our bargain compels it. Gjoll's mistress prepares a seat of honor for Baldr."

Odin, that dead-eyed sea-wolf beneath the Wayfarer's memories thrashed as if struck by a harpoon. The Wayfarer himself couldn't help but gape and stumble backward.

"Oh, yes, Wayfarer," Angrboda continued, emphasizing his name, even as she drifted closer to the barrier that had flared when she had tested it before. A hand's breadth away, she said, "The mead here is brewed for Baldr. Hel prepares a welcoming feast. The long benches have been dragged into her drab hall, now made bright with rings of gold and silver. She adds a tall chair atop her own platform to honor Ygg's bright, beautiful son. Eljudnir will, for a time, be warmed with gold's yellow glow."

Lit by the red dawn, her smile reminded the Wayfarer of the bloody froth that lingered on the ocean after those scaly-backed monsters had eaten his shipmates. As if she could sense the turmoil within him, her smile widened.

"That's not possible," the Wayfarer said. "All know that bright Baldr cannot be harmed."

She laughed. "Of course it's possible. All things die. Aesir. Jotunn. Everyone and everything eventually sets sail upon the Gjoll."

The Wayfarer brandished his staff as if it were a spear. Golden flames erupted from its tip. "How? How does the Valfather's son die?"

"A twig." She giggled. Her eyes lingered on the staff just as the smile lingered on her face. "The merest branch cut from the golden bough. Far-famed will that branch become."

The Wayfarer shook his head. "What? You speak in riddles, witch."

But Odin knew exactly what Angrboda meant. He swam higher till the Wayfarer himself was little more than a threadbare sail. Odin urged the Wayfarer to say, "But who? Who would kill Baldr? Who wants him dead?"

"Oh come now, father of magic, I know you," Angrboda said. "I can sense you there below the surface of this dead wayfarer's memories. Clever, father of the slain—and it might have worked on some witch who hated you less. But show yourself, and let's end this game, for unwilling have I spoken. I would again be still."

Odin, the dead-eyed wolf of the sea flexed his tail and broached the surface of the Wayfarer's memories. Odin stepped from the Wayfarer's guise as one might step from shadow into light. The dead man's ragged clothes and cloak fell away as Odin's leathers and dark blue cloak reappeared. He kept only the broad-brimmed hat.

Back to the ship of the dead, Wayfarer. You served me well, and I will reward you for it.

Golden fire burned away the rude staff the Wayfarer had held, and Gungnir emerged. Odin drove the spear into the barren soil. Golden fire kindled in the grasses and raced out to find and merge with the patterns and runes he had carved earlier.

Angrboda flinched within the burning square. Her gaze darted from corner to corner, rune to rune. She had nowhere to go.

"And I know you, Angrboda, mother of three monsters," he said in a voice as hot as the flames he'd summoned. "I seek from you all the answers to my questions. Tell me this, who wields the branch? Who kills my son? Is it your husband?"

"Unwilling have I spoken. I would again be still." She set her jaw and glared defiantly at him. Dawn's red light pooled atop the hill's bare crown.

"You will speak, Angrboda! You will answer all my questions!" He raised Gungnir, and the golden flames tightened around Angrboda.

She squirmed from the heat, clutching herself tight. "Unwilling have I spoken. I would again be still."

He lowered Gungnir's blade toward her, and the golden flames embraced her like a lover. She collapsed, screaming, a writhing tangle of spectral limbs.

"Does Loki kill my son?" he thundered. "Speak, witch, and the agony ends."

He let her burn for the space of nine heartbeats. Her shrieks reverberated atop the bare hill. Then he grounded Gungnir, and the golden flames retreated to circle like wolves around her.

Angrboda gasped and hunched in on herself, clutching her tattered clothing to her along with the swirling mists. She pushed herself up and met Odin's eye. Her voice was husky with pain. "Your eldest son by Frigg wields the far-famed branch."

Odin staggered away from the specter and the golden fire. He stared unseeing at the tops of the trees, at the rainswept, distant mountains to the north. His eyes moved westward toward the windswept sea, whitecaps just visible—that same sea over which the ship of the dead sailed.

Hodr would kill Baldr?

She turned away, cupping bare elbows in trembling fingers. The mists flowed in toward her. Her dead flesh, blackened from the flames, began knitting itself back together. "Unwilling have I spoken. I would again be still."

Her words barely registered. Hodr would kill his brother? It couldn't be true—must not be true. Why would he kill his brother? Because Baldr was protected and he was not? Because he lost his eyes yet Baldr lost nothing? How had he even learned Baldr's secret? No one knew it except Frigg and himself.

No, Angrboda had to be lying. He spun back and lowered Gungnir. The flames rushed in, ravenous wolves.

Her screams echoed as she thrashed and burned.

"Tell me the truth, witch!"

He withdrew the predatory golden flames and she lay still, breathing heavily among the tendrils of mist that wriggled across the blackened circle.

She pushed herself up on scorched limbs. The morning mist slithered toward her; her scorched flesh grew whole. Her dress, what was left of it, shifted like a limp sail. Head lowered, her voice in tatters, she whispered, "Unwillingly have I spoken, Ygg, but every word of it was true. You know the power both of your summoning and our bargain."

She met his gaze. "And know that I saw through your disguise almost immediately. Why do you think I agreed to hearing your Wayfarer's tale? I wanted you to know in this moment that my words were true—were twice true. Three times true."

He said nothing. Even if she was lying about seeing through his disguise, his power and their agreement ensured anything she said had to be true. She'd spoken cryptically, nastily, but her meaning was clear.

Hodr would kill Baldr.

He stared unseeing at the mist that continued to flow toward Angrboda, hiding her bare, burned flesh and helping it heal.

Hodr must have figured out—somehow—that the mistletoe harbored Baldr's spirit. He also must have figured out a way to turn a fragile plant into a weapon.

But that was the how.

The *why* escaped him. Was it because Hodr had been blinded while his brother was spared? Or was it that Hodr resented—hated— that his father and mother preferred their firstborn over him?

Odin dismissed the golden flames and pulled his power back from the runes. "One last question before I allow you to rest, mother of grief. In your vision of what's to come, who wins vengeance for this deed?"

Angrboda rose to her feet, clutching the remnants of her soiled, burned dress to her. Venom tinged her words. "You would hear the rest of my prophecy?"

"Of course I want to hear the rest." How else could he stop it from occurring.

His missing eye throbbed, and something furtive danced in the edges of that eye's sight. The eye he'd sacrificed was beginning to open.

Learn the future. Stop it. Change it. Whatever was necessary. He'd need three nights—fewer, if he pushed—to return to Gladsheim, but since he had no further need of a disguise he could call Huginn and

Muninn and send them ahead to Frigg with what he'd learned. He could shout till he lost his voice—perhaps that drunk fool would hear. Either way, Frigg could protect Baldr—and send someone to Ifington to stop Hodr.

His heart began to pound again, not with fury as it had moments before, but with hope. Even so, that feeling was nearly swamped by confusion when Angrboda spoke again.

"Rind's son—your son Vahle—at one night old will win vengeance for your dead son. He will not wash his hands nor comb his hair till he brings the slayer of Baldr to the flames."

Odin stared at her. This was the rest? Who was Rind? He would have a son by her?

He opened his mouth to demand more, but she spoke first.

"You've had your prophecy, son of Burr. I will say no more. No matter what you do. Ride home now." She drew herself up, the mist pooling about her bare feet, her eyes flashing like knives. "And be proud, Ygg, for no one shall seek me again till my lover wanders free from his bonds, and his cousins, the devourers, come to the last strife."

Angrboda raised a hand, but not in farewell. "May your path home be long and fraught with peril, oathbreaker."

Too late he realized what all those tendrils of mist she'd pulled in had been. Even as he raised Gungnir, a dull throbbing struck him in the head. He staggered. His hands grew heavy, as if he'd spent a day plying the oars.

He had been deceived. The mists may have healed her but she now used them for a much more terrible purpose.

A cloud passed before Sól; gloom fell like a net over the hilltop. Over his mind. A black bird in the trees squawked and clattered up into the dull air. The beat of its wings sounded like laughter.

He used Gungnir to steady himself and looked up at Angrboda. She stood, half naked, pale flesh still burned and scorched, mist pooling about her feet and flowing from her to him. She wore a look of triumphant smug hatred.

"What did you do, witch? You can't bind me. Not in life, and certainly not in death."

"No, I can't—but I didn't need to bind you, Ygg, just delay you." A triumphant smile spread across her face.

He spoke a rune word that rumbled like distant thunder. "Back to your barrow, witch!"

She flinched and scuttled back into her dank barrow.

He looked up, seeking Sól, but she was lost behind the heavy pall of gray skies. His head throbbed, and his feet dragged in the dead grasses. White mist dragged at his boots. His shoulders hunched beneath the burden of the colorless clouds.

He leaned heavily on Gungnir. He just needed to reach Sleipnir. Then she could carry him to... to where, again? Gladsheim. Yes. Home.

Sleipnir rose like a gray cliff before him. She whinnied as he placed a hand on her neck and brought the reins back over her head.

"Let's ride quickly, Sleipnir, back to..."

A heavy, cold rain began to fall. The man settled his broad-brimmed hat more firmly on his head, set one foot in the stirrup, and hauled himself up onto the giant horse.

The horse shook her mane and pranced. Dead grasses and white mist twined their way around her legs.

"Easy now, girl," the man said, thumping her neck.

He clucked his heavy tongue, and the gray horse started forward, picking a muddy road through a dark forest. That was the way back to...

Where was he headed?

Anywhere would do.

For he was a wayfarer and this gray horse, his ship.

80

Hodr

"So all it did was knock him off his feet?" Lopt said, laughter in his voice.

Hodr smiled at the memory. "Not just off his feet but through the wall behind him. My mother was not happy."

"And it didn't hurt him?"

"Not at all. When he stepped back through the hole in the wall, grinning, all the folk in the hall started chanting his name." His smile soured. "Afterward, Thor just laughed, clapped Baldr on the shoulder —which nearly knocked him down again—and went back to drinking."

Lopt laughed. "What company you grew up in, Jarl. Was every Midwinter like that?"

"No, my mother would've tossed Thor out if he'd broken the wall again. They spent a drafty fortnight in that hall before it was fixed."

"But that's a tradition, right? Throwing things at Baldr?"

Hodr nodded, his smile fading. "It became one, yes. But only once with Thor and Mjolnir."

"Does everyone participate?"

"It's not as popular as it was, but there's always some who do. There's more to the celebration that goes on before that, too, which usually means folk are too drunk to hit anything by the time Baldr stands on the stump."

Lopt shook his head with a grin as he steered the unladen cart back toward the way house he said he frequented in Gladsheim. It was in the lower tier, not far from where the Einherjar maintained a small fort inside the walls.

It was slow going. The streets were packed with people making their last preparations before the three-night Midwinter festival. Animals were being fed, children cared for, guests welcomed, and firewood stacked. Many were helping finish the long stands that held the food and drink which were provided by the jarls to all comers at the festival. Still others were setting up the various games – stone and axe throwing, archery, skating on the river, wrestling and, of course, drinking.

"In my village, it's the same as this," Lopt said, sweeping one arm to encompass the preparations, "but on a much smaller scale. Once my father grew wealthy enough, he started paying for skalds to come. They sang many songs—and they're the reason I know of you, Jarl."

Hodr nodded to show he'd heard. Memories far more vivid than the sight his new spear provided swamped him of the great hall in Gladsheim, up there on the high center hill, strung with decorations inside and out, its tall columns of polished, carved wood glowing gold in the torchlight. As if he were there again he heard the clatter of weapons falling to the floor, the cheers, laughter and song. He saw again those who danced and pounded the tables for more roasted boar and bitter ale—as well as the ring of warriors who formed a cheering, clapping circle around his brother.

"Jarl?" Lopt asked.

He shook his head and realized the cart had stopped. Spear in hand, he saw the pale light cast by the torches and braziers, as well as the dim outlines of the way house, its stable, and the small yard for the horses.

"My mind was elsewhere," he said, stepping down from the cart. "Let's eat and hopefully rest. Tomorrow will be a busy day. And stop calling me that. Especially here."

81

Vidar

Vidar's strength was failing. Another drop of spittle struck his chest and burned the skin beneath. That he'd lasted this long surprised him. The matron's horns, despite being gripped tight in his hands, dug a burning furrow in his shoulder and dragged a line of pain toward this throat. He'd gotten his legs up between himself and her broad chest. But her weight was too much. She'd bent him nearly double.

You are weak, little cousin, came the whisper from his emerald-eyed fylgja.

Despite his surprise at her speaking to him he growled, I'm not weak.

She laughed at him with the voice of a geyser's hiss.

Venom sizzled on his cheek, just below his eye. Heartbeats remained. After her pack broke the shield wall, the snow bear matron had swatted Garilon aside and leaped atop Vidar. He'd only just succeeded in getting his hands and legs up to stop her from goring him. If not for the cliff behind him, he'd be dead.

Your weakness is good, his fylgja whispered, fangs gnashing.

He coughed, breathing in the hot reek of the matron's breath swamped him. Her spittle dripped on him and one of her golden eyes was locked on his.

He pushed against the matron, roaring with the effort. He bought himself a knife's length of breathing room. But the matron just bore down harder. She probably could have disengaged or maybe gutted him with her hind legs, but she seemed to be enjoying this.

His grip slipped and her horn crept a finger-joint closer.

Your father would have broken that thing by now. Yet here you lay.

I'm not my father.

Too true, his fylgja said, prowling back and forth. The green glow of her eyes shimmered and undulated like the lights of Ymir's Breath above Utgard's mountains. The runes binding her to him, delicate as a fish's breath, glowed like a ship's wake.

He met her gaze. *Why do you speak to me now?*

His arms trembled, the matron's breath was hot on his face. She licked his cheek and left a long sizzling trail behind.

Is it because I'm about to die?

His fylgja grinned.

But won't you die too, bound as you are?

Better death than this. She met his eyes and, deliberately, lifted her chin. The blue bindings pulsed there, encircling her neck just like the same runes encircled his own.

I can't undo my father's magic. We are bound, one to the other.

She laughed. *This? It's a mockery of what such a joining should be.*

There is another way?

She sat on her haunches, as tall as he was, staring back at him as if she was considering.

I only became a baresark because my father convinced me that it was necessary. You and I are one. You must realize I speak the truth.

Even if she didn't, Vidar showed her. He flung out memory's net and, hand over hand, dragged in the conversation in which his father had convinced him to become a baresark. *Gladsheim needs such warriors, such leaders,* Odin had said, *especially if we mean to settle new lands—and hold what is ours.*

Vidar showed her the memory of his dismay at learning that to become a baresark he must have a spirit bound to his own.

Do you see that? Feel it as I do?

The disir stared at him, eyes burning bright. Why could she see into him but he couldn't into her? There should be a balance to the bond between them.

His grip slipped again and the matron's horn crept still closer to his neck. Her hot, thick rotten breath quickened. She must sense him failing...because he was so very close to death.

My death now means yours too, doesn't it? Is that better than continuing as we are?

His fylgja cocked her head and swatted her tail. He pictured a river breaking its banks.

I told you, I can't unmake these runes. This is my father's magic.

Not true.

It is true.

She shook her head.

Pain burned like seawater in his eyes. The matron had finally lost interest. Her muscles bunched and she shoved one of her horns deep into his shoulder.

He screamed. Pain swept him toward his fylgja. Green eyes glowing, she spread her jaws and he tumbled into them.

More stars than he had ever seen on even the blackest nights opened before him, below him, around him. He splashed into them, a current caught him, tossed him like a leaf in frothy rapids.

His death wouldn't end her—couldn't end her. He'd been a fool to think it might. His death must mean her release. And when he died, perhaps she'd return to this milky river that roared with a voice louder than the snow bear matron above him.

His fylgja spoke again, her voice floating beside him on the starry river. *Your father saw this and more.*

Open-mouthed, he stared at the expanse into which he'd fallen— the great tree, Yggdrasil, its spreading branches above and its immense trunk, and its roots, shadowed and dark, and yet he somehow saw something moving within that darkness, maggots gnawing on a carcass.

A never-ending cascade of white-green mist flowing from above, colliding with a stream of red-yellow, roiling fire blossoming from below. And where they met, the maelstrom roared and churned. From it flew eleven rivers of stars and glinting metal and showers of ice and chunks of rock.

His fylgja's emerald cat eyes appeared before him, wide open, the vertical slits white and filled with stars. *How do you think your father killed Ymir? We taught him.*

What?

She gestured with her feline head toward the vortex, spinning below him. Around him. Above him. Yggdrasil's upper limbs shone golden, mountain peaks at dawn.

He'd never thought about it. His father was like the tree before him. He just...was.

He told me that he hung on Yggdrasil, a sacrifice, himself to himself, and that he strode upon death's shores.

He did. But that was only part of what he did.

I don't understand.

Do you want to?

Pain pounded in his ears. Understand? He nearly laughed. The torrent of fire raging upward into the spinning, churning Cauldron cast off a dozen streams of Muspell's sparks that shot slowly toward Yggdrasil's roots. Something shifted within the darkness, something that clung to the roots, and devoured those sparks whole.

He shook his head and tumbled backward, a stone dangling from a string. *Of course I want to, but I need your help now—to save myself and my warband.*

I will help. But she lifted her chin again, exposing the fetter that glimmered like a bird's spittle. Her intent was clear.

The tattoos on his wrists pulsed in time with his quickening heart-beat. *I won't be changed again, not as you did before. What assurance do I have?*

As much as your father gave me.

Pain blossomed in his shoulder and dragged him back into his flesh. He found it hard to breathe; his face was buried in the matron's thick pelt, matted with blood and gore.

Help me now, or I die.

Vidar met the fylgja's flat green gaze, opened his mind and she leaped toward him.

Like a bowstring, Vidar snapped back, himself to himself. His chest burned with venom. The matron's horn was buried deep in his shoulder. One of her yellow-slitted eyes, bigger than his palm, bored into his. He could see the fine scaly texture of her black skin beneath the long, white-gray matted fur. He had both hands on her horn, his forearm against her lower jaw; his legs pressed against her straining neck and chest. Every muscle trembled with the effort of keeping her at bay. His skin sizzled and burned with every drop of slobber from her jaws. Her hot breath smelled like rotten eggs; he felt her low rumbling growl in his belly.

Are you ready? his fylgja asked.

Past ready.

Vidar's limbs thrummed like the deepest-toned string on Bragi's harp as his fylgja extended her limbs through his. The note swelled, till he felt scoured by the cold, rushing waters of a mighty flood that swept his pain away.

In its absence, his wounds and burns might as well not exist. And if they didn't exist, there was no reason to lie pinned beneath this stinking beast's foul body.

He shoved the matron's head up. Surprise flared in her eye. His shoulder squelched as the horn pulled free. But he felt no pain. His arm worked. He stood. The matron, stunned perhaps, didn't react.

Had she been smaller, she would have dangled from his hands like an unruly hound. But she was twice his height and many times his bulk. She thrashed her head from side to side, broke his grip, and stumbled sideways. A moment later she was up on all fours, her head level with his chest. She rushed in, horns slashing right and left to spill his guts.

Faster than he'd ever been able to, except once, Vidar dodged. Her horns merely ripped another ragged line across his ruined armor.

That moment, where horn met armor, stretched taut, like those moments between a dream and waking up when he was never quite sure which was which.

His fylgja shrieked and he chose—for now he had a choice—to let her cry pass through his lips. It felt very good. Right, even. His body thrummed.

He unsheathed his knife, somehow still there in its sheath at the small of his back, and buried the long blade in the hollow between the matron's corded shoulder muscles and neck.

The matron bellowed. Vidar sawed his blade in the wound, widening it. He was bloodied to the elbow; her blood was on his face, in his mouth, and it tasted very good.

His knife ground against bone, so he sawed it back and forth until something parted like a taut rope.

She screamed again and whipped her head sideways and knocked him away, skidding across the icy, rocky ground. He squelched against something soft, but leaped to a fighting crouch, one arm up to defend or strike, but his other dangled like a broken tree limb.

She dies, his fylgja whispered.

It was true. The matron weaved and staggered like Heimdall after a long night in the hall. Except she vomited blood and venom.

Are you ready?

For what?

You'll feel your body's pain when I leave.

You're leaving me?

Everything feeds, cousin. Or would you have me eat as we did before?

Memories sprouted like weeds: Jotunn breastplates split open, the stink of shit and blood in clean winter air.

He shook his head.

The matron gave a long, undulating cry, staggered backward, and fell heavily on one side. The bronzed hilt of his knife protruding from her neck like a woman's brooch.

Prepare yourself.

And then his fylgja was gone—she leaped out of him and into the matron's wound.

Once his fylgja departed the hole in his shoulder burned like a forge fire. A thousand other agonies made their voices heard—burns and cuts, his ribs, the meat of both thighs. He'd hurt less when he'd sparred with Thor. Vidar toppled to one side like a chopped-down tree.

Bodies covered the reddened ground between himself and the matron. He forced himself up to his elbow, then up higher, bracing himself with a hand that squelched in a puddle of red snow. More bodies showed themselves, white eyes stark and bright and staring.

The matron screamed once more, shuddered, and lay still. His fylgja remained hidden.

Bodies lay strewn all around. The soft thing that had halted his slide was Jalla's corpse, one arm gone at the shoulder, the other flung wide, axe in her dead fist, half her face a venom-scorched black sizzle of what it had been. One of her eyes stared accusingly at him.

He staggered up and away and then tripped and fell over another body behind him.

His sob...his failure...was as vicious, as vile a wound as the rent he'd carved in the matron's side.

The pack of snow bears were retreating, leaping up the ravine wall to disappear behind the sharp stones and glinting ice. They fled because he killed their matron.

Where would he flee now that she had slaughtered his warband?

His wounded shoulder and arm threw waves of pain that made it hard to think much less move.

"Jarl," a voice came from behind him. Garilon's voice.

He swung toward the sound and took in Garilon's stern face, bloody and scorched by venom, armor ragged, one bloody fist gripped tight around the haft of a wicked axe. A dozen of his warband gathered behind him.

He grinned, relieved to see that he hadn't led his warband to complete slaughter, then he stumbled, swayed...a ship's mast in a gale...and fell.

82

Frigg

The procession through Gladsheim worried Frigg. Baldr would first be carried around the Lower Tier, then the Middle Tier, and then the Upper Ring. During that entire time – from midday to midnight – even a one-eyed graybeard could strike that target. She winced at that thought, since her absent husband Odin partly fit that description. Still, the thought of Baldr prominently at risk worried her. There were only so many wardens she could have posted along the route and close to Baldr before the folk noticed and began to think it strange.

But Yelena was loose and was involved in the cutting out of the heart of the mistletoe in which they'd hidden Baldr's spirit. And since Yelena was a shapeshifter, she could be anyone or anywhere. Loki, too, was a suspect, along with Angrboda, Loki's dead wife. Odin had left to interrogate Angrboda's spirit, but had not yet returned despite having promised, as he always did, to return before the Midwinter festivals began. Which were imminent. And where was Odin? Nowhere to be found, even by Heimdall.

She swore to herself and pushed those thoughts from her mind.

Focus on what she *could* control. On her fingers, she listed the measures she'd taken. The Great Hall, which is where Baldr's procession would arrive, was locked down—side doors barred, and wardens posted.

Mistletoe itself could not be turned into a weapon, not by any means she knew. Odin might know a way, but he wasn't here.

She pushed back the wave of anger and resentment that bubbled up at that thought. It didn't help.

What might is the task she given Hermod—make sure nothing wooden in the hall could be pried loose and used against Baldr. Hermod had made triply sure that was the case.

She'd also told Fimafeng that no weapons of any kind would be permitted into the hall itself. Instead, stones would be thrown during the ritual, stored in barrels set before her platform and moved only when it was time to begin.

What else was there to do?

She'd already persuaded Heimdall to watch, and she'd alerted Tyr. But no other jarls would be present this Midwinter. Not unusual, but this year she would've liked the extra eyes. Especially since Yelena had killed Gulfinn—she'd foreseen his death. And that worried her.

It wasn't that Gulfinn's passing was necessarily linked to any time that overlapped with her vision of Baldr burning in a flaming ship. But combined with Yelena, the cut mistletoe, and her other visions... Klakki being killed by Jotunn spears was just one example...but she'd also heard nothing about Vidar or his journey into Utgard. Heimdall couldn't find him, which wasn't that unusual given the low gray clouds and snowstorms that almost always covered those lands, but still, it was another burden on her shoulders. A burden that she bore alone.

She was on edge. She wanted to scream, to tear her hair, to curl up under a warm blanket and let someone else handle it. But there was no one else.

Instead, she paced back and forth in the room behind the platform in the Great Hall. She stared into the hearth, enjoying the heat and the snap and pop of the logs. Until the vision of Baldr burning in the ship surfaced in her mind.

What else? What was she missing? Other than death playing out in flames above the heads of everyone she set eyes on...

She snorted. Fire and death; death and fire. No matter where she looked.

If they could only find that shapeshifting bitch who'd savaged Baldr's mistletoe, that would help. But how could they find a shapeshifter in a city in which so many thousands lived and was home to many more thousands who'd come to celebrate Midwinter.

Questions hung in her mind like decorations. Why hadn't the witch cut and burned all of Baldr's mistletoe? Why hadn't she burned the tree? Or the entire grove? And how had she figured out where Baldr's spirit had been hidden or even known what Frigg had done?

Who was the mistress the witch had referred to? Frigg's gut twisted. Angrboda seemed possible, but Loki's first wife had been dead a long time, too long for this young witch to have learned from directly. Unless Yelena was older than she looked which, as a shapeshifter, was not impossible. Or perhaps Angrboda had formed a coven before she died and passed her hatred for Odin and the Aesir down to them.

"Mother?"

Frigg looked up to see her daughter clad in full armor, sword strapped to one side, axe to the other. No doubt she wore a knife at the small of her back. Hermod's dark golden hair was gathered into a tight braid and doubled upon itself. She looked much older and more serious than she should at twenty-five years. She hadn't even eaten her first fruit.

"The hall is locked and I've done what I can to check Baldr's route for anything suspicious or potentially harmful," Hermod said. "I'll walk the route again tomorrow morning and recheck the hall to make sure my hidden marks haven't been disturbed."

"Excellent. Thank you, Hermod."

"So will you tell me why we're taking all these precautions? I know it's because of some threat to Baldr, but…"

"But he can't be hurt or killed, so what's the point?" She wanted to say that might not be as true as they thought. Instead, she continued, "You saw what the Sons did at the docks. The precautions aren't so much for Baldr as they are for everyone. We can't have a battle break out in the middle of the hall."

Although it wouldn't be the first time.

Hermod hitched up her sword belt and forced the pommel down so she could sit comfortably. "Any word from Father?"

Frigg shook her head. "Nothing. Heimdall still can't see him, either."

"He has time to keep his promise," Hermod said with all the confidence of a child who barely knew her father.

"Yes, he does."

"But you don't think he will, do you?"

Her smile felt lopsided and forced. "Midwinter starts tomorrow. Three nights out, three nights back puts him back tonight."

"There's still time," Hermod repeated. Then, with a note of hesitation in her voice, she added, "Mother?"

It was that hesitation, the uncertainty, that made her look up.

Hermod flashed a nervous smile. "How much danger are we actually in?"

Frigg straightened up. "Danger? I'm not sure—"

"Mother, please, I'm not the child I was when Father left. There's more going on than just a possible threat on my brother's life. That witch you found killed Gulfinn and then escaped. Ráta tore Yelena's home apart looking for some clue as to where she might have gone. And since he returned, Father's barely been home for more than a handful of nights…he was nearly killed at Ithavoll, then he lost his eye…. And then there's the attack on Háls… those fools setting the ships on fire…. And having spent so much time patrolling the city these last few days, it almost feels like we're in a dry bonfire that's ready to be kindled. So, how much danger are we actually in?"

Hermod had grown up. She had a choice. She could feel it in the air like a weight pressing down on her chest. Either treat her youngest as if she were still a child, or tell her the truth.

"You remember I told you we'd all sit down and tell you everything?"

Hermod nodded.

"Well, that time has come."

83

Hodr

With the heat of torches warming his face, Hodr stared off into the evening chill, savoring the sights granted by the spear Lopt had given him. He held a cooling horn nearly full of mulled wine. He had no taste for its heavy spices and sickly sweetness, but he kept holding it so Lopt or passing strangers wouldn't press another into his hand.

Last night, they'd delivered the smith's last shipment of weapons to a bored-looking Einherjar. Since morning, they'd been wandering the many streets Gladsheim had added in the fifty-odd winters he'd been gone. Not only had the lowest tier bulged past the wall like a fat man's belly beyond his belt, but the second tier had several new districts packed with longhouses around what had become a bustling marketplace. The upper tier, where they now stood, had sprouted new buildings beneath the dominating presence of both the Great Hall and Heimdall's tower above.

And in his limited, dim sight, all he could really see beyond a few spear length's distance were moving, swaying shadowy men and women who passed along the road or huddled around the warmth of the hundreds of torches that lined the roads, and the braziers and bonfires that marked nearly every intersection. A small army of thralls must be needed to keep them all blazing away.

Lopt jabbered at him, laughed, and took a long pull from his own horn of wine.

Hodr smiled, raised his horn in reply, and faked a sip. The sickly-sweet spicy smell turned his stomach.

It wasn't the city he remembered. It wasn't a city he even liked very much, not tonight, at least, not on Midwinter when the number of folk inside the walls numbered more than the fleas on wild hound's back.

A sharp cackle from up the line drew his attention. The heat from the nearby torches grew hotter on his face. Someone staggered out of line and vomited.

The Great Hall loomed before him. This line was simply to get in. They'd stood here, shuffling slowly forward for the last eitt and more. All to get packed in and stand shoulder to shoulder with his fellow Aesir when he could simply have walked up, shown his arm ring and been escorted to his father. He could've done so at the gate. Lopt had certainly urged him to, but he wasn't ready.

And, if he were honest, that's really why he stood here, half freezing half sweating. Better to present himself tomorrow, after all the attention on his brother died down.

A clump of drunken, singing shadows bobbled past, soon lost in the general, celebratory din.

Lopt staggered backward into him. Hodr fumbled to steady the sodden fool—he shouldn't have agreed to any of this—but Lopt's strong, hot hand gripped his elbow.

Unbidden, a sweet memory of Nanna—skin pale as cream, long golden hair tinged sunset red, and eyes the color of new grass beneath a spring snow—surfaced. There'd been a time when he and his brother had almost fought over her.

He shook the memory off as he shoved Lopt away.

"Apologies, my friend, I wasn't looking, fool that I am," Lopt said. "The line's moved forward a few paces. You must not have seen—er, heard—their footsteps above all this, eh?"

Hodr shrugged. "My mind was elsewhere."

"No doubt looking forward to seeing your father and mother again, eh? And your brother, of course."

"Not seeing, so much." He stepped forward before the grumbles of "Look alive there!" behind him in line became angrier.

"Ah, yes. My apologies, Jarl. You get around so well it's easy to forget your, uh, condition."

Aside from the cloth tied around his eyes. In a low voice, he said, "I've told you, don't use my title."

Lopt swore. "I just keep doing it, don't I? It happens when I'm nervous. I get forgetful. My wife used to say, 'Lopt, you're a grown man. A successful one. No need to be nervous around folk.' But this here situation is entirely different. Meeting the Alfather and Hár Frigg? Baldr and Nanna? And many of the other jarls, I'd expect. Who wouldn't be nervous?"

The smith slapped his hand down on Hodr's and squeezed warmly, giving him a friendly shake. "Maybe I'll go get another horn of wine. I could use a little more, just to steady myself. How about you?"

"No, I'm fine, thanks."

Hodr listened to him crunch away across the packed snow. And then he focused on the chill breeze and the soft roar of the torches rather than the voices hammering all around him.

Moments later, Lopt's footsteps returned. He drank noisily. "Do you know where they got these spices for the mulled wine? I tell you, they're delicious."

A man in front of them, who seemed to be waiting for someone to return, answered. "I heard the Alfather brought back a dozen packets of exotic stuff from the south."

"That's where Jarl Baldr's district is, right?" Lopt said, a slight slur adding a sibilance to his words.

The man laughed. "Further south than that—still looking for his brothers, they say."

"There are people further south?" Lopt asked. Hodr heard him smack his lips. "Well, I don't mind saying, I hope he goes back soon. This is really excellent stuff."

The stranger laughed. Hodr saw him reach out and thump Lopt on the shoulder.

The line shuffled forward a few more paces.

"So now that you've seen the line, Lopt," he said, "how much farther do we have to go?"

The smith's lips smacked again. "Hard to tell, since the line curves and goes over the rise. Not sure where the hall's entrance is. But at least a hundred or so people in front of us."

The great hall, the largest in the city, could hold five times that number and servants besides. Hodr remembered climbing its tall columns, carved to resemble trees, to jump and swing from the rafters and beams. He used to bring food stolen from the kitchens beside the hall and then scramble up high to enjoy it.

"I was wondering—not that I mind enjoying the streets of Gladsheim or the evening air—but why haven't you"—Lopt cleared his throat, stepped closer, and continued in a whisper—"you know, just walked up and announced yourself?"

The same, entirely fair, question asked yet again. He discarded a few nasty responses before saying, "I left on bad terms. I'm not overeager to present myself. And now that I'm here, I'm wondering if I shouldn't have waited until after Midwinter. Not the best time to surprise everyone."

Lopt staggered as he reached out to grip Hodr's arm in one strong, hot hand. "I totally understand. If you prefer, we can head back down and find a spot in one of the other halls. I'm only here because of you, after all."

Hodr grunted, met the smith's gaze with his blind face, and nodded. "We have some time still before I have to decide."

"Whatever you want is fine with me." Lopt lifted his cup in a salute, burped, and took another drink. "Just happy to be here. Tell this story for winters to come!"

He took a sip of his own wine, hoping to counter the dryness in his mouth. It tasted better cold. Though it seemed a good plan to encourage the smith to get so drunk that he'd have to escort him back to their way house. Meeting his parents could wait a night or so. Alara knew where he'd gone and that it might be some weeks before he returned.

A new voice, loud, bored, and familiar rang out above the din of conversation around him. "... all weapons must be left by the entrance. None permitted inside."

His fingers tightened reflexively around the spear. Yes, this meeting should happen another night.

84

Vidar

"All along the far ridge?" Vidar asked, leaning back into the dubious shelter of the tall boulder.

"That's what I'd do." Garilon tugged the cowl of his hood up.

They now stood at the top of the ravine that just a few nights earlier they had marched out of. Unlike that first night in Utgard, the sky overhead was the dense white-gray wool of low-hanging clouds from which blew a squall of snow and ice. Bitter gusts of wind shrieked through the jagged rocks and ice. The only benefit of the storm was that it prevented the Jotunn warriors, who must be lying in wait for them, from using the short, black recurved bows they favored.

"If we could spare a couple warriors, we could get some idea of what's ahead," Garilon continued.

Vidar heard the clipped tone and unspoken concluding phrase: *but there's not enough of us left*. But Garilon's face, hollow-cheeked with exhaustion and hunger, was devoid of expression.

I will go.

Go where?

Scout ahead.

You can do that?

In answer, his fylgja leaped from him and vanished into the storm. Apparently, now that he had given up controlling her through the runes, she could go where she chose.

"I'll take care of it," he said with a shrug he regretted as pain returned to his wounded shoulder.

How far can you go? he asked, not sure if she had to be present within him in order to hear him.

I'm not entirely sure.

Garilon opened his mouth to ask but then seemed to realize that an unusual method of scouting was being undertaken.

Do you have a name? Vidar asked his fylgja.

Of course.

When nothing further came, he asked, *May I know it?*

In time, you may.

He suppressed a frown and adjusted the rough sling his left arm was in. "This may take a while. Might as well rest."

So together, he and Garilon crunched back through the knee-deep snow, buffeted by random gusts, his ankles almost rolling with every other step on the uneven ground. They stepped behind the lumpen line of boulders, mounded with snow and ice, where the warband hid. Once tucked in among the boulders, the wind's shriek dropped to a dull moan, and it grew oddly warmer.

His twenty-seven remaining fighters, mostly unwounded, had used their shields to mound the heavy, packable snow into walls and then, using groups of spears as columns with shields balanced on top had formed a makeshift roof.

These warriors of his, these stout-hearted men and women, had all taken turns carrying him through the night as his fylgja worked her magic within him to quicken the healing of his wounds. Sadly, he'd no seidr left to similarly aid his warriors.

Those who were still awake nodded respectfully to him as he entered. They were all in a big huddle, leaning against each other for warmth. The fuel for the witchstoves had been used up. He didn't deserve their respect. He'd broken his warband as casually as a child breaks a toy.

He'd needed to know what was going on. Why the Jotunn had attacked. The worst part was, he still didn't know. He'd seen *something* at the frozen lake, but what exactly? Only the Jotunn knew. Nor had he learned anything about how the doorways worked—only that they existed. All he'd really succeeded in doing was get his warband slaughtered.

There are two dozen archers up here tucked in among the rocks above the doorway.

Well, that settled that. Jotunn. *Any idea what tribe they're with?*

Let me ask them.

Wait, what? Don't—

That was a joke.

Vidar shook his head and rubbed his tired eyes with one hand. *Can you tell me how exactly you even know what a joke is?*

A better question is how you know what a joke is.

Garilon thumped down opposite him.

"There are a couple of dozen archers in the rocks above the doorway," Vidar said.

The kjolr took the news as if he'd expected it. His eyes flicked sideways to the line of huddled warriors, dwelled there for a moment, and then returned to meet Vidar's gaze. And held it, steadily. For too long.

Anger rushed in, nearly swamping what he knew to be true—that his decisions had led to the destruction of his warband. But he'd had to do it. His father would have made the same decision. They had to know what was happening and why the Jotunn had attacked. If he had leaned too heavily on Garilon's advice they might never have reached that frozen lake or seen the Jotunn at work. Maybe he didn't know *exactly* what they were doing, but now he knew that something was happening about which they knew nothing.

Look at him again, his fylgja said as she settled back into him. His body warmed as she did.

So, he looked again—and reconsidered. Maybe Garilon's expression had been more appraising than accusatory, more an unasked question than anything. Maybe the question had been: Was it worth the lives spent? And maybe there was another question there, as well: What will you do now?

He blew out a breath and rubbed his eyes. Then he pushed himself up to his feet. Who could say? Perhaps the Norns, if they ever spoke.

Tell me of those you scouted. Can we kill them? he asked.

Yes, unless one such as we is among them.

That's possible? I mean, the Jotunn can do—become—what we are?

Of course.

Will I be able to use my arm?

It wasn't broken and I did encourage your flesh to heal.

It is somewhat better.

He wondered if he would make the wound worse by using it. He lifted his arm from the sling and let it hang, throbbing, small jabs of pain alternating with longer, more generous doses.

When we fight, it won't pain you.

Ignoring the look Garilon directed at him, he felt at the small of his back for his knife. Gone, of course. He'd left it in the matron.

And you're that confident that even wounded as I am, we'll be able to kill them all?

And feed on them, remember.

Yes, that was also part of our bargain. Answer me.

His fylgja smiled up at him from deep within himself. *What happened to the matron after I lent you my strength? There's a reason your father bound disir to Aesir.*

Fair enough. She extended her limbs through his and her strength flooded in. The cold vanished, as did the pain in his shoulder. His sight grew clearer, sharper.

He extended an open hand to Garilon. "I'll need your knife. I'll be back when the archers are dealt with."

Garilon dragged a nearby snow-crusted bag toward him. He dug in it and presented something to Vidar. "Use these instead. We paid for 'em."

In each hand, Garilon held one of the long, black-tipped horns that had once belonged to the matron. The base of each bore the ragged marks of an axe.

85

Hodr

"All weapons must be left by the entrance. None permitted inside."

Hodr recognized the voice. It was Fimafeng, his family's thrall and longtime steward. He hunched his shoulders and turned slowly away from the loud, old man's voice. Doing so meant he faced a bright torch—which he could see and feel—so he shuffled a little sideways to put Lopt between himself and the approaching steward.

Fimafeng had been a younger man when Hodr had left Gladsheim, blind and angry. It was possible he wouldn't recognize him, but it was also safer not to risk it. Lopt himself had guessed at Hodr's identity, so it wouldn't be hard for Fimafeng—who knew Hodr well—to recognize Odin's blind, spear-carrying son.

Fimafeng's voice grew louder still. "We celebrate with stones this year, fresh from the river bed. Smooth and round. Guaranteed to fly straight. And don't worry, there's more than enough to drink if you find your aim too accurate."

A general cheer followed the last statement. Hodr swore at himself. Had he left even a few moments earlier, he could've have avoided this entire situation. Stepping out of line now would only draw attention to himself.

Fimafeng's raw, old man's voice was nearer still. It grated on his ears. The man's throat had to burn with every word. "But you must leave your weapons by the door. The women won't fight, not tonight, eh? No one will touch them—the weapons, I mean. Knives are fine, so long as they stay in their scabbards. Until later, of course."

Ribald laughs and jeers followed that remark.

Spear in hand, Hodr slowly angled himself still further away till the torch's heat was on one side of his exchanging the torches' heat for the night sky's empty cold.

Lopt brayed laughter at something, staggered backward, and bumped into Hodr who stumbled into the men behind them. Drinking horns clattered against the stones beneath their feet.

Shouting—"you spilled my ale" and "get me another you bastard" —the men shoved Hodr and he staggered forward into Lopt who himself shouted, "My fault entirely, my good karls, I will happily fetch you more drinks!"

"Everything all right here?" Fimafeng said. He was right in front of them.

Hodr realized now that Lopt's accidental bump had turned him back toward the street; the torchlight he'd avoided now fell full upon him even as Lopt squatted to retrieve the horns he'd indirectly knocked from the men's hands while continuing to babble slurred apologies to those he'd jostled.

Hodr guessed that he hadn't been recognized—at least not yet— because Fimafeng was focused on the bumbling smith's antics. So, very slowly, Hodr sidled forward and edged sideways toward the cool darkness in between the torches.

"Yes, everything's fine, just my clumsy old hands, that's all." Lopt stood, stumbled backward and bumped into Hodr yet again. "Seems I need a new drink—and one for all my friends here who've suffered for my clumsiness."

Thanks to the gray sight granted by his spear, it seemed that

Fimafeng's remained focused on Lopt and those around him. So, Hodr froze, hoping to remain unnoticed.

"It happens, but don't let it come to drawn blades," Fimafeng said, his tone more bored than angry. He jerked a thumb back the way he'd come. "The drinks stall just over the rise is closest."

"Thank you, sir," Lopt said. To Hodr, he said, "I'll go fetch a pair of drinks."

Fimafeng stepped back, giving Lopt space, and looked directly at Hodr. He watched puzzlement furrow Fimafeng's brow, then the old thrall's jaw dropped and he gasped in recognition. Hodr's stomach fell. Thanks to the stupid, clumsy smith, he'd no choice but to face his father tonight.

"Jarl Hodr, is that you?" Fimafeng said, raising one hand to cut the torch's glare.

Lopt seemed to freeze in mid-stride, perhaps wondering what he should do—or maybe the bastard felt guilty that it was his clumsiness that had revealed Hodr's presence.

Hodr forced his lips into what he hoped was a smile. "Fimafeng! I thought I recognized your voice."

"It is you!" Fimafeng exclaimed, surprise turning to delight. "But why are you waiting in line? Come with me. I'll escort you right up to the hall."

Hodr waved a hand. "No, no. No need for that. I'm happy to wait my turn along with these good folk."

Fimafeng snorted. "Hár Frigg would have my ears if I left you waiting out here. And after so long, too. You've hardly changed from the young man I remember, unlike me, eh?" He gestured. "Come on, then. The Almother—and your sister and brother—will be delighted you've arrived. Hermod especially, I think. You may not recognize her after all these winters! Fights like Thor, I tell you."

Hodr could not help but hear the gasps and shocked expletives of those sober enough to overhear their conversation. The murmurs rolled in afterward, low waves eroding the beach: "Rán, take me, but it's true, the Alfather did have a blind son" and "Who's that?" and "Why that's the hero of the Old Bridge?" and "You mean that actually happened?" and "'Course it did you dimwit!" and "What's a son of the Alfather doing out here with us?"

Hodr took a deep breath, forced his shoulders to relax, and stepped toward Fimafeng, making a show of tapping the spear before him.

It seemed he would be seeing his family tonight after all. "Too kind of you, Fimafeng. My friend here, smith Lopt, will be joining me."

A momentary pause, and then Fimafeng said, "Well, of course, welcome, my good smith. If you'll both follow me, please."

Lopt's hot fingers dug into Hodr's elbow and, in a low voice, he said, "I am so very sorry about that, jar—I mean, Hodr."

**

Raucous laughter spilled out through the hall's entryway. The broad, tall doors bound with iron and decorated with gold and silver towered on either side of him as if he were walking down into the earth rather than into a hall full of celebrating Aesir. Astride the laughter's back, rode the heat from the cooking fires, the roasting of boar and snow-deer and fish, the sweat of hundreds and the yeasty tang of beers and ales. He felt ill—not just at the thought of going into the hall, at once so familiar and so foreign, but at the prospect of confronting his father...not to mention the rest of his family.

"Just a moment more, Jarl Hodr," Fimafeng said, returning from inside the hall. "I've informed Hár Frigg that you're here; she asked that you be shown in directly. We're just waiting for the doorway to clear."

Fimafeng gestured for the pair of wardens on either side of the doors to step forward and bar the path. "Keep everyone out until I come back."

Hodr's hand grew sweatier on his spear. He dumped the dregs of his unfinished wine on the dirt, tucked the horn behind his belt, and tugged his overtunic straight. Then he switched the spear to his other hand and wiped his sweaty palm on his chest. Any minute now, he'd be standing before his family.

"Ready, Jarl?" Fimafeng asked, a genuine smile on his face. "I know it's been a very long time, but they are delighted to see you."

Hodr swallowed, ignored the sweat beading on his forehead, and forced a smile. "My thanks, Fimafeng."

To Lopt, he said, "Wait here. It's best I meet everyone alone. I'll send Fimafeng back for you."

"Of course, Jarl." Lopt's words sounded a little slurred. He clutched Hodr's elbow with hot fingers that brought new sweat to Hodr's armpits. "I look forward to being introduced to your family— and I'm terrified at the prospect."

His sickly, drunken belch did little to settle Hodr's nerves.

Hodr jerked his elbow free and stepped into the hall's wet heat. The celebratory din had dulled into background noise, the steady slap of water against a ship's sides, even as his heart pounded in his ears.

Tapping the boards before him with his spear, he focused on the details of his surroundings. The entryway was a spear's length long and wide, and—wait, the boards were new. When he'd last been here, the hall's floor had been packed dirt strewn with ashes.

A sharp intake of breath cut through the background noise. His mother. He heard a pair of rushed steps, and then he was crushed in his brother's embrace. He barely kept hold of his spear.

In his ear, Baldr whispered, "I'm so glad you're back, Hodr. We've missed you."

He felt a smile forming on his lips as he returned Baldr's embrace. His breath became shaky, as if he'd been hit in the stomach.

Baldr released him and stepped back, keeping one hand on his shoulder.

"Baldr, I just wanted to apologize for—"

His brother's hand tightened warmly on his shoulder and, like Sól herself shouldering up over the mountains, he felt the kindness of his smile. Baldr made a dismissive gesture with his free hand. "All in the past, Hodr. It's just good that you're back."

Hodr could dimly see his brother beckoning someone to come closer. "And here's someone who's been dying to see you again."

Hodr heard the hesitant scuff of boot leather before the strong, clean-lined face of a young woman swam into hazy view. Her hair was pulled into a warrior's braid.

She smiled shyly at him. "Do you remember me, Hodr?"

He cocked his head, matching her voice to the memory of a young woman's. "Forget you? Never!"

She hugged him, strongly enough to creak his ribs. She was tall, like him, and smelled of oil and skymetal, just like the young woman she'd been. Hermod had been so fascinated with weapons and armor that even as a child she'd practiced beside him with toy swords, shields, and spears. She kissed his cheek, held him tighter, then retreated.

"So you've finally returned to us, Hodr," his mother said, her voice rolling in like a warm ocean wave. "And to think your sister and I were just talking about you."

When she stepped into the shadows of his sight, her eyes were black pits, but he could see her bright smile and wide-open arms. What hit him harder was the relief and happiness that throbbed in her voice. And when she embraced him, he couldn't help but bury his face in her shoulder. He couldn't cry, but he still wept, shoulders heaving as he held his mother tight.

When he pulled away, she let him go. Baldr and Hermod both watched,

Her hands came up to rest lightly on his cheeks. "I am so very happy that you're back, Hodr. It's been far too long." She ran her thumbs across the cloth tied round his eyes and then rested her hands on his shoulders. "After tonight, we'll have time to sit and talk. I want to hear all about this Alara of yours."

Hodr's mouth sagged open. His mother smiled kindly and gave him a little shake. "Your father's not the only one keeping an eye on you. She seems good for you, but I'll want to meet her just the same."

"She's wonderful, and the main reason I'm here," he said, smiling. "Where is father?"

Baldr shook his head and a look, like a small cloud drifting past the sun, crossed his face before he shook it away. "He'll be back soon, I'm sure. He'll be sorry to have missed your homecoming."

His mother edged back, one hand lingering on his shoulder before falling away. Worry entered her voice. "He rode down to the Gjoll's shores looking for answers to a question that's troubled us for months now. He said he'd be back before now, but..."

Before the silence grew, Hermod spoke. "There's been a lot going on. I'll walk with you to a table and tell you about it."

"I'd enjoy that," Hodr said, feeling a smile spread across his face. He raised the spear slightly and jerked a thumb back toward the open door. "I should give this over. Fimafeng was very insistent that all weapons should be set aside."

"Nonsense. You need it," Baldr said. "Keep it with you."

"Better to not have an exception made for me, I think," he replied. He tapped the spear, following it the few steps to the wall. "And besides, Hermod will get me seated. And when her duties pull her away, I've a friend who can help me. He was kind enough to bring me here. He also crafted this spear and gave it to me, but that's a long story too. May I introduce him?"

"We want to hear all about what you've been doing," his mother said. "And I'm sure Hermod shares my curiosity over Alara. Tomorrow we'll sit together and talk, just the four of us, assuming your father isn't back."

Her voice became cooler and more distant. "But for tonight, please show my son's friend in, Fimafeng. Any friend of his is a friend of ours."

86

Vidar

Vidar felt the thump of sorcery an instant before the cliff before him rumbled and shook. He skidded to a halt and threw his arms out wide. Behind him, the warband stumbled to a halt. The entrance to the Asgard doorway yawned black before them, several dozen spear lengths away.

He'd already killed, with his fylgja's help, the Jotunn archers who'd intended to ambush his warband. His fylgja had eaten well. He'd then returned to his warband, what was left of them, and led them in a shambling run back to their only way out—the doorway back to the mines beneath Hálsberg.

Snow and ice from atop the cliff thundered down, burying the entrance to the doorway. The thud stilled the air for a moment. Apparently, he hadn't cleared the way well enough. Shamans lingered, and given what he'd fought less than a night ago, snow bears lurked, along with the full strength of at least one Jotunn warband.

"Turn about. Keep it nice and tight," Garilon called out, his breath a cloud around his face. "And keep your eyes open. All directions. Don't break the line."

Vidar turned to look at Garilon standing tall, one hand pressed against his side, in the middle of a shield wall that was a dim memory of what it had been a few days earlier. Thanks to his mistakes. The remaining twenty-seven braced themselves, spears lowering, round shields overlapping, ice crunching beneath their boots.

"Kjolr, that's mostly snow and ice," Vidar said, jerking a thumb over his shoulder. "If half dig and scrape while the other half fight..."

Wind keened through the silence.

"You heard your Jarl," Garilon shouted, "Get to work."

***

Vidar flinched backward fast enough so that the snow bear's claws only tore burning furrows across his belly instead of spilling his guts on the snow. Another bear crowded in beside the first, jaws slavering venom, eager for an opening.

Vidar surged forward, slammed his shoulder into the beast's side, its musky, coarse hair making his flesh crawl. Its ribs broke and he shoved it away, limbs and clubbed tail flailing.

A handful of arrows hammered into his back. He spun and saw six Jotunn sprinting toward him, spears lowered.

A giant's hammer struck his lower back and he arched backward —flung up and over the gray-white fur of the second snow bear, the one he'd stupidly put his back to when the arrows had hit him. As he tumbled through the air, a line of fire opened on his thigh and his blood flowed.

He crashed into the frozen, rocky earth, blood hot and coppery in his mouth. The snow bear hissed, sucking in air. He knew that sound too well—she was about to spit venom.

Get up, his fylgja screamed into his mind. She poured fresh strength into him, a waterfall filling a lake.

Thanks to her, Vidar threw himself sideways into a diving roll that let him avoid most of the beast's venom. Even so, some of the venom pattered against his tattered armor and sizzled through it to burn his skin.

Coming up into a crouch, a Jotunn jabbed in the chest with his spear. The long wooden shaft flexed in the Jotunn's hands, but the skymetal point didn't puncture his skin. A second spear's blade struck him below one eye, and his head snapped back from the impact but it, too, didn't draw blood or even pain.

And then the rest of the Jotunn were on him, spears jabbing and pulling back to thrust again. Each strike was stronger than the last as they braced themselves and, grunting, threw their weight into each hit. They fought as a unit, just as the Aesir themselves did. Despite their precision, the sharp, cold points dimpled his skin but didn't cut him.

But of course these Jotunn would have figured out that he was a baresark. They knew their steel couldn't hurt him. The rhythm was meant to keep him distracted and pinned down so that the shaman could marshal more snow bears to send against him.

He blocked a pair of thrusts with a forearm, Vidar looked into the bearded, brown faces of the Jotunn. Their eyes gleamed like gems while their breath frosted in the air, ice crusting on their dark beards. Young warriors, and fierce. Shorter than himself, and burly.

To one side, Vidar glimpsed another four snow bears in the distance, shambling closer. The fifth, the one that had spat venom at him, circled to menace his flank.

He heard the shouts of his own warband, followed by a triple burst from Vithi's silvered horn, Vidar realized, as well, that he had let these beasts and spearmen do too good a job of separating him from his warband.

But they'd also given him a little too long to catch his breath. Like a parched man dipping cupped hands into a river, he caught up more of his fylgja's apparently unending strength and drank deeply.

This time the striking spears moved like a lazy ripple in a tall sail. He shuffled in, trapped several of the spear shafts between his left arm and side, and knocked the others spears up and away. He set his feet, braced his right hand against the trapped spears and, with another throat-tearing shout, pivoted.

Caught off guard—and how could they not be, he'd dodged and

struck far too quickly—the warriors who spears he'd trapped slammed sideways into those beside them.

Vidar darted into the gap in their line. He broke the neck of the Jotunn on his right with a single, hammering strike. He dropped the trapped spears and shuffled into a punch that broke another warrior's ribs, flung him backward and knocked down the remaining Jotunn on his right.

Now Vidar stood in a small open space. The Jotunn on his left fumbled to get their shields in front of them while ripping axes from their broad leather belts. The four additional snow bears were much closer now, their shambling, sideways run deceptively quick. And behind him, the venom-spitter hissed in a preparatory breath.

Meanwhile, thirty yards distant, the bulk of the attacking Jotunn warband pressed hard against the turtled clump of his own remaining warriors. If he didn't help now, he'd get the rest of his warband killed.

Vidar stooped, ripped free the axe strapped to the dead Jotunn's belt, and sprinted toward his warriors.

87

Hodr

Hermod found Hodr a spot near the raised platform where the rest of his family, aunts and uncles sat, Hodr spoke with Hermod for a short time—more shouted, really, given how loud the hall was—but now that the smith had joined them she'd grown reticent, had a thrall bring new tankards of ale and heaping platters of roast boar and fish and fresh-baked bread, and returned to her seat on the raised platform to sit beside Baldr, Nanna, and their mother.

Hodr knew Nanna was present because he caught a whiff of her wildflower scent on an eddy in the hall's hot air. It lacked the power over him it once had—Alara's influence, no doubt.

"You must be thrilled your long-delayed reunion went as well as it did," Lopt said, back yet again on the same topic. His words tumbled out like coins from a purse. "I liked your mother. Strong and hard, like winter, but kindness there, too. And such gentleness in your brother's face. Was he really a doughty warrior long ago? I also see the resemblance in your sister, though she's lovelier than you, I think, not that you'll mind me saying it. Tall and willowy like her mother, but without that hard edge experience brings. Your brother's wife is such a contrast with both of them

—more like a cloud at sunset, brushed with yellows and light reds."

Hodr tried to focus on the raucous folk around them rather than on Lopt's voice. Was he trying to impress? Or was he just nervous and drunk? Either way, the fancy words rang false and he didn't want to hear them anymore. But for a man who'd never been in the company of the realm's jarls, maybe it was the only way the smith could be expected to act. So maybe he should be a little more understanding. A little more tolerant, like Baldr would no doubt be.

And sitting here, having finally returned—and having received such a warm welcome—Hodr found it hard to resent the smith much less anything else. Not his lack of sight nor the attention on his brother nor all the praise Lopt heaped on him.

He had his own life now. It had taken him fifty winters to find it and to find a woman who loved him. But he'd found them both. Just the thought of getting back to Alara warmed him.

And who knew what the Norns had carved for him? With the smith's spear, maybe he could try to be a warrior again. Or maybe he could become Jarl of Ifington—with all the trade passing through it was a big enough to warrant a full jarldom.

If his father agreed to give Yggdrasil's fruits to Alara and the children she bore him, maybe becoming jarl would work out. But if his father didn't agree, well, he'd return to Alara and live a full, happy life with her and then, when he was old, gray and bent-backed, he'd board the ship that would take him down the Gjoll and pass back into the Gap. All those here in this hall had that doom set for them.

Except for his family.

Deep voices called for folk to make the circle wider. Like the flap of a wet sail, the crowd lurched into motion. Wood scraped on wood. The floor planks creaked and flexed, a rumbling as of a massive barrel reached his ears. Must be the ancient, scarred stump being rolled in. The procession would be getting close, then.

Hodr cocked an ear. Yes, just there. The mournful sound of the flutes drifted in. He stood.

Lopt's knees popped as he rose beside him. "What's happening?"

"The procession is outside. The last warrior will fall before Rán, and she'll step inside."

"Your brother is stepping down from his chair!" Hodr heard a note of eagerness in Lopt's voice. "He's taking off his clothes?"

He nodded. "Everything but his breechcloth."

The floor boomed; plates and cups rattled and rolled.

"The tree stump's in the center of a circle, in the wide space between the fire pits," Lopt exclaimed.

Indeed it was. This hall had been built with a broad belly to not only serve as the gathering place of Gladsheim—for a very long time every Aesir had eaten, drank and celebrated here. It was only in the last hundred or so winters that it mostly hosted Gladsheim's wealthier residents.

The deep booming of the drums filled the hall while the flutes sang their airy counterpoint. Booted feet tramped in. Those in the hall began to stomp in rhythm with the drums.

Lopt gasped at the same time everyone else in the hall did. From the smell of hot blood, Hodr knew what the smith was seeing. "Isn't this ritual conducted in Ifington?"

"Not on this scale," the smith stammered, sounding awed.

Hodr pictured the ritual in his mind. A blood- and gore-soaked young woman, naked, eyes wild from whatever herbs Idunn's priestesses fed her, cavorted on a wide platform that rippled with blue silks as if she rode the ocean itself rather than on the shoulders of a dozen burly young warriors.

Tonight, she was Rán, death herself, come among them. She thrust with a spear in one hand, to slay those who displeased her, and a green net in the other to drag them down and down to her home beneath the waves.

The crowd cheered. Lopt laughed aloud. Baldr, pale, naked flesh daubed with gold and blue pigments, would have stepped onto the tree stump as Aegir himself, at least tonight, to defend his people, the Aesir, from the ever-hungry Rán.

The stench of blood and offal hung heavy in the air. Lopt coughed and said, "So much blood!"

"A thousand or more animals died to bring us this feast," Hodr said. "Plenty of blood and guts to spread around."

Now the pounding of the drums swelled, grew harsher, evoking the sound of battle itself, of axes against shields, of churning waves grinding longships against a rocky coast, while the flutes sang of life, conjuring images of grass pushing up beneath snow, of purple flowers opening in green fields, of white clouds passing swiftly away after a storm.

Hodr remembered this part well. As a boy, he'd loved being terrified by this ritual. From atop her sea-like platform, Rán thrust out with her spear, spinning, twisting and jumping in a way that would get you killed on the battlefield, and then hurling out her net and dragging it back in as if she'd caught a corpse.

Young girls spent the summer months training and competing for the role of Rán, but deathless Baldr had played Aegir's part since before he'd taken his first bite of Yggdrasil's fruit. His invariable presence lent Gladsheim's Midwinter ceremony a far different tenor than any other he'd ever seen.

The pounding drums and shrieking flutes were close now, along with the heady stink of blood. The planks trembled and shook. Hodr steadied himself on the table behind him. In his mind he was back in his last battle, the one that had blinded him, but he shoved it away, gritted his teeth and steadied himself.

The net swished above his head. Blood pattered across his face. Lopt shouted and sang and leaped in place only to stagger backward into Hodr, jostling free still more memories of this event from when he'd had eyes to see.

As a boy, and then a young man, he'd been enthralled by the lithe naked young woman and then horrified by the blood and stink of death. More than once he'd spent the night with Rán after the ritual was over. He'd come to love that almost as much as he'd loved the actual deadly dance of spears. Up until a snow bear had spat venom into his face.

Yet he also remembered how even back then the older warriors, veterans of one skirmish or battle or war, depending—he'd seen

more than a hundred of these Midwinter rituals in Gladsheim alone
—would draw back from the young, naked woman, soaked in blood,
who whirled a net above her head and jabbed with a spear in time to
the music pouring from the pounding drums, shrilling flutes, and
dancing harps, while the young warriors, fresh, perhaps, from bloodless, cold patrols of the Breach would be drawn in, laughing as they
pretended to dodge Rán's spear or duck beneath her net.

The procession circled toward the hall's center and the stump
beside which Baldr would now be standing. The flutes changed their
tone, becoming seductive like Aegir's imagined voice. Lilting. The
drums and harps eased off, still present, still loud, but subservient to
the flute's songs. The music conjured visions of a warm field bathed
in light.

"Put down your spear," they sang. "Lay aside your net. For me. I'll
show you there's more to life than death."

And as they sang, Hodr saw it clearly in his memories, Baldr
stepped up onto the stump.

The drums, Rán's voice, beat like waves upon rocks, a counterpoint to the flute's argument.

Death is the end, the drums pounded. *As sure as the tides, as sure as
my spear driven through flesh.*

And yet from death, new life, the flutes argued.

All come to me, the drums roared.

But to you from me, the flutes sang.

I end you, the drums beat.

And I begin you, the flutes rejoiced. *But set all that aside. For one
night, lie here with me.*

The crowd roared out in horror as this young Rán, as bloody and
angry as the one cavorting in his memory, screamed her denial of
Aegir's offer. Her answer was a hurled spear, a promise flying faster
than wind-tossed spray.

Hodr saw it in his mind's eye. The long, low arc, aimed perfectly,
flat, swift and deadly. Aegir, arms wide and welcoming, chest
exposed, a sunny smile on his face. The spear struck his breastbone.
He grunted with the impact, knocked back a step.

But the spear bounced off and Aegir stood unhurt, no mark upon his skin. Aegir snatched the spear from the air and broke it over his knee and held the broken pieces above his head.

The crowd went wild—screaming, shouting, dancing, crying—while the flutes soared in triumph and the harps joined the song. The drums beat on, more quietly, cowed, perhaps, as the ocean after a terrible gale. Not subservient, never that, but won over.

And so it was done, mostly. Aegir had triumphed. Life proved stronger than Death. Rán, beaten, would drift in and succumb to him.

The crowd, inflamed by the music, kept up their din. Beside him, Lopt screamed as enthusiastically as everyone else.

But Hodr did not. Nor did his family, he suspected.

In much older days, this ritual involved the physical culmination of what the pounding drums and shrilling flutes merely suggested. But as the Aesir had grown more sophisticated in their longhouses and walled cities, Rán's surrender had become a symbolic kiss and embrace. Which was just as well, since even he, without a thread of seidr in his veins, felt the primal magic of this ritual.

As did many others since Hodr assumed that now, as in nights past, the men and women were pairing off, stumbling out into the night to enact their own ritual.

Hodr sipped his drink.

"That was unbelievable," Lopt said, grabbing Hodr's shoulder in one strong, hot hand and shaking him. "Thank you for bringing me. What I've seen all my life pales in comparison."

A flush passed through Hodr and his stomach burbled. He shook Lopt's hand off. "Just wait. It gets better."

The barrels of stones were being rolled out, the tremendous thunder drowning out even the crowd's persistent roar.

"Is this when—" Lopt began, excitedly.

"Indeed," Hodr said loudly. "In years past, you were allowed to throw pretty much any weapon at Aegir—when the role was played by my brother, of course. I'm not sure why my mother restricted it to stones this year."

"Will you participate?" Lopt asked. "People are gathering round."

He laughed. "I'd be lucky to hit the far wall."

Lopt's hot, strong hand squeezed his shoulder again. "I'll guide your aim and tell you exactly where to throw."

The dull thud of stone against flesh and the laughter that followed said that this part of the ritual had begun. Not that it had much reverence to it. The flute's lilted above the dull roar of the crowd and the drums' steady, rolling rumble.

A flush came over Hodr. He put his cup down; must be the ale. Lopt's grip loosened on his shoulder. He had wanted to come back here and make peace with his family. Maybe participating would help show that.

Hodr smiled. "Sure, why not. Good way to start off my first night back in Gladsheim."

Lopt clapped him on the back. "I'll be right back."

Feeling hot, Hodr tugged open the collar of his overtunic and sat on the table. He found a cup and took a small sip to wet his suddenly dry throat. This was wine, sweet and cool. It eased the drumming in his head, but the heat of Lopt's hand on his shoulder lingered, and the pattern his thumb had traced. Pattern?

Laughter and shouts, grunts and shoving, the smacking of lips, the clatter of cups on tables, the rattle of rocks on the floor crowded in on his thoughts as if he were the one at the center of the circle. The flutes shrieked and he winced; the pounding drums made his heart beat faster.

He dropped his cup and rubbed at his temples. He worked his jaw and, with a pop, the noise drew back like a prowling cat.

"Here you go, Jarl," Lopt said, leaning in close to speak in his ear. The smith pressed something into his hand. It felt like the spear the smith had given him. Behind the smith's dark face and shadowy form, people drifted like fog over water.

"How did you get this? My mother said—"

A bright smile broke out on Lopt's face, shimmering like the air above a sunlit rock. "What? That's not your spear, my friend. I just brought you a stone."

Mouth dry, Hodr felt the cool, smooth surface of a river stone in his hand. His thumb found a shallow groove like wood grain and ran along it. The rock felt slightly slick, as if it were coated in the oil he used to hone his spear's blade.

He rubbed the side of his head.

"It's not your spear, Jarl Hodr, it's just a rock," Lopt repeated.

Hodr turned toward the smith. The man's eyes burned like forge coals. Lopt gripped his shoulder, and his thumb dug into the muscle till it hurt and then eased off to trace a quick pattern once, twice, a third time.

"Of course it's a rock," Hodr said. He grinned at the smith. "Must be the wine. I'm not used to it."

"And the heat in here, hot as my forge, I tell you," Lopt said, his eyes glowing like an ingot fresh from the flames.

The smith's grip on his shoulder tightened, and he leaned in. "Put your hand on my shoulder, Jarl. I'll guide you through the crowd."

Hodr nodded.

With Lopt beside him, Hodr entered the press of onlookers surrounding his brother. The music pounded and shrieked; Hodr's breathed heavily, almost feeling like he needed to vomit. Lopt kept pushing him forward, through the chanting, dancing, singing crowd. They clapped and swayed with the music, laughed when a stone clattered to the ground and cheered as another thudded against Baldr's flesh.

And then, the crowd parted. Lopt stopped walking. Before him lay open space; nothing and no one stood between himself and his brother. The stone in his right hand felt heavy, oily still, with that long grain his thumb kept tracing.

Voice clanging like a hammer on an anvil, Lopt said, "Your brother's directly in front of you. Twelve paces away, standing on a stump. Call to him, son of Odin. Get him to turn toward you."

Lopt's hot hand slid from Hodr's shoulder to his elbow. Hodr called out. "Baldr!"

Baldr turned, his bare back and shoulders gleaming. Hodr ran his thumb up and down the long grain in the oily stone. His sight dimmed, and his blood roared.

Lopt's thumb dug into his elbow, traced a pattern and withdrew. "Say what you came to say, my friend. And then let go of all the jealousy and pain and hatred as you throw your stone. Remember, it can't hurt him."

"No, it can't," Hodr repeated.

Baldr smiled and spread his arms. Over the music, he called out, "I'm glad you're home again, Hodr. It's been too long, my brother."

88

Frigg

"It's been too long, my brother," Baldr called out, his voice floating above the din. Baldr's happiness spread like warmth from a fire—when he laughed, the folk did, too.

Frigg allowed herself to smile, despite her worries over the witch Yelena who could be anyone here, assuming she was willing to become a man. The reverse was of course possible: Long ago, Odin had become a woman, as had Loki.

Her smile faded as her eyes flicked from the throwing ritual to each of the hall's doors. No wolves. No ravens. No husband. Another broken promise added to the pile.

At least Tyr was in the hall, along with Bragi and Idunn. Heimdall stood his post as he'd promised, and as the wardens had confirmed. He hadn't reported any issues anywhere in Asgard.

It was odd that Loki and his wife Sigyn, along with their boys, were not present—they'd been here for every Midwinter since Odin's departure—but it was just as well given the suspicion she couldn't help but treat Loki with and at least she didn't have to pretend to enjoy Sigyn's company. It was conceivable, too, that Loki was here but shapeshifted. Much as Yelena might be here.

Frigg cast another suspicious eye across the hundreds gathered in the hall. She refused to dwell on the vision-flames that kindled over the heads of many. So far, Midwinter had passed by—nearly— without any major problems, aside from the usual drunken brawls. Baldr had passed safely through the entire city and now he was here, in the hall, where she had controlled everything she could control.

Nanna gasped. Her daughter had covered her mouth with one hand, green eyes wide, and was pointing at Baldr.

Hodr stood opposite Baldr just inside the wide circle of Aesir surrounding his brother. Hodr held a stone; his arm was drawing back. What was Nanna seeing that she wasn't?

Frigg's gaze ran the inner arc of the circle surrounding Baldr. Nothing appeared amiss. The Aesir were swaying and dancing, some in place, some beginning to move sideways as the music stirred them like a ladle in a pot. Something flickered in the corner of her eye.

She looked back at Hodr, his arm almost fully back in the throwing position. But something wasn't quite right.

Nanna screamed unintelligibly, flew out of her chair, across the table, and all but dove into the throng of people below the raised platform on which they stood.

Frigg looked back at Hodr, to his hand holding the rock. It was the wrong grip for throwing a stone, but the right grip for a spear.

She shook her head and squinted.

Just as a fish could seem to jump out of the reflected image of a tree in the water, so too did the long spear in Hodr's hand leap into Frigg's sight.

How had he gotten that spear? And why had it looked like a stone?

"No. Stop!" Frigg was on her feet before she realized she'd moved. Her voice rang from the rafters, but it was too late.

Hodr's arm rushed forward and the dark-tipped spear blurred through the air. Her eyes skipped to Baldr. He stood smiling, hands up in invitation.

The spear split his chest with a sound that broke her world. Everything stopped, shocked into stillness.

Baldr staggered backward. His hands came up to grip the spear that sprouted from his chest. Blood flowed reluctantly around the long spear. Apologetically.

Screaming, Nanna clawed frantically at the bewildered Aesir revelers between herself and her dying husband.

Across the gulf between them, filled with the bobbing jumble of Aesir heads, Frigg watched Baldr look up from his chest. He stared up at the ceiling, his eyes losing focus and blood bubbling from his lips. He gave an inaudible cough, and his face went slack. The pain etched into his handsome features vanished—that was, thanks to her, the first physical pain he had ever felt.

Golden Baldr dropped backwards like a felled tree.

In that moment, the vision of Baldr aboard the flaming ship roared to life as if it were a sail cut loose to fly before a gale. And that sail burned brighter than Baldr ever had. Frigg staggered back as if the heat were real.

The vision-flames leaped from head to head above the crowd. Disaster consumed the guests as if they were kindling for the conflagration. At first, the visions made some sense—a life stomped out beneath a Jotunn's boots, another speared like her son, yet another devoured by a beast. But as the visions roared through the hall, they grew jumbled. Yellows and reds and oranges, whites and blues. Death upon death, juxtaposed, layered in a midwinter bonfire that only Rán would extinguish.

Sound burst back into the room like an avalanche. Hodr's confused face vanished beneath a landslide of raised arms and fists. She tried to make out the vision above his head but lost it amid the dozens of other deaths.

Frigg met Tyr's eyes—he was already out of his seat and moving —and called above the roar of the crowd, "Don't let them kill Hodr."

He nodded once, quick and sharp, then bulled his way into the crowd.

"Hermod," she said, looking past Nanna's collapsed body into her daughter's horrified face. "Go with Tyr. Get Baldr. Bring him here."

Hermod blinked, eyes wide, tears welling up, unmoving.

Frigg took a step toward her and jabbed a hand toward the crowd. "Move, Hermod. Get Baldr."

Was that her voice? So controlled. So cold.

"Ráta, go with her," she said. The big baresark leaped to obey.

The hall vibrated like a string on Bragi's harp. She closed her eyes for a moment but opened them again when blackness whirled sickeningly around her.

She found herself backed up against one of the hall's columns, palms pressed against her temples. The wolf's head carvings tore into her back. She pushed off the column and stepped back to the platform's edge, as if it were a ship's prow and she the figurehead.

Tyr moved through the crowd, clubbing aside those who moved too slowly. He was nearly at the dense pack that had closed in around Hodr.

She reached up and touched her face. No tears yet. No time for them. There would be too much time for that later.

Hermod and Ráta were right behind Tyr, following the open path he'd made. An open ring stood around the spot where Baldr must lay.

Slowly, her mind made sense of a ripped-throated sound behind her. The wail swelled in volume. It was Nanna. Fire within fire within fire raged above her daughter's head. She knelt on the floor, back hunched, rocking and wailing, knocking her forehead against the wood. Her keening was loud even above the hall's din.

Baldr dead and Hodr, if he wasn't already, soon would be. Everyone had seen him murder his brother. She'd have to allow him to be executed. She wanted to collapse, but she could not. She would not. There was no time for wailing or visions now. She and Odin had missed something. Something that someone else had figured out. But who? Hodr? That felt as wrong as the murder she just witnessed. But if that witch Yelena could charm Harald and Klakki, then maybe she had also charmed Hodr.

Eir fell to her knees beside Nanna and wrapped her arms around her, head sideways on Nanna's convulsing back, providing what comfort she could. Too little. Not enough.

Frigg looked back out over the crowd, ignoring the vision flames that reached high above the tightly packed folk in the hall. More fire within fire; dark flickers of movement in those visions.

"Eir," Frigg said. She didn't hear. How could she? Frigg could barely hear her own thoughts. Frigg stepped forward, bent, and touched the chief valkyr's shoulder. "Eir."

Eir looked up, tears flowing down her face, eyes red. A wine cup behind her on the floor leaked dark wine into the darker wood. "Get Nanna out of here. Give her something to make her sleep—not too deep. Stay with her, please."

Eir nodded and tried to pull Nanna to her feet but couldn't. It wasn't that Nanna was resisting, but she was oblivious to everything around her.

Frigg strode to the side of the platform where Hamnen, a warden, stood slack-jawed. The man's gaze was as vacant as if the black-feathered arrow that sprouted from his chest in the vision above his head had already killed him.

She grabbed his shoulder and shook him. She pointed at Nanna and Eir. "Hamnen! Carry Hár Nanna to wherever Eir commands. Guard the door. Let none but myself or Eir in to see her. Do not let her leave. Do you understand?"

Hamnen nodded, tears streaking his face.

"Go, then." She slapped his shoulder, palm stinging from the impact.

She touched her own face and found that it was still dry. She should have been crying.

Tyr was striding back, Hodr's limp body over one shoulder. Faces black with rage, the crowd followed.

Every few paces, Tyr spun slowly, his bared sword keeping open a wide circle around him. Naked rage twisted his face. In the fires above his head, he stood before a tremendous hound, bloody froth on its muzzle; in the distance, a black ship advanced, its prow rising and falling on choppy seas.

Frigg closed her eyes for a moment. The noise in the hall boomed like the sea in a narrow fjord and the sickening blackness threatened.

As soon as she felt Tyr and his burden step onto the platform, she opened her eyes.

As if the platform were the shore, the crowd crashed against it.

Frigg nodded her thanks to Tyr and ushered him past her. She held up both hands to the crowd, palms outward, as if she alone could hold back their tide. Their voices crashed over her, demanding she turn Hodr over to them.

In the lull of the crowd's gathering breath, she called to Heimdall, knowing that unless Baldr's murder had turned the watchman back to his cups, he would hear her. "Sound your horn. Quickly."

She turned back to the crowd. A pair of stocky, long-bearded merchants had advanced into the empty space between the platform and the crowd.

She pointed at them. "Get back."

They hesitated, glancing at one another.

Beyond the crowd, Hermod's waving hand caught her eye. A covered body lay on a table before her. Ráta stood between the body and the crowd, arms wide, her expression brutally sober.

But it wasn't just a body. It was her son's body. And still she wasn't crying.

Several Einherjar stepped in from the side door and began clearing a path by shoving tables and benches out of the way, along with folk too dazed to move.

The roar of voices swelled in front of her. The pair of merchants rode it forward, the red ribbons laced through their beards seeming more like streaming blood than harmless affectations.

Frigg was about to warn them off again when a wall of sound fell on her. She staggered. The flames in the iron sconces blew out, and dust filtered down from the rafters. She clapped her hands to her ears, but it did nothing to lessen the sound. She resisted the urge to sink to her knees like Nanna had, instead letting the horn's voice pass over and around her as if she were a river rock.

Heimdall had heard. Gjallarhorn was more than simply loud. Its voice resonated from the deep, rumbling growl of a bear's chest to a note higher and sharper than the peaks of the northern range. Sharper than the spear that split Baldr's chest.

And like the seed of grief in her heart, that mournful note grew till it seemed like it would never stop.

89

Vidar

Sound had lost all meaning for Vidar—the worn voices of his exhausted warriors, the roars of snow bears, the grunts and snarls of attacking Jotunn—all of it merged into the singular grind of an axe's edge dragged across a sharpening stone.

Perhaps he was being sharpened. The calm, analytical portion of his mind drifted like one of his father's ravens above the battlefield. Dozens of Jotunn corpses lay stinking and steaming at his feet, right alongside the snow bears he'd broken or ripped open with their own matriarch's horns. Were it not for Garilon, standing tall and strong, a ship's unbroken mainmast, shouting orders, Vidar knew all his warriors would be dead. He himself would be dead were it not for his fylgja's undiminished, raging strength. She could break him as easily as a flooding river could break its banks. And if she did, she'd be free.

So why didn't she break him?

A rumbling growl reached him as he floated, or so it seemed, far above the carnage. He kicked the snow bear; it was, indeed, dead. The growl changed to the clang of hammer on metal, the rasp of sword against sword.

The raven that was his mind dove toward the ground, talons

outstretched. The rasp of metal upon metal became, the pounding of rain against sail, of waves against the shore, and then the rumble of a landslide.

He dropped into his flesh, thrumming with the power of his fylgja. The falling snow rippled as it fell, like a cloak shaken out or Vithi's tall grasses before a building storm.

Then the sound of a horn struck him. It could only be one horn. He hadn't heard that singular note since the Last War.

This was Heimdall's horn. Something was wrong.

The Gjallarhorn was only ever sounded when something truly dire was happening. It meant that all the jarls should come immediately to Gladsheim. He would happily leave if not for the trouble he himself was in. He laughed aloud, enjoying the irony.

He turned to shout at Garilon, but the kjolr had sunk to one knee, eyes tight shut and hands covering his ears to dampen the power of Gjallarhorn's voice. Beside him, his warriors had done the same, weapons dropped into the bloody snow.

The Jotunn warriors were similarly incapacitated. The snow bears had fled like whipped hounds.

A part of him wanted to leap forward and tear apart every Jotunn before him. It would be easy. His fylgja thrilled to that idea. But then thought's raven landed on the upper branches of his mind.

His reason reasserted its strength.

He must return to Asgard. Killing these several dozen Jotunn might help his warband now, but they were in Utgard. More Jotunn must be close—the rest of this warband, certainly, and maybe more. And once the Gjallarhorn fell silent, the Jotunn warriors would reform and attack while their shaman would reassert control over however many snow bears were left.

He glanced back at the tunnel his warband had been digging through the snow and ice the Jotunn had collapsed from the cliff above. How far had they gotten? Using his fylgja's strength, he could finish the tunnel and hold it while the remnants of his warband retreated.

Vidar looked inward and met the eyes of his fylgja, greener than Vithi's spring grasses.

There's no glory in this, only necessity. Will you help?

In answer, she stretched, and her strength pounded through him like a surging river.

He snatched up a discarded shield, and sprinted toward the tunnel.

90

Vafthrudnir

Vafthrudnir bolted upright, hands pressed over his ears, awakened, startled by the hungry howling of wolves right outside his tent. Heart pounding, his first thought was that Ygg's wolves had found him again. His wife Um nudged him with her elbow and, with terrified eyes, looked a question at him. Her ears were also covered. He drew in a deep breath, the tent's air was stale and warm, but he didn't smell wolf.

The sound roughened, more like a draugr trying to escape its barrow—or the screaming of a mad seidkonur riding a roof—then it deepened and grew as mournful as a battlefield full of dying Jotunn.

He knew the sound now. How could he have forgotten? It was Goldtooth's horn. He'd heard it blown before. Three times. The first sounding had filled the slack sails of the *nearly* defeated Aesir army. The second winding marked the abduction of Idunn and the fruits she warded while the third had marked the start of the Last War.

This was the fourth time. Loki had succeeded.

Vafthrudnir's vision blurred as he fought back the unexpected sob that would unman him. Um frowned, not understanding, until sadness bloomed in her eyes like summer's last, fragile flowering.

They sat that way for a dozen heartbeats, unmoving, not touching, simply looking at each other. Tears fell from her eyes; he held his in.

Another dozen heartbeats later, he realized his ears were merely ringing. He removed his hands. Silence had returned to Jotunheim.

Well, comparative silence. The heavy fabric and hides of their tents dulled most everyday noises, but not the uproar that followed the Gjallarhorn. Everyone had heard it, but unlike Vafthrudnir, they didn't know what it meant.

War had begun. His people were terrified at the prospect, but they didn't know the plan—not all of them, anyway. And many of those here would indeed die, but only so that their kinsmen could live. Because an Aesir had been murdered.

He rolled from their furs and began dressing.

Um clapped her hands to get his attention. "Where are you going?" she asked in the hand speech.

He tugged on his breeches and tied the fastening. His fingers moved in reply. "The Skrymir will want to discuss what just woke us."

"So the plan reaped it's sad harvest, then?"

He nodded.

Her head fell forward into her hands, long black hair obscuring her face. Her shoulders shook.

He pulled on a shirt and a heavier wool tunic. His shoulder ached where it always did, every morning, since the Skrymir had hauled him down from the tree. That old pain had been joined by the new ache mirroring where Freyja had wounded him and Fimbulthul alike.

He sat to pull thick wool socks on but instead embraced Um, both for himself and for her, rocking slightly until Um pulled away.

She smiled sadly, reached out, and wiped a tear from his cheek. Her fingers danced in the Jotunn speech. "I'm glad to see your tears. He did try to help us."

But for a wan smile, he didn't reply. He leaned into her and hugged her again, tightly, burying his face in the soft fragrance of her hair.

Perhaps they could have done it differently. Baldr had been kind over the last twenty winters. But Ygg's hatred reached back far longer. There was no mercy in Ygg's heart, so there could be none in his own. Loki's vengeance was a tool. A means to an end. He didn't like using it —a knife in Ygg's back would have been better—but only fools refused to use the weapons at hand, especially in a fight to the death.

And now that the deed was done?

He clung harder to Um, and she to him. It was hard to stay here, in the present, and not remember the long-ago death of his first wife. Her old, weathered hands had clutched his until they shuddered as her spirit's bright spark rode winter's breath back to the Roaring Cauldron.

Images of the frozen Jotunn he'd sent into the depths of Utgard's many lakes—the same ones he'd pulled out over the last fifteen winters—floated up into his mind, their faces just below the surface. Most of those faces were young Jotunn who should have lived long, fruitful lives but had instead slept beneath the cold waters.

At least they had another chance. Many would die beneath Aesir spears, but many more would live. And not in this wasteland, either, where a living child hadn't been born in nearly ten winters. All those would-be mothers and fathers would have another chance, too.

He pulled back, cupped her face between his hands, kissed her gently, and whispered, "I have to go. You'll be here when I return?"

"Depends how long you're gone. At midday, I'll be working with the seidkonur, but I'll be back by the evening meal." She managed the last word without a laugh. Calling it a meal was a joke—boiled water flavored with what roots they could scrounge. Some oats. A few fish each week. All the Jotunn, here in Utgard at least, ate like that.

He pulled the inner tent flap back to duck through, she called to him.

He glanced back, expecting to meet her dark eyes, but she was staring at the spot where their empty cradle had once stood. When she did face him, her expression was fierce. "No pity."

Vafthrudnir nodded and left, his cheeks dry once more.

91

Odin

The Wanderer patted his horse's neck as she drank from the brook. It burbled and trickled over the stones and broken branches that comprised its bed. He yawned just thinking about a bed. He rubbed his eye. He was hungry, but there was nothing to eat in the wet, cold, gray forest. His horse snorted, shook her mane and snorted again.

Why did he think of his horse as a she? His hand thumped against her doubled shoulder joint and the thick cords of muscle, sinew, and smooth gray hide. The rain drummed on the wide brim of his hat, pattered on his shoulders, ran off his legs and down into his boots.

Shivering, he tipped his head back and drank the rain. The rain fell harder. Louder, like arrows slamming into shields or feet pounding on hard packed earth. A sail, rattling against the shrouds.

Odd thoughts. Memories, maybe, of a dream. All he'd ever done was wander. He rested the butt of his spear in a stirrup, cradled it in the crook of one arm, lifted his hat and ran his other hand through damp hair, slicking it back from his forehead. His fingers caught on a strap that ran round his head. He followed it down to a patch over his eye. That eye pounded, like drums calling warriors to arms. No, not drums. A horn.

He spotted something dark swinging on long arms among distant branches. Rain ran into his eye, his sight blurred and his mind drifted away. He rubbed his eye till vision returned, clicked his tongue and his horse lurched into motion.

She took maybe a dozen steps forward in an odd, doubled rhythm, pulling hooves through a muck that sucked at them like an old man at his teeth. He counted the hoofbeats, dull though they were, all eight of them.

Eight? He was more tired than he thought.

The rhythm of the hooves drummed away the brook's trickling. Thunder boomed and rolled overhead. He smiled at the sound; it kindled something fierce and hot in his heart.

His horse's hooves banged and scraped against stone. He'd found the road. Had he been looking for a road? If so, where was he going? Where had he come from?

Thunder split the sky, rain drummed, wind howled, the spear in his hand grew warm. A spear? His eye ached beneath its patch.

The spear twitched in his hand. His horse whinnied and stomped the road. That spot between his shoulders itched. The Wanderer looked behind him. Mist draped the trees like the heavy coils of Loki's son. Loki? That name stirred familiar feelings, but the mist slunk forward and his thoughts slipped away again.

His eyes swept across the gray trunks and dark leaves and naked fingers of branches. There was that shape again, swinging closer. Watching.

The horn screamed again, like warriors beside him in the shield wall.

He'd stood in the wall. In many walls. His horse snorted and pawed the ground. He rocked in the saddle, swearing, clinging to its horn like he might a ship's gunwale during a storm. Not just a horse, a sleek mare. Tall and swift. The spear in his hand swayed.

He focused on the horn's call, throbbing in the air, clawing at his mind like a bear at a tree. He shivered again.

If he'd plunged his head into a barrel full of ice and kept his eye open, that gray-black bottom is what the sky above him looked like. His thoughts were sluggish, like ice-cold fingers. The rain grew heavier, colder. But he focused on the horn's voice, the sharp sliding of steel against steel.

Or like the ice of a frozen lake on a sad gray day—and he'd fallen into the lake and sank slowly down and down till Rán's nets clutched at his feet.

Perhaps he had fallen in. Or been thrown in.

In his mind, he pushed off the bottom of the barrel...or the lake... or wherever he was...and struggled upward toward the long, drawn-out screech of a woman's sorrow. He'd made widows of many.

That was a true thought.

Lightning darted across the sky above. He swam more strongly upward. Now he saw thick ice above him. He ran his fingers across it, scrabbling without sound as he looked for a weakness. The ice slashed him and red ribbons of blood billowed around him.

The old wound in his side burned; his missing eye pounded like a war drum. Again, those were true thoughts.

He shoved against the jagged ice and floated backward. He clenched his jaw, and curled bloodied hands into fists and swam back at the ice, twisted, and then slammed his feet into the rough underside. He drifted away again, but the burning in his side became a fire, and his rage kindled.

At last, it kindled.

Thwarted?

No.

Not him.

Not ever.

Inside his mind, his spear swayed into his hands, her blade a bright promise. He thrust upward with his spear. The ice shattered and tumbled down around him.

I am Odin.

He shivered like a longship striking an iceberg. He pitched

forward in Sleipnir's saddle, hands seizing its pommel. Gungnir fell away like a broken mast, vanishing into the depths.

I am Odin!

The screaming, shrieking, rumbling voice that reverberated throughout the gray, wet forest was Heimdall's horn. Something had happened—

The horn's pitch grew higher and thinner, as if the author of its voice was running out of breath, till it died away. Odin's ears rang hollow in the now silent forest.

Understanding crashed in like a wave. There were many reasons why Heimdall might have sounded the horn. But Odin knew, in his heart, precisely why that horn's singular voice rang out. He had failed.

His son Baldr was dead.

92

Loki

Loki worked his jaw; his ears popped as his hearing returned. He rode the hall's roof, tucked away in the shadow of the spread-winged eagle set above the door.

When he saw Goldtooth again, he would ram that horn of his so far up—

He peered down at the huge crowd gathered below, but he needn't have worried. No one was looking up. There wasn't much room to gather among the big buildings on Gladsheim's central hilltop, but there was enough room for the hundreds who'd been inside the hall to mingle with the many more hundreds who'd been outside enjoying the festival.

Everyone knew something had happened. They'd all heard the scream of that blasted horn, after all, but only some knew what actually happened. Their confusion, their fear, was glorious. Even up here he could feel it...taste it, like sweet wine.

And when the Jotunn came knocking on Gladsheim's gates, they would again hear that horn and he would be another step closer to fulfilling his promise to Ygg.

He'd already accomplished the first part of his plan. He'd

murdered Baldr—not directly, perhaps, but it was even sweeter that he'd duped Ygg's blind, disaffected son into the deed. What better way to begin tearing down Ygg than destroying two of his sons.

Old Lopt had proven useful, just as the thousand other shapes he'd worn and discarded, and however many more he would wear before his children were free and avenged. Before his dead wife was avenged.

The ache for revenge floated on his mind's current like an empty skiff. He would heap bodies into it, set it ablaze, and send it, burning, toward Gladsheim.

For now, though, the skiff of his thoughts thumped against the dock of recent memory—watching Hodr's arm come back to throw, Mistilteinn's dark tip just slightly behind Hodr's other outstretched hand. Such a beautiful weapon, Mistilteinn. And it had flown so true. The time he'd spent learning at Eitri's forge had been well spent.

The skiff of his thoughts drifted away from the imaginary dock. Caught in the eddies of memory, he saw again the shock on Baldr's face as he stared down at the length of wood sprouting from his chest before he toppled over dead. How he hated that perfect son of the imperfect father. Loki's children had been cast out long before they had the chance to thrive in the sun—all because those filthy, scratching hens spoke against them. And his brother...by their mutual blood oath...had listened to them.

He forced his jaw to unclench. Rage and hate were fine, but not now. He had to remain calm. Clear-headed. There was much more to do.

Easier thought than done, as the skiff of his thoughts, spun in the current of his rage and he glimpsed Frigg rising, eyes widening as she realized that something in her hall was very, very wrong. It hadn't been easy crafting a spear almost entirely from mistletoe, but he'd had a hundred winters to practice before he'd needed to hack the heart from Baldr's mistletoe. The trickiest part had been making the wooden blade look and feel like skymetal to a blind warrior's hands. But oil, paints, inlays, and those Jotunn runes cut by Vafthrudnir had done the trick.

The skiff of his thoughts drifted further out into the sea of his memories. Dark coils undulated beneath the surface and lifted from the sea, black scales glinting in Máni's cool light. In this memory, froth streamed from the heavy horns on his son's massive head. His jaws parted in what only a father or a mother's eye could tell was a sleepy smile.

The yellow, snake-like eyes, bigger than a shield, blinked slowly and sleepily, and, as Ygg's charm took hold, sagged shut. There'd been no hate in his son's eyes, no anger—unlike his mother whose gaze flashed like a storm every time she looked at Loki—just sadness.

As Jorm slipped beneath the waves, Loki had wept in rage and fury and hopelessness—and then leaped overboard, becoming a sea-snake himself, and followed Jorm down and down and down until his son's immense coils—he was longer than three longships at that time —slumped into the sea floor like a ship's anchor rope cut free. And so Ygg had taken Jorm.

And this night, Loki had taken Baldr and Hodr in long overdue repayment. Soon, Jorm would be fully avenged and freed from his long sleep. He would make sure of it.

Through that memory, another place arose—a rocky island, long white beaches, thick green forests and cool, wet air. In the center of that island, his second son, the great wolf, struggled against the long thread that bound him to the yellowed knob of Ymir's ancient bones fixed with Ygg's seidr into the island's rocky spine.

Fenrir pulled continually against the thread he'd been duped by Tyr into accepting around his neck. Blood ran through his thickly matted fur, joining older, dried blood. A howl rolled like a river from his son's foaming jaws. Only an unquenchable thirst for revenge stopped Fenrir from removing his own head, because that thread, thinner than a fish's breath, would never slip nor break nor otherwise part. Eitri and his sons had crafted it, after all.

Fenrir would be avenged. He would make sure of it.

Loki clenched his fists. He was tempted to strike now. He could probably take Goldtooth unawares and kill him, given all the confusion. He rubbed his eyes, till the tears were gone. He couldn't risk it.

Goldtooth would die, but Ygg must die first. And Ygg wasn't here. Nor did he know where Ygg was.

So instead, he glared up at the moon, a morsel dangled over the teeth of the eastern mountains. Just one more memory to dwell on, then. A cloud drifted across Máni's face. Through some trick of his mind, the cloud's soft, puffy lines withered, becoming instead the harsh lines of a corpse long in a barrow. Slowly, deliberately, the cloud turned toward Loki, half its untouched, pale and whole—too much like his dead wife's visage—yet also unique in its beauty. Yet half was gaunt and mottled with a blue-black stain, like blood spilled on a new dress. It was his daughter's face, Hel's face, her smile sad and lonely.

Then that smile sank behind the mountain of bone where his son howled and that mountain then sank beneath waves that shimmered like scales and all that was left was his anger and fear and sadness. Loki shuddered with a bone-deep chill that had nothing to do with the night air.

"Soon," he whispered to the night.

"Soon," he promised the folk below him, "I will set such a fire that the heavens themselves will burn."

93

Frigg

The spear that killed her son lay on the table before her. The light of a dozen witchlamps pooled about her, making longs shadows of the carved posts. An untouched cup of wine stood by her elbow.

Frigg had sent her thralls into one of the nearby longhouses, but Nanna—dosed with a sleeping draft—slept on Frigg's bed. Now that she was alone, still alone—but she shoved that thought, and where Odin was to the back of her mind—she had time to be quiet and think.

Not that she wanted to, not with this wicked thing in front of her. She ran her fingers lightly along the spear. She'd already wiped it clean and burned the rags.

A lighter, golden strip had been spliced to the darker, stronger wood of the spear shaft. She recognized the runes etched into the leaf-shaped blade and carved into the shaft. She also knew the oils rubbed into the wooden blade and the dark paints used to color the runes. And she knew it's secret name, for it could only have one Mist-ilteinn, in the Old Tongue. Mistletoe in today's.

That lighter strip of wood and the long, leaf-shaped wooden blade was the golden bough...the very mistletoe in which she had hidden her son's spirit. And because of that, for all his long life, Baldr had suffered no injury. Until now, at the hand of his own brother.

Silence rang in her ears. The roof creaked in the building winter wind. The central hearth's flames popped and crackled.

She slammed her fist against the table. The spear jumped, rolled and clattered to the floor. Her full cup toppled, dark red wine flowed and pooled on the table till it began dripping from the edges to patter on the floor.

She hadn't seen Baldr's blood pooling on the floor of the great hall. She couldn't have, not from where she had stood. But this growing puddle must have been what it looked like.

Frigg sobbed and smashed the table again and again. Wine splashed all over her face and chest, into her mouth. She'd fought warriors, killed warriors...men her size and bigger. Their hot blood has splashed on her just as this cool, sweet wine had.

"Mother?" Hermod asked, her voice quiet, nearly the little girl's voice it had once been.

Frigg froze. She was red to the shoulders, her hands stained and her sleeves, sky-blue moments ago, was now bruised like the evening sky after a storm.

She stared at her ruined dress and laughed, the sound harsh and wild and maybe even a little mad. How many dresses had she ruined in the last week. Two? Three?

Hermod laid a gentle hand on her shoulder. Her golden-brown hair, normally so carefully kept in warrior's braids was a frizzy cloud around her tanned, tear-streaked face. In the witchlamps' glow, Hermod's eyes were red-rimmed and blood-shot. She looked far older than she should. She'd wrapped herself in a heavy wool blanket.

Sweet Aegir, she had been selfish. Frigg pulled Hermod into a hug and rocked her gently back and forth, their heads side by side. She smoothed her daughter's hair. Not too old that she couldn't still comfort her, but too old for it to actually work. Hermod had seen battle and death, and she would again, but she'd just seen her own brother murder her other brother.

Frigg drew Hermod down to sit in the one of the two oak armchairs beside the hearth.

Hermod looked over her shoulder at the spear lying on the floor, it's tip in the pool of wine. "That's it, then?" Her voice was distant.

Mistilteinn. The name echoed in Frigg's mind.

"Yes. Sorry. I shouldn't have brought it here." Except that she'd needed to understand what manner of weapon had killed her son.

"It's just a thing. A weapon." Hermod shrugged. "Why'd he do it?"

And there it was. The question that circled around and around in Frigg's mind like a carrion bird. Why. Why. Why.

Frigg stood and stepped out of her ruined dress. "I don't know."

Hermod didn't reply.

"I'll be right back," Frigg said, holding the stained dress and motioning toward her sleeping room.

Hermod shrugged and stared into the fire. As she did, the flames of a vision began to kindle above Hermod's head. Of course it would happen now. She did not want to see her daughter's future death. Not now. Not ever.

She closed her eyes breathed in slowly. Her old shaman had taught her to control the visions. *You can decide when to see what the storm wants you to see. The storm is not your foe, little one. It chose you for this gift, to see...at least in a small way...how it sees. Ask it to withdraw and it will. For a time.*

So, she asked, and the storm did not impose itself upon her. But the vision-flames still formed above Hermod's head.

Fine, Frigg said to herself, *but at least let me change first.*

The sense of forbearance persisted, so Frigg tiptoed into her bedroom, Nanna a dark, still shape beneath the blankets, and pulled a sleeping gown from her wardrobe—green, with subtle, silvery lines that glinted in the low light. She returned to Hermod, stomach clenching as she braced herself for the vision.

This one was different than the others. Hermod stood...

... tall in the vision, armed with axe and shield. But from the way her shoulders slumped, she seemed tired. A familiar raven landed on her shoulder. Hermod turned back to the battlefield, the dead lying like

harvested wheat left to rot. Beyond Hermod, a silvery river glinted like ice. Ships were trapped in the ice, many were burning, still others seemed to have run aground, while a pair of longships...one with yellowed strakes like old nail...were locked together, warriors clashed upon their decks. From the other side of the river, thousands upon thousands of warriors streamed down from a chopped-down forest to the river's edge. And beyond them, taller than the hill on which Gladsheim stood, a black wolf slavered.

"Mother? What is it?"

Frigg blinked the vision away.

Hermod had taken a step forward, one hand reaching from beneath the blanket.

"What? Just...lost in thought for a moment." Frigg smiled and bent to pull on her gown.

"Your underdress is stained, too," Hermod said.

She sighed, handed the gown to Hermod, and pulled off the underdress. She scrubbed her body with it, balled it up, and flung it back toward her sleeping room.

"We were right to worry that father wouldn't return, weren't we?"

Frigg knew well enough what Hermod was about to say—that maybe if Odin had been here, Baldr might still be alive. Maybe Odin could have stopped Hodr. But the Norns had cut and painted the runes signifying Baldr's death, which meant that Odin couldn't have stopped it any more than she'd been able to. And yet the Norns had also promised that if Baldr's spirit were protected, then he could not be killed. She could only see two possibilities: they had either lied or not told the whole of what they saw.

"I believed him when he said he'd be back in time, Hermod," she said. "I expect something happened to him, particularly since Heimdall wasn't able to find him."

"But what could happen to *him*?"

"That *is* the question, isn't it?"

She pulled the underdress on, shivering as she did. What could stop Odin? That thing, that spirit, beneath the Urdarbrunnr had badly hurt him. Maybe it had struck again. Or perhaps something equally deadly had emerged from the cold shadows lining the road down to the Gjoll.

If Odin wasn't back by tomorrow evening, she would fly to the High Seat and look for him herself. If she could find him, she would send Thor to rescue him.

But what of Hodr?

She'd have to preserve his life so that he could be questioned. Which meant staving off the execution the folk of Gladsheim would no doubt demand. Part of her wanted Hodr punished, of course she did...he'd murdered his own brother...but she simply could not understand why. He'd been gone for so long and had seemed so at peace with himself and his life—and she knew that from watching him from afar. It made no sense that he threw it all away.

"I don't know where your father is. But you and I, Hermod, we're here. We'll deal with this. We'll be brave, both for ourselves and for the folk of Gladsheim."

"But, Mother, it was Hodr who—"

Frigg rose and embraced daughter. "I know, Hermod. I don't know why he did it. It doesn't make sense. But we'll find out why."

And if needs must, he'll pay for what he did, she promised herself.

She leaned back and brushed a stray golden sheaf of Hermod's hair back behind one ear. "But you and I, Hermod, we must be brave while we grieve. Everyone heard Heimdall's horn. Everyone knows something awful happened, but only our enemies know exactly what happened."

She looked directly into her daughter's eyes. "We must show them —show everyone—that we are still strong."

PLEASE LET ME KNOW WHAT YOU THOUGHT

I hope you enjoyed the story.

Consider purchasing the sequel, Dark Grows the Sun, which is also available on Amazon.

Narration

You can also listen to the narration of Kinsmen Die.

https://media.rss.com/fensalirpodcast-kinsmendie/feed.xml

Please leave a review on Amazon!

I can't overstate how important your reviews are to making sure other people get a chance to read my story. I'd love to hear your thoughts — positive, negative or anything in between.

Kinsmen Die

Dark Grows the Sun

Contact me directly

mattbishopwrites@gmail.com

https://www.facebook.com/mattbishopwrites

ACKNOWLEDGEMENTS AND THANKS

Jen, without your love and support, this book would not have been written. Emmett and Maeve: Thanks for understanding, without quite getting it, what "Daddy's writing" meant—and continues to mean.

Special thanks to my brother, Andy, for his feedback and support during the first couple years of my writer's journey. Some of the stuff you slogged through was truly cringe worthy.

Trevor and Kim: Thanks for beta reading the book. It's changed a lot since then thanks, in no small part, to your frank commentary.

Kevin and Matt: Thanks for your enthusiasm. It helped fill the tank.